ALSO BY JONATHAN FRANZEN

# FREEDOM

# FREEDOM

## JONATHAN FRANZEN

FARRAR, STRAUS AND GIROUX   NEW YORK

Farrar, Straus and Giroux
18 West 18th Street, New York 10011

Library of Congress Cataloging-in-Publication Data
Franzen, Jonathan.
    Freedom / Jonathan Franzen. — 1st ed.
        p.   cm.
    I. Title.

  PS3556.R352F74 2010
  813'.54—dc22

                                2010010273

ISBN: 978-0-312-60084-6

Designed by Jonathan D. Lippincott

www.fsgbooks.com

10   9   8   7   6   5   4   3   2   1

For their help with this book, the author is particularly grateful to Kathy Chetkovich and Elisabeth Robinson; to Joel Baker, Bonnie and Cam Blodgett, Scott Cheshire, Rolland Comstock, Nick Fowler, Sarah Graham, Charlie Herlovic, Tom Hjelm, Lisa Leonard, David Means, George Packer, Deanna Shemek, Brian Smith, Lorin Stein, and David Wallace; and to the American Academy in Berlin and Cowell College of the University of California, Santa Cruz.

To Susan Golomb and Jonathan Galassi

Go together,
You precious winners all; your exultation
Partake to everyone.  I, an old turtle,
Will wing me to some withered bough, and there
My mate, that's never to be found again,
Lament till I am lost.

—*The Winter's Tale*

# GOOD NEIGHBORS

The news about Walter Berglund wasn't picked up locally—he and Patty had moved away to Washington two years earlier and meant nothing to St. Paul now—but the urban gentry of Ramsey Hill were not so loyal to their city as not to read the *New York Times*. According to a long and very unflattering story in the *Times*, Walter had made quite a mess of his professional life out there in the nation's capital. His old neighbors had some difficulty reconciling the quotes about him in the *Times* ("arrogant," "high-handed," "ethically compromised") with the generous, smiling, red-faced 3M employee they remembered pedaling his commuter bicycle up Summit Avenue in February snow; it seemed strange that Walter, who was greener than Greenpeace and whose own roots were rural, should be in trouble now for conniving with the coal industry and mistreating country people. Then again, there had always been something not quite right about the Berglunds.

Walter and Patty were the young pioneers of Ramsey Hill—the first college grads to buy a house on Barrier Street since the old heart of St. Paul had fallen on hard times three decades earlier. They paid nothing for their Victorian and then killed themselves for ten years renovating it. Early on, some very determined person torched their garage and twice broke into their car before they got the garage rebuilt. Sunburned bikers descended on the vacant lot across the alley to drink Schlitz and grill knockwurst and rev engines at small hours until Patty went outside in sweatclothes and said, "Hey, you guys, you know what?" Patty frightened nobody, but she'd been a standout athlete in high school and college and possessed a jock sort of fearlessness. From her first day in the neighborhood, she was helplessly conspicuous. Tall, ponytailed, absurdly young, pushing a stroller past stripped cars and broken beer bottles and barfed-upon old snow, she might have been carrying all the hours of her day in the string bags that hung from her stroller. Behind her you could see the baby-encumbered preparations for a morning of baby-encumbered errands; ahead of her, an afternoon of public radio, the *Silver Palate Cookbook*, cloth diapers, drywall compound, and latex paint; and then *Goodnight Moon*, then zinfandel. She was already fully the thing that was just starting to happen to the rest of the street.

In the earliest years, when you could still drive a Volvo 240 without feeling self-conscious, the collective task in Ramsey Hill was to relearn certain life skills that your own parents had fled to the suburbs specifically to unlearn, like how to interest the local cops in actually doing their job, and how to protect a bike from a highly motivated thief, and when to bother rousting a drunk from your lawn furniture, and how to encourage feral cats to shit in somebody else's children's sandbox, and how to determine whether a public school sucked too much to bother trying to fix it. There were also more contemporary questions, like, what about those cloth diapers? Worth the bother? And was it true that you could still get milk delivered in glass bottles? Were the Boy Scouts OK politically? Was bulgur really necessary? Where to recycle batteries? How to respond when a poor person of color accused you of destroying her neighborhood? Was it true that the glaze of old Fiestaware contained dangerous amounts of lead? How elaborate did a kitchen water filter actually need to be? Did your 240 sometimes not go into overdrive when you pushed the overdrive button? Was it better to offer panhandlers food, or nothing? Was it possible to raise unprecedentedly confident, happy, brilliant kids while working full-time? Could coffee beans be ground the night before you used them, or did this have to be done in the morning? Had anybody in the history of St. Paul ever had a positive experience with a roofer? What about a good Volvo mechanic? Did your 240 have that problem with the sticky parking-brake cable? And that enigmatically labeled dashboard switch that made such a satisfying Swedish click but seemed not to be connected to anything: what *was* that?

For all queries, Patty Berglund was a resource, a sunny carrier of sociocultural pollen, an affable bee. She was one of the few stay-at-home moms in Ramsey Hill and was famously averse to speaking well of herself or ill of anybody else. She said she expected to be "beheaded" someday by one of the windows whose sash chains she'd replaced. Her children were "probably" dying of trichinosis from pork she'd undercooked. She wondered if her "addiction" to paint-stripper fumes might be related to her "never" reading books anymore. She confided that she'd been "forbidden" to fertilize Walter's flowers after what had happened "last time." There were people with whom her style of self-deprecation didn't sit well—who detected a kind of condescension in it, as if Patty, in exaggerating her own minor defects, were too obviously trying to spare the feelings of less accomplished homemakers. But most people found her humility sincere or at least amusing, and it was in any case hard to resist a woman whom your own children liked so much and who remembered not only their birthdays but yours, too, and came to your back door with a plate of cookies or a card or some lilies of the valley in a little thrift-store vase that she told you not to bother returning.

It was known that Patty had grown up back East, in a suburb of New York City, and had received one of the first women's full scholarships to play basketball at Minnesota, where, in her sophomore year, according to a plaque on the wall of Walter's home office, she'd made second-team all-American. One strange thing about Patty, given her strong family orientation, was that she had no discernible connection to her roots. Whole seasons passed without her setting foot outside St. Paul, and it wasn't clear that anybody from the East, not even her parents, had ever come out to visit. If you inquired point-blank about the parents, she would answer that the two of them did a lot of good things for a lot of people, her dad had a law practice in White Plains, her mom was a politician, yeah, a New York State assemblywoman. Then she would nod emphatically and say, "Yeah, so, that's what they do," as if the topic had been exhausted.

A game could be made of trying to get Patty to agree that somebody's behavior was "bad." When she was told that Seth and Merrie Paulsen were throwing a big Halloween party for their twins and had deliberately invited every child on the block except Connie Monaghan, Patty would only say that this was very "weird." The next time she saw the Paulsens in the street, they explained that they had tried *all summer* to get Connie Monaghan's mother, Carol, to stop flicking cigarette butts from her bedroom window down into their twins' little wading pool. "That is really weird," Patty agreed, shaking her head, "but, you know, it's not Connie's fault." The Paulsens, however, refused to be satisfied with "weird." They wanted *sociopathic*, they wanted *passive-aggressive*, they wanted *bad*. They needed Patty to select one of these epithets and join them in applying it to Carol Monaghan, but Patty was incapable of going past "weird," and the Paulsens in turn refused to add Connie to their invite list. Patty was angry enough about this injustice to take her own kids, plus Connie and a school friend, out to a pumpkin farm and a hayride on the afternoon of the party, but the worst she would say aloud about the Paulsens was that their meanness to a seven-year-old girl was very weird.

Carol Monaghan was the only other mother on Barrier Street who'd been around as long as Patty. She'd come to Ramsey Hill on what you might call a patronage-exchange program, having been a secretary to somebody high-level in Hennepin County who moved her out of his district after he'd made her pregnant. Keeping the mother of your illegitimate child on your own office payroll: by the late seventies, there were no longer so many Twin Cities jurisdictions where this was considered consonant with good government. Carol became one of those distracted, break-taking clerks at the city license bureau while somebody equivalently well-connected in St. Paul was hired in reverse across the river. The rental house on Barrier Street, next door to the Berglunds, had presumably been included in the deal; otherwise it was hard to see why Carol would have consented to live in what was then still basically a slum. Once a week, in summer, an empty-eyed kid in a Parks Department jumpsuit came by at dusk in an unmarked 4x4 and ran a mower around her lawn, and in winter the same kid materialized to snow-blow her sidewalk.

By the late eighties, Carol was the only non-gentrifier left on the block. She smoked Parliaments, bleached her hair, made lurid talons of her nails, fed her daughter heavily processed foods, and came home very late on Thursday nights ("That's Mom's night out," she explained, as if every mom had one), quietly letting herself into the Berglunds' house with the key they'd given her and collecting the sleeping Connie from the sofa where Patty had tucked her under blankets. Patty had been implacably generous in offering to look after Connie while Carol was out working or shopping or doing her Thursday-night business, and Carol had become dependent on her for a ton of free babysitting. It couldn't have escaped Patty's attention that Carol repaid this generosity by ignoring Patty's own daughter, Jessica, and doting inappropriately on her son, Joey ("How about another smooch from the lady-killer?"), and standing very close to Walter at neighborhood functions, in her filmy blouses and her cocktail-waitress heels, praising Walter's home-improvement prowess and shrieking with laughter at everything he said; but for many years the worst that Patty would say of Carol was that single moms had a hard life and if Carol was sometimes weird to her it was probably just to save her pride.

To Seth Paulsen, who talked about Patty a little too often for his wife's taste, the Berglunds were the super-guilty sort of liberals who needed to forgive everybody so their own good fortune could be forgiven; who lacked the courage of their privilege. One problem with Seth's theory was that the Berglunds weren't all that privileged; their only known asset was their house, which they'd rebuilt with their own hands. Another problem, as Merrie Paulsen pointed out, was that Patty was no great progressive and certainly no feminist (staying home with her birthday calendar, baking those goddamned birthday cookies) and seemed altogether allergic to politics. If you mentioned an election or a candidate to her, you could see her struggling and failing to be her usual cheerful self—see her becoming agitated and doing too much nodding, too much yeah-yeahing. Merrie, who was ten years older than Patty and looked every year of it, had formerly been active with the SDS in Madison and was now very active in the craze for Beaujolais nouveau. When Seth, at a dinner party, mentioned Patty for the third or fourth time, Merrie went nouveau red in the face and declared that there was *no* larger consciousness, *no* solidarity, *no* political substance, *no* fungible structure, *no* true communitarianism in Patty Berglund's supposed neighborliness, it was all just regressive housewifely bullshit, and, frankly, in Merrie's opinion, if you were to scratch below the nicey-nice surface you might be surprised to find something rather hard and selfish and competitive and Reaganite in Patty; it was obvious that the only things that mattered to her were her children and her house—*not* her neighbors, *not* the poor, *not* her country, *not* her parents, not even her own husband.

And Patty was undeniably very into her son. Though Jessica was the more obvious credit to her parents—smitten with books, devoted to wildlife, talented at flute, stalwart on the soccer field, coveted as a babysitter, not so pretty as to be morally deformed by it, admired even by Merrie Paulsen—Joey was the child Patty could not shut up about. In her chuckling, confiding, self-deprecating way, she spilled out barrel after barrel of unfiltered detail about her and Walter's difficulties with him. Most of her stories took the form of complaints, and yet nobody doubted that she adored the boy. She was like a woman bemoaning her gorgeous jerky boyfriend. As if she were proud of having her heart trampled by him: as if her openness to this trampling were the main thing, maybe the only thing, she cared to have the world know about.

"He is being such a little shit," she told the other mothers during the long winter of the Bedtime Wars, when Joey was asserting his right to stay awake as late as Patty and Walter did.

"Is it tantrums? Is he crying?" the other mothers asked.

"Are you kidding?" Patty said. "I *wish* he cried. Crying would be normal, and it would also stop."

"What's he doing, then?" the mothers asked.

"He's questioning the basis of our authority. We make him turn the lights out, but his position is that he shouldn't have to go to sleep until we turn our own lights out, because he's exactly the same as us. And, I swear to God, it is like clockwork, every fifteen minutes, I swear he's lying there staring at his alarm clock, every fifteen minutes he calls out, 'Still awake! I'm still awake!' In this tone of *contempt*, or sarcasm, it's *weird*. And I'm begging Walter not to take the bait, but, no, it's a quarter of midnight again, and Walter is standing in the dark in Joey's room and they're having another argument about the difference between adults and children, and whether a family is a democracy or a benevolent dictatorship, until finally it's *me* who's having the meltdown, you know, lying there in bed, whimpering, 'Please stop, please stop.'"

Merrie Paulsen wasn't entertained by Patty's storytelling. Late in the evening, loading dinner-party dishes into the dishwasher, she remarked to

Seth that it was hardly surprising that Joey should be confused about the distinction between children and adults—his own mother seemed to suffer from some confusion about which of the two she was. Had Seth noticed how, in Patty's stories, the discipline always came from Walter, as if Patty were just some feckless bystander whose job was to be cute?

"I wonder if she's actually in love with Walter, or not," Seth mused optimistically, uncorking a final bottle. "Physically, I mean."

"The subtext is always 'My son is extraordinary,'" Merrie said. "She's always complaining about the length of his attention span."

"Well, to be fair," Seth said, "it's in the context of his stubbornness. His infinite patience in defying Walter's authority."

"Every word she says about him is some kind of backhanded brag."

"Don't *you* ever brag?" Seth teased.

"Probably," Merrie said, "but at least I have some minimal awareness of how I sound to other people. And my sense of self-worth is not bound up in how extraordinary our kids are."

"You are the perfect mom," Seth teased.

"No, that would be Patty," Merrie said, accepting more wine. "I'm merely very good."

Things came, Patty complained, too easily to Joey. He was golden-haired and pretty and seemed innately to possess the answers to every test a school could give him, as though multiple-choice sequences of As and Bs and Cs and Ds were encoded in his very DNA. He was uncannily at ease with neighbors five times his age. When his school or his Cub Scout pack forced him to sell candy bars or raffle tickets door to door, he was frank about the "scam" that he was running. He perfected a highly annoying smile of condescension when faced with toys or games that other boys owned but Patty and Walter refused to buy him. To extinguish this smile, his friends insisted on sharing what they had, and so he became a crack video gamer even though his parents didn't believe in video games; he developed an encyclopedic familiarity with the urban music that his parents were at pains to protect his preteen ears from. He was no older than eleven or twelve when, at the dinner table, according to Patty, he accidentally or deliberately called his father "son."

"Oh-ho did that not go over well with Walter," she told the other mothers.

"That's how the teenagers all talk to each other now," the mothers said. "It's a rap thing."

"That's what Joey said," Patty told them. "He said it was just a word and not even a bad word. And of course Walter begged to differ. And I'm sitting there thinking, 'Wal-ter, Wal-ter, don't-get into-it, point-less to ar-gue,' but, no, he has to try to explain how, for example, even though 'boy' is not a bad word, you still can't say it to a grown man, especially not to a black man, but, of course, the whole problem with Joey is he refuses to recognize any distinction between children and grownups, and so it ends with Walter saying there won't be any dessert for him, which Joey then claims he doesn't even want, in fact he doesn't even *like* dessert very much, and I'm sitting there thinking, 'Wal-ter, Wal-ter, don't-get into-it,' but Walter can't help it—he has to try to *prove* to Joey that in fact Joey really *loves* dessert. But Joey won't accept any of Walter's evidence. He's totally lying through his teeth, of course, but he claims he's only ever taken seconds of dessert because it's conventional to, not because he actually likes it, and poor Walter, who can't stand to be lied to, says, 'OK, if you don't like it, then how about a *month* without dessert?' and I'm thinking, 'Oh, Wal-ter, Wal-ter, this-isn't going-to end-well,' because Joey's response is, 'I will go a *year* without dessert, I will never eat dessert *again*, except to be polite at somebody else's house,' which, bizarrely enough, is a credible threat—he's so stubborn he could probably do it. And I'm like, 'Whoa, guys, time-out, dessert is an important food group, let's not get carried away here,' which immediately undercuts Walter's authority, and since the whole argument has been about his authority, I manage to undo anything positive he's accomplished."

The other person who loved Joey inordinately was the Monaghan girl, Connie. She was a grave and silent little person with the disconcerting habit of holding your gaze unblinkingly, as if you had nothing in common. She was an afternoon fixture in Patty's kitchen, laboring to mold cookie dough into geometrically perfect spheres, taking such pains that the butter liquefied and made the dough glisten darkly. Patty formed eleven balls for every one of Connie's, and when they came out of the oven Patty never failed to ask Connie's permission to eat the one "truly outstanding" (smaller, flatter, harder) cookie. Jessica, who was a year older than Connie, seemed content to cede the kitchen to the neighbor girl while she read books or played with her terrariums. Connie posed no kind of threat to somebody as well rounded as Jessica. Connie had no notion of wholeness—was all depth and no breadth. When she was coloring, she got lost in saturating one or two areas with a felt-tip pen, leaving the rest blank and ignoring Patty's cheerful urgings to try some other colors.

Connie's intensive focus on Joey was evident early on to every local mother except, seemingly, Patty, perhaps because Patty herself was so focused on him. At Linwood Park, where Patty sometimes organized athletics for the kids, Connie sat by herself on the grass and fashioned clover-flower rings for nobody, letting the minutes stream past her until Joey took his turn at bat or moved the soccer ball down the field and quickened her interest momentarily. She was like an imaginary friend who happened to be visible. Joey, in his precocious self-mastery, seldom found it necessary to be mean to her in front of his friends, and Connie, for her part, whenever it became clear that the boys were going off to be boys, knew enough to fall back and dematerialize without reproach or entreaty. There was always tomorrow. For a long time, there was also always Patty, down on her knees among her vegetables or up on a ladder in a spattered wool shirt, attending to the Sisyphean work of Victorian paint maintenance. If Connie couldn't be near Joey she could at least be useful to him by keeping his mother company in his absence. "What's the homework situation?" Patty would ask her from the ladder. "Do you want some help?"

"My mom's going to help me when she gets home."

"She's going to be tired, it's going to be late. You could surprise her and get it done right now. You want to do that?"

"No, I'll wait."

When exactly Connie and Joey started fucking wasn't known. Seth Paulsen, without evidence, simply to upset people, enjoyed opining that Joey had been eleven and Connie twelve. Seth's speculation centered on the privacy afforded by a tree fort that Walter had helped Joey build in an ancient crab apple in the vacant lot. By the time Joey finished eighth grade, his name was turning up in the neighbor boys' replies to strenuously casual parental inquiries about the sexual behavior of their schoolmates, and it later seemed probable that Jessica had been aware of something by the end of that summer—suddenly, without saying why, she became strikingly disdainful of both Connie and her brother. But nobody ever saw them actually hanging out by themselves until the following winter, when the two of them went into business together.

According to Patty, the lesson that Joey had learned from his incessant arguments with Walter was that children were compelled to obey parents because parents had the money. It became yet another example of Joey's extraordinariness: while the other mothers lamented the sense of entitlement with which their kids demanded cash, Patty did laughing caricatures of Joey's chagrin at having to beg Walter for funds. Neighbors who hired Joey knew him to be a surprisingly industrious shoveler of snow and raker of leaves, but Patty said that he secretly hated the low wages and felt that shoveling an adult's driveway put him in an undesirable relation to the adult. The ridiculous moneymaking schemes suggested in Scouting publications—selling magazine subscriptions door to door, learning magic tricks and charging admission to magic shows, acquiring the tools of taxidermy and stuffing your neighbors' prizewinning walleyes—all similarly reeked either of vassalage ("I am taxidermist to the ruling class") or, worse, of charity. And so, inevitably, in his quest to liberate himself from Walter, he was drawn to entrepreneurship.

Somebody, maybe even Carol Monaghan herself, was paying Connie's tuition at a small Catholic academy, St. Catherine's, where the girls wore uniforms and were forbidden all jewelry except one ring ("simple, all-metal"), one watch ("simple, no jewels"), and two earrings ("simple, all-metal, half-inch maximum in size"). It happened that one of the popular ninth-grade girls at Joey's own school, Central High, had come home from a family trip to New York City with a cheap watch, widely admired at lunch hour, in whose chewable-looking yellow band a Canal Street vendor had thermo-embedded tiny candy-pink plastic letters spelling out a Pearl Jam lyric, DON'T CALL ME DAUGHTER, at the girl's request. As Joey himself would later recount in his college-application essays, he had immediately taken the initiative to research the wholesale source of this watch and the price of a thermo-embedding press. He'd invested four hundred dollars of his own savings in equipment, had made Connie a sample plastic band (READY FOR THE PUSH, it said) to flash at St. Catherine's, and then, employing Connie as a courier, had sold personalized watches to fully a quarter of her schoolmates, at thirty dollars each, before the nuns wised up and amended the dress code to forbid watchbands with embedded text. Which, of course—as Patty told the other mothers—struck Joey as an outrage.

"It's not an outrage," Walter told him. "You were benefiting from an artificial restraint of trade. I didn't notice you complaining about the rules when they were working in your favor."

"I made an investment. I took a risk."

"You were exploiting a loophole, and they closed the loophole. Couldn't you see that coming?"

"Well, why didn't you warn me?"

"I did warn you."

"You just warned me I could lose money."

"Well, and you didn't even lose money. You just didn't make as much as you hoped."

"It's still money I should have had."

"Joey, making money is not a *right*. You're selling junk those girls don't really need and some of them probably can't even afford. That's why Connie's school has a dress code—to be fair to everybody."

"Right—everybody but *me*."

From the way Patty reported this conversation, laughing at Joey's innocent indignation, it was clear to Merrie Paulsen that Patty still had no inkling of what her son was doing with Connie Monaghan. To be sure of it, Merrie probed a little. What did Patty suppose Connie had been getting for her trouble? Was she working on commission?

"Oh, yeah, we told him he had to give her half his profits," Patty said. "But he would've done that anyway. He's always been protective of her, even though he's younger."

"He's like a brother to her . . ."

"No, actually," Patty joked, "he's a lot nicer to her than that. You can ask Jessica what it's like to be his sibling."

"Ha, right, ha ha," Merrie said.

To Seth, later that day, Merrie reported, "It's amazing, she truly has no idea."

"I think it's a mistake," Seth said, "to take pleasure in a fellow parent's ignorance. It's tempting fate, don't you think?"

"I'm sorry, it's just too funny and delicious. You'll have to do the non-gloating for the two of us and keep our fate at bay."

"I feel bad for her."

"Well, forgive me, but I'm finding it hilarious."

Toward the end of that winter, in Grand Rapids, Walter's mother collapsed with a pulmonary embolism on the floor of the ladies' dress shop where she worked. Barrier Street knew Mrs. Berglund from her visits at Christmastime, on the children's birthdays, and on her own birthday, for which Patty always took her to a local masseuse and plied her with licorice and macadamia nuts and white chocolate, her favorite treats. Merrie Paulsen referred to her, not unkindly, as "Miss Bianca," after the bespectacled mouse matron in the children's books by Margery Sharp. She had a crepey, once-pretty face and tremors in her jaw and her hands, one of which had been badly withered by childhood arthritis. She'd been worn out, physically wrecked, Walter said bitterly, by a lifetime of hard labor for his drunk of a dad, at the roadside motel they'd operated near Hibbing, but she was determined to remain independent and look elegant in her widowed years, and so she kept driving her old Chevy Cavalier to the dress shop. At the news of her collapse, Patty and Walter hurried up north, leaving Joey to be supervised by his disdainful older sister. It was soon after the ensuing teen fuckfestival, which Joey conducted in his bedroom in open defiance of Jessica, and which ended only with the sudden death and funeral of Mrs. Berglund, that Patty became a very different kind of neighbor, a much more sarcastic neighbor.

"Oh, Connie, yes," her tune went now, "such a nice little girl, such a quiet little harmless girl, with such a sterling mom. You know, I hear Carol has a new boyfriend, a real studly man, he's like half her age. Wouldn't it be terrible if they moved away now, with everything Carol's done to brighten our lives? And Connie, wow, I'd sure miss her too. Ha ha. So quiet and nice and grateful."

Patty was looking a mess, gray-faced, poorly slept, underfed. It had taken her an awfully long time to start looking her age, but now at last Merrie Paulsen had been rewarded in her wait for it to happen.

"Safe to say she's figured it out," Merrie said to Seth.

"Theft of her cub—the ultimate crime," Seth said.

"Theft, exactly," Merrie said. "Poor innocent blameless Joey, stolen away by that little intellectual powerhouse next door."

"Well, she is a year and a half older."

"Calendrically."

"Say what you will," Seth said, "but Patty really loved Walter's mom. She's got to be hurting."

"Oh, I know, I know. Seth, I know. And now I can honestly be sad for her."

Neighbors who were closer to the Berglunds than the Paulsens reported that Miss Bianca had left her little mouse house, on a minor lake near Grand Rapids, exclusively to Walter and not to his two brothers. There was said to be disagreement between Walter and Patty about how to handle this, Walter wanting to sell the house and share the proceeds with his brothers, Patty insisting that he honor his mother's wish to reward him for being the good son. The younger brother was career military and lived in the Mojave, at the Air Force base there, while the older brother had spent his adult life advancing their father's program of drinking immoderately, exploiting their mother financially, and otherwise neglecting her. Walter and Patty had always taken the kids to his mother's for a week or two in the summer, often bringing along one or two of Jessica's neighborhood friends, who described the property as rustic and woodsy and not too terrible bugwise. As a kindness, perhaps, to Patty, who appeared to be doing some immoderate drinking of her own—her complexion in the morning, when she came out to collect the blue-wrapped *New York Times* and the green-wrapped *Star-Tribune* from her front walk, was all Chardonnay Splotch—Walter eventually agreed to keep the house as a vacation place, and in June, as soon as school let out, Patty took Joey up north to help her empty drawers and clean and repaint while Jessica stayed home with Walter and took an enrichment class in poetry.

Several neighbors, the Paulsens not among them, brought their boys for visits to the lakeside house that summer. They found Patty in much better spirits. One father privately invited Seth Paulsen to imagine her suntanned and barefoot, in a black one-piece bathing suit and beltless jeans, a look very much to Seth's taste. Publicly, everyone remarked on how attentive and unsullen Joey was, and what a good time he and Patty seemed to be having. The two of them made all visitors join them in a complicated parlor game they called Associations. Patty stayed up late in front of her mother-in-law's TV console, amusing Joey with her intricate knowledge of syndicated sixties and seventies sitcoms. Joey, having discovered that their lake was unidentified on local maps—it was really just a large pond, with one other house on it—had christened it Nameless, and Patty pronounced the name tenderly, sentimentally, "our Nameless Lake." When Seth Paulsen learned from one of the returning fathers that Joey was working long hours up there, cleaning gutters and cutting brush and scraping paint, he wondered whether Patty might be paying Joey a solid wage for his services, whether this might be part of the deal. But nobody could say.

As for Connie, the Paulsens could hardly look out a Monaghan-side window without seeing her waiting. She really was a very patient girl, she had the metabolism of a fish in winter. She worked evenings busing tables at W. A. Frost, but all afternoon on weekdays she sat waiting on her front stoop while ice-cream trucks went by and younger children played, and on weekends she sat in a lawn chair behind the house, glancing occasionally at the loud, violent, haphazard tree-removal and construction work that her mother's new boyfriend, Blake, had undertaken with his non-unionized buddies from the building trades, but mostly just waiting.

"So, Connie, what's interesting in your life these days?" Seth asked her from the alley.

"You mean, apart from Blake?"

"Yes, apart from Blake."

Connie considered briefly and then shook her head. "Nothing," she said.

"Are you bored?"

"Not really."

"Going to movies? Reading books?"

Connie fixed Seth with her steady, we-have-nothing-in-common gaze. "I saw *Batman*."

"What about Joey? You guys have been pretty tight, I bet you're missing him."

"He'll be back," she said.

Once the old cigarette-butt issue had been resolved—Seth and Merrie admitted to having possibly exaggerated the summerlong tally of butts in the wading pool; to having possibly overreacted—they'd discovered in Carol Monaghan a rich source of lore about local Democratic politics, which Merrie was getting more involved with. Carol matter-of-factly told hair-raising stories of the unclean machine, of buried pipelines of slush, of rigged bids, of permeable firewalls, of interesting math, and got a kick out of Merrie's horror. Merrie came to cherish Carol as a fleshly exemplum of the civic corruption Merrie intended to combat. The great thing about Carol was that she never seemed to change—kept tarting up on Thursday evenings for whoever, year after year after year, keeping alive the patriarchal tradition in urban politics.

And then, one day, she did change. There was already quite a bit of this going around. The city's mayor, Norm Coleman, had morphed into a Republican, and a former pro wrestler was headed toward the governor's mansion. The catalyst in Carol's case was the new boyfriend, Blake, a goateed young backhoe operator she'd met across the counter at the license bureau, and for whom she dramatically changed her look. Out went the complicated hair and escort-service dresses, in came snug pants, a simple shag cut, and less makeup. A Carol nobody had ever seen, an actually happy Carol, hopped buoyantly from Blake's F-250 pickup, letting anthem rock throb up and down the street, and slammed the passenger-side door with a mighty push. Soon Blake began spending nights at her house, shuffling around in a Vikings jersey with his work boots unlaced and a beer can in his fist, and before long he was chainsawing every tree in her back yard and running wild with a rented backhoe. On the bumper of his truck were the words I'M WHITE AND I VOTE.

The Paulsens, having recently completed a protracted renovation of their own, were reluctant to complain about the noise and mess, and Walter, on the other side, was too nice or too busy, but when Patty finally came home, late in August, after her months in the country with Joey, she was practically unhinged in her dismay, going up and down the street, door to door, wild-eyed, to vilify Carol Monaghan. "Excuse me," she said, "what happened here? Can somebody tell me what happened? Did somebody declare war on trees without telling me? Who is this Paul Bunyan with the truck? What's the story? Is she not renting anymore? Are you allowed to annihilate the trees if you're just renting? How can you tear the back wall off a house you don't even own? Did she somehow buy the place without our knowing it? How could she do that? She can't even change a lightbulb without calling up my husband! 'Sorry to bother you at the dinner hour, Walter, but when I flip this light switch nothing happens. Do you mind coming over right away? And while you're here, hon, can you help me with my taxes? They're due tomorrow and my nails are wet.' How could this person get a mortgage? Doesn't she have Victoria's Secret bills to pay? How is she even allowed to have a boyfriend? Isn't there some fat guy over in Minneapolis? Shouldn't somebody maybe get the word out to the fat guy?"

Not until Patty reached the door of the Paulsens, far down on her list of go-to neighbors, did she get some answers. Merrie explained that Carol Monaghan was, in fact, no longer renting. Carol's house had been one of several hundred that the city housing authority had come to own during the blight years and was now selling off at bargain prices.

"How did I not know this?" Patty said.

"You never asked," Merrie said. And couldn't resist adding: "You never seemed particularly interested in government."

"And you say she got it cheap."

"Very cheap. It helps to know the right people."

"How do *you* feel about that?"

"I think it sucks, both fiscally and philosophically," Merrie said. "That's one reason I'm working with Jim Schiebel."

"You know, I always loved this neighborhood," Patty said. "I loved living here, even at the beginning. And now suddenly everything looks so dirty and ugly to me."

"Don't get depressed, get involved," Merrie said, and gave her some literature.

"I wouldn't want to be Walter right now," Seth remarked as soon as Patty was gone.

"I'm frankly glad to hear that," Merrie said.

"Was it just me, or did you hear an undertone of marital discontent? I mean, helping Carol with her taxes? You know anything about that? I thought that was very interesting. I hadn't heard about that. And now he's failed to protect their pretty view of Carol's trees."

"The whole thing is so Reaganite-regressive," Merrie said. "She thought she could live in her own little bubble, make her own little world. Her own little dollhouse."

The add-on structure that rose out of Carol's back-yard mud pit, weekend by weekend over the next nine months, was like a giant utilitarian boat shed with three plain windows punctuating its expanses of vinyl siding. Carol and Blake referred to it as a "great-room," a concept hitherto foreign to Ramsey Hill. Following the cigarette-butt controversy, the Paulsens had installed a high fence and planted a line of ornamental spruces that had since grown up enough to screen them from the spectacle. Only the Berglunds' sight lines were unobstructed, and before long the other neighbors were avoiding conversation with Patty, as they never had before, because of her fixation on what she called "the hangar." They waved from the street and called out hellos but were careful not to slow down and get sucked in. The consensus among the working mothers was that Patty had too much time on her hands. In the old days, she'd been great with the little kids, teaching them sports and domestic arts, but now most of the kids on the street were teenagers. No matter how she tried to fill her days, she was always within sight or earshot of the work next door. Every few hours, she emerged from her house and paced up and down her back yard, peering over at the great-room like an animal whose nest had been disturbed, and sometimes in the evening she went knocking on the great-room's temporary plywood door.

"Hey, Blake, how's it going?"

"Going just fine."

"Sounds like it! Hey, you know what, that Skilsaw's pretty loud for eight-thirty at night. How would you feel about knocking off for the day?"

"Not too good, actually."

"Well, how about if I just ask you to stop, then?"

"I don't know. How about you letting me get my work done?"

"I'd actually feel pretty bad about that, because the noise is really bothering us."

"Yeah, well, you know what? Too bad."

Patty had a loud, involuntary, whinnylike laugh. "Ha-ha-ha! Too bad?"

"Yeah, listen, I'm sorry about the noise. But Carol says there was about five years of noise coming out of your place when you were fixing it up."

"Ha-ha-ha. I don't remember her complaining."

"You were doing what you had to do. Now I'm doing what I have to do."

"What you're doing is really ugly, though. I'm sorry, but it's kind of hideous. Just—horrible and hideous. Honestly. As a matter of pure fact. Not that that's really the issue. The issue is the Skilsaw."

"You're on private property and you need to leave now."

"OK, so I guess I'll be calling the cops."

"That's fine, go ahead."

You could see her pacing in the alley then, trembling with frustration. She did repeatedly call the police about the noise, and a few times they actually came and had a word with Blake, but they soon got tired of hearing from her and did not come back until the following February, when somebody slashed all four of the beautiful new snow tires on Blake's F-250 and Blake and Carol directed officers to the next-door neighbor who'd been phoning in so many complaints. This resulted in Patty again going up and down the street, knocking on doors, ranting. "The obvious suspect, right? The mom next door with a couple of teenage kids. Hard-core criminal me, right? Lunatic me! He's got the biggest, ugliest vehicle on the street, he's got bumper stickers that offend pretty much anybody who's not a white supremacist, but, God, what a mystery, who else but me could want to slash his tires?"

Merrie Paulsen was convinced that Patty was, in fact, the slasher.

"I don't see it," Seth said. "I mean, she's obviously suffering, but she's not a liar."

"Right, except I didn't actually notice her saying she didn't do it. You have to hope she's getting good therapy somewhere. She sure could use it. That and a full-time job."

"My question is, where is Walter?"

"Walter is killing himself earning his salary so she can stay home all day and be a mad housewife. He's being a good dad to Jessica and some sort of reality principle to Joey. I'd say he has his hands full."

Walter's most salient quality, besides his love of Patty, was his nice-ness. He was the sort of good listener who seemed to find everybody else more interesting and impressive than himself. He was preposterously fair-skinned, weak in the chin, cherubically curly up top, and had worn the same round wireframes forever. He'd begun his career at 3M as an at-torney in the counsel's office, but he'd failed to thrive there and was shunted into outreach and philanthropy, a corporate cul-de-sac where niceness was an asset. On Barrier Street he was always handing out great free tickets to the Guthrie and the Chamber Orchestra and telling neigh-bors about encounters he'd had with famous locals such as Garrison Keil-lor and Kirby Puckett and, once, Prince. More recently, and surprisingly, he'd left 3M altogether and become a development officer for the Nature Conservancy. Nobody except the Paulsens had suspected him of harbor-ing such reserves of discontent, but Walter was no less enthusiastic about nature than he was about culture, and the only outward change in his life was his new scarcity at home on weekends.

This scarcity may have been one reason he didn't intervene, as he might have been expected to, in Patty's battle with Carol Monaghan. His response, if you asked him point-blank about it, was to giggle nervously. "I'm kind of a neutral bystander on that one," he said. And a neutral by-stander he remained all through the spring and summer of Joey's sopho-more year and into the following fall, when Jessica went off to college in the East and Joey moved out of his parents' house and in with Carol, Blake, and Connie.

The move was a stunning act of sedition and a dagger to Patty's heart—the beginning of the end of her life in Ramsey Hill. Joey had spent July and August in Montana, working on the high-country ranch of one of Walter's major Nature Conservancy donors, and had returned with broad, manly shoulders and two new inches of height. Walter, who didn't ordinarily brag, had vouchsafed to the Paulsens, at a picnic in August, that the donor had called him up to say how "blown away" he was by Joey's fearlessness and tirelessness in throwing calves and dipping sheep. Patty, however, at the same picnic, was already vacant-eyed with pain. In June, before Joey went to Montana, she'd again taken him up to Nameless Lake to help her improve the property, and the only neighbor who'd seen them there described a terrible afternoon of watching mother and son lacerate each other over and over, airing it all in plain sight, Joey mocking Patty's mannerisms and finally calling her "stupid" to her face, at which Patty had cried out, "Ha-ha-ha! Stupid! God, Joey! Your maturity just never ceases to amaze me! Calling your mother stupid in front of other people! That's just so attractive in a person! What a big, tough, independent man you are!"

By summer's end, Blake had nearly finished work on the great-room and was outfitting it with such Blakean gear as PlayStation, Foosball, a refrigerated beer keg, a large-screen TV, an air-hockey table, a stained-glass Vikings chandelier, and mechanized recliners. Neighbors were left to imagine Patty's dinner-table sarcasm regarding these amenities, and Joey's declarations that she was being stupid and unfair, and Walter's angry demands that Joey apologize to Patty, but the night when Joey defected to the house next door didn't need to be imagined, because Carol Monaghan was happy to describe it, in a loud and somewhat gloating voice, to any neighbor sufficiently disloyal to the Berglunds to listen to her.

"Joey was *so* calm, *so* calm," Carol said. "I swear to God, you couldn't melt butter in his mouth. I went over there with Connie to support him and let everybody know I'm totally in favor of the arrangement, because, you know Walter, he's so considerate, he's going to worry it's an imposition on me. And Joey was totally responsible like always. He just wanted to be on the same page and make sure all the cards are on the table. He explained how he and Connie had discussed things with me, and I told Walter—because I knew he'd be concerned about this—I told him groceries were not a problem. Blake and I are a family now and we're happy to feed one more, and Joey's also very good about the dishes and garbage and being neat, and plus, I told Walter, he and Patty used to be so generous to Connie and give her meals and all. I wanted to acknowledge that, because they really were generous when I didn't have my life together, and I've never been anything but grateful for that. And Joey's just so responsible and calm. He explains how, since Patty won't even let Connie in the house, he really doesn't have any other choice if he wants to spend time with her, and I chime in and say how totally in support of the relationship I am—if only all the other young people in this world were as responsible as those two, the world would be a much better place—and how much more preferable it is for them to be in my house, safe and responsible, instead of sneaking around and getting in trouble. I'm so grateful to Joey, he'll always be welcome in my house. I said that to them. And I know Patty doesn't like me, she's always looked down her nose at me and been snooty about Connie. I know that. I know a thing or two about the things Patty's capable of. I knew she was going to throw some kind of fit. And so her face gets all twisted, and she's like, 'You think he *loves* your daughter? You think he's *in love* with her?' In this high little voice. Like it's impossible for somebody like Joey to be in love with Connie, because I didn't go to college or whatever, or I don't have as big a house or come from New York City or whatever, or I have to work an honest-to-Christ forty-hour full-time job, unlike her. Patty's so full of disrespect for me, you can't believe it. But Walter I thought I could talk to. He really is a sweetie. His face is beet red, I think because he's embarrassed, and he says, 'Carol, you and Connie need to leave so we can talk to Joey privately.' Which I'm fine with. I'm not there to make trouble, I'm not a troublemaking person. Except then Joey says no. He says he's not asking permission, he's just informing them about what he's going to do, and there's nothing to discuss. And that's when Walter loses it. Just loses it. He's got tears running down his face he's so upset—and I can understand that, because Joey's his youngest, and it's not Walter's fault Patty is so unreasonable and mean to Connie that Joey can't stand to live with them anymore. But he starts yelling at the top of his lungs, like, YOU ARE SIXTEEN YEARS OLD AND YOU ARE NOT GOING ANYWHERE UNTIL YOU FINISH HIGH SCHOOL. And Joey's just smiling at him, you couldn't melt butter in his mouth. Joey says it's not against the law for him to leave, and anyway he's only moving next door. Totally reasonable. I wish I'd been one percent as smart and cool when I was sixteen. I mean, he's just a great kid. It made me feel kind of bad for Walter, because he starts yelling all this stuff about how he's not going to pay for Joey's college, and Joey's not going to get to go back to Montana next summer, and all he's asking is that Joey come to dinner and sleep in his own bed and be a part of the family. And Joey's like, 'I'm still part of the family,' which, by the way, he never said he wasn't. But Walter's stomping around the kitchen, for a couple of seconds I think he's actually going to hit him, but he's just totally lost it, he's yelling, GET OUT, GET OUT, I'M SICK OF IT, GET OUT, and then he's gone and you can hear him upstairs in Joey's room, opening up

Joey's drawers or whatever, and Patty runs upstairs and they start scream- ing at each other, and Connie and I are hugging Joey, because he's the one reasonable person in the family and we feel so sorry for him, and that's when I know for sure it's the right thing for him to move in with us. Walter comes stomping downstairs again and we can hear Patty screaming like a maniac—she's totally lost it—and Walter starts yelling again, DO YOU SEE WHAT YOU'RE DOING TO YOUR MOTHER? Because it's all about Patty, see, she's always got to be the victim. And Joey's just standing there shaking his head, because it's so obvious. Why would he want to live in a place like this?"

Although some neighbors did undoubtedly take satisfaction in Patty's reaping the whirlwind of her son's extraordinariness, the fact remained that Carol Monaghan had never been well liked on Barrier Street, Blake was widely deplored, Connie was thought spooky, and nobody had ever really trusted Joey. As word of his insurrection spread, the emotions pre- vailing among the Ramsey Hill gentry were pity for Walter, anxiety about Patty's psychological health, and an overwhelming sense of relief and gratitude at how normal their own children were—how happy to accept parental largesse, how innocently demanding of help with their home- work or their college applications, how compliant in phoning in their af- terschool whereabouts, how divulging of their little day-to-day bruisings, how reassuringly predictable in their run-ins with sex and pot and al- cohol. The ache emanating from the Berglunds' house was sui generis. Walter—unaware, you had to hope, of Carol's blabbing about his night of "losing it"—acknowledged awkwardly to various neighbors that he and Patty had been "fired" as parents and were doing their best not to take it too personally. "He comes over to study sometimes," Walter said, "but right now he seems more comfortable spending his nights at Carol's. We'll see how long that lasts."

"How's Patty taking all this?" Seth Paulsen asked him.

"Not well."

"We'd love to get you guys over for dinner some night soon."

"That would be great," Walter said, "but I think Patty's going up to my mom's old house for a while. She's been fixing it up, you know."

"I'm worried about her," Seth said with a catch in his voice.

"So am I, a little bit. I've seen her play in pain, though. She tore up her knee in her junior year and tried to play another two games on it."

"But then didn't she have, um, career-ending surgery?"

"It was more a point about her toughness, Seth. About her playing through pain."

"Right."

Walter and Patty never did get over to the Paulsens for dinner. Patty was absent from Barrier Street, hiding out at Nameless Lake, for long stretches of the winter and spring that followed, and even when her car was in the driveway—for example, at Christmastime, when Jessica returned from college and, according to her friends, had a "blow-out fight" with Joey which resulted in his spending more than a week in his old bedroom, giving his formidable sister the proper holiday she wanted—Patty eschewed the neighborhood get-togethers at which her baked goods and affability had once been such welcome fixtures. She was sometimes seen receiving visits from fortyish women who, based on their hairstyles and the bumper stickers on their Subarus, were thought to be old basketball teammates of hers, and there was talk about her drinking again, but this was mostly just a guess, since, for all her friendliness, she had never made an actual close friend in Ramsey Hill.

By New Year's, Joey was back at Carol and Blake's. A large part of that house's allure was presumed to be the bed he shared with Connie. He was known by his friends to be bizarrely and militantly opposed to masturbation, the mere mention of which never failed to elicit a condescending smile from him; he claimed it was an ambition of his to go through life without resorting to it. More perspicacious neighbors, the Paulsens among them, suspected that Joey also enjoyed being the smartest person in the house. He became the prince of the great-room, opening its pleasures to everyone he favored with his friendship (and making the unsupervised beer keg a bone of contention at family dinners all over the neighborhood). His manner with Carol verged unsettlingly close to flirtation, and Blake he charmed by loving all the things that Blake himself loved, especially Blake's power tools and Blake's truck, at the wheel of which he learned how to drive. From the annoying way he smiled at his schoolmates' enthusiasm for Al Gore and Senator Wellstone, as if liberalism were a weakness on a par with self-abuse, it seemed he'd even embraced some of Blake's politics. He worked construction the next summer instead of returning to Montana.

And everybody had the sense, fairly or not, that Walter—his niceness—was somehow to blame. Instead of dragging Joey home by the hair and making him behave himself, instead of knocking Patty over the head with a rock and making her behave herself, he disappeared into his work with the Nature Conservancy, where he'd rather quickly become the state chapter's executive director, and let the house stand empty evening after evening, let the flower beds go to seed and the hedges go unclipped and the windows go unwashed, let the dirty urban snow engulf the warped GORE LIEBERMAN sign still stuck in the front yard. Even the Paulsens lost interest in the Berglunds, now that Merrie was running for city council. Patty spent all of the following summer away at Nameless Lake, and soon after her return—a month after Joey went off to the University of Virginia under financial circumstances that were unknown on Ramsey Hill, and two weeks after the great national tragedy—a FOR SALE sign went up in front of the Victorian into which she and Walter had poured fully half their lives. Walter had already begun commuting to a new job in Washington. Though housing prices would soon be rebounding to unprecedented heights, the local market was still near the bottom of its post-9/11 slump. Patty oversaw the sale of the house, at an unhappy price, to an earnest black professional couple with twin three-year-olds. In February, the two Berglunds went door to door along the street one final time, taking leave with polite formality, Walter asking after everybody's children and conveying his very best wishes for each of them, Patty saying little but looking strangely youthful again, like the girl who'd pushed her stroller down the street before the neighborhood was even a neighborhood.

"It's a wonder," Seth Paulsen remarked to Merrie afterward, "that the two of them are even still together."

Merrie shook her head. "I don't think they've figured out yet how to live."

# MISTAKES WERE MADE
Autobiography of Patty Berglund
by Patty Berglund
(Composed at Her Therapist's Suggestion)

# Chapter 1: Agreeable

If Patty weren't an atheist, she would thank the good Lord for school athletic programs, because they basically saved her life and gave her a chance to realize herself as a person. She is especially grateful to Sandra Mosher at North Chappaqua Middle School, Elaine Carver and Jane Nagel at Horace Greeley High School, Ernie and Rose Salvatore at the Gettysburg Girls Basketball Camp, and Irene Treadwell at the University of Minnesota. It was from these wonderful coaches that Patty learned discipline, patience, focus, teamwork, and the ideals of good sportsmanship that helped make up for her morbid competitiveness and low self-esteem.

Patty grew up in Westchester County, New York. She was the oldest of four children, the other three of whom were more like what her parents had been hoping for. She was notably Larger than everybody else, also Less Unusual, also measurably Dumber. Not actually dumb but relatively dumber. She grew up to be 5'9½" which was almost the same as her brother and numerous inches taller than the others, and sometimes she wished she could have gone ahead and been six feet, since she was never going to fit into the family anyway. Being able to see the basket better and to post up in traffic and to rotate more freely on defense might have rendered her competitive streak somewhat less vicious, leading to a happier life post-college; probably not, but it was interesting to think about. By the time she got to the collegiate level, she was usually one of the shorter players on the floor, which in a funny way reminded her of her position in her family and helped keep adrenaline at peak levels.

Patty's first memory of doing a team sport with her mother watching is also one of her last. She was attending ordinary-person Sports day camp at the same complex where her two sisters were doing extraordinary-person Arts day camp, and one day her mother and sisters showed up for the late innings of a softball game. Patty was frustrated to be standing in left field while less skilled girls made errors in the infield and she waited around for somebody to hit a ball deep. She started creeping in shallower and shallower, which was how the game ended. Runners on first and second. The batter hit a bouncing ball to the grossly uncoordinated short-stop, whom Patty ran in front of so she could field the ball herself and run and tag out the lead runner and then start chasing the other runner, some sweet girl who'd probably reached first on a fielding error. Patty bore down straight at her, and the girl ran squealing into the outfield, leaving the base path for an automatic out, but Patty kept chasing her and applied the tag while the girl crumpled up and screamed with the apparently horrible pain of being lightly touched by a glove.

Patty was aware that it was not her finest hour of sportsmanship. Something had come over her because her family was watching. In the family station wagon, in an even more quavering voice than usual, her mother asked her if she had to be quite so . . . *aggressive.* If it was necessary to be, well, to be so *aggressive.* Would it have hurt Patty to share the ball a little with her teammates? Patty replied that she hadn't been getting ANY balls in left field. And her mother said: "I don't mind if you play sports, but only if it's going to teach you cooperation and community-mindedness." And Patty said, "So send me to a REAL camp where I won't be the only good player! I can't cooperate with people who can't catch the ball!" And her mother said: "I'm not sure it's a good idea to be encouraging so much aggression and competition. I guess I'm not a sports fan, but I don't see the fun in defeating a person just for the sake of defeating them. Wouldn't it be much more fun to all work together to cooperatively build something?"

Patty's mother was a professional Democrat. She is even now, at the time of this writing, a state assemblywoman, the Honorable Joyce Emerson, known for her advocacy of open space, poor children, and the Arts.

Paradise for Joyce is an open space where poor children can go and do Arts at state expense. Joyce was born Joyce Markowitz in Brooklyn in 1934 but apparently disliked being Jewish from the earliest dawn of consciousness. (The autobiographer wonders if one reason why Joyce's voice always trembles is from struggling so hard all her life to not sound like Brooklyn.) Joyce got a scholarship to study liberal Arts in the woods of Maine where she met Patty's exceedingly Gentile dad whom she married at All Souls Unitarian Universalist Church on the Upper East Side of Manhattan. In the autobiographer's opinion, Joyce had her first baby before she was emotionally prepared for motherhood, although the autobiographer herself perhaps ought not to cast stones in this regard. When Jack Kennedy got the Democratic nomination, in 1960, it gave Joyce a noble and stirring excuse to get out of a house that she couldn't seem to help filling up with babies. Then came civil rights, and Vietnam, and Bobby Kennedy—more good reasons to be out of a house that wasn't nearly big enough for four little kids plus a Barbadian nanny in the basement. Joyce went to her first national convention in 1968 as a delegate committed to dead Bobby. She served as county party treasurer and later chairman and organized for Teddy in 1972 and 1980. Every summer, all day long, herds of volunteers tramped in and out through the house's open doors carrying boxes of campaign gear. Patty could practice dribbling and layups for six hours straight without anybody noticing or caring.

Patty's father, Ray Emerson, was a lawyer and amateur humorist whose repertory included fart jokes and mean parodies of his children's teachers, neighbors, and friends. A torment he particularly enjoyed inflicting on Patty was mimicking the Barbadian, Eulalie, when she was just out of earshot, saying, "Stop de game now, stop de playin," etc., in a louder and louder voice until Patty ran from the dinner table in mortification and her siblings shrieked with excitement. Endless fun could also be had ridiculing Patty's coach and mentor Sandy Mosher, whom Ray liked to call Saaaandra. He was constantly asking Patty whether Saaaandra had had any gentlemen callers lately or maybe, tee hee, tee hee, some *gentlelady* callers? Her siblings chorused: Saaaandra, Saaaandra! Other amusing methods of tormenting Patty were to hide the family dog, Elmo, and pretend that Elmo had been euthanized while Patty was at late basketball practice. Or tease Patty about certain factual errors she'd made many years earlier—ask her how the kangaroos in *Austria* were doing, and whether she'd seen the latest novel by the famous contemporary writer Louisa May Alcott, and whether she still thought funguses were part of the animal kingdom. "I saw one of Patty's funguses chasing a truck the other day," her father would say. "Look, look at me, this is how Patty's fungus chases a truck."

Most nights her dad left the house again after dinner to meet with poor people he was defending in court for little or no money. He had an office across the street from the courthouse in White Plains. His free clients included Puerto Ricans, Haitians, Transvestites, and the mentally or physically Disabled. Some of them were in such bad trouble he didn't even make fun of them behind their backs. As much as possible, though, he found their troubles amusing. In tenth grade, for a school project, Patty sat in on two trials that her dad was part of. One was a case against an unemployed Yonkers man who drank too much on Puerto Rican Day, went looking for his wife's brother, intending to cut him with a knife, but couldn't find him and instead cut up a stranger in a bar. Not just her dad but the judge and even the prosecutor seemed amused by the defendant's haplessness and stupidity. They kept exchanging little not-quite-winks. As if misery and disfigurement and jail time were all just a lower-class sideshow designed to perk up their otherwise boring day.

On the train ride home, Patty asked her dad whose side he was on.

"Ha, good question," he answered. "You have to understand, my client is a liar. The victim is a liar. And the bar owner is a liar. They're all liars. Of course, my client is entitled to a vigorous defense. But you have to try to serve justice, too. Sometimes the P.A. and the judge and I are working together as much as the P.A. is working with the victim or I'm working with the defendant. You've heard of our adversarial system of justice?"

"Yes."

"Well. Sometimes the P.A. and the judge and I all have the same adversary. We try to sort out the facts and avoid a miscarriage. Although don't, uh. Don't put that in your paper."

"I thought sorting out facts was what the grand jury and the jury are for."

"That's right. Put that in your paper. Trial by a jury of your peers. That's important."

"But most of your clients are innocent, right?"

"Not many of them deserve as bad a punishment as somebody's trying to give them."

"But a lot of them are completely innocent, right? Mommy says they have trouble with the language, or the police aren't careful about who they arrest, and there's prejudice against them, and lack of opportunity."

"All of that is entirely true, Pattycakes. Nevertheless, uh. Your mother can be somewhat dewy-eyed."

Patty minded his ridiculing less when her mother was the butt of it.

"I mean, you saw those people," he said to her. "Jesus Christ. El ron me puso loco."

An important fact about Ray's family was that it had a lot of money. His mom and dad lived on a big ancestral estate out in the hills of northwest New Jersey, in a pretty stone Modernist house that was supposedly designed by Frank Lloyd Wright and was hung with minor works by famous French Impressionists. Every summer, the entire Emerson clan gathered by the lake at the estate for holiday picnics which Patty mostly failed to enjoy. Her granddad, August, liked to grab his oldest granddaughter around the belly and sit her down on his bouncing thigh and get God only knows what kind of little thrill from this; he was certainly not very respectful of Patty's physical boundaries. Starting in seventh grade, she also had to play doubles with Ray and his junior partner and the partner's wife, on the grandparental clay tennis court, and be stared at by the junior partner, in her exposing tennis clothes, and feel self-conscious and confused by his ocular pawing.

Like Ray himself, her granddad had bought the right to be privately eccentric by doing good public legal works; he'd made a name for himself defending high-profile conscientious objectors and draft evaders in three wars. In his spare time, which he had much of, he grew grapes on his property and fermented them in one of his outbuildings. His "winery" was called Doe Haunch and was a major family joke. At the holiday picnics, August tottered around in flipflops and saggy swim trunks, clutching one of his crudely labeled bottles, refilling the glasses that his guests had discreetly emptied into grass or bushes. "What do you think?" he asked. "Is it good wine? Do you like it?" He was sort of like an eager boy hobbyist and sort of like a torturer intent on punishing every victim equally. Citing

European custom, August believed in giving children wine, and when the young mothers were distracted with corn to shuck or competitive salads to adorn, he watered his Doe Haunch Reserve and pressed it on kids as young as three, gently holding their chins, if necessary, and pouring the mixture into their mouths, making sure it went down. "You know what that is?" he said. "That's wine." If a child then began to act strangely, he said: "What you're feeling is called being drunk. You drank too much. You're drunk." This with a disgust no less sincere for being friendly. Patty, always the oldest of the kids, observed these scenes with silent horror, leaving it to a younger sibling or cousin to sound the alarm: "Grand-daddy's getting the little kids drunk!" While the mothers came running to scold August and snatch their kids away, and the fathers tittered dirtily about August's obsession with female deer hindquarters, Patty slipped into the lake and floated in its warmest shallows, letting the water stop her ears against her family.

Because here was the thing: at every picnic, back up in the kitchen of the stone house, there was always a bottle or two of fabulous old Bordeaux from August's storied cellar. This wine was put out at Patty's father's insistence, at unknown personal cost of wheedling and begging, and it was always Ray who gave the signal, the subtle nod, to his brothers and to any male friend he'd brought along, to slip away from the picnic and follow him. The men returned a few minutes later with big bubble-bowled glasses filled to the brim with an amazing red, Ray also carrying a French bottle with maybe one inch of wine left in it, to be divided among all the wives and other less favored visitors. No amount of pleading could induce August to fetch another bottle from his cellar; he offered, instead, more Doe Haunch Reserve.

And it was the same every year at Christmastime: the grandparents driving over from New Jersey in their late-model Mercedes (August traded in his old one every year or two), arriving at Ray and Joyce's overcrowded ranch house an hour before the hour that Joyce had implored them not to arrive before, and distributing insulting gifts. Joyce famously, one year, received two much-used dish towels. Ray typically got one of those big art books from the Barnes & Noble bargain table, sometimes with a $3.99 sticker still on it. The kids got little pieces of plastic Asian-made crap: tiny travel alarm clocks that didn't work, coin purses stamped with the name of a New Jersey insurance agency, frightening crude Chinese finger puppets, assorted swizzle sticks. Meanwhile, at August's alma mater, a library with his name on it was being built. Because Patty's siblings were outraged by the grandparental tightfistedness and compensated by making outrageous demands for parental Christmas booty—Joyce was up until 3 a.m. every Christmas Eve, wrapping presents selected from their endless and highly detailed Christmas lists—Patty went the other way and decided not to care about anything but sports.

Her granddad had once been a true athlete, a college track star and football tight end, which was probably where her height and reflexes came from. Ray also had played football but in Maine for a school that could barely field a team. His real game was tennis, which was the one sport Patty hated, although she was good at it. She believed that Björn Borg was secretly weak. With very few exceptions (e.g., Joe Namath) she wasn't impressed with male athletes in general. Her specialty was crushes on popular boys enough older or better-looking to be totally unrealistic choices. Being a very agreeable person, however, she went on dates with practically anybody who asked. She thought shy or unpopular boys had a hard life, and she took pity on them insofar as humanly possible. For some reason, many were wrestlers. In her experience, wrestlers were brave, taciturn, geeky, beetle-browed, polite, and not afraid of female jocks. One of them confided to her that in middle school she'd been known to him and his friends as the She-Monkey.

As far as actual sex goes, Patty's first experience of it was being raped at a party when she was seventeen by a boarding-school senior named Ethan Post. Ethan didn't do any sports except golf, but he had six inches of height and fifty pounds on Patty and provided discouraging perspectives on female muscle strength as compared to men's. What he did to Patty didn't strike her as a gray-area sort of rape. When she started fighting, she fought hard, if not too well, and only for so long, because she was drunk for one of the first times ever. She'd been feeling so wonderfully free! Very probably, in the vast swimming pool at Kim McClusky's, on a beautiful warm May night, Patty had given Ethan Post a mistaken impression. She was far too agreeable even when she wasn't drunk. In the pool, she must have been giddy with agreeability. Altogether, there was much to blame herself for. Her notions of romance were like Gilligan's Island:

"as primitive as can be." They fell somewhere between Snow White and Nancy Drew. And Ethan undeniably had the arrogant look that attracted her at that point in time. He resembled the love interest from a girls' novel with sailboats on the cover. After he raped Patty, he said he was sorry "it" had been rougher than he'd meant "it" to be, he was sorry about that.

It was only after the piña coladas wore off, early the next morning, in the bedroom which, being such an agreeable person, Patty shared with her littler sister so that their middle sister could have her own room to be Creative and messy in: only then did she get indignant. The indignity was that Ethan had considered her such a nothing that he could just rape her and then take her home. And she was *not* such a nothing. She was, among other things, already, as a junior, the all-time single-season record holder for assists at Horace Greeley High School. A record she would again demolish the following year! She was also first-team All State in a state that *included Brooklyn and the Bronx.* And yet a golfing boy she hardly even knew had thought it was OK to rape her.

To avoid waking her little sister, she went and cried in the shower. This was, without exaggeration, the most wretched hour of her life. Even today, when she thinks of people who are oppressed around the world and victims of injustice, and how they must feel, her mind goes back to that hour. Things that had never occurred to her before, such as the injustice of an oldest daughter having to share a room and not being given Eulalie's old room in the basement because it was now filled floor to ceiling with outdated campaign paraphernalia, also the injustice of her mother being so enthralled about the middle daughter's thespian performances but never going to any of Patty's games, occurred to her now. She was so indignant she almost felt like talking to somebody. But she was afraid to let her coach or teammates know she'd been drinking.

How the story came out, in spite of her best efforts to keep it buried, was that Coach Nagel got suspicious and spied on her in the locker room after the next day's game. Sat Patty down in her office and confronted her regarding her bruises and unhappy demeanor. Patty humiliated herself by immediately and sobbingly confessing to all. To her total shock, Coach then proposed taking her to the hospital and notifying the police. Patty had just gone three-for-four with two runs scored and several outstanding defensive plays. She obviously wasn't greatly harmed. Also, her parents were political friends of Ethan's parents, so that was a nonstarter. She dared to hope that an abject apology for breaking training, combined with Coach's pity and leniency, would put the matter to rest. But oh how wrong she was.

Coach called Patty's house and got Patty's mother, who, as always, was breathless and running out to a meeting and had neither time to talk nor yet the moral wherewithal to admit that she didn't have time to talk, and Coach spoke these indelible words into the P.E. Dept.'s beige telephone: "Your daughter just told me that she was raped last night by a boy named Ethan Post." Coach then listened to the phone for a minute before saying, "No, she just now told me . . . That's right . . . Just last night . . . Yes, she is." And handed Patty the telephone.

"Patty?" her mother said. "Are you—all right?"

"I'm fine."

"Mrs. Nagel says there was an incident last night?"

"The incident was I was raped."

"Oh dear, oh dear, oh dear. Last night?"

"Yes."

"I was home this morning. Why didn't you say something?"

"I don't know."

"Why, why, why? Why didn't you say something to me?"

"Maybe it just didn't seem like such a big deal right then."

"So but then you did tell Mrs. Nagel."

"No," Patty said. "She's just more observant than you are."

"I hardly saw you this morning."

"I'm not blaming you. I'm just saying."

"And you think you might have been . . . It might have been . . ."

"Raped."

"I can't believe this," her mother said. "I'm going to come and get you."

"Coach Nagel wants me to go to the hospital."

"Are you not all right?"

"I already said. I'm fine."

"Then just stay put, and don't either of you do anything until I get there."

Patty hung up the phone and told Coach that her mother was coming.

"We're going to put that boy in jail for a long, long time," Coach said.

"Oh no no no no no," Patty said. "No, we're not."

"Patty."

"It's just not going to happen."

"It will if you want it to."

"No, actually, it won't. My parents and the Posts are political friends."

"Listen to me," Coach said. "That has nothing to do with anything. Do you understand?"

Patty was quite certain that Coach was wrong about this. Dr. Post was a cardiologist and his wife was from big money. They had one of the houses that people such as Teddy Kennedy and Ed Muskie and Walter Mondale made visits to when they were short of funds. Over the years, Patty had heard much tell of the Posts' "back yard" from her parents. This "back yard" was apparently about the size of Central Park but nicer. Conceivably one of Patty's straight-A, grade-skipping, Arts-doing sisters could have brought trouble down on the Posts, but it was absurd to imagine the hulking B-student family jock making a dent in the Posts' armor.

"I'm just never going to drink again," she said, "and that will solve the problem."

"Maybe for you," Coach said, "but not for somebody else. Look at your arms. Look what he did. He'll do that to somebody else if you don't stop him."

"It's just bruises and scratches."

Coach here made a motivational speech about standing up for your teammates, which in this case meant all the young women Ethan might ever meet. The upshot was that Patty was supposed to take a hard foul for the team and press charges and let Coach inform the New Hampshire prep school where Ethan was a student, so he could be expelled and denied a diploma, and that if Patty didn't do this she would be letting down her team.

Patty began to cry again, because she would almost rather have died than let a team down. Earlier in the winter, with the flu, she'd played most of a half of basketball before fainting on the sideline and getting fluids intravenously. The problem now was that she hadn't been with her own team the night before. She'd gone to the party with her field-hockey friend Amanda, whose soul was apparently never going to be at rest until she'd induced Patty to sample piña coladas, vast buckets of which had been promised at the McCluskys'. El ron me puso loca. None of the other girls at the McCluskys' swimming pool were jocks. Almost just by showing up there, Patty had betrayed her real true team. And now she'd been punished for it. Ethan hadn't raped one of the fast girls, he'd raped Patty, because she didn't belong there, she didn't even know how to drink.

She promised Coach to give the matter some thought.

It was shocking to see her mother in the gym and obviously shocking to her mother to find herself there. She was wearing her everyday pumps and resembled Goldilocks in daunting woods as she peered around uncertainly at the naked metal equipment and the fungal floors and the clustered balls in mesh bags. Patty went to her and submitted to embrace. Her mother being much smaller of frame, Patty felt somewhat like a grandfather clock that Joyce was endeavoring to lift and move. She broke away and led Joyce into Coach's little glass-walled office so that the necessary conference could be had.

"Hi, I'm Jane Nagel," Coach said.

"Yes, we've—met," Joyce said.

"Oh, you're right, we did meet once," Coach said.

In addition to her strenuous elocution, Joyce had strenuously proper posture and a masklike Pleasant Smile suitable for nearly all occasions public and private. Because she never raised her voice, not even in anger (her voice just got shakier and more strained when she was mad), her Pleasant Smile could be worn even at moments of excruciating conflict.

"No, it was more than once," she said now. "It was several times."

"Really?"

"I'm quite sure of it."

"That doesn't sound right to me," Coach said.

"I'll be outside," Patty said, closing the door behind her.

The parent-coach conference didn't last long. Joyce soon came out on clicking heels and said, "Let's go."

Coach, standing in the doorway behind Joyce, gave Patty a significant look. The look meant *Don't forget what I said about teamwork.*

Joyce's car was the last one left in its quadrant of the visitor lot. She put the key in the ignition but didn't turn it. Patty asked what was going to happen now.

"Your father's at his office," Joyce said. "We'll go straight there."

But she didn't turn the key.

"I'm sorry about this," Patty said.

"What I don't understand," her mother burst out, "is how such an outstanding athlete as you are—I mean, how could Ethan, or whoever it was—"

"Ethan. It was Ethan."

"How could anybody—or Ethan," she said. "You say it's pretty definitely Ethan. How could—if it's Ethan—how could he have . . . ?" Her mother hid her mouth with her fingers. "Oh, I wish it had been almost anybody else. Dr. and Mrs. Post are such good friends of—good friends of so many good things. And I don't know Ethan well, but—"

"I hardly know him at all!"

"Well then how could this happen!"

"Let's just go home."

"No. You have to tell me. I'm your mother."

Hearing herself say this, Joyce looked embarrassed. She seemed to realize how peculiar it was to have to remind Patty who her mother was. And Patty, for one, was glad to finally have this doubt out in the open. If Joyce was her mother, then how had it happened that she hadn't come to the first round of the state tournament when Patty had broken the all-time Horace Greeley girls' tournament scoring record with 32 points? Somehow everybody else's mother had found time to come to that game.

She showed Joyce her wrists.

"*This* is what happened," she said. "I mean, part of what happened."

Joyce looked once at her bruises, shuddered, and then turned away as if respecting Patty's privacy. "This is terrible," she said. "You're right. This is terrible."

"Coach Nagel says I should go to the emergency room and tell the police and tell Ethan's headmaster."

"Yes, I know what your coach wants. She seems to feel that castration might be an appropriate punishment. What I want to know is what *you* think."

"I don't know what I think."

"If you want to go to the police now," Joyce said, "we'll go to the police. Just tell me if that's what you want."

"I guess we should tell Dad first."

So down the Saw Mill Parkway they went. Joyce was always driving Patty's siblings to Painting, Guitar, Ballet, Japanese, Debate, Drama, Piano, Fencing, and Mock Court, but Patty herself seldom rode with Joyce anymore. Most weekdays, she came home very late on the jock bus. If she had a game, somebody else's mom or dad dropped her off. If she and her friends were ever stranded, she knew not to bother calling her parents but to go ahead and use the Westchester Cab dispatcher's number and one of the twenty-dollar bills that her mother made her always carry. It never occurred to her to use the twenties for anything but cabs, or to go anywhere after a game except straight home, where she peeled aluminum foil off her dinner at ten or eleven o'clock and went down to the basement to wash her uniform while she ate and watched reruns. She often fell asleep down there.

"Here's a hypothetical question," Joyce said, driving. "Do you think it might be enough if Ethan formally apologized to you?"

"He already apologized."

"For—"

"For being rough."

"And what did you say?"

"I didn't say anything. I said I wanted to go home."

"But he did apologize for being rough."

"It wasn't a real apology."

"All right. I'll take your word for it."

"I just want him to know I *exist*."

"Whatever *you* want—sweetie."

Joyce pronounced this "sweetie" like the first word of a foreign language she was learning.

As a test or a punishment, Patty said: "Maybe, I guess, if he apologized in a really sincere way, that might be enough." And she looked carefully at her mother, who was struggling (it seemed to Patty) to contain her excitement.

"That sounds to me like a nearly ideal solution," Joyce said. "But only if you really think it would be enough for you."

"It wouldn't," Patty said.

"I'm sorry?"

"I said it wouldn't be enough."

"I thought you just said it would be."

Patty began to cry again very desolately.

"I'm sorry," Joyce said. "Did I misunderstand?"

"HE RAPED ME LIKE IT WAS NOTHING. I'M PROBABLY NOT EVEN THE FIRST."

"You don't know that, Patty."

"I want to go to the hospital."

"Look, here, we're almost at Daddy's office. Unless you're actually hurt, we might as well—"

"But I already know what he'll say. I know what he'll want me to do."

"He'll want to do whatever's best for you. Sometimes it's hard for him to express it, but he loves you more than anything."

Joyce could hardly have made a statement Patty more fervently longed to believe was true. Wished, with her whole being, was true. Didn't her dad tease her and ridicule her in ways that would have been simply cruel if he didn't secretly love her more than anything? But she was seventeen now and not actually dumb. She knew that you could love somebody more than anything and still not love the person all that much, if you were busy with other things.

There was a smell of mothballs in her father's inner sanctum, which he'd taken over from his now-deceased senior partner without redoing the carpeting and curtains. Where exactly the mothball smell came from was one of those mysteries.

"What a rotten little shit!" was Ray's response to the tidings his daughter and wife brought of Ethan Post's crime.

"Not so little, unfortunately," Joyce said with a dry laugh.

"He's a rotten little shit punk," Ray said. "He's a bad seed!"

"So do we go to the hospital now?" Patty said. "Or to the police?"

Her father told her mother to call Dr. Sipperstein, the old pediatrician, who'd been involved in Democratic politics since Roosevelt, and see if he was available for an emergency. While Joyce made this call, Ray asked Patty if she knew what rape was.

She stared at him.

"Just checking," he said. "You do know the actual legal definition."

"He had sex with me against my will."

"Did you actually say no?"

" 'No,' 'don't,' 'stop.' Anyway, it was obvious. I was trying to scratch him and push him off me."

"Then he is a despicable piece of shit."

She'd never heard her father talk this way, and she appreciated it, but only abstractly, because it didn't sound like him.

"Dave Sipperstein says he can meet us at five at his office," Joyce reported. "He's so fond of Patty, I think he would have canceled his dinner plans if he'd had to."

"Right," Patty said, "I'm sure I'm number one among his twelve thousand patients." She then told her dad her story, and her dad explained to her why Coach Nagel was wrong and she couldn't go to the police.

"Chester Post is not an easy person," Ray said, "but he does a lot of good in the county. Given his, uh, given his position, an accusation like this is going to generate extraordinary publicity. Everyone will know who the accuser is. Everyone. Now, what's bad for the Posts is not your concern. But it's virtually certain you'll end up feeling more violated by the pretrial and the trial and the publicity than you do right now. Even if it's pleaded out. Even with a suspended sentence, even with a gag order. There's still a court record."

Joyce said, "But this is all for *her* to decide, not—"

"Joyce." Ray stilled her with a raised hand. "The Posts can afford any lawyer in the country. And as soon as the accusation is made public, the worst of the damage to the defendant is over. He has no incentive to speed things along. In fact, it's to his advantage to see that your reputation suffers as much as possible before a plea or a trial."

Patty bowed her head and asked what her father thought she should do.

"I'm going to call Chester now," he said. "You go see Dr. Sipperstein and make sure you're OK."

"And get him as a witness," Patty said.

"Yes, and he could testify if need be. But there isn't going to be a trial, Patty."

"So he just gets away with it? And does it to somebody else next weekend?"

Ray raised both hands. "Let me, ah. Let me talk to Mr. Post. He might be amenable to a deferred prosecution. Kind of a quiet probation. Sword over Ethan's head."

"But that's *nothing*."

"Actually, Pattycakes, it's quite a lot. It'd be your guarantee that he won't do this to someone else. Requires an admission of guilt, too."

It did seem absurd to imagine Ethan wearing an orange jumpsuit and sitting in a jail cell for inflicting a harm that was mostly in her head anyway. She'd done wind sprints that hurt as bad as being raped. She felt more beaten up after a tough basketball game than she did now. Plus, as a jock, you got used to having other people's hands on you—kneading a cramped muscle, playing tight defense, scrambling for a loose ball, taping an ankle, correcting a stance, stretching a hamstring.

And yet: the feeling of injustice itself turned out to be strangely physical. Even realer, in a way, than her hurting, smelling, sweating body. Injustice had a shape, and a weight, and a temperature, and a texture, and a very bad taste.

In Dr. Sipperstein's office she submitted to examination like a good jock. After she'd put her clothes back on, he asked if she'd ever had intercourse before.

"No."

"I didn't think so. What about contraception? Did the other person use it?"

She nodded. "That's when I tried to get away. When I saw what he had."

"A condom."

"Yes."

All this and more Dr. Sipperstein jotted down on her chart. Then he took off his glasses and said, "You're going to have a good life, Patty. Sex is a great thing, and you'll enjoy it all your life. But this was not a good day, was it?"

At home, one of her siblings was in the back yard doing something like juggling with screwdrivers of different sizes. Another was reading Gibbon unabridged. The one who'd been subsisting on Yoplait and radishes was in the bathroom, changing her hair color again. Patty's true home amid all this brilliant eccentricity was a foam-cushioned, mildewed, built-in bench in the TV corner of the basement. The fragrance of Eulalie's hair oil still lingered on the bench years after Eulalie had been let go. Patty took a carton of butter-pecan ice cream down to the bench and answered no when her mother called down to ask if she was coming up for dinner.

Mary Tyler Moore was just starting when her father came down after his martini and his own dinner and suggested that he and Patty go for a drive. At that point in time, Mary Tyler Moore comprised the entirety of Patty's knowledge of Minnesota.

"Can I watch this show first?" she said.

"Patty."

Feeling cruelly deprived, she turned off the television. Her dad drove them over to the high school and stopped under a bright light in the parking lot. They unrolled their windows, letting in the smell of spring lawns like the one she'd been raped on not many hours earlier.

"So," she said.

"So Ethan denies it," her dad said. "He says it was just roughhousing and consensual."

The autobiographer would describe the girl's tears in the car as coming on like a rain that starts unnoticeably but surprisingly soon soaks everything. She asked if her dad had spoken to Ethan directly.

"No, just his father, twice," he said. "I'd be lying if I said the conversation went well."

"So obviously Mr. Post doesn't believe me."

"Well, Patty, Ethan's his son. He doesn't know you as well as we do."

"Do you believe me?"

"Yes, I do."

"Does Mommy?"

"Of course she does."

"Then what do I do?"

Her dad turned to her like an attorney. Like an adult addressing another adult. "You drop it," he said. "Forget about it. Move on."

"What?"

"You shake it off. Move on. Learn to be more careful."

"Like it never even happened?"

"Patty, the people at the party were all friends of his. They're going to say they saw you get drunk and be aggressive with him. They'll say you were behind a shed that wasn't more than thirty feet from the pool, and they didn't hear anything untoward."

"It was really noisy. There was music and shouting."

"They'll also say they saw the two of you leaving later in the evening and getting into his car. And the world will see an Exeter boy who's going to Princeton and was responsible enough to use contraceptives, and gentleman enough to leave the party and drive you home."

The deceptive little rain was wetting the collar of Patty's T-shirt.

"You're not really on my side, are you," she said.

"Of course I am."

"You keep saying 'Of course,' 'Of course.'"

"Listen to me. The P.A. is going to want to know why you didn't scream."

"I was embarrassed! Those weren't my friends!"

"But do you see that this is going to be hard for a judge or a jury to understand? All you would have had to do was scream, and you would have been safe."

Patty couldn't remember why she hadn't screamed. She had to admit that, in hindsight, it seemed bizarrely agreeable of her.

"I fought, though."

"Yes, but you're a top-tier student athlete. Shortstops get scratched and bruised all the time, don't they? On the arms? On the thighs?"

"Did you tell Mr. Post I'm a virgin? I mean, was?"

"I didn't consider that any of his business."

"Maybe you should call him back and tell him that."

"Look," her dad said. "Honey. I know it's horrendously unfair. I feel terrible for you. But sometimes the best thing is just to learn your lesson and make sure you never get in the same position again. To say to yourself, 'I made a mistake, and I had some bad luck,' and then let it. Let it, ah. Let it drop."

He turned the ignition halfway, so that the panel lights came on. He kept his hand on the key.

"But he committed a crime," Patty said.

"Yes, but better to, uh. Life's not always fair, Pattycakes. Mr. Post said he thought Ethan might be willing to apologize for not being more gentlemanly, but. Well. Would you like that?"

"No."

"I didn't think so."

"Coach Nagel says I should go to the police."

"Coach Nagel should stick to her dribbling," her dad said.

"Softball," Patty said. "It's softball season now."

"Unless you want to spend your entire senior year being publicly humiliated."

"Basketball is in the winter. Softball is in the spring, when the weather's warmer?"

"I'm asking you: is that really how you want to spend your senior year?"

"Coach Carver is basketball," Patty said. "Coach Nagel is softball. Are you getting this?"

Her dad started the engine.

As a senior, instead of being publicly humiliated, Patty became a real player, not just a talent. She all but resided in the field house. She got a three-game basketball suspension for putting a shoulder in the back of a New Rochelle forward who'd elbowed Patty's teammate Stephanie, and she still broke every school record she'd set the previous year, plus nearly broke the scoring record. Augmenting her reliable perimeter shooting was a growing taste for driving to the basket. She was no longer on speaking terms with physical pain.

In the spring, when the local state assemblyman stepped down after long service and the party leadership chose Patty's mother to run as his replacement, the Posts offered to co-host a fund-raiser in the green luxury of their back yard. Joyce sought Patty's permission before she accepted the offer, saying she wouldn't do anything that Patty wasn't comfortable with, but Patty was beyond caring what Joyce did, and told her so. When the candidate's family stood for the obligatory family photo, no grief was given to Patty for absenting herself. Her look of bitterness would not have helped Joyce's cause.

# Chapter 2: Best Friends

Based on her inability to recall her state of consciousness in her first three years at college, the autobiographer suspects she simply didn't have a state of consciousness. She had the sensation of being awake but in fact she must have been sleepwalking. Otherwise it's hard to understand how, to take one example, she became intense best friends with a disturbed girl who was basically her stalker.

Some of the fault—although the autobiographer hates to say it—may lie with Big Ten athletics and the artificial world it created for participating students, for boys especially, but also, even in the late 1970s, for girls. Patty went out to Minnesota in July for special jock summer camp followed by special, early, jocks-only freshman orientation, and then she lived in a jock dorm, made exclusively jock friends, ate exclusively at jock tables, cluster-danced at parties with her jock teammates, and was careful never to sign up for a class without plenty of other jocks to sit with and (time permitting) study with. Jocks didn't absolutely have to live this way, but the majority at Minnesota did, and Patty went even more overboard with Total Jockworld than most, because she could! Because she'd finally escaped from Westchester! "You should go *wherever you want*," Joyce had said to Patty, by which she'd meant: it is grotesque and repulsive to attend a mediocre state school like Minnesota when you have great offers from Vanderbilt and Northwestern (which are also more flattering to me).

"This is entirely *your* personal decision, and we will support you in *whatever you decide*," Joyce had said, by which she'd meant: don't blame me and Daddy when you ruin your life with stupid decisions. Joyce's transparent aversion to Minnesota, along with Minnesota's distance from New York, was a key factor in Patty's deciding to go there. Looking back now, the autobiographer sees her younger self as one of those miserable adolescents so angry at her parents that she needed to join a cult where she could be nicer and friendlier and more generous and subservient than she could bring herself to be at home anymore. Her cult just happened to be basketball.

The first of the nonjocks to lure her out of this cult and become important to her was the disturbed girl Eliza, who Patty, of course, initially had no idea was disturbed. Eliza was exactly half pretty. Her head started out gorgeous on top and got steadily worse-looking the lower down you looked. She had wonderfully thick and curly brown hair and amazing huge eyes, and then a cute enough little button nose, but then around her mouth her face got smooshed up and miniature in a disturbing sort of preemie way, and she had very little chin. She was always wearing baggy corduroys that slid down on her hips, and tight short-sleeved shirts that she bought in Boys departments at thrift stores and buttoned only the middle buttons of, and red Keds, and a big avocado-green shearling coat. She smelled like an ashtray but tried not to smoke around Patty unless they were outside. In an irony then invisible to Patty but now plenty visible to the autobiographer, Eliza had a lot in common with Patty's arty little sisters. She owned a black electric guitar and a dear small amp, but the few times Patty convinced her to play it in her presence Eliza became furious with her, which almost never happened otherwise (at least not at first). She said Patty was making her feel pressured and self-conscious and this was why she kept fucking up after only a few bars of her song. She ordered Patty to not be so obviously listening, but even when Patty turned away and pretended to read a magazine it wasn't good enough. Eliza swore that the minute Patty was out of the room again she'd be able to play her song perfectly. "But now? Forget it."

"I'm sorry," Patty said. "I'm sorry I do that to you."

"I can play this song amazingly when you're not listening."

"I know, I know. I'm sure you can."

"It's just a fact. It doesn't matter if you believe me."

"But I do believe you!"

"I'm *saying*," Eliza said, "it doesn't *matter* if you believe me, because my ability to play this song amazingly when you're not listening is simply an objective fact."

"Maybe try a different song," Patty pleaded.

But Eliza was already yanking the plugs out. "Stop. OK? I don't want your reassurance."

"Sorry, sorry, sorry," Patty said.

She'd first seen Eliza in the only class where a jock and a poet were likely to meet, Introductory Earth Science. Patty came and went to this particular huge class with ten other freshwomen jocks, a herd of girls mostly even taller than herself, all wearing maroon Golden Gopher track-suits or plain gray sweats, everybody's hair at various stages of damp. There were some smart girls in the herd, including the autobiographer's lifelong friend Cathy Schmidt who later became a public defender and was once nationally televised on *Jeopardy!* for two nights, but the over-heated lecture hall and those tracksuits and the damp hair and the near-ness of other tired jock bodies never failed to give Patty a contact dullness. A contact low.

Eliza liked to sit in the row behind the jocks, directly behind Patty but slouched down so deep in her seat that only her voluminous dark curls were visible. Her first words to Patty were spoken into her ear from be-hind, at the start of a class. She said, "You're the best."

Patty turned to see who was speaking and saw lots of hair. "I'm sorry?"

"I saw you play last night," the hair said. "You're brilliant and beautiful."

"Wow, thank you so much."

"They need to start giving you more minutes."

"Funnily enough, ha ha, I have the exact same opinion."

"You need to *demand* that they give you more minutes. OK?"

"Right, we've got so many great players on the team, though. It's not my decision."

"Yeah, but you're the best," the hair said.

"Wow, thank you so much for the compliment!" Patty answered brightly, to end things. At the time, she believed that it was because she was selflessly team-spirited that direct personal compliments made her so uncomfortable. The autobiographer now thinks that compliments were like a beverage she was unconsciously smart enough to deny herself even one drop of, because her thirst for them was infinite.

After the lecture ended, she enveloped herself in her fellow jocks and took care not to look back at the person with the hair. She assumed it was just a strange coincidence that an actual fan of hers had sat down right behind her in Earth Science. There were fifty thousand students at the U., but probably less than five hundred of them (not counting former players and friends or family of current players) considered women's athletic events a viable entertainment option. If you were Eliza and you wanted to sit directly behind the Gophers' bench (so that Patty, as she came off the court, couldn't help seeing you and your hair as you bent over a notebook), all you had to do was show up fifteen minutes before game time. And then, after the final buzzer and the ritual low-fiving line, it was the easiest thing in the world to intercept Patty near the locker-room door and hand her a piece of notebook paper and say to her: "Did you ask for more minutes, like I told you to?"

Patty still didn't know this person's name, but the person obviously knew hers, because the word PATTY was written on the notebook paper about a hundred times, in crackling cartoon letters with concentric pencil outlines to make them look like shouts echoing in the gym, as if a whole wild crowd were chanting her name, which could not have been further from reality, given that the gym was usually ninety percent empty and Patty was first-year and averaging less than ten minutes a game, i.e., was not exactly a household word. The crackling penciled shouts filled up the entire sheet of paper except for a small sketch of a player dribbling. Patty could tell the player was supposed to be her, because it was wearing her number and because who else would be drawn on a page covered with the word PATTY? Like everything Eliza did (as Patty learned soon enough), the drawing was half super-skilled and half clumsy and bad. The way the player's body was low to the ground and violently slanting as she made a sharp turn was excellent, but the face and head were like some generic female in a first-aid booklet.

Looking at the piece of paper, Patty had a preview of the falling sensation she would have a few months later after eating hash brownies with Eliza. Something very wrong and creepy but hard to defend herself against.

"Thank you for this drawing," she said.

"Why aren't they playing you more?" Eliza said. "You were on the bench practically the whole second half."

"Once we got the big lead—"

"You're brilliant and they bench you? I don't understand that." Eliza's curls were thrashing like a willow tree in heavy winds; she was quite exercised.

"Dawn and Cathy and Shawna got some good minutes," Patty said. "They did great holding the lead."

"But you're so much better than them!"

"I should go shower now. Thanks again for the drawing."

"Maybe not this year, but next year, at the latest, everybody's going to want a piece of you," Eliza said. "You're going to attract attention. You need to start learning how to protect yourself."

This was so ridiculous that Patty had to stop and set her straight. "Too much attention is not a problem people have in women's basketball."

"What about men? Do you know how to protect yourself from men?"

"What do you mean?"

"I mean, do you have good judgment when it comes to men?"

"Right now I don't have much time for anything except sports."

"You don't seem to understand how amazing you are. And how dangerous that is."

"I understand I'm good at sports."

"It's sort of a miracle you're not already getting taken advantage of."

"Well, I don't drink, which helps a lot."

"Why don't you drink?" Eliza pursued immediately.

"Because I can't when I'm in training. Not even one sip."

"You're in training every day of the year?"

"Well, and I had a bad drinking experience in high school, so."

"What happened—somebody rape you?"

Patty's face burned and assumed five different expressions all at once. "Wow," she said.

"Yes? Is that what happened?"

"I'm going to go shower."

"You see, this is exactly what I'm talking about!" Eliza cried with great excitement. "You don't know me at all, we've been talking for all of two minutes, and you basically just told me you're a rape survivor. You're completely unprotected!"

Patty was too alarmed and ashamed, at that moment, to spot the flaws in this logic.

"I can protect myself," she said. "I'm doing just fine."

"Sure. OK." Eliza shrugged. "It's your safety, not mine."

The gym echoed with the thunk of heavy switches as banks of lights went out.

"Do you play sports?" Patty asked, to make up for not having been more agreeable.

Eliza looked down at herself. She was wide and blady in the pelvis and somewhat pigeon-toed, with tiny Kedded feet. "Do I look like it?"

"I don't know. Badminton?"

"I hate gym," Eliza said, laughing. "I hate all sports."

Patty laughed, too, in her relief at having got the subject changed, although she was now quite confused.

"I didn't even 'throw like a girl' or 'run like a girl,'" Eliza said. "I refused to run or throw, period. If a ball landed in my hands, I just waited until somebody came and took it away. When I was supposed to run, like, to first base, I would stand there for a second and then maybe walk."

"God," Patty said.

"Yeah, I almost didn't get my diploma because of it," Eliza said. "The only reason I graduated was that my parents knew the school psychologist. I ended up getting credit for riding a bike every day."

Patty nodded uncertainly. "You love basketball, though, right?"

"Yeah, that's right," Eliza said. "Basketball is pretty fascinating."

"Well, so, you definitely don't hate sports. It sounds like what you really hate is gym."

"You're right. That's right."

"Well, so anyway."

"Yeah, so anyway, are we going to be friends?"

Patty laughed. "If I say yes, I'm just proving your point about how I'm not careful enough with people I barely know."

"That sounds like a no, then."

"How about we just wait and see?"

"Good. That's very careful of you—I like that."

"You see? You see?" Patty was laughing again already. "I'm more careful than you thought!"

The autobiographer has no doubt that if Patty had been more conscious of herself and paying any halfway decent kind of attention to the world around her, she wouldn't have been nearly as good at college basketball. Success at sports is the province of the almost empty head. Reaching a vantage point from which she could have seen Eliza for what she was (i.e., disturbed) would have messed with her game. You don't get to be an 88-percent free-throw shooter by giving deep thought to every little thing.

Eliza turned out not to like any of Patty's other friends and didn't even try to hang out with them. She referred to them collectively as "your lesbians" or "the lesbians" although half of them were straight. Patty very quickly came to feel that she lived in two mutually exclusive worlds. There was Total Jockworld, where she spent the vast majority of her time and where she would rather flunk a psychology midterm than skip going to the store and assembling a care package and taking it to a teammate who'd sprained an ankle or was laid up with the flu, and then there was dark little Elizaworld, where she didn't have to bother trying to be so good. The only point of contact between the worlds was Williams Arena, where Patty, when she sliced through a transitional defense for an easy layup or a no-look pass, experienced an extra little rush of pride and pleasure if Eliza was there watching. Even this point of contact was short-lived, because the more time Eliza spent with Patty the less she seemed to remember how interested in basketball she was.

Patty had always had friends plural, never anything intense. Her heart gladdened when she saw Eliza waiting outside the gym after practice, she knew it was going to be an instructive evening. Eliza took her to movies with subtitles and made her listen very carefully to Patti Smith recordings ("I love that you have the same name as my favorite artist," she said, disregarding the different spelling and the fact that Patty's actual legal name was Patrizia, which Joyce had given her to be different and Patty was embarrassed to say aloud) and loaned her books of poetry by Denise Levertov and Frank O'Hara. After the basketball team finished with a record of 8 wins and 11 losses and a first-round tournament elimination (despite Patty's 14 points and numerous assists), Eliza also taught her to really, really like Paul Masson Chablis.

What Eliza did with the rest of her free time was somewhat hazy. There seemed to be several "men" (i.e., boys) in her life, and she sometimes referred to concerts she'd gone to, but when Patty expressed curiosity about these concerts Eliza said first Patty had to listen to all the mix tapes Eliza made her; and Patty was having some difficulty with these mix tapes. She did like Patti Smith, who seemed to understand how she'd felt in the bathroom on the morning after she was raped, but the Velvet Underground, for example, made her lonely. She once admitted to Eliza that her favorite band was the Eagles, and Eliza said, "There's nothing wrong with that, the Eagles are great," but you sure didn't see any Eagles records in Eliza's dorm room.

Eliza's parents were big-deal Twin Cities psychotherapists and lived out in Wayzata, where everybody was rich, and she had an older brother, a junior at Bard College, whom she described as peculiar. When Patty asked, "Peculiar in what way?" Eliza answered, "In every way." Eliza herself had patched together a high-school education at three different local academies and was enrolled at the U. because her parents refused to subsidize her if she wasn't in school. She was a B student in a different way than Patty was a B student, which was to get the same B in everything. Eliza got A-pluses in English and Ds in everything else. Her only known interests besides basketball were poetry and pleasure.

Eliza was determined to get Patty to try pot, but Patty was extremely protective of her lungs, and this was how the brownie thing came about. They'd driven out in Eliza's Volkswagen Bug to the Wayzata house, which was full of African sculpture and empty of the parents, who were at a weekend conference. The idea had been to make a fancy Julia Child dinner, but they drank too much wine to succeed at this and ended up eating crackers and cheese and making the brownies and ingesting what must have been massive amounts of drug. Part of Patty was thinking, for the entire sixteen hours she was messed up, "I am *never* going to do this again." She felt like she'd broken training so badly that she would never be able to make it whole again, a very desolate feeling indeed. She was also fearful about Eliza—she suddenly realized that she had some kind of weird crush on Eliza and that it was therefore of paramount importance to sit motionless and contain herself and not discover that she was bisexual. Eliza kept asking her how she was, and she kept answering, "I am just fine, thank you," which struck them as hilarious every time. Listening to the Velvet Underground, Patty understood the group much better, they were a very *dirty* musical group, and their dirtiness was comfortingly similar to how she was feeling out there in Wayzata, surrounded by African masks. It was a relief to realize, as she became less stoned, that even while very stoned she'd managed to contain herself and Eliza hadn't touched her: that nothing lesbian was ever going to happen.

Patty was curious about Eliza's parents and wanted to stick around the house and meet them, but Eliza was adamant about this being a very bad idea. "They're the love of each other's lives," she said. "They do everything together. They have matching offices in the same suite, and they co-author all their papers and books, and they do joint presentations at conferences, and they can never *ever* talk about their work at home, because of patient confidentiality. They even have a tandem bicycle."

"So?"

"So they're strange and you're not going to like them, and then you're not going to like me."

"My parents aren't so great, either," Patty said.

"Trust me, this is different. I know what I'm talking about."

Driving back into the city in the Bug, with the warmthless Minnesota spring sun behind them, they had their first sort-of fight.

"You have to stay here this summer," Eliza said. "You can't go away."

"That's not very realistic," Patty said. "I'm supposed to work in my dad's office and be in Gettysburg in July."

"Why can't you stay here and go to your camp from here? We can get jobs and you can go to the gym every day."

"I have to go home."

"But why? You hate it there."

"If I stay here I'll drink wine every night."

"No, you won't. We'll have strict rules. We'll have whatever rules you like."

"I'll be back in the fall."

"Can we live together then?"

"No, I already promised Cathy I'd be in her quad."

"You can tell her your plans changed."

"I can't do that."

"This is crazy! I hardly ever see you!"

"I see you more than practically anybody. I love seeing you."

"Then why won't you stay here this summer? Don't you trust me?"

"Why wouldn't I trust you?"

"I don't know. I just can't figure out why you'd rather work for your dad. He did not take care of you, he did not protect you, and I will. He doesn't have your best interests at heart, and I do."

It was true that Patty's spirits sagged at the thought of going home, but it seemed necessary to punish herself for eating hash brownies. Her dad had also been making an effort with her, sending her actual handwritten letters ("We miss you on the tennis court") and offering her the use of her grandmother's old car, which he didn't think her grandmother ought to be driving anymore. After a year away, she was feeling remorseful about having been so cold to him. Maybe she'd made a mistake? And so she went home for the summer and found that nothing had changed and she had not made a mistake. She watched TV till midnight, got up at seven every morning and ran five miles, and spent her days highlighting names in legal documents and looking forward to the day's mail, which more often than not contained a long typewritten letter from Eliza, saying how much she missed her, and telling stories about her "lecherous" boss at the revival-house movie theater where she was working in the ticket booth, and exhorting her to write back immediately, which Patty did her best to do, using old letterhead stationery and the Selectric in her dad's mothball-smelling office.

In one letter Eliza wrote, *I think we need to make rules for each other for protection and self-improvement.* Patty was skeptical about this but wrote back with three rules for her friend. *No smoking before dinnertime. Get exercise every day and develop athletic ability.* And *Attend all lectures and do all homework for ALL classes (not just English).* No doubt she should have been disturbed by how different Eliza's rules for her turned out to be—*Drink only on Saturday night and only in Eliza's presence; No going to mixed parties except accompanied by Eliza;* and *Tell Eliza EVERYTHING*—but something was wrong with her judgment and she instead felt excited to have such an intense best friend. Among other things, having this friend gave Patty armor and ammunition against her middle sister.

"So, how's life in Minn-e-soooo-tah?" a typical encounter with the sister began. "Have you been eating lots of *corn?* Have you seen Babe the Blue Ox!? Have you been to *Brainerd?*"

You might think that Patty, being a trained competitor and three and a half years older than the sister (though only two years ahead of her in school), would have developed ways of handling the sister's demeaning silliness. But there was something congenitally undefended about Patty's heart—she never ceased to be shocked by the sister's lack of sisterliness. The sister also really was Creative and therefore skilled at coming up with unexpected ways to render Patty speechless.

"Why do you always talk to me in that weird voice?" was Patty's current best defense.

"I was just asking you about life in good old Minn-e-soooo-tah."

"You *cackle*, is what you do. It's like a *cackle*."

This was met with a glittery-eyed silence. Then: "It's the Land of Ten Thousand Lakes!"

"Please just go away."

"Do you have a boyfriend out there?"

"No."

"A girlfriend?"

"*No.* Although I did make a really great friend."

"You mean the one who's sending you all the letters? Is she a jock?"

"No. She's a poet."

"Wow." The sister seemed a tiny bit interested. "What's her name?"

"Eliza."

"Eliza Doolittle. She sure does write an awful lot of letters. Are you positive she's not your girlfriend?"

"She's a writer, OK? A really interesting writer."

"One hears whispers from the locker room, is all. The fungus that dare not speak its name."

"You're so disgusting," Patty said. "She has like three different boyfriends, she's very cool."

"Brainerd, Minn-e-soooo-tah," was the sister's reply. "You have to send me a postcard of Babe the Blue Ox from Brainerd." She went away singing "I'm Getting Married in the Morning" with much vibrato.

The following fall, back at school, Patty met the boy named Carter who became, for want of a better word, her first boyfriend. It now seems to the autobiographer anything but accidental that she met him immediately after she'd obeyed Eliza's third rule and told her that a guy she knew from the gym, a sophomore from the wrestling team, had asked her out to dinner. Eliza had wanted to meet the wrestler first, but there were limits even to Patty's agreeability. "He seems like a really nice guy," she said.

"I'm sorry, but you're still on probation guywise," Eliza said. "You thought the person who raped you was a nice guy."

"I'm not sure I actually formed that particular thought. I was just excited he was interested in me."

"Well, and now here's somebody else who's interested in you."

"Yes, but I'm sober."

They'd compromised by agreeing that Patty would go to Eliza's off-campus room (her reward from her parents for having worked a summer job) directly after dinner, and that if she wasn't there by ten o'clock then Eliza would come looking for her. When she got to the off-campus house, around nine-thirty, after a none too scintillating dinner, she found Eliza in her top-floor room with the boy named Carter. They were at opposite ends of her sofa, with their stockinged feet sole to sole on the center cushion, and were pushing each other's pedals in what might or might not have been a sister-and-brotherly way. The new DEVO album was playing on Eliza's stereo.

Patty faltered in the doorway. "Maybe I should leave the two of you alone?"

"Oh God, no no no no no, we want you here," Eliza cried. "Carter and I are ancient history, aren't we?"

"Very ancient," Carter said with dignity and, Patty thought later, mild irritation. He swung his feet down onto the floor.

"An extinct volcano," Eliza said as she leaped up to make introductions. Patty had never seen her friend with a boy before, and she was struck by how altered her personality was—her face was flushed, she stumbled over words and steadily emitted somewhat artificial giggles. It seemed to have slipped her mind that Patty had come over to be debriefed about her dinner. Everything was about Carter, a friend from one of her high schools who was taking time off from college and working at a bookstore and going to shows. Carter had extremely straight and interestingly tinted dark hair (henna, it turned out), beautiful long-lashed eyes (mascara, it turned out), and no notable physical flaws except for his teeth, which were jumbled and strangely small and pointed (basic middle-class child maintenance such as orthodontia had fallen through the cracks of his parents' bitter divorce, it turned out). Patty immediately liked that he didn't seem self-conscious about his teeth. She was setting about making a good impression on him, trying to prove herself worthy of being Eliza's friend, when Eliza stuck a huge goblet of wine in her face.

"No, thank you," Patty said.

"But it's Saturday night," Eliza said.

Patty wanted to point out that the rules did not *oblige* her to drink on Saturday, but in Carter's presence she got an objective glimpse of how odd these rules of Eliza's were, and how odd it was, for that matter, that she had to report to Eliza on her dinner with the wrestler. And so she changed her mind and drank the wine and then another enormous gobletful and felt warm and excellent. The autobiographer is mindful of how dull it is to read about someone else's drinking, but sometimes it's pertinent to the story. When Carter got up to leave, around midnight, he offered Patty a ride back to her dorm, and at the door of her building he asked if he could kiss her good night ("It's OK," she specifically thought, "he's a friend of Eliza's"), and after they'd made out for a while, standing in the cold October air, he asked if he could see her the next day, and she thought, "Wow, this guy moves *fast*."

To give credit where credit is due: that winter was the best athletic season of her life. She had no health issues, and Coach Treadwell, after giving her a tough lecture about being less unselfish and more of a leader, started her at guard in every single game. Patty herself was amazed at how slow-motion the bigger opposing players suddenly were, how easy it was to just reach out and steal the ball from them, and how many of her jump shots went in, game after game. Even when she was being double-teamed, which happened more and more often, she felt a special private connection with the basket, always knowing exactly where it was and always trusting that she was its favorite player on the floor, the best at feeding its circular mouth. Even off the court she existed in the zone, which felt like a kind of preoccupied pressure behind her eyebrows, an alert drowsiness or focused dumbness that persisted no matter what she was doing. She slept wonderfully that whole winter and never quite woke up. Even when she was elbowed in the head, or mobbed at the buzzer by happy teammates, she hardly felt it.

And her thing with Carter was part of this. Carter was perfectly uninterested in sports and appeared not to mind that, during peak weeks, she had no more than a few hours total for him, sometimes just enough to have sex in his apartment and run back to campus. In certain respects, even now, this seems to the autobiographer an ideal relationship, though admittedly less ideal when she allows herself a realistic guess about how many other girls Carter was having sex with during the six months Patty thought of him as her boyfriend. Those six months were the first of the two indisputably happy periods in Patty's life, when everything just clicked. She loved Carter's uncorrected teeth, his genuine humility, his skillful petting, his patience with her. He had many sterling qualities, Carter did! Whether he was giving her some excruciatingly gentle technical pointer about sex or confessing to his utter lack of career plans ("I'm probably best qualified to be some kind of quiet blackmailer"), his voice was always soft and swallowed and self-deprecating—poor corrupt Carter did not think well of himself as a member of the human race.

Patty herself continued to think well of him, hazardously well, until the Saturday night in April when she came back early from Chicago, where she and Coach Treadwell had flown for the all-American luncheon and award ceremony (Patty had been named second-team at guard), to surprise Carter at the party he was having for his birthday. From the street, she could see lights on in his apartment, but she had to ring his bell four times, and the voice that finally answered on the intercom was Eliza's.

"*Patty?* Aren't you in Chicago?"

"I'm home early. Buzz me up."

There was a crackling on the intercom, followed by a silence so long that Patty rang the doorbell two more times. Finally Eliza, in Keds and shearling coat, came running down the stairs and out the door. "Hi, hi, hi, hi!" she said. "I can't believe you're here!"

"Why didn't you buzz me up?" Patty said.

"I don't know, I thought I'd come down and see you, things are crazy up there, I thought I'd come down so we can talk." Eliza was bright-eyed and her hands were fidgeting wildly. "There's a lot of drugs up there, why don't we just go somewhere else, it's so great to see you, I mean, hey, hi! How are you? How was Chicago? How was the luncheon?"

Patty was frowning. "You're saying I can't go up and see my boyfriend?"

"Well, no, but, no, but—boyfriend? That's kind of a strong word, don't you think? I thought he was just Carter. I mean, I know you like him, but—"

"Who else is up there?"

"Oh, you know, other people."

"Who?"

"Not somebody you know. Hey, let's go somewhere else, OK?"

"Like who, though?"

"He didn't think you were coming back till tomorrow. You guys are having dinner tomorrow, right?"

"I flew back early to see him."

"Oh my God, you're not in love with him, are you? We really need to talk about protecting yourself better, I thought you guys were just having fun, I mean, you literally never used the word 'boyfriend,' which I ought to have known about, right? And if you don't tell me everything, I can't protect you. You sort of broke a rule, don't you think?"

"You haven't followed my rules, either," Patty said.

"Because, I swear to God, this is not what you think it is. I am your friend. But there's somebody else here who's definitely not your friend."

"A girl?"

"Look, I'll make her go away. We'll get rid of her and then the three of us can party." Eliza giggled. "He got really, really, really excellent coke for his birthday."

"Wait a minute. It's just the three of you? That's the party?"

"It's so great, it's so great, you've got to try it. Your season's over, right? We'll get rid of her and you can come up and party. Or we can go to my place instead, just you and me, if you'll wait one second I'll get some drugs and we can go to my place. You've got to try it. You won't understand if you don't try it."

"Leave Carter with somebody else and go do hard drugs with you. That sounds like a real plan."

"Oh God, Patty, I'm so sorry. It's not what you think. He said he was having a party, but then he got the coke and he changed his plan a little bit, and then it turned out he only wanted me here because the other person wouldn't come over if it was just the two of them."

"You could have left," Patty said.

"We were already partying, which if you'd try it you'd understand why I didn't leave. I swear to you that's the only reason I'm here."

The night did not end, as it should have, with a cooling or cessation of Patty's friendship with Eliza but instead with Patty swearing off Carter and apologizing for not having told Eliza more about her feelings for him, and with Eliza apologizing for not having paid closer attention to her and promising to follow her own rules better and not do any more hard drugs. It's now clear to the autobiographer that an available twosome and a white anthill of powder on the nightstand would have been exactly Carter's notion of an outstanding birthday treat for himself. But Eliza was so frantic with remorse and worry that she told her lies with great conviction, and the very next morning, before Patty had had a waking hour to think things over and conclude that her supposed best friend had done something twisted with her supposed boyfriend, Eliza showed up all a-panting at the door of Patty's quad, wearing her idea of running clothes (a Lena Lovich T-shirt, knee-length boxing shorts, black socks, Keds), to report that she'd just jogged three lengths around the quarter-mile track and to insist that Patty teach her some calisthenics. She was afire with a plan for them to study together every evening, afire with affection for Patty and fear of losing her; and Patty, having opened her eyes painfully to Carter's nature, went ahead and closed them to Eliza's.

Eliza's full-court press continued until Patty agreed to live in Minneapolis for the summer with her, at which point Eliza became scarcer again and lost interest in fitness. Patty spent much of that hot summer alone in a roachy sublet in Dinkytown, feeling sorry for herself and experiencing low self-esteem. She couldn't understand why Eliza had been so hell-bent on living with her if she was going to come home most nights at 2 a.m. or not come home at all. Eliza did, it was true, keep suggesting to Patty that she try new drugs or go to shows or find a new person to sleep with, but Patty was temporarily disgusted by sex and permanently by drugs and cigarette smoke. Plus her summer job in the P.E. Department paid barely enough to cover the rent, and she refused to emulate Eliza and beg her parents for cash infusions, and so she felt more and more inadequate and lonely.

"Why are we friends?" she finally said one night when Eliza was punking herself up for another outing.

"Because you're brilliant and beautiful," Eliza said. "You're my favorite person in the world."

"I'm a jock. I'm boring."

"No! You're Patty Emerson, and we're living together, and it's great."

These were literally her words, the autobiographer remembers them vividly.

"But we don't *do* anything," Patty said.

"What do you want to do?"

"I'm thinking of going home to my parents' for a while."

"What? Are you kidding? You don't like them! You've got to stay here with me."

"But you're gone practically every night."

"Well, let's start doing more things together."

"But you know I don't want to do those kinds of things."

"Well, let's go to a movie, then. We'll go to a movie right now. What do you want to see? Do you want to see *Days of Heaven?*"

And so began another of Eliza's full-court presses which lasted just long enough to get Patty over the hump of the summer and make sure she didn't flee. It was during this third honeymoon of double features and wine spritzers and wearing out the grooves of Blondie albums that Patty began to hear about the musician Richard Katz. "Oh my God," Eliza said,

"I think I might be in love. I think I might have to start being a good girl. He's so big, it's like being rolled over by a neutron star. It's like being erased with a giant eraser."

The giant eraser had just graduated from Macalester College, was working demolition, and had formed a punk band called the Traumatics which Eliza was convinced were going to be huge. The only thing confounding her idealization of Katz was his choice of friends. "He lives with this nerdy hanger-on guy Walter," she said, "this kind of straitlaced groupie, it's weird, I don't get it. At first I thought he was Katz's manager or something, but he's way too uncool for that. I come out of Katz's room in the morning and there's *Walter* at the kitchen table with this big fruit salad he's made. He's reading the *New York Times* and the first thing he asks me is whether I've seen any *good theater* lately. You know, like, plays. It's totally Odd Couple. You've got to meet Katz to understand how weird it is."

Few circumstances have turned out to be more painful to the autobiographer, in the long run, than the dearness of Walter and Richard's friendship. Superficially, at least, the two of them were an odder couple than even Patty and Eliza. Some genius in the Macalester College housing office had put a heartbreakingly responsible Minnesota country boy in the same freshman dorm room as a self-absorbed, addiction-prone, unreliable, street-smart guitar player from Yonkers, New York. The only thing the housing-office person could have known for sure they had in common was being financial-aid students. Walter had fair coloration and a stalky build, and though taller than Patty he was nowhere near as tall as Richard, who was 6'4" and heavy-shouldered and as dark-complected as Walter was light. Richard bore a strong resemblance (noticed and remarked on, over the years, by many more people than just Patty) to the Libyan dictator Muammar el-Qaddafi. He had the same black hair, the same tan pockmarked cheeks, the same satisfied-strongman-reviewing-the-troops-and-rocket-launchers mask of a smile,* and he looked about fifteen years older than his friend. Walter resembled the officious "student

*Patty didn't see a picture of Qaddafi until some years after college, and even then, though struck immediately by his resemblance to Richard Katz, she didn't make anything special of the fact that Libya seemed to her to have the world's cutest head of state.

manager" that high-school teams sometimes have, the unathletic kid who assists the coaches and wears a jacket and necktie to games and gets to stand on the sideline with a clipboard. Jocks tend to tolerate this kind of manager because he's invariably a deep student of the game, and this seemed to be one element of the Walter-Richard nexus, because Richard, irritable and unreliable though he was in most respects, was helplessly serious about his music, and Walter had the connoisseurial equipment necessary to be a fan of stuff like Richard's. Later, as Patty got to know them better, she saw that they were maybe not so different underneath—that both were struggling, albeit in very different ways, to be good people.

Patty met the eraser on a muggy August Sunday morning when she returned from her run and found him sitting on the living-room sofa, diminishing it with his largeness, while Eliza showered in their unspeakable bathroom. Richard was wearing a black T-shirt and reading a paperback novel with a big *V* on the cover. His first words to Patty, uttered only after she'd filled a glass with iced tea and was standing there all sweat-soaked, drinking it, were: "And what are you."

"I beg your pardon?"

"What are you doing here."

"I *live* here," she said.

"Right, I see that." Richard looked her over carefully, piece by piece. It felt to her as if, with each new piece of her that his eyes alit on, she was being further tacked to the wall behind her, so that, when he was done looking over all of her, she had been rendered entirely two-dimensional and fastened to the wall. "Have you seen the scrapbook?" he said.

"Um. Scrapbook?"

"I'll show it to you," he said. "You'll be interested."

He went into Eliza's room, came back and handed Patty a three-ring binder, and sat down again with his novel as if he'd forgotten she was there. The binder was the old-fashioned kind with a pale-blue cloth cover, on which the word PATTY was inked in block letters. It contained, as far as Patty could tell, every picture of her ever published in the sports pages of the *Minnesota Daily*; every postcard she'd ever sent Eliza; every photo strip the two of them had ever squeezed into a booth for; and every flash snapshot of them being stoned on the brownie weekend. The book seemed a little weird and intense to Patty, but mostly it made her feel sad for Eliza—sad and sorry to have questioned how much she really cared about her.

"She's an odd little girl," Richard remarked from the sofa.

"Where did you find this?" Patty said. "Do you always go snooping in people's things when you sleep over?"

He laughed. "*J'accuse!*"

"Well, do you?"

"Cool your jets. It was right behind the bed. In plain sight, as the cops say."

The noise of Eliza's showering had stopped.

"Go put it back," Patty said. "Please."

"I figured you'd be interested," Richard said, not stirring from the sofa.

"Please go put this back where you found it."

"I'm getting the sense you don't have a corresponding scrapbook of your own."

"Right now, please."

"Very odd little girl," Richard said, taking the binder from her. "That's why I asked what your story was."

The fakeness of Eliza's way with men, the steady leakage of giggles, the gushing and the hair-tossing, was something a friend of hers could quickly come to hate. Her desperateness to please Richard became mingled in Patty's mind with the weirdness of the scrapbook and the extreme neediness it evidenced, and it made her, for the first time, somewhat embarrassed to be Eliza's friend. Which was odd, since Richard seemed unembarrassed to be sleeping with her, and why should Patty have cared what he thought of their friendship anyway?

It was almost her last day in the roachpit when she next saw Richard. He was on the sofa again, sitting with his arms folded and tapping his booted right foot heavily and wincing while Eliza stood and played her guitar the only way Patty had ever heard her play it: uncertainly. "Get in the slot," he said. "Tap your foot." But Eliza, who was perspiring with concentration, stopped playing altogether as soon as she realized Patty was there.

"I can't play in front of her."

"Sure you can," Richard said.

"Actually she can't," Patty said. "I make her nervous."

"Interesting. Why is that?"

"I have no idea," Patty said.

"She's too supportive," Eliza said. "I can feel her willing me to succeed."

"That's very bad of you," Richard said to Patty. "You need to will her to fail."

"OK," Patty said. "I want you to fail. Can you do that? You seem to be pretty good at it."

Eliza looked at her in surprise. Patty was surprised with herself, too. "Sorry, I'm going in my room now," she said.

"First let's see her fail," Richard said.

But Eliza was unstrapping and unplugging.

"You need to practice with a metronome," Richard told her. "Do you have a metronome?"

"This was a really bad idea," Eliza said.

"Why don't *you* play something?" Patty said to Richard.

"Some other time," he said.

But Patty was recalling the embarrassment she'd felt when he produced the scrapbook. "One song," she said. "One *chord*. Play one chord. Eliza says you're amazing."

He shook his head. "Come to a show sometime."

"Patty doesn't go to shows," Eliza said. "She doesn't like the smoke."

"I'm an athlete," Patty said.

"Right, so we've seen," Richard said, giving her a significant look. "Basketball star. What are you—forward? Guard? I have no idea what constitutes tall in a chick."

"I'm not considered tall."

"And yet you are quite tall."

"Yes."

"We were just about to leave," Eliza said, standing up.

"You look like *you* could have played basketball," Patty told Richard.

"Good way to break a finger."

"That's actually not true," she said. "It hardly ever happens."

This was not an interesting or plot-advancing thing to have said, she sensed it immediately, how Richard didn't actually give a shit about her playing basketball.

"Maybe I'll go to one of your shows," she said. "When's the next one?"

"You can't go, it's too smoky for you," Eliza said unpleasantly.

"It's not going to be a problem," Patty said.

"Really? That's news."

"Bring earplugs," Richard said.

In her room, after she heard them go out, Patty began to cry for reasons she felt too desolate to fathom. The next time she saw Eliza, thirty-six hours later, she apologized for having been such a bitch, but Eliza was in excellent spirits by then and told her not to worry about it, she was thinking about selling her guitar and was happy to take Patty to hear Richard.

His next show was on a weeknight in September, at a poorly ventilated club called the Longhorn, where the Traumatics were opening for the Buzzcocks. Practically the first person Patty saw when she and Eliza arrived was Carter. He was standing with a headlock on a grotesquely pretty blond girl in a sequined minidress. "Oh shit," Eliza said. Patty waved bravely to Carter, who flashed his bad teeth and ambled toward her, a picture of affability, with the sequins in tow. Eliza put her head down and pulled Patty away through a knot of cigarette-puffing male punks and up against the stage. Here they found a fair-haired boy who Patty guessed was Richard's famous roommate even before Eliza said, in a loud monotone, "Hello Walter how are you."

Not knowing Walter yet, Patty had no idea how unusual it was that he returned this greeting with a cold nod rather than a friendly midwestern smile.

"This is my best friend Patty," Eliza said to him. "Can she stand here with you for a second while I go backstage?"

"I think they're about to emerge," Walter said.

"Just for one second," Eliza said. "Just watch out for her. OK?"

"Why don't we all go back there together," Walter said.

"No, you need to hold my place here," Eliza told Patty. "I'll be right back."

Walter watched unhappily as she burrowed off through bodies and disappeared. He didn't look nearly as nerdy as Eliza had led Patty to expect—he was wearing a V-necked sweater and had an overgrown curly mop of reddish blond hair and looked like what he was, i.e., a first-year law student—but he did stand out among the punks with their mutilated hair and garments, and Patty, who was suddenly self-conscious about her own clothes, which she'd always liked until one minute ago, was grateful for his ordinariness.

"Thank you for standing here with me," she said.

"I think we'll be standing here for quite a while now," Walter said.

"It's nice to meet you."

"Nice to meet you, too. You're the basketball star."

"That's me."

"Richard told me about you." He turned to her. "Do you do a lot of drugs?"

"No! God. Why?"

"Because your friend does."

Patty didn't know what to do with her facial expression. "Not around me she doesn't."

"Well, that's what she's going backstage for."

"OK."

"I'm sorry. I know she's your friend."

"No, it's interesting to know that."

"She seems to be very well funded."

"Yeah, she gets it from her parents."

"Right, the parents."

Walter seemed so preoccupied with Eliza's disappearance that Patty fell silent. She was feeling morbidly competitive again. She was barely even aware yet of being interested in Richard, and still it struck her as unfair that Eliza might be using more than just herself, her native half-pretty self—that she might be using parental resources—to hold Richard's attention and buy access to him. How dumb about life Patty was! How far behind other people! And how ugly everything on the stage looked! The naked cords, and the cold chrome of the drums, and the utilitarian mikes, and the kidnapper's duct tape, and the cannonlike spotlights: it all looked so hard core.

"Do you go to a lot of shows?" Walter said.

"No, never. Once."

"Did you bring some earplugs?"

"No. Do I need them?"

"Richard's very loud. You can use mine. They're almost new."

From his shirt pocket he produced a baggie containing two whitish foam-rubber larvae. Patty looked down at them and did her best to smile nicely. "No, thank you," she said.

"I'm a very clean person," he said earnestly. "There's no health risk."

"But then you won't have any for yourself."

"I'll tear them in half. You'll want to have something for protection."

Patty watched him carefully divide the earplugs. "Maybe I'll just hold them in my hand and wait and see if I need them," she said.

They stood there for fifteen minutes. Eliza finally came slithering and wiggling back and looking radiant just as the houselights dimmed and the audience surged against the stage. The first thing Patty did was drop the earplugs. There was altogether a lot more jostling than the situation seemed to call for. A fat person in leather barged into her back and knocked her against the stage. Eliza was already tossing her hair and hopping in anticipation, and so it fell to Walter to push the fat guy back and give Patty room to stand up straight.

The Traumatics who came running out onto that stage consisted of Richard, his lifelong bass player Herrera, and two skinny boys who looked barely out of high school. Richard was more of a showman then than he came to be later, when it seemed clear that he was never going to be a star and so it was better to be an anti-star. He bounced on his toes, did lurching little half pirouettes with his hand on the neck of his guitar, and so forth. He informed the audience that his band was going to play every song it knew, and that this would take twenty-five minutes. Then he and the band went totally haywire, churning out a vicious assault of noise that Patty couldn't hear any sort of beat in. The music was like food too hot to have any taste, but the lack of beat or melody didn't stop the central knot of male punks from pogoing up and down and shoulder-checking each other and stomping at every available female ankle. Trying to stay out of their way, Patty got separated from both Walter and Eliza. The noise was just unbearable. Richard and two other Traumatics were screaming into their microphones, *I hate sunshine! I hate sunshine!*, and Patty, who rather liked sunshine, brought her basketball skills to bear on making an immediate escape. She drove into the crowd with her elbows high and emerged from the scrum to find herself face-to-face with Carter and his glittery girl and kept right on moving until she was standing on the sidewalk in warm and fresh September air, under a Minnesota sky that astonishingly still had twilight in it.

She lingered at the door of the Longhorn, watching Buzzcocks fans arrive late and waiting to see if Eliza would come looking for her. But it was Walter, not Eliza, who came looking.

"I'm fine," she told him. "This just turned out not to be my cup of tea."

"Can I take you home?"

"No, you should go back. You could tell Eliza I'm getting home by myself, so she doesn't worry."

"She's not looking very worried. Let me take you home."

Patty said no, Walter insisted, she insisted no, he insisted yes. Then she realized he didn't have a car and was offering to ride the bus with her, and she insisted no all over again, and he insisted yes. He much later said that he'd already been falling for her while they stood at the bus stop, but no equivalent symphony could be heard in Patty's head. She was feeling guilty about abandoning Eliza and regretting that she'd dropped the earplugs and hadn't stayed to see more of Richard.

"I feel like I sort of failed a test there," she said.

"Do you even like this kind of music?"

"I like Blondie. I like Patti Smith. I guess basically no, I don't like this kind of music."

"So is it permissible to ask why you came?"

"Well, Richard invited me."

Walter nodded as if this had private meaning for him.

"Is Richard a nice person?" Patty asked.

"Extremely!" Walter said. "I mean, it all depends. You know, his mom ran away when he was little, and became a religious nut. His dad was a postal worker and a drinker who got lung cancer when Richard was in high school. Richard took care of him until he died. He's a very loyal person, although maybe not so much with women. He's actually not that nice to women, if that's what you're asking."

Patty had already intuited this and for some reason did not feel put off by the news of it.

"And what about you?" Walter said.

"What about me?"

"Are you a nice person? You seem like it. And yet . . ."

"And yet?"

"I hate your friend!" he burst out. "I don't think she's a good person. Actually, I think she's quite horrible. She's a liar and she's mean."

"Well, she's my best friend," Patty said huffily. "She's not horrible to me. Maybe you guys just got off on the wrong foot."

"Does she always take you to places and leave you standing there while she does coke with somebody else?"

"No, as a matter of fact, that's never happened before."

Walter said nothing, just stood stewing in his dislike. No bus was in sight.

"Sometimes it makes me feel really, really good, how into me she is," Patty said after a while. "A lot of the time she's not. But when she is . . ."

"I can't imagine it's hard to find people who are into you," Walter said.

She shook her head. "There's something wrong with me. I love all my other friends, but I feel like there's always a wall between us. Like they're all one kind of person and I'm another kind of person. More competitive and selfish. Less good, basically. Somehow I always end up feeling like I'm pretending when I'm around them. I don't have to pretend anything with Eliza. I can just be myself and still be *better* than her. I mean, I'm not dumb. I can see she's a fucked-up person. But some part of me loves being around her. Do you sometimes feel like that with Richard?"

"No," Walter said. "He's actually very unpleasant to be around, a lot of the time. There's just something I loved about him at very first sight, when we were freshmen. He's totally dedicated to his music, but he's also intellectually curious. I admire that."

"That's because you're probably a genuinely nice person," Patty said. "You love him for himself, not for how he makes you feel. That's probably the difference between you and me."

"But you seem like a genuinely nice person!" Walter said.

Patty knew, in her heart, that he was wrong in his impression of her. And the mistake she went on to make, the really big life mistake, was to go along with Walter's version of her in spite of knowing that it wasn't right. He seemed so certain of her goodness that eventually he wore her down.

When they finally got back to campus, that first night, Patty realized she'd been talking about herself for an hour without noticing that Walter was only asking questions, not answering them. The idea of trying to be nice in return and take an interest in him now seemed simply tiring, because she wasn't attracted to him.

"Can I call you sometime?" he said at the door of her dorm.

She explained that she wasn't going to be very social in the next months, due to training. "But it was incredibly sweet of you to take me home," she said. "I really appreciate it."

"Do you like theater? I have some friends I go to theater with. It wouldn't have to be a date or anything."

"I'm just so busy."

"This is a great city for theater," he persisted. "I bet you'd really enjoy it."

Oh Walter: did he know that the most intriguing thing about him, in the months when Patty was getting to know him, was that he was Richard Katz's friend? Did he notice how, every time Patty saw him, she contrived to find nonchalant ways to lead the conversation around to Richard? Did he have any suspicion, that first night, when she agreed to let him call her, that she was thinking of Richard?

Inside, upstairs, she found a phone message from Eliza on her door. She sat in her room with her eyes watering from the smoke in her hair and clothes until Eliza called again on the hall telephone, with club noise in the background, and upbraided her for scaring the shit out of her by disappearing.

"You were the one who disappeared," Patty said.

"I was just saying hi to Richard."

"You were gone like half an hour."

"What happened to Walter?" Eliza said. "Did he leave with you?"

"He took me home."

"Ew, gross. Did he tell you how much he hates me? I think he's really jealous of me. I think he's got some kind of thing for Richard. Maybe a gay thing."

Patty looked up and down the hallway to make sure nobody was listening. "Are you the one who got the drugs for Carter on his birthday?"

"What? I can't hear you."

"Were you the one who got that stuff that you and Carter were doing on his birthday?"

"I can't hear you!"

"THAT COKE ON CARTER'S BIRTHDAY. DID YOU BRING HIM THAT?"

"No! God! Is that why you left? Is that what you're upset about? Is that what Walter told you?"

Patty, jaw trembling, hung up the phone and went and showered for an hour.

There ensued yet another press from Eliza, but this one was half-hearted because she was pursuing Richard now as well. When Walter made good on his threat to call Patty, she found herself inclined to see him, both for his connection to Richard and for the frisson of being disloyal to Eliza. Walter was too tactful to bring up Eliza again, but Patty was always aware of his opinion of her friend, and some virtuous part of her enjoyed getting out and doing something cultural instead of drinking wine spritzers and listening to the same records over and over. She ended up seeing two plays and a movie with Walter that fall. Once her season started, she also saw him sitting by himself in the stands, red-faced, enjoying himself, and waving whenever she looked his way. He took to calling her the day after games to rave about her performance and display the kind of nuanced understanding of strategy which Eliza had never even bothered to try to fake. If he didn't reach her and had to leave a message, Patty had the additional frisson of calling him back and hoping she might talk to Richard instead, but Richard, alas, seemed never to be home when Walter wasn't.

In the tiny gaps between the blocks of time she spent answering Walter's questions, she managed to learn that he came from Hibbing, Minnesota, and that he was helping pay for law school by working part-time as a rough carpenter for the same contractor who employed Richard as a laborer, and that he had to get up at four every morning to do his studying. He always started yawning around 9 p.m., which Patty, with her own busy schedule, appreciated when she went out with him. They were joined, as he had promised, by three female friends of his from high school and college, three intelligent and creative girls whose weight problems and wide-strapped dresses would have provoked acid commentary from Eliza had she ever met them. It was from this adoring troika that Patty began to learn how miraculously worthy Walter was.

According to his friends, Walter had grown up living in cramped quarters behind the office of a motel called the Whispering Pines, with an alcoholic father, an older brother who regularly beat him up, a younger brother who studiously copied the older brother's ridicule of him, and a mother whose physical handicaps and low morale so impaired her performance as the motel's housekeeper and night manager that during high season, in the summer, Walter often cleaned rooms all afternoon and then checked in late arrivals while his father was drinking with his VFW buddies and his mother slept. This was in addition to his regular family job of helping his dad maintain the physical plant, doing everything from sealing the parking lot to snaking drains to repairing the boiler. His dad depended on his help, and Walter provided it in perennial hope of winning his dad's approval, which his friends said was impossible, however, because Walter was too sensitive and intellectual and not enough into hunting and trucks and beer (which the brothers were). Despite working what amounted to a full-time year-round unpaid job, Walter had also managed to star in school plays and musicals, inspire lifelong devotion in numerous childhood friends, learn cooking and basic sewing from his mother, pursue his interest in nature (tropical fish; ant farms; emergency care for orphaned nestlings; flower pressing), and graduate valedictorian. He got an Ivy League scholarship offer but instead went to Macalester, close enough to Hibbing to take a bus up on weekends and help his mom combat the motel's encroaching decay (the dad apparently now had emphysema and was useless). Walter had dreamed of being a film director or even an actor but instead was studying law at the U. because, as he reportedly had put it, "Somebody in the family needs to have an actual income."

Perversely—since she wasn't attracted to Walter—Patty felt competitive and vaguely offended by the presence of other girls on what could have been dates, and she was gratified to notice that it was she, not they, who made his eyes glow and his unstoppable blush come out. She did like to be the star, Patty did. Under pretty much all circumstances. At the last play they saw, in December at the Guthrie, Walter arrived just before curtain time, all snow-covered, with paperback Christmas presents for the other girls and, for Patty, an enormous poinsettia that he'd carried on the bus and through slushy streets and had difficulty checking at the coat counter. It was clear to everyone, even to Patty, that giving the other girls interesting books while giving her a plant was intended as the opposite of disrespectful. The fact that Walter wasn't investing his enthusiasm in some slimmer version of his nice, adoring friends, but rather in Patty, who applied her intelligence and creativity mainly to thinking up newly nonchalant-seeming ways of mentioning Richard Katz, was mystifying and alarming but also, undeniably, flattering. After the show, Walter carried the poinsettia all the way back to her dorm for her, on the bus and through further slush. The card attached to it, which she opened in her room, said *For Patty, with great affection, from her admiring fan.*

It was right around then that Richard got around to dumping Eliza. He was apparently quite the brutal dumper. Eliza was beside herself when she called Patty with the news, wailing that "the faggot" had turned Richard against her, that Richard wasn't giving her a *chance*, and that Patty had to help her and arrange a meeting with him, he refused to speak to her or open the door of his apartment or—

"I've got finals," Patty said coolly.

"You can go over there and I'll go with you," Eliza said. "I just need to see him and explain."

"Explain what?"

"That he has to give me a chance! That I deserve a hearing!"

"Walter isn't gay," Patty said. "That's just something you made up in your head."

"Oh my God, he's turned you against me, too!"

"No," Patty said. "That's not how it is."

"I'm coming over now and we can make a plan."

"I've got my history final in the morning. I need to study."

Patty now learned that Eliza had stopped going to classes six weeks earlier, because she was so into Richard. He'd *done* this to her, she'd given up everything for him, and now he'd hung her out to dry and she had to keep her parents from finding out that she was failing everything, she was coming over to Patty's dorm now and Patty had to stay right there and wait for her, so they could make a plan.

"I'm really tired," Patty said. "I have to study and then sleep."

"I can't believe it! He's turned you both against me! My two favorite people in the world!"

Patty managed to get off the phone, hurried to the library, and stayed there until it closed. She was certain that Eliza would be waiting outside her dorm, smoking cigarettes and determined to keep her awake half the night. She dreaded paying these wages of friendship but was also resigned to it, and so it was strangely disappointing to return to her dorm and see no trace of Eliza. She almost felt like calling her, but her relief and her tiredness outweighed her guilt.

Three days went by without word from Eliza. The night before Patty left for Christmas vacation, she finally called Eliza's number to make sure everything was OK, but the phone rang and rang. She flew home to Westchester in a cloud of guilt and worry that grew thicker with each of her failed attempts, from the phone in her parents' kitchen, to make contact with her friend. On Christmas Eve she went so far as to call the Whispering Pines Motel in Hibbing, Minnesota.

"This is a great Christmas present!" Walter said. "Hearing from you."

"Oh, well, thank you. I'm actually calling about Eliza. She's sort of disappeared."

"Count yourself lucky," Walter said. "Richard and I finally had to unplug our phone."

"When was that?"

"Two days ago."

"Oh, well, that's a relief."

Patty stayed talking to Walter, answering his many questions, describing her siblings' mad Yuletide acquisitiveness, and her family's annual humiliating reminders of how amusingly old she'd been before she stopped believing in Santa Claus, and her father's bizarre sexual and scatological repartee with her middle sister, and the middle sister's "complaints" about how unchallenging her freshman course work at Yale was, and her mother's second-guessing of her decision, twenty years earlier, to stop celebrating Hanukkah and other Jewish holidays. "And how are things with you?" Patty asked Walter after half an hour.

"Fine," he said. "My mom and I are baking. Richard's playing checkers with my dad."

"That sounds nice. I wish I were there."

"I wish you were, too. We could go snowshoeing."

"That sounds really nice."

It genuinely did, and Patty could no longer tell whether it was Richard's presence that made Walter appealing or whether he might be appealing for his own sake—for his ability to make whatever place he was in seem like a homey place to be.

The dreadful call from Eliza came on Christmas night. Patty answered it on the extension in the basement, where she was watching an NBA game by herself. Before she could even apologize, Eliza herself apologized for her silence and said that she'd been busy seeing doctors. "They say I have leukemia," she said.

"No."

"I'm starting treatments after New Year's. My parents are the only other ones who know, and you can't tell anyone. You especially can't tell Richard. Will you swear you won't tell anyone?"

Patty's cloud of guilt and worry now condensed into a storm of sentiment. She wept and wept and asked Eliza if she was *sure*, if the doctors were *sure*. Eliza explained that she'd been feeling increasingly draggy as the fall went on, but she hadn't wanted to tell anyone, because she was afraid Richard would dump her if it turned out she had mono, but finally she'd felt so crappy that she went to see a doctor, and the verdict had come back two days earlier: leukemia.

"Is it the bad kind?"

"They're all bad."

"But the kind you can get better from?"

"There's a good chance the treatments will help," Eliza said. "I'll know more in a week."

"I'll come back early. I can stay with you."

But Eliza, oddly enough, no longer wanted Patty staying with her.

Regarding the Santa Claus business: the autobiographer has no sympathy with lying parents, and yet there are degrees to this. There are lies you tell a person who's being given a surprise party, lies told in a spirit of fun, and then there are lies you tell a person to make them look foolish for believing them. One Christmas, as a teenager, Patty became so upset about being teased for her unnaturally long-lived childhood belief in Santa (which had persisted even after two younger siblings lost it) that she refused to leave her room for Christmas dinner. Her dad, coming in to plead with her, for once stopped smiling and told her seriously that the family had preserved her illusions because her innocence was beautiful and they specially loved her for it. This was both a welcome thing to hear and obvious bullshit belied by the pleasure everybody took in teasing her. Patty believed that parents have a duty to teach their children how to recognize reality when they see it.

Suffice it to say that Patty, in her many winter weeks of playing Florence Nightingale to Eliza—trudging through a blizzard to bring her soup, cleaning her kitchen and bathroom, staying up late with her and watching TV when she should have been sleeping before games, sometimes falling asleep with her arms around her emaciated friend, submitting to extreme endearments ("You're my darling angel," "Seeing your face is like being in heaven," etc., etc.), and refusing, all the while, to return Walter's phone calls and explain why she didn't have time to hang out with him anymore—failed to notice any number of red flags. No, Eliza said, this particular chemotherapy wasn't the kind that made people's hair fall out. And, no, it wasn't possible to schedule treatments at times when Patty was available to take her home from the clinic. And, no, she didn't want to give up her apartment and stay with her parents, and, yes, the parents came to visit all the time, it was just coincidence that Patty never saw them, and, no, it was not unusual for cancer patients to give themselves anti-emetics with a hypodermic needle such as the one Patty noticed on the floor underneath Eliza's nightstand.

Arguably the biggest red flag was the way she, Patty, avoided Walter. She saw him at two games in January and spoke to him briefly, but he missed a bunch of games after that, and her conscious reason for not returning his many later phone messages was that she was embarrassed to admit how much of Eliza she was seeing. But why should it have been embarrassing to be caring for a friend stricken with cancer? And likewise: how hard would it have been, when she was in fifth grade, to open her ears to her schoolmates' cynicism regarding Santa Claus, if she'd had the least bit of interest in learning the truth? She threw away the big poinsettia plant even though it still had life in it.

Walter finally caught up with her at the end of February, late on the snowy day of the Gophers' big game against UCLA, its highest-ranked opponent of the season. Patty was already ill-disposed toward the world that day, owing to a morning phone conversation with her mother, whose birthday it was. Patty had resolved not to babble about her own life and discover yet again that Joyce wasn't listening and didn't give a shit about the ranking of her team's opponent, but she hadn't even had a chance to exercise this self-restraint, because Joyce was so excited about Patty's middle sister, who had tried out for the lead role in an Off Broadway revival of *The Member of the Wedding* at her Yale professor's special urging and had landed the part of understudy, which was apparently a huge deal that might result in the sister's taking time off from Yale and living at home and pursuing drama full-time; and Joyce had been in raptures.

When Patty glimpsed Walter rounding the bleak brick corner of Wilson Library, she turned and hurried away, but he came running after her. Snow had collected on his big fur hat; his face was as red as a navigational beacon. Although he tried to smile and be friendly, his voice was shaking when he asked Patty whether she'd gotten any of his phone messages.

"I've just been so busy," she said. "I'm really sorry I didn't call you back."

"Is it something I *said*? Did I somehow offend you?"

He was hurt and angry and she hated it.

"No, no, not at all," she said.

"I would have called even more except I didn't want to keep bothering you."

"Just really, really busy," she murmured as the snow fell.

"The person who answers your phone started sounding really annoyed with me, because I kept leaving the same message."

"Well, her room's right next to the phone, so. You can understand that. She takes a lot of messages."

"I *don't* understand," Walter said, nearly crying. "Do you want me to leave you alone? Is that it?"

She hated scenes like this, she hated them.

"I'm truly just very busy," she said. "And I actually have a big game tonight, so."

"No," Walter said, "there's something wrong. What is it? You look so unhappy!"

She didn't want to mention the conversation with her mother, because she was trying to get her head into a game zone and it was best not to dwell on these things. But Walter so desperately insisted on an explanation—insisted in a way that went beyond his own feelings, insisted almost for the sake of *justice*—that she felt she had to say something.

"Look," she said, "you have to swear not to tell Richard," although she realized, even as she said it, that she'd never quite understood this prohibition, "but Eliza has leukemia. It's really terrible."

To her surprise, Walter laughed. "That doesn't seem likely."

"Well, it's true," she said. "Whether or not it seems likely to you."

"OK. And is she still doing heroin?"

A fact she'd seldom paid attention to before—that he was two years older than she was—suddenly made its presence felt.

"She has leukemia," Patty said. "I don't know anything about heroin."

"Even Richard knows enough not to do that stuff. Which, believe me, is saying something."

"I don't know anything about it."

Walter nodded and smiled. "Then you really are a sweet person."

"I don't know about that," she said. "But I've got to go eat now and get ready for the game."

"I can't see you play tonight," he said as she was turning to leave. "I wanted to, but Harry Blackmun's speaking. I have to go to that."

She turned back to him in irritation. "Not a problem."

"He's on the Supreme Court. He wrote *Roe v. Wade.*"

"I know that," she said. "My mom practically has a shrine to him that she burns incense at. You don't have to tell me who Harry Blackmun is."

"Right. Sorry."

The snow swirled between them.

"Right, so, I won't bother you anymore," Walter said. "I'm sorry about Eliza. I hope she's OK."

The autobiographer blames nobody but herself—not Eliza, not Joyce, not Walter—for what happened next. Like every player, she had suffered through plenty of cold shooting streaks and played her share of subpar games, but even on her worst nights she'd felt ensconced in something larger—in the team, in sportsmanship, in the idea that athletics *mattered*—and had drawn true comfort from the encouraging cries of her teammate sisters and their jinx-breaking raillery at halftime, the variations on themes of bricks and butterfingers, the stock phrases that she herself had yelled a thousand times before. She had always wanted the ball, because the ball had always saved her, the ball was what she knew for sure she had in life, the ball had been her loyal companion in her endless girlhood summers. And all the repetitious activities that people do in church which seem vapid or phony to nonbelievers—the low fives after every single basket, the lovecluster after every drained free throw, the high fives for every teammate coming off the court, the endless shriekings of "Way to go SHAWNA!" and "Way to play smart CATHY!" and "SWISH, WOO HOO, WOO HOO!"—had become such second nature to her and made such perfect sense, as necessary aids to unthinking high performance, that it would no sooner have occurred to her to be embarrassed by them than by the fact that running up and down the court made her sweat a lot. Female athletics was not all sweetness and light, of course. Underneath the hugs were festering rivalries and moral judgments and severe impatience, Shawna blaming Patty for feeding too many outlet passes to Cathy and not enough to her, Patty seething when the slow-witted reserve center Abbie Smith turned yet another possession into a jump ball that she then could not control, Mary Jane Rorabacker nursing an eternal grudge against Cathy for not inviting her to room with her and Patty and Shawna in sophomore year despite their having starred together at St. Paul Central, every starter feeling guiltily relieved when a promising recruit and potential rival underperformed under pressure, etc., etc., etc. But competitive sports was founded on a trick of devotion, a method of credence, and once it was fully drummed into you, in middle school or high school at the latest, you didn't have to wonder about anything important when you headed to the gym and suited up, you knew the Answer to the Question, the Answer was the Team, and any venial personal concerns were set aside.

It's possible that Patty, in her agitation following her encounter with Walter, forgot to eat enough. Definitely something was wrong from the minute she arrived at Williams Arena. The UCLA team was huge and physical, with three starters six feet or bigger, and Coach Treadwell's game plan was to wear them out on transition and let her smaller players, Patty especially, scurry and strike before the Bruins could get their defense set. On D the plan was to be extra aggressive and try to draw the Bruins' two big scorers into early foul trouble. The Gophers weren't expected to win, but if they did win they could move up into the top twenty in the unofficial national rankings—higher than they'd ever been during Patty's tenure. And so it was a very bad night for her to lose her religion.

She experienced a peculiar weakness at her core. She had her usual range of movement in her stretches, but her muscles felt somehow inelastic. Her teammates' loud pep grated on her nerves, and a tightness in her chest, a self-consciousness, inhibited her from shouting back at them. She succeeded in boxing out all thoughts about Eliza, but instead she found herself considering how, although her own career would be forever over after another season and a half, her middle sister could go on and be a famous actress all her life, and what a dubious investment of her own time and resources athletics had therefore been, and how blithely she'd ignored her mother's years of hinting to this effect. None of this, it's safe to say, was recommended as a way to be thinking before a big game.

"Just be yourself, be great," Coach Treadwell told her. "Who's our leader?"

"I'm our leader."

"Louder."

"*I'm* our leader."

"Louder!"

"I'M our leader."

If you've ever played team sports, you'll know that Patty immediately felt stronger and more centered and leaderly for saying this. Funny how the trick works—the transfusion of confidence through simple words. She was fine doing warm-ups and fine shaking hands with the Bruins' captains and feeling their appraising eyes on her, knowing they'd been told she was a big scoring threat and the Gophers' director on offense; she stepped into her rep for success as if it were a suit of armor. Once you're in the game, though, and you start hemorrhaging confidence, transfusion from the sidelines isn't possible. Patty scored one basket on an easy fast-break layup, and that was basically the end of her night. As early as the second minute, she could tell from the lump in her throat that she was going to suck as she had never sucked before. Her Bruin counterpart had two inches and thirty pounds and ungodly amounts of vertical leap on her, but the problem wasn't only physical or even mainly physical. The problem was the defeat in her heart. Instead of burning competitively with the injustice of the Bruins' size advantage, and relentlessly pursuing the ball, as Coach had told her to do, she felt defeated by injustice: felt sorry for herself. The Bruins tried out a full-court press and discovered that it worked spectacularly. Shawna rebounded and passed Patty the ball, but she got trapped in the corner and gave it up. She got the ball again and fell out of bounds. She got the ball again and faked it directly into the hands of a defender, as if making a little present. Coach called a time-out and told her to station herself farther up the court on transition; but Bruins were waiting for her there. A long pass went off her hands and into the seats. Fighting the lump in her throat, trying to get mad, she got a foul for charging. She had no spring in her jump shot. She turned the ball over twice in the paint, and Coach took her out to have a word.

"Where's my girl? Where's my leader?"

"I don't have it tonight."

"You absolutely have it, you just have to find it. It's in there. Find it."

"OK."

"Scream at me. Let it out."

Patty shook her head. "I don't want to let it out."

Coach, crouching, peered up into her face, and Patty, with great effort of will, forced herself to meet her eyes.

"Who's our leader?"

"I am."

"Shout it."

"I can't."

"You want me to bench you? Is that what you want?"

"No!"

"Then get out there. We need you. Whatever it is, we can talk about it later. OK?"

"OK."

This new transfusion poured straight into the hemorrhage without circulating even once through Patty's body. For the sake of her teammates, she stayed in the game, but she reverted to her old habit of being selfless, of following plays instead of leading them, of passing instead of shooting, and then to her even older habit of lingering around the perimeter and taking long jumpers, some of which might have fallen on another night, but not that night. How hard it is to hide on a basketball court! Patty got beaten on defense again and again, and each defeat seemed to make the next one more likely. What she was feeling became a lot more familiar to her later in her life, when she made the acquaintance of serious depression, but on that February night it was a hideous novelty to feel the game swirling around her, totally out of her control, and to intuit that the significance of everything that happened, every approach and retreat of the ball, every heavy thud of her feet on the floor, every new moment of trying to guard a fully focused and determined Bruin, every teammate's hearty halftime whap on the shoulder, was her own badness and the emptiness of her future and the futility of struggle.

Coach finally sat her down for good midway through the second half, with the Gophers trailing by 25. She revived a little as soon as she was safely benched. She found her voice and exhorted her teammates and high-fived them like an eager rookie, reveling in the abasement of being reduced to a cheerleader in a game she should have starred in, embracing the shame of being too-delicately consoled by her pitying teammates. She felt she fully deserved to be abased and shamed like this, after how she'd stunk. Wallowing in this shit was the best she'd felt all day.

Afterward, in the locker room, she endured Coach's sermon with closed ears and then sat on a bench and sobbed for half an hour. Her friends were considerate enough to let her just do this.

In her down parka and her Gophers stocking cap, she went to Northrop Auditorium, hoping the Blackmun lecture might somehow still be going on there, but the building was dark and locked. She thought of returning to her hall and calling Walter, but she realized that what she really wanted now was to break training and get trashed on wine. She walked through snowy streets to Eliza's apartment, and here she realized that what she *really* wanted was to scream abusive things at her friend.

Eliza, on the intercom, objected that it was late and she was tired.

"No, you have to let me up," Patty said. "This is non-optional."

Eliza let her in and then lay down on her sofa. She was wearing pajamas and listening to some kind of throbbing jazz. The air was thick with lethargy and old smoke. Patty stood by the sofa, bundled in her parka, snow melting off her sneakers, and watched how slowly Eliza was breathing and how long it took for the impulse to speak to be effectuated—various random facial muscle movements gradually becoming a little less random and finally gathering into a murmured question: "How was your game."

Patty didn't answer. After a while, it became apparent that Eliza had forgotten about her.

There didn't seem to be much point in screaming abusive things at her right now, so Patty ransacked the apartment instead. The drug stuff came to light immediately, right on the floor at the head of the sofa—Eliza had simply dropped a throw pillow over it. At the bottom of a nest of poetry journals and music magazines on Eliza's desk was the blue three-ring binder. As far as Patty could tell, nothing had been added to it since the summer. She sifted through Eliza's papers and bills, looking for something medical, but didn't find anything. The jazz record was playing on repeat. Patty turned it off and sat down on the coffee table with the scrapbook and the drug stuff on the floor in front of her. "Wake up," she said.

Eliza squeezed her eyes shut tighter.

Patty shoved her leg. "Wake up."

"I need a cigarette. The chemo really knocked me out."

Patty pulled her upright by the shoulder.

"Hey," Eliza said, with a murky smile. "Nice to see you."

"I don't want to be your friend anymore," Patty said. "I don't want to see you anymore."

"Why not?"

"I just don't."

Eliza closed her eyes and shook her head. "I need you to help me," she said. "I've been taking drugs because of the pain. Because of the cancer. I wanted to tell you. But I was too embarrassed." She tilted sideways and lay back down.

"You don't have cancer," Patty said. "That's just a lie you made up because you have some crazy idea about me."

"No, I have leukemia. I definitely have leukemia."

"I came over to tell you in person, as a courtesy. But now I'm going to leave."

"No. You have to stay. I have a drug problem you have to help me with."

"I can't help you. You'll have to go to your parents."

There was a long silence. "Get me a cigarette," Eliza said.

"I hate your cigarettes."

"I thought you understood about parents," Eliza said. "About not being the person they wanted."

"I don't understand anything about you."

There was another silence. Then Eliza said, "You know what's going to happen if you leave, don't you? I'm going to kill myself."

"Oh, that's a great reason to stay and be friends," Patty said. "That sounds like a lot of fun for both of us."

"I'm just saying that's probably what I'll do. You're the only thing I have that's beautiful and real."

"I'm not a thing," Patty said righteously.

"Have you ever seen somebody shoot up? I've gotten pretty good at it."

Patty took the syringe and the drugs and put them in the pocket of her parka. "What's your parents' telephone number?"

"Don't call them."

"I'm going to call them. It's non-optional."

"Will you stay with me? Will you come visit me?"

"Yes," Patty lied. "Just tell me their number."

"They ask about you all the time. They think you're a good influence on my life. Will you stay with me?"

"Yes," Patty lied again. "What's their number?"

When the parents arrived, after midnight, they wore the grim looks of people interrupted in their enjoyment of a long respite from dealing with exactly this sort of thing. Patty was fascinated to finally meet them, but this feeling was evidently not reciprocated. The father had a full beard and deep-set dark eyes, the mother was petite and wearing high-heeled leather boots, and together they gave off a strong sexual vibe that reminded Patty of French movies and of Eliza's comments about their being the love of each other's life. Patty wouldn't have minded receiving a few words of apology for unleashing their disturbed daughter on unsuspecting third parties such as herself, or a few words of gratitude for taking their daughter off their hands these past two years, or a few words of acknowledgment of whose money had subsidized the latest crisis. But as soon as the little nuclear family was together in the living room, there unfolded a weird diagnostic drama in which there seemed to be no role at all for Patty.

"So which drugs," the father said.

"Um, smack," Eliza said.

"Smack, cigarettes, booze. What else? Anything else?"

"A little coke sometimes. Not so much now."

"Anything else?"

"No, that's all."

"And what about your friend? Is she using, too?"

"No, she's a huge basketball star," Eliza said. "I *told* you. She's totally straight and great. She's *amazing*."

"Did she know you were using?"

"No, I told her I had cancer. She didn't know anything."

"How long did that go on?"

"Since Christmas."

"So she believed you. You created an elaborate lie that she believed." Eliza giggled.

"Yes, I believed her," Patty said.

The father didn't even glance her way. "And what's this," he said, holding up the blue binder.

"That's my Patty Book," Eliza said.

"Appears to be some sort of obsessional scrapbook," the father said to the mother.

"So she said she was going to leave you," the mother said, "and then you said you were going to kill yourself."

"Something like that," Eliza admitted.

"This is quite obsessional," the father commented, flipping pages.

"Are you actually suicidal?" the mother said. "Or was that just a threat to keep your friend from leaving?"

"Mostly a threat," Eliza said.

"Mostly?"

"OK, I'm not actually suicidal."

"And yet you're aware that we have to take it seriously now," the mother said. "We have no choice."

"You know, I think I'm going to go now," Patty said. "I've got class in the morning, so."

"What kind of cancer did you pretend to have?" the father said. "Where in the body was it situated?"

"I said it was leukemia."

"In the blood, then. A fictitious cancer in your blood."

Patty put the drug stuff on the cushion of an armchair. "I'll just leave this right here," she said. "I really do have to be going."

The parents looked at her, looked at each other, and nodded.

Eliza stood up from the sofa. "When will I see you? Will I see you tomorrow?"

"No," Patty said. "I don't think so."

"Wait!" Eliza ran over and seized Patty by the hand. "I fucked everything up, but I'll get better, and then we can see each other again. OK?"

"Yes, OK," Patty lied as the parents moved in to pry their daughter off her.

Outside, the sky had cleared and the temperature had fallen to near zero. Patty drove breath after breath of cleanness down deep into her lungs. She was free! She was free! And, oh, how she wished she could go back now and play the game against UCLA again. Even at one in the morning, even with nothing in her stomach, she felt ready to excel. She sprinted down Eliza's street in sheer exhilaration at her freedom, hearing Coach's words in her ears for the first time, three hours after they'd been spoken, hearing her say how it was just one game, how everybody had bad games, how she'd be herself again tomorrow. She felt ready to dedicate herself more intensely than ever to staying fit and improving her skills, ready to see more theater with Walter, ready to say to her mother, "That's really great news about The Member of the Wedding!" Ready to be an all-around better person. In her exhilaration, she ran so blindly that she didn't see the black ice on the sidewalk until her left leg had slipped grue-somely out sideways behind her right leg and she'd ripped the shit out of her knee and was lying on the ground.

There's not a lot to say about the six weeks that followed. She had two surgeries, the second one following an infection from the first, and be-came an ace crutch-user. Her mother flew out for the first operation and treated the hospital staff as if they were midwestern yokels of question-able intelligence, causing Patty to apologize for her and be especially agreeable whenever she was out of the room. When it turned out that Joyce might have been right not to trust the doctors, Patty felt so cha-grined that she didn't even tell her about the second operation until the day before it happened. She assured Joyce that there was no need to fly out again—she had tons of friends to look after her.

Walter Berglund had learned from his own mother how to be atten-tive to women with ailments, and he took advantage of Patty's extended incapacitation to reinsert himself into her life. On the day after her first surgery, he appeared with a four-foot-tall Norfolk pine and suggested that she might prefer a living plant to cut flowers that wouldn't last. After that, he managed to see Patty almost every day except on weekends, when he was up in Hibbing helping his parents, and he quickly endeared him-self to her jock friends with his niceness. Her homelier friends appreci-ated how much more intently he listened to them than all the guys who couldn't see past their looks, and Cathy Schmidt, her brightest friend, de-clared Walter smart enough to be on the Supreme Court. It was a novelty in Female Jockworld to have a guy in their midst who everybody felt so natural and relaxed around, a guy who could hang out in the lounge dur-ing study breaks and be one of the girls. And everybody could see that he was crazy about Patty, and everybody but Cathy Schmidt agreed that this was a most excellent thing.

Cathy, as noted, was sharper than the rest. "You're not really into him, are you," she said.

"I sort of am," Patty said. "But also sort of not."

"So . . . the two of you are not . . ."

"No! Nothing. I probably never should have told him I was raped. He got all squirrelly when I told him that. All . . . *tender* and . . . *nursey* and . . . *upset*. And now it's like he's waiting for written permission, or for me to make the move. Which, the crutches probably aren't helping there, either. But it's like I'm being followed around by a really nice, well-trained dog."

"That's not so great," Cathy said.

"No. It's not. But I can't get rid of him, either, because he's incredibly nice to me, and I really do love talking to him."

"You're sort of into him."

"Exactly. Maybe even somewhat more than sort of. But—"

"But not wildly more."

"Exactly."

Walter was interested in everything. He read every word of the newspaper and *Time* magazine, and in April, once Patty was semi-ambulatory again, he began inviting her to lectures and art films and documentaries that she otherwise would not have dreamed of going to. Whether it was because of his love or because of the void in her schedule created by her injury, this was the first time that a person had ever looked through her jock exterior and seen lights on inside. Although she felt inferior to Walter in pretty much every category of human knowledge except sports, she was grateful to him for illuminating that she actually had opinions and that her opinions could differ from his. (This was a refreshing contrast to Eliza, who, if you'd asked her who the current U.S. president was, would have laughed and claimed to have no idea and put another record on her stereo.) Walter burned with all sorts of earnest and peculiar views—he hated the pope and the Catholic Church but approved of the Islamic revolution in Iran, which he hoped would lead to better energy conservation in the United States; he liked China's new population-control policies and thought the U.S. should adopt something similar; he cared less about the Three Mile Island nuclear mishap than about the low price of gasoline and the need for high-speed rail systems that would render the passenger car obsolete; etc., etc.—and Patty found a role in obstinately approving of things he disapproved of. She especially enjoyed disagreeing with him about the Subjugation of Women. One afternoon near the end of the semester, over coffee at the Student Union, the two of them had a memorable talk about Patty's Primitive Art professor, whose lectures she approvingly described to Walter by way of giving him a subtle hint about what she found lacking in his personality.

"Yuck," Walter said. "This sounds like one of those middle-aged profs who can't stop talking about sex."

"Well, but he's talking about fertility figures," Patty said. "It's not his fault if the only sculpture we have from fifty thousand years ago is about sex. Plus he's got a white beard, and that's enough to make me feel sorry for him. I mean, think about it. He's up there, and he's got all these dirty things he wants to say about 'young ladies today,' you know, and our 'scrawny thighs,' and all, and he knows he's making us uncomfortable, and he knows he has this beard and he's middle-aged and we're all, you know, younger. But he can't help saying things anyway. I think that would be so hard. Not being able to help humiliating yourself."

"But it's so offensive!"

"And also," Patty said, "I think he's actually really into thunder thighs. I think that's what it's really about: he's into the Stone Aged thing. You know: fat. Which is sweet and kind of heartbreaking, that he's so into ancient art."

"But aren't you offended, as a feminist?"

"I don't really think of myself as a feminist."

"That's unbelievable!" Walter said, reddening. "You don't support the ERA?"

"Well, I'm not very political."

"But the whole reason you're here in Minnesota is you got an athletic scholarship, which couldn't even have happened five years ago. You're here because of feminist federal legislation. You're here because of Title Nine."

"But Title Nine's just basic fairness," Patty said. "If half your students are female, they should be getting half the athletic money."

"That's feminism!"

"No, it's basic fairness. Because, like, Ann Meyers? Have you heard of her? She was a big star at UCLA and she just signed a contract with the NBA, which is ridiculous. She's like five-six and a girl. She's never going to play. Men are just better athletes than women and always will be. That's why a hundred times more people go to see men's basketball than women's basketball—there's so much more that men can do athletically. It's just dumb to deny it."

"But what if you want to be a doctor, and they don't let you into medical school because they'd rather have male students?"

"That would be unfair, too, although I don't want to be a doctor."

"So what *do* you want?"

Sort of by default, because her mother was so relentless in promoting impressive careers for her daughters, and also because her mother had been, in Patty's opinion, a substandard parent, Patty was inclined to want to be a homemaker and an outstanding mother. "I want to live in a beautiful old house and have two children," she told Walter. "I want to be a really, really great mom."

"Do you want a career, too?"

"Raising children would be my career."

He frowned and nodded.

"You see," she said, "I'm not very interesting. I'm not nearly as interesting as your other friends."

"That's so untrue," he said. "You're incredibly interesting."

"Well, that's very nice of you to say, but I don't think it makes much sense."

"I think there's so much more inside you than you give yourself credit for."

"I'm afraid you're not very realistic about me," Patty said. "I bet you can't actually name one interesting thing about me."

"Well, your athletic ability, for starters," Walter said.

"Dribble dribble. That's real interesting."

"And the way you think," he said. "The fact that you think that that hideous prof is sweet and heartbreaking."

"But you disagree with me about that!"

"And the way you talk about your family. The way you tell stories about them. The fact that you're so far away from them and having your own life here. That's all incredibly interesting."

Patty had never been around a man so obviously in love with her. What he and she were secretly talking about, of course, was Walter's desire to put his hands on her. And yet the more time she spent with him, the more she was coming to feel that even though she wasn't nice—or maybe *because* she wasn't nice; because she was morbidly competitive and attracted to unhealthy things—she was, in fact, a fairly interesting person. And Walter, by insisting so fervently on her interestingness, was definitely making progress toward making himself interesting to her in turn.

"If you're so feminist," she said, "why are you best friends with Richard? Isn't he kind of disrespectful?"

Walter's face clouded. "Definitely, if I had a sister, I'd make sure she never met him."

"Why?" Patty said. "Because he'd treat her badly? Is he bad to women?"

"He doesn't mean to be. He likes women. He just goes through them pretty quickly."

"Because we're interchangeable? Because we're just objects?"

"It's not political," Walter said. "He's in favor of equal rights. It's more like this is his addiction, or one of them. You know, his dad was such a drunk, and Richard doesn't drink. But it's the same thing as emptying your whole liquor cabinet down the drain, after a binge. That's the way he is with a girl he's done with."

"That sounds horrible."

"Yeah, I don't particularly like it in him."

"But you're still friends with him, even though you're a feminist."

"You don't stop being loyal to a friend just because they're not perfect."

"No, but you try to help them be a better person. You explain why what they're doing is wrong."

"Is that what you did with Eliza?"

"OK, you have a point there."

The next time she spoke to Walter, he finally asked her out on an actual movie-and-a-dinner date. The movie (this was very Walter) turned out to be a free one, a black-and-white Greek-language thing called *The Fiend of Athens*. While they sat in the Art Department cinema, surrounded by empty seats, waiting for the movie to start, Patty described her plan for the summer, which was to stay with Cathy Schmidt at her parents' house in the suburbs, continue physical therapy, and prepare for a comeback next season. Out of the blue, in the empty cinema, Walter asked her if she might instead want to live in the room being vacated by Richard, who was moving to New York City.

"Richard's leaving?"

"Yeah," Walter said, "New York is where all the interesting music is happening. He and Herrera want to reconstitute the band and try to make it there. And I've still got three months on the lease."

"Wow." Patty composed her face carefully. "And I would live in his room."

"Well, it wouldn't be his room anymore," Walter said. "It would be yours. It's an easy walk to the gym. I'm thinking it would be a lot easier than commuting all the way from Edina."

"And so you're asking me to *live* with you."

Walter blushed and avoided her eyes. "You'd have your own room, obviously. But, yes, if you ever wanted to have dinner and hang out, that would be great, too. I think I'm somebody you can trust to be respectful of your space but also be there if you wanted company."

Patty peered into his face, struggling to understand. She felt a combination of (a) offended, and (b) very sorry to hear that Richard was leaving. She *almost* suggested to Walter that he had better kiss her first, if he was going to be asking her to live with him, but she was so offended that she didn't feel like being kissed at that moment. And then the cinema lights went down.

As the autobiographer remembers it, the plot of *The Fiend of Athens* concerned a mild-mannered Athenian accountant with horn-rimmed glasses who is walking to work one morning when he sees his own picture on the front page of a newspaper, with the headline FIEND OF ATHENS STILL AT LARGE. Athenians in the street immediately start pointing at him and chasing him, and he's on the brink of being apprehended when he's rescued by a gang of terrorists or criminals who mistake him for their fiendish leader. The gang has a bold plan to do something like blow up the Parthenon, and the hero keeps trying to explain to them that he's just a mild-mannered accountant, not the Fiend, but the gang is so counting on his help, and the rest of the city is so intent on killing him, that there finally comes an amazing moment when he whips off his glasses *and becomes their fearless leader*—the Fiend of Athens! He says, "OK, men, this is how the plan is going to work."

Patty watched the movie seeing Walter in the accountant and imagining him whipping his glasses off like that. Afterward, over dinner at Vescio's, Walter interpreted the movie as a parable of Communism in postwar Greece and explained to Patty how the United States, in need of NATO partners in southeast Europe, had long sponsored political repression over there. The accountant, he said, was an Everyman figure who comes to accept his responsibility to join in the violent struggle against right-wing repression.

Patty was drinking wine. "I don't agree with that at all," she said. "I think it's about how the main character never had a real life, because he was so responsible and timid, and he had no idea what he was actually capable of. He never really got to be alive until he was mistaken for the Fiend. Even though he only lived a few days after that, it was OK for him to die because he'd finally really done something with his life, and realized his potential."

Walter seemed astonished by this. "That was a totally pointless way to die, though," he said. "He didn't accomplish anything."

"But then why did he do it?"

"Because he felt solidarity with the gang that saved his life. He realized that he had a responsibility to them. They were the underdogs, and they needed him, and he was loyal to them. He died for his loyalty."

"God," Patty marveled. "You really are quite amazingly worthy."

"That's not how it feels," Walter said. "I feel like the stupidest person on earth sometimes. I *wish* I could cheat. I *wish* I could be totally self-focused like Richard, and try to be some kind of artist. And it's not because I'm worthy that I can't. I just don't have the constitution for it."

"But the accountant didn't think he had the constitution for it, either. He surprised himself!"

"Yes, but it wasn't a realistic movie. The picture in the newspaper didn't just look like the actor, it *was him*. And if he'd just given himself up to the authorities, he could have straightened everything out eventually. The mistake he made was to start running. That's why I'm saying it was a parable. It wasn't a realistic story."

It felt strange to Patty to be drinking wine with Walter, since he was a teetotaler, but she was in a fiendish mood and had quickly put away quite a lot. "Take your glasses off," she said.

"No," he said. "I won't be able to see you."

"That's OK. It's just me. Just Patty. Take them off."

"But I love seeing you! I love looking at you!"

Their eyes met.

"Is that why you want me to live with you?" Patty said.

He blushed. "Yes."

"Well, so, maybe we should go look at your apartment, so I can decide."

"Tonight?"

"Yes."

"You're not tired?"

"No. I'm not tired."

"How's your knee feeling?"

"My knee is feeling just fine, thank you."

For once, she was thinking of Walter only. If you'd asked her, as she crutched her way down 4th Street through the soft and conducive May air, whether she was half-hoping to run into Richard at the apartment, she would have answered no. She wanted sex *now*, and if Walter had had one ounce of sense he would have turned away from the door of his apartment as soon as he heard TV noise on the other side of it—would have taken her somewhere else, anywhere else, back to her own room, anywhere. But Walter believed in true love and was apparently fearful of laying a hand on Patty before he was sure his was reciprocated. He led her right on into the apartment, where Richard was sitting in the living room with his bare feet up on the coffee table, a guitar across his lap, and a spiral notebook beside him on the sofa. He was watching a war movie and working on a jumbo Pepsi and spitting tobacco juice into a 28-ounce tomato can. The room was otherwise neat and uncluttered.

"I thought you were at a show," Walter said.

"Show sucked," Richard said.

"You remember Patty, right?"

Patty shyly crutched herself into better view. "Hi, Richard."

"Patty who is not considered tall," Richard said.

"That's me."

"And yet you are quite tall. I'm glad to see Walter finally lured you over here. I was beginning to fear it would never happen."

"Patty's thinking of living here this summer," Walter said.

Richard raised his eyebrows. "Really."

He was thinner and younger and sexier than she remembered. It was terrible how suddenly she wanted to deny that she'd been thinking of living here with Walter or expecting to go to bed with him that night. But there was no denying the evidence of her standing there. "I'm looking for someplace convenient to the gym," she said.

"Of course. Makes sense."

"She was hoping to see your room," Walter said.

"Room's a bit of a mess right now."

"You say that as if there were times when it's not a mess," Walter said with a happy laugh.

"There are periods of relative unmessiness," Richard said. He extinguished the TV with an extended toe. "How's your little friend Eliza?" he asked Patty.

"She's not my friend anymore."

"I told you that," Walter said.

"I wanted it from the horse's mouth. She's a fucked-up little chick, isn't she? The extent of it wasn't immediately apparent, but, man. It became apparent."

"I made the same mistake," Patty said.

"Only Walter saw the truth from day one. The Truth About Eliza. That's not a bad title."

"I had the advantage of her hating me at first sight," Walter said. "I could see her more clearly."

Richard closed his notebook and spat brown saliva into his can. "I will leave you kids alone."

"What are you working on?" Patty asked.

"The usual unlistenable shit. I was trying to do something with this chick Margaret Thatcher. The new prime minister of England?"

"Chick is a far-fetched word for Margaret Thatcher," Walter said. "Dowager is more like it."

"How do you feel about the word 'chick'?" Richard asked Patty.

"Oh, I'm not a picky person."

"Walter says I shouldn't use it. He says it's demeaning, although, in my experience, the chicks themselves don't seem to mind."

"It makes you sound like you're from the sixties," Patty said.

"It makes him sound Neanderthal," Walter said.

"The Neanderthals reportedly had very large craniums," Richard said.

"So do oxen," Walter said. "And other cud-chewing animals."

Richard laughed.

"I didn't think anybody but baseball players chewed tobacco anymore," Patty said. "What's it like?"

"You're free to try some, if you're in the mood to vomit," Richard said, standing up. "I'm going to head back out. Leave you guys alone."

"Wait, I want to try it," Patty said.

"Really not a good idea," Richard said.

"No, I definitely want to try it."

The mood she'd been in with Walter was irreparably broken, and now she was curious to see if she had the power to make Richard stay. She'd finally found her opportunity to demonstrate what she'd been trying to explain to Walter since the night they first met—that she wasn't a good enough person for him. It was also, of course, an opportunity for Walter to whip off his glasses and behave fiendishly and drive away his rival. But Walter, then as ever, only wanted Patty to have what she wanted.

"Let her try it," he said.

She gave him a grateful smile. "Thank you, Walter."

The chew was mint-flavored and burned her gums shockingly. Walter brought her a coffee mug to spit in, and she sat on the sofa like an experimental subject, waiting for the nicotine to take effect, enjoying the attention. But Walter was paying attention to Richard, too, and as her heart began to race she flashed on Eliza's contention that Walter had a thing for his friend; she remembered Eliza's jealousy.

"Richard's excited about Margaret Thatcher," Walter said. "He thinks she represents the excesses of capitalism that will inevitably lead to its self-destruction. I'm guessing he's writing a love song."

"You know me well," Richard said. "A love song to the lady with the hair."

"We disagree about the likelihood of a Marxist Revolution," Walter explained to Patty.

"Mm," she said, spitting.

"Walter thinks the liberal state can self-correct," Richard said. "He thinks the American bourgeoisie will voluntarily accept increasing restrictions on its personal freedoms."

"I have all these great ideas for songs that Richard inexplicably keeps rejecting."

"The fuel-efficiency song. The public-transportation song. The nationalized-health-care song. The baby-tax song."

"It's pretty much virgin territory, in terms of rock-song content," Walter said.

"Two Kids Good, Four Kids Bad."

"Two Kids Good—*No* Kids Better."

"I can already see the masses taking to the streets."

"You just have to become unbelievably famous," Walter said. "Then people will listen."

"I'll make a note to do that." Richard turned to Patty. "How you doing there?"

"Mm!" she said, ejecting the wad into the coffee mug. "I see what you mean about the vomiting."

"Try not to do it on the couch."

"Are you all right?" Walter said.

The room was swimming and pulsing. "I can't believe you enjoy this," Patty said to Richard.

"And yet I do."

"Are you all right?" Walter asked her again.

"I'm fine. Just need to sit very still."

She in fact felt quite sick. There was nothing to be done but stay on the sofa and listen to Walter and Richard banter and joust about politics and music. Walter, with great enthusiasm, showed her the Traumatics' seven-inch single and compelled Richard to play both sides of it on the stereo. The first song was "I Hate Sunshine," which she'd heard at the club in the fall, and which now seemed to her the sonic equivalent of absorbing too much nicotine. Even at low volume (Walter, needless to say, was pathologically considerate of his neighbors), it gave her a sick, dready sensation. She could feel Richard's eyes on her while she listened to his dire baritone singing voice, and she knew she hadn't been mistaken about the way he'd looked at her the other times she'd seen him.

Around eleven o'clock, Walter began to yawn uncontrollably.

"I'm so sorry," he said. "I have to take you home now."

"I'm fine walking by myself. I've got my crutches for self-defense."

"No," he said. "We'll take Richard's car."

"No, you need to go to sleep, you poor thing. Maybe Richard can drive me. Can you do that for me?" she asked him.

Walter closed his eyes and sighed miserably, as if he'd been pushed past his limits.

"Sure," Richard said. "I'll drive you."

"She needs to see your room first," Walter said, his eyes still closed.

"Be my guest," Richard said. "Its condition speaks for itself."

"No, I want the guided tour," Patty said, giving him a pointed look.

The walls and ceiling of his room were painted black, and the punk disorder that Walter's influence had suppressed in the living room here vented itself with a vengeance. There were LPs and LP sleeves everywhere, along with several cans of spit, another guitar, overloaded bookshelves, a mayhem of socks and underwear, and tangled dark bedsheets that it was interesting and somehow not unpleasant to think that Eliza had been vigorously erased in.

"Nice cheerful color!" Patty said.

Walter yawned again. "Obviously I'll be repainting it."

"Unless Patty prefers black," Richard said from the doorway.

"I'd never thought of black," she said. "Black is interesting."

"Very restful color, I find," Richard said.

"So you're moving to New York," she said.

"I am."

"That's exciting. When?"

"Two weeks."

"Oh, that's when I'm going out there, too. It's my parents' twenty-fifth anniversary. Some sort of horrible Event is planned."

"You're from New York?"

"Westchester County."

"Same as me. Though presumably a different part of Westchester."

"Well, the suburbs."

"Definitely a different part than Yonkers."

"I've seen Yonkers from the train a bunch of times."

"Exactly my point."

"So are you driving to New York?" Patty said.

"Why?" Richard said. "You need a ride?"

"Well, maybe! Are you offering one?"

He shook his head. "Have to think about it."

Poor Walter's eyes were falling shut, he literally was not seeing this negotiation. Patty herself was breathless with the guilt and confusion of it and crutched herself speedily toward the front door, where, at a distance, she called out a thank-you to him for the evening.

"I'm sorry I got so tired," he said. "Are you sure I can't drive you home?"

"I'll do it," Richard said. "You go to bed."

Walter definitely looked miserable, but it might only have been his exhaustion. Out on the street, in the conducive air, Patty and Richard walked in silence until they got to his rusty Impala. Richard seemed to take care not to touch her while she got herself seated and handed him her crutches.

"I would have thought you'd have a van," she said when he was sitting beside her. "I thought all bands had vans."

"Herrera has the van. This is my personal conveyance."

"This is what I'd be riding to New York in."

"Yeah, listen." He put the key in the ignition. "You need to fish or cut bait here. Do you understand me? It's not fair to Walter otherwise."

She looked straight ahead through the windshield. "What isn't fair?"

"Giving him hope. Leading him on."

"That's what you think I'm doing?"

"He's an extraordinary person. He's very, very serious. You need to take some care with him."

"I know that," she said. "You don't have to tell me that."

"Well, so, what did you come over here for? It seemed to me—"

"What? What did it seem to you?"

"It seemed to me like I was interrupting something. But then, when I tried to get away . . ."

"God, you really *are* a jerk."

Richard nodded as if he couldn't care less what she thought of him, or as if he were tired of stupid women saying stupid things to him. "When I tried to get away," he said, "you seemed not to want to take the hint. Which is fine, that's your choice. I just want to make sure you know you're kind of tearing Walter apart."

"I really don't want to talk about this with you."

"Fine. We won't talk about it. But you've been seeing a lot of him, right? Practically every day, right? For weeks and weeks."

"We're friends. We hang out."

"Nice. And you know the situation in Hibbing."

"Yes. His mom needs help with the hotel."

Richard smiled unpleasantly. "That's what you know?"

"Well, and his dad's not well, and his brothers aren't doing anything."

"And that's what he's told you. That's the extent of it."

"His dad has emphysema. His mom has disabilities."

"And he's working construction twenty-five hours a week and pulling down As in law school. And there he is, every day, with all that time to hang out with you. How nice for you, that he has so much free time. But you're a good-looking chick, you deserve it, right? Plus you've got your terrible injury. That *and* being good-looking: that earns you the right not to even ask him any questions."

Patty was burning with her feeling of injustice. "You know," she said unsteadily, "he talks about what a jerk you are to women. He talks about that."

This seemed not to interest Richard in the slightest. "I'm just trying to understand this in the context of your being such pals with wee Eliza," he said. "It's making more sense to me now. It didn't when I first saw you. You seemed like a nice suburban girl."

"So I'm a jerk, too. Is that what you're saying? I'm a jerk and you're a jerk."

"Sure. Whatever you like. I'm Not OK, You're Not OK. Whatever. I'm just asking you *not* to be a jerk to Walter."

"I'm not!"

"I'm simply telling you what I see."

"Well, you see wrong. I really like Walter. I really care about him."

"And yet you're apparently unaware that his dad's dying of liver disease and his older brother's in jail for vehicular assault and his other brother's spending his Army paychecks making payments on his vintage Corvette. And Walter's averaging about four hours of sleep while you're being friends and hanging out, just so you can come over here and flirt with me."

Patty became very quiet.

"It's true I didn't know all of that," she said after a while. "All of that information. But you shouldn't be friends with him if you've got a problem with people flirting with you."

"Ah. So it's my fault. I getcha."

"Well, I'm sorry, but it kind of is."

"I rest my case," Richard said. "You need to get your thoughts straightened out."

"I'm aware that I need to do that," Patty said. "But you're still being a jerk."

"Look, I'll drive you to New York, if that's what you want. Two jerks on the road. Could be fun. But if that's what you want, you need to do me a favor and stop stringing Walter along."

"Fine. Please take me home now."

Due perhaps to the nicotine, she spent that entire night sleeplessly replaying the evening in her head, trying to do as Richard had demanded and get her thoughts straight. But it was an odd mental kabuki, because even as she was circling around and around the question of what kind of person she was and what her life was ultimately going to look like, one fat fact sat fixed and unchanging at the center of her: she wanted to take a road trip with Richard and, what's more, she was going to do it. The sad truth was that their talk in the car had been a tremendous excitement and relief to her—an excitement because Richard was exciting and a relief because, finally, after months of trying to be somebody she wasn't, or wasn't quite, she'd felt and sounded like her unpretended true self. This was why she knew she'd find a way to take the road trip. All she had to do now was surmount her guilt about Walter and her sorrow about not being the kind of person he and she both wished she were. How right he'd been to go slow with her! How smart he was about her inner dubiousness! When she considered how right and smart he was about her, she felt all the sadder and guiltier about disappointing him, and was plunged back into the roundabout of indecision.

And then, for almost a week, she didn't hear from him. She suspected he was keeping his distance at Richard's suggestion—that Richard had given him a misogynistic lecture about the faithlessness of women and the need to protect his heart better. In her imagination, this was both a valuable service for Richard to perform and a terrible disillusioning thing to do to Walter. She couldn't stop thinking of Walter carrying large plants for her on buses, the poinsettia redness of his cheeks. She thought of the nights when, in her dorm lounge, he'd been trapped by the Hall Bore, Suzanne Storrs, who combed her hair sideways over her head with the part way down one side of it, just above her ear, and how he'd listened patiently to Suzanne's sour droning about her diet and the hardships of inflation and the overheating of her dorm room and her wide-ranging disappointment with the university's administrators and professors, while Patty and Cathy and her other friends laughed at *Fantasy Island*: how Patty, ostensibly incapacitated by her knee, had declined to stand up and rescue Walter from Suzanne, for fear that Suzanne would then come over and inflict her boringness on everybody else, and how Walter, though perfectly capable of joking with Patty about Suzanne's shortcomings, and though undoubtedly mindful of how much work he had to do and how early he had to get up in the morning, allowed himself to be trapped again on other evenings, because Suzanne had taken a shine to him and he felt sorry for her.

Suffice it to say that Patty couldn't quite bring herself to cut bait. They didn't communicate again until Walter called from Hibbing to apologize for his silence and report that his dad was in a coma.

"Oh, Walter, I miss you!" she exclaimed although this was *exactly* the sort of thing Richard would have urged her not to say.

"I miss you, too!"

She bethought herself to ask for details about his dad's condition, even though it only made sense to be a good questioner if she was intending to proceed with him. Walter spoke of liver failure, pulmonary edema, a shitty prognosis.

"I'm so sorry," she said. "But listen. About the room—"

"Oh, you don't have to decide about that now."

"No, but you need an answer. If you're going to rent it to somebody else—"

"I'd rather rent it to you!"

"Well, yes, and I might want it, but I have to go home next week, and I was thinking of riding to New York with Richard. Since that's when he's driving."

Any worries that Walter might not grasp the import here were dispelled by his sudden silence.

"Don't you already have a plane ticket?" he said finally.

"It's the refundable kind," she lied.

"Well, that's fine," he said. "But, you know, Richard's not very reliable."

"No, I know, I know," she said. "You're right. I just thought I might save some money, which I could then apply to the rent." (A compounding of the lie. Her parents had bought the ticket.) "I'll definitely pay the rent for June no matter what."

"That doesn't make any sense if you're not going to live there."

"Well, I probably will, is what I'm saying. I'm just not positive yet."

"OK."

"I really want to. I'm just not positive. So if you find another renter, you should probably go with them. But definitely I'll cover June."

There was another silence before Walter, in a discouraged voice, said he had to get off the phone.

Energized by having achieved this difficult conversation, she called Richard and assured him that she'd done the necessary bait-cutting, at which point Richard mentioned that his departure date was somewhat uncertain and there were a couple of shows in Chicago that he was hoping to stop and see.

"Just as long as I'm in New York by next Saturday," Patty said.

"Right, the anniversary party. Where is it?"

"It's at the Mohonk Mountain House, but I only need to get to Westchester."

"I'll see what I can do."

It's not so fun to be on a road trip with a driver who considers you, and perhaps all women, a pain in the ass, but Patty didn't know this until she'd tried it. The trouble started with the departure date, which had to be moved up for her. Then a mechanical issue with the van delayed Herrera, and since it was Herrera's friends in Chicago whom Richard had been planning to stay with, and since Patty had not been part of that deal in any case, there promised to be awkwardness there. Patty also wasn't good at computing distances, and so, when Richard was three hours late in picking her up and they didn't get away from Minneapolis until late afternoon, she didn't understand how late they would be arriving in Chicago and how important it was to make good time on I-94. It wasn't *her* fault they'd started late. She didn't consider it excessive to ask, near Eau Claire, for a bathroom stop, and then, an hour later, near nowhere, for some dinner. This was her road trip and she intended to enjoy it! But the back seat was full of equipment that Richard didn't dare let out of his sight, and his own basic needs were satisfied by his plug (he had a big spit can on the floor), and although he didn't criticize how much her crutches slowed and complicated everything she did, he also didn't tell her to relax and take her time. And all across Wisconsin, every minute of the way, in spite of his curtness and his barely suppressed irritation with her entirely reasonable human needs, she could feel the almost physical pressure of his interest in *fucking*, and this didn't help the mood in the car much, either. Not that she wasn't greatly attracted to him. But she needed a modicum of time and breathing space, and even taking into account her youth and inexperience the autobiographer is embarrassed to report that her means of buying this time and space was to bring the conversation around, perversely, to Walter.

At first, Richard didn't want to talk about him, but once she got him going she learned a lot about Walter's college years. About the symposia he'd organized—on overpopulation, on electoral-college reform—that hardly any students had attended. About the pioneering New Wave music show he'd hosted for four years on the campus radio station. About his petition drive for better-insulated windows in Macalester's dorms. About the editorials he'd written for the college paper regarding, for example, the food trays he processed in his job on the dish belt: how he'd calculated how many St. Paul families could be fed with a single night's waste, and how he'd reminded his fellow students that other human beings had to deal with the gobs of peanut butter they left smeared on everything, and how he'd grappled philosophically with his fellow students' habit of putting three times too much milk on their cold cereal and then leaving brimming bowls of soiled milk on their trays: did they somehow think milk was a free and infinite commodity like water, with no environmental strings attached? Richard recounted all this in the same protective tone he'd taken with Patty two weeks earlier, a tone of strangely tender regret on Walter's behalf, as if he were wincing at the pain Walter brought upon himself in butting up against harsh realities.

"Did he have girlfriends?" Patty asked.

"He made poor choices," Richard said. "He fell for the impossible chicks. The ones with boyfriends. The arty ones moving in a different kind of circle. There was one sophomore he didn't get over all senior year. He gave her his Friday-night radio slot and took a Tuesday afternoon. I found out about that too late to stop it. He rewrote her papers, took her to shows. It was terrible to watch, the way she worked him. She was always turning up in our room inopportunely."

"How funny," Patty said. "I wonder why that was."

"He never heeds my warnings. He's very obstinate. And you wouldn't necessarily guess it about him, but he always goes for good-looking. For pretty and well-formed. He's ambitious that way. It didn't lead to happy times for him in college."

"And this girl who kept showing up in your room. Did you like her?"

"I didn't like what she was doing to Walter."

"That's kind of a theme of yours, isn't it?"

"She had shit taste and a Friday-night slot. At a certain point, there was only one way to get the message across to him. About what kind of chick he was dealing with."

"Oh, so you were doing him a favor. I get it."

"Everybody's a moralist."

"No, seriously, I can see why you don't respect us. If all you ever see, year after year, is girls who want you to betray your best friend. I can see that's a weird situation."

"I respect you," Richard said.

"Ha-ha-ha."

"You've got a good head. I wouldn't mind seeing you this summer, if you want to give New York a try."

"That doesn't seem very workable."

"I'm merely saying it would be nice."

She had about three hours to entertain this fantasy—staring at the taillights of the traffic rushing down and down toward the great metropolis, and wondering what it would be like to be Richard's chick, wondering if a woman he respected might succeed in changing him, imagining herself never going back to Minnesota, trying to picture the apartment they might find to live in, savoring the thought of unleashing Richard on her contemptuous middle sister, picturing her family's consternation at how cool she'd become, and imagining her nightly erasure—before they landed in the reality of Chicago's South Side. It was 2 a.m. and Richard couldn't find Herrera's friends' building. Rail yards and a dark, haunted river kept blocking their way. The streets were deserted except for gypsy cabs and occasional Scary Black Youths of the kind one read about.

"A map would have been helpful," Patty said.

"It's a numbered street. Shouldn't be that hard."

Herrera's friends were artists. Their building, which Richard finally located with a cab driver's help, looked uninhabited. It had a doorbell dangling from two wires that unexpectedly were functional. Somebody moved aside a piece of canvas covering a front window and then came down to air grievances with Richard.

"Sorry, man," Richard said. "We got held up unavoidably. We just need to crash for a couple of nights."

The artist was wearing cheap, saggy underpants. "We just started taping that room today," he said. "It's pretty wet. Herrera said something about coming on the weekend?"

"He didn't call you yesterday?"

"Yeah, he called. I told him the spare room's a fucking mess."

"Not a problem. We're grateful. I've got some stuff to bring in."

Patty, being useless for carrying things, guarded the car while Richard slowly emptied it. The room they were given was heavy with a smell that she was too young to recognize as drywall mud, too young to find domestic and comforting. The only light was a glaring aluminum dish clamped to a mud-strafed ladder.

"Jesus," Richard said. "What do they have, chimpanzees doing drywalling?"

Underneath a dusty and mud-spattered pile of plastic drop cloths was a bare, rust-stained double mattress.

"Not up to your usual Sheraton standards, I'm guessing," Richard said.

"Are there sheets?" Patty said timidly.

He went rummaging in the main space and came back with an afghan, an Indian bedspread, and a velveteen pillow. "You sleep here," he said. "They've got a couch I can use."

She threw him a questioning look.

"It's late," he said. "You need to sleep."

"Are you sure? There's plenty of room here. A couch is going to be too short for you."

She was bleary, but she wanted him and was carrying the necessary gear, and she had an instinct to get the deed done right away, get it irrevocably on the books, before she had time to think too much and change her mind. And it was many years, practically half a lifetime, before she learned and was duly confounded by Richard's reason for suddenly turning so gentlemanly that night. At the time, in the mud-humid construction site, she could only assume she'd somehow been mistaken about him, or that she'd turned him off by being a pain in the ass and useless at carrying things.

"There's something that passes for a bathroom out there," he said. "You might have better luck than I did finding a light switch."

She gave him a yearning look from which he turned away quickly, purposefully. The sting and surprise of this, the strain of the drive, the stress of arrival, the grimness of the room: she killed the light and lay down in her clothes and wept for a long time, taking care to keep it inaudible, until her disappointment dissolved in sleep.

The next morning, awakened at six o'clock by ferocious sunlight, and rendered thoroughly cross by then waiting hours and hours for anybody else to stir in the apartment, she really did become a pain in the ass. That whole day represented something of a lifetime nadir of agreeability. Herrera's friends were physically uncouth and made her feel one inch tall for not getting their hip cultural references. She was given three quick chances to prove herself, after which they brutally ignored her, after which, to her relief, they left the apartment with Richard, who came back alone with a box of doughnuts for breakfast.

"I'm going to work on that room today," he said. "Makes me sick to see the shitty work they're doing. You feel like doing some sanding?"

"I was thinking we could go to the lake or something. I mean, it's so hot in here. Or maybe a museum?"

He regarded her gravely. "You want to go to a museum."

"Just something to get out and enjoy Chicago."

"We can do that tonight. Magazine's playing. You know Magazine?"

"I don't know anything. Isn't that obvious?"

"You're in a bad mood. You want to hit the road."

"I don't want to do anything."

"If we get the room cleaned up, you'll sleep better tonight."

"I don't care. I just don't feel like sanding."

The kitchen area was a nauseating, never-cleaned sty that smelled like a mental illness. Sitting on the couch where Richard had slept, Patty tried to read one of the books she'd brought along in hopes of impressing him, a Hemingway novel which the heat and the smell and her tiredness and the lump in her throat and the Magazine albums that Richard was playing made it impossible to concentrate on. When she got just intolerably hot, she went into the room where he was plastering and told him she was going for a walk.

He was shirtless, his chest hair flat and straight with running sweat. "Not a great neighborhood for that," he said.

"Well, maybe you'll come with me."

"Give me another hour."

"No, forget it," she said, "I'll just go by myself. Do we have a key to this place?"

"You really want to go out by yourself on crutches?"

"Yes, unless you want to come with me."

"Which, as I just said, I would do in an hour."

"Well, I don't feel like waiting an hour."

"In that case," Richard said, "the key is on the kitchen table."

"Why are you being so mean to me?"

He shut his eyes and seemed to count silently to ten. It was obvious how much he disliked women and the things they said.

"Why don't you take a cold shower," he said, "and wait for me to finish."

"You know, yesterday, for a while, it seemed like you were liking me."

"I do like you. I'm just doing some work here."

"Fine," she said. "Work."

The streets in the afternoon sun were even hotter than the apartment. Patty swung herself along at a considerable clip, trying not to cry too obviously, trying to appear as if she knew where she was going. The river, when she came to it, looked more benign than it had in the night, looked merely weedy and polluted rather than evil and all-swallowing. On the other side of it were Mexican streets festooned for some imminent or recent Mexican holiday, or maybe just permanently festooned. She found an air-conditioned taqueria where she was stared at but not harassed and could sit and drink a Coke and wallow in her girlish misery. Her body so wanted Richard, but the rest of her could see that she'd made a Mistake in coming along with him: that everything she'd hoped for from him and Chicago had been a big fat fantasy in her head. Phrases familiar from high-school Spanish, *lo siento* and *hace mucho calor* and *¿qué quiere la señora?*, kept surfacing in the surrounding hubbub. She summoned courage and ordered three tacos and devoured them and watched innumerable buses roll by outside the windows, each trailing a wake of shimmering filth. Time passed in a peculiar manner which the autobiographer, with her now rather abundant experience of murdered afternoons, is able to identify as *depressive* (at once interminable and sickeningly swift; chock-full second-to-second, devoid of content hour-by-hour), until finally, as the workday ended, groups of young laborers came in and began to pay too much attention to her, talking about her *muletas*, and she had to leave.

By the time she'd retraced her steps, the sun was an orange orb at the end of the east-west streets. Her intention, as she now allowed herself to realize, had been to stay out long enough to make Richard very worried about her, and in this she seemed completely to have failed. Nobody was home at the apartment. The walls of her room were nearly finished, the floor carefully swept, the bed neatly made up for her with real sheets and pillows. On the Indian bedspread was a note from Richard, in microscopic capital letters, giving her the address of a club and directions on how to take the El there. It concluded: WORD OF WARNING: I HAD TO BRING OUR HOSTS ALONG.

Before deciding whether to go out, Patty lay down for a short nap and was awakened many hours later, in great disorientation, by the return of Herrera's friends. She hopped, one-legged, into the main room and there learned, from the most disagreeable of them, the underpanted one from the night before, that Richard had gone off with some other people and had asked that Patty be told not to wait up for him—he'd be back in plenty of time to get her to New York.

"What time is it now?" she said.

"About one o'clock."

"In the morning?"

Herrera's friend leered at her. "No, there's a total eclipse of the sun."

"And where is Richard?"

"He went off with a couple of girls he met. He didn't say where."

As noted, Patty was bad at computing driving distances. To get to Westchester in time to go with her family to the Mohonk Mountain House, she and Richard would have had to leave Chicago at five o'clock that morning. She slept long past that and awoke to gray and stormy weather, a different city, a different season. Richard was still nowhere in sight. She ate stale doughnuts and turned some pages of Hemingway until it was eleven and even she could see that the math wasn't going to work.

She bit the bullet and called her parents, collect.

"Chicago!" Joyce said. "I can't believe this. Are you near an airport? Can you catch a plane? We thought you'd be here by now. Daddy wants to get an early start, with all the weekend traffic."

"I messed up," Patty said. "I'm really sorry."

"Well, can you get there by tomorrow morning? The big dinner isn't until tomorrow night."

"I'll try really hard," Patty said.

Joyce had been in the state assembly for three years now. If she had not gone on to enumerate to Patty all the relatives and family friends converging on Mohonk for this important tribute to a marriage, and the tremendous excitement with which Patty's three siblings were anticipating the weekend, and how greatly honored she (Joyce) felt by the outpouring of sentiment from literally all four corners of the country, it's possible that Patty would have done what it took to get to Mohonk. As things were, though, a strange peace and certainty settled over her while she listened to her mother. Light rain had begun to fall on Chicago; good smells of quenched concrete and Lake Michigan were carried inside by the wind stirring the canvas curtains. With an unfamiliar lack of resentment, a newly cool eye, Patty looked into herself and saw that no harm or even much hurt would come to anyone if she simply skipped the anniversary. Most of the work had already been done. She saw that she was almost free, and to take the last step felt kind of terrible, but not terrible in a bad way, if that makes any sense.

She was sitting by a window, smelling the rain and watching the wind bend the weeds and bushes on the roof of a long-abandoned factory, when the call from Richard came.

"Very sorry about this," he said. "I'll be there within the hour."

"You don't have to hurry," she said. "It's already way too late."

"But your party's tomorrow night."

"No, Richard, that was the dinner. I was supposed to be there *today*. Today by five o'clock."

"Shit. Are you kidding me?"

"Did you really not remember that?"

"It's a little mixed up in my head at this point. I'm somewhat short on sleep."

"OK, well, anyway. There's no hurry at all. I think I'm going to go home now."

And go home she did. Pushed her suitcase down the stairs and followed with her crutches, flagged a gypsy cab on Halstead Street, and took one Greyhound bus to Minneapolis and another to Hibbing, where Gene Berglund was dying in a Lutheran hospital. It was about forty degrees and pouring rain on the vacant small-hour streets of downtown Hibbing. Walter's cheeks were rosier than ever. Outside the bus station, in his father's cigarette-reeking gas-guzzler, Patty threw her arms around his neck and took the plunge of seeing how he kissed, and was gratified to find he did it very nicely.

# Chapter 3: Free Markets Foster Competition

On the chance that, regarding Patty's parents, a note of complaint or even outright blame has crept into these pages, the autobiographer here acknowledges her profound gratitude to Joyce and Ray for at least one thing, namely, their never encouraging her to be Creative in the Arts, the way they did with her sisters. Joyce and Ray's neglect of Patty, however much it stung when she was younger, seems more and more benign when she considers her sisters, who are now in their early forties and living alone in New York, too eccentric and/or entitled-feeling to sustain a long-term relationship, and still accepting parental subsidies while struggling to achieve an artistic success that they were made to believe was their special destiny. It turns out to have been better after all to be considered dumb and dull than brilliant and extraordinary. This way, it's a pleasant surprise that Patty is even a little bit Creative, rather than an embarrassment that she isn't more so.

A great thing about the young Walter was how much he wanted Patty to win. Where Eliza had once mustered unsatisfying little driblets of partisanship on her behalf, Walter gave her full-bore infusions of hostility toward anybody (her parents, her siblings) who made her feel bad. And since he was so intellectually honest in other areas of life, he had excellent credibility when he criticized her family and signed on with her questionable programs of competing with it. He may not have been exactly what she wanted in a man, but he was unsurpassable in providing the rabid fandom which, at the time, she needed even more than romance.

It's easy now to see that Patty would have been well advised to take some years to develop a career and a more solid post-athletic identity, get some experience with other kinds of men, and generally acquire more maturity before embarking on being a mother. But even though she was finished as an intercollegiate player, there was still a shot clock in her head, she was still in the buzzer's thrall, she needed more than ever to keep winning. And the way to win—her obvious best shot at defeating her sisters and her mother—was to marry the nicest guy in Minnesota, live in a bigger and better and more interesting house than anybody else in her family, pop out the babies, and do everything as a parent that Joyce hadn't. And Walter, despite being an avowed feminist and an annually renewing Student-level member of Zero Population Growth, embraced her entire domestic program without reservation, because she really *was* exactly what he wanted in a woman.

They got married three weeks after her college graduation—almost exactly a year after she'd taken the bus to Hibbing. It had fallen to Walter's mom, Dorothy, to frown and express concern, in her soft and tentative and nevertheless quite stubborn way, about Patty's determination to be married at the Hennepin County courthouse instead of in a proper wedding hosted by her parents in Westchester. Wouldn't it be better, Dorothy softly wondered, to include the Emersons? She understood that Patty wasn't close to her family, but, still, mightn't she later come to regret excluding them from such a momentous occasion? Patty tried to paint Dorothy a picture of what a Westchester wedding would be like: two hundred or so of Joyce and Ray's closest friends and Joyce's biggest-ticket campaign contributors; pressure from Joyce on Patty to select her middle sister as the maid of honor and to let her other sister do an interpretive dance during the ceremony; unbridled champagne intake leading Ray to make some joke about lesbians within earshot of Patty's basketball friends. Dorothy's eyes welled up a little, maybe in sympathy with Patty or maybe in sadness at Patty's coldness and harshness on the subject of her family. Wouldn't it be possible, she softly persisted, to insist on a small private ceremony in which everything would be exactly how Patty wanted it?

Not the least of Patty's reasons to avoid a wedding was the fact that Richard would have to be Walter's best man. Her thinking here was partly obvious and partly had to do with her fear of what would happen if Richard ever met her middle sister. (The autobiographer will now finally man up and say the sister's name: Abigail.) It was bad enough that Eliza had had Richard; to see him hooking up with Abigail, even for one night, would have just about finished Patty off. Needless to say, she didn't mention this to Dorothy. She said she guessed she just wasn't a very ceremonial person.

As a concession, she did take Walter to meet her family in the spring before she married him. It pains the autobiographer to admit that she was a tiny bit embarrassed to let her family see him, and, worse, that this may have been another reason why she didn't want a wedding. She loved him (and *does* love him, *does* love him) for qualities that made abundant sense to her in their two-person private world but weren't necessarily apparent to the sort of critical eye that she was sure her sisters, Abigail in particular, would train on him. His nervous giggle, his too-readily reddening face, his very niceness: these attributes were dear to her in the larger context of the man. A source of pride, even. But the unkind part of her, which exposure to her family always seemed to bring out in force, couldn't help regretting that he wasn't six-foot-four and very cool.

Joyce and Ray, to their credit, and perhaps in their secret relief that Patty had turned out to be heterosexual (secret because Joyce, for one, stood ready to be strenuously Welcoming to Difference), were on their very best behavior. Hearing that Walter had never been to New York, they became gracious ambassadors to the city, urging Patty to take him to museum exhibitions that Joyce herself had been too busy in Albany to have seen, and then meeting up with them for dinner at *Times*-approved restaurants, including one in SoHo, which was then still a dark and exciting neighborhood. Patty's worry that her parents would make fun of Walter gave way to the worry that Walter would take their side and not see why they were unbearable to her: would begin to suspect that the real problem was Patty, and would lose that blind faith in her goodness which already, in less than a year with him, she had rather desperately come to count on.

Thankfully Abigail, who was a high-end restaurant hound and insisted on turning several of the dinners into awkward fivesomes, was in peak disagreeable form. Unable to imagine people gathering for some reason besides listening to her, she prattled about the world of New York theater (by definition an unfair world since she had made no progress in it since her understudy breakthrough); about the "sleazy slimeball" Yale professor with whom she'd had insuperable Creative differences; about some friend of hers named Tammy who'd self-financed a production of *Hedda Gabler* in which she (Tammy) had brilliantly starred; about hangovers and rent control and disturbing third-party sexual incidents that Ray, refilling and refilling his own wineglass, demanded every prurient detail of. Midway through the final dinner, in SoHo, Patty got so fed up with Abigail's shanghaiing of the attention that ought to have been lavished on Walter (who had politely attended to every word of Abigail's) that she flat-out told her sister to shut up and let other people talk. There ensued a bad interval of silent manipulation of tableware. Then Patty, making comical gestures of drawing water from a well, got Walter talking about himself. Which was a mistake, in hindsight, because Walter was passionate about public policy and, not knowing what real politicians are like, believed that a state assemblywoman would be interested in hearing his ideas.

He asked Joyce if she was familiar with the Club of Rome. Joyce confessed that she was not. Walter explained that the Club of Rome (one of whose members he'd invited to Macalester for a lecture two years earlier) was devoted to exploring the limits of growth. Mainstream economic theory, both Marxist and free-market, Walter said, took for granted that economic growth was always a positive thing. A GDP growth rate of one or two percent was considered modest, and a population growth rate of one percent was considered desirable, and yet, he said, if you compounded these rates over a hundred years, the numbers were terrible: a world population of eighteen billion and world energy consumption ten times greater than today's. And if you went *another* hundred years, with steady growth, well, the numbers were simply impossible. So the Club of Rome was seeking more rational and humane ways of putting the brakes on growth than simply destroying the planet and letting everybody starve to death or kill each other.

"The Club of Rome," Abigail said. "Is that like an Italian Playboy Club?"

"No," Walter said quietly. "It's a group of people who are challenging our preoccupation with growth. I mean, everybody is so obsessed with growth, but when you think about it, for a mature organism, a growth is basically a cancer, right? If you have a growth in your mouth, or a growth in your colon, it's bad news, right? So there's this small group of intellectuals and philanthropists who are trying to step outside our tunnel vision and influence government policy at the highest levels, both in Europe and the Western Hemisphere."

"The Bunnies of Rome," Abigail said.

"Nor-*fock*-a Virginia!" Ray said in a grotesque Italian accent.

Joyce loudly cleared her throat. *En famille*, when Ray became silly and dirty because of wine, she could simply retreat into her private Joycean reveries, but in her future son-in-law's presence she had no choice but to be embarrassed. "Walter is talking about an interesting idea," she said. "I'm not particularly familiar with this idea, or with this . . . club. But it's certainly a very provocative perspective on our world situation."

Walter, not seeing the little neck-slicing gesture that Patty was making, pressed on. "The whole reason we need something like the Club of Rome," he said, "is that a rational conversation about growth is going to have to begin outside the ordinary political process. Obviously you know this yourself, Joyce. If you're trying to get elected, you can't even talk about *slowing* the growth rate, let alone reversing it. It's total political poison."

"Safe to say," Joyce said with a dry laugh.

"But *somebody* has to talk about it, and try to influence policy, because otherwise we're going to kill the planet. We're going to choke on our own multiplication."

"Speaking of choking, Daddy," Abigail said, "is that your private bottle there, or can we have some, too?"

"We'll get another," Ray said.

"I don't think we need another," Joyce said.

Ray raised his Joyce-stilling hand. "Joyce—just—just—calm down. We're fine here."

Patty, with a frozen smile, sat looking at the glamorous and plutocratic parties at other tables in the restaurant's lovely discreet light. There was, of course, nowhere better in the world to be than New York City. This fact was the foundation of her family's satisfaction with itself, the platform from which all else could be ridiculed, the collateral of adult sophistication that bought them the right to behave like children. To be Patty and sitting in that SoHo restaurant was to confront a force she had not the slightest chance of competing with. Her family had claimed New York and was never going to budge. Simply never coming here again—just forgetting that restaurant scenes like this even existed—was her only option.

"You're not a wine drinker," Ray said to Walter.

"I'm sure I could become one if I wanted," Walter said.

"This is a very nice amarone, if you want to try a little."

"No, thank you."

"You sure?" Ray waved the bottle at Walter.

"Yes he's sure!" Patty cried. "He's only said it every night for the last four nights! Hello? Ray? Not *everybody* wants to be drunk and disgusting and rude. Some people actually enjoy having an adult conversation instead of making sex jokes for two hours."

Ray grinned as if she'd been amusing. Joyce unfolded her half-glasses to examine the dessert menu while Walter blushed and Abigail, with a spastic neck-twist and a sour frown, said, " 'Ray'? 'Ray'? We call him 'Ray' now?"

The next morning, Joyce quaveringly told Patty: "Walter is much more—I don't know if the right word is conservative, or what, I guess not exactly conservative, although, actually, from the standpoint of democratic process, and power flowing upward from the people, and prosperity for all, not exactly *autocratic*, but, in a way, yes, almost conservative—than I'd expected."

Ray, two months later, at Patty's graduation, with a poorly suppressed snicker, said to Patty: "Walter got so red in the face about that growth stuff, my God, I thought he was going to have a *stroke*."

And Abigail, six months after that, at the only Thanksgiving that Patty and Walter were ever foolish enough to celebrate in Westchester, said to Patty: "How are things going with the *Club of Rome*? Have you guys joined the *Club of Rome* yet? Have you learned the passwords? Have you sat in the leather chairs?"

Patty, at LaGuardia Airport, sobbing, said to Walter: "I hate my family!"

And Walter valiantly replied: "We'll make our own family!"

Poor Walter. First he'd set aside his acting and filmmaking dreams out of a sense of financial obligation to his parents, and then no sooner had his dad set him free by dying than he teamed up with Patty and set aside his planet-saving aspirations and went to work for 3M, so that Patty could have her excellent old house and stay home with the babies. The whole thing happened almost without discussion. He got excited about the plans that excited her, he threw himself into renovating the house and defending her against her family. It wasn't until years later—after Patty had begun to Disappoint him—that he became more forgiving of the other Emersons and insisted that she was the lucky one, the only Emerson to escape the shipwreck and survive to tell the tale. He said that Abigail, who'd been left stranded to scavenge emotional meals on an island of great scarcity (Manhattan Island!), should be forgiven for monopolizing conversations in her attempt to feed herself. He said that Patty should pity her siblings, not blame them, for not having had the strength or the luck to get away: for being so hungry. But this all came much later. In the early years, he was so fired up about Patty, she could do no wrong. And very nice years they were.

Walter's own competitiveness wasn't family-oriented. By the time she met him, he'd already won that game. At the poker table of being a Berglund, he'd been dealt every ace except maybe looks and ease with women. (His older brother—who is currently on his third young wife, who is working hard to support him—got that particular ace.) Walter not only knew about the Club of Rome and read difficult novels and appreciated Igor Stravinsky, he could also sweat a copper pipe joint and do finish carpentry and identify birds by their songs and take good care of a problematic woman. He was so much his family's winner that he could afford to make regular voyages back to help the others.

"I guess now you're going to have to see where I grew up," he'd said to Patty outside the Hibbing bus station, after she'd aborted the road trip with Richard. They were in his dad's Crown Victoria, which they'd fogged up with their hot and heavy breathing.

"I want to see your room," Patty said. "I want to see everything. I think you're a wonderful person!"

Hearing this, he had to kiss her for another long while before resuming his anxiety. "Be that as it may," he said, "I'm still embarrassed to take you home."

"Don't be embarrassed. You should see *my* home. It's a freak show."

"Yeah, well, this is not anything as interesting as that. This is just your basic Iron Range squalor."

"So let's go. I want to see it. I want to sleep with you."

"That sounds great," he said, "but I think my mom might be uncomfortable with it."

"I want to sleep *near* you. And then I want to have breakfast with you."

"That we can arrange."

In truth, the scene at the Whispering Pines was sobering to Patty and touched off a moment of doubt about what she'd done by coming to Hibbing; it unsettled that self-contained state of mind in which she'd run to a guy who physically didn't do for her what his best friend did. The motel wasn't so bad from the outside, and there was a non-depressing number of cars in the parking lot, but the living quarters, behind the office, were indeed a long way from Westchester. They lit up a whole previously invisible universe of privilege, her own suburban privilege; she had an unexpected pang of homesickness. The floors were spongily carpeted and sloped perceptibly toward the creek in back. In the living/dining area was a hubcap-sized, extensively crenellated ceramic ashtray within easy reach of the davenport where Gene Berglund had read his fishing and hunting magazines and watched whatever programming the motel's antenna (rigged, as she saw the next morning, to the top of a decapitated pine tree behind the septic field) was able to pull down from stations in the Twin Cities and Duluth. Walter's little bedroom, which he'd shared with his younger brother, was at the bottom of the downslope and permanently damp with creek vapors. Running down the middle of the carpeting was a line of gummy residue from the duct tape that Walter had put down as a child to demarcate his private space. Paraphernalia from his striving childhood were still ranged along the far wall: Boy Scout handbooks and awards, a complete set of abridged presidential biographies, a partial set of World Book Encyclopedia volumes, skeletons of small animals, an empty aquarium, stamp and coin collections, a scientific thermometer/barometer with wires leading out a window. On the room's warped door was a yellowed homemade No Smoking sign, lettered in red crayon, its N and its S unsteady but tall in their defiance.

"My first act of rebellion," Walter said.

"How old were you?" Patty said.

"I don't know. Maybe ten. My little brother had bad asthma."

Outside, the rain was coming down hard. Dorothy was asleep in her room, but Walter and Patty were both still buzzing with lust. He showed her the "lounge" that his dad had operated, the impressive stuffed walleye mounted on the wall, the birch-plywood bar that he'd helped his dad build. Until recently, when he had to be hospitalized, Gene had stood smoking and drinking behind this bar in the late afternoon, waiting for his friends to get off work and give him business.

"So this is me," Walter said. "This is where I come from."

"I love that you come from here."

"I'm not sure what you mean by that, but I'll take it."

"Just that I admire you so much."

"That's good. I guess." He went to the front desk and looked at keys. "How does Room 21 sound to you?"

"Is it a good room?"

"It's very much like all the other rooms."

"I'm twenty-one years old. So it's perfect."

Room 21 was full of faded and abraded surfaces that, in lieu of being refurbished, had been subjected to decades of vigorous scouring. The creek-dampness was noticeable but not overwhelming. The beds were low and standard sized, not queen.

"You don't have to stay if you don't want," Walter said, setting her bag down. "I can take you back to the station in the morning."

"No! This is fine. I'm not here for vacation. I'm here to see you, and to try to be useful."

"Right. I'm just worried that I'm not actually what you want."

"Oh, well, worry no more."

"Well, I'm still worried."

She made him lie down on a bed and tried to reassure him with her body. Soon enough, though, his worry boiled up again. He righted himself and asked her why she'd gone on the road trip with Richard. It was a question she'd allowed herself to hope he wouldn't ask.

"I don't know," she said. "I guess I wanted to see what a road trip was like."

"Hm."

"There was something I had to see about. That's the only way I can explain it. There was something I had to find out. And I found it out, and now I'm here."

"What did you find out?"

"I found out where I wanted to be, and who I wanted to be with."

"Well, that was quick."

"It was a stupid mistake," she said. "He's got a way of looking at a person, as I'm sure you know. It takes a while for a person to sort out what she actually wants. Please don't blame me for that."

"I'm just impressed that you sorted it out so quickly."

She had an impulse to start crying, and yielded to it, and Walter for a while became his best comforting self.

"He wasn't nice to me," she said through tears. "And you're the opposite of that. And I so, so, so need the opposite of that right now. Can you please be nice?"

"I can be nice," he said, stroking her head.

"I swear you won't be sorry."

These were exactly her words, in the autobiographer's sorry recollection.

Here's something else the autobiographer vividly remembers: the violence with which Walter then grabbed her shoulders and rolled her onto her back and loomed over her, pressing himself between her legs, with an utterly unfamiliar look on his face. It was a look of rage, and it became him. It was like curtains suddenly parting on something beautiful and manly.

"*This is not about you*," he said. "Do you get that? I love every bit of you. Every inch of you. Every *inch*. From the minute I saw you. Do you get that?"

"Yes," she said. "I mean, thank you. I kind of had that sense, but it's really good to hear."

He wasn't done, though.

"Do you understand that I have a . . . a . . ." He searched for words. "A problem. With Richard. I have a *problem*."

"What problem?"

"I don't trust him. I love him, but I don't trust him."

"Oh, God," Patty said, "you should definitely trust him. He obviously cares about you, too. He's incredibly protective of you."

"Not always."

"Well, he was with me. Do you realize how much he admires you?"

Walter stared down at her furiously. "Then why did you go with him? Why was he in Chicago with you? What the *fuck*? I don't understand!"

Hearing him say fuck, and seeing how horrified he seemed by his own anger, she began to cry again. "God, please, God, please, God, please," she said, "I'm here. OK? I'm here for you! And nothing happened in Chicago. Truly nothing."

She pulled him closer, pulled hard on his hips. But instead of touching her breasts or taking her jeans down, as Richard surely would have, he stood up and began pacing Room 21.

"I'm not sure this is right," he said. "Because, you know, I'm not stupid. I have eyes and ears, I'm not *stupid*. I really don't know what to do now."

It was a relief to hear that he wasn't stupid about Richard; but she felt she'd run out of ways to reassure him. She simply lay there on the bed, listening to the rain on the roof, aware that she could have avoided this whole scene by never getting in a car with Richard; aware that she deserved some punishment. And yet it was hard not to imagine better ways for things to have gone. It was all such a foretaste of the late-night scenes of later years: Walter's beautiful rage going wasted while she wept and he punished her and apologized for punishing her, saying that they were both exhausted and it was very late, which indeed it was: so late that it was early.

"I'm going to take a bath," she said finally.

He was sitting on the other bed, his face in his hands. "I'm sorry," he said. "This is truly not about you."

"Actually, you know what? That is not my very favorite thing to keep hearing."

"I'm sorry. Believe it or not, I mean something nice by it."

"And 'sorry' is not really high on my list at this point, either."

Without taking his hands from his face, he asked if she needed help with the bath.

"I'm fine," she said, although it was something of a production to bathe with her braced and bandaged knee propped up outside the water. When she emerged from the bathroom in her pajamas, half an hour later, Walter appeared not to have moved a muscle. She stood in front of him, looking down at his fair curls and narrow shoulders. "Listen, Walter," she said. "I can leave in the morning if you want. But I need to get some sleep now. You should go to bed, too."

He nodded.

"I'm sorry I went to Chicago with Richard. It was my idea, not his. You should blame me, not him. But right now? You're making me feel kind of shitty."

He nodded and stood up.

"Kiss me good night?" she said.

He did, and it was better than fighting, so much better that soon they were under the covers and turning off the lamp. Daylight was leaking in around the curtains—dawn in May came early in the north country.

"I know essentially nothing about sex," Walter confessed.

"Oh, well," she said, "it's not very complicated."

And so began the happiest years of their life. For Walter, especially, it was a very giddy time. He took possession of the girl he wanted, the girl who could have gone with Richard but had chosen him instead, and then, three days later, at the Lutheran hospital, his lifelong struggle against his father ended with his father's death. (To be dead is to be as beaten as a dad can get.) Patty was with Walter and Dorothy at the hospital that morning, and was moved by their tears to do some crying of her own, and it felt to her, as they drove back to the motel in near-silence, that she was already practically married.

In the motel parking lot, after Dorothy had gone inside to lie down, Patty watched Walter do a strange thing. He sprinted from one end of the lot to the other, leaping as he ran, bouncing on his toes before he turned around and ran some more. It was a glorious clear morning, with a steady strong breeze from the north, the pine trees along the creek literally whispering. At the end of one of his sprints, Walter hopped up and down and then turned away from Patty and started running down Route 73, way down around the bend and out of sight, and was gone for an hour.

That next afternoon, in Room 21, in broad daylight, with the windows open and the faded curtains billowing, they laughed and cried and fucked with a joy whose gravity and innocence it fairly wrecks the autobiographer to think back on, and cried some more and fucked some more and lay next to each other with sweating bodies and full hearts and listened to the sighing of the pines. Patty felt like she'd taken some powerful drug that wasn't wearing off, or like she'd fallen into an incredibly vivid dream that she wasn't waking up from, except that she was fully aware, from second to second to second, that it wasn't a drug or a dream but just life happening to her, a life with only a present and no past, a romance unlike any romance she'd imagined. Because Room 21! How could she have imagined Room 21? It was such a sweetly clean old-fashioned room, and Walter such a sweetly clean old-fashioned person. And she was 21 and could feel her 21ness in the young, clean, strong wind that was blowing down from Canada. Her little taste of eternity.

More than four hundred people came out for his dad's funeral. On Gene's behalf, without even having known him, Patty was proud of the huge turnout. (It helps to die early if you want a big funeral.) Gene had been a hospitable guy who liked to fish and hunt and hang out with his buddies, most of them veterans, and who'd had the misfortune of being alcoholic and poorly educated and married to a person who invested her hopes and dreams and best love in their middle son, rather than in him. Walter would never forgive Gene for having worked Dorothy so hard at the motel, but frankly, in the autobiographer's opinion, although Dorothy was incredibly sweet, she was also definitely one of those martyr types. The after-funeral reception, in a Lutheran function hall, was Patty's total-immersion crash course in Walter's extended family, a festival of Bundt cake and determination to see the bright side of everything. All five of Dorothy's living siblings were there, as was Walter's older brother, newly released from jail, with his trampy-pretty (first) wife and their two little kids, and so was their taciturn younger brother in his Army dress uniform. The only important person missing, really, was Richard.

Walter had called him with the news, of course, though even this had been complicated, since it involved tracking down Richard's ever-elusive bass player, Herrera, in Minneapolis. Richard had just arrived in Hoboken, New Jersey. After giving Walter his telephonic condolences, he said that he was wiped out financially and sorry he couldn't make it to the funeral. Walter assured him this was totally fine, and then proceeded for several years to hold it against Richard that he hadn't made the effort, which was not entirely fair, given that Walter had already secretly been mad at Richard and hadn't even *wanted* him at the funeral. But Patty knew better than to be the one to point this out.

When they made their New York trip, a year later, she suggested that Walter look Richard up and spend an afternoon with him, but Walter pointed out that he had twice called Richard in recent months while Richard had not initiated *any* calls to him. Patty said, "But he's your best friend," and Walter said, "No, *you're* my best friend," and Patty said, "Well, then, he's your best male friend, and you should look him up." But Walter insisted it had always been like this—that he'd always felt more like the pursuer than the pursued; that there was a kind of brinksmanship between them, a competition not to be the first to blink and show need—and he was sick of it. He said this wasn't the first time Richard had done his disappearing act. If he still wanted to be friends, Walter said, then maybe, for once, he could trouble himself to do the calling. Though Patty suspected that Richard might still be feeling sheepish about the Chicago episode and trying not to intrude on Walter's domestic bliss, and that it might therefore behoove Walter to assure him he was still welcome, she again knew better than to push.

Where Eliza imagined a gay thing between Walter and Richard, the autobiographer now sees a sibling thing. Once Walter had outgrown being sat on and punched in the head by his older brother and sitting on his younger brother and punching *his* head, there was no satisfactory competition to be found in his own family. He'd needed an extra brother to love and hate and compete with. And the eternally tormenting question for Walter, as the autobiographer sees it, was whether Richard was the little brother or the big brother, the fuckup or the hero, the beloved damaged friend or the dangerous rival.

As with Patty, Walter claimed to have loved Richard at first sight. It had happened on his first night at Macalester, after his dad had dropped him off and hurried to get back to Hibbing, where Canadian Club was calling to him from the lounge. Walter had sent Richard a nice letter in the summer, using an address provided by the housing office, but Richard hadn't written back. On one of the beds in their dorm room was a guitar case, a cardboard carton, and a duffel bag. Walter didn't see the owner of this minimal luggage until after dinner, at a dorm hall meeting. It was a moment he later described to Patty many times: how, standing in a corner, apart from everybody else, there was a kid he couldn't take his eyes off, a very tall acned person with a Jewfro and an Iggy Pop T-shirt who looked nothing like the other freshmen and didn't laugh, didn't even smile politely, at the jokey orientative spiel their R.A. was giving them. Walter himself had great compassion for people attempting to be funny, and laughed loudly to reward them for their effort, and yet he instantly knew he wanted to be friends with the tall unsmiling person. He hoped this was his roommate, and it was.

Remarkably enough, Richard liked him. It started with the accident of Walter's having come from the town Bob Dylan grew up in. Back in their room, after the meeting, Richard plied him with questions about Hibbing, what the scene there was like, and whether Walter had personally known any Zimmermans. Walter explained about the motel being several miles outside town, but the motel itself impressed Richard, as did the fact that Walter was a full-scholarship student with an alcoholic dad. Richard said he hadn't written back to Walter because his own dad had died of lung cancer five weeks earlier. He said that since Bob Dylan was an asshole, the beautifully pure kind of asshole who made a young musician want to be an asshole himself, he'd always imagined that Hibbing was an asshole-filled kind of place. Downy-cheeked Walter, sitting in that dorm room, eagerly listening to his new roommate and trying hard to impress him, was a vivid refutation of this theory.

Already, that first night, Richard made comments about girls which Walter never forgot. He said he was unfavorably impressed with the high percentage of overweight chicks at Macalester. He said he'd spent the afternoon walking the surrounding streets, trying to figure out where the townie chicks hung out. He said he'd been astonished by how many people had smiled and said hello to him. Even the good-looking chicks had smiled and said hi. Was it like this in Hibbing, too? He said that, at his dad's funeral, he'd gotten to know a very hot cousin of his who was unfortunately only thirteen and was now sending him letters about her adventures in masturbation. Although Walter never needed much of a push in the direction of solicitude toward women, the autobiographer can't help thinking about the polarizing specialization of achievement that comes with sibling rivalry, and wondering if Richard's obsession with scoring might have given Walter an additional incentive not to compete on that particular turf.

Important fact: Richard had no relationship with his mom. She hadn't even come to his dad's funeral. By Richard's own account to Patty (much later), the mom was an unstable person who eventually became a religious nut but not before making life hellish for the guy who'd got her pregnant at nineteen. Richard's dad had been a saxophone player and bohemian in Greenwich Village. The mom was a tall, rebellious WASP girl of good family and bad self-control. After four raucous years of drinking and serial infidelity, she stuck Mr. Katz with the job of raising their son (first in the Village, later in Yonkers) while she went off to California and found Jesus and brought forth four more kids. Mr. Katz quit playing music but not, alas, drinking. He ended up working for the postal service and never remarrying, and it's safe to say that his various young girlfriends, in the years before drink fully ruined him, did little to provide the stabilizing maternal presence that Richard needed. One of them robbed their apartment before disappearing; another relieved Richard of his virginity while babysitting him. Soon after that episode, Mr. Katz sent Richard to spend a summer with his stepfamily, but he lasted less than a week with them. On his first day in California, the entire family gathered around him and joined hands to give thanks to God for his safe arrival, and apparently things got only wackier from there.

Walter's parents, who were merely social churchgoers, opened their home to the tall orphan. Dorothy was especially fond of Richard—may, indeed, have had a demure little Dorothyish thing for him—and encouraged him to spend his vacations in Hibbing. Richard needed little encouragement, having nowhere else to go. He delighted Gene by showing interest in shooting guns and more generally by not being the sort of "hoity-toity" person Gene had been afraid that Walter would take up with, and he impressed Dorothy by pitching in with chores. As previously noted, Richard had a strong (if highly intermittent) wish to be a good person, and he was scrupulously polite to people, like Dorothy, whom he considered Good. His manner with her, as he questioned her about some ordinary casserole she'd made, asking where she'd found the recipe and where a person learned about balanced diets, struck Walter as fake and condescending, since the chances of Richard ever actually buying groceries and making a casserole himself were nil, and since Richard reverted to his ordinary hard self as soon as Dorothy was out of the room. But Walter was in competition with him, and though Walter may not have excelled at picking up townie chicks, the province of listening to women with sincere attentiveness most definitely *was* his turf, and he guarded it fiercely. The autobiographer thus considers herself more reliable than Walter regarding the authenticity of Richard's respect for goodness.

What was unquestionably admirable in Richard was his quest to better himself and fill the void created by his lack of parenting. He'd survived childhood by playing music and reading books of his own idiosyncratic choosing, and part of what attracted him to Walter was Walter's intellect and work ethic. Richard was deeply read in certain areas (French existentialism, Latin American literature), but he had no method, no system, and was genuinely in awe of Walter's intellectual focus. Though he paid Walter the respect of never treating him with the hyper-politeness he reserved for those he considered Good, he loved hearing Walter's ideas and pressing him to explain his unusual political convictions.

The autobiographer suspects there was also a perverse *competitive* advantage for Richard in befriending an uncool kid from the north country. It was a way of setting himself apart from the hipsters at Macalester who came from more privileged backgrounds. Richard disdained these hipsters (including the female ones, though this didn't preclude fucking them when opportunities arose) with the same intensity as the hipsters themselves disdained people like Walter. The Bob Dylan documentary *Don't Look Back* was such a touchstone for both Richard and Walter that Patty eventually rented it and watched it with Walter, one night when the kids were little, so that she could see the famous scene in which Dylan outshone and humiliated the singer Donovan at a party for cool people in London, purely for the pleasure of being an asshole. Though Walter felt sorry for Donovan—and, what's more, felt bad about himself for not wanting to be more like Dylan and less like Donovan—Patty found the scene thrilling. The breathtaking nakedness of Dylan's competitiveness! Her feeling was: Let's face it, victory is very sweet. The scene helped her understand why Richard had preferred to hang out with unmusical Walter, rather than the hipsters.

Intellectually, Walter was definitely the big brother and Richard his follower. And yet, for Richard, being smart, like being good, was just a sideshow to the main competitive effort. This was what Walter had in mind when he said he didn't trust his friend. He could never shake the feeling that Richard was hiding stuff from him; that there was a dark side of him always going off in the night to pursue motives he wouldn't admit to; that he was happy to be friends with Walter as long as it was understood that he was the top dog. Richard was especially unreliable whenever a girl entered the picture, and Walter resented these girls for being even momentarily more compelling than he was. Richard himself never saw it this way, because he tired of girls so quickly and always ended up kicking them to the curb; he always came back to Walter, whom he didn't get tired of. But to Walter it seemed *disloyal* of his friend to put so much energy into pursuing people he didn't even like. It made Walter feel weak and small to be forever available for Richard to come back to. He was tormented by the suspicion that he loved Richard more than Richard loved him, and was doing more than Richard to make the friendship work.

The first big crisis came during their senior year, two years before Patty met them, when Walter was smitten with the evil sophomore personage named Nomi. To hear Richard tell it (as Patty once did), the situation was straightforward: his sexually naïve friend was being exploited by a worthless female who wasn't into him, and Richard finally took it upon himself to demonstrate her worthlessness. According to Richard, the girl wasn't worth competing over, she was just a mosquito to be slapped. But Walter saw things very differently. He got so angry with Richard that he refused to speak to him for weeks. They were sharing a two-room double of the sort reserved for seniors, and every night when Richard came in through Walter's room, on his way to his own more private room, he stopped to engage in one-sided conversations that a disinterested observer would probably have found amusing.

Richard: "Still not speaking to me. This is remarkable. How long is this going to last?"

Walter: silence.

Richard: "If you don't want me to sit down and watch you read, just say the word."

Walter: silence.

Richard: "Interesting book? You don't seem to be turning the pages."

Walter: silence.

Richard: "You know what you're being? You're being like a girl. This is what girls do. This is bullshit, Walter. This is kind of pissing me off."

Walter: silence.

Richard: "If you're waiting for me to apologize, it's not going to happen. I'll tell you that right now. I'm sorry you're hurt, but my conscience is clear."

Walter: silence.

Richard: "You do understand, don't you, that you're the only reason I'm even still here. If you'd asked me four years ago, what are the odds of me graduating from college, I would have said small to nonexistent."

Walter: silence.

Richard: "Seriously, I'm a little disappointed."

Walter: silence.

Richard: "OK. Fuck it. Be a girl. I don't care."

Walter: silence.

Richard: "Look. If I had a drug problem and you threw away my drugs, I'd be pissed off at you, but I'd also understand that you were trying to do me a favor."

Walter: silence.

Richard: "Admittedly not a perfect analogy, in that I actually, so to speak, used the drugs, instead of just throwing them away. But if you were prone to crippling addiction, whereas I was just doing something recreational, on the theory that it's a shame to waste good drugs . . ."

Walter: silence.

Richard: "All right, so it's a dumb analogy."

Walter: silence.

Richard: "That was funny. You should be laughing at that."

Walter: silence.

So, at any rate, the autobiographer imagines it, based on the later testimony of both parties. Walter maintained his silence until Easter vacation, when he went home alone and Dorothy managed to extract the reason he hadn't brought Richard along with him. "You have to take people the way they are," Dorothy told him. "Richard's a good friend, and you should be loyal to him." (Dorothy was big on loyalty—it lent meaning to her not so pleasant life—and Patty often heard Walter quoting her admonition; he seemed to attach almost scriptural significance to it.) He pointed out that Richard himself had been extremely *disloyal* in stealing a girl Walter cared about, but Dorothy, who herself perhaps had fallen under the Katzian spell, said she didn't believe that Richard had done it deliberately to hurt him. "It's good to have friends in life," she said. "If you want to have friends, you have to remember that nobody's perfect."

An additional vexing wrinkle to the girl issue was the fact that the ones Richard attracted were almost invariably big music fans,* and that Walter, being Richard's oldest and biggest fan, was in bitter competition with them. Girls who otherwise might have been friendly to a lover's best friend, or at least tolerant of him, found it necessary to be frosty to Walter, because serious fans always need to feel uniquely connected to the object of their fandom; they jealously guard those points of connection, however tiny or imaginary, that justify the feeling of uniqueness. Girls understandably considered it impossible to be any more connected to Richard than locked in coitus with him, mingling actual fluids. Walter seemed to them merely a pestering small insect of irrelevance, even though it was *Walter* who had turned Richard on to Anton von Webern and Benjamin Britten, it was *Walter* who had given Richard a political framework for his angriest early songs, it was *Walter* whom Richard actually loved in a meaningful way. And it was bad enough to be treated with such consistent frostiness by sexy girls, but even worse was Walter's suspicion—confessed to Patty in the years when they'd kept no secrets from each other—that he was at root no different than any of those girls: that he, too, was a kind of parasite on Richard, trying to feel cooler and better about himself by means of his unique connection to him. And, worst of all, his suspicion that Richard knew it, and was made all the lonelier by it, and all the more guarded.

---

*It occurred to Patty, on the bus ride from Chicago to Hibbing, that maybe the reason Richard had spurned her was that she wasn't into his music and he was annoyed by this. Not that there was anything she could have done about it.

The situation was especially toxic in the case of Eliza, who wasn't content to ignore Walter but went out of her way to make him feel bad. How, Walter wondered, could Richard keep sleeping with a person so deliberately nasty to his best friend? Walter was grownup enough by then not to do the silence thing, but he did stop making meals for Richard, and the main reason he kept going to Richard's gigs was to show his displeasure with Eliza, and, later, to try to shame Richard into not using the coke she was keeping him supplied with. Of course there was no shaming Richard into anything. Not then, not ever.

The particulars of their conversations about Patty are, sadly, unknown, but the autobiographer is pleased to think they were nothing like their conversations about Nomi or Eliza. It's possible that Richard urged Walter to be more assertive with her, and that Walter replied with some guff about her having been raped or being on crutches, but there are few things harder to imagine than other people's conversations about yourself. What Richard was privately feeling about Patty did eventually become clearer to her—the autobiographer is getting to that, albeit rather slowly. For now, it's enough to note that he migrated to New York and stayed there, and that for a number of years Walter was so busy building his own life with Patty that he hardly even seemed to miss him.

What was happening was that Richard was becoming more Richard and Walter more Walter. Richard settled in Jersey City, decided it was finally safe to experiment with social drinking, and then, after a period he later described as "fairly dissolute," decided, no, not so safe after all. As long as he'd lived with Walter, he'd avoided the alcohol that had ruined his dad, used coke only when other people were paying, and moved forward steadily with his music. On his own, he was a mess for quite a while. It took him and Herrera three years to get the Traumatics reconstituted, with the pretty, damaged blonde Molly Tremain sharing the vocals, and to put out their first LP, *Greetings from the Bottom of the Mine Shaft*, with the tiniest of labels. Walter went to see the band play at the Entry when they came through Minneapolis, but he was home again with Patty and the infant Jessica, carrying six copies of the LP, by ten-thirty in the evening. Richard had developed a day-job niche in building urban rooftop decks for the sort of Lower Manhattan gentry who got a contact cool from hanging out with artists and musicians, i.e., didn't mind if their deck-builder's workday began at 2 p.m. and ended a few hours later, and if it therefore took him three weeks to do a five-day job. The band's second record, *In Case You Hadn't Noticed*, attracted no more notice than the first, but its third, *Reactionary Splendor*, was released by a less-tiny label and got mentioned on several year-end Best Ten lists. This time, when Richard came through Minnesota, he phoned in advance and was able to spend an afternoon at Patty and Walter's house with the polite but bored and mostly silent Molly, who either was or wasn't his girlfriend.

That afternoon—to the surprisingly small extent that the autobiographer remembers it—was especially nice for Walter. Patty had her hands full with the kids and with her attempts to induce Molly to utter polysyllables, but Walter was able to show off all the work he was doing on the house, and the beautiful and energetic offspring he'd conceived with Patty, and to watch Richard and Molly eat the best meal of their entire tour, and, no less important, to acquire rich data from Richard about the alternative-music scene, data that Walter would put to good use in the months that followed, buying the records of every artist Richard had mentioned, playing them while he renovated, impressing male neighbors and colleagues who fancied themselves musically hip, and feeling that he had the best of both worlds. The state of their rivalry was very satisfactory to him that day. Richard was poor and subdued and too thin, and his woman was peculiar and unhappy. Walter, now unquestionably the big brother, could relax and enjoy Richard's success as a piquant and hipness-enhancing accessory to his own.

At that point, the only thing that could have thrown Walter back into the bad ways he'd felt in college, when he'd been tormented by his sense of *losing* to the person he loved too much not to care about beating, would have been some bizarre pathological sequence of events. Things at home would have had to sour very badly. Walter would have had to have terrible conflicts with Joey, and fail to understand him and earn his respect, and generally find himself replicating his relationship with his own dad, and Richard's career would have had to take an unexpected latter-day turn for the better, and Patty would have had to fall violently in love with Richard. What were the chances of all that happening?

Alas, not zero.

One hesitates to ascribe too much explanatory significance to sex, and yet the autobiographer would be derelict in her duties if she didn't devote an uncomfortable paragraph to it. The regrettable truth is that Patty had soon come to find sex sort of boring and pointless—the same old sameness—and to do it mostly for Walter's sake. And, yes, undoubtedly, to not do it very well. There just usually seemed to be something else she'd rather have been doing. Most often, she would rather have been sleeping. Or a distracting or mildly worrisome noise would be coming from one of the kids' rooms. Or she would be mentally counting how many entertaining minutes of a West Coast college basketball game would still remain when she was finally allowed to turn the TV back on. But even just basic chores of gardening or cleaning or shopping could seem delicious and urgent in comparison to fucking, and once you got it in your head that you needed to relax in a hurry and be fulfilled in a hurry so you could get downstairs and plant the impatiens that were wilting in their little plastic boxes, it was all over. She tried taking shortcuts, tried preemptively doing Walter with her mouth, tried telling him she was sleepy and he should just go ahead and have his fun and not worry about her. But poor Walter was constituted to care about his own satisfaction less than hers, or at least to predicate his on hers, and she could never seem to figure out a nice way of explaining what a bad position this put her in, because, when you got right down to it, it entailed telling him she didn't want him the way he wanted her: that craving sex with her mate was one of the things (OK, the main thing) she'd given up in exchange for all the good things in their life together. And this turned out to be a rather difficult admission to make to a man you loved. Walter tried everything he could think of to make sex better for her except the one thing that might conceivably have worked, which was to stop worrying about making it better for her and just bend her over the kitchen table some night and have at her from behind. But the Walter who could have done this wouldn't have been Walter. He was what he was, and he wanted what he was to be what Patty wanted. He wanted things to be mutual! And so the drawback of sucking him was that he always then wanted to go down on her, which made her incredibly ticklish. Eventually, after years of resisting, she managed to get him to stop trying altogether. And felt terribly guilty but also *angry* and *annoyed* to be made to feel like such a failure. The tiredness of Richard and Molly, on the afternoon they came to visit, seemed to Patty the tiredness of people who'd been up all night fucking, and it says a lot about her state of mind at that point, about the deadness of sex to her, about the totality of her immersion in being Jessica and Joey's mother, that she didn't even envy them for it. Sex seemed to her a diversion for young people with nothing better to do. Certainly neither Richard nor Molly looked uplifted by it.

And then the Traumatics were gone—on to their next gig, in Madison, and then on to releasing further wryly titled records that a certain kind of critic and about five thousand other people in the world liked to listen to, and doing small-venue gigs attended by scruffy, well-educated white guys who were no longer as young as they used to be—while Patty and Walter pursued their mostly very absorbing workaday life, in which the weekly thirty minutes of sexual stress was a chronic but low-grade discomfort, like the humidity in Florida. The autobiographer does acknowledge the possible connection between this small discomfort and the large mistakes that Patty was making as a mother in those years. Where Eliza's parents, once upon a time, had erred in being too much into each other and not enough into Eliza, Patty can probably be said to have made the opposite error with Joey. But there are so many other, non-parental errors to be related in these pages that it seems just inhumanly painful to dwell on her mistakes with Joey as well; the autobiographer fears that it would make her lie down on the floor and never get up.

What happened first was that Walter and Richard became great friends again. Walter knew a lot of people, but the voice he most wanted to come home and hear on their answering machine was Richard's, saying things like, "Yo, Jersey City here. Wondering if you can make me feel better about the situation in Kuwait. Give me a call." Both from the frequency of Richard's phonings and from the less defended way he spoke to Walter now—telling him he didn't know anybody else like him and Patty, that they were his lifeline to a world of sanity and hope—Walter finally got it through his head that Richard genuinely liked and needed him and wasn't just passively consenting to be his friend. (This was the context in which Walter gratefully cited his mom's advice about loyalty.) Whenever another tour brought the Traumatics through town, Richard made time to stop by the house, usually alone. He took particular interest in Jessica, whom he held to be a Genuinely Good Soul in the mold of her grand-mother, and plied her with earnest questions about her favorite writers and her volunteer work at the local soup kitchen. Though Patty could have wished for a daughter who was more like her, and for whom her own wealth of experience with mistake-making would have been a comforting resource, she was mostly very proud to have a daughter so wise about the way the world worked. She enjoyed seeing Jessica through Richard's ad-miring eyes, and when he and Walter then went out together, it made Patty feel secure to see the two guys getting into the car, the great guy she'd married and the sexy one she hadn't. Richard's affection for Walter made her feel better about Walter herself; his charisma had a way of rati-fying anything it touched.

One notable shadow was Walter's disapproval of Richard's situation with Molly Tremain. She had a beautiful voice but was a depressed or possibly bipolar person and spent massive amounts of time alone in her Lower East Side apartment, doing freelance copyediting at night and sleeping away her days. Molly was always available when Richard wanted to come over, and Richard claimed that she was fine with being his part-time lover, but Walter couldn't shake the suspicion that their relationship was founded on misunderstandings. Over the years, Patty extracted from Walter various disturbing things that Richard had said to him in private, including "Sometimes I think my purpose on earth is to put my penis in the vaginas of as many women as I can" and "The idea of having sex with the same person for the rest of my life feels like death to me." Walter's suspicion that Molly secretly believed he would outgrow these senti-ments turned out to be correct. Molly was two years older than Richard, and when she suddenly decided that she wanted a baby before it was too late, Richard was compelled to explain why this was never going to hap-pen. Things between them quickly got so awful that he dumped her alto-gether and she in turn quit the band.

It happened that Molly's mother was a longtime Arts editor at the *New York Times*, a fact that may explain why the Traumatics, despite rec-ord sales in the low four digits and audiences in the high two digits, had received several full write-ups in the *Times* ("Consistently Original, Perennially Unheard Of," "Undaunted by Indifference, the Traumatics

Soldier On") plus brief reviews of each of their records after *In Case You Hadn't Noticed*. Coincidentally or not, *Insanely Happy*—their first record without Molly and, as it turned out, their last—was ignored not only by the *Times* but even by the free weekly city papers that had long been a bastion of Traumatic support. What had happened, as Richard theorized over an early supper with Walter and Patty when the band dragged itself through the Twin Cities yet again, was that he'd been buying press attention on credit all along, without realizing it, and that the press had finally concluded that familiarity with the Traumatics was never going to be necessary to anyone's cultural literacy or street credibility, and so there was no reason to extend him further credit.

Patty, carrying earplugs, went along with Walter to the show that night. The Sick Chelseas, a foursome of assonant local girls barely older than Jessica, opened for the Traumatics, and Patty found herself trying to guess which of the four Richard had been hitting on backstage. She wasn't feeling jealous of the girls, she was feeling sad for Richard. It was finally sinking in, with both her and Walter, that in spite of being a good musician and a good writer Richard was not having the best life: had not actually been kidding with all his self-deprecation and avowals of admiration and envy of her and Walter. After the Sick Chelseas finished playing, their late-adolescent friends seeped out of the club and left behind no more than thirty die-hard Traumatics fans—white, male, scruffy, and even less young than they used to be—to hear Richard's deadpan banter ("We want to thank you guys for coming to this 400 Bar and not the other, more popular 400 Bar . . . We seem to have made the same mistake ourselves") and then a rollicking rendition of their new record's title song—

*What tiny little heads up in those big fat SUVs!*
*My friends, you look insanely happy at the wheel!*
*And the Circuit City smiling of a hundred Kathy Lees!*
*A wall of Regis Philbins! I tell you I'm starting to feel*
*INSANELY HAPPY! INSANELY HAPPY!*

and, later, an interminable and more typically repellent song, "TCBY," consisting mostly of guitar noise reminiscent of razor blades and broken glass, over which Richard chanted poetry—

*They can buy you*
*They can butcher you*

*Tritely, cutely branded yogurt*
*The cat barfed yesterday*

*Techno cream, beige yellow*
*Treat created by yes-men*

*They can bully you*
*They can bury you*

*Trampled choked benighted youth*
*Taught consumerism by yahoos*

*This can't be the country's best*
*This can't be the country's best*

and finally his slow, country-sounding song, "Dark Side of the Bar," which dampened Patty's eyes with sadness for him—

*There's an unmarked door to nowhere*
*On the dark side of the bar*
*And all I ever wanted was*
*To be lost in space with you*
*The reports of our demise*
*Pursue us through the vacuum*
*We took a wrong turn at the pay phones*
*We were never seen again*

The band was good—Richard and Herrera had been playing together for almost twenty years—but it was hard to imagine any band being good enough to overcome the desolation of the too-small house. After a single encore, "I Hate Sunshine," Richard didn't exit to the side of the stage but simply parked his guitar on a stand, lit a cigarette, and hopped down to the floor.

"You guys were nice to stay," he said to the Berglunds. "I know you've got to get up early."

"It was great! You were great!" Patty said.

"Seriously, I think this is your best record yet," Walter said. "These are terrific songs. It's another big step forward."

"Yeah." Richard, distracted, was scanning the back of the club, looking to see if any of the Sick Chelseas were lingering. Sure enough, one was. Not the conventionally pretty bassist whom Patty would have put her money on, but the tall and sour and disaffected-looking drummer, which of course made more sense as soon as Patty thought about it. "There's somebody waiting to talk to me," Richard said. "You're probably going to want to head right home, but we can all go out together if you want."

"No, you go," Walter said.

"Really wonderful to hear you play, Richard," Patty said. She put a friendly hand on his arm and then watched him walk over to the sour drummer.

On the way home to Ramsey Hill, in the family Volvo, Walter raved about the excellences of *Insanely Happy* and the debased taste of an American public that turned out by the millions for the Dave Matthews Band and didn't even know that Richard Katz *existed*.

"Sorry," Patty said. "Remind me again what's wrong with Dave Matthews?"

"Basically everything, except technical proficiency," Walter said.

"Right."

"But maybe especially the banality of the lyrics. 'Gotta be free, so free, yeah, yeah, yeah. Can't live without my freedom, yeah, yeah.' That's pretty much every song."

Patty laughed. "Do you think Richard was going to go have sex with that girl?"

"I'm sure he was going to go try," Walter said. "And, probably, succeed."

"I didn't think they were very good. Those girls."

"No, they weren't. If Richard has sex with her, it won't be a referendum on their talent."

At home, after checking on the kids, she put on a sleeveless top and little cotton shorts and came after Walter in bed. This was very unusual of her, but thankfully not so unheard-of as to provoke comment and examination; and Walter needed no persuading to oblige her. It wasn't a big deal, just a little late-evening surprise, and yet in autobiographical retrospect it now looks almost like the high point of their life together. Or maybe, more accurately, the endpoint: the last time she remembers feeling safe and secure in being married. Her closeness to Walter at the 400 Bar, the recollection of the scene of their very first meeting, the ease of being with Richard, their friendly warmth as a couple, the simple pleasure of having such an old and dear friend, and then afterward the rare treat, for both of them, of her sudden intense desire to feel Walter inside her: *the marriage was working.* And there seemed to be no compelling reason for its not continuing to work, maybe even work better and better.

A few weeks later, Dorothy collapsed at the dress store in Grand Rapids. Patty, sounding like her own mother, expressed concern to Walter about the hospital care she was getting, and was tragically vindicated when Dorothy went into multiple organ failure and died. Walter's grief was both over-general, encompassing not merely his loss of her but the stunted dimensions of her entire life, and somewhat muted by the fact that her death was also a relief and liberation to him—an end to his responsibility for her, a cutting of his main tether to Minnesota. Patty was surprised by the intensity of her own grief. Like Walter, Dorothy had always believed the best about her, and Patty was sorry that for someone as generous-spirited as Dorothy an exception couldn't have been made to the rule that everybody ultimately dies alone. That Dorothy in her eternally trusting niceness had had to pass through death's bitter door unaccompanied: it just pierced Patty's heart.

She was pitying herself, too, of course, as people always do in pitying others for their solitary dying. She attended to the funeral arrangements in a mental state whose fragility the autobiographer hopes at least partly explains her poor handling of her discovery that an older neighbor girl, Connie Monaghan, had been preying on Joey sexually. The litany of the mistakes that Patty proceeded to make in the wake of this discovery would exceed the current length of this already long document. The autobiographer is still so ashamed of what she did to Joey that she can't begin to make a sensible narrative out of it. When you find yourself in the alley behind your neighbor's house at three in the morning with a box cutter in your hand, destroying the tires of your neighbor's pickup truck, you can plead insanity as a legal defense. But is it a moral one?

For the defense: Patty had tried, at the outset, to warn Walter about the kind of person she was. She'd *told* him there was something wrong with her.

For the prosecution: Walter was appropriately wary. Patty was the one who tracked him down in Hibbing and threw herself at him.

For the defense: But she was trying to be good and make a good life! And then she forsook all others and worked hard to be a great mom and homemaker.

For the prosecution: Her motives were bad. She was competing with her mom and sisters. She wanted her kids to be a reproach to them.

For the defense: She loved her kids!

For the prosecution: She loved Jessica an appropriate amount, but Joey she loved way too much. She knew what she was doing and she didn't stop, because she was mad at Walter for not being what she really wanted, and because she had bad character and felt she deserved compensation for being a star and a competitor who was trapped in a housewife's life.

For the defense: But love just happens. It wasn't *her* fault that every last thing about Joey gave her so much pleasure.

For the prosecution: It was her fault. You can't love cookies and ice cream inordinately and then say it's not your fault you end up weighing three hundred pounds.

For the defense: But she didn't know that! She thought she was doing the right thing by giving her kids the attention and the love her own parents hadn't given her.

For the prosecution: She did know it, because Walter told her, and told her, and told her.

For the defense: But Walter couldn't be trusted. She thought she had to stick up for Joey and be the good cop because Walter was the bad cop.

For the prosecution: The problem wasn't between Walter and Joey. The problem was between Patty and Walter, and she knew it.

For the defense: She loves Walter!

For the prosecution: The evidence suggests otherwise.

For the defense: Well, in that case, Walter doesn't love her, either. He doesn't love the real her. He loves some wrong idea of her.

For the prosecution: That would be convenient if only it were true. Unfortunately for Patty, he didn't marry her in spite of who she was, he married her because of it. Nice people don't necessarily fall in love with nice people.

For the defense: It isn't fair to say she doesn't love him!

For the prosecution: If she can't behave herself, it doesn't matter if she loves him.

Walter knew that Patty had cut the tires of their horrible neighbor's horrible truck. They never talked about it, but he knew. The fact that they never talked about it was how she knew he knew. The neighbor, Blake, was building a horrible addition on the back of the house of his horrible girlfriend, Connie Monaghan's horrible mother, and Patty that winter was finding it expedient to drink a bottle or more of wine every evening, and then waking up in a sweat of anxiety and rage in the middle of the night, and stalking the first floor of the house in pounding-hearted lunacy. There was a stupid smugness to Blake which in her sleep-deprived state she equated with the stupid smugness of the special prosecutor who'd made Bill Clinton lie about Monica Lewinsky and the stupid smugness of the congressmen who'd recently impeached him for it. Bill Clinton was the rare politician who didn't seem sanctimonious to Patty—who didn't pretend to be Mr. Clean—and she was one of the millions of American women who would have slept with him in a heartbeat. Flattening horrible Blake's tires was the least of the blows she felt like striking in her president's defense. This is in no way intended to exculpate her but simply to elucidate her state of mind.

A more direct irritant was the fact that Joey, that winter, was pretending to admire Blake. Joey was too smart to *genuinely* admire Blake, but he was going through an adolescent rebellion that required him to like the very things that Patty most hated, in order to drive her away. She probably deserved this, owing to the thousand mistakes she'd made in loving him too much, but, at the time, she wasn't feeling like she deserved it. She was feeling like she was being lashed in the face with a bullwhip. And because of certain monstrously mean things she'd seen that she was capable of saying to Joey, on several occasions when he'd baited her out of her self-control and she'd lashed back at him, she was doing her best to vent her pain and anger on safer third parties, such as Blake and Walter.

She didn't think she was an alcoholic. She wasn't an alcoholic. She was just turning out to be like her dad, who sometimes escaped his family by drinking too much. Once upon a time, Walter had positively *liked* that she enjoyed drinking a glass or two of wine after the kids were in bed. He said he'd grown up being nauseated by the smell of alcohol and had learned to forgive it and love it on her breath, because he loved her breath, because her breath came from deep inside her and he loved the inside of her. This was the sort of thing he used to say to her—the sort of avowal she couldn't reciprocate and was nevertheless intoxicated by. But once the one or two glasses turned into six or eight glasses, everything changed. Walter needed her sober at night so she could listen to all the things he thought were morally defective in their son, while she needed not to be sober so as not to have to listen. It wasn't alcoholism, it was self-defense.

And here: here is an actual serious personal failing of Walter's: he couldn't accept that Joey wasn't like him. If Joey had been shy and diffident with girls, if Joey had enjoyed playing the role of child, if Joey had wanted a dad who could teach him things, if Joey had been helplessly honest, if Joey had sided with underdogs, if Joey had loved nature, if Joey had been indifferent to money, he and Walter would have gotten along famously. But Joey, from infancy onward, was a person more in the mold of Richard Katz—effortlessly cool, ruggedly confident, totally focused on getting what he wanted, impervious to moralizing, unafraid of girls—and Walter carried all his frustration and disappointment with his son to Patty and laid it at her feet, as if she were to blame. He'd been begging her for fifteen years to back him up when he tried to discipline Joey, to help him enforce the household prohibitions on video games and excess TV and music that degraded women, but Patty couldn't help loving Joey just the way he was. She admired and was amused by his resourcefulness in evading prohibitions: he seemed to her quite the incredible boy. An A student, a hard worker, popular at school, wonderfully entrepreneurial. Maybe, if she'd been a single mother, she would have worried more about disciplining him. But Walter had taken over that job, and she'd allowed herself to feel she had an amazing friendship with her son. She hung on his wicked impressions of teachers he didn't like, she gave him uncensored salacious gossip from the neighborhood, she sat on his bed with her knees gathered in her arms and stopped at nothing to get him laughing; not even Walter was off-limits. She didn't feel she was being unfaithful to Walter when she made Joey laugh at his eccentricities—his teetotaling, his insistence on bicycling to work in blizzards, his defenselessness against bores, his hatred of cats, his disapproval of paper towels, his enthusiasm for difficult theater—because these were all things she herself had learned to love in him, or at least to find quaintly amusing, and she wanted Joey to see Walter her way. Or so she rationalized it, since, if she'd been honest with herself, what she really wanted was for Joey to be delighted by her.

She didn't see how he could possibly be *loyal and devoted* to the neighbor girl. She thought that Connie Monaghan, sneaky little competitor that she was, had managed to get some kind of filthy little momentary hold on him. She was disastrously slow to grasp the seriousness of the Monaghan menace, and in the months when she was underestimating Joey's feelings for the girl—when she thought that she could simply freeze Connie out and make lighthearted fun of her trashy mom and her mom's boneheaded boyfriend, and that Joey would soon enough be laughing at them, too—she managed to undo fifteen years of effort to be a good mom. She fucked it up royally, Patty did, and then proceeded to become quite unhinged. She had terrible fights with Walter in which he blamed her for making Joey ungovernable and she was unable to defend herself properly, because she wasn't allowed to speak the sick conviction in her heart, which was that Walter had ruined her friendship with her son. By sleeping in the same bed with her, by being her husband, by claiming her for the grownup side, Walter had made Joey believe that Patty was in the enemy camp. She hated Walter for this, and resented the marriage, and Joey moved out of the house and in with the Monaghans and made everybody pay in bitter tears for their mistakes.

Though this barely scratches the surface, it's already more than the autobiographer intended to say about those years, and she will now bravely move on.

One small benefit of having the house to herself was that Patty could listen to whatever music she wanted, especially to the country music that Joey had cried out in pain and revulsion at the merest sound of, and that

Walter, with his college-radio tastes, could tolerate only a narrow and mostly vintage playlist of: Patsy Cline, Hank Williams, Roy Orbison, Johnny Cash. Patty loved all of those singers herself, but she loved Garth Brooks and the Dixie Chicks no less. As soon as Walter left for work in the morning, she cranked up the volume to a level incompatible with thinking, and steeped herself in heartbreaks enough like her own to be comforting and enough different to be sort of funny. Patty was strictly a lyrics-and-stories gal—Walter had long ago given up on interesting her in Ligeti and Yo La Tengo—and never tired of cheating men and strong women and the indomitable human spirit.

At the very same time, Richard was forming Walnut Surprise, his new alt-country band, with three kids whose combined age wasn't much greater than his own. Richard might have persisted with the Traumatics, and launched further records into the void, were it not for a strange accident that could only have befallen Herrera, his old friend and bassist, whose dishevelment and disorganization made Richard look like the man in the gray flannel suit in comparison. Deciding that Jersey City was too bourgeois (!) and not depressing enough, Herrera had moved up to Bridgeport, Connecticut, and settled in a slum there. One day he went to a rally in Hartford for Ralph Nader and other Green Party candidates and assembled a spectacle that he called the Dopplerpus, which consisted of a rented carnival octopus ride on whose tentacles he and seven friends sat and played dirges on portable amps while the ride flung them around and distorted their sound interestingly. Herrera's girlfriend later told Richard that the Dopplerpus had been "amazing" and a "huge hit" with the "more than a hundred" people who'd attended the rally, but afterward, when Herrera was packing up, his van started rolling down a hill, and Herrera chased after it and reached in through the window and grabbed the steering wheel, which swung the van alongside a brick wall and pancaked him. He somehow finished packing up and drove back to Bridgeport, coughing blood, and there nearly expired of a ruptured spleen, five broken ribs, a broken clavicle, and a punctured lung before his girlfriend got him to a hospital. The accident, following the disappointments of *Insanely Happy*, seemed like a cosmic sign to Richard, and since he couldn't live without making music, he'd teamed up with a young fan of his who played killer pedal steel guitar, and Walnut Surprise was born.

Richard's personal life was in scarcely better shape than Walter and Patty's. He had lost several thousand dollars on the last Traumatics tour and had "loaned" the uninsured Herrera further thousands for medical expenses, and his domestic situation, as he described it on the phone to Walter, was collapsing. What had made his whole existence workable, for nearly twenty years, was the big ground-floor Jersey City apartment for which he paid a rent so low as to be literally nominal. Richard could never be bothered to get rid of things, and his apartment was big enough that he didn't have to. Walter had been to it on one of his trips to New York and reported that the hall outside Richard's door was filled with junk stereo equipment, mattresses, and surplus parts for his pickup truck, and that the rear courtyard was filling up with supplies and leftovers from his deck-building business. Best of all, there was a room in the basement directly beneath his apartment where the Traumatics had been able to practice (and, later, record) without unduly disturbing the other tenants. Richard had always taken care to remain on good terms with them, but in the wake of his breakup with Molly he'd made the dreadful mistake of going a step further and getting involved with one of them.

At the time, it hadn't seemed like a mistake to anyone but Walter, who considered himself uniquely qualified to detect the bullshit in his friend's dealings with women. When Richard said, on the phone, that the time had come to put childish things behind him and sustain a real relationship with a grownup woman, warning bells had gone off in Walter's head. The woman was an Ecuadoran named Ellie Posada. She was in her late thirties and had two kids whose father, a limousine driver, had been struck and killed when his car broke down on the Pulaski Skyway. (It did not escape Patty's attention that, although Richard poked plenty of very young girls for fun, the women he actually had longer-term relationships with were his own age or even older.) Ellie worked for an insurance agency and lived across the hall from Richard. For a nearly a year, he gave Walter upbeat reports on how unexpectedly well her kids were taking to him and he to them, and how great Ellie was to come home to, and how uninteresting women who weren't Ellie had become to him, and how he hadn't eaten so well or felt so healthy since he'd lived with Walter, and (this really set Walter's alarm bell ringing) how fascinating the insurance business turned out to be. Walter told Patty that he could hear something tellingly abstracted, or theoretical, or far away, in Richard's tone of voice during this ostensibly happy year, and it came as no surprise to him when Richard's nature finally caught up with him. The music he'd started making with Walnut Surprise turned out to be even more fascinating than the insurance business, and the skinny chicks in his young bandmates' orbit turned out to be not so uninteresting after all, and Ellie turned out to be a strict constructionist when it came to exclusive sexual contracts, and before long he was afraid to come home at night to his own building, because Ellie was lying in ambush for him. Soon after that, Ellie organized the building's other tenants to complain about his egregious appropriation of their communal space, and his hitherto absent landlord sent him stern letters by certified mail, and Richard found himself homeless, at the age of forty-four, in midwinter, with maxed-out credit cards and a $300 monthly storage bill for all his crap.

Now came Walter's finest hour as Richard's big brother. He offered him a way to live rent-free, devote himself in solitude to songwriting, and make some good money while he got his life sorted out. Walter had inherited from Dorothy her sweet little house on a lake near Grand Rapids. He had plans for some major interior and exterior improvements which, since he'd quit 3M and joined the Nature Conservancy, he'd despaired of finding time to do himself, and he proposed that Richard come out and live in the house, get a good start on the kitchen renovation, and then, when the snow melted, put a big deck on the back of the house, overlooking the lake. Richard would get thirty dollars an hour, plus free electricity and heat, and could do the work on his own schedule. And Richard, who was in a low place, and who (as he later told Patty, with touching plainness) had come to consider the Berglunds the closest thing he had to family, took only one day to think it over before accepting the offer. For Walter, his assent was further sweet confirmation that Richard really loved him. For Patty, well, the timing was dangerous.

Richard stopped with his overloaded old Toyota pickup for a night in St. Paul on his way up north. Patty was already into a bottle by the time he arrived, at three in the afternoon, and did not acquit herself well as a hostess. Walter did the cooking while she drank for the three of them. It was as if he and she both had just been waiting to see their old friend so they could vent their conflicting versions of why Joey, instead of joining them for dinner, was playing air hockey with a right-wing dolt next door. Richard, flummoxed, kept stepping outside to smoke cigarettes and fortify himself for the next round of Berglund fraughtness.

"It's going to be fine," he said, coming inside again. "You guys are great parents. It's just, you know, when a kid's got a big personality, there can be big dramas of individuation. It takes time to work these things out."

"*God,*" Patty said. "Where did you get so wise?"

"Richard is one of those bizarre people who actually still read books and think about things," Walter said.

"Right, unlike me, I know." She turned to Richard. "Every once in a while it happens that I don't read every single book he recommends. Sometimes I decide to just—skip it. I believe that is the subtext here. My substandard intellect."

Richard gave her a hard look. "You should cool it with the drinking," he said.

He might as well have punched her in the sternum. Where Walter's disapproval actively fed her misbehavior, Richard's had the effect of catching her out in her childishness, of exposing her unattractiveness to daylight.

"Patty's in a lot of pain," Walter said quietly, as if to warn Richard that his loyalty still lay, however unaccountably, with her.

"You can drink all you want as far as I'm concerned," Richard said. "I'm just saying, if you want the kid to come home, it might help to have your house in order."

"I'm not even sure I *want* him home at this point," Walter said. "I'm kind of enjoying the respite from his contempt."

"So, let's see, then," Patty said. "We've got individuation for Joey, we've got relief for Walter, but then, for Patty, what? What does she get? Wine, I guess. Right? Patty gets wine."

"Whoa," Richard said. "Little bit of self-pity there?"

"For God's sake," Walter said.

It was terrible to see, through Richard's eyes, what she'd been turning into. From twelve hundred miles away it had been easy to smile at Richard's love troubles, his eternal adolescence, his failed resolutions to put childish things behind him, and to feel that here, in Ramsey Hill, a more adult sort of life was being led. But now she was in the kitchen with him—his height, as always, a breathtaking surprise to her, his Qaddafian features weathered and deepened, his mass of dark hair graying handsomely—and he illuminated in a flash what a self-absorbed little child she'd been able to remain by walling herself inside her lovely house. She'd run from her family's babyishness only to be just as big a baby herself. She didn't have a job, her kids were more grownup than she was, she hardly even had *sex*. She was ashamed to be seen by him. All these years, she'd treasured her memory of their little road trip, kept it locked up securely in some deep interior place, letting it age like a wine, so that, in some symbolic way, the thing that might have happened between them stayed alive and grew older with the two of them. The nature of the possibility altered as it aged in its sealed bottle, but it didn't go bad, it remained potentially drinkable, it was a kind of reassurance: rakish Richard Katz had once invited her to move to New York with him, and she'd said no. And now she could see that this wasn't how things worked at all. She was forty-two and drinking herself red-nosed.

She stood up carefully, trying not to wobble, and poured a half-dead bottle down the drain. She set her empty glass in the sink and said that she was going upstairs to lie down for a while, and that the men should go ahead and eat.

"Patty," Walter said.

"I'm fine. I'm really fine. I just had too much to drink. I might come down again later. I'm sorry, Richard. It's so wonderful to see you. I'm just in a bit of a state."

Though she loved their house on the lake, and had been retreating there for weeks at a time by herself, she didn't go there once during the spring Richard spent working on it. Walter found time to go up for several long weekends and help out, but Patty was too embarrassed. She stayed home and got herself in shape: took Richard's advice about the drinking, started running and eating again, gained enough weight to fill in the most haggard of the lines that had been forming in her face, and generally acknowledged realities about her physical appearance which she'd been ignoring in her fantasy world. One reason she'd resisted any kind of makeover was that her hateful neighbor Carol Monaghan had undergone one when her hateful boy-toy Blake appeared on the scene. Anything Carol did was definitionally anathema to Patty, but she humbled herself and followed

Carol's example. Lost the ponytail, saw a colorist, got an age-appropriate haircut. She was making an effort to see more of her old basketball friends, and they rewarded her by telling her how much better she looked.

Richard had intended to return to the East by the end of May, but, being Richard, he was still working on the deck in mid-June when Patty went up to enjoy some weeks in the country. Walter went along for the first four days, on his way to a money-tree-shaking V.I.P. fishing trip that a major Nature Conservancy donor was hosting at his deluxe "camp" in Saskatchewan. To make up for her poor showing in the winter, Patty was a whirlwind of hospitality at the lake house, cooking up splendid meals for Walter and Richard while they hammered and sawed in the back yard. She was proudly sober the whole time. In the evening, without Joey in the house, she had no interest in TV. She sat in Dorothy's favorite armchair, reading *War and Peace* at Walter's long-standing recommendation, while the men played chess. Thankfully for all concerned, Walter was better than Richard at chess and usually won, but Richard was dogged and kept asking for another game, and Patty knew that this was hard on Walter— that he was straining very hard to win, getting himself wound up, and would need hours to fall asleep afterward.

"More of this clotting-of-the-middle shit," Richard said. "You're always tying up the middle. I hate that."

"I'm a clotter of the middle," Walter affirmed in a voice breathless with the suppression of competitive glee.

"It drives me crazy."

"Well, because it's effective," Walter said.

"It's only effective because I don't have enough discipline to make you pay for it."

"You play a very entertaining game. I never know what's coming."

"Yeah, and I keep losing."

The days were bright and long, the nights startlingly cool. Patty loved early summer in the north, it took her back to her first days in Hibbing with Walter. The crisp air and moist earth, the conifer smells, the morning of her life. She felt she'd never been younger than she'd been at twenty-one. It was as if her Westchester childhood, though chronologically prior, had somehow taken place in a later and more fallen time. Inside the house was a faint pleasant musty smell reminiscent of Dorothy.

Outside was the lake that Joey and Patty had decided to call Nameless, newly melted, dark with bark and needles, reflecting bright fair-weather clouds. In summer, deciduous trees hid the only other nearby house, which a family named Lundner used on weekends and in August. Between the Berglunds' house and the lake was a grassy hillock with a few mature birch trees, and when the sun or a breeze discouraged mosquitoes Patty could lie on the grass with a book for hours and feel completely apart from the world, except for the rare airplane overhead and the even rarer car passing on the unpaved county road.

The day before Walter left for Saskatchewan, her heart began to race. It was just a thing her heart was doing, this racing. The next morning, after she drove Walter to the airstrip in Grand Rapids and returned to the house, it was racing so much that an egg slipped out of her hand and fell on the floor while she was making pancake batter. She put her hands on the counter and took deep breaths before kneeling down to clean it up. The finish work in the kitchen had been left for Walter to do at some later date, but grouting the new tile floor ought to have been within Richard's capabilities, and he hadn't gotten to it yet. On the plus side, as he'd told them, he'd taught himself to play the banjo.

Though the sun had been up for four hours, it was still fairly early morning when he emerged from his bedroom in jeans and a T-shirt advertising his support for Subcomandante Marcos and the liberation of Chiapas.

"Buckwheat pancakes?" Patty said brightly.

"Sounds great."

"I could fry you some eggs if you'd rather."

"I like a good pancake."

"Easy enough to do some bacon, too."

"I wouldn't say no to bacon."

"OK! Pancakes and bacon it will be."

If Richard's heart was racing also, he gave no sign of it. She stood and watched him put away two stacks of pancakes, holding his fork in the civilized grip that she happened to know Walter had taught him as a freshman at college.

"What are your plans for the day?" he asked her with low to moderate interest.

"Gosh. I hadn't thought about it. Nothing! I'm on vacation. I think I'm going to do nothing this morning, and then make you some lunch."

He nodded and ate, and it occurred to her that she was a person who dwelt in fantasies with essentially no relation to reality. She went to the bathroom and sat on the closed toilet lid, her heart racing, until she heard Richard go outside and begin handling lumber. There's a hazardous sadness to the first sounds of someone else's work in the morning; it's as if stillness experiences pain in being broken. The first minute of the workday reminds you of all the other minutes that a day consists of, and it's never a good thing to think of minutes as individuals. Only after other minutes have joined the naked, lonely first minute does the day become more safely integrated in its dayness. Patty waited for this to happen before she left the bathroom.

She took *War and Peace* out to the grassy knoll, with the vague ancient motive of impressing Richard with her literacy, but she was mired in a military section and kept reading the same page over and over. A melodious bird that Walter had despaired of teaching her the proper name of, a veery or a vireo, grew accustomed to her presence and began to sing in a tree directly above her. Its song was like an idée fixe that it couldn't get out of its little head.

How she felt: as if a ruthless and well-organized party of resistance fighters had assembled under cover of the darkness of her mind, and so it was *imperative* not to let the spotlight of her conscience shine anywhere near them, not even for one second. Her love of Walter and her loyalty to him, her wish to be a good person, her understanding of Walter's lifelong competition with Richard, her sober appraisal of Richard's character, and just the all-around shittiness of sleeping with your spouse's best friend: these superior considerations stood ready to annihilate the resistance fighters. And so she had to keep the forces of conscience fully diverted. She couldn't even allow herself to consider how she was dressing—she had to instantly deflect the thought of putting on a particular flattering sleeveless item before taking midmorning coffee and cookies out to Richard, she had to flick that thought right away from her—because the tiniest hint of ordinary flirting would attract the searchlight, and the spectacle it illuminated would be just too revolting and shameful and pathetic. Even if Richard wasn't disgusted by it, she herself would be. And if he noticed it and called her out on it, the way he'd called her out on her drinking: disaster, humiliation, the worst.

Her pulse, however, knew—and was telling her with its racing—that she would probably not have another chance like this. Not before she was fully over the hill physically. Her pulse was registering her keen covert awareness that the fishing camp in Saskatchewan could only be reached by biplane, radio, or satellite phone, and that Walter would not be calling her in the next five days unless there was an emergency.

She left Richard's lunch on the table and drove to the nearby tiny town of Fen City. She could see how easily she could have a traffic accident, and became so lost in imagining herself killed and Walter sobbing over her mutilated body and Richard stoically comforting him that she almost ran the only stop sign in Fen City; she dimly heard the screaming of her brakes.

It was all in her head, it was all in her head! The only thing that gave her any hope was how well she was concealing her own inner turmoil. She'd been maybe a little abstracted and shaky in the last four days, but infinitely better behaved than she'd been in February. If she herself was managing to keep her dark forces hidden, it stood to reason that Richard might have corresponding dark forces that he was doing just as good a job of hiding. But this was a tiny sliver of hope indeed; it was the way insane people lost in fantasies reasoned.

She stood in front of the Fen City Co-op's meager selection of domestic beers, the Millers and the Coorses and the Budweisers, and tried to make a decision. Held a sixpack in her hand as if she might be able to judge in advance, through the aluminum of the cans, how she would feel if she drank it. Richard had told her to cool it with the drinking; she'd been ugly to him drunk. She reshelved the sixpack and wrenched herself away to less compelling parts of the store, but it was hard to plan dinner when you felt like throwing up. She returned to the beer shelves like a bird repeating its song. The various beer cans had different decorations but all contained the identical weak low-end brew. It occurred to her to drive to Grand Rapids and buy some actual wine. It occurred to her to drive back to the house without buying anything at all. But then where would she be? A weariness set in as she stood and vacillated: a premonition that none of the possible impending outcomes would bring enough relief or pleasure to justify her current heart-racing wretchedness. She saw, in other words, what it meant to have become a deeply unhappy person. And yet the autobiographer now envies and pities the younger Patty standing there in the Fen City Co-op and innocently believing that she'd reached the bottom: that, one way or another, the crisis would be resolved in the next five days.

A chubby teenage girl at the cash register had taken an interest in her paralysis. Patty gave her a lunatic smile and went and got a plastic-wrapped chicken and five ugly potatoes and some humble, limp leeks. The only thing worse than inhabiting her anxiety undrunk, she decided, would be to be drunk and still inhabiting it.

"I'm going to roast a chicken for us," she told Richard when she got home.

Flecks of sawdust were resting in his hair and eyebrows and sticking to his sweaty, broad forehead. "That's very nice of you," he said.

"Deck's looking really great," she said. "It's a wonderful improvement. How much longer do you think it's going to take?"

"Couple of days, maybe."

"You know, Walter and I can finish it up ourselves if you want to get back to New York. I know you meant to be back there by now."

"It's good to see a job finished," he said. "It won't be more than a couple of days. Unless you're wanting to be alone here?"

"Do I want to be alone here?"

"I mean, it's a lot of noise."

"Oh, no, I like construction noise. It's very comforting somehow."

"Unless it's your neighbors."

"Well, I hate those neighbors, so that's different."

"Right."

"So maybe I'll get working on that chicken."

She must have betrayed something in the way she said that, because Richard gave her a little frown. "You OK?"

"No no no," she said, "I love being up here. I love it. This is my favorite place in the world. It doesn't *solve* anything, if you know what I mean. But I love getting up in the morning. I love smelling the air."

"I meant are you OK with my being here."

"Oh, totally. God. Yes. Totally. Yah! I mean, you know how Walter loves you. I feel like we've been friends with you for so long, but I've hardly ever really talked to you. It's a nice opportunity. But you truly shouldn't feel you have to stay, if you want to get back to New York. I'm so used to being alone up here. It's fine."

This speech seemed to have taken her a very long time to get to the end of. It was followed by a brief silence between them.

"I'm just trying to hear what you're actually saying," Richard said. "Whether you actually want me here or not."

"God," she said, "I keep saying it, don't I? Didn't I just say it?"

She could see his patience with her, his patience with a female, reach its end. He rolled his eyes and picked up a section of two-by-four. "I'm going to wrap up here and then go for a swim."

"It's going to be cold."

"Every day a little bit less so."

Going back into the house, she experienced a cramp of envy of Walter, who was allowed to tell Richard that he loved him, and who wanted nothing destabilizing in return, nothing worse than to be loved himself. How easy men had it! She felt in comparison like a bloated sedentary spider, spinning her dry web year after year, waiting. She suddenly understood how the girls of years ago had felt, the girls of college who'd resented Walter's free pass with Richard and been irritated by his pesky presence. She saw Walter, for a moment, as Eliza had seen him.

I might have to do it, I might have to do it, I might have to do it, she said to herself while washing the chicken and assuring herself that she didn't actually mean it. She heard a splash from the lake and watched Richard swimming out in tree shadow toward water still gilded with afternoon light. If he really hated sunshine, the way he claimed to in his old song, northern Minnesota in June was a trying place to be. The days lasted so long that you found yourself surprised the sun wasn't running low on fuel by the end of them. Just kept burning and burning. She yielded to an impulse to grab herself between the legs, to test the waters, for the shock of it, in lieu of going for a swim herself. Am I alive? Do I possess a body?

There were very odd angles in her cutting of the potatoes. They looked like some kind of geometric brainteaser.

Richard, after his shower, came into the kitchen in a textless T-shirt that must have been bright red some decades earlier. His hair was momentarily subdued, a youthful shiny black.

"You changed your look this winter," he remarked to Patty.

"No."

"What do you mean, 'no'? Your hair's different, you look great."

"Really hardly any different. Just a tiny bit different."

"And—possibly put on a little weight?"

"No. Well. A little."

"You look good with it. You look better not so skinny."

"Is that a nice way of saying I've gotten fat?"

He shut his eyes and grimaced as if trying to remain patient. Then he opened his eyes and said, "Where is this bullshit coming from?"

"Ah?"

"Do you want me to leave? Is that it? There's this weird phony thing you're doing that gives me the impression you're not comfortable with me here."

The roasting chicken smelled like something of the sort she used to eat. She washed her hands and dried them, rummaged in the back of an unfinished cabinet, and found a bottle of cooking sherry covered with construction dust. She filled a juice glass with it and sat down at the table. "OK, frankly? I'm a little nervous around you."

"Don't be."

"I can't help it."

"You have no reason to be."

This was what she hadn't wanted to hear. "I'm having this one glass," she said.

"You've mistaken me for somebody who gives a shit how much you drink."

She nodded. "OK. Good. That helps to know."

"You've been wanting a drink this whole time? Jesus. Have a drink."

"Doing just that."

"You know, you're a very strange person. I mean that as a compliment."

"So taken."

"Walter got very, very lucky."

"Ho, well, that's the unfortunate thing, isn't it. I'm not sure he sees it that way anymore."

"Oh, he does. Believe me, he does."

She shook her head. "I was going to say that I don't think he likes the things that are strange about me. He likes the good strange all right, but he's none too happy about the bad strange, and the bad strange is mostly what he gets these days. I was going to say that it's ironic that *you*, who don't seem to mind the bad strange, are not the person I'm married to."

"You wouldn't want to be married to me."

"No, I'm sure it would be very bad. I've heard the stories."

"I'm sorry to hear that, though not surprised."

"Walter tells me everything."

"I'm sure he does."

Out on the lake a duck was quacking about something. Mallards nested in the reedy far corner of it.

"Did Walter ever tell you I slashed Blake's snow tires?" Patty said.

Richard raised his eyebrows, and she told him the story.

"That's really fucked up," he said admiringly, when she'd finished.

"I know. Isn't it?"

"Does Walter know this?"

"Um. Good question."

"I take it you don't tell him everything."

"Oh, God, Richard, I don't tell him anything."

"You really could, I think. You might find he knows a lot more than you think he does."

She took a deep breath and asked what kinds of secret things Walter knew about her.

"He knows you're not happy," Richard said.

"I really don't think that requires great powers of discernment. What else?"

"He knows you blame him for Joey moving out of the house."

"Oh, that," she said. "That I have more or less told him. That doesn't really count."

"OK. So why don't you tell me. Besides the fact that you're a tire-slasher, what does he not know about you?"

When Patty considered this question, all she could see was the great emptiness of her life, the emptiness of her nest, the pointlessness of her existence now that the kids had flown. The sherry had made her sad. "Why don't you sing me a song while I get dinner on the table. Will you do that?"

"I don't know," Richard said. "Feels a little weird."

"Why?"

"I don't know. Just feels weird."

"You're a singer. That's what you do. You sing."

"I guess I've never had the sense that you particularly like what I sing."

"Sing me 'Dark Side of the Bar.' I love that song."

He sighed and bowed his head and crossed his arms and seemed to fall asleep.

"What?" she said.

"I think I'm going to leave tomorrow, if that's all right with you."

"OK."

"There's not more than two days' work left. The deck's already usable as is."

"OK." She stood up and put the sherry glass in the sink. "Can I ask why, though? I mean, it's really nice having you here."

"It's just better if I go."

"OK. Whatever's best. I think it's another ten minutes with the chicken, if you want to set the table for us."

He didn't stir from the table.

"Molly wrote that song," he said, after a while. "I really had no business recording it. It was a very schmucky thing of me to do. Deliberate, calculated schmuckiness on my part."

"It's really sad and pretty. What were you supposed to do? Not use it?"

"Basically, yeah. Not use it. That would have been the nice thing."

"I'm sorry about the two of you. You guys were together a long time."

"We were and we weren't."

"Right, I know that, but still."

He sat brooding while she set the table, tossed the salad, and carved the chicken. She hadn't thought she would have any appetite, but once she took a bite of chicken she remembered that she hadn't eaten a thing since the evening before, and that her day had started at five in the morning. Richard also ate, silently. At a certain point, their silence became remarkable and thrilling, and then, a while after that, exhausting and discouraging. She cleared the table, put away the leftovers, washed the dishes, and saw that Richard had removed himself to the little screen porch to smoke cigarettes. The sun was finally gone, but the sky was still bright. Yes, she thought, it was better if he left. Better, better, better.

She went out on the screen porch. "Thinking of going to bed now and doing some reading," she said.

Richard nodded. "Sounds good. I'll see you in the morning."

"The evenings are so long," she said. "The light just doesn't want to die."

"This has been a great place to be. You guys are very generous."

"Oh, that's all Walter. It didn't actually occur to me to offer it to you."

"He trusts you," Richard said. "If you trust him, everything will be fine."

"Oh, well, maybe, maybe not."

"Do you not want to be with him?"

It was a good question.

"I don't want to lose him," she said, "if that's what you mean. I don't spend my time thinking about leaving him. I'm kind of counting the days till Joey finally gets sick of the Monaghans. He's still got a full year of high school."

"Not sure exactly what the point of that is."

"Just that I'm still committed to my family."

"Good. It's a great family."

"Right, so I'll see you in the morning."

"Patty." He put out his cigarette in the commemorative Danish Christmas bowl of Dorothy's that he was using as an ashtray. "I'm not going to be the person who wrecks my best friend's marriage."

"No! God! Of course not!" She was nearly weeping with disappointment. "I mean, really, Richard, I'm sorry, but what did I say? I said I'm going to bed and I'll see you in the morning. That's all I said! I said I care about my family. That's exactly what I said."

He gave her a very impatient and skeptical look.

"Seriously!"

"OK, sure," he said. "I didn't mean to presume anything. I was just trying to figure out the tension here. You may recall we had a conversation like this once before."

"I do recall that, yes."

"So I thought it was better to mention it than not mention it."

"That's fine. I appreciate it. You're a really good friend. And you shouldn't feel you have to leave tomorrow on my account. Nothing to be afraid of here. No reason to run away."

"Thanks. I might leave anyway, though."

"That's fine."

And she went inside to Dorothy's bed, which Richard had been using until she and Walter arrived to kick him out of it. Cool air was coming out of the places where it had hidden during the long day, but blue twilight was persisting in every window. It was dream light, insane light, it refused to go away. She turned a lamp on to diminish it. The resistance fighters had been exposed! The jig was up! She lay in her flannel pajamas and re-played everything she'd said in the last hours and was appalled by nearly all of it. She heard the toilet's tuneful resonance as Richard emptied his bladder into it, and then the flush, and the tuneful water in the pipes, and the water pump laboring briefly in a lower voice. For sheer respite from herself, she picked up *War and Peace* and read for a long time.

The autobiographer wonders if things might have gone differently if she hadn't reached the very pages in which Natasha Rostov, who was obviously meant for the goofy and good Pierre, falls in love with his great cool friend Prince Andrei. Patty had not seen this coming. Pierre's loss unfolded, as she read it, like a catastrophe in slow motion. Things probably would not have gone any differently, but the effect those pages had on her, their pertinence, was almost psychedelic. She read past midnight, absorbed now even by the military stuff, and was relieved to see, when she turned the lamp off, that the twilight finally was gone.

In her sleep, at some still-dark hour after that, she rose from the bed and let herself into the hall and then into Richard's bedroom and crawled into bed with him. The room was cold and she pressed herself close to him.

"Patty," he said.

But she was sleeping and shook her head, resisting awakening, and there was no holding out against her, she was very determined in her sleep. She spread herself over and around him, trying to maximize their contact, feeling big enough to cover him entirely, pressing her face into his head.

"Patty."

"Mm."

"If you're sleeping, you need to wake up."

"No, I'm asleep . . . I'm sleeping. Don't wake me up."

His penis was struggling to escape his shorts. She rubbed her belly against it.

"I'm sorry," he said, squirming beneath her. "You have to wake up."

"No, don't wake me up. Just fuck me."

"Oh, Jesus." He tried to get away from her, but she followed him amoebically. He grabbed her wrists to keep her at bay. "People who aren't conscious: believe it or not, I draw the line there."

"Mm," she said, unbuttoning her pajamas. "We're both asleep. We're both having really great dreams."

"Yes, but people wake up in the morning, and they remember their dreams."

"But if they're only dreams . . . I'm having a dream. I'm going back to sleep. You go to sleep, too. You fall asleep. We'll both be asleep . . . and then I'll be gone."

That she could say all this, and not only say it but remember it very clearly afterward, does admittedly cast doubt on the authenticity of her sleep state. But the autobiographer is *adamant* in her insistence that she was not awake at the moment of betraying Walter and feeling his friend split her open. Maybe it was the way she was emulating the fabled ostrich and keeping her eyes firmly shut, or maybe the fact that she afterward retained no memory of specific pleasure, only an abstract awareness of the deed that had been done, but if she performs a thought experiment and imagines a phone ringing in the middle of the deed, the state she imagines being shocked into is one of awakeness, from which it logically follows that, in the absence of any ringing phone, the state she was in was a sleeping one.

Only after the deed was done did she wake up, in some alarm, and bethink herself, and betake herself quickly back to her own bed. The next thing she knew, there was light in the windows. She heard Richard getting up and peeing in the bathroom. She strained to decipher the sounds he then made—whether he was packing up his truck or going back to work. It sounded like he was going back to work! When she finally summoned the courage to come out of hiding, she found him kneeling behind the house, sorting a pile of scrap lumber. There was sun but it was a dim disk in thin clouds. A change in the weather was ruffling the surface of the lake. Without all the dazzle and dapple, the woods looked sparser and emptier.

"Hey, good morning," Patty said.

"Morning," Richard said, not looking up at her.

"Have you had breakfast? How about some breakfast? Can I make you some eggs?"

"I had some coffee, thanks."

"I'll make you some eggs"

He stood up and put his hands on his hips and surveyed the lumber, still not looking at her. "I'm straightening this up for Walter, so he knows what we've got here."

"OK."

"It's going to take me a couple hours to pack up. You should just go about your day."

"OK. Do you need any help?"

He shook his head.

"And you're sure no breakfast?"

To this he made no response of any sort.

There came to her, with curious vividness, a kind of PowerPoint list of names in descending order of their owners' goodness, topped naturally by Walter's, which was followed closely by Jessica's and more distantly by Joey's and Richard's, and then, way down in the cellar, in lonely last place, her own ugly name.

She took coffee to her room and sat listening to the sounds of Richard's organizing, the rattle of nails being boxed, the rumble of tool chests. Late in the morning she ventured forth to ask if he might at least stay and have some lunch before he left. He assented, though not in a friendly way. She was too frightened to feel like crying, so she went and boiled some eggs for egg salad. Her plan or hope or fantasy, to the extent that she'd allowed herself to be conscious of having one, had been that Richard would forget his intention to leave that day, and that she would sleepwalk again the next night, and that everything would be pleasant and unspoken again the next day, and then more sleepwalking, and then another pleasant day, and then Richard would load up his truck and go back to New York, and much later in life she would recall the amazing intense dreams she'd had for a couple of nights at Nameless Lake, and safely wonder if anything had happened. This old plan (or hope, or fantasy) was now in tatters. Her new plan called for her to try very hard to forget the night before and pretend it hadn't happened.

One thing the new plan can safely be said *not* to have included was leaving lunch half-eaten on the table and then finding her jeans on the floor and the crotch of her bathing suit wedged painfully to one side while he banged her into ecstasy against the innocently papered wall of Dorothy's old living room, in full daylight and as wide awake as a human being could be. No mark was left on the wall there, and yet the spot remained clear and distinct forever after. It was a little coordinate of the universe permanently charged and altered by its history. It became, that spot, a quiet third presence in the room with her and Walter on the weekends they later spent alone here. This seemed to her, in any case, the first time in her life she'd properly had sex. A real eye-opener, as it were. She was henceforth done for, though it took some time to know this.

"OK, so," she said when she was sitting on the floor with her head against the spot where her butt had been. "So, that was interesting."

Richard had put his pants back on and was pacing around for no purpose. "I'm just going to go ahead and smoke inside your house if you don't mind."

"I think, under the circumstances, an exception will be granted."

The day had turned fully overcast, with a cold breeze moving in through the screens and the screen door. All birdsong had ceased, and the lake seemed desolate. Nature waiting for the chill to pass.

"What are you wearing a bathing suit for anyway?" Richard said, lighting up.

Patty laughed. "I'd thought I might go for a swim after you left."

"It's freezing."

"Well, not a long swim, obviously."

"Just a little mortification of the flesh."

"Exactly."

The cold breeze and the smoke of Richard's Camel were mixing like joy and remorse. Patty started laughing again for no reason and then found something funny to say.

"You may suck at chess," she said, "but you're definitely winning at the other game."

"Shut the fuck up," Richard said.

She couldn't quite gauge his tone of voice, but, fearing that it was angry, she struggled to stop laughing.

Richard sat down on the coffee table and smoked with great determination. "We have to never do this again," he said.

Another snicker broke out of her; she couldn't help it. "Or maybe just a couple more times and then never again."

"Yeah, where does that get us?"

"Conceivably the itch would be scratched, and that would be that."

"Not the way it works, in my experience."

"Well, I guess I have to defer to your experience, don't I? Having none myself."

"Here's the choice," Richard said. "We stop now, or you leave Walter. And since the latter is not acceptable, we stop now."

"Or, third possibility, we could not stop and I could just not tell him."

"I don't want to live that way. Do you?"

"It's true that two of the three people he loves most in the world are you and me."

"The third being Jessica."

"It's some consolation," Patty said, "that she would hate me for the rest of my life and totally side with him. He would always have that."

"That's not what he wants, and I'm not going to do it to him."

Patty laughed again, at the thought of Jessica. She was a very good and painfully earnest and strenuously mature young person whose exasperation with Patty and Joey—her feckless mom, her ruthless brother—was seldom so extreme as not to seem comical. Patty liked her daughter a great deal and would in fact, realistically, be devastated to forfeit her good opinion. But she still couldn't help being amused by Jessica's opprobrium. It was part of how the two of them got along; and Jessica was too absorbed in her own seriousness to be bothered by it.

"Hey," she said to Richard, "do you think it's possible you're homosexual?"

"You ask that now?"

"I don't know. It's just that sometimes guys who have to screw a million women are trying to prove something. Disprove something. And it's sounding to me like you care more about Walter's happiness than you do about mine."

"Trust me on this one. I have no interest in kissing Walter."

"No, I know. I know. But there's still something I mean by that. I mean, I'm sure you'd get tired of me very soon. You'd see me naked when I'm forty-five, and you'd be thinking, Hmm. Do I still want this? I don't think so! Whereas Walter you never have to get tired of, because you don't feel like kissing him. You can just be close to him forever."

"This is D. H. Lawrence," Richard said impatiently.

"Yet another author I need to read."

"Or not."

She rubbed her tired eyes and her abraded mouth. She was, all in all, very happy with the turn things had taken.

"You're really excellent with tools," she said with another snicker.

Richard began to pace again. "Try to be serious, OK? Try hard."

"This is our time right now, Richard. That's all I'm saying. We have a couple of days, and we either use them or we don't. They're going to be over soon either way."

"I made a mistake," he said. "I didn't think it through. I should have taken off yesterday morning."

"All but one part of me would have been glad if you did. Admittedly, that one part is a fairly important part."

"I like seeing you," he said. "I like being around you. It makes me happy to think of Walter being with you—you're that kind of person. I thought it would be OK to stay a couple of extra days. But it was a mistake."

"Welcome to Pattyland. Mistakeland."

"It didn't occur to me that you would sleepwalk."

She laughed. "That was kind of a brilliant stroke, wasn't it?"

"Jesus. Cool it, OK? You're annoying me."

"Yeah, but the great thing is it doesn't even matter. What's the worst that can happen now? You'll be annoyed with me and leave."

He looked at her then, and he smiled, and the room filled (metaphorically) with sunshine. He was, in her opinion, a very beautiful man.

"I do like you," he said. "I like you a lot. I always liked you."

"Same back at you."

"I wanted you to have a good life. Do you understand? I thought you were a person who was actually worthy of Walter."

"And so that's why you went off that night in Chicago and never came back."

"It wouldn't have worked in New York. It would have ended badly."

"If you say so."

"I do say so."

Patty nodded. "So you actually wanted to sleep with me that night."

"Yeah. A lot. But not just sleep with you. Talk to you. Listen to you. That was the difference."

"Well, I guess that's nice to know. I can cross that worry off my list now, twenty years later."

Richard lit another cigarette and they sat there for a while, separated by a cheap old Oriental rug of Dorothy's. There was a sighing in the trees, the voice of an autumn that was never far away in northern Minnesota.

"This is potentially kind of a hard situation, then, isn't it," Patty finally said.

"Yes."

"Harder than I perhaps realized."

"Yes."

"Arguably better of me not to have sleepwalked."

"Yes."

She began to cry for Walter. They had spent so few nights apart over the years that she'd never had a chance to miss him and appreciate him the way she missed him and appreciated him now. This was the beginning of a terrible confusion of the heart, a confusion that the autobiographer is still suffering from. Already, there at Nameless Lake, in the unchanging overcast light, she could see the problem very clearly. She'd fallen for the one man in the world who cared as much about Walter and felt as protective of him as she did; anybody else could have tried to turn her against him. And even worse, in a way, was the responsibility she felt toward Richard, in knowing that he had nobody else like Walter in his life, and that his loyalty to Walter was, in his own estimation, one of the few things besides music that saved him as a human being. All this, in her sleep and selfishness, she had gone and jeopardized. She'd taken advantage of a person who was messed up and susceptible but nevertheless trying hard to maintain some kind of moral order in his life. And so she was crying for Richard, too, but even more for Walter, and for her own unlucky, wrongdoing self.

"It's good to cry," Richard said, "although I can't say I've ever tried it myself."

"It's kind of a bottomless pit, once you get into it," Patty snuffled. She was feeling suddenly cold in her bathing suit, and physically unwell. She went and put her arms around Richard's warm, broad shoulders, and lay down with him on the Oriental rug, and so the long bright gray afternoon went.

Three times, altogether. One, two, three. Once sleeping, once violently, and then once with the full orchestra. Three: pathetic little number. The autobiographer has now spent quite a bit of her mid-forties counting and recounting, but it never adds up to more than three.

There is otherwise not much to relate, and most of what remains consists of further mistakes. The first of these she committed in concert with Richard while they were still lying on the rug. They decided together—agreed—that he should leave. They decided quickly, while they were sore and spent, that he should leave now, before they got themselves in any deeper, and that they would both then give the situation careful thought and come to a sober decision, which, if it should turn out to be negative, would only be more painful if he stayed any longer.

Having made this decision, Patty sat up and was surprised to see that the trees and the deck were soaked. The rain was so fine that she hadn't heard it on the roof, so gentle that it hadn't trickled in the gutters. She put on Richard's faded red T-shirt and asked if she could keep it.

"Why do you want my shirt?"

"It smells like you."

"That's not considered a plus in most quarters."

"I just want one thing that's yours."

"All right. Let's hope it turns out to be the only thing."

"I'm forty-two," she said. "It would cost me twenty thousand dollars to get pregnant. Not to burst your bubble or anything."

"I'm very proud of my zero batting average. Try not to wreck it, OK?"

"And what about me?" she said. "Should I be worried that I've brought some disease into the house?"

"I've had all my shots, if that's what you're asking. I'm usually paranoically careful."

"I bet you say that to all the girls."

And so on. It was all very chummy and chatty, and in the lightness of the moment she told him that he had no excuse now not to sing her a song, before he left. He unpacked his banjo and plucked away while she made sandwiches and wrapped them in foil.

"Maybe you should spend the night and get an early start in the morning," she called to him.

He smiled as if refusing to dignify this with an answer.

"Seriously," she said. "It's raining, it's going to get dark."

"No chance," he said. "Sorry. You will never be trusted again. It's something you're just going to have to live with."

"Ha-ha-ha," she said. "Why aren't you singing? I want to hear your voice."

To be nice to her, he sang "Shady Grove." He had become, over the years, in defiance of initial expectations, a skilled and fairly nuanced vocalist, and he was so big-chested that he could really blow your house down.

"OK, I'm seeing your point," she said when he finished. "This isn't making things any easier for me."

Once you get musicians going, though, they hate to stop. Richard tuned his guitar and sang three country songs that Walnut Surprise later recorded for *Nameless Lake*. Some of the lyrics were barely more than nonsense syllables, to be discarded and replaced with vastly better ones, but Patty was still so affected and excited by his singing, in a country mode she recognized and loved, that she began to shout in the middle of the third song, "STOP! OK! ENOUGH! STOP! ENOUGH! OK!" But he wouldn't stop, and his absorption in his music made her feel so lonely and abandoned that she began to cry raggedly and finally to become so hysterical that he had no choice but to stop singing—though he was still unmistakably pissed off by the interruption!—and try, unsuccessfully, to calm her.

"Here are your sandwiches," she said, dumping them into his arms, "and there's the door. We said you were leaving, and so you're leaving. OK? Now! I mean it! *Now*. I'm sorry I asked you to sing, MY FAULT AGAIN, but let's try to learn from our mistakes, OK?"

He took a deep breath and drew himself up as if to deliver some pronouncement, but his shoulders slumped and he let the big statement escape from his lungs unspoken.

"You're right," he said, irritably. "I don't need this."

"We made a good decision, don't you think?"

"Probably we did, yeah."

"So go."

And he went.

And she became a better reader. At first in desperate escapism, later in search of help. By the time Walter returned from Saskatchewan, she'd dispatched the remainder of *War and Peace* in three marathon reading days. Natasha had promised herself to Andrei but was then corrupted by the wicked Anatole, and Andrei went off in despair to get himself mortally wounded in battle, surviving only long enough to be nursed by Natasha and forgive her, whereupon excellent old Pierre, who had done some growing up and deep thinking as a prisoner of war, stepped forward to present himself as Natasha's consolation prize; and lots of babies followed. Patty felt she'd lived an entire compressed lifetime in those three days, and when her own Pierre returned from the wilderness, badly sunburned despite religious slatherings of maximum-strength sunblock, she was ready to try to love him again. She picked him up in Duluth and debriefed him on his days with nature-loving millionaires, who had apparently opened their wallets wide for him.

"It's incredible," Walter said when they got home and he saw the almost-finished deck. "He's here four months and he can't do the last eight hours of work."

"I think he was sick of the woods," Patty said. "I told him he should just go back to New York. He wrote some great songs here. He was ready to go."

Walter frowned. "He played you songs?"

"Three," she said, turning away from him.

"And they were good?"

"Really good." She walked down toward the lake, and Walter followed her. It wasn't hard to keep her distance from him. Only at the very beginning had they been one of those couples who embraced and locked lips at every homecoming.

"You guys got along OK?" Walter asked.

"It was a little awkward. I was glad when he left. I had to drink a big glass of sherry the one night he was here."

"That's not so bad. One glass."

Part of the deal she'd struck with herself was to tell Walter no lies, not even tiny ones; to speak no words that couldn't narrowly be construed as truth.

"I've been reading a *ton*," she said. "I think *War and Peace* is actually the best book I've ever read."

"I'm jealous," Walter said.

"Ah?"

"Getting to read that book for the first time. Having whole days to do it."

"It was great. I feel kind of altered by it."

"You seem a little altered, actually."

"Not in a bad way, I hope."

"No. Just different."

In bed with him that night, she took off her pajamas and was relieved to find she wanted him more, not less, for what she'd done. It was fine, having sex with him. There was nothing so wrong with it.

"We need to do this more," she said.

"Any time. Literally any time."

They had a sort of second honeymoon that summer, fueled by her contrition and sexual botheration. She tried hard to be a good wife, and to please her very good husband, but a full accounting of the success of her efforts must include the e-mails that she and Richard began to exchange within days of his departure, and the permission she somehow gave him, a few weeks after that, to get on a plane to Minneapolis and go up to Nameless Lake with her while Walter was hosting another V.I.P. trip in the Boundary Waters. She immediately deleted the e-mail with Richard's flight information, as she'd deleted all the others, but not before memorizing the flight number and arrival time.

A week before the date, she repaired to the lake in solitude and gave herself entirely to her derangement. It consisted of getting stumbling drunk every evening, awakening later in panic and remorse and indecision, then sleeping through the morning, then reading novels in a suspended state of false calm, then jumping up and pacing for an hour or more in the vicinity of the telephone, trying to decide whether to call Richard and tell him not to come, and finally opening a bottle to make the whole thing go away for a few hours.

Slowly the remaining days ticked down toward zero. On the last night, she got vomiting drunk, fell asleep in the living room, and was jolted back to consciousness at a predawn hour. To get her hands and her arms to stop shaking enough to dial Richard's number, she had to lie down on the still-ungrouted kitchen floor.

She reached his voice mail. He had found a new, smaller apartment a few blocks from his old one. All she could picture of this new place was a larger version of the black room of the apartment he'd once shared with Walter, the apartment she'd displaced him from. She dialed again, and again got his voice mail. She dialed a third time, and Richard answered.

"Don't come," she said. "I can't do it."

He said nothing, but she could hear him breathing.

"I'm sorry," she said.

"Why don't you call me again in a couple of hours. See how you feel in the morning."

"I've been throwing up. Been vomiting."

"I'm sorry to hear that."

"Please don't come. I promise I'll stop bothering you. I think I just needed to push it to the limit before I could see that I can't do it."

"I guess that makes sense."

"It's the right thing, isn't it?"

"Probably. Yeah. It probably is."

"I can't do it to him."

"Then good. I won't come."

"It's not that I don't want you to come. I'm just asking you not to."

"I will do what you want."

"No, God, listen to me. I'm asking you to do what I *don't* want."

Possibly, in Jersey City, New Jersey, he was rolling his eyes at this. But she knew that he wanted to see her, he was ready to take a plane in the morning, and the only way they could agree definitively that he shouldn't come was to prolong the conversation for two hours, going around and around, performing the unresolvable conflict, until they both felt so dirtied and exhausted and sick of themselves and sick of each other that the prospect of getting together became genuinely unappetizing.

Not least among the ingredients of Patty's misery, when they finally hung up, was her sense of wasting Richard's love. She knew him to be a man supremely irritated by female bullshit, and the fact that he'd put up with two nonstop hours of hers, which was about 119 minutes more than he was constituted to put up with, filled her with gratitude and sorrow about the *waste*, the *waste*. The waste of his love.

Which led her—it almost goes without saying—to call him again twenty minutes later and drag him through a somewhat shorter but even more wretched version of the first call. It was a small preview of what she later did in a more extended way with Walter in Washington: the harder she worked to exhaust his patience, the more patience he showed, and the more patience he showed, the harder it was to let go of him. Fortunately Richard's patience with her, unlike Walter's, was nowhere close to infinite. He finally just hung up on her, and he didn't answer when she called yet again, an hour later, shortly before the time she figured he had to leave for Newark Airport to catch his flight.

Despite having hardly slept, and despite having thrown up what little she'd eaten the day before, she felt immediately fresher and clearer and more energetic. She cleaned the house, read half of a Joseph Conrad novel Walter had recommended, and didn't buy any more wine. When Walter came back from the Boundary Waters, she cooked a beautiful dinner and threw her arms around his neck and—a rarity—made him actually squirm a little with the intensity of her affection.

What she should have done then was find a job or go back to school or become a volunteer. But there always seemed to be something in the way. There was the possibility that Joey would relent and move back home for his senior year. There was the house and garden she'd neglected in her year of drunkenness and depression. There was her cherished freedom to go up to Nameless Lake for weeks at a time whenever she felt like it. There was a more general freedom that she could see was killing her but she was nonetheless unable to let go of. There was Parents' Weekend at Jessica's college in Philadelphia, which Walter couldn't attend but was delighted that Patty showed an interest in attending, since he sometimes worried that she and Jessica weren't close enough. And then there were the weeks leading up to that Parents' Weekend, weeks of e-mails to and from Richard, weeks of imagining the Philadelphia hotel room in which they were going to spend *one day and one night* off the radar. And then there were the months of serious depression after Parents' Weekend.

She'd flown to Philadelphia on a Thursday, in order to spend, as she carefully told Walter, an actual day on her own as a tourist. Taking a cab to the city center, she was pierced unexpectedly by regret for not doing exactly that: not walking the streets as an independent adult woman, not cultivating an independent life, not being a sensible and curious tourist instead of a love-chasing madwoman.

Unbelievable as it may sound, she had not been alone at a hotel since her time in Room 21, and she was very impressed with her plushly mod room at the Sofitel. She examined all the amenities carefully while she waited for Richard to arrive, and then examined them again as the appointed hour came and went. She tried to watch television but could not. She was a pile of nervous pulp by the time the phone finally rang.

"Something's come up," Richard said.

"All right. OK. Something's come up. OK." She went to the window and looked at Philadelphia. "What was it? Somebody's skirt?"

"Cute," Richard said.

"Oh, just give me a little time," she said, "and I'll give you every cliché in the book. We haven't even started on jealousy yet. This is, like, Minute One of jealousy."

"There's nobody else."

"*Nobody?* There's been *nobody?* God, even I've been worse-behaved than that. In my own little marital way."

"I didn't say there haven't been any. I said there isn't one."

She pressed her head against the window. "I'm sorry," she said. "This is just making me feel too old, too ugly, too stupid, too jealous. I can't stand to hear what's coming out of my mouth."

"He called me this morning," Richard said.

"Who?"

"Walter. I should have let it ring, but I picked up. He said he'd gotten up early to take you to the airport, and he was missing you. He said things have been really good with you guys. 'Happiest in many years,' I believe his phrase was."

Patty said nothing.

"Said you were going out to see Jessica, Jessica secretly very happy about this, although worried that you might say something weird and embarrass her, or that you're not going to like her new boyfriend. Walter all in all extremely happy that you're doing this for her."

Patty fidgeted there by the window, struggling to listen.

"Said he was feeling bad about some of the things he'd said to me last winter. Said he didn't want me to have the wrong idea about you. Said last winter was terrible, because of Joey, but things are much better now. 'Happiest in many years.' I'm pretty sure that was the phrase."

Some combination of gagging and sobbing produced a ridiculous painful burp from Patty.

"What was *that?*" Richard said.

"Nothing. Sorry."

"So, anyway."

"Anyway."

"I decided not to go."

"Right. I understand. Of course."

"Good, then."

"But why don't you just come down anyway. I mean, since I'm here. And then I can go back to my incredibly happy life, and you can go back to New Jersey."

"I'm just telling you what he said."

"My incredibly, incredibly happy life."

Oh, the temptations of self-pity. So sweet to her, so irresistible to give voice to, and so ugly to him. She could hear precisely the moment she'd gone a step too far. If she'd kept her cool, she might have charmed and cajoled him into coming down to Philadelphia. Who knows? She might never have gone home again. But she fucked everything up with self-pity. She could hear him grow cooler and more distant, which made her feel even sorrier for herself, and so on, and so forth, until finally she had to get off the phone and give herself entirely to the other sweetness.

Where did the self-pity come from? The inordinate volume of it? By almost any standard, she led a luxurious life. She had all day every day to figure out some decent and satisfying way to live, and yet all she ever seemed to get for all her choices and all her freedom was more miserable. The autobiographer is almost forced to the conclusion that she pitied herself for being so free.

That evening in Philadelphia, there was a brief dismal episode: she went down to the hotel bar with the intention of picking somebody up. She quickly discovered that the world is divided into people who know how to be comfortable by themselves on a bar chair and people who do not. Also, the men just looked too *stupid*, and for the first time in a long while she started thinking about how it felt to be drunk and raped, and went back up to her mod room to enjoy further paroxysms of self-pity.

The next morning, she took a commuter train out to Jessica's college in a state of neediness from which no good could come. Although she'd tried, for nineteen years, to do everything for Jessica that her own mother hadn't done for her—had never missed a game of hers, had bathed her in approval, had familiarized herself with the intricacies of her social life, had been her partisan in every little hurt and disappointment, had involved herself deeply in the drama of her college applications—there was, as noted, an absence of true closeness. This was due partly to Jessica's self-sufficient nature and partly to Patty's overdoing things with Joey. It was to Joey, not Jessica, that she'd gone with her overflowing heart. But the door to Joey was closed and locked now, due to her mistakes, and she arrived on the beautiful Quaker campus not caring about Parents' Weekend. She just wanted some private time with her daughter.

Unfortunately, Jessica's new boyfriend, William, couldn't take a hint. William was a good-natured blond Californian soccer player whose own parents weren't visiting. He followed Patty and Jessica to lunch, to Jessica's afternoon art-history lecture, and to Jessica's dorm room, and when Patty then pointedly offered to take Jessica to dinner in the city, Jessica replied that she'd already made a local dinner reservation for three. At the restaurant, Patty listened stoically while Jessica prodded William to describe the charitable organization he'd founded while still in high school— some grotesquely worthy program wherein poor Malawian girls had their educations sponsored by soccer clubs in San Francisco. Patty had little choice but to keep drinking wine. Midway through her fourth glass, she decided that William needed to know that she herself had once excelled at intercollegiate sports. Since Jessica declined to supply the fact that she'd been second-team all-American, she was obliged to supply it herself, and since this sounded like bragging she felt she had to undercut it by telling the story of her *groupie*, which led to Eliza's drug habits and lies about leukemia, and to the wrecking of her knee. She was speaking loudly and, she thought, entertainingly, but William, instead of laughing, kept glancing nervously at Jessica, who was sitting with her arms crossed and looking morose.

"And the point is what?" she said finally.

"Nothing," Patty said. "I'm just telling you what things were like when I was in college. I didn't realize you weren't interested."

"I'm interested," William was kind enough to say.

"What's interesting to me," Jessica said, "is that I'd never heard any of this."

"I've never told you about Eliza?"

"No. That must have been Joey."

"I'm sure I've talked about it."

"No, Mom. Sorry. You haven't."

"Well, anyway, now I'm talking about it, although maybe I've said enough."

"Maybe!"

Patty knew she was behaving badly, but she couldn't help it. Seeing Jessica and William's tenderness with each other, she thought of herself at nineteen, thought of her mediocre schooling and her sick relationships with Carter and Eliza, and regretted her life, and pitied herself. She was falling into a depression that deepened precipitously the following day, when she returned to the college and endured a tour of its sumptuous grounds, a luncheon on the lawn of the president's house, and an afternoon colloquium ("Performing Identity in a Multivalent World") attended by scores of other parents. Everyone looked radiantly better-adjusted than she was feeling. The students all seemed cheerfully competent at everything, no doubt including sitting comfortably in a bar chair, and all the other parents seemed so proud of them, so thrilled to be their friends, and the college itself seemed immensely proud of its wealth and its altruistic mission. Patty really had been a good parent; she'd succeeded in preparing her daughter for a happier and easier life than her own; but it was clear from the other families' very body language that she hadn't been a great mom in the ways that counted most. While the other mothers and daughters walked shoulder to shoulder on the paved pathways, laughing or comparing cell phones, Jessica walked on the grass one or two steps ahead of Patty. The only role she offered Patty that weekend was to be impressed with her fabulous school. Patty did her utmost to play this role, but finally, in an access of depression, she sat down on one of the Adirondack chairs that dotted the main lawn and begged Jessica to come to dinner with her in the city without William, who, mercifully, had had a game that afternoon.

Jessica stood at some distance and regarded her guardedly. "William and I need to study tonight," she said. "Normally I would have been studying all yesterday and today."

"I'm sorry I kept you from that," Patty said with depressive sincerity.

"No, it's fine," Jessica said. "I really wanted you to be here. I really wanted you to see where I'm spending four years of my life. It's just that the workload's pretty intense."

"No, of course. It's great. It's great that you can handle that. I'm so proud of you. I really am, Jessica. I think the world of you."

"Well, thank you."

"It's just—how about if we go to my hotel room? It's a really fun room. We can order room service and watch movies and drink from the minibar. I mean, *you* can drink from the minibar, I'm not going to drink tonight. But just to have a girls' night, just the two of us, for one night. You can study the whole rest of the fall."

She kept her eyes on the ground, awaiting Jessica's judgment. She was painfully aware of proposing something new for them.

"I really think I'd better work," Jessica said. "I already promised William."

"Oh, please, though, Jessie. One night's not going to kill you. It would mean a lot to me."

When Jessica did not reply to this, Patty forced herself to look up. Her daughter was gazing with desolate self-control at the main college building, on an outside wall of which Patty had noticed a stone graven with words of wisdom from the Class of 1920: USE WELL THY FREEDOM.

"Please?" she said.

"No," Jessica said, not looking at her. "No! I don't feel like it."

"I'm sorry I drank too much and said those stupid things last night. I wish you'd let me make it up to you."

"I'm not trying to punish you," Jessica said. "It's just, you obviously don't like my school, you obviously don't like my boyfriend—"

"No, he's fine, he's nice, I do like him. It's just that I came here to see you, not him."

"Mom, I make your life so easy for you. Do you have any idea how easy? I don't do drugs, I don't do any of the shit that Joey does, I don't embarrass you, I don't create scenes, I never did *any* of that—"

"I know! And I am truly grateful for it."

"OK, but then don't complain if I have my own life and my own friends and don't feel like suddenly rearranging everything for you. You get all the benefits of me taking care of myself, the least you can do is not make me feel guilty about it."

"Jessie, though, we're talking about one night. It's silly to make such a big deal of it."

"Then don't make a big deal of it."

Jessica's self-control and coolness toward her seemed to Patty a just punishment for how rule-bound and cold to her mother she herself had been at nineteen. She was feeling so bad about herself, indeed, that almost any punishment would have seemed appropriate to her. Saving her tears for later—feeling as if she didn't *deserve* whatever emotional advantage she might have gained by crying, or by running off in a sulk to the train station—she exercised her own self-control and ate an early dining-hall dinner with Jessica and her roommate. She behaved like a grownup even though she felt that Jessica was the real grownup of the two of them.

Back in St. Paul, she continued her plunge down the mental-health mine shaft, and there were no more e-mails from Richard. The autobiographer wishes she could report that Patty didn't send him any e-mails, either, but it should be clear by now that her capacity for error, agonizing, and self-humiliation is boundless. The one message she feels OK about sending was written after Walter gave her the news that Molly Tremain had killed herself with sleeping pills in her Lower East Side apartment. Patty was her best self in that e-mail and hopes that it's how Richard remembers her.

The rest of the story of what Richard was doing that winter and spring has been told elsewhere, notably in *People* and *Spin* and *Entertainment Weekly* after the release of *Nameless Lake* and the emergence of a "cult" of Richard Katz. Michael Stipe and Jeff Tweedy were among the worthies who came forward to endorse Walnut Surprise and confess to having been longtime closet Traumatics listeners. Richard's scruffy, well-educated white male fans may not have been so young anymore, but quite a few of them were now influential senior Arts editors.

As for Walter, the resentment you feel when your favorite unknown band suddenly goes on everybody's playlist was multiplied by a thousand. Walter was proud, of course, that the new record was named after Dorothy's lake, and that so many of the songs had been written in that house. Richard had also mercifully crafted the lyrics of each song so that the "you" in them, who was Patty, could be mistaken for dead Molly; this was the angle that he directed interviewers to take, knowing that Walter read and saved every scrap of press his friend ever got. But Walter was mostly disappointed and hurt by Richard's moment in the sun. He said he understood why Richard hardly ever called him anymore, he understood that

Richard had a lot on his plate now, but he didn't really understand it. The true state of their friendship was turning out to be exactly as he'd always feared. Richard, even when he seemed to be most down, was never really down. Richard always had his secret musical agenda, an agenda that did not include Walter, and was always ultimately making his case directly to his fans, and keeping his eyes on the prize. A couple of minor music journalists were diligent enough to phone Walter for interviews, and his name could be found in some out-of-the-way places, most of them online, but Richard, in the interviews that Walter read, referred to him simply as "a really good college friend," and none of the big magazines mentioned him by name. Walter wouldn't have minded getting a little more credit for having been so morally and intellectually and even financially supportive of Richard, but what really hurt him was how little he seemed to matter to Richard, compared to how much Richard mattered to him. And Patty of course couldn't offer him her best proof of how much he actually did matter to Richard. When Richard managed to find time to connect with him on the phone, Walter's hurt poisoned their conversations and made Richard that much less inclined to call again.

And so Walter became competitive. He'd been lulled into believing himself the big brother, and now Richard had set him straight yet again. Richard may have privately sucked at chess and long-term relationships and good citizenship, but he was publicly loved and admired and celebrated for his tenacity, his purity of purpose, his gorgeous new songs. It all made Walter suddenly hate the house and the yard and the small Minnesotan stakes he'd sunk so much of his life and energy into; Patty was shocked by how bitterly he belittled his own accomplishments. Within weeks of the release of *Nameless Lake*, he was flying to Houston for his first interview with the megamillionaire Vin Haven, and a month after that he began to spend his work weeks in Washington, D.C. It was obvious to Patty, if not to Walter himself, that his resolve to go to Washington and create the Cerulean Mountain Trust and become a more ambitious international player was fueled by competition. In December, when Walnut Surprise played with Wilco at the Orpheum on a Friday night, he didn't even fly back to St. Paul in time to see them.

Patty gave that show a miss herself. She couldn't bear to listen to the new record—couldn't get past the past tense of the second song—

*There was nobody like you*
*For me. Nobody*
*I live with nobody. Love*
*Nobody. You were that body*
*That nobody was like*
*You were that body*
*That body for me*
*There was nobody like you*

and so she did her best to follow Richard's lead and relegate him to the past. There was something exciting, something almost Fiend of Athens, in Walter's new energy, and she succeeded in hoping that the two of them might begin life afresh in Washington. She still loved the house on Nameless Lake, but she was done with the house on Barrier Street, which hadn't been enough to hold Joey. She visited Georgetown for one afternoon, on a pretty blue fall Saturday when a Minnesotan wind was tossing the turning trees, and said, yeah, OK, I can do this. (Was she also conscious of the proximity of the University of Virginia, where Joey had just enrolled? Was her grasp of geography maybe not as bad as she'd always thought?) Incredibly, it was not until she actually arrived for good in Washington— not until she was crossing Rock Creek in a taxi with two suitcases—that she remembered how much she'd always hated politics and politicians. She walked into the house on 29th Street and saw, in a heartbeat, that she'd made yet another mistake.

# 2004

# MOUNTAINTOP REMOVAL

When it became unavoidable that Richard Katz return to the studio with his eager young bandmates and start recording a second Walnut Surprise album—when he'd exhausted all modes of procrastination and flight, first playing every receptive city in America and then touring progressively more remote foreign countries, until his bandmates rebelled at adding Cyprus to their Turkish trip, and then breaking his left index finger while fielding a paperback copy of Samantha Power's seminal survey of world genocide flung too violently by the band's drummer, Tim, across a hotel room in Ankara, and then retreating solo to a cabin in the Adirondacks to score a Danish art film and, in his utter boredom with the project, seeking out a coke dealer in Plattsburgh and taking 5,000 euros of Danish government arts funding up his nose, and then going AWOL for a stretch of costly dissipation in New York and Florida which didn't end until he was busted in Miami for DWI and possession, and then checking himself into the Gubser Clinic in Tallahassee for six weeks of detox and snide resistance to the gospel of recovery, and then recuperating from the shingles he'd taken insufficient care to avoid contracting during a chicken-pox outbreak at the Gubser, and then performing 250 hours of agreeably mindless community service at a Dade County park, and then simply refusing to answer his phone or check his e-mail while he read books in his apartment on the pretext of shoring up his defenses against the chicks and drugs that his bandmates all seemed able to enjoy without too seriously overdoing it—he sent Tim a postcard and told him to tell the others that he was dead broke and going back to building rooftop decks full-time; and the rest of Walnut Surprise began to feel like idiots for having waited.

Not that it mattered, but Katz really was broke. Income and outlays had more or less balanced during the band's year and a half of touring; whenever there'd been danger of a surplus, he'd upgraded their hotels and bought drinks for bars full of fans and strangers. Though *Nameless Lake* and the newly kindled consumer interest in old Traumatics recordings had brought him more money than his previous twenty years of work combined, he'd managed to blow every dime of it in his quest to relocate the self he'd misplaced. The most traumatic events ever to befall the longtime front man of the Traumatics had been (1) receiving a Grammy nomination, (2) hearing his music played on National Public Radio, and (3) deducing, from December sales figures, that *Nameless Lake* had made the perfect little Christmas gift to leave beneath tastefully trimmed trees in several hundred thousand NPR-listening households. The Grammy nomination had been a particularly disorienting embarrassment.

Katz had read extensively in popular sociobiology, and his understanding of the depressive personality type and its seemingly perverse persistence in the human gene pool was that depression was a successful adaptation to ceaseless pain and hardship. Pessimism, feelings of worthlessness and lack of entitlement, inability to derive satisfaction from pleasure, a tormenting awareness of the world's general crappiness: for Katz's Jewish paternal forebears, who'd been driven from shtetl to shtetl by implacable anti-Semites, as for the old Angles and Saxons on his mother's side, who'd labored to grow rye and barley in the poor soils and short summers of northern Europe, feeling bad all the time and expecting the worst had been natural ways of equilibrating themselves with the lousiness of their circumstances. Few things gratified depressives, after all, more than really bad news. This obviously wasn't an optimal way to live, but it had its evolutionary advantages. Depressives in grim situations handed down their genes, however despairingly, while the self-improvers converted to Christianity or moved away to sunnier locales. Grim situations were Katz's niche the way murky water was a carp's. His best years with the Traumatics had coincided with Reagan I, Reagan II, and Bush I; Bill Clinton (at least pre-Lewinsky) had been something of a trial for him. Now came Bush II, the worst regime of all, and he might well have started making music again, had it not been for the accident of success. He flopped around on the ground, heavily carplike, his psychic gills straining futilely to extract dark sustenance from an atmosphere of approval and plenitude. He was at once freer than he'd been since puberty and closer than he'd ever been to suicide. In the last days of 2003, he went back to building decks.

He was lucky with his first two clients, a couple of private-equity boys who were into the Chili Peppers and didn't know Richard Katz from Ludwig van Beethoven. He sawed and nail-gunned on their roofs in relative peace. Not until his third job, begun in February, did he have the misfortune of working for people who thought they knew who he was. The building was on White Street between Church and Broadway, and the client, an independently rich publisher of art books, owned the entire Traumatics oeuvre in vinyl and seemed hurt that Katz didn't remember seeing his face in various sparse crowds at Maxwell's, in Hoboken, over the years.

"There are so many faces," Katz said. "I'm bad with faces."

"That night when Molly fell off the stage, we all had drinks afterward. I still have her bloody napkin somewhere. You don't remember?"

"Drawing a blank. Sorry."

"Well, anyway, it's been great to see you getting some of the recognition you deserve."

"I'd rather not talk about that," Katz said. "Let's talk about your roof instead."

"Basically, I want you to be creative and bill me," the client said. "I want to have a deck built by Richard Katz. I can't imagine you're going to be doing this for long. I couldn't believe it when I heard you were in business."

"Some rough idea of square footage and preference in materials would nevertheless be useful."

"Really anything. Just be creative. It doesn't even matter."

"Bear with me, though, and pretend it does," Katz said. "Because if it really doesn't matter, I'm not sure I—"

"Cover the roof. OK? Make it vast." The client seemed annoyed with him. "Lucy wants to have parties up here. That's one reason we bought this place."

The client had a son, Zachary, a Stuy High senior and hipster-in-training and apparently something of a guitarist, who came up to the roof after school on Katz's first day of work and, from a safe distance, as if Katz were a lion on a chain, peppered him with questions calculated to demonstrate his own knowledge of vintage guitars, which Katz considered a particularly tiresome commodity fetish. He said as much, and the kid went away annoyed with him.

On Katz's second day of work, while he was transporting lumber and Trex boards roofward, Zachary's mother, Lucy, waylaid him on the third-floor landing and offered, unsolicited, her opinion that the Traumatics had been the kind of adolescently posturing, angst-mongering boy group that never interested her. Then she waited, with parted lips and a saucy challenge in her eyes, to see how her presence—the drama of being her—was registering. In the way of such chicks, she seemed convinced of the originality of her provocation. Katz had encountered, practically verbatim, the same provocation a hundred times before, which put him in the ridiculous position now of feeling bad for being unable to pretend to be provoked: of pitying Lucy's doughty little ego, its flotation on a sea of aging-female insecurity. He doubted he could get anywhere with her even if he felt like trying, but he knew that her pride would be hurt if he didn't make at least a token effort to be disagreeable.

"I know," he said, propping Trex against a wall. "That's why it was such a breakthrough for me to produce a record of authentic adult feeling which women, too, could appreciate."

"What makes you think I liked *Nameless Lake*?" Lucy said.

"What makes you think I care?" Katz gamely rejoined. He'd been up and down the stairs all morning, but what really exhausted him was having to perform himself.

"I liked it OK," she said. "It was maybe just a teeny bit overpraised."

"I'm at a loss to disagree with you," Katz said.

She went away annoyed with him.

In the eighties and nineties, to avoid undercutting his best selling point as a contractor—the fact that he was making unpopular music deserving of financial support—Katz had been all but required to behave unprofessionally. His bread-and-butter clientele had been Tribeca artists and movie people who'd given him food and sometimes drugs and would have questioned his artistic commitment if he'd shown up for work before midafternoon, refrained from hitting on unavailable females, or finished on schedule and within budget. Now, with Tribeca fully annexed by the financial industry, and with Lucy lingering on her DUX bed all morning, sitting cross-legged in a tank top and sheer bikini underpants while she read the *Times* or talked on the phone, waving up at him through the skylight whenever he passed it, her barely clothed bush and impressive thighs sustainedly observable, he became a demon of professionalism and Protestant virtue, arriving promptly at nine and working several hours past nightfall, trying to shave a day or two off the project and get the hell out of there.

He'd returned from Florida feeling equally averse to sex and to music. This sort of aversion was new to him, and he was rational enough to recognize that it had everything to do with his mental state and little or nothing to do with reality. Just as the fundamental sameness of female bodies in no way precluded unending variety, there was no rational reason to despair about the sameness of popular music's building blocks, the major and minor power chords, the 2/4 and the 4/4, the A-B-A-B-C. Every hour of the day, somewhere in greater New York, some energetic young person was working on a song that would sound, at least for a few listenings—maybe for as many as twenty or thirty listenings—as fresh as the morning of Creation. Since receiving his walking papers from Florida Probations and taking leave of his large-titted Parks Department supervisor, Marta Molina, Katz had been unable to turn on his stereo or touch an instrument or imagine letting anybody else into his bed, ever again. Hardly a day went by without his hearing an arresting new sound leaking from somebody's basement practice room or even (it could happen) from the street doors of a Banana Republic or a Gap, and without his seeing, on the streets of Lower Manhattan, a young chick who was going to change somebody's life; but he'd stopped believing this somebody could be him.

Then came a freezing Thursday afternoon, a sky of uniform grayness, a light snow that made the downtown skyline's negative space less negative, blurring the Woolworth Building and its fairy-tale turrets, gently slanting in the weather's tensors down the Hudson and out into the dark Atlantic, and distancing Katz from the scrum of pedestrians and traffic four stories below. The melty wetness of the streets nicely raised the treble of the traffic's hiss and negated most of his tinnitus. He felt doubly enwombed, by the snow and by his manual labor, as he cut and fitted Trex into the intricate spaces between three chimneys. Midday turned to twilight without his thinking once of cigarettes, and since the interval between cigarettes was how he was currently sectioning his days into swallowable bites, he had the feeling that no more than fifteen minutes had passed between his eating of his lunchtime sandwich and the sudden, unwelcome looming-up of Zachary.

The kid was wearing a hoodie and the sort of low-cut skinny pants that Katz had first observed in London. "What do you think of Tutsi Picnic?" he said. "You into them?"

"Don't know 'em," Katz said.

"No way! I can't believe that."

"And yet it's the truth," Katz said.

"What about the Flagrants? Aren't they awesome? That thirty-seven-minute song of theirs?"

"Haven't had the pleasure."

"Hey," Zachary said, undiscouraged, "what do you think about those psychedelic Houston bands that were recording on Pink Pillow in the late sixties? Some of their sound really reminds me of your early stuff."

"I need the piece of material you're standing on," Katz said.

"I thought some of those guys might be influences. Especially Peshawar Rickshaw."

"If you could just raise your left foot for a second."

"Hey, can I ask you another question?"

"And this saw will be making some noise now."

"Just one other question."

"All right."

"Is this part of your musical process? Going back to work at your old day job?"

"I hadn't really thought about it."

"See, because my friends at school are asking. I told them I thought this was part of your process. Like, maybe you were reconnecting with the working man to gather material for your next record."

"Do me a favor," Katz said, "and tell your friends to have their parents call me if they want a deck built. I'll work anywhere below Fourteenth and west of Broadway."

"Seriously, is that why you're doing this?"

"The saw is very loud."

"OK, but one more question? I swear this is my last question. Can I do an interview with you?"

Katz revved the saw.

"Please?" Zachary said. "There's this girl in my class that's totally into *Nameless Lake*. It would be really helpful, in terms of getting her to talk to me, if I could digitally record one short interview and put it up online."

Katz set down the saw and regarded Zachary gravely. "You play guitar and you're telling me you have trouble interesting girls in you?"

"Well, this particular one, yeah. She's got more mainstream taste. It's been a real uphill battle."

"And she's the one you've got to have, can't live without."

"Pretty much."

"And she's a senior," Katz said by old calculating reflex, before he could tell himself not to. "Didn't skip any grades or anything."

"Not that I know of."

"Her name?"

"Caitlyn."

"Bring her over after school tomorrow."

"But she's not going to believe you're here. That's why I want to do the interview, to prove you're here. Then she'll want to come over and meet you."

Katz was two days short of eight weeks of celibacy. For the previous seven weeks, abjuring sex had seemed like the natural complement to staying clean of drugs and alcohol—one form of virtue buttressing the other. Not five hours ago, glancing down through the skylight at Zachary's exhibitionist mother, he'd felt uninterested to the point of mild nausea. But now, all at once, with divinatory clarity, he saw that he would be falling one day short of the eight-week mark: would be giving himself over to the meticulous acquisition of Caitlyn, obliterating the numberless moments of consciousness between now and tomorrow night by imagining the million subtly different faces and bodies that she might turn out to possess, and then exercising his mastery and enjoying the fruits of such exercise, all in the arguably worthy service of squishing Zachary and disillusioning an eighteen-year-old fan with "mainstream" taste. He saw that he'd simply made a virtue of being uninterested in vice.

"Here's the deal," he said. "You set it up, think up your little questions, and I'll be down in a couple of hours. But I need to see results tomorrow. I need to see this isn't just some bullshit of yours."

"Awesome," Zachary said.

"You hear what I'm saying, though, right? I'm done interviewing. If I make an exception, we need results."

"I swear she's going to want to come over. She's definitely going to want to meet you."

"Good, then go contemplate what a large favor I'm doing you. I'll be down around seven."

Darkness had fallen. The snow had dwindled to a flurry, and the nightly nightmare of Holland Tunnel traffic had commenced. All but two of the city's subway lines, as well as the indispensable PATH train, converged within three hundred yards of where Katz stood. This was still the pinch point of the world, this neighborhood. Here was the World Trade Center's floodlit cicatrix, here the gold hoard of the Federal Reserve, here the Tombs and the Stock Exchange and City Hall, here Morgan Stanley and American Express and the windowless monoliths of Verizon, here stirring views across the harbor toward distant Liberty in her skin of green oxide. The stout female and wiry male bureaucrats who made the city function were crowding Chambers Street with brightly colored small umbrellas, heading home to Queens and Brooklyn. For a moment, before he turned his work lights on, Katz felt almost happy, almost familiar to himself again; but by the time he was packing up his tools, two hours later, he was aware of all the ways in which he already hated Caitlyn, and what a strange, cruel universe it was that made him want to fuck a chick because he hated her, and how badly this episode, like so many others before it, was going to end, and what a waste it would make of his accumulated clean time. He hated Caitlyn additionally for this waste.

And yet it was important that Zachary be squished. The kid had been given his own practice room, a cubical space lined with eggshell foam and scattered with more guitars than Katz had owned in thirty years. Already, for pure technique, to judge from what Katz had overheard in his comings and goings, the kid was a more hotdog soloist than Katz had ever been or ever would be. But so were a hundred thousand other American high-school boys. So what? Rather than thwarting his father's vicarious rock ambitions by pursuing entomology or interesting himself in financial derivatives, Zachary dutifully aped Jimi Hendrix. Somewhere there had been a failure of imagination.

The kid was waiting in his practice room with an Apple laptop and a printed list of questions when Katz came in, his nose running and his frozen hands aching in the indoor warmth. Zachary indicated the folding chair he was to sit in. "I was wondering," he said, "if you could start by playing a song and then maybe play another when we're done."

"No, I won't do that," Katz said.

"One song. It would be really cool if you would."

"Just ask me your questions, all right? This is fairly humiliating already."

Q: So, Richard Katz, it's been three years since *Nameless Lake*, and exactly two years since Walnut Surprise was up for a Grammy. Can you tell me a little bit about how your life has changed since then?

A: I can't answer that question. You have to ask me better questions.

Q: Well, maybe you can tell me a little about your decision to go back to work as a manual laborer. Do you feel blocked artistically?

A: Really need to take a different tack here.

Q: OK. What do you think of the MP3 revolution?

A: Ah, revolution, wow. It's great to hear the word "revolution" again. It's great that a song now costs exactly the same as a pack of gum and lasts exactly the same amount of time before it loses its flavor and you have to spend another buck. That era which finally ended whenever, yesterday—you know, that era when we pretended rock was the scourge of conformity and consumerism, instead of its anointed handmaid—that era was really irritating to me. I think it's good for the honesty of rock and roll and good for the country in general that we can finally see Bob Dylan and Iggy Pop for what they really were: as manufacturers of wintergreen Chiclets.

Q: So you're saying rock has lost its subversive edge?

A: I'm saying it never had any subversive edge. It was always wintergreen Chiclets, we just enjoyed pretending otherwise.

Q: What about when Dylan went electric?

A: If you're going to talk about ancient history, let's go back to the French Revolution. Remember when, I forget his name, but that rocker who wrote the "Marseillaise," Jean Jacques Whoever—remember when his song started getting all that airplay in 1792, and suddenly the peasantry rose up and overthrew the aristocracy? *There* was a song that changed the world. Attitude was what the peasants were missing. They already had everything else—humiliating servitude, grinding poverty, unpayable debts, horrific working conditions. But without a song, man, it added up to nothing. The sansculotte style was what really changed the world.

Q: So what's the next step for Richard Katz?

A: I'm getting involved in Republican politics.

Q: Ha ha.

A: Seriously. Getting nominated for a Grammy was such an un-expected honor, I feel duty bound to make the most of it in this critical election year. I've been given the opportunity to partici-pate in the pop-music mainstream, and manufacture Chiclets, and help try to persuade fourteen-year-olds that the look and feel of Apple Computer products is an indication of Apple Com-puter's commitment to making the world a better place. Because making the world a better place is cool, right? And Apple Com-puter must be way more committed to a better world, because iPods are so much cooler-looking than other MP3 players, which is why they're so much more expensive and incompatible with other companies' software, because—well, actually, it's a little unclear why, in a better world, the very coolest products have to bring the very most obscene profits to a tiny number of residents of the better world. This may be a case where you have to step back and take the long view and see that getting to have your own iPod is itself the very thing that makes the world a better place. And that's what I find so refreshing about the Republican Party. They leave it up to the individual to decide what a better world might be. It's the party of liberty, right? That's why I can't under-stand why those intolerant Christian moralists have so much in-fluence on the party. Those people are very antichoice. Some of them are even opposed to the worship of money and material goods. I think the iPod is the true face of Republican politics, and I'm in favor of the music industry really getting out in front on this one, and becoming more active politically, and standing up proud and saying it out loud: We in the Chiclet-manufacturing business are not about social justice, we're not about accurate or objectively verifiable information, we're not about meaningful labor, we're not about a coherent set of national ideals, we're not about wisdom. We're about choosing what WE want to listen to and ignoring everything else. We're about ridiculing people who have the bad manners not to want to be cool like us. We're about giving ourselves a mindless feel-good treat every five minutes. We're about the relentless enforcement and exploitation of our intellectual-property rights. We're about persuading ten-year-old children to spend twenty-five dollars on a cool little silicone iPod case that it costs a licensed Apple Computer subsidiary thirty-nine cents to manufacture.

Q: Seriously, though. There was a very strong antiwar mood at last year's Grammys. Many of the nominees were very outspoken. Do you think successful musicians have a responsibility to be role models?

A: Me me me, buy buy buy, party party party. Sit in your own little world, rocking, with your eyes closed. What I've been trying to say is that we already *are* perfect Republican role models.

Q: If that's the case, then why was there a censor at the awards last year, making sure that nobody spoke out against the war? Are you saying Sheryl Crow is a Republican?

A: I hope so. She seems like such a nice person, I'd hate to think she was a Democrat.

Q: She's been very vocally antiwar.

A: Do you think George Bush actually hates gay people? Do you think he personally gives a shit about abortion? Do you think Dick Cheney really believes Saddam Hussein engineered 9/11? Sheryl Crow is a chewing-gum manufacturer, and I say that as a longtime chewing-gum manufacturer myself. The person who cares what Sheryl Crow thinks about the war in Iraq is the same person who's going to buy an obscenely overpriced MP3 player because Bono Vox is shilling for it.

Q: But there's a place for leaders in a society, too, right? Wasn't that what corporate America was trying to suppress at the Grammys? The voices of potential leaders of an antiwar movement?

A: You want the CEO of Chiclets to be a leader in the fight against tooth decay? Use the same advertising methods to sell gum and tell the world that gum is bad for you? I know I just made a crack about Bono, but he has more integrity than the rest of the music world combined. If you made a fortune selling Chiclets, you might as well go ahead and sell overpriced iPods, too, and get even richer, and then use your money and your status to get entrée to the White House and try to do some actual hands-on good in Africa. Like: be a man, suck it up, admit that you like being part of the ruling class, and that you believe in the ruling class, and that you'll do whatever it takes to consolidate your position in it.

Q: Are you saying you supported the invasion of Iraq?

A: I'm saying, if invading Iraq had been the kind of thing that a person like me supported, it never would have happened.

Q: Let's get back to Richard Katz the person for a minute.

A: No, let's turn your little machine off. I think we're done here.

"That was great," Zachary said, pointing and clicking. "That was perfect. I'm going to put this up right now and send the link to Caitlyn."
"You have her e-mail address?"
"No, but I know who does."
"Then I'll see you both after school tomorrow."
Katz made his way down Church Street toward the PATH train under a familiar cloud of post-interview remorse. He wasn't worried about having given offense; his business was giving offense. He was worried about having sounded pathetic—too transparently the washed-up talent

whose only recourse was to trash his betters. He strongly disliked the person he'd just demonstrated afresh that he unfortunately was. And this, of course, was the simplest definition of depression that he knew of: strongly disliking yourself.

Back in Jersey City, he stopped at the gyro joint that provided three or four of his dinners every week, departed with a heavy stinking bag of lowest-grade meats and pita, and climbed the stairs to his apartment, which he'd been away from so much in the last two and a half years that it seemed to have turned against him, to no longer wish to be his place. A little bit of coke could have changed that—could have restored the apartment's lost luster of friendliness—but only for a few hours, or at most a few days, after which it would make everything much worse. The one room he still halfway liked was the kitchen, whose harsh fluorescent lighting suited his mood. He sat down at his ancient enamel-top table to distract himself from the taste of his dinner by reading Thomas Bernhard, his new favorite writer.

Behind him, on a counter crowded with unwashed dishes, his landline rang. The readout said WALTER BERGLUND.

"Walter, my conscience," Katz said. "Why are you bothering me now?"

He was tempted, in spite of himself, to pick up, because he'd lately found himself missing Walter, but he remembered, in the nick of time, that this could just as easily be Patty calling from their home phone. He'd learned from his experience with Molly Tremain that you shouldn't try to save a drowning woman unless you were ready to drown yourself, and so he'd stood and watched from a pier while Patty floundered and cried for help. Any way she might be feeling now was a way he didn't want to hear about. The great benefit of touring *Nameless Lake* to death—toward the end, he'd been able to entertain long trains of thought while performing, able to review the band's finances and contemplate the scoring of new drugs and experience remorse about his latest interview without losing the beat or skipping a verse—had been the emptying of all meaning from the lyrics, the permanent severing of his songs from the state of sadness (for Molly, for Patty) in which he'd written them. He'd gone so far as to believe the touring had exhausted the sadness itself. But there was no way he was going to touch the phone while it was ringing.

He did, however, check his voice mail.

*Richard? It's Walter—Berglund. I don't know if you're there, you're probably not even in the country, but I'm wondering if you might be around tomorrow. I'm going up to New York on business, and I have a little proposal for you. Sorry about the late notice. I'm mostly just saying hi. Patty says hi, too. Hope everything's OK with you!*

To delete this message, press 3.

It was two years since Katz had heard from Walter. As the silence had lengthened, he'd begun to think that Patty, in a moment of stupidity or misery, had confessed to her husband what had happened at Nameless Lake. Walter, with his feminism, his infuriating reverse double standard, would quickly have forgiven Patty and left Katz alone to bear the blame for the betrayal. It was a funny thing about Walter: circumstances kept conspiring to make Katz, who otherwise feared nobody, feel lessened and intimidated by him. In renouncing Patty, sacrificing his own pleasure and brutally disappointing her in order to preserve her marriage, he'd risen momentarily to the level of Walter's excellence, but all he'd gotten for his trouble was envy of his friend for his unexamined possession of his wife. He'd tried to pretend that he was doing the Berglunds a favor by ceasing communication with them, but mainly he just hadn't wanted to hear that they were happy and securely married.

Katz couldn't have said exactly why Walter mattered to him. No doubt part of it was simply an accident of grandfathering: of forming an attachment at an impressionable age, before the contours of his personality were fully set. Walter had slipped into his life before he'd shut the door on the world of ordinary people and cast his lot with misfits and dropouts. Not that Walter was so ordinary himself. He was at once hopelessly naïve and very shrewd and dogged and well-informed. And then there was the complication of Patty, who, although she'd long tried hard to pretend otherwise, was even less ordinary than Walter, and then the further complication of Katz's being no less attracted to Patty than Walter was, and arguably *more* attracted to Walter than Patty was. This was definitely a weird one. No other man had warmed Katz's loins the way the sight of Walter did after long absence. These groinal heatings were no more about literal sex, no more homo, than the hard-ons he got from a long-anticipated first snort of blow, but there was definitely something deep-chemical there. Something that insisted on being called love. Katz had enjoyed seeing the Berglunds as their family grew, enjoyed knowing them, enjoyed knowing they were out there in the Midwest, having a good life that he could drop in on when he wasn't feeling great. And then he'd wrecked it by letting himself spend a night alone in a summer house with a former basketball player who was skilled at scooting through narrow lanes of opportunity. What had been his diffusely warm world of domestic refuge had collapsed, overnight, into the hot, hungry microcosm of Patty's cunt. Which he still couldn't believe he'd had such cruelly fleeting access to.

*Patty says hi, too.*

"Yeah, fuck that," Katz said, eating gyro. But as soon as he'd replaced his appetite with a deep gastric unease about his means of satisfying it, he returned Walter's call. Luckily, Walter himself answered.

"What's up," Katz said.

"What's up with *you?*" Walter countered with giddy niceness. "It seems like you've been everywhere."

"Yeah, really singing the body electric. Heady times here."

"Tripping the light fantastic."

"Exactly. In a Dade County jail cell."

"Yeah, I read about that. What on earth were you doing in Florida anyway?"

"South American chick I mistook for a human being."

"I figured it was all part of the fame thing," Walter said. "'Fame requires every sort of excess.' I remembered we used to talk about that."

"Well, fortunately, I'm past having to deal with it. I've stepped off the bus."

"What do you mean?"

"I'm building decks again."

"Decks? Are you kidding? That's crazy! You should be out trashing hotel rooms and recording your most repellent fuck-you songs ever."

"Tired moves, man. I'm doing the only honorable thing I can think of."

"But that's such a waste!"

"Be careful what you say. You might offend me."

"Seriously, Richard, you're a great talent. You can't just stop because people happened to like one of your records."

"'Great talent.' That's like calling somebody a genius at tic-tac-toe. We're talking about pop music here."

"Wow, wow, wow," Walter said. "This is not what I expected to be hearing. I thought you'd be finishing a record and getting ready for more touring. I would have called you sooner if I'd known you were building decks. I was trying not to bother you."

"You never have to feel that."

"Well, I never heard from you, I figured you were busy."

"Mea culpa," Katz said. "How are you guys doing? Everything OK with you?"

"More or less. You know we moved to Washington, right?"

Katz closed his eyes and flogged his neurons to produce a confirming memory of this. "Yes," he said. "I think I knew that."

"Well, things have gotten somewhat complex here, it turns out. In fact, that's what prompted me to call. I have a proposal for you. Do you have some time tomorrow afternoon? On the late side?"

"Late afternoon's no good. How about morning?"

Walter explained that he was meeting Robert Kennedy Jr. at noon and had to return to Washington in the evening for a flight to Texas on Saturday morning. "We could talk on the phone now," he said, "but my assistant really wants to meet you. She's the one you'd be working with. I'd rather not steal her thunder by saying anything now."

"Your assistant," Katz said.

"Lalitha. She's incredibly young and brilliant. She actually lives right upstairs from us. I think you'll like her a lot."

The brightness and excitement in Walter's voice, the hint of guilt or thrill in the word "actually," did not escape Katz's notice.

"Lalitha," he said. "What kind of name is that?"

"Indian. Bengali. She grew up in Missouri. She's actually very pretty."

"I see. And what's her proposal about?"

"Saving the planet."

"I see."

Katz suspected that Walter was calculatedly dangling this Lalitha as bait, and it irritated him to be thought so easily manipulated. And yet—knowing Walter to be a man who didn't call a female pretty without good reason—he was manipulated, he was intrigued.

"Let me see if I can rearrange some things tomorrow afternoon," he said.

"Fantastic," Walter said.

What would be would be and what would not would not. In Katz's experience, it seldom hurt to make chicks wait. He called White Street and informed Zachary that the meeting with Caitlyn would have to be postponed.

The following afternoon, at 3:15, only fifteen minutes late, he strode into Walker's and saw Walter and the Indian chick waiting at a corner table. Before he even reached the table, he knew he had no chance with her. There were eighteen words of body language with which women signified availability and submission, and Lalitha was using a good twelve of them at once on Walter. She looked like a living illustration of the phrase *hanging on his words*. As Walter rose from the table to embrace Katz, the girl's eyes remained fixed on Walter; and this was indeed a weird twist for the universe to have taken. Never before had Katz seen Walter in studly mode, turning a pretty head. He was wearing a good dark suit and had gained some middle-aged bulk. There was a new breadth to his shoulders, a new projection to his chest. "Richard, Lalitha," he said.

"Very nice to meet you," Lalitha said, loosely shaking his hand and adding nothing about being honored or excited, nothing about being a huge fan.

Katz sank into a chair feeling sucker-punched by a damning recognition: contrary to the lies he'd always told himself, he wanted Walter's women not in spite of his friendship but because of it. For two years, he'd been consistently oppressed by avowals of fandom, and now suddenly he was disappointed not to receive one of these avowals from Lalitha, because of the way she was looking at Walter. She was dark-skinned and complexly round and slender. Round-eyed, round-faced, round-breasted; slender in the neck and arms. A solid B-plus that could be an A-minus if she would work for extra credit. Katz pushed a hand through his hair, brushing out bits of Trex dust. His old friend and foe was beaming with unalloyed delight at seeing him again.

"So what's up," he said.

"Well, a lot," Walter said. "Where to begin?"

"That's a nice suit, by the way. You look good."

"Oh, you like it?" Walter looked down at himself. "Lalitha made me buy it."

"I kept telling him his wardrobe sucked," the girl said. "He hadn't bought a new suit in ten years!"

She had a subtle subcontinental accent, percussive, no-nonsense, and she sounded proprietary of Walter. If her body hadn't been speaking of such anxiousness to please, Katz might have believed she already owned him.

"You look good yourself," Walter said.

"Thank you for lying."

"No, it's good, it's kind of a Keith Richards look."

"Ah, now we're being honest. Keith Richards looks like a wolf dressed up in a grandmother's bonnet. That headband?"

Walter consulted Lalitha. "Do you think Richard looks like a grandmother?"

"No," she said with a curt, round O sound.

"So you're in Washington," Katz said.

"Yeah, it's sort of a strange situation," Walter said. "I work for a guy named Vin Haven who's based in Houston, he's a big oil-and-gas guy. His wife's dad was an old-school Republican. Served under Nixon, Ford, and Reagan. He left her a mansion in Georgetown that they hardly ever used. When Vin set up the Trust, he put the offices on the ground floor and sold Patty and me the second and third floors at a price below market. There's also a little maid's apartment on the top floor where Lalitha's been living."

"I have the third-best commute in Washington," Lalitha said. "Walter's is even better than the president's. We all share the same kitchen."

"Sounds cozy," Katz said, giving Walter a significant look that seemed not to register. "And what is this Trust?"

"I think I told you about it the last time we talked."

"I was doing so many drugs there for a while, you're going to have to tell me everything at least twice."

"It is the Cerulean Mountain Trust," Lalitha said. "It's a whole new approach to conservation. It's Walter's idea."

"Actually, it was Vin's idea, at least to begin with."

"But the really original ideas are all Walter's," Lalitha assured Katz.

A waitress (nothing special, already known to Katz and dismissed from consideration) took orders for coffee, and Walter launched into the story of the Cerulean Mountain Trust. Vin Haven, he said, was a very unusual man. He and his wife, Kiki, were passionate bird-lovers who happened also to be personal friends of George and Laura Bush and Dick and Lynne Cheney. Vin had accumulated a nine-figure fortune by profitably losing money on oil and gas wells in Texas and Oklahoma. He was now getting on in years, and, having had no children with Kiki, he'd decided to blow more than half his total wad on the preservation of a single bird species, the cerulean warbler, which, Walter said, was not only a beautiful creature but the fastest-declining songbird in North America.

"Here's our poster bird," Lalitha said, taking a brochure from her briefcase.

The warbler on its cover looked nondescript to Katz. Bluish, small, unintelligent. "That's a bird all right," he said.

"Just wait," Lalitha said. "It's not about the bird. It's much bigger than that. You have to wait and hear Walter's vision."

Vision! Katz was beginning to think that Walter's real purpose in arranging this meeting had simply been to inflict on him the fact of his being *adored* by a rather pretty twenty-five-year-old.

The cerulean warbler, Walter said, bred exclusively in mature temperate hardwood forests, with a stronghold in the central Appalachians. There was a particularly healthy population in southern West Virginia, and Vin Haven, with his ties to the nonrenewable energy industry, had seen an opportunity to partner with coal companies to create a very large, permanent private reserve for the warbler and other threatened hardwood species. The coal companies had reason to fear that the warbler would soon be listed under the Endangered Species Act, with potentially deleterious effects on their freedom to cut down forests and blow up mountains. Vin believed that they could be persuaded to help the warbler, to keep the bird off the Threatened list and garner some much-needed good press, as long as they were allowed to continue extracting coal. And this was how Walter had landed the job as executive director of the Trust. In Minnesota, working for the Nature Conservancy, he'd forged good relationships with mining interests, and he was unusually open to constructive engagement with the coal people.

"Mr. Haven interviewed half a dozen other candidates before Walter," Lalitha said. "Some of them stood up and walked out on him, right in the middle of the interviews. They were so closed-minded and afraid of being criticized! Nobody else but Walter could see the potential for some-body who was willing to take a big risk and not care so much about conventional wisdom."

Walter grimaced at this compliment, but he was clearly pleased by it. "Those people all had better jobs than I did. They had more to lose."

"But what kind of environmentalist cares more about saving his job than saving land?"

"Well, a lot of them do, unfortunately. They have families and responsibilities."

"But so do you!"

"Face it, man, you're just too excellent," Katz said, not kindly. He was still holding out hope that Lalitha, when they stood up to leave, would prove to be big in the butt or thick in the thighs.

To help save the cerulean warbler, Walter said, the Trust was aiming to create a hundred-square-mile roadless tract—Haven's Hundred was its working nickname—in Wyoming County, West Virginia, surrounded by a larger "buffer zone" open to hunting and motorized recreation. To be able to afford both the surface and mineral rights to such a large single parcel, the Trust would first have to permit coal extraction on nearly a third of it, via mountaintop removal. This was the prospect that had scared off the other applicants. Mountaintop removal as currently practiced was ecologically deplorable—ridgetop rock blasted away to expose the underlying seams of coal, surrounding valleys filled with rubble, biologically rich streams obliterated. Walter, however, believed that properly managed reclamation efforts could mitigate far more of the damage than people realized; and the great advantage of fully mined-out land was that nobody would rip it open again.

Katz was remembering that one of the things he'd missed about Walter was good discussion of actual ideas. "But don't we want to leave the coal underground?" he said. "I thought we hated coal."

"That's a longer discussion for another time," Walter said.

"Walter has some excellent original thoughts on fossil fuels versus nuclear and wind," Lalitha said.

"Suffice it to say that we're *realistic* about coal," Walter said.

Even more exciting, he continued, was the money the Trust was pouring into South America, where the cerulean warbler, like so many other

North American songbirds, spent its winters. The Andean forests were disappearing at a calamitous rate, and for the last two years Walter had been making monthly trips to Colombia, buying up big parcels of land and coordinating with local NGOs that encouraged ecotourism and helped peasants replace their wood-burning stoves with solar and electric heating. A dollar still went fairly far in the southern hemisphere, and the South America half of the Pan-American Warbler Park was already in place.

"Mr. Haven hadn't planned to do anything in South America," Lalitha said. "He'd completely neglected that part of the picture until Walter pointed it out to him."

"Apart from everything else," Walter said, "I thought there could be some educational benefit in creating a park that spanned two continents. To drive home the fact that everything's interconnected. We're eventually hoping to sponsor some smaller reserves along the warbler's migratory route, in Texas and Mexico."

"That's good," Katz said dully. "That's a good idea."

"*Really* good idea," Lalitha said, gazing at Walter.

"The thing is," Walter said, "the land is disappearing so fast that it's hopeless to wait for governments to do conservation. The problem with governments is they're elected by majorities that don't give a shit about biodiversity. Whereas billionaires do tend to care. They've got a stake in keeping the planet not entirely fucked, because they and their heirs are going to be the ones with enough money to enjoy the planet. The reason Vin Haven started doing conservation on his ranches in Texas was that he likes to hunt the bigger birds and look at the little ones. Self-interest, yeah, but a total win-win. In terms of locking up habitat to save it from development, it's a lot easier to turn a few billionaires than to educate American voters who are perfectly happy with their cable and their Xboxes and their broadband."

"Plus you don't actually want three hundred million Americans running around your wilderness areas anyway," Katz said.

"Exactly. It wouldn't be wilderness anymore."

"So basically you're telling me you've gone over to the dark side."

Walter laughed. "That's right."

"You need to meet Mr. Haven," Lalitha said to Katz. "He's really an interesting character."

"Being friends with George and Dick would seem to tell me everything I need to know."

"No, Richard, it doesn't," she said. "It doesn't tell you everything."

Her charming pronunciation of the O in "no" made Katz want to keep contradicting her. "And the guy's a hunter," he said. "He probably even hunts with Dick, right?"

"As a matter of fact, he does hunt with Dick sometimes," Walter said. "But the Havens eat what they kill, and they manage their land for wildlife. The hunting is not the problem. The Bushes aren't the problem, either. When Vin comes to town, he goes to the White House to watch Longhorns games, and at halftime he works on Laura. He's got her interested in seabirds in Hawaii. I think we're going to see some action there soon. The Bush connection per se is not the problem."

"So what is the problem?" Katz said.

Walter and Lalitha exchanged uneasy glances.

"Well, there are several," Walter said. "Money is one of them. Given how much we're pouring into South America, it would really have helped to get some public funding in West Virginia. And the mountaintop-removal issue turns out to be a real tar baby. The local grassroots groups have all demonized the coal industry and especially MTR."

"MTR is mountaintop removal," Lalitha said.

"The *New York Times* gives Bush-Cheney a total free pass on Iraq but keeps running these fucking editorials about the evils of MTR," Walter said. "Nobody state, federal, or private wants to touch a project that involves sacrificing mountain ridges and displacing poor families from their ancestral homes. They don't want to hear about forest reclamation, they don't want to hear about sustainable green jobs. Wyoming County is very, very empty—the total number of families directly impacted by our plan is less than two hundred. But the whole thing gets turned into evil corporations versus the helpless common man."

"It is so stupid and unreasonable," Lalitha said. "They won't even *listen* to Walter. He has really good news about reclamation, but people just close their ears when we walk into a room."

"There's this thing called the Appalachian Regional Reforestation Initiative," Walter said. "Are you at all interested in the details?"

"I'm interested in watching the two of you talk about them," Katz said.

"Well, very briefly, what's given MTR such a bad name is that most surface-rights owners don't insist on the right sort of reclamation. Before a coal company can exercise its mineral rights and tear down a mountain, it has to put up a bond that doesn't get refunded until the land's been restored. And the problem is, these owners keep settling for these barren, flat, subsidence-prone pastures, in the hope that some developer will come along and build luxury condos on them, in spite of their being in the middle of nowhere. The fact is, you can actually get a very lush and biodiverse forest if you do the reclamation right. Use four feet of topsoil and weathered sandstone instead of the usual eighteen inches. Take care not to compact the soil too much. And then plant the right mixture of fast- and slow-growing tree species in the right season. We've got evidence that forests like that might actually be *better* for warbler families than the second-growth forests they replace. So our plan isn't just about preserving the warbler, it's about creating an advertisement for doing things right. But the environmental mainstream doesn't want to talk about doing things right, because doing things right would make the coal companies look less villainous and MTR more palatable politically. And so we couldn't get any outside money, and we've got public opinion trending against us."

"But the problem with going it alone," Lalitha said, "was that we were either looking at a much smaller park, too small to be a stronghold for the warbler, or at making too many concessions to the coal companies."

"Which really are somewhat evil," Walter said.

"And so we couldn't ask too many questions about Mr. Haven's money."

"It sounds like you've got your hands full," Katz said. "If I were a billionaire, I'd be taking out my checkbook right now."

"There's even worse, though," Lalitha said, her eyes strangely glittering.

"Are you bored yet?" Walter said.

"Not at all," Katz said. "I'm frankly a little starved for intellectual stimulus."

"Well, the problem is, unfortunately, that Vin has turned out to have some other motives."

"Rich people are like little babies," Lalitha said. "Fucking little *babies.*"

"Say that again," Katz said.

"Say what?"

"Fucking. I like the way you pronounce it."

She blushed; Mr. Katz had gotten through to her.

"Fucking, fucking, fucking," she said happily, for him. "I used to work at the Conservancy, and when we'd have our annual gala, the rich people were happy to buy a table for twenty thousand dollars, but only if they got their gift bag at the end of the night. The gift bags were full of worthless garbage donated by somebody else. But if they didn't get their gift bags, they wouldn't donate twenty thousand again the next year."

"I need your assurance," Walter said to Katz, "that you won't mention any of this to anybody else."

"So assured."

The Cerulean Mountain Trust, Walter said, had been conceived in the spring of 2001, when Vin Haven had traveled to Washington to participate in the vice president's notorious energy task force, the one whose invite list Dick Cheney was still spending taxpayer dollars to defend against the Freedom of Information Act. Over cocktails one night, after a long day of task-forcing, Vin had spoken to the chairmen of Nardone Energy and Blasco and sounded them out on the subject of cerulean warblers. Once he'd convinced them that their legs weren't being pulled—that Vin was actually serious about saving a non-huntable bird—an agreement in principle had been reached: Vin would go shopping for a huge tract of land whose core would be opened to MTR but then reclaimed and made forever wild. Walter had known about this agreement when he took the job as the Trust's executive director. What he hadn't known—had discovered only recently—was that the vice president, during that same week in 2001, had privately mentioned to Vin Haven that the president intended to make certain regulatory and tax-code changes to render natural-gas extraction economically feasible in the Appalachians. And that Vin had proceeded to buy large bundles of mineral rights not only in Wyoming County but in several other parts of West Virginia that were either coalless or had been mined out. These big purchases of seemingly useless rights might have raised a red flag, Walter said, if Vin hadn't been able to claim that he was safeguarding possible future preserve sites for the Trust.

"Long story short," Lalitha said, "he was using us for cover."

"Keeping in mind, of course," Walter said, "that Vin really does love birds and is doing great things for the cerulean warbler."

"He just wanted his little gift bag also," Lalitha said.

"His not-so-little gift bag, as it turns out," Walter said. "This is still mostly under the radar, so you probably haven't heard about it, but West Virginia's about to get the shit drilled out of it. Hundreds of thousands of acres that we all assumed were permanently preserved are now in the process of being destroyed as we sit here. In terms of fragmentation and disruption, it's as bad as anything the coal industry's done. If you own the mineral rights, you can do whatever the fuck you want to exercise them, even on public land. New roads everywhere, thousands of wellheads, noisy equipment running night and day, blazing lights all night."

"And meanwhile your boss's mineral rights are suddenly a lot more valuable," Katz said.

"Exactly."

"And now he's selling off the land he was pretending to buy for you?"

"Some of it, yeah."

"Incredible."

"Well, he is still spending a ton of money. And he'll be taking steps to mitigate the impact of drilling where he still owns the rights. But he's had to sell a lot of rights to cover some big expenses that we were hoping not to have, if public opinion had gone our way. The bottom line is, he never intended the true cost of his investment in the Trust to be as big as I'd originally thought."

"In other words, you got played."

"I got played, a little bit. We're still getting the Warbler Park, but I got played. And please don't ever mention any of this to anyone."

"So what does this mean?" Katz said. "I mean, besides my having been right about friends of Bush being evil."

"It means that Walter and I have become rogue employees," Lalitha said with her strange glittering look.

"Not rogue," Walter corrected quickly. "Don't say rogue. We're not rogue."

"No, in fact, we are fairly rogue."

"I like the way you say 'rogue,' too," Katz remarked to her.

"We still really like Vin," Walter said. "Vin's one-of-a-kind. We just feel like, since he wasn't entirely straight with us, there's no need for us to be entirely straight with him."

"We have some maps and charts to show you," Lalitha said, digging in her briefcase.

The early crowd at Walker's, the van drivers and the cops from the precinct house around the corner, were filling the tables and laying siege to the bar. Outside, in the durable late-winter light of a February afternoon, streets were clogging with Friday tunnel traffic. In a parallel universe, dim with unreality, Katz was still up on the roof at White Street, flirting purposefully with nubile Caitlyn. She seemed hardly worth the bother now. Although he could take or leave nature, Katz couldn't help envying Walter for taking on Bush's cronies and trying to beat them at their own game. Compared to manufacturing Chiclets, or building decks for the contemptible, it seemed *interesting.*

"I took the job in the first place," Walter said, "because I couldn't sleep at night. I couldn't stand what was happening to the country. Clinton had done less than zero for the environment. Net fucking negative. Clinton just wanted everybody to party to Fleetwood Mac. 'Don't stop thinking about tomorrow?' Bull*shit.* Not thinking about tomorrow was exactly what he did environmentally. And then Gore was too much of a wimp to let his green flag fly, and too nice a guy to fight dirty in Florida. I was still halfway OK as long as I was in St. Paul, but I kept having to drive all over the state for the Conservancy, and it was like having acid thrown in my face every time I passed the city limits. Not just the industrial farming but the sprawl, the sprawl, the sprawl. Low-density development is the *worst.* And SUVs everywhere, snowmobiles everywhere, Jet Skis everywhere, ATVs everywhere, two-acre lawns everywhere. The goddamned green monospecific chemical-drenched lawns."

"Here are the maps," Lalitha said.

"Yeah, these show the fragmentation," Walter said, handing Katz two laminated maps. "This one is undisturbed habitat in 1900, this one's undisturbed habitat in 2000."

"Prosperity will do that," Katz said.

"The development was so stupidly done, though," Walter said. "We still might have enough land for other species to survive if it wasn't all so fragmented."

"Nice fantasy, I agree," Katz said. In hindsight, he supposed it was inevitable that his friend would become one of those people who carried around laminated literature. But he was still surprised by what an *angry* crank Walter had become in the last two years.

"This was what was keeping me awake at night," Walter said. "This fragmentation. Because it's the same problem everywhere. It's like the internet, or cable TV—there's never any center, there's no communal agreement, there's just a trillion little bits of distracting noise. We can never sit down and have any kind of sustained conversation, it's all just cheap trash and shitty development. All the real things, the authentic things, the honest things are dying off. Intellectually and culturally, we just bounce around like random billiard balls, reacting to the latest random stimuli."

"There's some pretty good porn on the internet," Katz said. "Or so I'm told."

"I wasn't accomplishing anything systemic in Minnesota. We were just gathering little bits of disconnected prettiness. There are approximately six hundred breeding bird species in North America, and maybe a third of them are getting clobbered by fragmentation. Vin's idea was that if two hundred really rich people would each pick one species, and try to stop the fragmentation of their strongholds, we might be able to save them all."

"The cerulean warbler is a very choosy little bird," Lalitha said.

"It breeds in treetops in mature deciduous forest," Walter said. "And then, as soon as the babies can fly, the family moves down into the understory for safety. But the original forests were all cut down for timber and charcoal, and the second-growth forests don't have the right kind of understory, and they're all fragmented with roads and farms and subdivisions and coal-mining sites, which makes the warbler vulnerable to cats and raccoons and crows."

"And so, before you know it, no more cerulean warblers," Lalitha said.

"That does sound tough," Katz said. "Although it is just one bird."

"Every species has an inalienable right to keep existing," Walter said.

"Sure. Of course. I'm just trying to figure out where this is coming from. I don't remember you caring about birds when we were in college. Back then, as I recall, it was more about overpopulation and the limits to growth."

Walter and Lalitha again exchanged glances.

"Overpopulation is exactly what we want you to help us with," Lalitha said.

Katz laughed. "Doing my best with that already."

Walter was shuffling through some laminated charts. "I started walking it back," he said, "because I still wasn't sleeping. You remember Aristotle and the different kinds of causes? Efficient and formal and final? Well, nest-predation by crows and feral cats is an efficient cause of the warbler's decline. And fragmentation of the habitat is a formal cause of *that*. But what's the final cause? The final cause is the root of pretty much every problem we have. The final cause is too many damn people on the planet. It's especially clear when we go to South America. Yes, per capita consumption is rising. Yes, the Chinese are illegally vacuuming up resources down there. But the real problem is population pressure. Six kids per family versus one point five. People are desperate to feed the children that the pope in his infinite wisdom makes them have, and so they trash the environment."

"You should come with us to South America," Lalitha said. "We drive along these little roads, there's terrible exhaust from bad engines and too-cheap gasoline, the hillsides are all denuded, and the families all have eight or ten children, it's really sickening. You should come along with us sometime and see if you like what you see down there. Because it's coming soon to a theater near you."

Crackpot, Katz thought. Hot little crackpot.

Walter handed him a laminated bar chart. "In America alone," he said, "the population's going to rise by fifty percent in the next four decades.

Think about how crowded the exurbs are already, think about the traffic and the sprawl and the environmental degradation and the dependence on foreign oil. And then add fifty percent. And that's just America, which can theoretically sustain a larger population. And then think about global carbon emissions, and genocide and famine in Africa, and the radicalized dead-end underclass in the Arab world, and overfishing of the oceans, illegal Israeli settlements, the Han Chinese overrunning Tibet, a hundred million poor people in nuclear Pakistan: there's hardly a problem in the world that wouldn't be solved or at least tremendously alleviated by having fewer people. And yet"—he gave Katz another chart—"we're going to add another three billion by 2050. In other words, we're going to *add* the equivalent of the world's entire population when you and I were putting our pennies in UNICEF boxes. Any little things we might do now to try to save some nature and preserve some kind of quality of life are going to get overwhelmed by the sheer numbers, because people can change their consumption habits—it takes time and effort, but it can be done—but if the population keeps increasing, nothing else we do is going to matter. And yet *nobody* is talking about the problem publicly. It's the elephant in the room, and it's killing us."

"This is all sounding more familiar," Katz said. "I'm remembering some rather lengthy discussions."

"I was definitely into it in college. But then, you know, I did some breeding myself."

Katz raised his eyebrows. *Breeding* was an interesting way of speaking of one's wife and children.

"In my own way," Walter said, "I guess I was part of a larger cultural shift that was happening in the eighties and nineties. Overpopulation was definitely part of the public conversation in the seventies, with Paul Ehrlich, and the Club of Rome, and ZPG. And then suddenly it was gone. Became just unmentionable. Part of it was the Green Revolution—you know, still plenty of famines, but not apocalyptic ones. And then population control got a terrible name politically. Totalitarian China with its one-child policy, Indira Gandhi doing forced sterilizations, American ZPG getting painted as nativist and racist. The liberals got all scared and silent. Even the Sierra Club got scared. And the conservatives, of course, never gave a shit in the first place, because their entire ideology is selfish short-term interest and God's plan and so forth. And so the problem became this cancer that you know is growing inside you but you decide you're just not going to think about."

"And this has what to do with your cerulean warbler?" Katz said.

"It has *everything* to do with it," Lalitha said.

"Like I said," Walter said, "we've decided to take some liberties with interpreting the mission of the Trust, which is to ensure the survival of the warbler. We keep walking the problem back, walking it back. And what we finally arrive at, in terms of a final cause or an unmoved mover, in 2004, is the fact that it's become totally toxic and uncool to talk about reversing population growth."

"And so I ask Walter," Lalitha said, "who is the coolest person you know?"

Katz laughed and shook his head. "Oh, no. No, no, no."

"Listen, Richard," Walter said. "The conservatives won. They turned the Democrats into a center-right party. They got the entire country singing 'God Bless America,' stress on *God*, at every single major-league baseball game. They won on every fucking front, but they especially won culturally, and *especially* regarding babies. In 1970 it was cool to care about the planet's future and not have kids. Now the one thing everyone agrees on, right and left, is that it's beautiful to have a lot of babies. The more the better. Kate Winslet is pregnant, hooray hooray. Some dimwit in Iowa just had octuplets, hooray hooray. The conversation about the idiocy of SUVs stops dead the minute people say they're buying them to protect their precious babies."

"A dead baby's not a pretty thing," Katz said. "I mean, presumably you guys aren't advocating infanticide."

"Of course not," Walter said. "We just want to make having babies more of an embarrassment. Like smoking's an embarrassment. Like being obese is an embarrassment. Like driving an Escalade would be an embarrassment if it weren't for the kiddie argument. Like living in a four-thousand-square-foot house on a two-acre lot should be an embarrassment."

" 'Do it if you have to,' " Lalitha said, " 'but don't expect to be congratulated anymore.' That's the message we need to spread."

Katz looked into her crackpot eyes. "You don't want kids yourself."

"No," she said, holding his gaze.

"You're, what, twenty-five?"

"Twenty-seven."

"You might feel differently in five years. The oven timer goes off around age thirty. At least that's been my experience with women."

"It won't be mine," she said and widened, for emphasis, her already very round eyes.

"Kids are beautiful," Walter said. "Kids have always been the meaning of life. You fall in love, you reproduce, and then your kids grow up and fall in love and reproduce. That's what life was always *for*. For pregnancy. For more life. But the problem now is that more life is still beautiful and meaningful on the individual level, but for the world as a whole it only means more death. And not nice death, either. We're looking at losing half the world's species in the next hundred years. We're facing the biggest mass extinction since at least the Cretaceous-Tertiary. First we'll get the utter wipeout of the world's ecosystems, then mass starvation and/or disease and/or killings. What's still 'normal' at the individual level is heinous and unprecedented at the global level."

"It's like the problem with Katz," it sounded like Lalitha said.

"Moi?"

"Kitty cats," she said. "C-A-T-S. Everybody loves their kitty cat and lets it run around outside. It's just one cat—how many birds can it kill? Well, every year in the U.S. one *billion* songbirds are murdered by domestic and feral cats. It's one of the leading causes of songbird decline in North America. But no one gives a shit because they love their own individual kitty cat."

"Nobody wants to think about it," Walter said. "Everybody just wants their normal life."

"We want you to help us get people thinking about it," Lalitha said. "About overpopulation. We don't have the resources to do family planning and women's education overseas. We're a species-oriented conservation group. So what can we do for leverage? How do we get governments and NGOs to quintuple their investment in population control?"

Katz smiled at Walter. "Did you tell her we've already been through this? Did you tell her about the songs you used to try to get me to write?"

"No," Walter said. "But do you remember what you used to say? You said that nobody cared about your songs because you weren't famous."

"We've been Googling you," Lalitha said. "There's a very impressive list of well-known musicians who say they admire you and the Traumatics."

"The Traumatics are dead, honey. Walnut Surprise is also dead."

"So here's the proposal," Walter said. "However much money you're making building decks, we'll pay you a good multiple of, for however long you want to work for us. We're imagining some sort of summer music-and-politics festival, maybe in West Virginia, with a bunch of very cool headliners, to raise awareness of population issues. All focused entirely on young people."

"We're ready to advertise summer internships to college students all over the country," Lalitha said. "Also in Canada and Latin America. We can fund twenty or thirty internships with Walter's discretionary fund. But first we need to make the internships look like something very cool to do. Like *the* thing for the very cool kids to do this summer."

"Vin's very hands-off in terms of my discretionary fund," Walter said. "As long as we put a cerulean warbler on our literature, I can do whatever I want."

"But it has to happen fast," Lalitha said. "Kids are already making up their minds about this summer. We need to reach them in the next few weeks."

"We'd need your name and your image at a minimum," Walter said. "If you could do some video for us, better yet. If you could write us some songs, even better. If you could make some calls to Jeff Tweedy, and Ben Gibbard, and Jack White, and find us some people to work on the festival pro bono, or sponsor it commercially, best of all."

"Also great if we can tell potential interns they'll be getting to work with you directly," Lalitha said.

"Even just the promise of some minimal contact with them would be fantastic," Walter said.

"If we could put on the poster, 'Join rock legend Richard Katz in Washington this summer' or something like that," Lalitha said.

"We need to make it cool, and we need to make it viral," Walter said.

Katz, as he endured this bombardment, was feeling sad and remote. Walter and the girl seemed to have snapped under the pressure of thinking in too much detail about the fuckedness of the world. They'd been seized by a notion and talked each other into believing in it. Had blown a bubble that had then broken free of reality and carried them away. They didn't seem to realize they were dwelling in a world with a population of two.

"I don't know what to say," he said.

"Say yes!" Lalitha said, glittering.

"I'm going to be in Houston for a couple of days," Walter said, "but I'll send you some links, and we can talk again on Tuesday."

"Or just say yes now," Lalitha said.

Their hopeful expectancy was like an unbearably bright lightbulb. Katz turned away from it and said, "I'll think about it."

On the sidewalk outside Walker's, taking leave of the girl, he ascertained that there was nothing wrong with her lower body, but it didn't seem to matter now, it only added to his sadness about Walter. The girl was going to Brooklyn to see a college friend of hers. Since Katz could just as easily take the PATH from Penn Station, he walked with Walter toward Canal Street. Ahead of them, in the gathering twilight, were the friendly glowing windows of the world's most overpopulated island.

"God, I love New York," Walter said. "There is something so profoundly wrong with Washington."

"Plenty of things wrong here, too," Katz said, sidestepping a high-speed mom-and-stroller combo.

"But at least this is an actual place. Washington's all abstraction. It's about access to power and nothing else. I mean, I'm sure it's fun if you're living next door to Seinfeld, or Tom Wolfe, or Mike Bloomberg, but living next door to them isn't what New York is *about*. In Washington people literally talk about how many feet away from John Kerry's house their own house is. The neighborhoods are all so blah, the only thing that turns people on is proximity to power. It's a total fetish culture. People get this kind of orgasmic shiver when they tell you they sat next to Paul Wolfowitz at a conference or got invited to Grover Norquist's breakfast. Everybody's obsessing 24/7, trying to position themselves in relation to power. Even the black scene has something wrong with it. It's got to be more discouraging to be poor black in Washington than anywhere else in the country. You're not even scary. You're just an afterthought."

"I will remind you that Bad Brains and Ian MacKaye came out of D.C."

"Yeah, that was some weird historical accident."

"And yet we did admire them in our youth."

"God, I love the New York subway!" Walter said as he followed Katz down to the uric uptown platform. "This is the way human beings are supposed to live. High density! High efficiency!" He cast a beneficent smile upon the weary subway riders.

It occurred to Katz to ask about Patty, but he felt too gutless to say her name. "So is this chick single, or what?" he said.

"Who, Lalitha? No. She's had the same boyfriend since college."

"He lives with you, too?"

"No, he's in Nashville. He was in med school in Baltimore, and now he's doing his internship."

"And yet she stayed behind in Washington."

"She's very invested in this project," Walter said. "And, frankly, I think the boyfriend's on his way out. He's very old-school Indian. He threw a huge, huge fit when she didn't move to Nashville with him."

"And what did you advise her?"

"I tried to get her to stand up for herself. He could have matched somewhere in Washington if he'd really wanted to. I told her she didn't have to sacrifice everything for his career. She and I've got a kind of father-daughter thing. Her parents are very conservative. I think she appreciates working for somebody who believes in her and doesn't just see her as somebody's future wife."

"And just so we're clear," Katz said, "you're aware that she's in love with you?"

Walter blushed. "I don't know. Maybe a little bit. I actually think it's more like an intellectual idealization. More father-daughter."

"Yeah, dream on, buddy. You expect me to believe you've never imagined those eyes shining up at you while her head's bobbing on your lap?"

"Jesus, no. I try not to imagine things like that. Especially not with an employee."

"But maybe you don't always succeed in not imagining it."

Walter glanced around to see if anyone on the platform was listening, and lowered his voice. "Aside from everything else," he said, "I think there's something objectively demeaning about a woman on her knees."

"Why don't you try it sometime and let her be the judge of that."

"Well, because, Richard," Walter said, still blushing, but also laughing unpleasantly, "I happen to understand that women are wired differently than men."

"Whatever happened to gender equality? I seem to recall that you were into that."

"I just think, if you ever had a daughter yourself, you might see the woman's side with a little more sympathy."

"You've named my best reason for not wanting a daughter."

"Well, if you did have one, you might let yourself recognize the actually-not-terribly-hard-to-recognize fact that very young women can get their desire and their admiration and their love for a person all mixed up, and not understand—"

"Not understand what?"

"That to the guy they're just an object. That the guy might only be wanting to get his, you know, his, you know"—Walter's voice dropped to a whisper—"his dick sucked by somebody young and pretty. That that might be his only interest."

"Sorry, not computing," Katz said. "What's wrong with being admired? This is not computing at all."

"I really don't want to talk about it."

An A train arrived, and they crowded onto it. Almost immediately, Katz saw the light of recognition in the eyes of a college-age kid standing by the opposite doors. Katz lowered his head and turned away, but the kid had the temerity to touch him on the shoulder. "I'm so sorry," he said, "but you're the musician, right? You're Richard Katz."

"Perhaps not sorrier than I am," Katz said.

"I'm not going to bother you. I just wanted to say I really love your stuff."

"OK, thanks, man," Katz said, his eyes on the floor.

"Especially the older stuff, which I'm just starting to get into. *Reactionary Splendor*? Oh, my God. It is so fucking brilliant. It's on my iPod right now. Here, I'll show you."

"That's OK. I believe you."

"Oh, sure, no, of course. Of course. I'm sorry to bother you. I'm just a huge fan."

"Don't worry about it."

Walter was following this exchange with a facial expression as ancient as the college parties that he'd been masochistic enough to attend with Katz, an expression of wonderment and pride and love and anger and the loneliness of the invisible, none of it agreeable to Katz, not in college and even less so now.

"It must be very strange to be you," Walter said as they exited at 34th Street.

"I have no other way of being to compare it to."

"It's got to feel great, though. I don't believe that at some level you don't love it."

Katz considered the question honestly. "It's more like a situation where I would hate the absence of the thing but I don't like the thing itself, either."

"I think *I* would like it," Walter said.

"I think you would, too."

Unable to grant Walter fame, Katz walked with him all the way up to the Amtrak status board, which was showing a forty-five-minute delay for his southbound Acela.

"I strongly believe in trains," Walter said. "And I routinely pay the price."

"I'll wait with you," Katz said.

"No need, no need."

"No, let me buy you a Coke. Or did D.C. finally make you a drinker?"

"No, still teetotaling. Which is such a stupid word."

To Katz, the train's delay was a sign that the subject of Patty was destined to be broached. When he broached it, however, in the station bar, to the nerve-grating sounds of an Alanis Morissette song, Walter's eyes grew hard and distant. He drew breath as if to speak, but no words came out.

"Must be a little odd for you guys," Katz prompted. "Having the girl upstairs and your office downstairs."

"I don't know what to say to you, Richard. I really don't know what to tell you."

"You guys getting along? Patty doing anything interesting?"

"She's working at a gym in Georgetown. Does that count as interesting?" Walter shook his head grimly. "I've been living with a depressed person for a very long time now. I don't know why she's so unhappy, I don't know why she can't seem to get out of it. There was a little while, around the time we moved to Washington, when she seemed to be doing better. She'd seen a therapist in St. Paul who got her started on some kind of writing project. Some kind of personal history or life journal that she was very mum and secretive about. As long as she was working on that, things weren't so bad. But for the last two years they've been pretty much all bad. The plan had been for her to look for a job as soon as we got to Washington, and start some kind of second career, but it's a little tough at her age with no marketable skills. She's very smart and very proud, and she couldn't stand being rejected and couldn't stand being entry-level. She tried volunteering, doing afterschool athletics with the D.C. schools, but that didn't work out, either. I finally got her to try an antidepressant, which I think would have helped her if she'd stuck with it, but she didn't like the way it made her feel, and she really was pretty unbearable while she was on it. It gave her kind of a crankhead personality, and she quit before they got the cocktail adjusted right. And so finally, last fall, I more or less forced her to get a job. Not for my sake—I'm way overpaid, and Jessica's out of school now, and Joey's not my dependent anymore. But she had so much free time, I could see that it was killing her. And the job she chose to get was working at the reception counter of a gym. I mean, it's a perfectly nice gym—one of my board members goes there, and at least one of my bigger donors. And there she is, there's my wife, who's one of the smartest people I know, scanning their membership cards and telling them to have a great workout. She's also got a pretty serious exercise addiction going. She works out at least an hour a day, minimum—she *looks* great. And then she comes home at eleven with takeout, and if I'm in town we eat together, and she asks me why I'm still not having sex with my assistant. Sort of like what you just did, only not as graphically. Not as directly."

"Sorry. I didn't realize."

"How could you? Who would think? I tell her the same thing every time, which is that she's the person I love, she's the person I want. And then we change the subject. Like, for the last couple of weeks—I think mainly to drive me crazy—she's been talking about getting a boob job. It makes me want to cry, Richard. I mean, there is *nothing* wrong with her. Nothing on the outside. It's totally crazy. But she says she's going to die soon and she thinks it might be interesting, before she dies, to see what it's like to have some chest. She says it might help her to have some goal to be saving up her money for, now that . . ." Walter shook his head.

"Now that what."

"Nothing. She was doing something else with her money, before, that I thought was very bad."

"Is she sick? Is there a medical problem?"

"No. Not physically. By dying soon I think she means in the next forty years. The way we're all going to die soon."

"I'm really sorry, man. I had no idea."

A navigational beacon in Katz's black Levi's, a long-dormant transmitter buried by a more advanced civilization, was sparking back to life. Where he ought to have felt guilty, he instead was getting hard. Oh, the clairvoyance of the dick: it could see the future in a heartbeat, leaving the brain to play catch-up and find the necessary route from occluded present to preordained outcome. Katz could see that Patty, in the seemingly random life-meanderings that Walter had just described to him, had in fact deliberately been trampling symbols in a cornfield, spelling out a message unreadable to Walter at ground level but clear as could be to Katz at great height. IT'S NOT OVER, IT'S NOT OVER. The parallels between his life and hers were really almost eerie: a brief period of creative productivity, followed by a major change that turned out to be a disappointment and a mess, followed by drugs and despair, followed by the taking of a stupid job. Katz had been assuming that his situation was simply that success had wrecked him, but it was also true, he realized, that his worst years as a songwriter had precisely coincided with his years of estrangement from the Berglunds. And, yes, he hadn't given much thought to Patty in the last two years, but he could feel now, in his pants, that this was mainly because he'd assumed their story was over.

"How do Patty and the girl get along?"

"They don't speak," Walter said.

"So not buddies."

"No, I'm saying they literally don't speak to each other. Each of them knows when the other's usually in the kitchen. They go out of their way to avoid each other."

"And which one started that?"

"I don't want to talk about it."

"OK."

On the station bar's sound system, "That's What I Like About You" was playing. It seemed to Katz the perfect soundtrack for the neon Bud Light signage, the fake leaded-glass lampshades, the durably polyurethaned crap furniture with its embedded commuter grime. He was still reasonably safe from hearing one of his own songs played in a place like this, but he knew it was a safety only of degree, not of category.

"Patty's decided she doesn't like anybody under thirty," Walter said. "She's formed a prejudice against an entire generation. And, being Patty, she's very funny on the subject. But it's gotten pretty vicious and out of control."

"Whereas you seem quite taken with the younger generation," Katz said.

"All it takes to disprove a general law is one counterexample. I've got at least two great ones in Jessica and Lalitha."

"But not Joey?"

"And if there are two," Walter said, as if he hadn't even heard his son's name, "there are bound to be a lot more. That's the premise of what I want to do this summer. Trust that young people still have brains and a social conscience, and then give them something to work with."

"You know, we're very different, you and me," Katz said. "I don't do vision. I don't do belief. And I'm impatient with the kiddies. You remember that about me, right?"

"I remember that you're often wrong about yourself. I think you believe in a lot more than you give yourself credit for. You've got a whole cult following because of your integrity."

"Integrity's a neutral value. Hyenas have integrity, too. They're pure hyena."

"So, what, should I not have called you?" Walter said with a tremor in his voice. "Part of me didn't want to bother you, but Lalitha talked me into it."

"No, it's good you called. It's been too long."

"I think I figured you'd outgrown us or something. I mean, I know I'm not a cool person. I figured you were done with us."

"Sorry, man. I just got really busy."

But Walter was becoming upset, nearly tearful. "It almost seemed like you were embarrassed by me. Which I understand, but it still doesn't feel very good. I thought we were friends."

"I said I was sorry," Katz said. He was angered both by Walter's emotion and by the irony or injustice of needing to apologize, *twice*, for having tried to do him a favor. It was generally his policy never to apologize at all.

"I don't know what I expected," Walter said. "But maybe some acknowledgment of the fact that Patty and I helped you. That you wrote all those songs in my mother's house. That we're your oldest friends. I'm not going to dwell on this, but I want to clear the air and let you know what I've been feeling, so I don't have to feel it anymore."

The angry stirring of Katz's blood was of a piece with the divinations of his dick. I'm going to do you a different kind of favor now, old friend, he thought. We're going to finish some unfinished business, and you and the girl will thank me for it.

"It's good to clear the air," he said.

# WOMANLAND

Growing up in St. Paul, Joey Berglund had received numberless assurances that his life was destined to be a lucky one. The way star halfbacks talk about a great open-field run, the sense of cutting and weaving at full speed through a defense that moved in slow motion, the entire field of play as all-visible and instantaneously graspable as a video game at Rookie level, was the way every facet of his life had felt for his first eighteen years. The world had given unto him, and he was fine with taking. He arrived as a first-year student in Charlottesville with the ideal clothes and haircut and found that the school had paired him with a perfect roommate from NoVa (as the locals called the Virginia suburbs of D.C.). For two and a half weeks, college looked like it would be an extension of the world as he had always known it, only better. He was so convinced of this—took it so much for granted—that on the morning of September 11 he actually left his roommate, Jonathan, to monitor the burning World Trade Center and Pentagon while he hurried off to his Econ 201 lecture. Not until he reached the big auditorium and found it all but empty did he understand that a really serious glitch had occurred.

Try as he might, in the weeks and months that followed, he could not recall what he'd been thinking as he'd crossed the semi-deserted campus. It was highly uncharacteristic of him to be so clueless, and the deep chagrin he'd then experienced, on the steps of the Chemistry Building, became the seed of his intensely *personal* resentment of the terrorist attacks.

Later, as his troubles began to mount, it would seem to him as if his very good luck, which his childhood had taught him to consider his birthright, had been trumped by a stroke of higher-order bad luck so wrong as not even to be real. He kept waiting for its wrongness, its fraudulence, to be exposed, and for the world to be set right again, so that he could have the college experience he'd expected. When this failed to happen, he was gripped by an anger whose specific object refused to come into focus. The culprit, in hindsight, seemed *almost* like bin Laden, but not quite. The culprit was something deeper, something not political, something structurally malicious, like the bump in a sidewalk that trips you and lands you on your face when you're out innocently walking.

In the days after 9/11, everything suddenly seemed extremely stupid to Joey. It was stupid that a "Vigil of Concern" was held for no conceivable practical reason, it was stupid that people kept watching the same disaster footage over and over, it was stupid that the Chi Phi boys hung a banner of "support" from their house, it was stupid that the football game against Penn State was canceled, it was stupid that so many kids left Grounds to be with their families (and it was stupid that everybody at Virginia said "Grounds" instead of "campus"). The four liberal kids on Joey's hall had endless stupid arguments with the twenty conservative kids, as if anybody cared what a bunch of eighteen-year-olds thought about the Middle East. A stupidly big fuss was made about the students who'd lost relatives or family friends in the attacks, as if the other kinds of horrible death that were constantly occurring in the world mattered less, and there was stupid applause when a vanful of upperclassmen solemnly departed for New York to give succor to the Ground Zero workers, as if there weren't enough people in New York to do the job. Joey just wanted normal life to return as fast as possible. He felt as if he'd bumped his old Discman against a wall and knocked its laser out of a track he'd been enjoying and into a track he didn't recognize or like and also couldn't make stop playing. Before long, he was so lonely and isolated and hungry for familiar things that he made the rather serious mistake of giving Connie Monaghan permission to take a Greyhound bus to visit him in Charlottesville, thereby undoing a summer's worth of spadework to prepare her for their inevitable breakup.

All summer, he'd labored to impress on Connie the importance of not getting together for at least nine months, so as to test their feelings for each other. The idea was to develop independent selves and see if these independent selves were still a good match, but to Joey this was no more a "test" than a high-school chemistry "experiment" was research. Connie would end up staying in Minnesota while he pursued a business career and met girls who were more exotic and advanced and connected. Or so he'd imagined before 9/11.

He was careful to schedule Connie's visit while Jonathan was at home in NoVa for a Jewish holiday. She spent the entire weekend camped out on Joey's bed with her overnight bag beside her on the floor, zipping her things back inside it as soon as she was done with them, as if trying to minimize her footprint. While Joey endeavored to read Plato for a Monday-morning class, she pored over the faces in his first-year facebook and laughed at the ones with odd expressions or unfortunate names. Bailey Bodsworth, Crampton Ott, Taylor Tuttle. By Joey's reliable count, they had sex eight times in forty hours, stoning themselves repeatedly on the hydroponic bud she'd brought along. When it came time to take her back to the bus station, he loaded a bunch of new songs onto her MP3 player for the punishing twenty-hour return trip to Minnesota. The sorry truth was that he felt responsible for her, knew he needed to break up with her anyway, and couldn't think how.

At the bus station, he raised the subject of her education, which she'd promised to pursue but somehow, in her obdurate way, without explanation, hadn't.

"You need to start taking classes in January," he told her. "Start at Inver Hills and then maybe transfer to the U. next year."

"OK," she said.

"You're really smart," he said. "You can't just keep being a waitress."

"OK." She looked away desolately at the line forming by her bus. "I'll do it for you."

"Not for me. For you. Like you promised."

She shook her head. "You just want me to forget about you."

"Not true, not true at all," Joey said, although it was fairly true.

"I'll go to school," she said. "But it's not going to make me forget about you. Nothing's going to make me forget about you."

"Right," he said, "but we still need to find out who we are. We both need to do some growing."

"I already know who I am."

"Maybe you're wrong, though. Maybe you still need to—"

"No," she said. "I'm not wrong. I only want to be with you. That's all I want in my life. You're the best person in the world. You can do anything you want, and I can be there for you. You'll own lots of companies, and I can work for you. Or you can run for president, and I'll work for your campaign. I'll do the things that nobody else will do. If you need somebody to break the law, I'll do that for you. If you want children, I'll raise them for you."

Joey was aware of needing his wits about him to reply to this rather alarming declaration, but he was unfortunately still somewhat stoned.

"Here's the thing I want you to do," he said. "I want you to get a college education. Like, for example," he unwisely added, "if you were going to work for me, you'd need to know a lot of different stuff."

"That's why I said I'd go to school *for you*," Connie said. "Weren't you listening?"

He was beginning to see, as he hadn't in St. Paul, that things' prices weren't always evident at first glance: that the really big ballooning of the interest charges on his high-school pleasures might still lie ahead of him.

"We'd better get in line," he said. "If you want a good seat."

"OK."

"Also," he said, "I think we should go at least a week without calling. We need to get back to being more disciplined."

"OK," she said, and walked obediently toward the bus. Joey followed with her overnight bag. He at least didn't have to worry about her making any scenes. She'd never been a compromiser of him, never an insister on sidewalk hand-holding, never a clinger, a pouter, a reproacher. She saved up all her ardor for when they were alone, she was a specialist like that. When the bus doors opened, she stabbed him with one burning look and then handed her bag to the driver and boarded. There was no bullshit about waving through the window or making kissy faces. She put earphones in her ears and slouched down out of sight.

There was no bullshit in the weeks that followed, either. Connie obediently refrained from calling him, and as the national fever began to break and autumn deepened on the Blue Ridge, lingering with hay-colored sunshine and rich smells of warm lawn and turning leaf, Joey attended blowout Cavalier football losses and worked out at the gym and gained numerous pounds of beer weight. He gravitated socially to hall mates from prosperous families who believed in carpet bombing the Islamic world until it learned to behave itself. He wasn't right-wing himself but was comfortable with those who were. Reaming Afghanistan wasn't exactly what his sense of dislocation demanded, but it was close enough to afford some satisfaction.

Only when enough beer had been consumed to bring a group conversation around to sex did he feel isolated. His thing with Connie was too intense and strange—too *sincere*; too muddled with love—to be fungible as coin of bragging. He disdained but also envied his hall mates for their communal bravado, their porny avowals of what they wanted to do to the choicest babes in the facebook or had supposedly done, in isolated instances, while wasted, and seemingly without regret or consequence, to various wasted girls at their academies and prep schools. His hall mates' yearnings still largely centered on the blow job, which Joey apparently was totally alone in considering little more than a glorified jerkoff, an amusement for the parking lot at lunch hour.

Masturbation itself was a demeaning dissipation whose utility he was nevertheless learning to value as he sought to wean himself from Connie. His preferred venue for release was the Handicapped bathroom in the science library at whose Reserve desk he collected $7.65 an hour for reading textbooks and the *Wall Street Journal* and occasionally fetching texts for science nerds. Landing a work-study job at the Reserve desk had seemed to him yet another confirmation that he was destined to be fortunate in life. He was astonished that the library still possessed printed matter of such rarity and widespread interest that it had to be guarded in separate stacks and not allowed to leave the building. There was no way it wouldn't all be digitized within the next few years. Many of the reserved texts were written in formerly popular foreign languages and illustrated with sumptuous color plates; the nineteenth-century Germans had been especially industrious cataloguers of human knowledge. It could even dignify masturbation, a little bit, to use a century-old German sexual-anatomy atlas as an auxiliary to it. He knew that sooner or later he would need to break his silence with Connie, but at the end of each evening, after employing the paddle-handled Handicapped faucets to wash his gametes and prostatic fluids down the drain, he decided to risk waiting one more day, until finally, late one evening, at the Reserve desk, on the very day he'd realized that he'd probably waited one day too long, he got a call from Connie's mother.

"Carol," he said amiably. "Hello."

"Hello, Joey. You probably know why I'm calling."

"No, actually, I don't."

"Well, you've just about broken our little friend's heart, is why."

Stomach lurching, he retreated to the privacy of the stacks. "I was going to call her tonight," he told Carol.

"Tonight. Really. You were going to call her tonight."

"Yes."

"Why do I not believe you?"

"I don't know."

"Well, she's gone to bed, so it's good you didn't call. She went to bed without eating. She went to bed at seven."

"Good thing I didn't call, then."

"This isn't funny, Joey. She's very depressed. You've given her a depression and you need to stop messing around. Do you understand? My daughter isn't some dog that you can tie to a parking meter and then forget about."

"Maybe you should get her an antidepressant."

"She's not your pet that you can leave in the back seat with the windows rolled up," Carol said, warming to her metaphor. "We're part of your life, Joey. I think we deserve a little more than the nothing you've been giving us. This has been a very frightening fall for all concerned, and you have been *absent.*"

"You know, I do have classes to attend, and so forth."

"Too busy for a five-minute phone call. After three and a half weeks of silence."

"I really was going to call her tonight."

"Never mind Connie even," Carol said. "Leave Connie out of it for a minute. You and I lived together like a family for almost two years. I never thought I'd hear myself saying this, but I'm starting to get an idea of what you put your mom through. Seriously. I never understood how cold you are until this fall."

Joey directed a smile of pure oppression at the ceiling. There had always been something not quite right about his interactions with Carol. She was what the prep-school boys on his hall and the fraternity brothers who were rushing him were wont to call a MILF (an acronym that, in Joey's opinion, sounded faintly cretinous for its omission of the T for "to"). Although he was generally a very sound sleeper, there had occasionally been nights, during the period of his residency at the Monaghans, when he'd awakened in Connie's bed with strange anxious premonitions of himself: as the unwitting and horrified trespasser of his sister's bed, for example, or as the accidental shooter of a nail into Blake's forehead with Blake's nail gun, or, strangest of all, as the towering crane at a major Great Lakes dockyard, his horizontal member swinging heavy containers off the deck of a mother ship and gently depositing them on a smaller, flatter barge. These visions tended to follow moments of inappropriate connection with Carol—the glimpse of her bare butt through the nearly closed door of her and Blake's bedroom; the complicit wink she gave Joey pursuant to a dinner-table belch from Blake; the lengthy and explicit rationale she presented to him (illustrated with vivid stories from her own careless youth) for putting Connie on the Pill. Since Connie was constitutionally incapable of being displeased with Joey, it had fallen to her mother to register her discontents. Carol was Connie's garrulous organ, her straight-talking advocate, and Joey had sometimes had the sense, on weekend nights when Blake was out with buddies, of being the sandwiched party in a virtual threesome, Carol's mouth running and running with all the things that Connie wouldn't say, Connie then silently doing with Joey all the things that Carol couldn't do, and Joey jolting awake in the wee hours with a sense of entrapment in something not quite right. Mom I'd Like Fuck.

"So what am I supposed to do?" he said.

"Well, for starters, I want you to be a more responsible boyfriend."

"I'm not her boyfriend. We're on hiatus."

"What is hiatus? What does that mean?"

"It means we're experimenting with being apart."

"That's not what Connie tells me. Connie tells me you want her to go to school so she can learn administrative skills and be your assistant in your endeavors."

"Look," Joey said. "Carol. I was stoned when I said that. I mistakenly said the wrong thing while stoned on the incredibly strong pot that Connie buys."

"You think I don't know she smokes pot? You think Blake and I don't have noses? You're not telling me anything I don't know. All you do is make yourself look like a bad boyfriend when you try to snitch on her."

"My point is that I said the wrong thing. And I haven't had a chance to correct myself, because we agreed not to talk for a while."

"And whose responsibility is that? You know you're like a god to her. Literally like a god, Joey. You tell her to hold her breath, she'll hold her breath until she faints. You tell her to sit in a corner, she'll sit in a corner until she keels over with starvation."

"Well, and whose fault is that?" Joey said.

"It's yours."

"No, Carol. It's yours. You're the parent. You're the one whose house she's living in. I just came along."

"Yeah, and now you're going your own way, without taking responsibility. After being all but married to her. After being part of our family."

"Whoa. Whoa. Carol. I'm a freshman in college. Do you understand that? I mean, the weirdness of even having this conversation?"

"I understand that when I was one year older than you are now, I had a baby girl and was having to make my own way in the world."

"And how's that working out for you?"

"Not too bad, as a matter of fact. I wasn't going to tell you this, because it's still early on, but since you ask, Blake and I are going to have a little baby. Our little family's about to get a little bigger."

It took Joey a moment to compute that she was telling him that she was pregnant.

"Listen," he said, "I'm still at work. I mean, congratulations and all. I'm just busy at this particular moment."

"Busy. Right."

"I promise I'll call her tomorrow afternoon."

"No, I'm sorry," Carol said, "that won't do it. You need to come out right away and spend some time with her."

"That's not an option."

"Then come for a week at Thanksgiving. We'll have a nice family Thanksgiving, all four of us. It'll give her something to look forward to, and you can see for yourself how depressed she is."

Joey had been planning to spend the holiday in Washington with his roommate, Jonathan, whose older sister, a junior at Duke, either photographed misleadingly well or was somebody not to miss meeting in person. The sister's name was Jenna, which in Joey's mind connected her to the Bush twins and all the partying and loose morals that the Bush name connoted.

"I don't have money for a flight," he said.

"You can take a bus, just like Connie. Or is the bus not good enough for Joey Berglund?"

"I also have other plans."

"Well, you better change your plans," Carol said. "Your girlfriend of the last four years is seriously depressed. She cries for hours, she doesn't eat. I've had to talk to her boss at Frost's to keep her from getting fired, because she can't remember orders, she gets confused, she never smiles. She may be getting high at work, I wouldn't be surprised. Then she comes home and goes straight to bed and stays there. When she has her afternoon shifts, I have to drive all the way home on my lunch break to make sure she's up and gets dressed for work, because she won't answer the phone. Then I have to drive her to Frost's and make sure she goes inside. I tried to send Blake to do it for me, but she won't talk to him anymore or do anything he says. Sometimes I think she's trying to wreck my relationship with him, just to be spiteful, because you're gone. When I tell her to see the doctor, she says she doesn't need a doctor. When I ask her what she's trying to prove, and what her plan is for her life, she says her plan is to be with you. That's her only plan. So whatever your own little Thanksgiving plan is, you better change it."

"I said I would call her tomorrow."

"Do you honestly think you can use my daughter as a sex buddy for four years and then just walk away when it suits you? Is that really what you think? She was a *child* when you started having relations with her."

Joey thought of the momentous day in his old tree fort when Connie had rubbed the crotch of her cutoff shorts and then taken his somewhat smaller hand and shown him where to touch her: how little persuading he'd required. "I was a child, too, of course," he said.

"Hon, you were never a child," Carol said. "You were always so cool and self-possessed. Don't think I didn't know you when you were a little baby. You never even cried! I never saw anything like it in my whole life. You wouldn't even cry when you stubbed your toe. Your face would wrinkle up but you wouldn't make a peep."

"No, I cried. I definitely remember crying."

"You used her, you used me, you used Blake. And now you think you can just turn your back on us and walk away? You think that's how the world works? You think we're all just here for your personal pleasure?"

"I'll try to get her to see a doctor for a prescription. But, Carol, you know, this is a really strange conversation we're having. Not a good kind of conversation."

"Well, you better get used to it, because we're going to be having it again tomorrow, and the next day, and the next day after that, until I hear you're coming for Thanksgiving."

"I'm not coming for Thanksgiving."

"Well, then, you better get used to hearing from me."

After the library closed, he went out into the chilly night and sat on a bench outside his dorm, caressing his phone and trying to think of somebody to call. In St. Paul he'd made it clear to all his friends that his thing with Connie was off-limits conversationally, and in Virginia he'd kept it a secret. Almost everybody in his dorm communicated with their parents daily, if not hourly, and although this did make him feel unexpectedly grateful to his own parents, who had been far cooler and more respectful of his wishes than he'd been able to appreciate as long as he lived next door to them, it also touched off something like a panic. He'd asked for his freedom, they'd granted it, and he couldn't go back now. There had been a brief spate of familial phoning after 9/11, but the talk had mostly been impersonal, his mom amusingly ranting about how she couldn't stop watching CNN even though she was convinced that watching so much CNN was harming her, his dad taking the opportunity to vent his long-standing hostility to organized religion, and Jessica flaunting her knowledge of non-Western cultures and explaining the legitimacy of their beef with U.S. imperialism. Jessica was at the very bottom of the list of people whom Joey would call in distress. Maybe, if she were his last living acquaintance and he'd been arrested in North Korea and were willing to endure a stern lecture: maybe then.

As if to reassure himself that Carol had been wrong about him, he wept a little in the darkness, on his bench. Wept for Connie in her misery, wept for having abandoned her to Carol—for not being the person who could save her. Then he dried his eyes and called his own mother, whose telephone Carol could probably have heard ringing if she'd stood by a window and listened closely.

"Joseph Berglund," his mother said. "I seem to remember that name from somewhere."

"Hi, Mom."

Immediately a silence.

"Sorry I haven't called in a while," he said.

"Oh, well," she said, "there's really nothing much happening around here except anthrax scares, a very unrealistic realtor trying to sell our house, and your dad flying back and forth to Washington. You know they make everybody flying into Washington stay in their seat for an hour before they land there? It seems like kind of a weird regulation. I mean, what are they thinking? The terrorists are going to cancel their evil plan because the seat-belt sign is on? Dad says they're barely even airborne when the stewardesses start warning everybody to use the bathroom right away, before it's too late. And then they start handing out whole cans of drinks."

She sounded like a nattering older lady, not the vital force he still imagined when he allowed himself to think of her. He had to squeeze his eyes shut to avert renewed weeping. Everything he'd done with regard to her in the last three years had been calculated to foreclose the intensely personal sort of talks they'd had when he was younger: to get her to *shut up*, to train her to contain herself, to make her stop pestering him with her overfull heart and her uncensored self. And now that the training was complete and she was obediently trivial with him, he felt bereft of her and wanted to undo it.

"Am I allowed to ask if all is well with you?" she said.

"Everything is well with me."

"Life's good in the former slave states?"

"Very good. The weather's been beautiful."

"Right, that's the advantage of growing up in Minnesota. Everywhere you go now, the weather will be nicer."

"Yep."

"Are you making lots of new friends? Meeting lots of people?"

"Yep."

"Well, good good good. Good good good. It's nice of you to call, Joey. I mean, I know you don't have to, so it's nice that you did. You have some real fans here back at home."

A herd of male first-years burst out of the dorm and onto the lawn, their voices amplified by beer. "Jo-eeee, Jo-eeee," they lowed affectionately. He nodded to them in cool acknowledgment.

"Sounds like you've got some fans there, too," his mother said.

"Yep."

"My popular boy."

"Yep."

Another silence fell as the herd headed off to fresh watering holes. Joey felt a pang of disadvantage, watching them go. He was already nearly a month ahead of his budgeted fall-semester spending. He didn't want to be the poor kid who drank only one beer while everybody else was having six, but he didn't want to look like a freeloader, either. He wanted to be dominant and generous; and this required funds.

"How's Dad liking his new job?" he made an effort to ask his mother.

"I think he's liking it OK. It's sort of driving him insane. You know: suddenly having lots of somebody else's money to spend on fixing all the things he thinks are wrong with the world. He used to be able to complain that nobody was fixing them. Now he actually has to try to fix them himself, which is impossible, of course, since we're all going to hell in a handbasket. He sends me e-mails at three in the morning. I don't think he's sleeping much."

"And what about you? How are you?"

"Oh, well, it's nice of you to ask, but you don't really want to know."

"Sure I do."

"No, trust me, you don't. And don't worry, I'm not saying that in a mean way. It's not a reproach. You've got your life and I've got mine. It's all good good good."

"No, but, like, what do you do all day?"

"Actually, FYI," his mother said, "that can be a somewhat awkward question to ask a person. It's sort of like asking a childless couple why they don't have any children, or an unmarried person why they aren't married. You have to be careful with certain kinds of questions that may seem perfectly innocuous to you."

"Hm."

"I'm sort of in limbo right now," she said. "It's hard to make any big changes in my life when I know I'm going to be moving. I did start a little creative-writing project, for my private amusement. I also have to keep the house looking like a bed-and-breakfast in case a realtor stops by with a potential mark. I spend a lot of time making sure the magazines are nicely fanned."

Joey's feeling of bereavement was giving way to irritation, because, no matter how much she denied that she was doing it, she couldn't seem to help reproaching him. These moms and their reproaches, there was no end to it. He called her for a little support, and the next thing he knew, he was falling short of providing support to her.

"So how are you on money?" she said, as if sensing his irritation. "Do you have enough money?"

"It's a little tight," he admitted.

"I bet!"

"Once I'm a resident here, tuition will go way down. It's just this first year that's really hard."

"Do you want me to send you some money?"

He smiled in the darkness. He liked her, in spite of everything; he couldn't help it. "I thought Dad said there wasn't going to be any money."

"Dad doesn't necessarily have to know every little thing."

"Well, and the school won't consider me a state resident if I'm taking anything from you."

"The school doesn't have to know everything, either. I could send you a check made out to Cash, if that would help you."

"Yeah, and then what?"

"Then nothing. I promise. No strings attached. I'm saying you've already made your point with Dad. There's no need to take on horrible debt at high interest, just to keep proving a point you already made."

"Let me think about it."

"Why don't I put a check in the mail to you. Then you can decide on your own if you want to cash it or not. You won't have to discuss it with me."

He smiled again. "Why are you doing this?"

"Well, you know, Joey, believe it or not, I want you to have the life you want to have. I've had some free time for asking myself questions while I've been fanning magazines on the coffee table, and whatnot. Like, if you were to tell me and Dad you never wanted to see us again, for the rest of your life, would I still want you to be happy?"

"That is a bizarre hypothetical question. It has no bearing on reality."

"That's nice to hear, but it's not my point. My point is that we all think we know the answer to the question. Parents are programmed to want the best for their kids, regardless of what they get in return. That's what love is supposed to be like, right? But in fact, if you think about it, that's kind of a strange belief. Given what we know about the way people really are. Selfish and shortsighted and egotistical and needy. Why should being a parent, just in and of itself, somehow confer superior-personhood on everybody who tries it? Obviously it doesn't. I've told you a little bit about my own parents, for example—"

"Not very much," Joey said.

"Well, maybe sometime I'll tell you more, if you ask me nicely. But my point is that I've given some real thought to this question of love, regarding you. And I've decided—"

"Mom, do you mind if we talk about something else?"

"I've decided—"

"Or, actually, maybe some other day? Next week or something? I've got a lot of stuff to do here before I go to bed."

A silence of injury descended in St. Paul.

"I'm sorry," he said. "It's just really late, and I'm tired and I still have stuff to do."

"I was simply explaining," his mother said in a much lower voice, "why I'm going to send a check."

"Right, thank you. That's nice of you. I guess."

In an even smaller and more injured voice, his mother thanked him for calling and hung up.

Joey looked around the lawn for some bushes or an architectural cranny where he might cry unobserved by passing posses. Seeing none, he ran inside his dorm and, blindly, as if needing to barf, veered into the first john he came to, on a hall not his own, and locked himself into a stall and sobbed with hatred of his mother. Somebody was showering in a cloud of deodorant soap and mildew. A big smiling-faced erection, soaring like Superman, spurting droplets, was Sharpied on the stall's rust-pocked door. Beneath it somebody had written *SCORE NOW OR TAKE A CHIT.*

The nature of his mother's reproach wasn't simple the way Carol Monaghan's was. Carol, unlike her daughter, was not too bright. Connie had a wry, compact intelligence, a firm little clitoris of discernment and sensitivity to which she gave Joey access only behind closed doors. When she and Carol and Blake and Joey used to have dinner together, Connie would eat with her eyes lowered and seem lost in her own strange thoughts, but afterward, alone with Joey in their bedroom, she could reproduce every last deplorable detail of Carol and Blake's dinner-table behavior. She once asked Joey if he'd noticed that the point of almost every utterance of Blake's was how stupid other people were and how superior and put-upon he, Blake, was. According to Blake, the morning's KSTP weather forecast had been stupid, the Paulsens had put their recycling barrel in a stupid place, the seat-belt beeper in his truck was stupid not to shut off after sixty seconds, the commuters driving the speed limit on Summit Avenue were stupid, the stoplight at Summit and Lexington was stupidly timed, his boss at work was stupid, the city building code was stupid. Joey began to laugh while Connie continued, with implacable recall, to list examples: the new TV remote was stupidly designed, the NBC prime-time schedule had been stupidly rearranged, the National League was stupid for not adopting the designated-hitter rule, the Vikings were stupid for letting Brad Johnson and Jeff George get away, the moderator of the second presidential debate had been stupid not to press Al Gore on what a liar he was, Minnesota was stupid to make its hardworking citizens pay for free *top-of-the-line* medical care for Mexican illegals and welfare cheats, free *top-of-the-line* medical care—

"And you know what?" Connie said finally.

"What?" Joey said.

"You never do that. You really are smarter than other people, so you never have to call them stupid."

Joey accepted her compliment uncomfortably. For one thing, he was getting a strong whiff of competition from the direct comparison of him and Blake—an unsettling sense of being a pawn or a prize in some complicated mother-daughter struggle. And although it was true that he'd checked a lot of judgments at the door when he'd moved in with the Monaghans, he had formerly declared all manner of things to be stupid, in particular his mother, who had come to seem to him a font of endless, nerve-grating asininity. Now Connie seemed to be suggesting that what made people complain about stupidity was their own stupidity.

In truth, the only thing his mother had been guilty of being stupid about was Joey himself. Granted, it had also seemed very dumb of her to be, for example, so disrespectful of Tupac, whose best stuff Joey considered unarguably genius-level work, or so hostile toward *Married with Children*, whose own stupidity was so calculated and extreme that it was flat-out brilliant. But she would never have attacked *Married with Children* if Joey hadn't been so devoted to watching it in reruns, she would never have stooped to doing her embarrassingly off-base caricatures of Tupac if Joey hadn't admired him so much. The actual root cause of her stupidity was her wish for Joey to keep on being her little boy-pal: to continue being more entertained and fascinated by his mother than by great TV or a bona-fide genius rap star. This was the sick heart of her dumbness: she was *competing*.

Eventually he'd become desperate enough to drive it into her head that he didn't want to be her little boy-pal anymore. This hadn't even been his conscious plan, it was more like a by-product of his long-running irritation with his moralistic sister, whom he could think of no finer way to enrage and horrify than to invite a bunch of his friends over to his house and get drunk on Jim Beam while his parents were with his ailing grandmother in Grand Rapids, and then, the following night, to screw Connie extra-specially noisily against the wall that his bedroom shared with Jessica's, thereby inciting Jessica to crank up her intolerable Belle and Sebastian to club-level volumes and later, after midnight, to pound on his locked bedroom door with her virtuously white knuckles—

"God damn it, Joey! You stop this right now! *Right now*, do you hear me?"

"Hey, whoa, I'm doing you a favor here."

"*What?*"

"Aren't you sick of not telling on me? I'm doing you a favor! I'm giving you your chance!"

"I'm telling on you *now*. I'm going to call Dad *right now*."

"Go ahead! Didn't you just hear me? I said I was doing you a favor."

"You fucker. You smug little *fucker*. I'm calling Dad *right now*—" while Connie, stark naked, bloody-red of lip and nipple, sat holding her breath and looking at Joey with a mixture of fear and amazement and excitement and allegiance and delight which convinced him, like nothing before and few things since, that no rule or propriety or moral law mattered to her one-thousandth as much as being his chosen girl and partner in crime.

He hadn't expected his grandmother to die that week—she wasn't that old. By hurling shit into the fan one day before she passed, he'd put himself extremely in the wrong. Just *how* wrong was evidenced by the fact that he was never even yelled at. Up in Hibbing, at the funeral, his parents simply froze him out. He was left to stew separately in his guilt while the rest of his family joined together in a grief that he ought to have been experiencing with them. Dorothy had been the only grandparent in his life, and she'd impressed him, when he was still very young, by inviting him to handle her crippled hand and see that it was still a person's hand and nothing to be scared of. After that, he'd never objected to the kindnesses his parents had asked him to do for her when she was visiting. She was a person, maybe the only person, to whom he'd been one-hundred-percent good. And now suddenly she was dead.

Her funeral was followed by some weeks of respite from his mother, some weeks of welcome chilliness, but by and by she came after him again. She exploited the pretext of his frankness about Connie to become inappropriately frank with him in turn. She tried to make him her Designated Understander, and this turned out to be even worse than being her little boy-pal. It was devious and irresistible. It started with a confidence: she sat down on his bed one afternoon and launched into telling him how she'd been stalked in college by a drug-addicted pathological liar whom she'd nonetheless loved and his dad had disapproved of. "I had to tell somebody," she said, "and I didn't want to tell Dad. I was down getting my new driver's license yesterday, and I realized that she was in line ahead of me. I haven't seen her since the night I wrecked my knee. That's like twenty years? She's gained a lot of weight, but it was definitely her. And I got so frightened, seeing her. I realized I felt guilty."

"Why frightened?" he found himself saying, like Tony Soprano's shrink. "Why guilty?"

"I don't know. I ran out of there before she could turn around and see me. I still have to go back down for my license. But I was terrified that she was going to turn around and see me. I was terrified of what was going to happen. Because, you know, I am so not a lesbian. You have to believe that I would know it if I were—half my old friends are gay. And I definitely am not."

"Good to hear," he said with a nervous smirk.

"But I realized, yesterday, seeing her, that I'd been in love with her. And I was never able to deal with that. And now she has that kind of lithium heaviness—"

"What's lithium."

"For manic depression. Bipolar disease."

"Ah."

"And I totally abandoned her, because Dad hated her so much. She was suffering, and I never called her again, and I threw her letters away without opening them."

"But she lied to you. She was scary."

"I know, I know. But I still feel guilty."

She told him many other secrets in the months that followed. Secrets that proved to be like candy laced with arsenic. For a while, he actually considered himself *lucky* to have a mom who was so cool and forthcoming. He responded by disclosing various perversions and petty crimes of his classmates, trying to impress her with how much more jaded and debauched his peers were than young people in the seventies. And then one day, during a conversation about date rape, it had seemed natural enough for her to tell him how she herself had been date-raped as a teenager, and how he mustn't ever breathe a word of it to Jessica, because Jessica didn't understand her the way he did—nobody understood her the way he did. He'd lain awake in the nights following that conversation, feeling murderously angry at his mother's rapist, and outraged by the world's injustice, and guilty for every negative thing he'd ever said or felt about her, and privileged and important to be granted access to the world of grownup secrets. And then one morning he'd woken up hating her so violently that it made his skin crawl and his stomach turn to be in the same room with her. It was like a chemical transformation. As if there were arsenic leaching from his organs and his bone marrow.

What he'd been dismayed by tonight on the telephone was how completely *un*stupid she had sounded. This, indeed, was the substance of her reproach. She didn't seem to be very good at living her life, but it wasn't because she was stupid. Almost the opposite somehow. She had a comical-tragical sense of herself and seemed, moreover, genuinely apologetic for the way she was. And yet it all added up to a reproach of him. As if she were speaking some sophisticated but dying aboriginal language which it was up to the younger generation (i.e., Joey) to either perpetuate or be responsible for the death of. Or as if she were one of his dad's endangered birds, singing its obsolete song in the woods in the forlorn hope of some passing kindred spirit hearing it. There was her, and then there was the rest of the world, and by the very way she chose to speak to him she was reproaching him for placing his allegiance with the rest of the world. And who could fault him for preferring the world? He had his own life to try to live! The problem was that when he was younger, in his weakness, he'd let her see that he did understand her language and did recognize her song, and now she couldn't seem to help reminding him that those capacities were still inside him, should he ever feel like exercising them again.

Whoever was showering in the dormitory bathroom had stopped and was toweling off. The hall door opened and closed, opened and closed; a minty smell of tooth-brushing wafted over from the sinks and into Joey's stall. His crying had given him a boner that he now removed from his boxers and khakis and held on to for dear life. If he squeezed the base of it really hard, he could make the head of it huge and hideous and almost black with venous blood. He so much liked looking at it, so much enjoyed the feeling of protection and independence its repulsive beauty gave him, that he was reluctant to finish himself off and lose hold of that hardness. To walk around hard every minute of the day, of course, would be to be what people called a prick. Which was what Blake was. Joey didn't want to be like Blake, but he wanted even less to be his mother's Designated Understander. With silently spastic fingers, staring at his hardness, he came into the yawning toilet and immediately flushed it.

Upstairs, in his corner room, he found Jonathan reading John Stuart Mill and watching the ninth inning of a World Series game. "Very confounding situation here," Jonathan said. "I'm experiencing actual pangs of sympathy for the Yankees."

Joey, who never watched baseball by himself but was amenable to watching it with others, sat down on his bed while Randy Johnson dealt fastballs to a defeat-eyed Yankee. The score was 4–0. "They could still come back," he said.

"Not going to happen," Jonathan said. "And I'm sorry, but since when do expansion teams get to play in the Series after four seasons? I'm still trying to accept that Arizona even has a team."

"I'm glad you're seeing the light of reason finally."

"Don't get me wrong. There's still nothing sweeter than a Yankee loss, preferably by one run, preferably on a passed ball by Jorge Posada, the chinless wonder. But this is the one year you kind of want them to win anyway. It's a patriotic sacrifice we all have to make for New York."

"I want them to win every year," Joey said, although he didn't have strong feelings about it.

"Yeah, what's up with that? Aren't you supposed to like the Twins?"

"It's probably mostly because my parents hate the Yankees. My dad loves the Twins *because* they've got a tiny payroll, and naturally the Yankees are the enemy when it comes to payrolls. And my mom's just an anti–New York maniac in general."

Jonathan gave him an interested look. To date, Joey had disclosed very little about his parents, only enough to avoid seeming annoyingly mysterious about them. "Why does she hate New York?"

"I don't know. I guess because it's where she came from."

On Jonathan's TV, Derek Jeter lined out to second base, and the game was over.

"Very complex mix of emotions here," Jonathan said, turning it off.

"You know, I don't even know my grandparents?" Joey said. "My mom's really weird about them. My entire childhood, they came to see us once, for like forty-eight hours. The whole time, my mom was unbelievably neurotic and fake. We went to see them one other time, when we were in New York on vacation, and that was bad, too. I'd get these birthday cards three weeks late from them, and my mom would be, like, *cursing* them for being so late, even though it wasn't really their fault. I mean, how are they supposed to remember the birthday of somebody they never get to see?"

Jonathan was frowning thoughtfully. "Where in New York?"

"I don't know. Somewhere in the suburbs. My grandmother's a politician, in the state legislature or something. She's this nice, elegant Jewish lady who my mom apparently can't stand to be in the same room with."

"Whoa, say that again?" Jonathan sat up straight on his bed. "Your mom is Jewish?"

"I guess in some theoretical way."

"Dude, you're a Jew! I had no idea!"

"Only, like, one-quarter," Joey said. "It's really watered down."

"You could immigrate to Israel right now, no questions asked."

"My lifelong dream fulfilled."

"I'm just saying. You could be packing a Desert Eagle, or piloting one of those fighter jets, and dating a total sabra."

To illustrate his point, Jonathan opened his laptop and navigated to a site devoted to pictures of bronzed Israeli goddesses with high-caliber bandoliers crisscrossing their naked D-cup chests.

"Not my kind of thing," Joey said.

"I'm not that into it, either," Jonathan said, with perhaps less than complete honesty. "I'm just saying, if it *were* your kind of thing."

"Also, isn't there a problem with illegal settlements and Palestinians not having any rights?"

"Yes, there's a problem! The problem is being a tiny island of democracy and pro-Western government surrounded by Muslim fanatics and hostile dictators."

"Yeah, but that just means it was a stupid place to put the island," Joey said. "If the Jews hadn't gone to the Middle East, and if we didn't have to keep supporting them, maybe the Arab countries wouldn't be so hostile to us."

"Dude. Are you familiar with the Holocaust?"

"I know. But why didn't they go to New York instead? We would have let them in. They could have had their synagogues here, and so forth, and we could have had some kind of normal relationship with the Arabs."

"But the Holocaust happened in Europe, which was supposed to be civilized. When you lose half your world population to genocide, you stop trusting anybody to protect you except yourself."

Joey was uncomfortably aware that he was displaying attitudes more his parents' than his own, and that he was therefore about to lose an argument he didn't even care about winning. "Fine," he persisted nonetheless, "but why does that have to be *our* problem?"

"Because it's our business to support democracy and free markets wherever they are," Jonathan said. "That's the problem in Saudi Arabia—too many angry people with no economic prospects. That's how come bin Laden can recruit there. I totally agree with you about the Palestinians. That's just a giant fucking breeding ground for terrorists. That's why we have to try to bring freedom to all the Arab countries. But you don't start doing that by selling out the one working democracy in the entire region."

Joey admired Jonathan not only for his coolness but for having the confidence not to pretend to be stupid in order to maintain it. He managed the difficult trick of making it seem cool to be smart. "Hey," Joey said, to change the subject, "am I still invited to Thanksgiving?"

"Invited? You're doubly invited now. My family isn't the self-hating kind of Jewish. My parents really, really dig Jews. They will roll out the red carpet for you."

The following afternoon, alone in their room, and oppressed by not yet having made the promised call to Connie about seeing a doctor, Joey found himself opening Jonathan's computer and searching for pictures of his sister, Jenna. He didn't consider it snooping if he went straight to family photos that Jonathan had already shown him anyway. His roommate's excitement about his Jewishness seemed to presage a similarly warm reception on Jenna's part, and he copied the two most fetching pictures of her onto his own hard drive, altering the file extensions to make them un-findable by anyone but him, so that he could picture some concrete alternative to Connie before he made the dreaded call to her.

The female scene at school had not proved satisfactory thus far. Compared to Connie, the really attractive girls he'd met in Virginia all seemed to have been sprayed with Teflon, encased in suspicion of his motives. Even the prettiest ones wore too much makeup and overly formal clothes and dressed for Cavaliers games as if they were the Kentucky Derby. It was true that certain second-tier girls, at parties where they'd drunk too much, had given him to understand he was a boy to whom hookups were available. But for whatever reason, whether because he was a wuss or because he hated shouting over music or because he thought too highly of himself or because he was unable to ignore how stupid and annoying too much alcohol made a girl, he'd formed an early prejudice against these parties and their hookups and decided that he much preferred hanging out with other guys.

He sat holding his phone for a long time, for maybe half an hour, while the sky in the windows grayed toward rain. He waited for so long and in such a stupor of reluctance that it was almost like Zen archery when his thumb, of its own accord, hit the speed-dial for Connie's number and the ringing dragged him forward into action.

"Hey!" she answered in a cheerful ordinary voice, a voice he realized he'd been missing. "Where are you?"

"I'm in my room."

"What's it doing there?"

"I don't know. It's kind of gray."

"God, it was *snowing* here this morning. It's already winter."

"Yeah, listen," he said. "Are you OK?"

"Me?" She seemed surprised by the question. "Yes. I miss you every minute of the day, but I'm getting used to that."

"I'm sorry I went so long without calling."

"That's OK. I love talking to you, but I understand why we need to be more disciplined. I was just working on my Inver Hills application. I also signed up to take the SAT in December, like you suggested."

"Did I suggest that?"

"If I'm going to go to real school in the fall, like you said, it's what I need to do. I bought a book on how to study for it. I'm going to study three hours every day."

"So you're really OK."

"Yes! How are you?"

Joey struggled to reconcile Carol's account of Connie with how clear and collected she was sounding. "I talked to your mom last night," he said.

"I know. She told me."

"She said she's pregnant?"

"Yes, a blessed event is coming our way. I think it's going to be twins."

"Really? Why?"

"I don't know. It's just my sense. That it's going to be especially horrible in some way."

"The whole conversation was actually pretty weird."

"She's been spoken to now," Connie said. "She won't be calling you again. If she does, let me know, and I'll make it stop."

"She said you were very depressed," Joey blurted out.

This brought a sudden silence, total in the black-hole way that only Connie could make a silence.

"She said you're sleeping all day and not eating enough," Joey said. "She sounded really worried about you."

After another silence, Connie said, "I was a little bit depressed for a while. But it was none of Carol's business. And now I'm doing better."

"But maybe you need an antidepressant or something?"

"No. I'm doing much better."

"Well, that's great," Joey said, although he felt that it was somehow not great at all—that morbid weakness and clinginess on her part might have provided him with a viable escape route.

"So have you been sleeping with other people?" Connie said. "I thought that might be why you weren't calling."

"No! No. Not at all."

"It's OK with me if you do. I meant to tell you that last month. You're a guy, you have needs. I don't expect you to be a monk. It's just sex, who cares?"

"Well, the same goes for you," he said gratefully, sensing another possible escape route here.

"Except it's not going to happen with me," Connie said. "Nobody else sees me the way you do. I'm invisible to men."

"I don't believe that at all."

"No, it's true. Sometimes I try to be friendly, or even flirty, at the restaurant. But it's like I'm invisible. I don't really care anyway. I just want you. I think people sense that."

"I want you, too," he found himself murmuring, in contravention of certain safety guidelines he'd established for himself.

"I know," she said. "But guys are different, is all I'm saying. You should feel free."

"I've actually been jerking off a lot."

"Yeah, me, too. For hours and hours. Some days it's the only thing I feel like doing. That's probably why Carol thinks I'm depressed."

"But maybe you *are* depressed."

"No, I just like to come a lot. I think about you, and I come. I think about you some more, and then I come some more. That's all it is."

Very quickly the conversation devolved into phone sex, which they hadn't had since the earliest days, when they were sneaking around and whispering on phones in their respective bedrooms. It had become a lot more interesting in the meantime, because they knew how to talk to each other now. At the same time, it was as if they'd never had sex before—was cataclysmic that way.

"I wish I could lick it off your fingers," Connie said when they were finished.

"I'm licking it for you," Joey said.

"That's good. Lick it up for me. Does it taste good?"

"Yes."

"I swear I can taste it in my mouth."

"I can taste you, too."

"Oh, baby."

Which led immediately to further phone sex, a more nervous rendition, since Jonathan's afternoon class was ending and he might return soon.

"My baby," Connie said. "Oh, my baby. My baby, my baby, my baby."

Joey, as he climaxed again, believed that he was with Connie in her bedroom on Barrier Street, his arching back her arching back, his little breasts her little breasts. They lay breathing as one into their cell phones. He'd been wrong, the night before, when he'd told Carol that she, not he, was responsible for the way Connie was. He could feel now in his body how they'd made each other who they were.

"Your mom wants me to spend Thanksgiving with you guys," he said after a while.

"You don't have to do that," she said. "We agreed we were going to try to wait nine months."

"Well, she was kind of a bitch about it."

"That's her way. She's a bitch. But she's been spoken to, and it won't happen again."

"So you don't care either way?"

"You know what I want. Thanksgiving has nothing to do with it."

He had been hoping, for paradoxically opposing reasons, that Connie would join Carol in urging him to come back for the holiday. He was keen, on the one hand, to see her and to sleep with her, and, on the other hand, to find fault with her, so that he would have something to resist and break away from. What she was doing instead, with her cool clarity, was resetting a hook that for a while, in recent weeks, he'd managed to work halfway free of. Resetting it deeper than ever.

"I should probably get off the phone now," he said. "Jonathan's coming back."

"OK," Connie said, and let him go.

Their conversation had diverged so wildly from his expectations that he couldn't even remember now what he'd expected. He got up from his bed as if surfacing through a wormhole in the fabric of reality, his heart thudding, his vision altered, and paced around the room under the collective gaze of Tupac and Natalie Portman. He'd always liked Connie a lot. Always. And so why now, of all the inopportune moments, was he being gripped, as if for the first time, by such a titanic undertow of *really liking her*? How could it be, after years of having sex with her, years of feeling tender and protective of her, that he was only now getting sucked into such heavy waters of affection? Feeling connected to her in such a scarily consequential way? Why now?

It was wrong, it was wrong, he knew it was wrong. He sat down at his computer to view the pictures of Jonathan's sister and try to reestablish some order. Luckily, before he was able to get the file extensions changed back to JPG and be caught red-handed, Jonathan himself walked in.

"My man, my Jewish brother," he said, falling to his bed like a shooting victim. "'Sup?"

"'Sup," Joey said, hastily closing a graphical window.

"Whoa, Jesus, a *little* bit of chlorine in the air here? You been to the pool, or what?"

Joey almost, right then, told his roommate everything, the whole story of him and Connie right up to the present moment. But the dream world he'd been in, the nethery place of sexually merged identities, was receding quickly in the face of Jonathan's male presence.

"I don't know what you're talking about," he said with a smile.

"Crack a window, for God's sake. I mean, I like you and all, but I'm not ready to go all the way yet."

Taking Jonathan's complaint to heart, Joey did, after that, open the windows. He called Connie again the very next day, and again two days after that. He quietly shelved his sound arguments against too-frequent calling and fell gratefully on phone sex as a replacement for his solitary science-library masturbation, which now seemed to him a squalid aberration, embarrassing to recall. He succeeded in persuading himself that, as long as they avoided ordinary newsy chitchat and spoke only of sex, it was OK to exploit this loophole in his otherwise strict embargo on excess contact. As they continued to exploit it, however, and October became November and the days grew shorter, he realized that it was making their contact *all the deeper and realer* to hear Connie finally naming the things they'd done and the things she imagined them doing in the future. This deepening was somewhat strange, since all they were doing was getting each other off. But in hindsight it seemed to him as if, in St. Paul, Connie's silence had formed a kind of protective barrier: had given their couplings what politicians called deniability. To discover, now, that sex had been fully registering in her as language—as words that she could speak out loud—made her much realer to him as a person. The two of them could no longer pretend that they were just mute youthful animals mindlessly doing their thing. Words made everything less safe, words had no limits, words made their own world. One afternoon, as Connie described it, her excited clitoris grew to be eight inches long, a protruding pencil of tenderness with which she gently parted the lips of his penis and drove herself down to the base of its shaft. Another day, at her urging, Joey described to her the sleek warm neatness of her turds as they slid from her anus and fell into his open mouth, where, since these were only words, they tasted like excellent dark chocolate. As long as her words were in his ear, urging him on, he wasn't ashamed of anything. He returned to the wormhole three or four or even five times a week, disappeared into the world the two of them created, and later reemerged and shut the windows and went out to the dining hall or down to his dormitory lounge and effortlessly performed the shallow affability that college life required of him.

It was, as Connie had said, only sex. The permission she'd given him to pursue it elsewhere was very much on Joey's mind as he rode with Jonathan to NoVa for Thanksgiving. They were in Jonathan's Land Cruiser, which he'd received as a high-school graduation present and now parked off campus in open defiance of the first-year no-cars rule. It was Joey's impression, from movies and books, that much could happen quickly when college students were let loose at Thanksgiving. All fall, he'd taken care not to ask Jonathan any questions about his sister, Jenna, figuring that he had nothing to gain by arousing Jonathan's suspicions prematurely. But as soon as he mentioned Jenna in the Land Cruiser he saw that all his care had been for naught. Jonathan gave him a knowing look and said, "She's got a very serious boyfriend."

"No doubt."

"Or, no, sorry, I misspoke. I should have said that *she* is very serious about a boyfriend who in fact is ridiculous and a class-A jackass. I won't insult my own intelligence by asking why you're asking about her."

"I was just being polite," Joey said.

"Ha-ha. It was interesting, when she finally went away to college, I found out who my real friends were and which ones were only interested in coming over to my house as long as she was there. It turned out to be about fifty percent of them."

"I had the same problem, but not with my sister," Joey said, smiling at the thought of Jessica. "For me it was Foosball and air hockey and a beer keg." He proceeded, in the freedom of being on the road, to divulge to

Jonathan the circumstances of his last two years of high school. Jonathan listened attentively enough but seemed interested in only one part of the story, the part about his living with his girlfriend.

"And where is this person now?" he asked.

"In St. Paul. She's still at home."

"No shit," Jonathan said, very impressed. "But wait a minute. That girl Casey saw going into our room on Yom Kippur—that wasn't *her*, was it?"

"Actually, yes," Joey said. "We broke up, but we sort of had one little backslide."

"You fucking little liar! You told me that was just some hookup."

"No. All I said was I didn't want to talk about it."

"You *gave me to believe* it was a hookup. I can't believe you deliberately brought her out here when I was gone."

"Like I said, we had one backslide. We're broken up now."

"For real? You don't talk to her on the phone?"

"Just a tiny little bit. She's really depressed."

"I am impressed with what a sneaky little liar you turn out to be."

"I'm not a liar," Joey said.

"Said the liar. Do you have a picture of her on your computer?"

"No," Joey lied.

"Joey the secret stud," Jonathan said. "Joey the runaway. God damn. You're making more sense to me now."

"Right, but I'm still Jewish, so you still have to like me."

"I didn't say I didn't like you. I said you're making more sense. I could care less if you've got a girlfriend—I'm not going to tell Jenna. I'll just warn you right now that you're lacking the key to her heart."

"And what's that?"

"A job at Goldman Sachs. That's what her boyfriend has. His stated ambition is to be worth a hundred million at age thirty."

"Is he going to be at your parents'?"

"No, he's in Singapore. He just graduated last year, and they're already flying him to fucking Singapore for some billion-dollar round-the-clock something. She'll be pining alone at home, bro."

Jonathan's father was the founder and luminary president of a think tank devoted to advocating the unilateral exercise of American military supremacy to make the world freer and safer, especially for America and Israel. Hardly a week had passed, in October and November, without Jonathan pointing out to Joey an opinion piece in the *Times* or the *Journal* in which his father expounded on the menace of radical Islam. They'd also watched him on the *NewsHour* and Fox News. He had a mouth full of exceptionally white teeth that he flashed every time he started speaking, and he looked almost old enough to be Jonathan's grandfather. Besides Jonathan and Jenna, he had three much older children from earlier marriages, plus two former wives.

The house of his third marriage was in McLean, Virginia, on a sylvan cul-de-sac that was like a vision of where Joey wanted to live as soon as he got rich. Inside the house, whose floors were of fine-grained oak, there seemed to be no end of rooms looking out on a wooded ravine in which woodpeckers swooped among the mostly bare trees. Despite having grown up in a house he'd considered book-filled and tasteful, Joey was staggered by the quantity of hardcover books and by the obviously top quality of the multicultural swag that Jonathan's father had collected during distinguished foreign residencies. Just as Jonathan had been surprised to learn of Joey's adventures in high school, Joey was now surprised to see what high-class luxury his messy and somewhat crude-mannered roommate came from. The only real off note was the tackily ornate Judaica parked in various nooks and corners. Seeing Joey smirk at a notably monstrous silver-painted menorah, Jonathan assured him it was extremely old and rare and valuable.

Jonathan's mother, Tamara, who'd clearly once been a total babe and was still quite a bit of one, showed Joey the luxurious bedroom and bathroom that would be solely his. "Jonathan tells me you're Jewish," she said.

"Yes, apparently I am," Joey said.

"But not observant?"

"Not even conscious, actually, until a month ago."

Tamara shook her head. "I don't understand that," she said. "I know it's very common, but I will never understand it."

"It wasn't like I was Christian or anything, either," Joey said by way of excuse. "It was all part of the same nonissue."

"Well, you're very welcome with us. I think you might find it interesting to learn a little bit about your heritage. You'll find that Howard and I aren't particularly conservative. We just think it's important to be aware and always be remembering."

"They'll whip you right into shape," Jonathan said.

"Don't worry, it'll be a very gentle whipping," Tamara said with a milfy smile.

"That's great," Joey said. "I'm definitely up for anything."

As soon as they could, the two boys escaped to the basement rec room, whose amenities shamed even those in Blake and Carol's great-room. Tennis could practically have been played on the blue felt expanses of the mahogany pool table. Jonathan introduced Joey to a complicated, inter-minable, and frustrating game called Cowboy Pool that required a table without a central ball-collection mechanism. Joey was on the verge of suggesting a switch to air hockey, at which he was annihilatingly skilled, when the sister, Jenna, came downstairs. She acknowledged Joey, barely, from the pinnacle of her two-year age advantage, and began to speak of urgent family matters with her brother.

Joey suddenly understood, as never before, what people meant by "breathtaking." Jenna had the unsettling kind of beauty that relegated everything around her, even a beholder's basic organ functions, to after-thought status. Her figure and complexion and bone structure made the features that he'd so admired in other "pretty" girls now seem like crude approximations of beauty; even the pictures of her hadn't done her jus-tice. Her hair was thick and shining and strawberry blonde, and she was wearing an oversized Duke athletic jersey and flannel pajama bottoms, which, far from concealing her body's perfection, demonstrated its power to overcome the baggiest of clothes. Everything else that Joey rested his eyes on in the rec room was notable only for not being her—was all the same second-class blah. And yet, when he did steal a glance at her, his brain was too unsettled to even see much. The whole thing was weirdly tiring. There seemed to be no way to arrange his face that wasn't false and self-conscious. He was painfully aware of smirking stupidly at the floor while she and her amazingly unawed sibling bickered about the New York City shopping expedition she intended to make on Friday.

"You can't leave us the Cabriolet," Jonathan said. "Joey and I are go-ing to look like a couple of life partners in that thing."

Jenna's one evident defect was her voice, which was pinched and little-girly. "Yeah, right," she said. "A couple of life partners with jeans hanging halfway down their ass."

"I just don't see why you can't drive the Cabriolet to New York," Jonathan said. "You've driven it there before."

"Because Mom says I can't. Not on a holiday weekend. The Land Cruiser is safer. I'll bring it back on Sunday."

"Are you kidding? The Land Cruiser is a rollover machine. It's totally unsafe."

"Well, you can tell that to Mom. Tell her your freshman car's an unsafe rollover machine and that's why I can't take it to New York."

"Hey." Jonathan turned to Joey. "You want to go to New York for the weekend?"

"Sure!" Joey said.

"Just take the Cabriolet," Jenna said. "It won't hurt you for three days."

"No, this is great," Jonathan said. "We can all go to New York in the Land Cruiser and go shopping. You can help me find some pants that meet your standards."

"Reasons that's a nonstarter?" Jenna said. "Number one, you don't even have any place to stay."

"Why can't we crash with you at Nick's? Isn't he, like, in Singapore?"

"Nick's not going to want a bunch of freshman guys running around his apartment. Plus he might be back by Saturday night."

"Two is not a bunch. This would just be me and my incredibly tidy Minnesotan roommate."

"I am very tidy," Joey assured her.

"No doubt," she said with zero interest, from her pinnacle. Joey's presence nevertheless seemed to complicate her resistance—she couldn't be quite as dismissive to a stranger as she could to her own brother. "I really don't care," she said. "I'll ask Nick. But if he says no, you can't come."

As soon as she went back upstairs, Jonathan presented Joey with a palm to high-five. "New York, New York," he said. "I bet we can crash with Casey's family if Nick ends up being as big a dick as he usually is. They're on the Upper East Side somewhere."

Joey was just stunned by Jenna's beauty. He wandered into the area where she'd stood, which smelled faintly of patchouli. That he might get to spend an entire weekend in her vicinity, through the sheer happenstance of being Jonathan's roommate, felt like some kind of miracle.

"You, too, I see," Jonathan said, shaking his head sadly. "This is the story of my young life."

Joey felt himself reddening. "What I don't get is how you turned out to be so ugly."

"Ha, you know what they say about older parents. My dad was fifty-one when I was born. There was a crucial two years of genetic deterioration. Not every boy gets to be pretty like you."

"I didn't realize you had these feelings."

"What feelings? I only look for prettiness in girls, where it belongs."

"Fuck you, rich kid."

"Pretty boy, pretty boy."

"Fuck you. Let me kick your ass at air hockey."

"Just as long as kicking it is all you want to do."

Tamara's threat notwithstanding, there was blessedly little religious instruction, or invasive parental interaction of any kind, during Joey's stay in McLean. He and Jonathan installed themselves in the basement home theater, which had reclining seats and an eight-foot projection screen, and stayed up until 4 a.m. watching bad TV and casting aspersions on each other's heterosexuality. By the time they roused themselves on Thanksgiving, crowds of relatives were arriving at the house. Since Jonathan was obliged to speak to them, Joey found himself floating through the beautiful rooms like a helium molecule, devoting himself to arranging sight lines that Jenna might pass through or, better yet, alight in. The upcoming excursion to New York, which her boyfriend had surprisingly signed off on, was like money in the bank: he would have, at a minimum, two long car trips to make an impression on her. For now, he wanted only to accustom his eyes to her, to make looking less impossible. She was wearing a demure, high-necked dress, a *friendly* dress, and either was very adept at applying makeup or simply didn't wear much. He took note of her good manners, manifested in her patience with bald-pated uncles and face-lifted aunts who seemed to have a lot to say to her.

Before dinner was served, he slipped away to his bedroom to call St. Paul. Calling Connie was out of the question in his current state; shame about their filthy conversations, curiously absent throughout the fall, was creeping up on him now. His parents were a different matter, however, if only because of the checks of his mother's that he'd been cashing.

His dad answered the phone in St. Paul and spoke to him for no more than two minutes before handing him off to his mother, which Joey took as a kind of betrayal. He actually had a fair amount of respect for his dad—for the consistency of his disapproval; for the strictness of his principles—and he might have had even more if his dad hadn't been so deferential to his mother. Joey could have used some manly backup, but instead his dad kept passing him off to his mom and washing his hands of them.

"Hello, you," she said with a warmth that made him cringe. He immediately resolved to be hard with her, but, as happened so often, she wore him down with her humor and her cascading laugh. Before he knew it, he'd described the entire scene in McLean to her, excluding Jenna.

"A house full of Jews!" she said. "How interesting for you."

"You're a Jew yourself," he said. "And that makes me a Jew, too. And Jessica, too, and Jessica's kids if she has any."

"No, that's only if you've been drinking the Kool-Aid," his mother said. After three months in the East, Joey was able to hear that she had a bit of Minnesota accent. "You see," she said, "I think, when it comes to religion, you're only what you say you are. Nobody else can say it for you."

"But you don't have *any* religion."

"Exactly my point. That was one of the few things that my parents and I agreed on, bless their hearts. That religion is stoopid. Although apparently my sister now disagrees with me, which means that our record of disagreeing about absolutely everything is still unblemished."

"Which sister?"

"Your aunt Abigail. She's apparently deep into the Kabbalah and rediscovering her Jewish roots, such as they are. How do I know this, you ask? Because we got a *chain letter*, or e-mail actually, from her, about the Kabbalah. I thought it was pretty bad form, and so I actually e-mailed her back, to ask her please not to send me any more chain letters, and she e-mailed me back about her Journey."

"I don't even know what the Kabbalah is," Joey said.

"Oh, I'm sure she'd be happy to tell you all about it, if you ever want to be in touch with her. It's very Important and Mystical—I think Madonna's into it, which tells you pretty much all you need to know right there."

"Madonna's Jewish?"

"Yah, Joey, hence her name." His mother laughed at him.

"Well, anyway," he said, "I'm trying to keep an open mind about it. I don't feel like rejecting something I haven't even found out about yet."

"That's right. And who knows? It might even be useful to you."

"It might," he said coolly.

At the very long dinner table, he was seated on the same side as Jenna, which spared him a view of her and allowed him to concentrate on conversing with one of the bald uncles, who assumed that he was Jewish and regaled him with an account of his recent vacation-slash-business-trip in Israel. Joey pretended to be fluent and impressed with much that was utterly foreign to him: the Western Wall and its tunnels, the Tower of David, Masada, Yad Vashem. Delayed-action resentment of his mother, coupled with the fabulousness of the house and his fascination with Jenna and a certain unfamiliar feeling of genuine intellectual curiosity, was making him actually long to be more Jewish—to see what this kind of belonging might be like.

Jonathan and Jenna's father, at the far end of the table, was holding forth on foreign affairs at such commanding length that, little by little, the other conversations petered out. The turkeylike cords in his neck were more noticeable in the flesh than on TV, and it turned out to be the almost shrunken smallness of his skull that made his white, white smile so prominent. The fact that such a wizened person had sired the amazing Jenna seemed to Joey of a piece with his eminence. He spoke of the "new blood libel" that was circulating in the Arab world, the lie about there having been no Jews in the twin towers on 9/11, and of the need, in times of national emergency, to counter evil lies with benevolent half-truths. He spoke of Plato as if he'd personally received enlightenment at his Athenian feet. He referred to members of the president's cabinet by their first names, explaining how "we" had been "leaning on" the president to exploit this unique historical moment to resolve an intractable geopolitical deadlock and radically expand the sphere of freedom. In normal times, he said, the great mass of American public opinion was isolationist and know-nothing, but the terrorist attacks had given "us" a golden opportunity, the first since the end of the Cold War, for "the philosopher" (which philosopher, exactly, Joey wasn't clear on or had missed an earlier reference to) to step in and unite the country behind the mission that his philosophy had revealed as right and necessary. "We have to learn to be comfortable with stretching some facts," he said, with his smile, to an uncle who had mildly challenged him about Iraq's nuclear capabilities. "Our modern media are very blurry shadows on the wall, and the philosopher has to be prepared to manipulate these shadows in the service of a greater truth."

Between Joey's impulse to impress Jenna and its irruption in actual words there was only one short second of free-fall terror. "But how do you know it's the truth?" he called out.

All heads turned to him, and his heart began to pound.

"We never know for certain," Jenna's father said, doing his smile thing. "You're right about that. But when we discover that our understanding of the world, based on decades of careful empirical study by the very best minds, is in striking accordance with the inductive principle of universal human freedom, it's a good indication that our thinking is at least approximately on track."

Joey nodded eagerly, to show his total and profound agreement, and was surprised when, in spite of himself, he persisted: "But it seems like once we start lying about Iraq, we're no better than the Arabs with the lie about no Jews being killed on 9/11."

Jenna's father, not ruffled in the slightest, said, "You're a very bright young man, aren't you?"

Joey couldn't tell if this was supposed to be ironic.

"Jonathan says you're a very fine student," the old man continued gently. "And so I'm guessing you've already had the experience of being frustrated with people who aren't as bright as you are. People who are not only unable but *unwilling* to admit certain truths whose logic is self-evident to you. Who don't even seem to *care* that their logic is bad. Have you never been frustrated that way?"

"But that's because they're free," Joey said. "Isn't that what freedom is for? The right to think whatever you want? I mean, I admit, it's a pain in the ass sometimes."

Around the table, people chuckled at this.

"That's exactly right," Jenna's father said. "Freedom is a pain in the ass. And that's precisely why it's so imperative that we seize the opportunity that's been presented to us this fall. To get a nation of free people to let go of their bad logic and sign on with better logic, by whatever means are necessary."

Unable to bear another second of exposure, Joey nodded even more eagerly. "You're right," he said. "I see, you're right."

Jenna's father went on to unburden himself of further stretched facts and firm opinions that Joey heard hardly a word of. His body was throbbing with the excitement of having spoken up and being heard by Jenna. The feeling he'd misplaced all fall, the feeling of being a player, was coming back to him. When Jonathan stood up from the table, he rose unsteadily and followed him into the kitchen, where they collected enough undrunk wine to fill two sixteen-ounce tumblers for themselves.

"Dude," Joey said, "you can't mix red and white like that."

"It's rosé, dufus," Jonathan said. "Since when are you Mr. Oenophile?"

They took their brimming glasses down to the basement and consumed the wine over air hockey. Joey was still so throbbing that he hardly felt the effects, which proved fortunate when Jonathan's father came downstairs and joined them. "How about a little Cowboy Pool?" he said, rubbing his hands together. "I assume Jonathan's already taught you our house game?"

"Yeah, I totally suck at it," Joey said.

"It's the queen of all pool games, combining the best features of both billiards and pocket billiards," the old man said as he arranged the 1 ball, the 3 ball, and the 5 ball on their appointed spots. Jonathan seemed somewhat mortified by him, which interested Joey, since he tended to assume that only his own parents could truly mortify a person. "We have an additional special house rule that I'm willing to apply to myself tonight. Jonathan? What do you say? The rule is designed to prevent a highly skilled player from parking behind the 5 ball and running up the score. You boys will be allowed to do that, assuming you've mastered putting straight draw on the cue ball, whereas I will be obliged to shoot one billiard or sink one of the other balls each time I sink the 5."

Jonathan rolled his eyes. "Yeah, sounds good, Dad."

"Shall we shag?" his father said, chalking his cue.

Joey and Jonathan looked at each other and snickered explosively. The old man didn't even notice.

It pained Joey to suck so badly at a game, and the effects of the wine became apparent when the old man gave him a few pointers that only made him suck worse. Jonathan, meanwhile, was competing intensely, bearing down with a look of dead seriousness that Joey hadn't seen in him before. During one of his longer runs, his father took Joey aside and asked about his summer plans.

"That's a long way away," Joey said.

"Not so far at all, really. What are your areas of greatest interest?"

"I mostly need to make money, and stay in Virginia. I'm paying my own way through school."

"So Jonathan tells me. It's a remarkable ambition. And forgive me if I'm going too far here, but my wife says you're beginning to develop an interest in your heritage, after not being raised in faith. I don't know if that's at all a factor in your deciding to make your own way in the world, but if it is, I want to congratulate you on thinking for yourself and having the courage to do that. In time, you might even come back to lead your family in their own exploration."

"I'm definitely sorry I never learned anything about it."

The old man shook his head the same disapproving way his wife had. "We have the most marvelous and durable tradition in the world," he said. "I think for a young person today it ought to have a particular appeal, because it's all about personal choice. Nobody tells a Jew what he has to believe. You get to decide all of that for yourself. You can choose your very own apps and features, so to speak."

"Right, interesting," Joey said.

"And what are your other plans? Are you interested in a business career the way everybody else seems to be these days?"

"Yes, definitely. I'm thinking of majoring in econ."

"That's fine. There's nothing wrong with wanting to make money. Now, I didn't have to make my own money, although I don't mind saying I've done a pretty good job of managing what I was given. I owe a lot to my great-grandfather in Cincinnati, who came over here with nothing. He was given an opportunity in this country, which gave him the freedom to make the most of his abilities. That's why I've chosen to spend my life the way I have—to honor that freedom and try to ensure that the next American century be similarly blessed. Nothing wrong with making money, nothing at all. But there has to be something more in your life than that. You have to choose which side you're on, and fight for it."

"Absolutely," Joey said.

"There may be some good-paying summer jobs at the Institute this summer, if you're interested in doing something for your country. Our fund-raising's been off the charts since the attacks. Very gratifying to see. You could think about applying if you're so inclined."

"Definitely!" Joey said. He was sounding to himself like one of Socrates' young interlocutors, whose lines of dialogue, on page after page, consisted of variations on "Yes, unquestionably" and "Undoubtedly it must be so." "That sounds great," he said. "I'll definitely apply."

Putting too much draw on the cue ball, Jonathan scratched unexpectedly, thereby negating all the points he'd accumulated on his run. "Fuck!" he cried, and added, for good measure, "*Fuck!*" He banged his cue on the edge of the table; and there ensued an awkward moment.

"You have to be especially careful when you've run up a big score," his father said.

"I know that, Dad. *I know that.* I was *being* careful. I just got a little distracted by you guys' conversation."

"Joey, your turn?"

What was it about witnessing a friend's meltdown that made him uncontrollably want to smile? He had a wonderful sense of liberation, not having to interact with his own dad in these ways. He could feel more of his good luck returning with each passing moment. For Jonathan's sake, he was glad that he immediately missed his own next shot.

But Jonathan turned pissy on him anyway. After his father, twice victorious, went back upstairs, he began calling Joey a faggot in not-so-funny ways and finally said he didn't think that going to New York with Jenna was such a good idea.

"Why not?" Joey said, stricken.

"I don't know. I just don't feel like it."

"It's going to be awesome. We can try to get into Ground Zero and see what it looks like."

"That whole area's blocked off. You can't see anything."

"I also want to see where they film the *Today* show."

"It's stupid. It's just a window."

"Come on, it's New York. We've got to do this thing."

"Well, so go with Jenna then. That's what you want anyway, isn't it? Go to Manhattan with my sister, and then work for my dad next summer. And my mom's a big horse rider. Maybe you want to ride horses with her, too."

The one bad aspect of Joey's good fortune were the moments when it seemed to come at someone else's expense. Never having experienced envy himself, he was impatient with its manifestations in other people. In high school, more than once, he'd had to terminate friendships with kids who couldn't handle his having so many other friends. His feeling was: fucking grow up already. His friendship with Jonathan, however, was non-terminable, at least for the remainder of the school year, and although Joey was annoyed by his sulking he did keenly understand the pain of being a son.

"So, fine," he said. "We'll stay here. You can show me D.C. You want to do that instead?"

Jonathan shrugged.

"Seriously. Let's hang out in D.C."

Jonathan brooded about this for a while. Then he said, "You had him on the run, man. All that bullshit about the noble lie? You had him on the run, and then suddenly you got this shit-eating grin. You're such a fucking little faggot suck-up."

"Yeah, I didn't see you saying anything, either," Joey said.

"I've already been through it."

"Well then why should I go through it?"

"Because you haven't been through it yet. You haven't earned the right not to. You haven't fucking earned anything."

"Said the kid with the Land Cruiser."

"Look, I don't want to talk about it anymore. I'm going to go do some reading."

"Fine."

"I'll go to New York with you. I don't even care if you sleep with my sister. You probably deserve each other."

"What does that mean?"

"You'll find out."

"Let's just be friends, OK? I don't have to go to New York."

"No, we'll go," Jonathan said. "Pathetically enough, I really don't want to drive that Cabriolet."

Upstairs, in his turkey-smelling bedroom, Joey found a stack of books on the nightstand—Elie Wiesel, Chaim Potok, *Exodus*, *The History of the Jews*—and a note from Jonathan's father: *Some kindling for you. Feel free to keep or pass along. Howard.* Flipping through them, feeling both a deep lack of personal interest and a deepening respect for people who were interested, Joey became angry with his mother all over again. Her disrespect of religion seemed to him just more of her me me me: her competitive Copernican wish to be the sun around which all things revolved. Before he went to sleep, he dialed 411 and got a number for Abigail Emerson in Manhattan.

The next morning, while Jonathan was still sleeping, he called Abigail and introduced himself as her sister's son and said he was coming to New York. In response, his aunt cackled weirdly and asked him if he was good with plumbing.

"Beg pardon?"

"Things are going down but they're not staying down," Abigail said. "It's kind of like me after too much brandy." She proceeded to tell him about the low elevation and antiquated sewers of Greenwich Village, about her super's holiday plans, about the pros and cons of ground-floor courtyard apartments, and about the "pleasure" of returning at midnight on Thanksgiving and finding her neighbors' incompletely disintegrated flushings floating in her bathtub and washed up on the shores of her kitchen sink. "It's all verrrrrrry, very lovely," she said. "The perfect kickoff to a long weekend of no super."

"Well, so, anyway, I thought maybe we could meet up or something," Joey said. He was already having second thoughts about this, but his aunt now became responsive, as if her monologue had been a thing she'd just needed to flush from herself.

"You know," she said, "I've seen pictures of you and your sister. Verrrrrry handsome pictures, in your verrrrrry beautiful house. I think I might even recognize you on the street."

"Uh huh."

"My apartment is unfortunately not so beautiful at the moment. A little fragrant also! But if you'd like to meet me at my favorite café, and be served by the gayest waiter in the Village, who is my personal best male bud, I'd be verrrrry happy to. I can tell you all the things your mother doesn't want you to know about us."

This sounded good to Joey, and they made a date.

For the trip to New York, Jenna brought along a high-school friend, Bethany, whose looks were ordinary only by comparison. The two of them sat in back, where Joey could neither see Jenna nor, between the endless stereo whining of Slim Shady and Jonathan's chanting of his lyrics, make out what she and Bethany were talking about. The only interactions between back and front were Jenna's criticisms of her brother's driving. As if his hostility toward Joey the night before had been transmuted into road rage, Jonathan was tailgating at eighty and muttering abuse at less aggressive drivers; he seemed in general to be reveling in being an asshole. "Thank you for not killing us," Jenna said when the SUV had come to rest in a staggeringly expensive midtown parking garage and the music had blessedly ceased.

The trip soon proved to have all the makings of a bust. Jenna's boyfriend, Nick, shared a rambling, decaying apartment on 54th Street with two other Wall Street trainees who were also gone for the weekend. Joey wanted to see the city, and he wanted even more not to seem to Jenna like some little Eminem-listening juvie, but the living room was equipped with a huge plasma TV and late-model Xbox that Jonathan insisted he immediately join him in enjoying. "See you later, kids," Jenna said as she and Bethany went out to meet up with other friends. Three hours later, when Joey suggested taking a walk before it got too late, Jonathan told him not to be such a faggot.

"What is *wrong* with you?" Joey said.

"No, I'm sorry, what is wrong with *you*? You should have tagged along with Jenna if you wanted to do girl stuff."

Doing girl stuff in fact sounded rather appealing to Joey. He liked girls, he missed their company and the way they talked about things; he missed Connie. "You were the one who said you wanted to go shopping."

"What's the matter, are my pants not tight enough in the butt for you?"

"It also might be nice to get some dinner?"

"Right, somewhere romantic, just the two of us."

"New York pizza? Isn't it supposed to be the world's best pizza?"

"No, that's New Haven."

"OK, a deli then. New York deli. I'm starving."

"So go look in the fridge."

"You go look in the fucking fridge. I'm getting out of here."

"Yeah, fine. Do that."

"Will you be here when I get back? So I can get in?"

"Yes, honey."

With a lump in his throat, a girly nearness to tears, Joey went out into the night. Jonathan's loss of cool was extremely disappointing to him. He was suddenly sensible of his own superior maturity, and as he drifted through the late shopping crowds on Fifth Avenue he considered how he might convey this maturity to Jenna. He bought two Polish sausages from a street vendor and pushed into even thicker crowds at Rockefeller Center and watched the ice skaters and admired the enormous unlit Christmas tree, the stirring floodlit heights of the NBC tower. So he liked doing girl stuff, so what? It didn't make him a wuss. It just made him very lonely. Watching the skaters, feeling homesick for St. Paul, he called up Connie. She was on her shift at Frost's and could stay on the phone only long enough for him to tell her that he missed her, to describe where he was standing, and to say he wished he could show it to her.

"I love you, baby," she said.

"I love you, too."

The next morning, he got his chance with Jenna. She was apparently an early riser and had already been out to buy breakfast when Joey, rising early himself, wandered into the kitchen in a UVA T-shirt and paisley boxers. Finding her reading a book at the kitchen table, he felt pretty much stark-naked.

"I bought some bagels for you and my undeserving brother," she said.

"Thank you," he said, considering whether to go and put some pants on or just keep strutting his stuff. Since she showed no further interest in him, he decided to risk not dressing. But then, as he waited on a toasting bagel and stole glances at her hair and her shoulders and her bare, crossed legs, he began to get a boner. He was about to make his escape to the living room when she looked up and said, "I'm sorry, this book? This book is ungodly boring."

He took cover behind a chair. "What's it about?"

"I thought it was about slavery. Now I'm not even sure what it's about." She showed him two facing pages of dense prose. "The really funny thing? This is the second time I'm reading it. It's on like half the syllabuses at Duke. Syllabi. And I still can't figure out what the actual story is. You know, what actually happens to the characters."

"I read *Song of Solomon* for school last year," Joey said. "I thought it was pretty amazing. It's like the best novel I ever read."

She made a complicated face of indifference toward him and annoyance with her book. He sat down across the table from her, took a bite of bagel and chewed it for a while, chewed it some more, and finally realized that swallowing was going to be an issue. There was no hurry, however, since Jenna was still trying to read.

"What do you think's up with your brother?" he said when he'd managed to get a few bites down.

"What do you mean?"

"He's being kind of a jerk. Kind of immature. Don't you think?"

"Don't ask me. He's *your* friend."

She continued to stare at her book. Her disdainful imperviousness was identical to that of the top-tier girls at Virginia. The only difference was that she was even more attractive to him than those girls, and that he was close enough to her now to smell her shampoo. Underneath the table, in his boxers, his half-mast boner was pointing at her like a Jaguar's hood ornament.

"So what are you doing today?" he said.

She closed her book as if resigning herself to his continued presence. "Shopping," she said. "And there's a party in Brooklyn tonight. What about you?"

"Apparently nothing, since your brother doesn't want to leave the apartment. I have an aunt who I'm supposed to see at four, but that's it."

"I think it's harder for guys," Jenna said. "Being at home. My dad is *amazing*, and I'm fine with that, I'm fine with him being famous. But I think Jonathan always feels like he has to prove something."

"By watching TV for ten hours?"

She frowned and looked directly at Joey, possibly for the first time. "Do you even *like* my brother?"

"No definitely. He's just been weird since Thursday night. Like, the way he was driving yesterday? I thought you might have some insight."

"I think for him the biggest thing is wanting to be liked for his own sake. You know, and not because of who our dad is."

"Right," Joey said. And was inspired to add: "Or who his sister is."

She blushed! A small amount. And shook her head. "I'm not any-body."

"Ha ha ha," he said, blushing as well.

"Well, I'm certainly not like my dad. I don't have any big ideas, or any great ambition. I'm actually quite the selfish little person, when you get right down to it. A hundred acres in Connecticut, some horses and a full-time groom, and maybe a private jet, and I'll be all set."

Joey noted that it had taken no more than one allusion to her beauty to get her to open up and start talking about herself. And once the door had opened even just a millimeter, once he'd slipped through the crack in it, he knew what to do. How to listen and how to understand. It wasn't fake listening or fake understanding, either. It was Joey in Womanland. Before long, in the dirty winter light of the kitchen, as he took instruction from Jenna on how to dress a bagel properly, with lox and onions and capers, he was feeling not greatly more uncomfortable than he would have felt talking with Connie, or his mom, or his grandmother, or Connie's mom. Jenna's beauty was no less dazzling than ever, but his boner entirely subsided. He offered her some nuggets about his family situation, and in return she admitted that her own family wasn't too happy about her boyfriend.

"It's pretty crazy," she said. "I think that's one reason Jonathan wanted to come here, and why he won't leave the apartment. He thinks he's somehow going to interfere with me and Nick. Like if he gets in the way, and hovers around, he can make it stop."

"Why don't they like Nick?"

"Well, for one thing, he's Catholic. And he was varsity lacrosse. He's superbright, but not bright in the way they approve of." Jenna laughed. "I told him about my dad's think tank once, and the next time his frat had a party they put a sign on the keg that said Think Tank. I thought it was pretty hilarious. But it gives you an idea."

"Do you get drunk a lot?"

"No, I have the capacity of a flea. Nick stopped drinking, too, once he started working. He has like one Jack and Coke per week now. He's totally focused on getting ahead. He was the first person in his family to go to a four-year college, total opposite of my family, where you're an underachiever if you only have one PhD."

"And he's nice to you?"

She looked away with a shadow of something in her face. "I feel unbelievably safe with him. Like, I was thinking, if we'd been in the towers on September 11, even on a high floor, he would have found a way to get us out. He would have gotten us through, I just have that feeling."

"There were a lot of guys like that at Cantor Fitzgerald," Joey said. "Very tough traders. And they didn't get out."

"Well then they weren't like Nick," she said.

Seeing her close her mind like this, Joey wondered how hard he would have to make himself, and how much money he would have to earn, to even enter the running for the likes of her. His dick, in his boxers, bestirred itself again, as if to declare its upness for the challenge. But the softer parts of him, his heart and his brain, were awash in hopelessness at the enormity of it.

"I think I might go down to Wall Street and check it out today," he said.

"Everything's closed on Saturday."

"I just want to see what it looks like, since I might end up working there."

"No offense?" Jenna said, reopening her book. "You seem way too nice for that."

Four weeks later, Joey was back in Manhattan, housesitting for his aunt Abigail. All fall, he'd been stressing about where to stay during his Christmas vacation, since his two competing homes in St. Paul disqualified each other, and since three weeks was far too long to impose on the family of a new college friend. He'd vaguely planned on staying with one of his better high-school friends, which would have positioned him to pay separate visits to his parents and the Monaghans, but it turned out that Abigail was going to Avignon for the holidays to attend an international miming workshop and was worrying, herself, when she met him on Thanksgiving weekend, about who would stay in her Charles Street apartment and see to the complex dietary requirements of her cats, Tigger and Piglet.

The meeting with his aunt had been interesting, if one-sided. Abigail, though younger than his mother, looked considerably older in all respects except her clothes, which were tarty-teenage. She smelled like cigarettes, and she had a heartrending way of eating her slice of chocolate-mousse cake, parceling out each small bite for intensive savoring, as if it were the best thing that was going to happen to her that day. Such few questions as she asked Joey she answered for him before he could get a word in. Mostly she delivered a monologue, with ironic commentary and self-conscious interjections, that was like a train that he was permitted to hop onto and ride for a while, supplying his own context and guessing at many of the references. In her nattering, she seemed to him a sad cartoon version of his mother, a warning of what she might become if she wasn't careful.

Apparently, to Abigail, the mere fact of Joey's existence was a reproach that necessitated a lengthy accounting of her life. The traditional marriage-babies-house thing was not for her, she said, and neither was the shallow commercialized world of conventional theater, with its degrading rigged open calls and its casting directors who only wanted this year's model and had not the airy-fairiest notion of originality of expression, and neither was the world of stand-up, which she'd wasted a verrrrry long time trying to break into, working up great material about the *truth* of American suburban childhood, before realizing it was all just testosterone and potty humor. She denigrated Tina Fey and Sarah Silverman exhaustively and then extolled the genius of several male "artists" whom Joey decided must be mimes or clowns and with whom she declared herself lucky to be in ever-increasing contact, albeit still mainly via workshops. As she talked on and on, he found himself admiring her determination to survive without success of the sort still plausibly available to him. She was so dotty and self-involved that he was spared the annoyance of feeling guilty and could go straight to compassion. He perceived that, as the representative not only of his own but of her sister's superior good fortune, he could do his aunt no greater kindness than to let her justify herself to him, and to promise to come and see her perform at his earliest opportunity. For this she rewarded him with the housesitting offer.

His first days in the city, when he was going from store to store with his hall mate Casey, were like hyper-vivid continuations of the urban dreams he was having all night. Humanity coming at him from every direction. Andean musicians piping and drumming in Union Square. Solemn firefighters nodding to the crowd assembled by a 9/11 shrine outside a station house. A pair of fur-coated ladies ballsily appropriating a cab that Casey had hailed outside Bloomingdale's. Très hot middle-school girls wearing jeans under their miniskirts and slouching on the subway with their legs wide open. Cornrowed ghetto kids in ominous jumbo parkas, National Guard troops patrolling Grand Central with highly advanced weapons. And the Chinese grandmother hawking DVDs of films that hadn't even opened yet, the break-dancer who ripped a muscle or a tendon and sat rocking in pain on the floor of the 6 train, the insistent saxophone player to whom Joey gave five dollars to help him get to his gig, despite Casey's warning that he was being conned: each encounter was like a poem he instantly memorized.

Casey's parents lived in an apartment with an elevator that opened directly into it, a must-have feature, Joey decided, if he ever made it big in New York. He joined them for dinner on both Christmas Eve and Christmas, thereby shoring up the lies he'd told his parents about where he was staying for the holidays. Casey and his family were leaving for a ski trip in the morning, however, and Joey knew that he was wearing thin his welcome in any case. When he returned to Abigail's stale, cluttered apartment and found that Piglet and/or Tigger had vomited in several locations, in punitive feline protest of his long day's absence, he came up against the strangeness and dumbness of his plan to spend two entire weeks on his own.

He immediately made everything even worse by speaking to his mother and admitting that some of his plans had "fallen through" and he was housesitting for her sister "instead."

"In Abigail's apartment?" she said. "By yourself? Without her even speaking to me? In New York City? By yourself?"

"Yep," Joey said.

"I'm sorry," she said, "you have to tell her that's not acceptable. Tell her she has to call me right away. Tonight. Right away. Immediately. Non-optional."

"It's way too late for that. She's in France. It's OK, though. This is a very safe neighborhood."

But his mother wasn't listening. She was having words with his father, words Joey couldn't make out but which sounded somewhat hysterical. And then his dad was on the line.

"Joey? Listen to me. Are you there?"

"Where else would I be?"

"Listen to me. If you don't have the personal decency to come and spend a few days with your mother in a house that's meant so much to her and that you're never going to set foot in again, that's fine with me. That was your own terrible decision that you can repent at your leisure. And the stuff you left in your room, which we were hoping you'd come and deal with—we'll just give it to Goodwill, or let the garbagemen haul it away. That's your loss, not ours. But to be on your own in a city that you're too young to be on your own in, a city that's repeatedly been attacked by terrorists, and not just for a night or two but for *weeks*, is a recipe for making your mother anxious the entire time."

"Dad, it's a totally safe neighborhood. It's Greenwich Village."

"Well, you've ruined her holiday. And you're going to ruin her last days in this house. I don't know why I keep expecting more of you at this point, but you are being *brutally selfish* to a person who loves you more than you can even know."

"Why can't she say it herself, then?" Joey said. "Why do you have to say it? How do I even know it's true?"

"If you had one speck of imagination, you'd know it's true."

"Not if she never says it herself! If you've got a problem with me, why don't you tell me what *your* problem is, instead of always talking about her problems?"

"Because, frankly, I'm not as worried as she is," his father said. "I don't think you're as smart as you think you are, I don't think you're aware of all the dangers in the world. But I do think you're pretty smart and know how to take care of yourself. If you ever did get into trouble, I would hope we'd be the first people you'd call. Otherwise, you've made your choice in life, and there's nothing I can do about it."

"Well—thanks," Joey said with only partial sarcasm.

"Don't thank me. I have very little respect for what you're doing. I'm just recognizing that you're eighteen years old and free to do what you want. What I'm talking about is my personal disappointment that a child of ours can't find it in his heart to be kinder to his mother."

"*Why don't you ask her why not?*" Joey countered savagely. "*She knows why not!* She fucking *knows*, Dad. Since you're so wonderfully concerned about her happiness, and all, why don't you ask *her*, instead of bothering *me?*"

"Don't talk to me that way."

"Well then don't talk to *me* that way."

"All right, then, I won't."

His father seemed glad to let the subject drop, and Joey was also glad. He relished feeling cool and in control of his life, and it was disturbing to discover that there was this other thing in him, this reservoir of rage, this complex of family feelings that could suddenly explode and take control of him. The angry words he'd spoken to his father had felt pre-formed, as if there were an aggrieved second self inside him 24/7, ordinarily invisible but clearly fully sentient and ready to vent itself, at a moment's notice, in the form of sentences independent of his volition. It made him wonder who his real self was; and this was very disturbing.

"If you change your mind," his father said when they'd exhausted their limited supplies of Christmas chitchat, "I'm more than happy to buy you a plane ticket so you can come out here for a few days. It would mean the world to your mother. And to me, too. I would like that myself."

"Thanks," Joey said, "but, you know, I can't. I've got the cats."

"You can put them in a kennel, your aunt will be none the wiser. I'll pay for that, too."

"OK, maybe. Probably not, but maybe."

"All right, then, Merry Christmas," his father said. "Mom says Merry Christmas, too."

Joey heard her calling it in the background. *Why*, exactly, did she not get back on the line and say it to him directly? It seemed pretty damning of her. Another useless admission of her guilt.

Though Abigail's apartment wasn't tiny, there wasn't one square inch of it unoccupied by Abigail. The cats patrolled it like her plenipotentiaries, depositing hair everywhere. Her bedroom closet was densely packed with pants and sweaters in messy stacks that bunched up the hanging coats and dresses, and her drawers were unopenably stuffed. Her CDs were all unlistenable chanteuses and New Age burble, shelved in double rows and wedged sideways into every chink. Even her books were occupied with Abigail, covering topics like Flow, creative visualization, and the conquering of self-doubt. There was also all manner of mystical accessories, not just Judaica but Eastern incense burners and elephant-headed statuettes. The one thing there wasn't much in the way of was food. It was now occurring to Joey, as he paced the kitchen, that unless he wanted to eat pizza three times a day he would actually have to go to a grocery store and shop and cook for himself. Abigail's own food supplies consisted of rice cakes, forty-seven forms of chocolate and cocoa, and instant ramen noodles of the sort that satisfied him for ten minutes and then left him hungry in a new, gnawing way.

He thought of the spacious house on Barrier Street, he thought of his mother's outstanding cooking, he thought of caving in and accepting his father's offer of a plane ticket, but he was determined not to give his hidden self more opportunities to vent itself, and his only option for not continuing to think about St. Paul was to go to Abigail's brass bed and jerk off, and then to jerk off again while the cats yowled reproachfully outside the bedroom door, and then, still not satisfied, to boot up his aunt's computer, since he couldn't get internet on his own computer here, and seek out porn to jerk off to some more. In the way of such things, each free site he happened upon was linked to an even raunchier and more compelling one. Eventually one of these better sites started generating pop-up windows like some Sorcerer's Apprentice nightmare; it got so bad that he had to shut down the computer. Rebooting impatiently, his abused and sticky dick going limp in his hand, he found the system commandeered by hard-drive-overloading, keyboard-freezing alien software. Never mind that he'd infected his aunt's computer. Right now he couldn't get the one thing in the world he wanted, which was to see one more pretty female face distended with ecstasy, so that he could come for a fifth time and try to get a little sleep. He shut his eyes and stroked himself, struggling to summon up enough remembered images to get the job done, but the meowing of the cats was too distracting. He went to the kitchen and cracked open a bottle of brandy that he hoped wouldn't be too expensive to replace.

Awakening hungover late the next morning, he smelled what he hoped was just cat shit but proved, when he ventured into the cramped and infernally overheated bathroom, to be raw sewage. He called the super, Mr. Jiménez, who arrived two hours later with a wheeled grocery basket filled with plumbing tools.

"This ol' building gotta lotta problems," Mr. Jiménez said, shaking his head fatalistically. He told Joey to be sure to lower the bathtub drain stopper and firmly plug the sinks when he wasn't using them. These instructions were in fact on Abigail's list, along with complicated protocols of cat nourishment, but Joey, the day before, in his rush to escape the place and get to Casey's, had forgotten to follow them.

"Lotta, lotta problems," Mr. Jiménez said, using a plunger to nudge West Village waste back down the drain.

As soon as Joey was alone again and confronting afresh the specter of two weeks of solitude and brandy abuse and/or masturbation, he called Connie and told her he would pay for her bus ticket if she would come out and stay with him. She instantly agreed, except for the part about his paying; and his vacation was saved.

He hired a geek to fix his aunt's computer and reconfigure his own, he spent sixty dollars on prepared foods at Dean & DeLuca, and when he went to Port Authority and met Connie at her gate he didn't think he'd ever been happier to see her. In the previous month, mentally comparing her to the incomparable Jenna, he'd lost sight of how fine she was herself, in her slender, economical, ardent way. She was wearing an unfamiliar peacoat and walked right up to him and put her face against his face and her wide-open eyes against his eyes, as if pressing herself into a mirror. Some drastic all-organ melting occurred inside him. He was about to get laid about forty times, but it was more than that. It was as if the bus station and all the low-income travelers flowing around the two of them were equipped with Brightness and Color controls that were radically lowered by the mere presence of this girl he'd known forever. Everything seemed faint and far away as he led her through passages and halls that he'd seen in living color not thirty minutes earlier.

In the hours that followed, Connie made several somewhat alarming disclosures. The first came while they were riding the subway down to Charles Street and he asked her how she'd managed to get so much time off at the restaurant—whether she'd found people to cover her shifts.

"No, I just quit," she said.

"You *quit*? Isn't this sort of a bad time of year to do that to them?"

She shrugged. "You needed me here. I told you all you ever have to do is call me."

His alarm at this disclosure restored the brightness and color of the subway car. It was like the way his brain on pot would jolt back to present awareness after being lost in a deep stoned reverie: he could see that the other subway riders were leading their lives, pursuing their goals, and that he needed to take care to do this, too. Not get sucked too far into something he couldn't control.

Mindful of one of their crazier phone-sex episodes, in which the lips of her vagina had opened so fantastically wide that they covered his entire face, and his tongue was so long that its tip could reach her vagina's inscrutable inner end, he had shaved very carefully before leaving for Port

Authority. Now that the two of them were together in the flesh, however, these fantasies revealed their absurdity and were disagreeable to recall. In the apartment, instead of taking Connie straight to bed, as he'd done on the weekend in Virginia, he turned on the TV and checked the score of a college bowl game that meant nothing to him. It then seemed a matter of great urgency to check his e-mail and see if any of his friends had written in the last three hours. Connie sat with the cats on the sofa and waited patiently while his computer powered up.

"By the way," she said, "your mom says to say hi."

"*What?*"

"Your mom says hi. She was out chipping ice when I was leaving. She saw me with my bag and asked where I was going."

"And you *told* her?"

Connie's surprise was innocent. "Was I not supposed to? She told me to have a good time and to say hi to you."

"Sarcastically?"

"I don't know. Maybe it was, come to think of it. I was just happy she spoke to me at all. I know she hates me. But then I thought maybe she's finally starting to get used to me."

"I doubt it."

"I'm sorry if I said the wrong thing. You know I'd never say the wrong thing if I knew it was wrong. You know that, don't you?"

Joey stood up from his computer, trying not to be angry. "It's OK," he said. "It's not your fault. Or only a little bit your fault."

"Baby, are you ashamed of me?"

"No."

"Are you ashamed of the stuff we said on the phone? Is that what this is?"

"No."

"I actually am, a little bit. Some of it was pretty sick. I'm not sure I need to do that anymore."

"You were the one who started it!"

"I know. I know, I know. But you can't blame me for everything. You can only blame me for half of it."

As if to acknowledge the truth of this, he ran to where she was sitting on the sofa and knelt down at her feet, bowing his head and resting his hands on her legs. Up close to her jeans like this, her best tight jeans, he thought of the long hours she'd sat on a Greyhound bus while he was watching second-rate college bowl games and talking on the phone with friends. He was in trouble, he was falling into some unanticipated fissure in the ordinary world, and he couldn't bear to look up at her face. She rested her hands on his head and offered no resistance when, by and by, he pushed forward and pressed his face into her denim-sheathed zipper. "It's OK," she knew to say, stroking his hair. "It's going to be OK, baby. Everything's going to be OK."

In his gratitude, he peeled down her jeans and rested his closed eyes against her underpants, and then these, too, he pulled down so he could press his shaved lip and chin into her scratchy hair, which he noticed that she'd trimmed for him. He could feel one of the cats clambering onto his feet, seeking attention. Pussy, pussy.

"I just want to stay here for about three hours," he said, breathing her smell.

"You can stay there all night," she said. "I have no plans."

But then his telephone rang in his pants pocket. Taking it out to shut it off, he saw his old St. Paul number and felt like smashing the phone in his anger at his mother. He spread Connie's legs and attacked her with his tongue, delving and delving, trying to fill himself with her.

The third and most alarming of her disclosures came during a post-coital interlude at some later evening hour. Hitherto absent neighbors were tromping on the floor above the bed; the cats were yowling bitterly outside the door. Connie was telling him about the SAT, which he'd forgotten she was even going to take, and about her surprise at how much easier the real questions had been than the practice questions in her study books. She was feeling emboldened to apply to schools within a few hours of Charlottesville, including Morton College, which wanted midwestern students for geographical diversity and which she now thought she could get into.

This seemed all wrong to Joey. "I thought you were going to go to the U.," he said.

"I still might," she said. "But then I started thinking how much nicer it would be to be closer to you, so we could see each other on weekends. I mean, assuming everything goes well and we still want to. Don't you think that would be nice?"

Joey untangled his legs from hers, trying to get some clarity. "Definitely maybe," he said. "But, you know, private schools are incredibly expensive."

This was true, Connie said. But Morton offered financial aid, and she'd spoken to Carol about her educational trust fund, and Carol had admitted that there was still a lot of money in it.

"Like how much?" Joey said.

"Like a lot. Like seventy-five thousand. It might be enough for three years if I get financial aid. And then there's the twelve thousand that I've saved, and I can work summers."

"That's great," Joey compelled himself to say.

"I was just going to wait until I turned twenty-one, and take the cash. But then I thought about what you said, and I saw you were right about getting a good education."

"If you went to the U., though," Joey said, "you could get an education and still have the cash when you were done."

Upstairs, a television began to bark, and the tromping continued.

"It sounds like you don't want me near you," Connie said neutrally, without reproach, just stating a fact.

"No, no," he said. "Not at all. That might potentially be great. I'm just thinking practically."

"I already can't stand being in that house. And then Carol's going to have her babies, and it's going to get even worse. I can't be there anymore."

Not for the first time, he experienced an obscure resentment of her father. The man had been dead for a number of years now, and Connie had never had a relationship with him and rarely even alluded to his existence, but to Joey this had somehow made him even more of a male rival. He was the man who'd been there first. He'd abandoned his daughter and paid off Carol with a low-rent house, but his money had continued to flow and pay for Connie's Catholic schooling. He was a presence in her life that had nothing to do with Joey, and though Joey ought to have been glad that she had other resources besides himself—that he didn't have total responsibility for her—he kept succumbing to moral disapproval of the father, who seemed to Joey the source of all that was amoral in Connie herself, her strange indifference to rules and conventions, her boundless capacity for idolatrous love, her irresistible intensity. And now, on top of all that, Joey resented the father for making her far better off financially than he himself was. That she didn't care about money even one percent as much as he did only made it worse.

"Do something new to me," she said into his ear.

"That TV is really bothering me."

"Do the thing we talked about, baby. We can both listen to the same music. I want to feel you in my ass."

He forgot about the TV, the blood in his head drowned it out as he did what she had asked for. After the new threshold had been crossed, its resistances negotiated, its distinctive satisfactions noted, he went and washed himself in Abigail's bathroom and fed the cats and lingered in the living room, feeling the need to establish some distance, however feebly and belatedly. He roused his computer from its sleep, but there was only one new e-mail. It was from an unfamiliar address at duke.edu and had the subject header in town? Not until he'd opened it and begun reading did he fully comprehend that it had come from Jenna. Had been typed, character by character, by Jenna's privileged fingers.

> hello mr bergland. jonathan tells me you're in the big city, as am i. who knew how many football games there are to watch and how much money young bankers bet on them? not i, said the fly. you may still be doing christmas-y things like your blond protestant progenitors, but nick says to come over if you have questions about wall st, he's willing to answer them. i suggest you act now while his generous mood (and vacation!) lasts. apparently even goldman shuts down this time of year, who knew. your friend, jenna.

He read the message five times before it began to lose its savor. It seemed to him as clean and fresh as he was feeling dirty and red-eyed. Jenna was being either exceptionally thoughtful or, if she was trying to rub his nose in her tightness with Nick, exceptionally mean. Either way, he could see that he'd succeeded in making an impression on her.

Pot smoke came slipping from the bedroom, followed by Connie, as nude and light-footed as the cats. Joey closed the computer and took a hit from the joint that she held up to his face, and then another hit, and then another, and another, and another, and another, and another.

# THE NICE MAN'S ANGER

L ate on a dismal afternoon in March, in cold and greasy drizzle, Walter rode with his assistant, Lalitha, up from Charleston into the mountains of southern West Virginia. Although Lalitha was a fast and somewhat reckless driver, Walter had come to prefer the anxiety of being her passenger to the judgmental anger that consumed him when he was at the wheel—the seemingly inescapable sense that, of all the drivers on the road, only he was traveling at exactly the right speed, only he was striking an appropriate balance between too punctiliously obeying traffic rules and too dangerously flouting them. In the last two years, he'd spent a lot of angry hours on the roads of West Virginia, tailgating the idiotic slowpokes and then slowing down himself to punish the rude tailgaters, ruthlessly defending the inner lane of interstates from assholes trying to pass him on the right, passing on the right himself when some fool or cellphone yakker or sanctimonious speed-limit enforcer clogged the inner lane, obsessively profiling and psychoanalyzing the drivers who refused to use their turn signals (almost always youngish men for whom the use of blinkers was apparently an affront to their masculinity, the compromised state of which was already manifest in the compensatory gigantism of their pickups and SUVs), experiencing murderous hatred of the lane-violating coal-truck drivers who caused fatal accidents literally once a week in West Virginia, impotently blaming the corrupt state legislators who refused to lower the coal-truck weight limit below 110,000 pounds despite bounteous evidence of the havoc they wreaked, muttering "Unbelievable! Unbelievable!" when a driver ahead of him braked for a green light and then accelerated through yellow and left him stranded at red, boiling while he waited *a full minute* at intersections with no cross traffic visible *for miles*, and painfully swallowing, for Lalitha's sake, the invective he yearned to vent when stymied by a driver refusing to make a legal right turn on red: "Hello? Get a clue? The world consists of more than just you! Other people have reality! Learn to drive! Hello!" Better the adrenaline rush of Lalitha's flooring the gas to pass uphill-struggling trucks than the stress on his cerebral arteries of taking the wheel himself and remaining stuck behind those trucks. This way, he could look out at the gray matchstick Appalachian woods and the mining-ravaged ridges and direct his anger at problems more worthy of it.

Lalitha was in buoyant spirits as they sailed in their rental car up the big fifteen-mile grade on I-64, a phenomenally expensive piece of federal pork brought home by Senator Byrd. "I am so ready to celebrate," she said. "Will you take me celebrating tonight?"

"We'll see if there's a decent restaurant in Beckley," Walter said, "although I'm afraid it's not likely."

"Let's get drunk! We can go to the best place in town and have martinis."

"Absolutely. I will buy you one giant-assed martini. More than one, if you want."

"No but you, too, though," she said. "Just once. Make one exception, for the occasion."

"I think a martini might honestly kill me at this point in my life."

"One light beer, then. I'll have three martinis, and you can carry me to my room."

Walter didn't like it when she said things like this. She didn't know what she was saying, she was just a high-spirited young woman—just, actually, the brightest ray of light in his entire life these days—and didn't see that physical contact between employer and employee shouldn't be a joking matter.

"Three martinis would certainly give new meaning to the word 'headache ball' tomorrow morning," he said in lame reference to the demolition they were driving up to Wyoming County to witness.

"When was the last time you had a drink?" Lalitha said.

"Never. I've never had a drink."

"Not even in high school?"

"Never."

"Walter, that's incredible! You have to try it! It's so fun to drink sometimes. One beer won't make you an alcoholic."

"That's not what I'm worried about," he said, wondering, as he spoke, if this was true. His father and his older brother, who together had been the bane of his youth, were alcoholics, and his wife, who was fast becoming the bane of his middle age, had alcoholic proclivities. He'd always understood his own strict sobriety in terms of opposition to them—first, of wanting to be as unlike his dad and brother as possible, and then later of wanting to be as unfailingly kind to Patty as she, drunk, could be unkind to him. It was one of the ways that he and Patty had learned to get along: he always sober, she sometimes drunk, neither of them *ever* suggesting that the other change.

"What are you worried about, then?" Lalitha said.

"I guess I'm worried about changing something that's worked perfectly well for me for forty-seven years. If it's not broke, why fix it?"

"Because it's fun!" She jerked the wheel of the rental car to pass a semi wallowing in its own spray. "I'm going to order you a beer and make you take at least one sip to celebrate."

The northern hardwood forest south of Charleston was even now, on the eve of the equinox, a dour tapestry of grays and blacks. In another week or two, warm air from the south would arrive to green these woods, and a month after that those songbirds hardy enough to migrate from the tropics would fill them with their song, but gray winter seemed to Walter the northern forest's true native state. Summer merely an accident of grace that annually befell it.

In Charleston, earlier in the day, he and Lalitha and their local attorneys had formally presented the Cerulean Mountain Trust's industry partners, Nardone and Blasco, with the documents they needed to commence demolition of Forster Hollow and open up fourteen thousand acres of future warbler preserve for mountaintop removal. Representatives of Nardone and Blasco had then signed the towers of paper that Trust attorneys had been preparing for the last two years, officially committing the coal companies to a package of reclamation agreements and rights transfers that, taken together, would ensure that the mined-out land remain forever "wild." Vin Haven, the Trust's board chairman, had been "present" via teleconferencing and later called Walter directly on his cell to congratulate him. But Walter was feeling the opposite of celebratory. He'd finally succeeded in enabling the obliteration of dozens of sweet wooded hilltops and scores of miles of clear-running, biotically rich Class III, IV, and V streams. To achieve even this, Vin Haven had had to sell off $20 million in mineral rights, elsewhere in the state, to gas drillers poised to rape the land, and then hand over the proceeds to further parties whom Walter didn't like. And all for what? For an endangered-species "stronghold" that you could cover with a postage stamp on a road-atlas map of West Virginia.

Walter felt, himself, in his anger and disappointment with the world, like the gray northern woods. And Lalitha, who'd been born in the warmth of southern Asia, was the sunny person who brought a momentary kind of summer to his soul. The only thing he felt like celebrating tonight was that, having "succeeded" in West Virginia, they could now plunge forward with their overpopulation initiative. But he was mindful of his assistant's youth and hated to dampen her spirits.

"All right," he said. "I will try a beer, once. In your honor."

"No, Walter, in *your* honor. This was all your doing."

He shook his head, knowing she was specifically wrong about this. Without her warmth and charm and courage, the entire deal with Nardone and Blasco would probably have fallen through. It was true that he'd supplied the big ideas; but big ideas were all he seemed to have. Lalitha was in every other way the driver now. She was wearing a nylon shell, its thrown-back hood a basket filled with her lustrous black hair, over the pin-striped suit she'd put on for that morning's formalities. Her hands were at ten and two o'clock on the steering wheel, her wrists bare, her silver bracelets fallen down beneath the cuffs of her shell. Myriad were the things that Walter hated about modernity in general and car culture in particular, but the confidence of young women drivers, the autonomy they'd achieved in the last hundred years, was not among them. Gender equality, as expressed in the pressure of Lalitha's neat foot on the gas pedal, made him glad to be alive in the twenty-first century.

The most difficult problem he'd had to solve for the Trust had been what to do with the two hundred or so families, most of them very poor, who owned houses or trailers on small or smallish parcels of land within the Warbler Park's proposed boundaries. Some of the men still worked in the coal industry, either underground or as drivers, but most were out of a job and passed their time with guns and internal-combustion engines, supplementing their families' diets with game shot deeper in the hills and carried out on ATVs. Walter had moved quickly to buy out as many families as possible before the Trust attracted publicity; he'd paid as little as $250 an acre for certain hillside tracts. But when his attempts to woo the local environmentalist community backfired, and a scarily motivated activist named Jocelyn Zorn began to campaign against the Trust, there were still more than a hundred families holding out, most of them in the valley of Nine Mile Creek, which led up to Forster Hollow.

Excepting the problem of Forster Hollow, Vin Haven had found the perfect sixty-five thousand acres for the core reserve. The surface rights of ninety-eight percent of it were in the hands of just three corporations, two of them faceless and economically rational holding companies, the third wholly owned by a family named Forster which had fled the state more than a century ago and was now comfortably dissipating itself in coastal affluence. All three companies were managing the land for certified forestry and had no reason not to sell it to the Trust at a fair market rate. There was also, near the center of Haven's Hundred, an enormous, vaguely hourglass-shaped collection of very rich coal seams. Until now, nobody had mined these fourteen thousand acres, because Wyoming County was so remote and so hilly, even for West Virginia. One bad, narrow road, useless for coal trucks, wound up into the hills along Nine Mile Creek; at the top of the valley, situated near the hourglass's pinch point, was Forster Hollow and the clan and friends of Coyle Mathis.

Over the years, Nardone and Blasco had each tried and failed to deal with Mathis, earning his abiding animosity for their trouble. Indeed, a major piece of bait that Vin Haven had offered the coal companies, during the initial negotiations, was a promise to rid them of the problem of Coyle. "It's part of the magic synergy we got going here," Haven had told Walter. "We're a fresh player that Mathis's got no reason to hold a grudge against. Nardone in particular I bargained way down on the reclamation front by promising to take Mathis off its hands. A little bit of goodwill I found lying by the side of the road, simply by virtue of me not being Nardone, turns out to be worth a couple million."

If only!

Coyle Mathis embodied the pure negative spirit of backcountry West Virginia. He was consistent in disliking absolutely everybody. Being the enemy of Mathis's enemy only made you another of his enemies. Big Coal, the United Mine Workers, environmentalists, all forms of government, black people, meddling white Yankees: he hated all equally. His philosophy of life was *Back the fuck off or live to regret it.* Six generations of surly Mathises had been buried on the steep creek-side hill that would be among the first sites blasted when the coal companies came in. (Nobody had warned Walter about the cemetery problem in West Virginia when he took the job with the Trust, but he'd sure found out about it in a hurry.)

Knowing a thing or two about omnidirectional anger himself, Walter might still have managed to bring Mathis around if the man hadn't reminded him so much of his own father. His stubborn, self-destructive spite. Walter had prepared a fine package of attractive offers by the time he and Lalitha, after receiving no response to their numerous friendly letters, had driven the dusty road up the Nine Mile valley, uninvited, on a hot bright morning in July. He was willing to give the Mathises and their neighbors as much as $1,200 an acre, plus free land in a reasonably nice hollow on the southern margin of the preserve, plus relocation costs, plus state-of-the-art exhumation and reburial of all Mathis bones. But Coyle Mathis didn't even wait to hear the details. He said, "No, N-O," and added that he intended to be buried in the family cemetery and no man was going to stop him. And suddenly Walter was sixteen again and dizzy with anger. Anger not only with Mathis, for his lack of manners and good sense, but also, paradoxically, with Vin Haven, for pitting him against a man whose economic irrationality he at some level recognized and admired. "I'm sorry," he said as he stood profusely sweating on a rutted track, in hot sunshine, by the side of a junk-strewn yard that Mathis had pointedly not invited him to enter, "but that is just *stupid.*"

Lalitha, beside him, holding a briefcase full of documents that they'd imagined Mathis might actually sign, cleared her throat in explosive regret for this deplorable word.

Mathis, who was a lean and surprisingly handsome man in his late fifties, directed a delighted smile up at the green, insect-buzzing heights that surrounded them. One of his dogs, a whiskery mutt with a demented physiognomy, began to growl. "Stupid!" Mathis said. "That's a funny word to be using, mister. You almost done made my day there. Not every day I get called stupid. You might say people around here know better'n that."

"Look, I'm sure you're a very smart man," Walter said. "I was referring to—"

"I reckon I'm smart enough to count to ten," Mathis said. "How about you, sir? You look like you got some education. You know how to count to ten?"

"I, in fact, know how to count to twelve hundred," Walter said, "and I know how to multiply that by four hundred and eighty, and how to add two hundred thousand to the product. And if you would just take one minute to listen—"

"My question," Mathis said, "is can you do it backwards? Here, I'll get you started. Ten, nine . . ."

"Look, I'm very sorry I used the word stupid. The sun's a little bright out here. I didn't mean—"

"Eight, seven . . ."

"Maybe we'll come back another time," Lalitha said. "We can leave you some materials that you can read at your leisure."

"Oh, y'all reckon I can read, do you?" Mathis was beaming at them. All three of his dogs were growling now. "I believe I'm at six. Or was it five? Stupid old me, I done forgot already."

"Look," Walter said, "I sincerely apologize if I—"

"Four three two!"

The dogs, themselves apparently rather intelligent, advanced with flattened ears.

"We'll come back," Walter said, hastily retreating with Lalitha.

"I'll shoot your car if you do!" Mathis called after them merrily.

All the way back down the terrible road to the state highway, Walter loudly cursed his own stupidity and his inability to control his anger, while Lalitha, ordinarily a font of praise and reassurance, sat pensively in the passenger seat, brooding about what to do next. It was not an overstatement to say that, without Mathis's cooperation, all the other work they'd done to secure Haven's Hundred would be for naught. At the bottom of the dusty valley, Lalitha delivered her assessment: "He needs to be treated like an important man."

"He's a two-bit sociopath," Walter said.

"Be that as it may," she said—and she had a particularly charming Indian way of pronouncing this favorite phrase of hers, a clipped lilt of practicality that Walter never tired of hearing—"we're going to need to flatter his sense of importance. He needs to be the savior, not the sellout."

"Yeah, unfortunately, a sellout is the only thing we're asking him to be."

"Maybe if I went back up and talked to some of the women."

"It's a fucking patriarchy up here," Walter said. "Haven't you noticed?"

"No, Walter, the women are very strong. Why don't you let me talk to some of them?"

"This is a nightmare. A *nightmare*."

"Be that as it may," Lalitha said again, "I wonder if I should stay behind and try to talk to people."

"He's already said no to the offer. Categorically."

"We'll need a better offer, then. You'll have to talk to Mr. Haven about a better offer. Go back to Washington and talk to him. It's probably just as well if you don't go back up the hollow. But maybe I won't seem so threatening by myself."

"I can't let you do that."

"I'm not afraid of dogs. He'd set the dogs on you, but not on me, I don't think."

"This is just hopeless."

"Maybe, maybe not," Lalitha said.

Leaving aside her sheer bravery, as an unaccompanied dark-skinned woman, slight of build and alluring of feature, in returning to a poor-white place where she'd already been threatened with physical harm, Walter was struck, in the months that followed, by the fact that it was she, the suburban daughter of an electrical engineer, and not he, the small-town son of an angry drunk, who'd effected the miracle in Forster Hollow.

Not only did Walter lack the common touch; his entire personality had been formed in opposition to the backcountry he'd come from. Mathis, with his poor-white unreason and resentments, had offended Walter's very being: had blinded him with rage. Whereas Lalitha, having no experience with the likes of Mathis, had been able to go back with an open mind and a sympathetic heart. She'd approached the proud country poor the way she drove a car, as if no harm could possibly come to a person of such cheer and goodwill; and the proud country poor had granted her the respect they'd withheld from angry Walter. Her success made him feel inferior and unworthy of her admiration, and thus all the more grateful to her. Which then led him to a more general enthusiasm about young people and their capacity to do good in the world. And also—though he resisted conscious countenancing of it—to loving her far more than was advisable.

Based on the intelligence Lalitha gathered in her return to Forster Hollow, Walter and Vin Haven had crafted a new and outrageously expensive offer for its inhabitants. Simply offering them more cash, Lalitha said, wasn't going to do the trick. For Mathis to save face, he needed to be the Moses who led his people to a new promised land. Unfortunately, as far as Walter could tell, the people of Forster Hollow had negligible skills beyond hunting, engine repair, vegetable growing, herb gathering, and welfare-check cashing. Vin Haven nevertheless obligingly made inquiries within his wide circle of business friends and returned to Walter with one interesting possibility: body armor.

Until he'd flown to Houston and met Haven, in the summer of 2001, Walter had been unfamiliar with the concept of good Texans, the national news being so dominated by bad ones. Haven owned a large ranch in the Hill Country and an even larger one south of Corpus Christi, both of them lovingly managed to provide habitat for game birds. Haven was the Texan sort of nature lover who happily blasted cinnamon teal out of the sky but also spent hours raptly monitoring, via closed-circuit spycam, the development of baby barn owls in a nest box on his property, and could expertly rhapsodize about the scaling patterns on a winter-plumage Baird's sandpiper. He was a short, gruff, bullet-headed man, and Walter had liked him from the first minute of his initial interview. "A hundred-million-dollar ante for one passerine species," Walter had said. "That's an interesting allocation."

Haven had tilted his bullet head to one side. "You got a problem with it?"

"Not necessarily. But given that the bird's not even federally listed yet, I'm curious what your thinking is."

"My thinking is, it's my hundred million, I can spend it whatever way I like."

"Good point."

"The best science we got on the cerulean warbler shows populations declining at three percent a year for the last forty years. Just because it hasn't passed the threshold of federally threatened, you can still plot that line straight down toward zero. That's where it's going: to zero."

"Right. And yet—"

"And yet there's other species even closer to zero. I know that. And I hope to God somebody else is worrying about 'em. I often ask myself, would I slit my own throat if I was guaranteed I could save one species by slitting it? We all know one human life is worth more than one bird's life. But is my miserable little life worth a whole species?"

"Thankfully not a choice that anybody's being asked to make."

"In a sense, that's right," Haven said. "But in a bigger sense, it's a choice that everybody's making. I got a call from the director of National Audubon back in February, right after the inauguration. The man's named Martin Jay, if that ain't the damndest thing. Talk about the right name for the job. Martin Jay is wondering if I might arrange him a little meeting with Karl Rove at the White House. He says one hour is all he needs to persuade Karl Rove that making conservation a priority is a political winner for the new administration. So I say to him, I think I can get you an hour with Rove, but here's what you got to do for me first. You got to get a reputable independent pollster to do a survey of how important a priority the environment is for swing voters. If you can show Karl Rove some good-looking numbers, he's gonna be all ears. And Martin Jay falls all over himself saying thank you, thank you, fabuloso, consider it done. And I say to Martin Jay, there's just one little thing, though: before you commission that survey and let Rove see it, you might want to have a pretty good idea what the results are going to be. That was six months ago. I never heard from him again."

"You and I see very much eye to eye on the politics of this," Walter said.

"Kiki and I are working a little bit on Laura, whenever we can," Haven said. "Might be more promise in that direction."

"That's great, that's incredible."

"Don't hold your breath. I sometimes think W.'s more married to Rove than to Laura. Not that you heard that from me."

"But so why the cerulean warbler?"

"I like the bird. It's a pretty little bird. Weighs less than the first joint of my thumb and flies all the way to South America and back every year. That's a beautiful thing right there. One man, one species. Isn't that enough? If we could just round up six hundred and twenty other men, we'd have every North American breeder covered. If you were lucky enough to get the robin, you wouldn't even have to spend one penny to preserve it. Me, though, I like a challenge. And Appalachian coal country's one hell of a challenge. That's just something you're going to have to accept if you're going to run this outfit for me. You got to have an open mind about mountaintop-removal mining."

In his forty years in the oil-and-gas business, running a company called Pelican Oil, Vin Haven had developed relationships with pretty much everyone worth knowing in Texas, from Ken Lay and Rusty Rose to Ann Richards and Father Tom Pincelli, the "birding priest" of the lower Rio Grande. He was especially tight with the people at LBI, the oilfield-services giant which, like its archrival Halliburton, had expanded into one of the country's leading defense contractors under the administrations of Reagan and the elder Bush. It was LBI to which Haven turned for a solution to the problem of Coyle Mathis. Unlike Halliburton, whose former CEO was now running the nation, LBI was still scrambling for inside access to the new administration and thus particularly disposed to do a favor for a close personal friend of George and Laura.

An LBI subsidiary, ArDee Enterprises, had recently won a big contract to supply the high-grade body armor that American forces, as improvised explosive devices began exploding in every corner of Iraq, had belatedly discovered themselves in sore need of. West Virginia, which had cheap labor and a lax regulatory environment, and which had unexpectedly provided Bush-Cheney with their margin of victory in 2000—choosing the Republican candidate for the first time since the Nixon landslide of 1972—was viewed very favorably in the circles Vin Haven ran in. ArDee Enterprises was hastily constructing a body-armor plant in Whitman County, and Haven, catching ArDee before hiring for the factory had commenced, was able to secure a guarantee of 120 permanent jobs for the people of Forster Hollow in exchange for a package of concessions so generous that ArDee would be getting their labor practically for free. Haven promised Coyle Mathis, by way of Lalitha, to pay for free high-quality housing and job training for him and the other Forster Hollow families, and further sweetened the deal with a lump-sum payment to ArDee large enough to fund the workers' health insurance and retirement plans for the next twenty years. As for job security, it was enough to point to the declarations, issued by various members of the Bush administration, that America would be defending itself in the Middle East for generations to come. There was no foreseeable end to the war on terror and, ergo, no end to the demand for body armor.

Walter, who had a low opinion of the Bush-Cheney venture in Iraq and an even lower opinion of the moral hygiene of defense contractors, was uneasy about working with LBI and providing further ammunition for the lefty environmentalists who opposed him in West Virginia. But Lalitha was intensely enthusiastic. "It's *perfect*," she told Walter. "This way, we can be more than a model of science-based reclamation. We can also be a model of compassionate relocation and retraining of people displaced by endangered-species conservation."

"Kind of shitty luck, of course, for the people who sold out early," Walter said.

"If they're still struggling, we can offer them jobs, too."

"For an additional however many million."

"And the fact that it's patriotic is also perfect!" Lalitha said. "The people will be doing something to help their country in time of war."

"These people don't strike me as losing a lot of sleep over helping their country."

"No, Walter, you're wrong about that. Luanne Coffey has two sons in Iraq. She hates the government for not doing more to protect them. She and I actually talked about that. She hates the government, but she hates the terrorists even more. This is perfect."

And so, in December, Vin Haven flew into Charleston in his jet and personally accompanied Lalitha to Forster Hollow while Walter stayed simmering, with his anger and humiliation, in a motel room in Beckley. It had been no surprise to hear from Lalitha that Coyle Mathis was still given to lengthily riffing on what an arrogant, prissy-ass fool her boss was. She'd played the role of good cop to the hilt; and Vin Haven, who did have the common touch (as evidenced by his friendship with George W.), was apparently reasonably well tolerated in Forster Hollow as well. While a small band of protesters from outside the Nine Mile valley, led by nut-case Jocelyn Zorn, marched with placards (DON'T TRUST THE TRUST) outside the tiny elementary school where the meeting was held, all eighty families from the hollow signed away their rights and accepted, on the spot, eighty whopping certified checks drawn on the Trust's account in Washington.

And now, ninety days later, Forster Hollow was a ghost hamlet owned by the Trust and available for demolition at 6 a.m. tomorrow. Walter had seen no reason to attend the first morning of demolition, and had seen several reasons not to, but Lalitha was thrilled by the imminent removal of the last permanent structures in the Warbler Park. He'd lured her, in hiring her, with the vision of a hundred square miles entirely free of human taint, and she'd bought the vision big-time. Since she was the one who'd brought the vision to the brink of realization, he couldn't very well deny her the satisfaction of going to Forster Hollow. He wanted to give her every little thing he could, since he couldn't give her his love. He indulged her the way he'd often been tempted to indulge Jessica but had mostly refrained from, for the sake of good parenting.

Lalitha was hunched forward with anticipation as she drove the rental car into Beckley, where rain was falling more heavily.

"That road's going to be a mess tomorrow," Walter said, looking out at the rain and noting, with displeasure, the elderly sourness in his voice.

"We'll get up at four and take it slow," Lalitha said.

"Ha, that'll be a first. Have I ever seen you take a road slow?"

"I'm very excited, Walter!"

"I shouldn't even be here," he said sourly. "I should be doing that press conference tomorrow morning."

"Cynthia says Mondays are better for the news cycle," Lalitha said, referring to their press person, whose job, until now, had consisted mainly of avoiding contact with the press.

"I don't know which I'm dreading more," Walter said. "That nobody will show up, or that we'll have a room full of reporters."

"Oh, we definitely want the room full. This is really amazing news, if you explain it right."

"All I know is I'm dreading it."

Staying in hotels with Lalitha had become perhaps the hardest single part of their working relationship. In Washington, where she lived upstairs from him, she at least was on a different floor, and Patty was around to generally disturb the picture. At the Days Inn in Beckley, they fitted identical keycards into identical doors, fifteen feet from each other, and entered rooms whose identical profound drabness only a torrid illicit liaison could have overcome. Walter couldn't avoid thinking about how alone Lalitha was in her identical room. Part of his feeling of inferiority consisted of straightforward envy—envy of her youth; envy of her innocent idealism; envy of the simplicity of her situation, as compared to the impossibility of his—and it seemed to him that her room, though outwardly identical, was the room of fullness, the room of beautiful and allowable yearning, while his was the room of emptiness and sterile prohibition. He turned on CNN, for the blare of it, and watched a report on the latest carnage in Iraq while he undressed for a lonely shower.

The previous morning, before he'd left for the airport, Patty had appeared in the doorway of their bedroom. "Let me put it as plainly as possible," she said. "You have my permission."

"Permission for what?"

"You know what for. And I'm saying you have it."

He might almost have believed she meant this if the expression on her face hadn't been so ragged, and if she hadn't been wringing her hands so piteously as she spoke.

"Whatever you're talking about," he said, "I don't want your permission."

She'd looked at him beseechingly, and then despairingly, and left him alone. Half an hour later, on his way out, he'd tapped on the door of the little room where she did her writing and her e-mailing and, more and more frequently of late, her sleeping. "Sweetie," he said through the door. "I'll see you on Thursday night." When she gave no answer, he knocked again and went in. She was sitting on the foldout sofa, squeezing the fingers of one hand in the fist of the other. Her face was red, wrecked, tear-tracked. He crouched at her feet and held her hands, which were aging faster than the rest of her; were bony and thin-skinned. "I love you," he said. "Do you understand that?"

She nodded quickly, biting her lips, appreciative but unconvinced. "OK," she said in a whispery squeak. "You'd better go."

How many thousand more times, he wondered as he descended the stairs to the Trust offices, am I going to let this woman stab me in the heart?

Poor Patty, poor competitive lost Patty, who wasn't doing anything remotely brave or admirable in Washington, could not help noticing his admiration of Lalitha. The reason he couldn't let himself even think of loving Lalitha, let alone do anything about it, was Patty. It wasn't just that he respected the letter of marital law, it was also that he couldn't bear the idea of her knowing there was someone he thought more highly of than her. Lalitha *was* better than Patty. This was simply a fact. But Walter felt that he would sooner die than acknowledge this obvious fact to Patty, because, however much he might turn out to love Lalitha, and however unworkable his life with Patty had become, he loved Patty in some wholly other way, some larger and more abstract but nevertheless essential way that was about a lifetime of responsibility; about being a good person. If he were to fire Lalitha, literally and/or figuratively, she would cry for some months and then move on with her life and do good things with someone else. Lalitha was young and blessed with clarity. Whereas Patty, although she was often cruel to him and lately, more and more, had been shrinking from his caresses, still needed him to think the world of her. He knew this, because why else hadn't she left him? He knew it very, very well. There was an emptiness at Patty's center that it was his lot in life to do his best to fill with love. A slim flicker of hope in her which he alone could safeguard. And so, although his situation was already impossible and seemed to be getting more impossible every day, he had no choice but to persist in it.

Emerging from the motel shower, taking care not to glance at the egregious white middle-aged body in the mirror, he checked his Black-Berry and found a message from Richard Katz.

> Hey pardner, job's done up here. Do we meet in Washington now or what? Do I stay in a hotel or sleep on your sofa? I want such perks as I am due.
> All best to your beuatiful women. RK

Walter studied the message with an uneasiness of uncertain origin. Possibly it was just the typo's reminder of Richard's fundamental careless-ness, but possibly also the aftertaste of their meeting in Manhattan two weeks earlier. Although Walter had been very happy to see his old friend again, he'd been haunted afterward by Richard's insistence, in the restau-rant, that Lalitha repeat the word *fucking*, and by his subsequent insinua-tions about her interest in oral sex, and by the way that he himself, at the bar in Penn Station, had proceeded to badmouth Patty, which he *never* let himself do with anybody else. To be forty-seven and still trying to im-press his college roommate by denigrating his wife and spilling confi-dences better left unspilled: it was pathetic. Although Richard had seemed happy enough to see him, too, Walter couldn't shake the old familiar feel-ing that Richard was trying to impose his Katzian vision of the world on him and, thereby, defeat him. When, to Walter's surprise, before they parted, Richard had agreed to lend his name and likeness to the crusade against overpopulation, Walter had immediately called Lalitha with the great news. But only she had been able to savor it with complete enthusi-asm. Walter had boarded the train to Washington wondering if he'd done the right thing.

And why, in his e-mail, had Richard mentioned the *beauty* of Lalitha and Patty? Why send his best to them but not to Walter himself? Just an-other careless oversight? Walter didn't think so.

Down the road from the Days Inn was a steakhouse that was plastic to the core but equipped with a full bar. It was a ridiculous place to go, since neither Walter nor Lalitha ate cow, but the motel clerk had nothing better to recommend. In a plastic-seated booth, Walter touched the rim of his beer glass to Lalitha's gin martini, which she proceeded to make short work of. He signaled to their waitress for another and then suffered through perusal of the menu. Between the horrors of bovine methane, the lakes of watershed-devastating excrement generated by pig and chicken farms, the catastrophic overfishing of the oceans, the ecological nightmare of farmed shrimp and salmon, the antibiotic orgy of dairy-cow factories, and the fuel squandered by the globalization of produce, there was little he could ever order in good conscience besides potatoes, beans, and freshwater-farmed tilapia.

"Fuck it," he said, closing the menu. "I'm going to have the rib eye."

"Excellent, excellent celebrating," Lalitha said, her face already flushed. "I'm going to have the delicious grilled-cheese sandwich from the children's menu."

The beer was interesting. Unexpectedly sour and undelicious, like drinkable dough. After just three or four sips, seldom-heard-from blood vessels in Walter's brain were pulsing disturbingly.

"Got an e-mail from Richard," he said. "He's willing to come down and work with us on strategy. I told him he should come down for the weekend."

"Ha! You see? You didn't even think it was worth the bother of asking him."

"No, no. You were right about that."

Lalitha noticed something in his face. "Aren't you happy about it?"

"No, absolutely," he said. "In theory. There's just something I don't . . . trust. I guess basically I don't see why he's doing it."

"Because we were extremely persuasive!"

"Yeah, maybe. Or because you're extremely pretty."

She seemed both pleased and confused by this. "He's your very good friend, right?"

"Used to be. But then he got famous. And now all I can see are the parts of him I don't trust."

"What don't you trust about him?"

Walter shook his head, not wanting to say.

"Do you not trust him with *me*?"

"No, that would be very stupid, wouldn't it? I mean, what do I care what you do? You're an adult, you can look out for yourself."

Lalitha laughed at him, simply pleased now, not confused at all.

"I think he's very funny and charismatic," she said. "But I mostly just felt sorry for him. You know what I mean? He seems like one of those men who have to spend all their time maintaining an attitude, because they're weak inside. He's nothing like the man you are. All I could see when we were talking was how much he admires you, and how he was trying not to show it too much. Couldn't you see that?"

The degree of pleasure it brought Walter to hear this felt dangerous to him. He wanted to believe it, but he didn't trust it, because he knew Richard to be, in his own way, relentless.

"Seriously, Walter. That kind of man is very *primitive*. All he has is dignity and self-control and attitude. He only has one little thing, while you have everything else."

"But the thing he has is what the world wants," Walter said. "You've read all the Nexis stuff on him, you know what I'm talking about. The world doesn't reward ideas or emotions, it rewards integrity and coolness. And that's why I don't trust him. He's got the game set up so he's always going to win. In private, he may think he admires what we're doing, but he's never going to admit it in public, because he has to maintain his attitude, because that's what the world wants, and he knows it."

"Yes, but that's why it's so great that he'll be working with us. I don't *want* you to be cool, I don't like a cool man. I like a man like you. But Richard can help us communicate."

Walter was relieved when their waitress came to take their orders and terminated the pleasure of hearing why Lalitha liked him. But the danger only deepened as she drank her second martini.

"Can I ask a personal question?" she said.

"Ah—sure."

"The question is: do you think I should get my tubes tied?"

She'd spoken loudly enough for other tables to have heard, and Walter reflexively put a finger to his lips. He felt conspicuous enough already, felt glaringly urban, sitting with a girl of a different race amid the two varieties of rural West Virginians, the overweight kind and the really skinny kind.

"It just seems logical," she said more quietly, "since I know I don't want children."

"Well," he said, "I don't . . . I don't . . ." He wanted to say that, since Lalitha so seldom saw Jairam, her longtime boyfriend, pregnancy hardly seemed like a pressing worry, and that, if she ever did get pregnant accidentally, she could always have an abortion. But it seemed fantastically inappropriate to be discussing his assistant's tubes. She was smiling at him with a kind of woozy shyness, as if seeking his permission or fearing his disapproval. "I guess basically," he said, "I think Richard was right, if you remember what he said. He said people change their minds about these things. It's probably best to leave your options open."

"But what if I *know* that I'm right now, and my future self is the one I don't trust?"

"Well, you're not going to be your old self anymore, in the future. You're going to be your new self. And your new self might want different things."

"Then *fuck* my future self," Lalitha said, leaning forward. "If it wants to reproduce, I already have no respect for it."

Walter willed himself not to glance at the other diners. "Why is this even coming up now? You hardly even see Jairam anymore."

"Because Jairam wants children, that's why. He doesn't believe how serious I am about not wanting them. I need to show him, so he'll stop bothering me. I don't want to be his girlfriend anymore."

"I'm really not sure we should be discussing this kind of thing."

"OK, but who else can I talk to, then? You're the only one who understands me."

"Oh, God, Lalitha." Walter's head was swimming with beer. "I am so sorry. I am so sorry. I feel like I've led you into something I never meant to lead you into. You still have your whole life ahead of you, and I . . . I feel like I've led you into something."

This sounded all wrong. In trying to say something narrow, something specific to the problem of world population, he'd managed to sound like he was saying something broad about the two of them. Had seemed to be foreclosing a larger possibility that he wasn't ready to foreclose yet, even though he knew it wasn't actually a possibility.

"These are my own thoughts, not yours," Lalitha said. "You didn't put them in my head. I was just asking your advice."

"Well, and I guess my advice is don't do it."

"OK. Then I'm going to have another drink. Or do you advise me not to?"

"I do advise you not to."

"Please order me one anyway."

A chasm was opening in front of Walter, available for immediate jumping into. He was shocked by how quickly such a thing could open up in front of him. The only other time—or, no, no, no, the *only* time—he'd fallen in love, he'd taken the better part of a year before acting on it, and even then Patty had ended up doing most of the heavy lifting for him. Now it appeared that these things could be managed in a matter of *minutes*. Just a few more heedless words, another slug of beer, and God only knew . . .

"I just meant," he said, "that I might have led you too much into overpopulation. Into being crazy about it. With my own stupid anger, my own issues. I wasn't trying to say anything larger than that."

She nodded. Tiny pearls of tear were clinging to her eyelashes.

"I feel very fatherly toward you," he babbled.

"I understand."

But *fatherly* was also wrong—too foreclosing of the kind of love that it was still too painful to admit he was never going to allow himself.

"Obviously," he said, "I'm too young to be your father, or almost too young, besides which, in any case, you have your own father. I was really just referring to your having asked me for fatherly advice. To my having, as your boss, and as a considerably older person, a certain kind of . . . *solicitude* toward you. 'Fatherly' in that respect. Not in some sort of taboo respect."

This all sounded like patent nonsense even as he said it. His whole fucking problem was taboos. Lalitha, who seemed to know it, raised her lovely eyes and looked directly into his. "You don't have to love me, Walter. I can just love you. All right? You can't stop me from loving you."

The chasm widened dizzyingly.

"I do love you!" he said. "I mean—in a sense. A very definite sense. I definitely do. A lot. A whole lot, actually. OK? I just don't see where we can go with it. I mean, if we're going to keep working together, we absolutely can't be talking like this. This is already very, very, very, very bad."

"Yes, I know." She lowered her eyes. "And you're married."

"Yes, exactly! *Exactly.* And so there we are."

"There we are, yes."

"Let me see about your drink."

Love declared, disaster averted, he went looking for their waitress and ordered a third martini, heavy on the vermouth. His blush, which all his life had been a thing that constantly came and went, had now come without going. He lurched, hot-faced, into the men's room and attempted to pee. His need was at once pressing and difficult to connect to. He stood at the urinal, taking deep breaths, and was finally at the point of getting things flowing when the door swung open and somebody came in. Walter heard the guy washing his hands and drying them while he stood with burning cheeks and waited for his bladder to overcome its shyness. He was again on the verge of success when he realized that the guy at the sinks was lingering deliberately. He gave up on peeing, wasted water with an unnecessary flush, and zipped up his pants.

"You might want to see a doctor, pal, about your urinary difficulties," the guy at the sinks drawled sadistically. White, thirtyish, with hard living in his face, he was an exact match of Walter's profile of the kind of driver who didn't believe in turn signals. He stood near Walter's shoulder while Walter hastily washed his hands and dried them.

"Like the dark meat, do you?"

"What?"

"Said I seen what you doing with that nigger girl."

"She's *Asian*," Walter said, stepping around him. "If you'll excuse me—"

"Candy's dandy but liquor's quicker, ain't that right, pal?"

There was so much hatred in his voice that Walter, fearing violence, made his escape through the door without delivering a rejoinder. He hadn't thrown a punch or absorbed one in thirty-five years, and he suspected that a punching would feel far worse at forty-seven than it had at twelve. His whole body was vibrating with unreleased violence, his head reeling with injustice, as he sat down to an iceberg-lettuce salad in the booth.

"How's your beer?" Lalitha asked.

"It's interesting," he said, drinking the rest of it right down. His head felt liable to detach from his neck and drift up to the ceiling like a party balloon.

"I'm sorry if I said things I shouldn't have."

"Don't worry about it," he said. "I'm—" *in love with you, too. I'm horribly in love with you.* "I'm in a hard position, honey," he said. "I mean, not 'honey.' Not 'honey.' Lalitha. Honey. I'm in a hard position."

"Maybe you should have another beer," she said with a sly smile.

"You see, the thing is, I also love my wife."

"Yes of course," she said. But she wasn't even *trying* to help him out. She arched her back like a cat and stretched forward across the table, displaying the ten pale nails of her beautiful young hands on either side of his salad plate, inviting him to touch them. "I'm so drunk!" she said, smiling up at him wickedly.

He glanced around the plastic dining room to see if his bathroom tormentor might be witnessing this. The guy was not obviously in sight, nor was anybody else staring unduly. Looking down at Lalitha, who was snuggling her cheek against the plastic tabletop as if it were the softest of pillows, he recalled the words of Richard's prophecy. The girl on her knees, head bobbing, smiling up. Oh, the cheap clarity of Richard Katz's vision of the world. A surge of resentment cut through Walter's buzz and steadied him. To take advantage of this girl was Richard's way, not his.

"Sit up," he said sternly.

"In a minute," she murmured, wiggling her outstretched fingers.

"No, sit up now. We're the public face of the Trust, and we have to be aware of that."

"I think you might have to take me home, Walter."

"We need to get some food in you first."

"Mm," she said, smiling with closed eyes.

Walter stood up and ran down their waitress and asked to have their entrées boxed for takeout. Lalitha was still slumped forward, her half-finished third martini by her elbow, when he returned to the booth. He roused her and held her firmly by the upper arm as he led her outside and installed her in the passenger seat. Going back inside for the food, he encountered, in the glassed-in vestibule, his tormentor from the bathroom.

"Fucking dark-meat lover," the guy said. "Fucking spectacle. What the fuck you doin' around here?"

Walter tried to step around him, but the guy blocked his way. "Asked you a question," he said.

"Not interested," Walter said. He tried to push past but found himself shoved hard against the plate glass, shaking the framework of the vestibule. At that moment, before anything worse could happen, the inner door opened and the restaurant's hard-bitten hostess asked what was going on.

"This person's bothering me," Walter said, breathing hard.

"Fucking pervert."

"You going to have to take this off the premises," the hostess said.

"I ain't going nowhere. This pervo's the one that's leaving."

"Then go back to your table and sit down and don't use that kind of language with me."

"Can't even eat, he makes me so sick to my stomach."

Leaving the two of them to sort things out, Walter went inside and found himself in the crosshairs of the murderously hateful gaze emanating from a heavyset young blonde, clearly his tormentor's woman, who was alone at a table near the door. While he waited for his food, he wondered why it was tonight, of all the nights, that he and Lalitha had provoked this kind of hatred. They'd received a few stares now and then, mostly in smaller towns, but never anything like this. In fact, he'd been agreeably surprised by the number of black-white couples he'd seen in Charleston, and by the generally low priority of racism among the state's many ailments. Most of West Virginia was too white for race to be a forefront issue. He was forced to the conclusion that what had attracted the young couple's attention was the guilt, his own dirty guilt, that had radiated from his booth. They didn't hate Lalitha, they hated *him*. And he deserved it. When the food finally came out, his hands were shaking so much that he could hardly sign the credit-card slip.

Back at the Days Inn, he carried Lalitha in his arms through the rain and set her down outside her door. He had little doubt that she could have walked, but he wanted to indulge her earlier wish to be carried to her room. And it actually helped to have her in his arms like a child, it reminded him of his responsibilities. When she sat down on the bed and toppled over, he covered her with a bedspread the way he'd once covered Jessica and Joey.

"I'm going to go next door and eat dinner," he said, tenderly smoothing her hair from her forehead. "I'll leave yours here for you."

"No don't," she said. "Stay and watch TV. I'll sober up and we can eat together."

In this, too, he indulged her, locating PBS on cable and watching the tail end of the *NewsHour*—some discussion of John Kerry's war record whose irrelevance made him so nervous he could barely follow it. He could hardly stand to watch news of any sort anymore. Everything was moving too fast, too fast. He felt a stab of sympathy for the Kerry campaign, which now had less than seven months to turn the country's mood around and expose three years of high-tech lying and manipulation.

He himself had been under tremendous pressure to get the Trust's contracts with Nardone and Blasco signed before their initial agreement with Vin Haven expired, on June 30, and became subject to renegotiation. In his rush to deal with Coyle Mathis and beat the deadline, he'd had no choice but to sign off on the body-armor deal with LBI, exorbitant and distasteful though it was. And now, before anything could be reconsidered, the coal companies were rushing to wreck the Nine Mile valley and move into the mountains with their draglines, which they were free to do because one of Walter's few clear successes, in West Virginia, had been to get the MTR permits fast-tracked and persuade the Appalachian Environmental Law Center to remove the Nine Mile sites from its dilatory lawsuit. The deal was sealed, and Walter now needed to forget about West Virginia in any case and start work in earnest on his anti-population crusade—needed to get the intern program up and running before the nation's most liberal college kids all finalized their summer plans and went to work for the Kerry campaign instead.

In the two and a half weeks since his meeting in Manhattan with Richard, the world population had increased by 7,000,000. A *net* gain of seven million human beings—the equivalent of New York City's population—to clear-cut forests and befoul streams and pave over grasslands and throw plastic garbage into the Pacific Ocean and burn gasoline and coal and exterminate other species and obey the fucking pope and pop out families of twelve. In Walter's view, there was no greater force for evil in the world, no more compelling cause for despair about humanity and the amazing planet it had been given, than the Catholic Church, although, admittedly, the Siamese-twin fundamentalisms of Bush and bin Laden were running a close second these days. He couldn't see a church or a REAL MEN LOVE JESUS sign or a fish symbol on a car without his chest tightening with anger. In a place like West Virginia, this meant that he got angry pretty much every time he ventured into daylight, which no doubt contributed to his road rage. And it wasn't just religion, and it wasn't just the jumbo *everything* to which his fellow Americans seemed to feel uniquely entitled, it wasn't just the Walmarts and the buckets of corn syrup and the high-clearance monster trucks; it was the feeling that nobody else in the country was giving even *five seconds' thought* to what it meant to be packing another 13,000,000 large primates onto the world's limited surface every month. The unclouded serenity of his countrymen's indifference made him wild with anger.

Patty had recently suggested, as an antidote to road rage, that he distract himself with radio whenever he was driving a car, but to Walter the message of every single radio station was that nobody else in America was thinking about the planet's ruination. The God stations and the country stations and the Limbaugh stations were all, of course, actively cheering the ruination; the classic-rock and news-network stations continually made much ado about absolutely nothing; and National Public Radio was, for Walter, even worse. *Mountain Stage* and *A Prairie Home Companion*: literally fiddling while the planet burned! And worst of all were *Morning Edition* and *All Things Considered*. The NPR news unit, once upon a time fairly liberal, had become just another voice of center-right free-market ideology, describing even the slightest *slowing* of the nation's economic growth rate as "bad news" and deliberately wasting precious minutes of airtime every morning and evening—minutes that could have been devoted to raising the alarm about overpopulation and mass extinctions—on fatuously earnest reviews of literary novels and quirky musical acts like Walnut Surprise.

And TV: TV was like radio, only ten times worse. The country that minutely followed every phony turn of *American Idol* while the world went up in flames seemed to Walter fully deserving of whatever nightmare future awaited it.

He was aware, of course, that it was wrong to feel this way—if only because, for almost twenty years, in St. Paul, he hadn't. He was aware of the intimate connection between anger and depression, aware that it was mentally unhealthy to be so exclusively obsessed with apocalyptic scenarios, aware of how, in his case, the obsession was feeding on frustration with his wife and disappointment with his son. Probably, if he'd been truly alone in his anger, he couldn't have stood it.

But Lalitha was with him every step of the way. She ratified his vision and shared his sense of urgency. In his initial interview with her, she'd told him about the family trip she'd taken back to West Bengal when she was fourteen. She'd been exactly the right age to be not merely saddened and horrified but *disgusted* by the density and suffering and squalor of human life in Calcutta. Her disgust had pushed her, on her return to the States, into vegetarianism and environmental studies, with a focus, in college, on women's issues in developing nations. Although she'd happened to land a good job with the Nature Conservancy after college, her heart—like Walter's own when he was young—had always been in population and sustainability issues.

There was, to be sure, a whole other side of Lalitha, a side susceptible to strong, traditional men. Her boyfriend, Jairam, was thick-bodied and somewhat ugly but arrogant and driven, a heart surgeon in training, and Lalitha was by no means the first attractive young woman whom Walter had seen parking her charms with a Jairam type in order to avoid being hit on everywhere she went. But six years of Jairam's escalating nonsense seemed finally to be curing her of him. The only real surprise about the question she'd asked Walter tonight, the question about sterilization, was that she'd even felt the need to ask it.

Why, indeed, had she asked him?

He turned off the TV and paced her room to give the matter closer thought, and the answer came to him immediately: she'd been asking whether *he* might want to have a kid with her. Or maybe, more precisely, she'd been warning him that even if he wanted to, she might not.

And the sick thing was—if he was honest with himself—that he *did* want to have a baby with her. Not that he didn't adore Jessica and, in a more abstract way, love Joey. But their mother was suddenly feeling very far away to him. Patty was a person who probably hadn't even wanted very much to marry him, a person he'd first heard about from *Richard*, who had mentioned, one long-ago summer evening in Minneapolis, that the chick he was sleeping with was living with a basketball star who confounded his preconceptions of lady jocks. Patty had almost gone with Richard, and out of the gratifying fact that she hadn't—that she'd succumbed to Walter's love instead—had grown their entire life together, their marriage and their house and their kids. They'd always been a good couple but an odd couple; nowadays, more and more, they seemed simply ill matched. Whereas Lalitha was a genuine kindred spirit, a soul mate who wholeheartedly adored him. If they ever had a son, the son would be like him.

He continued to pace her room, greatly agitated. While his attention was diverted by drink and rednecks, the chasm at his feet had been growing wider and wider. He was now thinking about having *babies* with his assistant! And not even pretending that he wasn't! And this was all new within the last *hour*. He knew it was new because, when he'd advised her not to have her tubes tied, he truly had not been thinking of himself.

"Walter?" Lalitha said from the bed.

"Yeah, how are you doing?" he said, rushing to her side.

"I was thinking I might throw up, but now I'm thinking I won't have to."

"That's good!"

She was blinking up at him rapidly, with a tender smile. "Thank you for staying with me."

"Oh absolutely."

"How are you with your beer?"

"I don't even know."

Her lips were right there, her mouth was right there, and his heart seemed liable to crack his rib cage with its heaving. Kiss her! Kiss her! Kiss her! it was telling him.

And then his BlackBerry rang. Its ringtone was the song of the cerulean warbler.

"Take it," Lalitha said.

"Um..."

"No, take it. I'm happy lying here."

The caller was Jessica, it wasn't urgent, they talked every day. But seeing her name on the screenlet was enough to draw Walter back from the brink. He sat down on the other bed and answered.

"It sounds like you're walking," Jessica said. "Are you running somewhere?"

"No," he said. "Celebrating, actually."

"It sounds like you're on a *treadmill*, the way you're panting."

There was too little strength in his arm even to hold a phone up to his ear. He lay down on his side and told his daughter about the events of the morning and his various misgivings, which she did her best to reassure him about. He had come to appreciate the rhythm of their daily calls. Jessica was the one person in the world he allowed to ask him about himself before plying her with questions about her own life; she looked after him that way; she was the child who'd inherited his sense of responsibility. Although her ambition was still to be a writer, and she was currently working as a barely paid editorial assistant in Manhattan, she had a deep green streak and hoped to make environmental issues the focus of her future writing. Walter told her that Richard was coming down to Washington and asked her if she was still planning to join them on the weekend, to lend her valuable young intelligence to the discussions. She said she definitely was.

"And how was your day?" he said.

"Eh," she said. "My roommates didn't magically replace themselves with better roommates while I was at the office. I've got clothes piled around my door to keep the smoke out."

"You have to not let them smoke inside. You just have to tell them that."

"Right, I get outvoted, is the thing. They both just started. It's still possible they'll see how stupid it is and stop. In the meantime, I'm literally holding my breath."

"And how's work?"

"As usual. Simon gets ever skeazier. He's like a sebum factory. You have to wipe everything off after he's been around your desk. He was hanging around Emily's desk for like an hour today, trying to get her to go to a Knicks game with him. The senior editors get all these free tickets to stuff, including sporting events, for reasons unknown to me. I guess the Knicks must be fairly desperate to fill their luxury seats at this point. And Emily's like, how many hundred ways can I find to say no? I finally went over and started asking Simon about his *wife*. You know—wife? Three kids in Teaneck? Hello? Stop looking down Emily's shirt?"

Walter closed his eyes and tried to think of something to say.

"Dad? You there?"

"I'm here, yeah. How old is, um. Simon?"

"I don't know. Indeterminate. Probably not more than twice Emily's age. We speculate about whether he colors his hair. Sometimes the color seems to change a little, from week to week, but that could just be body-oil issues. I'm luckily not directly subordinate to him."

Walter was suddenly worried that he might cry.

"Dad? You there?"

"Yeah, yeah."

"It's just your cell goes so blank when you're not talking."

"Yeah, listen," he said, "it's terrific that you're coming for the weekend. I think we'll put Richard in the guest room. We're going to do a long meeting on Saturday and then a shorter one on Sunday. Try to hammer out a concrete plan. Lalitha's already got some great ideas."

"No doubt," Jessica said.

"That's great, then. We'll talk tomorrow."

"OK, I love you, Dad."

"I love you, too, sweetheart."

He let the phone slip from his hand and lay crying for a while, silently, shaking the cheap bed. He didn't know what to do, he didn't know how to live. Each new thing he encountered in life impelled him in a direction that fully convinced him of its rightness, but then the next new thing loomed up and impelled him in the opposite direction, which also felt right. There was no controlling narrative: he seemed to himself a purely reactive pinball in a game whose only object was to stay alive for staying alive's sake. To throw away his marriage and follow Lalitha had felt irresistible until the moment he saw himself, in the person of Jessica's older colleague, as another overconsuming white American male who felt entitled to more and more and more: saw the romantic imperialism of his falling for someone fresh and Asian, having exhausted domestic supplies.

Likewise the course he'd charted for two and a half years with the Trust, convinced of the soundness of his arguments and the rightness of his mission, only to feel, this morning, in Charleston, that he'd made nothing but horrible mistakes. And likewise the overpopulation initiative: what better way to live could there be than to throw himself into the most critical challenge of his time? A challenge that then seemed trumped-up and barren when he thought of his Lalitha with her tubes tied. How to live?

He was drying his eyes, pulling himself together, when Lalitha got up and came over and put a hand on his shoulder. She smelled of sweet respired martini. "My boss," she said softly, stroking his shoulder. "You're the best boss in the world. You're such a wonderful man. We'll get up in the morning and everything will be fine."

He nodded and sniffled and gasped a little. "Please don't get sterilized," he said.

"No," she said, stroking him. "I won't do that tonight."

"There's no hurry about anything. Everything has to slow down."

"Slow, slow, yes. Everything will be slow."

If she'd kissed him, he would have kissed her back, but she just kept stroking his shoulder, and eventually he was able to reconstruct some semblance of a professional self. Lalitha looked wistful but not too disappointed. She yawned and stretched her arms like a sleepy child. Walter left her with her sandwich and went next door with his steak, which he devoured with guilty savagery, holding it in his hands and tearing off pieces with his teeth, covering his chin with grease. He thought again of Jessica's oily, despoiling colleague Simon.

Sobered by this, and by the loneliness and sterility of his room, he washed his face and attended to e-mail for two hours, while Lalitha slept in her undespoiled room and dreamed of—what? He couldn't imagine. But he did feel that, by coming so close to the brink and then drawing back so awkwardly, they had inoculated themselves against the danger of coming so close again. And this was fine with him now. It was the way he knew how to live: with discipline and self-denial. He took comfort in how long it would be before they traveled together again.

Cynthia, his press person, had e-mailed him final drafts of the full press release and of the preliminary announcement that was going out at noon tomorrow, as soon as the demolition of Forster Hollow had commenced. There was also a terse, unhappy note from Eduardo Soquel, the Trust's point man in Colombia, confirming that he was willing to miss his eldest daughter's *quinceañera* on Sunday and fly to Washington. Walter needed Soquel by his side at the press conference on Monday, to emphasize the Pan-American nature of the park and highlight the Trust's successes in South America.

It wasn't unusual for big conservation land deals to be kept under wraps until they were finalized, but rare were the deals containing a bombshell on the order of fourteen thousand acres of forest being opened up to MTR. Back in late 2002, when Walter had merely *suggested* to the local environmental community that the Trust might allow MTR on its warbler preserve, Jocelyn Zorn had alerted every anti-coal reporter in West Virginia. A flurry of negative stories had resulted, and Walter had realized that he simply couldn't afford to take his full case to the public. The clock was ticking; there was no time for the slow work of educating the public and shaping its opinion. Better to keep his negotiations with Nardone and Blasco secret, better to let Lalitha convince Coyle Mathis and his neighbors to sign nondisclosure agreements, and wait for all the faits to be accomplis. But now the jig was up, now the heavy equipment was moving in. Walter knew he had to get out in front of the story and spin it his way, as a "success story" of science-based reclamation and compassionate relocation. And yet, the more he thought about it now, the more certain he became that the press was going to slaughter him for the MTR thing. He could be tied up for weeks with putting out fires. And meanwhile the clock was also running on his overpopulation initiative, which was all he really cared about now.

After rereading the press release, with deep unease, he checked his e-mail queue one last time and found a new message, from caperville @nytimes.com.

Hello, Mr. Berglund,

My name is Dan Caperville and I'm working on a story about land conservation in Appalachia. I understand the Cerulean Mountain Trust has recently closed a deal for the preservation of a large forested tract in Wyoming Co. WV. I'd love to talk about that with you at your earliest convenience . . .

What the fuck? How did the *Times* already know about this morning's signing? Walter was so unready to ponder this e-mail, under present circumstances, that he composed a reply immediately and fired it off before he had time to reconsider:

Dear Mr. Caperville,

Thank you so much for your query! I would love to talk to you about the exciting things the Trust has in the works. As it happens, I'm holding a press conference this coming Monday morning in Washington, announcing a major and very exciting new environmental initiative, which I hope you'll be able to attend. In consideration of your paper's stature, I can also send you an early copy of our press release on Sunday evening. If you're available to speak with me early Monday morning, in advance of the presser, I might be able to arrange that as well.

Looking forward to working with you—

Walter E. Berglund

Executive Director, Cerulean Mountain Trust

He copied everything to Cynthia and Lalitha, with the comment WTF?, and then paced the room in agitation, thinking how welcome a second beer would be right now. (One beer in forty-seven years, and already he felt like an addict.) The right thing to do now was probably to wake Lalitha, drive back to Charleston, catch the first morning flight out, move the press conference up to Friday, and get out in front of the story. But it seemed as if the world, the insane-making velocitous world, was conspiring to deprive him of *the only two things* he truly wanted now. Having already been deprived of kissing Lalitha, he at least wanted to spend the weekend planning the overpopulation initiative with her and Jessica and Richard, before dealing with the mess in West Virginia.

At ten-thirty, still pacing the room, he was feeling so deprived and anxious and sorry for himself that he called home to Patty. He wanted to get some credit for his fidelity, or maybe he just wanted to dump some anger on a person he loved.

"Oh, hi," Patty said. "I didn't expect to hear from you. Is everything OK?"

"Everything's *horrible*."

"I bet! It's hard to keep saying no when you want to say yes, isn't it?"

"Oh Jesus don't start," he said. "Please, for God's sake, do not start that tonight."

"Sorry. I was trying to be sympathetic."

"I've actually got a *professional* problem on my hands here, Patty. Not just some petty little personal emotional thing, believe it or not. A *serious professional difficulty* that I could use a bit of reassurance about. Somebody at the meeting this morning leaked something to the press, and I have to try to get out in front on a story I'm not sure I even want to be out in front on, because I was already feeling like I've fucked everything up here. Like all I've managed to do is release fourteen thousand acres to be blasted into a moonscape, and now the world has to be informed, and I don't even care about the project anymore."

"Right, well, actually," Patty said, "the moonscape stuff does sound sort of awful."

"Thank you! Thank you for the reassurance!"

"I was just reading an article about it in the *Times* this morning."

"Today?"

"Yeah, they actually mentioned your warbler, and how bad mountain-top removal is for it."

"Unbelievable! Today?"

"Yes, today."

"Fuck! Somebody must have seen the piece in the paper today and then called the reporter with the leak. I just heard from him half an hour ago."

"Well, anyway," Patty said, "I'm sure you know best, although moun-taintop removal does sound fairly horrible."

He clutched his forehead, feeling close to tears again. He couldn't believe he was getting this from his wife, at this hour, on this of all days. "Since when are you such a big fan of the *Times*?" he said.

"I'm just saying it sounds pretty bad. It doesn't even sound like there's any disagreement about how bad it is."

"You're the person who made fun of your mother for believing every-thing she read in the *Times*."

"Ha-ha-ha! I'm my mother now? Because I don't like mountaintop removal, I'm suddenly *Joyce*?"

"I'm just saying there are other aspects to the story."

"You think we should be burning more coal. Making it easier to burn more coal. In spite of global warming."

He slid his hand down over his eyes and pressed them until they hurt. "You want me to explain the reason? Should I do that?"

"If you want to."

"We're heading for a catastrophe, Patty. We are heading for a total collapse."

"Well, and, frankly, I don't know about you, but that's starting to sound like kind of a relief to me."

"I'm not talking about us!"

"Ha-ha-ha! I actually didn't get that. I truly didn't realize what you meant."

"I meant that world population and energy consumption are going to have to fall drastically at some point. We're way past sustainable even now. Once the collapse comes, there's going to be a window of opportunity for ecosystems to recover, but only if there's any nature left. So the big question is how much of the planet gets destroyed before the collapse. Do we completely use it up, and cut down every tree and sterilize every ocean, and then collapse? Or are there going to be some unwrecked strongholds that survive?"

"Either way, you and I will be long dead by then," Patty said.

"Well, before I'm dead, I'm trying to create a stronghold. A refuge. Something to help a couple of ecosystems make it past the pinch point. That's the whole project here."

"Like," she persisted, "there's going to be a worldwide plague, and there'll be this long line for the Tamiflu, or the Cipro, and you're going to make us be the very last two people in it. 'Oh, sorry, guys, darn, we *just* ran out.' We'll be nice and polite and agreeable, and then we'll be dead."

"Global warming is a huge threat," Walter said, declining the bait, "but it's still not as bad as radioactive waste. It turns out that species can adapt a lot faster than we used to think. If you've got climate change spread over a hundred years, a fragile ecosystem has a fighting chance.

But when the reactor blows up, everything's fucked immediately and stays fucked for the next five thousand years."

"So yay coal. Let's burn more coal. Rah, rah."

"It's complicated, Patty. The picture gets complicated when you consider the alternatives. Nuclear's a disaster waiting to happen overnight. There's *zero* chance of ecosystems recovering from an overnight disaster. Everybody's talking about wind energy, but wind's not so great, either. This idiot Jocelyn Zorn's got a brochure that shows the two choices—the *only* two choices, presumably. Picture A shows this devastated post-MTR desertscape, Picture B shows ten windmills in a pristine mountain landscape. And what's wrong with this picture? What's wrong is there are only ten windmills in it. Where what you actually need is ten *thousand* windmills. You need every mountaintop in West Virginia to be covered with turbines. Imagine being a migratory bird trying to fly through that. And if you blanket the state with windmills, you think it's still going to be a tourist attraction? And plus, to compete with coal, those windmills have to operate forever. A hundred years from now, you're still going to have the same old piss-ugly eyesore, mowing down whatever wildlife is left. Whereas the mountaintop-removal site, in a hundred years, if you reclaim it properly, it may not be perfect, but it's going to be a valuable mature forest."

"And you know this, and the newspaper doesn't," Patty said.

"That's right."

"And it's not possible you're wrong."

"Not about coal versus wind or nuclear."

"Well, maybe if you explain all this, the way you just did to me, then people will believe it and you won't have any problems."

"Do *you* believe it?"

"I don't have all the facts."

"But I have the facts, and I'm telling you! Why can't you believe me? Why can't you reassure me?"

"I thought that was Pretty Face's job. I'm kind of out of practice since she took over. She's so much better at it anyway."

Walter ended the conversation before it could take an even worse turn. He turned off all the lights and got ready for bed by the parking-lot glow in the windows. Darkness was the only available relief from his state of flayed misery. He drew the blackout curtains, but light still leaked in at the base of them, and so he stripped the spare bed and used the pillows and covers to block out as much of it as he could. He put on a sleep mask and lay down with a pillow over his head, but even then, no matter how he adjusted the mask, there remained a faint suggestion of stray photons beating on his tightly shut eyelids, a less than perfect darkness.

He and his wife loved each other and brought each other daily pain. Everything else he was doing in his life, even his longing for Lalitha, amounted to little more than flight from this circumstance. He and Patty couldn't live together and couldn't imagine living apart. Each time he thought they'd reached the unbearable breaking point, it turned out that there was still further they could go without breaking.

One thunderstormy night in Washington, the previous summer, he'd set out to check a box on his dishearteningly long personal to-do list by setting up an online banking account, which he'd been intending to do for several years. Since moving to Washington, Patty had pulled less and less of her weight in the household, not even shopping for groceries anymore, but she did still pay the bills and balance the family checkbook. Walter had never scrutinized the checkbook entries until, after forty-five minutes of frustration with the banking software, he had the figures glowing on his computer screen. His first thought, when he saw the strange pattern of monthly $500 withdrawals, was that some hacker in Nigeria or Moscow had been stealing from him. But surely Patty would have noticed this?

He went upstairs to her little room, where she was chattering happily with one of her old basketball friends—she still showered laughter and wit on the people in her life who weren't Walter—and gave her to understand that he wasn't leaving until she got off the phone.

"It was cash," she said when he showed her the printouts of account activity. "I wrote myself some checks for cash."

"Five hundred a month? Near the end of every month?"

"That's when I take my cash out."

"No, you take two hundred every couple of weeks. I know what your withdrawals look like. And there's also a fee for a certified check here. The fifteenth of May?"

"Yes."

"That sounds like a certified check, not cash."

Over in the direction of the Naval Observatory, where Dick Cheney lived, thunder was banging in an evening sky the color of Potomac water. Patty, on her little sofa, crossed her arms defiantly. "OK!" she said. "You caught me! Joey needed the whole summer rent up front. He's going to pay it back when he earns it, but he didn't have the cash in hand right then."

For the second summer in a row, Joey was working in Washington without living at home. His spurning of their help and hospitality was irritating enough to Walter, but even worse was the identity of his summer employer: a corrupt little start-up—backed financially (though this didn't mean much to Walter at the time) by Vin Haven's friends at LBI—that had won the no-bid contract to privatize the bread-baking industry in newly liberated Iraq. Walter and Joey had already had their big fight about it some weeks earlier, on the Fourth of July, when Joey had come over for a picnic and very belatedly divulged his summer plans. Walter had lost his temper, Patty had run and hidden in her room, and Joey had sat smirking his Republican smirk. His Wall Street smirk. As if indulging his stupid rube father, with his old-fashioned principles; as if he himself knew better.

"So there's a perfectly good bedroom here," Walter said to Patty, "but that's not good enough for him. That wouldn't be grownup enough. That wouldn't be cool enough. He might even have to ride a bus to work! With the little people!"

"He has to maintain his Virginia residency, Walter. And he's going to pay it back, OK? I knew what you'd say if I asked you, so I went ahead and did it without telling you. If you don't want me making my own decisions, you should confiscate the checkbook. Take away my bank card. I'll come to you and beg for money every time I need it."

"Every month! You've been sending money every month! To Mr. Independent!"

"I'm *lending* him some money. OK? His friends basically all have limitless funds. He's very frugal, but if he's going to make those connections, and be in that world—"

"That great frat-house world, full of the best sort of people—"

"He has a *plan*. He has a plan and he wants you to be impressed with him—"

"News to me!"

"It's just for clothes and socializing," Patty said. "He pays his own tuition, he pays his own room and board, and maybe, if you could ever forgive him for not being an identical copy of you in every way, you might see how similar you two are. You were supporting yourself the exact same way when you were his age."

"Right, except I wore the same three pairs of corduroys for four years of college, and I wasn't out drinking five nights a week, and I sure as hell wasn't getting any money from my mother."

"*Well, it's a different world now, Walter.* And maybe, just *maybe,* he understands better than you do what a person has to do to get ahead in it."

"Work for a defense contractor, get shitfaced every night with fratboy Republicans. That's really the only way to get ahead? That's the only option available?"

"You don't understand how scared these kids are now. They're under so much pressure. So they like to party hard—so what?"

The old mansion's air-conditioning was no match for the humidity pressing on it from outside. The thunder was becoming continuous and omnidirectional; the ornamental pear tree outside the window heaved its branches as if somebody were climbing in it. Sweat was running on every part of Walter's body not directly in contact with his clothes.

"It's interesting to hear you suddenly defending young people," he said, "since you're normally so—"

"I'm defending your *son,*" she said. "Who, in case you haven't noticed, is not one of the brainless flipflop wearers. He's considerably more interesting than—"

"I cannot *believe* you've been sending him drinking money! You know what it's exactly like? It's exactly like corporate welfare. All these supposedly free-market companies sucking on the tit of the federal government. 'We need to shrink the government, we don't want any regulations, we don't want any taxes, but, oh, by the way—' "

"This isn't sucking on *tits,* Walter," Patty said with hatred.

"I was speaking metaphorically."

"Well, I'm saying you picked an interesting metaphor."

"Well, and I picked it carefully. All these companies pretending to be so grownup and free-market when they're actually just big babies devouring the federal budget while everybody else starves. Fish and Wildlife has its budget cut year after year, another five percent every year. You go to their field offices, they're ghost offices now. There's no staff, there's no money for land acquisition, no—"

"Oh the precious fish. The precious wildlife."

"I CARE ABOUT THEM. Can you not understand that? Can you not respect that? If you can't respect that, what are you even living with me for? Why don't you just leave?"

"Because leaving is not the *answer*. My God, do you think I haven't thought about it? Taking my great skills and work experience and great middle-aged body out on the open market? I actually think it's wonderful what you're doing for your warbler—"

"Bullshit."

"So, OK, it's not my personal thing, but—"

"What *is* your thing? You don't *have* a thing. You sit around doing nothing, nothing, nothing, nothing, every day, and it's killing me. If you would actually go out and get a job, and earn an actual paycheck, or do something for another human being, instead of sitting in your room feeling sorry for yourself, you might feel less worthless, is what I'm saying."

"Fine, but, honey, nobody wants to pay *me* a hundred eighty thousand a year to save the warblers. It's nice work if you can get it. But I can't get it. You want me to make Frappuccinos at Starbucks? You think eight hours a day at Starbucks is going to make me feel like I'm worth something?"

"It might! If you would ever try it! Which you never have, in your entire life!"

"Oh, finally it comes out! Finally we're getting somewhere!"

"I never should have let you stay home. That was the mistake. I don't know why your parents never made you get a job, but—"

"*I had jobs!* God *damn* it, Walter." She tried to kick him and only by accident missed his knee. "I worked a whole horrible summer for my dad. And then you saw me at the U., you know I can do it. I worked two solid years there. Even when I was eight months' pregnant, I was still going in."

"You were hanging out with Treadwell and drinking coffee and watching game films. That's not a job, Patty. That's a favor from people who love you. First you worked for your dad, then you worked for your friends in the A.D."

"And sixteen hours a day at home for twenty years? Unpaid? Does that not count? Was that just a 'favor,' too? Raising your kids? Working on your house?"

"Those were things *you* wanted."

"You didn't?"

"For you. I wanted them for you."

"Oh, bullshit, bullshit, bullshit. You wanted them for you, too. You were competing with Richard the whole time, and you know it. The only reason you're forgetting it now is that it didn't work out so great. You're not *winning* anymore."

"Winning has nothing to do with it."

"Liar! You're just as competitive as I am, you just won't tell the truth about it. That's why you won't leave me alone. That's why I've got to get that precious job. Because I'm making you a *loser.*"

"I can't listen to this. This is some alternate reality."

"Well, whatever, don't listen, but I'm still on your team. And, believe it or not, I still want you to win. The reason I'm helping Joey is he's on our team, and I will help you, too. I will go out tomorrow, for your sake, and I will—"

"Not for my sake."

"YES, FOR YOUR SAKE. Don't you get it? I *have* no sake. I don't believe in anything. I don't have faith in anything. The team is all I've got. And so I'll get some kind of job for your sake, and then you can just leave me the hell alone, and let me send Joey however much money I make. You won't see so much of me anymore—you won't have to be so disgusted."

"I'm not disgusted."

"Well, that is beyond my comprehension."

"And you don't have to get a job if you don't want to."

"Yes, I do! It's pretty clear, isn't it? You've made it pretty clear."

"No. You don't have to do anything. Just be my Patty again. Just come back to me."

She cried then, torrentially, and he lay down with her. Fighting had become their portal to sex, almost the only way it ever happened anymore.

While the rain lashed and the sky flashed, he tried to fill her with self-worth and desire, tried to convey how much he needed her to be the person he could bury his cares in. It never quite worked, and yet, when they were done, there came a stretch of minutes in which they lay and held each other in the quiet majesty of long marriage, forgot themselves in shared sadness and forgiveness for everything they'd inflicted on each other, and rested.

The very next morning, Patty had gone out and looked for work. She came back in less than two hours and skipped into Walter's office, in the mansion's many-windowed "conservatory," to announce that the local Republic of Health had hired her as a front-desk greeter.

"I don't know about this," Walter said.

"What? Why not?" Patty said. "It's literally the only place in George-town that doesn't embarrass me or sicken me. And they had an opening! It's a very lucky thing."

"Front-desk greeter just doesn't seem appropriate, given your talents."

"Appropriate to who?"

"To people who might see you."

"And which people are these?"

"I don't know. People I might be hitting up for money, or legislative backing, or regulatory help."

"Oh, my God. Are you listening to yourself? Are you hearing what you just said?"

"Look, I'm trying to be honest with you. Don't punish me for being honest."

"I'm punishing you for your *content*, Walter, not your honesty. I mean! 'Not appropriate.' Wow."

"I'm saying you're too smart for an entry-level gym job."

"No, you're saying I'm too old. You wouldn't have a problem with Jessica working there for the summer."

"Actually, I'd be disappointed if that's all she wanted to do with her summer."

"Oh, good Lord, then. I truly cannot win. 'Any job is better than no job, or, but, no, sorry, wait, the job that you actually want and are well qualified for is *not* better than no job.'"

330

"OK, fine. Take it. I don't care."

"Thank you for not caring!"

"I just think you're selling yourself way short."

"Well, maybe it'll only be temporary," Patty said. "Maybe I'll get my realtor's license, like every other unemployable wife around here, and start selling squalid little crooked-floored town houses for two million dollars. 'In this very bathroom, in 1962, Hubert Humphrey had a large bowel movement, which, in recognition of this historic movement, the property has been placed on the National Registry, which explains the hundred-thousand-dollar premium its owners are demanding. There's also a small but rather nice azalea bush behind the kitchen window.' I can start wearing pinks and greens and a Burberry raincoat. I'll buy a Lexus SUV with my first big commission. It'll be much more appropriate."

"I said OK."

"Thank you, honey! Thank you for letting me take the job I want!"

Walter watched her stride out the door and stop by Lalitha's desk. "Hi, Lalitha," she said. "I just got a job. I'm going to work at my gym."

"That's nice," Lalitha said. "You like that gym."

"Yeah, but Walter thinks it's inappropriate. What do you think?"

"I think any honest work can bring a human being dignity."

"*Patty*," Walter called. "I said it was OK."

"See, now he's changed his mind," she said to Lalitha. "Before, he was saying it was inappropriate."

"Yes, I heard that."

"Right, ha-ha-ha, I'm sure you did. But it's important to pretend otherwise, OK?"

"Don't leave the door open if you don't want to be heard," Lalitha said coldly.

"We all have to work really hard on pretending."

Becoming a front-desk greeter at Republic of Health did for Patty's spirits everything Walter had hoped a job would do. Everything and, alas, more. Her depression immediately seemed to lift, but this only showed how misleading the word "depression" was, because Walter was certain that her old unhappiness and anger and despair were all still present beneath her bright and brittle new way of being. She spent her mornings in her room, worked the p.m. shift at the gym, and didn't get home until after ten. She began reading beauty and fitness magazines and noticeably using eye makeup. The sweatpants and baggy jeans that she'd been wearing in Washington, the sort of unconfining clothes that mental patients spend their days in, gave way to closer-fitting jeans that cost actual money.

"You look great," Walter said one evening, trying to be nice.

"Well, now that I have an income," she said, "I need something to spend it on, right?"

"You could always make charitable contributions to the Cerulean Mountain Trust instead."

"Ha-ha-ha!"

"Our need is great."

"I'm having fun, Walter. A tiny little bit of fun."

But she didn't really seem like she was having fun. She seemed like she was trying to hurt him, or spite him, or prove some kind of point. Walter began working out at Republic of Health himself, using a stack of free passes she'd given him, and he was unsettled by the intensity of the friendliness she directed at the members whose cards she scanned. She wore tiny-sleeved, provocatively sloganed Republic T-shirts (PUSH, SWEAT, LIFT) that highlighted her beautifully toned upper arms. Her eyes had a speed-freak glitter, and her laugh, which had always thrilled Walter, sounded false and ominous when he heard it echoing behind him in the Republic's foyer. She was giving it to everybody now, giving it indiscriminately, meaninglessly, to every member who walked in off Wisconsin Avenue. And then one day he noticed a breast-augmentation brochure on her desk at home.

"Jesus," he said, examining it. "This is obscene."

"Actually, it's a medical brochure."

"It's a *mental-illness* brochure, Patty. It's like a guide to how to become more mentally ill."

"Well, excuse me, I just thought it might be nice, for the short remainder of my comparative youth, to have a little bit of actual chest. To see what that might be like."

"You already *have* a chest. I adore your chest."

"Well, that's all very nice, dear, but in fact you don't get to make the decision, because it's not your body. It's mine. Isn't that what you've always said? You're the feminist in this household."

"Why are you doing this? I don't understand what you're doing with yourself."

"Well, maybe you should just leave if you don't like it. Have you considered that? It would solve the whole problem, like, instantly."

"Well, that's never going to happen, so—"

"I KNOW IT'S NEVER GOING TO HAPPEN."

"Oh! Oh! Oh! Oh!"

"So I might as well go ahead and buy myself some tits, to help make the years go by and give me something to save up my pennies for, is all I'm saying. I'm not talking about anything grotesquely large. You might even find you like 'em. Have you considered that?"

Walter was frightened by the long-term toxicity they were creating with their fights. He could feel it pooling in their marriage like the coal-sludge ponds in Appalachian valleys. Where there were really huge coal deposits, as in Wyoming County, the coal companies built processing plants right next to their mines and used water from the nearest stream to wash the coal. The polluted water was collected in big ponds of toxic sludge, and Walter had become so worried about having sludge impoundments in the middle of the Warbler Park that he'd tasked Lalitha with showing him how not to worry about it so much. This hadn't been an easy task, since there was no way around the fact that when you dug up coal you also unearthed nasty chemicals like arsenic and cadmium that had been safely buried for millions of years. You could try dumping the poison back down into abandoned underground mines, but it had a way of seeping into the water table and ending up in drinking water. It really was a lot like the deep shit that got stirred up when a married couple fought: once certain things had been said, how could they ever be forgotten again? Lalitha was able to do enough research to reassure Walter that, if the sludge was carefully sequestered and properly contained, it eventually dried out enough that you could cover it with crushed rock and topsoil and pretend it wasn't there. This story had become the sludge-pond gospel that he was determined to spread in West Virginia. He believed in it the same way he believed in ecological strongholds and science-based reclamation, because he had to believe in it, because of Patty. But now, as he lay and sought sleep on the hostile Days Inn mattress, between the scratchy Days Inn sheets, he wondered if any of it was true . . .

He must have drifted off at some point, because when the alarm rang, at 3:40, he felt cruelly yanked from oblivion. Another eighteen hours of waking dread and anger lay ahead of him. Lalitha knocked on his door at 4:00 sharp, looking fresh in casual jeans and hiking shoes. "I feel horrid!" she said. "How about you?"

"Horrid also. At least you don't look it, the way I do."

The rain had stopped in the night, giving way to a dense, south-smelling fog that was scarcely less wetting. Over breakfast, at a truck stop across the road, Walter told Lalitha about the e-mail from Dan Caperville at the *Times*.

"Do you want to go home now?" she said. "Do the press conference tomorrow morning?"

"I told Caperville I was doing it on Monday."

"You could tell him you changed it. Just get it out of the way, so we'll have the weekend free."

But Walter was so painfully exhausted that he couldn't imagine holding a press conference the next morning. He sat and suffered mutely while Lalitha, doing what he had lacked the courage to do the night before, read the *Times* article on her BlackBerry. "This is only twelve paragraphs," she said. "Not so bad."

"I guess that's why everybody else missed it and I had to hear about it from my wife."

"So you spoke to her last night."

Lalitha seemed to mean something by this, but he was too tired to figure out what. "I just wonder who did the leaking," he said. "And how much they leaked."

"Maybe your wife leaked it."

"Right." He laughed and then saw the hard look on Lalitha's face. "She wouldn't do a thing like that," he said. "She doesn't care enough, if nothing else."

"Hm." Lalitha took a bite of pancake and looked around the diner with the same hard, unhappy expression. She, of course, had every reason to be sore at Patty, and at Walter, this morning. To feel rejected and alone. But these were the first seconds in which he'd ever experienced anything like coldness from her; and they were dreadful. What he'd never understood about men in his position, in all the books he'd read and movies he'd seen about them, was clearer to him now: you couldn't keep expecting wholehearted love without, at some point, requiting it. There was no credit to be earned for simply being good.

"I just want to have our weekend meeting," he said. "If I can just have two days to work on overpopulation, I can face anything on Monday."

Lalitha finished her pancakes without speaking to him. Walter forced down some of his own breakfast as well, and they went out into the light-polluted dark morning. In the rental car, she adjusted the seat and mirrors, which he'd moved the night before. As she was reaching across herself to fasten her seat belt, he put an awkward hand on her neck and pulled her closer, bringing them eye to serious eye in the all-night roadside light.

"I can't go five minutes without you on my side," he said. "Not five minutes. Do you understand that?"

After a moment's thought, she nodded. Then, letting go of the seat belt, she placed her hands on his shoulders, gave him a solemn kiss, and drew back to gauge its effect. He felt as if he'd done his utmost now and could go no further on his own. He simply waited while, with a child's frown of concentration, she took his glasses off, set them on the dashboard, put her hands on his head, and touched her little nose to his. He was momentarily troubled by how similar her face and Patty's looked in extreme close-up, but all he had to do was close his eyes and kiss her and she was pure Lalitha, her lips pillowy, her mouth peach-sweet, her blood-filled head warm beneath her silky hair. He struggled against how wrong it felt to kiss somebody so young. He could feel her youth as a kind of fragility in his hands, and he was relieved when she drew back again to look at him, with shining eyes. He felt that some word of acknowledgment was called for now, but he couldn't stop staring at her, and she seemed to take this as an invitation to clamber across the gear shift and straddle him awkwardly on the bucket seat, so that he could take her fully in his arms. The *aggression* with which she kissed him then, the hungry abandon, brought him a joy so extreme that it blew up the ground beneath him. He was in free fall, everything he believed in was receding into darkness, and he began to cry.

"Oh, what is it?" she said.

"You have to go slow with me."

"Slow, slow, yes," she said, kissing his tears, wiping them with her satiny thumbs. "Walter, are you sad?"

"No, honey, the opposite."

"Then let me love you."

"OK. You can do that."

"Really OK?"

"Yes," he said, crying. "But we should probably hit the road."

"In a minute."

She put her tongue to his lips, and he opened them to let her in. There was more desire for him in her mouth than in Patty's entire body. Her shoulders, as he gripped them through her nylon shell, seemed to be all bone and baby fat and no muscle, all eager pliability. She straightened her back and bore down on him, pushing her hips into his chest; and he wasn't ready for it. He was closer now but still not fully there. His resistance the night before hadn't been simply a matter of taboo or principle, and his tears weren't all for joy.

Sensing this, Lalitha pulled away from him and studied his face. In response to whatever she saw in it, she climbed back into the other seat again and observed him from a greater distance. Now that he'd driven her away, he keenly wanted her again, but he had a dim recollection, from the stories he'd heard and read about men in his position, that this was the terrible thing about them: that it was known as stringing a girl along. He sat for a while in the changeless purple-toned streetlight, listening to the trucks on the interstate.

"I'm sorry," he said finally. "I'm still trying to figure out how to live."

"That's OK. You can have some time."

He nodded, taking note of the word *some*.

"Can I ask you one question, though?" she said.

"You can ask me a million questions."

"Well, just one for now. Do you think you might love me?"

He smiled. "Yes, I definitely think that."

"That's all I need, then." And she started the engine.

Somewhere above the fog, the sky was turning blue. Lalitha took the back roads out of Beckley at highly illegal speeds, and Walter was happy to gaze out the window and not think about what was happening to him, just inhabit the free fall. That the Appalachian hardwood forest was among the world's most biodiverse temperate ecosystems, home to a variety of tree species and orchids and freshwater invertebrates whose bounty the high plains and sandy coasts could only envy, wasn't readily apparent from the roads they were traveling. The land here had betrayed itself, its gnarly topography and wealth of extractable resources discouraging the egalitarianism of Jefferson's yeoman farmers, fostering instead the concentration of surface and mineral rights in the hands of the out-of-state wealthy, and consigning the poor natives and imported workers to the margins: to logging, to working in the mines, to scraping out pre- and then, later, post-industrial existences on scraps of leftover land which, stirred by the same urge to couple as had now gripped Walter and Lalitha, they'd overfilled with tightly spaced generations of too-large families. West Virginia was the nation's own banana republic, its Congo, its Guyana, its Honduras. The roads were reasonably picturesque in summer, but now, with the leaves still down, you could see all the scabby rock-littered pastures, the spindly canopies of young second growth, the gouged hillsides and mining-damaged streams, the spavined barns and paintless houses, the trailer homes hip-deep in plastic and metallic trash, the torn-up dirt tracks leading nowhere.

Deeper in the country, the scenes were less discouraging. Remoteness brought the relief of no people: no people meant more everything else. Lalitha swerved violently around a grouse on the road, a grouse greeter, an avian goodwill ambassador inviting appreciation of the brawnier forestation and less marred heights and clearer streams of Wyoming County. Even the weather was brightening for them.

"I want you," Walter said.

She shook her head. "Don't say anything else, OK? We still have work to do. Let's just do our jobs and then see."

He was tempted to make her stop at one of the little rustic picnic areas along Black Jewel Creek (of which the Nine Mile was a principal tributary), but it would be irresponsible, he thought, to lay a hand on her again until he was certain he was ready. Delay was bearable if gratification was assured. And the beauty of the land up here, the sweet spore-laden dampness of the early-spring air, was so assuring him.

It was after six by the time they reached the turnoff for Forster Hollow. Walter had expected to encounter heavy truck and earth-moving-equipment traffic on the Nine Mile road, but there wasn't a vehicle in sight. Instead they found deep tire and tractor chewings in the mud. Where the woods encroached, freshly broken branches were lying on the ground and dangling lamely from the overarching trees.

"Looks like somebody got here early," Walter said.

Lalitha was applying gas in fitful spurts, fishtailing the car in the mud, veering dangerously close to the road's edge to avoid the larger fallen branches.

"I almost wonder if they got here yesterday," Walter said. "I wonder if they misunderstood and brought the equipment in yesterday to get an early start."

"They did have the legal right, as of noon."

"But that's not what they told us. They told us six a.m. today."

"Yes, but they're coal companies, Walter."

They came to one of the narrowest pinches in the road and found it roughly bulldozed and chainsawed, the tree trunks pushed down into the ravine below. Lalitha revved the engine and shimmied and jounced across a hastily graded stretch of mud and stone and stump. "Glad this is a rental car!" she said as she accelerated zestfully onto the clearer road beyond.

Two miles farther up, at the boundary of property now belonging to the Trust, the road was blocked by a couple of passenger cars backed up in front of a chainlink gate being assembled by workers in orange vests. Walter could see Jocelyn Zorn and some of her women conferring with a hard-hatted manager who was holding a clipboard. In another, not too dissimilar world, Walter might have been friends with Jocelyn Zorn. She resembled the Eve in the famous altarpiece painting by van Eyck; she was pallid and dull-eyed and somewhat macrocephalic-looking in the highness of her hairline. But she had a fine, unsettling cool, an unflappability suggestive of irony, and was the sort of bitter salad green for which Walter ordinarily had a fondness. She came down the road to meet him and Lalitha as they were stepping out into the mud.

"Good morning, Walter," she said. "Can you explain what's going on here?"

"Looks like some road improvement," he said disingenuously.

"There's a lot of dirt going in the creek. It's already turbid halfway to the Black Jewel. I'm not seeing much in the way of erosion mitigation here. Less than none, actually."

"We'll talk to them about that."

"I've asked DEP to come up and have a look. I imagine they'll get here by June or so. Did you buy them off, too?"

Through the brown spatters on the bumper of the rearmost car Walter could read the message BEEN DONE BY NARDONE.

"Let's rewind a little bit, Jocelyn," he said. "Can we step back and look at the bigger picture?"

"No," she said. "I'm not interested in that. I'm interested in the dirt in the stream. I'm also interested in what's happening beyond the fence."

"What's happening is we're preserving sixty-five thousand acres of roadless woodland for eternity. We're securing unfragmented habitat for as many as two thousand breeding pairs of cerulean warbler."

Zorn lowered her dull eyes to the muddy ground. "Right. Your species of interest. It's very pretty."

"Why don't we all go somewhere else," Lalitha said cheerfully, "and sit down and talk about the bigger picture. We're on your side, you know."

"No," Zorn said. "I'm going to stay here for a while. I asked my friend from the *Gazette* to come up and have a look."

"Have you been talking to the *New York Times*, too?" it occurred to Walter to ask.

"Yes. They seemed pretty interested, actually. MTR's a magic term these days. That's what you're doing up there, isn't it?"

"We're having a press conference on Monday," he said. "I'm going to lay out the whole plan. I think, when you hear the details, you're going to be very excited. We can get you a plane ticket if you want to join us. I'd love to have you there. You and I could even have a little public dialogue, if you want to voice your concerns."

"In Washington?"

"Yes."

"Figures."

"That's where we're based."

"Right. It's where everything's based."

"Jocelyn, we have fifty thousand acres here that will never be touched in any way. The rest of it will be successional within a few years. I think we've made some very good decisions."

"I guess we disagree about that, then."

"Seriously think about joining us in Washington on Monday. And have your friend at the *Gazette* give me a call today." Walter gave Zorn a business card from his wallet. "Tell him we'd love to bring him to Washington, too, if he's interested."

From farther up in the hills came a murmur of thunder that sounded like blasting, probably up at Forster Hollow. Zorn put the business card in a pocket of her rain parka. "By the way," she said, "I've been talking to Coyle Mathis. I already know what you're doing."

"Coyle Mathis is legally barred from discussing it," Walter said. "I'm happy to sit down with you and talk about it myself, though."

"The fact that he's living in a brand-new five-bedroom ranch house in Whitmanville speaks for itself."

"That's a nice house, isn't it?" Lalitha said. "Much, much nicer than where he was."

"You might want to pay him a visit and see if he agrees with you about that."

"Anyway," Walter said, "you need to move your cars out of the way so we can get through."

"Hm," Zorn said, uninterested. "I guess you could call somebody to tow us, if there were cell reception here. Which there isn't."

"Oh, come on, Jocelyn." Walter's anger was outflanking his barricades against it. "Can we at least be adults about this? Acknowledge that we're fundamentally on the same side, even if we disagree about our methods?"

"Sorry, no," she said. "My method is to block the road."

Not trusting himself to say more, Walter strode up the hill and let Lalitha hurry after him. A flail, the whole morning was becoming a flail. The hard-hatted manager, who looked no older than Jessica, was explaining to the other women, with remarkable courtesy, why they needed to move their cars. "Do you have a radio?" Walter asked him abruptly.

"I'm sorry. Who are you?"

"I'm the director of the Cerulean Mountain Trust. We were expected at the top of the road at six o'clock."

"Right, sir. I'm afraid that's going to be a problem if these ladies don't move their cars."

"Well, then, how about radioing for somebody to come down and get us?"

"Out of range, unfortunately. These damned hollers are dead zones."

"OK." Walter took a deep breath. He could see a pickup parked beyond the gate. "Maybe you can run us up in your truck, then."

"I'm afraid I'm not authorized to leave the gate area."

"Well, then, lend it to us."

"I can't do that, either, sir. You're not insured for it on the work site. But if these ladies would just move aside for a sec, you'd be free to proceed in your own vehicle."

Walter turned to the women, none of whom looked younger than sixty, and smiled in vague supplication. "Please?" he said. "We're not with a coal company. We're conservationists."

"Conservationists my ass!" the oldest one said.

"No, seriously," Lalitha said in a soothing tone. "It would be to everyone's benefit if you would let us through. We're here to monitor the work and make sure it's being done responsibly. We're very much on your side, and we share your concerns about the environment. In fact, if one or two of you would like to come along with us—"

"I'm afraid that's not authorized," the manager said.

"Fuck the authorization!" Walter said. "We need to get through here! I *own* this fucking land! Do you understand that? *I own everything you can see here.*"

"How you likin' it?" the oldest woman said to him. "Doesn't feel so good now, does it? Being on the wrong side of the fence."

"You're more than free to walk in, sir," the manager said, "although it's a pretty far piece. I reckon you're looking at two hours with all the mud."

"Just lend me the truck, OK? I will indemnify you, or you can say I stole it, or whatever you like. Just lend me the fucking truck."

Walter felt Lalitha's hand on his arm. "Walter? Let's go sit in the car for a minute." She turned to the women. "We're very much on your side, and we appreciate your coming out to show your concern for this wonderful forest, which we're very dedicated to preserving."

"Interesting way you got of going about that," the oldest woman said.

As Lalitha led Walter back down toward the rental car, they could hear heavy equipment coming rumbling up the road behind it. The rumble became a roar which then resolved itself into a pair of giant, road-wide backhoes with mud-caked tractors. The driver of the front one left the engine coughing out fumes while he hopped down for a word with Walter.

"Sir, you're going to have to move your vehicle up ahead to where we can pass it."

"Does it look like I can do that?" he said wildly. "Is that what it fucking looks like to you?"

"I wouldn't know, sir. But we can't be backing up. Be near a mile back down to a turnout."

Before Walter could get even angrier, Lalitha took him by both arms and peered up fervently into his face. "You have to let me handle this. You're too upset now."

"I'm upset for good reason!"

"Walter. *Sit in the car.* Now."

He did as he was told. He sat for more than an hour, fiddling with his non-receiving BlackBerry and listening to the mindless waste of fossil fuels as the backhoe behind him idled. When the driver finally thought to turn it off, he heard a chorus of engines from farther back—another four or five heavy trucks and earthmovers were backed up now. Somebody needed to summon the state police to deal with Zorn and her zealots. In the meantime, incredibly, in deepest Wyoming County, he was stopped dead in traffic. Lalitha was running up and down the road, conferring with the various parties, doing her best to spread goodwill. To pass the time, Walter did mental tallies of what had gone wrong in the world in the hours since he'd awakened in the Days Inn. Net population gain: 60,000. New acres of American sprawl: 1,000. Birds killed by domestic and feral cats in the United States: 500,000. Barrels of oil burned worldwide: 12,000,000. Metric tons of carbon dioxide dumped into the atmosphere: 11,000,000. Sharks murdered for their fins and left floating finless in the water: 150,000 . . . The tallies, which he recalculated as the hour grew even later, brought him a strange spiteful satisfaction. There are days so bad that only their worsening, only a descent into an outright orgy of badness, can redeem them.

It was getting on toward nine o'clock when Lalitha returned to him. One of the drivers, she said, had found a spot two hundred yards back down the road where a passenger car could pull off and let the big equipment pass. The rearmost driver was going to back his truck all the way down to the highway and phone for the police.

"Do you want to try to walk up to Forster Hollow?" Walter said.

"No," Lalitha said, "I want us to leave immediately. Jocelyn has a camera. We don't want to be photographed anywhere near a police action."

There ensued half an hour of grinding gears and squawking brakes and black bursts of diesel smoke, followed by a further forty-five minutes of breathing the rear truck's foul exhaust as it inched backward down the valley. Out on the highway at last, in the freedom of the open road, Lalitha drove back toward Beckley at frantic speeds, flooring the gas on the shortest of straightaways, leaving rubber on the curves.

They were on the shabby outskirts of town when his BlackBerry sang its cerulean song, making official their return to civilization. The call was from a Twin Cities number, possibly familiar, possibly not.

"Dad?"

Walter frowned with astonishment. "Joey? Wow! Hello."

"Yeah, hey. Hello."

"Everything OK with you? I didn't even recognize your number, it's been so long."

The line seemed to go dead, as if the call had been dropped. Or maybe he'd said the wrong thing. But then Joey spoke again, in a voice like someone else's. Some quavering, tentative kid. "Yeah, so, anyway, Dad, um—do you have a second?"

"Go ahead."

"Yeah, well, so, I guess the thing is, I'm sort of in some trouble."

"What?"

"I said I'm in some trouble."

It was the kind of call that every parent dreaded getting; but Walter, for a moment, wasn't feeling like Joey's parent. He said, "Hey, so am I! So is everybody!"

# ENOUGH ALREADY

Within days of young Zachary's posting of their interview on his blog, Katz's cellular voice mailbox began to fill with messages. The first was from a pesty German, Matthias Dröhner, whom Katz vaguely recalled having struggled to fend off during Walnut Surprise's swing through the Fatherland. "Now that you are giving interviews again," Dröhner said, "I hope you'll be so kind as to give one to me, like you promised, Richard. You did promise!" Dröhner, in his message, didn't say how he'd come by Katz's cell number, but a good guess was via blogospheric leakage from the bar napkin of some chick he'd hit on while touring. He was undoubtedly now getting interview requests by e-mail as well, probably in much greater numbers, but he hadn't had the fortitude to venture online since the previous summer. Dröhner's message was followed by calls from an Oregonian chick named Euphrosyne; a bellowingly jovial music journalist in Melbourne, Australia; and a college radio DJ in Iowa City who sounded ten years old. All wanted the same thing. They wanted Katz to say again—but in slightly different words, so that they could post it or publish it under their own names—exactly what he'd already said to Zachary.

"That was golden, dude," Zachary told him on the roof on White Street, a week after the posting, while they were awaiting the arrival of Zachary's object of desire, Caitlyn. The "dude" form of address was new and irritating to Katz but entirely consonant with his experience of interviewers. As soon as he submitted to them, they dropped all pretense of awe.

"Don't call me dude," he said nevertheless.

"Sure, whatever," Zachary said. He was walking a long Trex board as if it were a balance beam, his skinny arms outstretched. The afternoon was fresh and blustery. "I'm just saying my hit-counter's going crazy. I'm getting hot-linked all over the world. Do you ever look at your fan sites?"

"No."

"I'm right up at the very top of the best one now. I can get my computer and show you."

"Really no need for that."

"I think there's a real hunger for people speaking truth to power. Like, there's a little minority now that's saying you sounded like an asshole and a whiner. But that's just the player-hating fringe. I wouldn't worry about it."

"Thanks for the reassurance," Katz said.

When the girl Caitlyn appeared on the roof, accompanied by a pair of female sidekicks, Zachary remained perched on his balance beam, too cool to make introductions, while Katz set down his nail gun and suffered examination by the visitors. Caitlyn was clad in hippie garb, a brocade vest and a corduroy coat such as Carole King and Laura Nyro had worn, and would certainly have been worthy of pursuit had Katz not, in the week since he'd seen Walter Berglund, become preoccupied again with Patty. Meeting a choice adolescent now was like smelling strawberries when you were hungry for a steak.

"What can I do for you girls?" he said.

"We baked you some banana bread," the pudgier sidekick said, brandishing a foil-wrapped loaf.

The other two girls rolled their eyes. "*She* baked you banana bread," Caitlyn said. "We had nothing to do with it."

"I hope you like *walnuts*," the baker girl said.

"Ah, I getcha," Katz said.

A confused silence fell. Helicopter rotors were pounding the lower Manhattan airspace, the wind doing funny things with the sound.

"We're just big fans of *Nameless Lake*," Caitlyn said. "We heard you were building a deck up here."

"Well, as you see, your friend Zachary's as good as his word."

Zachary was rocking the Trex board with his orange sneakers, affecting impatience to be alone with Katz again, and thus evincing some good basic pickup skills.

"Zachary's a great young musician," Katz said. "I wholeheartedly endorse him. He's a talent to watch."

The girls turned their heads toward Zachary with a kind of sad boredom.

"Seriously," Katz said. "You should get him to go downstairs with you and listen to him play."

"We're actually more into alt country," Caitlyn said. "Not so much boy rock."

"He's got some great country licks," Katz persisted.

Caitlyn squared her shoulders, aligning her posture like a dancer, and gazed at him steadily, as if to give him a chance to amend the indifference he was showing her. She clearly wasn't used to indifference. "Why are you building a deck?" she said.

"For fresh air and exercise."

"Why do you need exercise? You look pretty fit."

Katz felt very, very tired. To be unable to bring himself to play for even ten seconds the game that Caitlyn was interested in playing with him was to understand the allure of death. To die would be the cleanest cutting of his connection to the thing—the girl's *idea* of Richard Katz—that was burdening him. Away to the southwest of where they were standing stood the massive Eisenhower-era utility building that marred the nineteenth-century architectural vistas of almost every Tribecan loft-dweller. Once upon a time, the building had offended Katz's urban aesthetic, but now it pleased him by offending the urban aesthetic of the millionaires who'd taken over the neighborhood. It loomed like death over the excellent lives being lived down here; it had become something of a friend of his.

"Let's have a look at that banana bread," he said to the pudgy girl.

"I also brought you some wintergreen Chiclets," she said.

"Why don't I autograph the box for you, and you can keep it."

"That would be awesome!"

He took a Sharpie from a toolbox. "What's your name?"

"Sarah."

"It's great to meet you, Sarah. I'm going to take your banana bread home and have it for dessert tonight."

Caitlyn briefly, with something like *moral* outrage, observed this dissing of her pretty self. Then she walked over to Zachary, trailed by the other girl. And here, Katz thought, was a concept: instead of trying to fuck the girls he hated, why not simply snub them for real? To keep his attention on Sarah and away from the magnetic Caitlyn, he took out the tin of Skoal that he'd bought to give his lungs a break from cigarettes, and inserted a big pinch of it between gum and cheek.

"Can I try some of that?" the emboldened Sarah said.

"It'll make you sick."

"But, like, one shred?"

Katz shook his head and pocketed the tin, whereupon Sarah asked if she could fire the nail gun. She was like a walking advertisement of the late-model parenting she'd received: You have permission to ask for things! Just because you aren't pretty doesn't mean you don't! Your offerings, if you're bold enough to make them, will be welcomed by the world! In her own way, she was just as tiring as Caitlyn. Katz wondered if he'd been this tiring himself at eighteen, or whether, as it now seemed to him, his anger at the world—his perception of the world as a hostile adversary, worthy of his anger—had made him more interesting than these young paragons of self-esteem.

He let Sarah fire the nail gun (she shrieked at its recoil and nearly dropped it) and then sent her on her way. Caitlyn had been snubbed so effectively that she didn't even say good-bye but simply followed Zachary downstairs. Katz wandered over to the master-bedroom skylight in hopes of glimpsing Zachary's mother, but all he saw was the DUX bed, the Eric Fischl canvas, the flat-screen TV.

Katz's susceptibility to women over thirty-five was a source of some embarrassment. It felt sad and a little sick in the way it seemed to reference his own lunatic and absent mother, but there was no altering the basic wiring of his brain. The kiddies were perennially enticing and perennially unsatisfying in much the same way that coke was unsatisfying: whenever he was off it, he remembered it as fantastic and unbeatable and craved it, but as soon as he was on it again he remembered that it wasn't fantastic at all, it was sterile and empty: neuro-mechanistic, death-flavored. Nowadays especially, the young chicks were hyperactive in their screwing, hurrying through every position known to the species, doing this that and the other, their kiddie snatches too unfragrant and closely shaved to even register as human body parts. He remembered more detail from his few hours with Patty Berglund than he did from a decade's worth of kiddies. Of course, he'd known Patty forever and been attracted to her forever; long anticipation had certainly been a factor. But there was also just something intrinsically more human about her than about the youngsters. More difficult, more involving, more worth having. And now that his prophetic dick, his divining rod, was again pointing him in her direction, he was at a loss to recall why he hadn't taken fuller advantage of his opportunity with her. Some misguided notion of niceness, now incomprehensible to him, had prevented him from going to her hotel in Philadelphia and helping himself to more of her. Having betrayed Walter once, in the chilly middle of a northern night, he should have gone ahead and done it another hundred times and got it out of his system. The evidence of how much he'd wanted to do this was right there in the songs he'd written for *Nameless Lake*. He'd turned his ungratified desire into art. But now, having made that art and reaped its dubious rewards, he had no reason to keep renouncing a thing he still wanted. And if Walter were then, in turn, to feel entitled to the Indian chick, and stop being such a moralistic irritant, so much the better for all concerned.

He took a Friday-evening train to Washington from Newark. He still wasn't able to listen to music, but his non-Apple MP3 player was loaded with a track of pink noise—white noise frequency-shifted toward the bass end and capable of neutralizing every ambient sound the world could throw at him—and by donning big cushioned headphones and angling himself toward the window and holding a Bernhard novel close to his face, he was able to achieve complete privacy until the train stopped in Philly. Here a white couple in their early twenties, wearing white T-shirts and eating white ice cream from waxed-paper cups, settled into the newly vacated seats in front of him. The extreme white of their T-shirts seemed to him the color of the Bush regime. The chick immediately reclined her seat into his space, and when she finished her ice cream, a few minutes later, she tossed the cup and spoon back under her seat, where his feet were.

With a heavy sigh, he removed his headphones, stood up, and dropped the cup on her lap.

"Jesus!" she cried with scalding disgust.

"Hey, man, what the fuck?" her resplendently white companion said.

"You dropped this on my feet," Katz said.

"She didn't throw it on your *lap*."

"That is a pretty amazing accomplishment," Katz said. "To sound self-righteous about your girlfriend dropping a wet ice-cream container on somebody else's feet."

"This is a *public train*," the girl said. "You should take a private jet if you can't deal with other people."

"Yeah, I'll try to remember to do that next time."

The rest of the way to Washington, the couple kept lunging against their seat backs, attempting to push them past their limits and farther into his space. They didn't seem to have recognized him, but, if they had, they would surely soon be blogging about what an asshole Richard Katz was.

Although he'd played D.C. often enough over the years, its horizontality and vexing diagonal avenues never ceased to freak him out. He felt like a rat in a governmental maze here. For all he could tell from the back seat of his taxi, the driver was taking him not to Georgetown but to the Israeli embassy for enhanced interrogation. The pedestrians in every neighborhood all seemed to have taken the same dowdiness pills. As if individual style were a volatile substance that evaporated in the vacuity of D.C.'s sidewalks and infernally wide squares. The whole city was a monosyllabic imperative directed at Katz in his beat-up biker jacket. Saying: die.

The mansion in Georgetown had some character, however. As Katz understood it, Walter and Patty hadn't personally chosen this house, but it nevertheless reflected the excellent urban-gentry taste he'd come to expect of them. It had a slate roof and multiple dormers and high ground-floor windows looking out on something resembling an actual small lawn. Above the doorbell was a brass plate discreetly conceding the presence of THE CERULEAN MOUNTAIN TRUST.

Jessica Berglund opened the door. Katz hadn't seen her since she was in high school, and he smiled with pleasure at the sight of her all grown up and womanly. She seemed cross and distracted, however, and barely greeted him. "Hi, um," she said, "just come on back to the kitchen, OK?"

She glanced over her shoulder at a long parquet-floored hallway. The Indian girl was standing at the end of it. "Hi, Richard," she called, waving to him nervously.

"Just give me one second," Jessica said. She stalked down the hall, and Katz followed with his overnight bag, passing a large room full of desks and file cabinets and a smaller room with a conference table. The place smelled like warm semiconductors and fresh paper products. In the kitchen was a big French farmer's table that he recognized from St. Paul. "Excuse me for one second," Jessica said as she pursued Lalitha into a more executive-looking suite at the back of the house.

"*I'm* a young person," he heard her say there. "OK? I'm the young person here. Do you get it?"

Lalitha: "Yes! Of course. That's why it's so wonderful you came down. All I'm saying is I'm not so old myself, you know."

"You're twenty-seven!"

"That's not young?"

"How old were you when you got your first cell phone? When did you start going online?"

"I was in college. But, Jessica, listen—"

"There's a *big difference* between college and high school. There's an entirely different way that people communicate now. A way that people my age started learning much earlier than you did."

"I know that. We don't disagree about that. I really don't see why you're so angry at me."

"Why I'm angry? Because you have my dad thinking you're this great expert on young people, but you're *not* the great expert, as you just totally demonstrated."

"Jessica, I know the difference between a text and an e-mail. I misspoke because I'm tired. I hardly slept all week. It's not fair of you to make so much of this."

"Do you even *send* texts?"

"I don't have to. We have BlackBerrys, which do the same thing, only better."

"It is not the same thing! *God*. This is what I'm talking about! If you didn't grow up with cell phones in high school, you don't understand that your phone is very, very different from your e-mail. It's a totally different way of being in touch with people. I have friends who hardly even check their e-mail anymore. And if you and Dad are going to be targeting kids in college, it's really important that you understand that."

"OK, then. Be mad at me. Go ahead and be mad. But I still have work to do tonight, and you need to leave me alone now."

Jessica returned to the kitchen, shaking her head, her jaw set. "I'm sorry," she said. "You probably want to take a shower and have some dinner. There's a dining room upstairs that I think it's nice to actually use now and then. I got a, um." She looked around in great distraction. "I made a big dinner salad and some pasta I'll reheat. I also got some nice bread, the proverbial loaf of bread that my mother is apparently incapable of buying when a house full of people is coming for the weekend."

"Don't worry about me," Katz said. "I've still got part of a sandwich in my bag."

"No, I'll come up and sit with you. It's just that things are a little disorganized around here. This house is just . . . just . . . just . . ." She clenched her fingers and shook her hands. "Unnhh! This house!"

"Calm down," Katz said. "It's great to see you."

"How do they even *live* when I'm not here? That's what I don't understand. How the whole thing even functions at the basic level of taking the trash out." Jessica shut the kitchen door and lowered her voice. "God only knows what *she* eats. Apparently, from what my mom says, she subsists on Cheerios, milk, and cheese sandwiches. And bananas. But where are these foods? There's not even any *milk* in the fridge."

Katz made a vague gesture with his hands, to suggest that he could not be held responsible.

"And, you know, as it happens," Jessica said, "I know quite a bit about Indian regional cooking. Because a lot of my friends in college were Indian? And *years* ago, when I first came down here, I asked her if she could teach me how to do some regional cooking, like from Bengal, where she was born. I'm very respectful of people's traditions, and I thought we could make this nice big meal together, her and me, and actually sit down at the dining-room table like a family. I thought that might be cool, since she's Indian and I'm interested in food. And she laughed at me and said she couldn't even cook an egg. Apparently both her parents were engineers and never made a real meal in their lives. So there went *that* plan."

Katz was smiling at her, enjoying the seamless way that she combined and blended, in her compact unitary person, the personalities of her parents. She sounded like Patty and was outraged like Walter, and yet she was entirely herself. Her blond hair was pulled back and tied with a severity that seemed to stretch her eyebrows into the raised position, contributing to her expression of appalled surprise and irony. He wasn't the least bit attracted to her, and he liked her all the more for this.

"So where is everybody?" he said.

"Mom is at the gym, 'working.' And Dad, I don't actually know. Some meeting in Virginia. He told me to tell you he'll see you in the morning—he'd meant to be here tonight, but something came up."

"When's your mom getting home?"

"Late, I'm sure. You know, it's not at all obvious now, but she was actually a fairly great mom when I was growing up. You know, like, cooked? Made people feel welcome? Put flowers in a vase by the bed? Apparently that's all a thing of the past now."

In her capacity as emergency hostess, Jessica led Katz up a narrow rear staircase and showed him the big second-floor bedrooms that had been converted to living and dining and family rooms, the small room in which Patty had a computer and a foldout sofa, and then, on the third floor, the equally small room where he would sleep. "This is officially my brother's room," she said, "but I bet he hasn't spent ten nights in it since they moved here."

There was, indeed, no trace of Joey, just more of Walter and Patty's very tasteful furniture.

"How are things with Joey anyway?"

Jessica shrugged. "I'm the wrong person to ask."

"You guys don't talk?"

She looked up at Katz with her amusedly wide-open and somewhat protuberant eyes. "We talk sometimes, now and then."

"And what, then? What's the situation?"

"Well, he's become a Republican, so the conversations don't tend to be very pleasant."

"Ah."

"I put some towels out for you. Do you need a washcloth, too?"

"Never been a washcloth user, no."

When he went back downstairs, half an hour later, showered and wearing a clean T-shirt, he found dinner waiting for him on the dining table. Jessica sat down on the far side of it with her arms tightly folded—she was altogether a very tightly wound girl—and watched him eat. "Congratulations, by the way," she said, "on everything that's happened. It was very weird to suddenly start hearing you everywhere, and see you on everybody's playlist."

"What about you? What do you like to listen to?"

"I'm more into world music, especially African and South American. But I liked your record. I certainly recognized the lake."

It was possible that she meant something by this, also possible that she didn't. Could Patty have told her what had happened at the lake? Her and not Walter?

"So what's going on?" he said. "It sounded like you had a little problem with Lalitha."

Again the amused or ironical widening of her eyes.

"What?" he said.

"Oh, nothing. I'm just a little impatient with my family lately."

"I get the sense she's something of a problem for your parents."

"Mm."

"She seems great. Smart, energetic, committed."

"Mm."

"Is there something you want to tell me?"

"No! I just think she's kind of got her eyes on my dad. And it's kind of killing my mom. To watch that happening. I kind of feel like, when a person is married, you leave them alone, right? They're off-limits if they're married. Right?"

Katz cleared his throat, unsure where this was heading. "In theory, yes," he said. "But life gets complicated when you're older."

"It doesn't mean I have to like her, though. It doesn't mean I have to accept her. I don't know if you're aware that she's living right upstairs? She's here *all the time.* She's here more than my mom is. And I just don't think that's quite fair. My feeling is she needs to move out and get her own place. But I don't think my dad wants her to."

"And why doesn't he want that?"

Jessica smiled at Katz tightly, in a very unhappy way. "My parents have a lot of problems. Their marriage has a lot of problems. You don't have to be a psychic to see that. Like, my mom's been really depressed. For years. And she can't get out of it. But they love each other, I *know* they love each other, and it just really bothers me to see what's happening here. If she would just *leave*—I mean, Lalitha—if she would just leave, so my mom could have a chance again . . ."

"You and your mom are close?"

"No. Not really."

Katz ate in silence and waited to hear more. He seemed, luckily, to have caught Jessica in a mood to disclose things to the nearest bystander.

"I mean, she tries," she said. "But she's got a real gift for saying the wrong thing. She doesn't respect my judgment. Like, that I'm a basically intelligent adult who can think for herself? My boyfriend in college, he was incredibly sweet, and she was just horrible to him. It was like she was afraid I was going to marry him, and so she constantly had to be making fun of him. He was my first real boyfriend, and I just wanted to have some time to enjoy that, but she wouldn't leave it alone. There was this time when William and I came down for the weekend, to go to the museums and do a gay-marriage march. We were staying here, and she started asking him if he liked it when girls flashed their breasts at frat parties. She'd read some stupid article in the newspaper about boys shouting at girls to show their breasts. And I'm like, no, Mother, I'm not at Virginia. We don't have frats at my college, that's just some stupid Stone-Aged thing that kids do in the South, I don't go to Florida for spring break, we're not like the people in your stupid article. But she wouldn't leave it alone. She kept asking William how he felt about other girls' breasts. And kept acting surprised when he said he wasn't interested. She *knew* he was being sincere, not to mention incredibly embarrassed that his girlfriend's mother was talking about breasts, but she acted like she didn't believe him. To her, the whole thing was a joke. She wanted *me* to laugh at William. Who, yes, was a little hard to take sometimes. But, like, can I have a chance to figure that out for myself?"

"So she cares about you. She didn't want you marrying the wrong guy."

"I wasn't going to marry him! That's the thing!"

Katz's eyes were drawn to the breasts that were mostly concealed by Jessica's tightly crossed arms. She was small-chested like her mother but less well proportioned. What he was feeling now was that his love of Patty applied by extension to her daughter, minus the wish to fuck her. He could see what Walter had meant about her being a young person who gave an older person hope about the future. Her lights all seemed definitely to be on.

"You're going to have a good life," he said.

"Thank you."

"You've got a good head. It's great to see you again."

"I know, you too," she said. "I don't even remember the last time I saw you. Maybe in high school?"

"You were working in a soup kitchen. Your dad took me down to see you there."

"Right, my résumé-building years. I had about seventeen extracurricular activities. I was like Mother Teresa on speed."

Katz helped himself to more of the pasta, which had olives and some sort of salad green in it. Yes, arugula: he was back safely in the bosom of the gentry. He asked Jessica what she would do if her parents split up.

"Wow, I don't know," she said. "I hope they don't. Do you think they will? Is that what Dad says to you?"

"I wouldn't rule it out."

"Well, I guess I'll be joining the crowd then. Half of my friends are from broken homes. I just never saw it happening to us. Not until Lalitha came along."

"You know, it takes two to tango. You shouldn't blame her too much."

"Oh, believe me, I'll blame Dad, too. I will definitely blame him. I can hear it in his voice, and it's just really . . . confusing. Just *wrong*. Like, I always thought I knew him really well. But apparently I didn't."

"And what about your mom?"

"She's definitely unhappy about it, too."

"No, but what if she were the one to leave? How would you feel about that?"

Jessica's puzzlement at the question dispelled any notion that Patty had confided in her. "I don't think she would ever do that," she said. "Unless Dad made her."

"She's happy enough?"

"Well, Joey says she isn't. I think she's told Joey a lot of stuff she doesn't tell me. Or maybe Joey just makes stuff up to be unpleasant to me. I mean, she definitely makes fun of Dad, all the time, but that doesn't mean anything. She makes fun of everybody—I'm sure including me whenever I'm not around to hear it. We're all very amusing to her, and it definitely annoys the shit out of me. But she's really into her family. I don't think she can imagine changing anything."

Katz wondered if this could be true. Patty had told him herself, four years earlier, that she wasn't interested in leaving Walter. But the prophet in Katz's pants was insistently maintaining otherwise, and Joey was perhaps more reliable than his sister on the subject of their mother's happiness.

"Your mom's a strange person, isn't she."

"I feel bad for her," Jessica said, "whenever I'm not being mad at her. She's so smart, and she never really made anything of herself except being a good mom. The one thing I know for sure is *I'm* never going to stay home full-time with *my* kids."

"So you think you want kids. The world population crisis notwithstanding."

She widened her eyes at him and reddened. "Maybe one or two. If I ever meet the right guy. Which doesn't seem very likely to happen in New York."

"New York's a tough scene."

"God, thank you. Thank you for saying that. I have never in my life felt so smallened and invisible and totally dissed as in the last eight months. I thought New York was supposed to be this great dating scene. But the guys are all either losers, jerks, or married. It's *appalling*. I mean, I know I'm not a knockout or anything, but I think I'm at least worth five minutes of polite conversation. It's been eight months now, and I'm still waiting for those five minutes. I don't even want to go out anymore, it's so demoralizing."

"It's not you. You're a good-looking chick. You just may be too nice for New York. It's a pretty naked economy there."

"But how come there are so many girls like me? And no guys? Did the good guys all decide to go somewhere else?"

Katz cast his mind over the young males of his acquaintance in greater New York, including his former Walnut Surprise mates, and could think of not one whom he would trust on a date with Jessica. "The girls all come for publishing and art and nonprofits," he said. "The guys come for money and music. There's a selection bias there. The girls are good and interesting, the guys are all assholes like me. You shouldn't take it personally."

"I would just like to have *one* nice date."

He was regretting having told her she was good-looking. It had sounded faintly like a come-on, and he hoped she hadn't taken it that way. Unfortunately, it seemed as if she had.

"Are you really an asshole?" she said. "Or were you just saying that?"

The note of flirtatious provocation was alarming and needed to be nipped in the bud. "I came down here to do your dad a favor," he said.

"That doesn't sound like being an asshole," she said in a teasing tone.

"Trust me. It is." He gave her the hardest look he knew how to give a person, and he could see that it scared her a little.

"I don't understand," she said.

"I'm not your ally on the Indian front. I'm your enemy."

"What? Why? What do you care?"

"I told you. I'm an asshole."

"Jesus. OK, then." She looked at the tabletop with highly elevated eyebrows, confused and scared and pissed off all at once.

"This pasta is excellent, by the way. Thank you for making it."

"Sure. Take some salad, too." She stood up from the table. "I think I'm going to go upstairs and do some reading. Let me know if you need anything else."

He nodded, and she left the room. He felt bad for the girl, but his business in Washington was a dirty one, and there was no point in sugarcoating it. After he'd finished eating, he carefully surveyed Walter's vast book collection and even vaster collection of CDs and LPs, and then retreated upstairs to Joey's room. He wanted to be the person who walked into a room where Patty was, not the person waiting in a room she walked into. To be the person waiting was to be too vulnerable; it wasn't Katzian. Although he normally eschewed earplugs, for the veritable symphony they made of his tinnitus, he inserted some in his ears now, so as not to lie cravenly listening for footsteps and voices.

The next morning, he lingered in his room until nearly nine o'clock before descending the back staircase in search of breakfast. The kitchen was empty, but somebody, presumably Jessica, had made coffee and cut up fruit and set out muffins. A light spring rain was falling on the small back yard, its daffodils and jonquils, and the shoulders of the closely neighboring town houses. Hearing voices from the front of the mansion, Katz wandered down the hallway with coffee and a muffin and found Walter and Jessica and Lalitha, all scrubbed and morning-skinned and shower-haired, waiting for him in the conference room.

"Good, you're here," Walter said. "We can start."

"Didn't realize we were meeting so early."

"It's nine o'clock," Walter said. "This is a workday for us."

He and Lalitha were seated side by side near the middle of the big table. Jessica was way down at the farthest end with her arms crossed, tensely radiating skepticism and defendedness. Katz sat down across the table from the others.

"You sleep all right?" Walter said.

"Slept fine. Where's Patty?"

Walter shrugged. "She's not coming to the meeting, if that's what you mean."

"We're actually trying to accomplish something," Lalitha said. "We're not trying to spend the entire day laughing at how impossible it is to accomplish anything."

Whuff!

Jessica's eyes were darting from person to person, spectating. Walter, on closer inspection, had terrible circles under his eyes, and his fingers, on the tabletop, were doing something between trembling and tapping.

Lalitha looked a bit wrecked herself, her face bluish with dark-skinned pallor. Observing the relation of their bodies to each other, their deliberate angling-apart, Katz wondered if chemistry might already have done its work. They looked sullen and guilty, like lovers compelled to behave themselves in public. Or, conversely, like people who hadn't settled on terms yet and were unhappy with each other. The situation merited careful monitoring either way.

"So we'll start with the problem," Walter said. "The problem is that nobody dares make overpopulation part of the national conversation. And why not? Because the subject is a downer. Because it seems like old news. Because, like with global warming, we haven't quite reached the point where the consequences become undeniable. And because we sound like elitists if we try to tell poor people and uneducated people not to have so many babies. Having large families tracks inversely with economic status, and so does the age at which girls start having babies, which is just as damaging from a numbers perspective. You can cut the growth rate in half just by doubling the average age of first-time mothers from eighteen to thirty-five. That's one reason rats reproduce so much more than leopards do—because they reach sexual maturity so much sooner."

"Already a problem in that analogy, of course," Katz said.

"Exactly," Walter said. "It's the elitism thing again. Leopards are a 'higher' species than rats or bunnies. So that's another part of the problem: we turn poor people into rodents when we call attention to their high birth rates and their low age of first reproduction."

"I think the cigarette analogy is a good one," Jessica said from the far end of the table. It was clear that she'd gone to an expensive college and had learned to speak her mind in seminars. "People with money can get Zoloft and Xanax. So when you tax cigarettes, and alcohol too, you're hitting poor people the hardest. You're making the cheap drugs more expensive."

"Right," Walter said. "That's a very good point. And it applies to religion, too, which is another big drug for people who don't have economic opportunity. If we try to pick on religion, which is our real villain, we're picking on the economically oppressed."

"And guns also," Jessica said. "Hunting's also very low-end."

"Ha, tell that to Mr. Haven," Lalitha said in her clipped accent. "Tell that to Dick Cheney."

"No, actually, Jessica's right," Walter said.

Lalitha turned on him. "Really? I don't see it. What does hunting have to do with population?"

Jessica rolled her eyes impatiently.

This could be a long day, Katz thought.

"It's all circling around the same problem of personal liberties," Walter said. "People came to this country for either money or freedom. If you don't have money, you cling to your freedoms all the more angrily. Even if smoking kills you, even if you can't afford to feed your kids, even if your kids are getting shot down by maniacs with assault rifles. You may be poor, but the one thing nobody can take away from you is the freedom to fuck up your life whatever way you want to. That's what Bill Clinton figured out—that we can't win elections by running against personal liberties. Especially not against guns, actually."

That Lalitha nodded in submissive agreement to this, rather than sulking, made the situation clearer. She was still begging and Walter still withholding. And he was in his natural element, his personal fortress, when he was allowed to speak abstractly. He hadn't changed at all since his years at Macalester.

"The real problem, though," Katz said, "is free-market capitalism. Right? Unless you're talking about *outlawing* reproduction, your problem isn't civil liberties. The real reason you can't get any cultural traction with overpopulation is that talking about fewer babies means talking about limits to growth. Right? And growth isn't some side issue in free-market ideology. It's the entire essence. Right? In free-market economic theory, you have to leave stuff like the environment out of the equation. What was that word you used to love? 'Externalities'?"

"That's the word, all right," Walter said.

"I don't imagine the theory's changed much since we were in school. The theory is that there isn't any theory. Right? Capitalism can't handle talking about limits, because the whole point of capitalism is the restless growth of capital. If you want to be heard in the capitalist media, and communicate in a capitalist culture, overpopulation can't make any sense. It's literally nonsense. And that's your real problem."

"So maybe we should just call it a day, then," Jessica said drily. "Since there's nothing we can do."

"I didn't invent the problem," Katz said to her. "I'm just pointing it out."

"We know about the problem," Lalitha said. "But we're a pragmatic organization. We're not trying to overthrow the whole system, we're just trying to mitigate. We're trying to help the cultural conversation catch up with the crisis, before it's too late. We want to do with population the same thing Gore's doing with climate change. We have a million dollars in cash, and there are some very practical steps we can take right now."

"I'd actually be fine with overthrowing the whole system," Katz said. "You can go ahead and sign me up for that."

"The reason the system can't be overthrown in this country," Walter said, "is all about freedom. The reason the free market in Europe is tempered by socialism is that they're not so hung up on personal liberties there. They also have lower population growth rates, despite comparable income levels. The Europeans are all-around more rational, basically. And the conversation about rights in this country isn't rational. It's taking place on the level of emotion, and class resentments, which is why the right is so good at exploiting it. And that's why I want to get back to what Jessica said about cigarettes."

Jessica made a beckoning gesture, as if to say, Thank you!

From the hallway came the sound of somebody, Patty, moving around the kitchen in hard heels. Katz, wanting a cigarette, took Walter's empty coffee mug and prepared a plug of chew instead.

"Positive social change works top-down," Walter said. "The surgeon general issues his report, educated people read it, bright kids start to realize that smoking is stupid, not cool, and national smoking rates go down. Or Rosa Parks sits down on her bus, college students hear about it, they march in Washington, they take buses to the South, and suddenly there's a national civil-rights movement. We're now at a point where any reasonably educated person can understand the problem with population growth. So the next step is to make it cool for college kids to care about the issue."

While Walter held forth on the subject of college kids, Katz strained to hear what Patty was doing in the kitchen. The essential pussiness of his situation was coming home to him. The Patty he wanted was the Patty who didn't want Walter: the housewife who didn't want to be a housewife anymore; the housewife who wanted to fuck a rocker. But instead of just calling her up and saying he wanted her, he was sitting here like some college sophomore, indulging his old friend's intellectual fantasies. What was it about Walter that so knocked him off his game? He felt like a free-flying insect caught in a sticky web of family. He couldn't stop trying to be *nice* to Walter, because he liked him; if he hadn't liked him so much, he probably wouldn't have wanted Patty; and if he hadn't wanted her, he wouldn't have been sitting here pretending. What a mess.

And now her footsteps were coming down the hallway. Walter stopped speaking and took a deep breath, visibly bracing himself. Katz swiveled his chair toward the doorway; and there she was. The fresh-faced mom who had a dark side. She was wearing black boots and a snug red-and-black silk brocade skirt and a chic short raincoat in which she looked both great and not like herself. Katz couldn't remember ever seeing her in anything but jeans.

"Hi, Richard," she said, glancing in his general direction. "Hi, everybody. How's it going here?"

"We're just getting started," Walter said.

"Don't let me interrupt you, then."

"You're all dressed up," Walter said.

"Going shopping," she said. "Maybe I'll see you guys tonight if you're around."

"Are you making dinner?" Jessica said.

"No, I have to work till nine. I guess, if you want, I could stop for some food before I leave."

"That would be extremely helpful," Jessica said, "since we're going to be meeting all day."

"Well, and I would be happy to make dinner if I didn't have to work an eight-hour shift."

"Oh, never mind," Jessica said. "Just forget it. We'll go out or something."

"That does sound like the easiest thing," Patty agreed.

"So anyway," Walter said.

"Right, so anyway," she said. "I hope it's a really fun day for everybody."

Having thus speedily irritated, ignored, or disappointed each of the four of them, she proceeded down the hallway and out the front door. Lalitha, who had been clicking on her BlackBerry since the moment Patty appeared, looked the most obviously unhappy.

"Does she work seven days a week now, or what?" Jessica said.

"No, not usually," Walter said. "I'm not sure what this is about."

"It's always about something, though, isn't it," Lalitha murmured as she thumbed her device.

Jessica turned on her, instantly redirecting her pique. "Just let us know whenever you're done with your e-mail, OK? We'll just sit and wait until you're ready, OK?"

Lalitha, tight-lipped, continued to thumb.

"Maybe you can do that later?" Walter said gently.

She slapped the BlackBerry onto the table. "OK," she said. "Ready!"

As the nicotine coursed through Katz, he began to feel better. Patty had seemed defiant, and defiant was good. Nor had the fact of her *dressing up* escaped his attention. Dressing up for what reason? To present herself to him. And working both Friday and Saturday nights for what reason? To avoid him. Yes, to play the same hide-and-seek that he was playing with her. Now that she was gone, he could see her better, receive her signals without so much static, imagine placing his hands on that fine skirt of hers, and remember how she'd wanted him in Minnesota.

But meanwhile the problem of too much procreation: the first concrete task, Walter said, was to think of a name for their initiative. His own working idea was Youth Against Insanity, a private homage to "Youth Against Fascism," which he considered (and Katz agreed with him) one of the finer songs that Sonic Youth had ever recorded. But Jessica was adamant about picking a name that said yes rather than no. Something pro, not contra. "Kids my age are way more libertarian than you guys were," she explained. "Anything that smells like elitism, or not respecting somebody else's point of view, they're allergic to. Your campaign can't be about telling other people what not to do. It's got to be about this cool positive choice that *we're* all making."

Lalitha suggested the name The Living First, which hurt Katz's ears, and which Jessica shot down with withering scorn. And so they brainstormed the morning away, sorely missing, in Katz's opinion, the input of a professional P.R. consultant. They went through Lonelier Planet, Fresher Air, Rubbers Unlimited, Coalition of the Already Born, Free Space, Life Quality, Smaller Tent, and Enough Already! (which Katz rather liked but which the others said was still too negative; he filed it away as a possible future song or album title). They considered Feed the Living, Be Reasonable, Cooler Heads, A Better Way, Strength in Smaller Numbers, Less Is More, Emptier Nests, Joy of None, Kidfree Forever, No Babies on Board, Feed Yourself, Dare Not to Bear, Depopulate!, Two Cheers for People, Maybe None, Less Than Zero, Stomp the Brakes, Smash the Family, Cool Off, Elbow Room, More for Me, Bred Alone, Breather, Morespace, Love What's Here, Barren by Choice, Childhood's End, All Children Left Behind, Nucleus of Two, Maybe Never, and What's the Rush? and rejected all of them. To Katz, the exercise was an illustration of the general impossibility of the enterprise and the specific rancidness of prefabricated coolness, but Walter ran the discussion with an upbeat judiciousness that bespoke long years in the artificial world of NGOs. And, somewhat incredibly, the dollars he planned to spend were real.

"I say we go with Free Space," he said finally. "I like how it steals the word 'free' from the other side, and appropriates the rhetoric of the wide-open West. If this thing takes off, it can also be the name of a whole movement, not just our group. The Free Space movement."

"Am I the only one who's hearing 'free parking space'?" Jessica said.

"That's not such a bad connotation," Walter said. "We all know what it's like to have trouble finding a parking space. Fewer people on the planet, better parking opportunities? It's actually a very vivid everyday example of why overpopulation's bad."

"We need to see if Free Space is trademarked," Lalitha said.

"Fuck the trademark," Katz said. "Every phrase known to man is trademarked."

"We could put an extra space between the words," Walter said. "Sort of like the opposite of EarthFirst! and without the exclamation point. If we get sued on the trademark, we can build a case on the extra space. That plays, doesn't it? The Case for Space?"

"Better not to get sued at all, I think," Lalitha said.

In the afternoon, after sandwiches had been ordered and eaten and Patty had come home and gone out again without interacting with them

(Katz caught a quick glimpse of her black gym-greeter jeans as her legs receded down the hallway), the four-member advisory board of Free Space hammered out a plan for the twenty-five summer interns whom Lalitha had already set about attracting and hiring. She'd been envisioning a late-summer music and consciousness-raising festival on a twenty-acre goat farm now owned by the Cerulean Mountain Trust on the southern edge of its warbler reserve—a vision that Jessica immediately found fault with. Did Lalitha not understand *anything* about young people's new relationship with music? It wasn't enough just to bring in some big-name talent! They had to send twenty interns out to twenty cities across the country and have them organize *local* festivals—"A battle of the bands," Katz said. "Yes, exactly, twenty different local battles of the bands," Jessica said. (She had been frosty to Katz all day but seemed grateful for his help in squashing Lalitha.) By offering cash prizes, they would attract five great bands in each of the twenty cities, all competing for the right to represent their local music scene in a weekend-long battle of the bands in West Virginia, under the aegis of Free Space, with some big names there to do the final judging and lend their aura to the cause of reversing global population growth and making it uncool to have kids.

Katz, who even by his own standards had consumed colossal amounts of caffeine and nicotine, wound up in a nearly manic state in which he agreed to everything that was asked of him: writing special Free Space songs, returning to Washington in May to meet with the Free Space interns and aid in their indoctrination, making a surprise guest appearance at the New York battle of the bands, emceeing the Free Space festival in West Virginia, endeavoring to reconstitute Walnut Surprise so that it could perform there, and pestering big names to appear with him and join him on the final panel of judges. In his mind, he was doing nothing more than writing checks on an account with nothing in it, because, despite the actual chemical substances he'd ingested, the true substance of his state was a throbbing, single-minded focus on taking Patty away from Walter: this was the rhythm track, everything else was irrelevant high-end. Smash the Family: another song title. And once the family was smashed, he would not have to make good on any of his promises.

He was so revved up that when the meeting ended, toward five o'clock, and Lalitha went back to her office to begin effectuating their plans, and

Jessica disappeared upstairs, he consented to go out with Walter. He was thinking that this was the last time they would ever go out together. It happened that the suddenly hot band Bright Eyes, fronted by a gifted youngster named Conor Oberst, was playing a familiar venue in D.C. that night. The show was sold out, but Walter was keen to get backstage with Oberst and pitch Free Space to him, and Katz, flying high, made the somewhat abasing phone calls necessary to get a pair of passes at the door. Anything was better than hanging around the mansion, waiting for Patty to come home.

"I can't believe you're doing all these things for me," Walter said at the Thai restaurant, near Dupont Circle, where they stopped for dinner along the way.

"No problem, man." Katz picked up a skewer of satay, considered whether he could stomach it, and decided no. More tobacco was a very bad idea, but he took out his tin of it anyway.

"It's like we're finally getting around to doing the things we used to talk about in college," Walter said. "It really means a lot to me."

Katz's eyes restlessly roved the restaurant, alighting on everything but his friend. He had the sense that he had run right off a cliff, was still pumping his legs, but would be crashing very soon.

"You OK?" Walter said. "You seem kind of jumpy."

"No, I'm fine, fine."

"You don't seem fine. You've gone through a whole can of that shit today."

"Just trying not to smoke around you."

"Well, thank you for that."

Walter consumed all of the satay while Katz dribbled spit into his water glass, feeling momentarily calmed, in nicotine's false way.

"How are things with you and the girl?" he said. "I got kind of a weird vibe off you guys today."

Walter blushed and didn't answer.

"You sleeping with her yet?"

"Jesus, Richard! That is none of your business."

"Whoa, is that a yes?"

"No, it's a none-of-your-fucking-business."

"You in love with her?"

"Jesus! Enough already."

"See, I think that was a better name. Enough Already! With exclamation point. Free Space sounds like a Lynyrd Skynyrd song."

"Why are you so interested in seeing me sleep with her? What's that about?"

"I'm just going by what I see."

"Well, we're different, you and me. Do you get that? Do you understand that it's possible to have values higher than getting laid?"

"Yeah, I get that. In the abstract."

"Well, then, shut up about it, OK?"

Katz looked around impatiently for their waiter. He was in an evil mood, and everything Walter did or said was irritating him. If Walter was too pussy to make a play for Lalitha, if he wanted to keep being Mr. Righteous, it was nothing to Katz now. "Let's get the fuck out of here," he said.

"How about letting my entrée get here first? You may not be hungry, but I am."

"No, sure. Of course. My mistake."

His spirits began to crash an hour later, in the crush of young people at the doors of the 9:30 Club. Katz hadn't gone to a show as an actual audience member in several years, he hadn't gone to hear a kiddie idol since he'd been a kiddie himself, and he'd become so accustomed to the older crowd at Traumatics and Walnut Surprise events that he'd forgotten how very different a kiddie scene could be. How almost religious in its collective seriousness. Unlike Walter, who, in his culturally eager way, owned the entire Bright Eyes oeuvre and had tiresomely extolled it at the Thai restaurant, Katz knew the band only by osmotic repute. He and Walter were at least twice the age of everybody else at the club, the flat-haired boys and fashionably unskinny babes. He could feel himself being looked at and recognized, here and there, as they made their way onto the intermission-emptied floor, and he thought he could hardly have made a worse decision than to appear in public and to bestow, by his mere presence, approval on a band he knew next to nothing about. He didn't know which would be worse under these circumstances, to be outed and fawned over or to stand there in middle-aged obscurity.

"Do you want to try to get backstage?" Walter said.

"Can't do it, buddy. Not up to it."

"Just to make the introduction. It'll take one minute. I can follow up later with a proper pitch."

"Not up to it. I don't know these people."

The intermission mix, the choice of which was the headliner's prerogative, was impeccably quirky. (Katz, as a headliner, had always hated the posturing and gamesmanship and didacticism of choosing the mix, the pressure to prove himself groovy in his listening tastes, and had left it to his bandmates.) Roadies were setting out a great many mikes and instruments while Walter gushed about the Conor Oberst story: how he'd started recording at twelve, how he was still based in Omaha, how his band was more like a collective or a family than an ordinary rock group. Kiddies were streaming onto the floor from every portal, Bright-Eyed (what a fucking irritating youth-congratulating name for a band, Katz thought) and bushless-tailed. His feeling of having crashed did not consist of envy, exactly, or even entirely of having outlived himself. It was more like despair about the world's splinteredness. The nation was fighting ugly ground wars in two countries, the planet was heating up like a toaster oven, and here at the 9:30, all around him, were hundreds of kids in the mold of the banana-bread-baking Sarah, with their sweet yearnings, their innocent entitlement—to what? To emotion. To unadulterated worship of a superspecial band. To being left to themselves to ritually repudiate, for an hour or two on a Saturday night, the cynicism and anger of their elders. They seemed, as Jessica had suggested at the meeting earlier, to bear malice toward nobody. Katz could see it in their clothing, which bespoke none of the rage and disaffection of the crowds he'd been a part of as a youngster. They gathered not in anger but in celebration of their having found, as a generation, a gentler and more respectful way of being. A way, not incidentally, more in harmony with consuming. And so said to him: die.

Oberst took the stage alone, wearing a powder-blue tuxedo, strapped on an acoustic, and crooned a couple of lengthy solo numbers. He was the real deal, a boy genius, and thus all the more insufferable to Katz. His Tortured Soulful Artist shtick, his self-indulgence in pushing his songs past their natural limits of endurance, his artful crimes against pop convention: he was performing sincerity, and when the performance threatened to give sincerity the lie, he performed his sincere anguish over the difficulty of sincerity. Then the rest of the band came out, including three lovely young backup Graces in vampish dresses, and it was all in all a great show—Katz didn't stoop to denying it. He merely felt like the one stone-sober person in a room full of drunks, the one nonbeliever at a church revival. He was pierced by a homesickness for Jersey City, its belief-killing streets. It seemed to him he had some work to do there, in his own splintered niche, before the world ended entirely.

"What did you think?" Walter asked him giddily in the taxi afterward.

"I think I'm getting old," he said.

"I thought they were pretty great."

"A few too many songs about adolescent soap operas."

"They're all about belief," Walter said. "The new record's this incredible kind of pantheistic effort to keep believing in something in a world full of death. Oberst works the word 'lift' into every song. That's the name of the record, *Lifted*. It's like religion without the bullshit of religious dogma."

"I admire your capacity for admiring," Katz said. And added, as the taxi crawled through traffic at a complex diagonal intersection, "I don't think I can do this thing for you, Walter. I'm experiencing high levels of shame."

"Just do what you can. Find your own limits. If all you want to do is come down in May for a day or two and meet the interns, maybe have sex with one of them, that's fine with me. That would be a lot already."

"Thinking of going back to writing songs."

"That's great! That's wonderful news. I'd almost rather have you do that than work for us. Just stop building decks, for God's sake."

"Might need to keep building decks. Can't be helped."

The mansion was dark and quiet when they returned to it, a single light burning in the kitchen. Walter went straight up to bed, but Katz lingered for a while in the kitchen, thinking Patty might hear him and come down. Aside from everything else, he was now craving the company of someone with a sense of irony. He ate some cold pasta and smoked a cigarette in the back yard. Then he went up to the second floor and back to the little room of Patty's. From the pillows and blankets he'd seen on the foldout sofa the evening before, he had the impression that she slept in it. The door was closed and no light showed around its edges.

"Patty," he said in a voice she could have heard if she'd been awake. He listened carefully, enveloped in tinnitus.

"Patty," he said again.

His dick didn't believe for one second that she was sleeping, but it was possible that the door was closed on an empty room, and he had a curious reluctance to open it and see. He needed some small breath of encouragement or confirmation of his instincts. He went back down to the kitchen, finished the pasta, and read the *Post* and the *Times*. At two o'clock, still buzzing with nicotine, and beginning to be pissed off with her, he went back to her room, tapped on the door, and opened it.

She was sitting on the sofa in the dark, still wearing her black gym uniform, staring straight ahead, her hands clutching each other on her lap.

"Sorry," Katz said. "Is this OK?"

"Yes," she said, not looking at him. "But we should go downstairs."

There was an unfamiliar tightness in his chest as he descended the back staircase again, an intensity of sexual anticipation that he didn't think he'd felt since high school. Following him into the kitchen, Patty closed the door to the staircase behind her. She was wearing very soft-looking socks, the socks of somebody whose feet weren't so young and well-padded anymore. Even without the boost of shoes, her height was the same agreeable surprise it had always been to him. One of his own song lyrics popped into his head, the one about her body being the body for him. It had come to this for old Katz: he was being moved by his own lyrics. And the body for him was still very nice, not actively displeasing in any way: the product, surely, of many hours of sweating at her gym. In white block letters on the front of her black T-shirt was the word LIFT.

"I'm going to have some chamomile tea," she said. "Do you want some?"

"Sure. I don't think I've ever had chamomile tea."

"Ah, what a sheltered life you've lived."

She went out to the office and came back with two mugs of instantly hot water with tea-bag labels dangling.

"Why didn't you answer me when I went up the first time?" he said. "I've been sitting down here for two hours."

"I guess I was lost in thought."

"Did you think I was just going to go to bed?"

"I don't know. I was sort of thinking without thinking, if you know what I mean. But I understood that you would want to talk to me, and I knew I had to do it. And so here I am."

"You don't have to do anything."

"No, it's good, we should talk." She sat down across the farmer's table from him. "Did you guys have a good time? Jessie said you went to a concert."

"Us and about eight hundred twenty-one-year-olds."

"Ha-ha-ha! You poor thing."

"Walter enjoyed himself."

"Oh, I'm sure he did. He's quite the enthusiast about young people these days."

Katz was encouraged by the note of discontent. "I take it you're not?"

"Me? Safe to say no. I mean, my own children excepted. I do still like my own children. But the rest of them? Ha-ha-ha!"

Her thrilling, lifting laugh hadn't changed. Underneath her new haircut, though, underneath her eye makeup, she was looking older. It only went in one direction, aging, and the self-protective core of him, seeing it, was telling him to run while he still could. He'd followed an instinct in coming down here, but there was a big difference, he was realizing, between an instinct and a plan.

"What don't you like about them?" he said.

"Oh, well, where to begin?" Patty said. "How about the flipflop thing? I have some issues with their flipflops. It's like the world is their bedroom. And they can't even hear their own flap-flap-flapping, because they've all got their gadgets, they've all got their earbuds in. Every time I start hating my neighbors around here, I run into some G.U. kid on the sidewalk and suddenly forgive the neighbors, because at least they're adults. At least they're not running around in flipflops, advertising how much more laid-back and reasonable they are than us adults. Than uptight me, who would prefer not to look at people's bare feet on the subway. Because, really, who could object to seeing such beautiful toes? Such perfect toenails? Only a person who's too unluckily middle-aged to inflict the spectacle of her own toes on the world."

"I hadn't particularly noticed the flipflops."

"You really do lead a sheltered life, then."

Her tone was somehow rote and disconnected, not teasing in a way that he could work with. Denied encouragement, his sense of anticipation was waning. He was beginning to dislike her for not being in the state he'd imagined he would find her in.

"And the credit-card thing?" she said. "Using a credit card to buy one hot dog or one pack of gum? I mean, cash is so yesterday. Right? Cash actually requires you to add and subtract. You actually have to pay attention to the person who's giving you your change. Like, for one tiny little moment, you have to be less than one-hundred-percent cool and checked into your own little world. But not with a credit card you don't. You just blandly hand it over and blandly take it back."

"That's more like what the crowd was tonight," he said. "Nice kids, just a little self-absorbed."

"You'd better get used to it, though, right? Jessica says you're going to be up to your armpits in young people all summer."

"Yeah, maybe."

"It sounded more like definitely."

"Yeah, but I'm thinking of bailing. In fact, I already said so to Walter."

Patty stood up to put their tea bags in the sink and remained standing, her back to him. "So this might be your only visit," she said.

"That's right."

"Well, then, I suppose I should be sorry I didn't come down sooner."

"You could always come up and see me in the city."

"Right. If I'd ever been invited."

"You're invited now."

She wheeled around with narrowed eyes. "Don't play games with me, OK? I don't want to see that side of you. It actually sort of makes me sick. OK?"

He held her gaze, trying to show her that he meant it—trying to *feel* that he meant it—but this seemed only to exasperate her. She retreated, shaking her head, to a far corner of the kitchen.

"How are you and Walter getting along?" he said unkindly.

"None of your business."

"I keep hearing that. What does it mean?"

She blushed a little. "It means it's none of your business."

"Walter says not so great."

"Well, that's true enough. Mostly." She blushed again. "But you just worry about Walter, OK? Worry about your best friend. You already made your choice. You made it very clear to me which one of us's happiness you cared more about. You had your chance with me, and you chose him."

Katz could feel himself beginning to lose his cool, and it was highly unpleasant. A pressure between his ears, a rising anger, a need to argue. It was like suddenly being Walter.

"You drove me away," he said.

"Ha-ha-ha! 'Sorry, I can't go to Philadelphia even for one day, because of poor Walter'?"

"I said that for one minute. For thirty seconds. And you then proceeded, for the next *hour*—"

"To fuck it up. I know. I know I know I know. I know who fucked it all up. I know it was me! But, Richard, you *knew* it was harder for me. You could have thrown me a lifeline! Like, possibly, for that one minute, *not* talked about poor Walter and his poor tender feelings, but about *me* instead! That's why I'm saying you already made your choice. You may not have even known you were doing it, but that's what you did. So live with it now."

"Patty."

"I may be a fuckup, but if nothing else I've had some time to think in the last few years, and I've figured some things out. I have a little better idea of who you are, and how you work. I can imagine how hard it is for you that our little Bengali friend's not interested in you. How terrrrribly destabilizing for you. What a topsy-turvy world this turns out to be! What a total bad trip! I guess you could still try working on Jessica, but good luck with that. If you really find yourself at a loss, your best bet may be Emily in the development office. But Walter's not into her, so I don't imagine she'll be too interesting to you."

Katz's blood was up, he was all jittery-jangly. It was like coke cut heavily with nasty meth.

"I came down here for you," he said.

"Ha-ha-ha! I don't believe you. You don't even believe it yourself. You're such a bad liar."

"Why else would I come down here?"

"I don't know. Concern about biodiversity and sustainable population?"

He was remembering how unpleasant it had been to argue with her on the phone. How grossly unpleasant, how murderously trying to his patience. What he couldn't remember was why he'd put up with it. Something about the way she'd wanted him, the way she'd come after him. A way that was missing now.

"I've spent so much time being mad at you," she said. "Do you have any idea? I sent you all those e-mails that you never responded to, I had that whole humiliating one-sided conversation with you. Did you even read those e-mails?"

"Most of them."

"Ha. I don't know if that makes it worse or better. I guess it doesn't even matter, since it was all in my head anyway. I've spent three years wanting a thing I knew would never make me happy. But that didn't make me stop wanting it. You were like a bad drug I couldn't stop craving. My whole life was like a kind of mourning for some evil drug I knew was bad for me. It was literally not until yesterday, when I actually saw you, that I realized I didn't need the drug after all. It was suddenly like, 'What was I *thinking*? He's here for Walter.'"

"No," he said. "For you."

She wasn't even listening. "I feel so old, Richard. Just because a person isn't making good use of her life, it doesn't stop her life from passing. In fact, it makes her life pass all the quicker."

"You don't look old. You look great."

"Well, and that's what really counts, isn't it? I've become one of those women who put a ton of work into looking OK. If I can just go on and make a beautiful corpse, I'll have the whole problem pretty well licked."

"Come with me."

She shook her head.

"Just come with me. We'll go somewhere, and Walter can have his freedom."

"No," she said, "although it's nice to hear you finally say that. I can apply it retroactively to the last three years and make an even better fantasy out of what might have been. It'll enrich my already rather rich fantasy life. Now I can imagine staying home in your apartment while you do your world tour and fuck nineteen-year-olds, or going along with you and being you guys's den mother—you know, milk and cookies at three a.m.—or being your Yoko and letting everybody blame me for how washed-up and bland you've gotten, and then throwing horrible scenes and letting you find out, the slow way, how bad it is to have me in your life. That should be good for months and months of daydreaming."

"I don't understand what it is you want."

"Believe me, if I understood that myself, we wouldn't be having this conversation. I actually thought I did know what I wanted. I knew it wasn't a good thing, but I thought I knew. And now you're here, and it's like no time at all has passed."

"Except Walter's falling for the girl."

She nodded. "That's right. And you know what? That turns out to be quite extraordinarily painful to me. Quite devastatingly painful." Tears filled her eyes, and she turned quickly to hide the sight of them.

Katz had sat through some tearful scenes in his day, but this was the first time he'd had to watch a woman cry for love of somebody else. He didn't like it one bit.

"So he came home from West Virginia on Thursday night," Patty said. "I might as well tell you this, since we're old friends, right? He came home from West Virginia on Thursday night, and he came up to my room, and what happened, Richard, was like the thing I'd always wanted. *Always* wanted. My entire adult life. I hardly even recognized his face! It was like he'd lost his mind. But the only reason I was getting it was that he was already gone. It was like a little farewell. A little parting gift, to show me what I was never going to have again. Because I'd made him too miserable for too long. And now he's finally ready for something better, but he's not going to have it with me, because I made him too miserable for too long."

From what Katz was hearing, it sounded like he'd arrived forty-eight hours too late. Forty-eight hours. Incredible. "You can still have it," he said. "Make him happy, be a good wife. He'll forget the girl."

"Maybe." She touched the back of her hand to her eyes. "If I were a sane, whole person, that's probably what I'd be trying to do. Because, you know, I used to want to win. I used to be a fighter. But I've developed some kind of allergy to doing the sensible thing. I spend my life jumping out of my skin with frustration at myself."

"That's what I love about you."

"Oh, love now. Love. Richard Katz talking about love. This must be my signal that it's time to go to bed."

It was an exit line; he didn't try to stop her. So firm was his faith in his instincts, however, that when he went upstairs himself, ten minutes later, he was still imagining that he might find her waiting in his bed. What he found instead, sitting on his pillow, was a thick, unbound manuscript with her name on the first page. Its title was "Mistakes Were Made."

He smiled at this. Then he put a large plug of chew in his cheek and sat up reading, periodically spitting into a vase from the nightstand, until there was light in the window. He noted how much more interested he was in the pages about himself than in the other pages; it confirmed his long-standing suspicion that people ultimately only want to read about themselves. He noted further, with pleasure, that this self of his had genuinely fascinated Patty; it reminded him of why he liked her. And yet his clearest sensation, when he read the last page and let his now very watery wad plop into the vase, was of defeat. Not defeat by Patty: her writing skills were impressive, but he could hold his own in the self-expression department. The person who'd defeated him was Walter, because the document had obviously been written for Walter, as a kind of heartsick undeliverable apology to him. Walter was the star in Patty's drama, Katz merely an interesting supporting actor.

For a moment, in what passed for his soul, a door opened wide enough for him to glimpse his pride in its pathetic woundedness, but he slammed the door shut and considered how stupid he'd been to let himself want her. Yes, he liked the way she talked, yes, he had a fatal weakness for a certain smart depressive kind of chick, but the only way he knew to interact with a chick like that was to fuck her, walk away, come back and fuck her again, walk away again, hate her again, fuck her again, and so forth. He wished he could go back in time now and congratulate the self he'd been at twenty-four, in that foul squat on the South Side of Chicago, for having recognized that a woman like Patty was meant for a man like Walter, who, whatever his other sillinesses might be, had the patience and imagination to handle her. The mistake that Katz had made since then had been to keep returning to a scene in which he was bound to feel defeated. Patty's entire document attested to the exhausting difficulty of figuring out, in a scene like that, what was "good" and what wasn't. He was very good at knowing what was good *for him*, and this was normally enough for every purpose in his life. It was only around the Berglunds that he felt that it was not enough. And he was sick of feeling that; he was ready to be done with it.

"So, my friend," he said, "that's the end of you and me. You won that one, old buddy."

The light in the window was brightening. He went to the bathroom and flushed down his spit and the spent tobacco and then put the vase back where he'd found it. The clock radio showed 5:57. He packed up his things and went downstairs to Walter's office with the document and left it in the center of his desktop. A little parting gift. Somebody had to clear the air around here, somebody had to put an end to the bullshit, and Patty obviously wasn't up to it. And so she wanted Katz to do the dirty work? Well, fine. He was ready to be the nonpussy of the outfit. His job in life was to speak the dirty truth. To be the dick. He walked down the main hallway and out the front door, which had a spring-loaded lock. Its click, when he closed it behind him, sounded irrevocable. Good-bye to the Berglunds.

Humid air had arrived in the night, dewing the cars of Georgetown and moistening the off-kilter panels of Georgetown sidewalk. Birds were active in the budding trees; an early-departing jet was crackling across the pale spring sky. Even Katz's tinnitus seemed muted in the morning hush. *This is a good day to die!* He tried to remember who had said that. Crazy Horse? Neil Young?

Shouldering his bag, he walked downhill in the direction of sighing traffic and came eventually to a long bridge leading over to the center of American world domination. He stopped near the center of the bridge, looked down at a female jogger on the creek-side path far below, and tried to evaluate, from the intensity of the photonic interaction between her ass and his retinas, how good a day to die it really was. The height was great enough to kill him if he dove, and diving was definitely the way to do it. Be a man, go headfirst. Yes. His dick was saying yes to something

378

now, and this something was certainly not the wideish ass of the retreating jogger.

Had death, in fact, been his dick's message in sending him to Washington? Had he simply misunderstood its prophecy? He was pretty sure that nobody would miss him much when he was dead. He could free Patty and Walter of the bother of him, free himself of the bother of being a bother. He could go wherever Molly had gone before him, and his father before her. He peered down at the spot where he was likely to land, a much-trampled patch of gravel and bare dirt, and asked himself whether this nondescript bit of land was worthy of killing him. Him the great Richard Katz! Was it worthy?

He laughed at the question and continued across the bridge.

Back in Jersey City, he took arms against the sea of junk in his apartment. Opened the windows to the warm air and did spring cleaning. Washed and dried every dish, threw out bales of useless paper, and manually deleted three thousand pieces of spam from his computer, stopping repeatedly to inhale the marsh and harbor and garbage smells of the warmer months in Jersey City. After dark, he drank a couple of beers and unpacked his banjo and guitars, ascertaining that the torque in the neck of his Strat hadn't magically fixed itself in its months in its case. He drank a third beer and called the drummer of Walnut Surprise.

"Hello, dickhead," Tim said. "Good to finally hear from you—*not.*"

"What can I say," Katz said.

"How about, 'I'm really sorry for being a total loser and disappearing on you and telling fifty different lies.' Dickhead."

"Yeah, well, regrettably, there was some stuff I had to attend to."

"Right, being a dickhead is really time-consuming. What the fuck are you even calling me for?"

"Wondered how things are going with you."

"You mean, apart from you being a total loser and fucking us over in fifty different ways and lying to us constantly?"

Katz smiled. "Maybe you can write out your grievances and present them to me in written form, so we can talk about something else now."

"I already did that, asshole. Have you checked your e-mail in the last year?"

"Well, just give me a call then, if you feel like it, later. My phone's operative again."

"Your phone is operative again! That's a good one, Richard. How's your computer? Is that operative again, too?"

"Just saying I'm around if you want to call."

"And just go fuck yourself is all I'm saying."

Katz set down his phone feeling good about the conversation. He thought it unlikely that Tim would have bothered abusing him if he had something better than Walnut Surprise in the works. He drank one last beer, ate one of the killer mirtazapines that a script-happy doctor in Berlin had given him, and slept for thirteen hours.

He woke to a blazing hot afternoon and took a walk in his neighborhood, checking out females dressed in this year's style of skimpy clothes, and bought some actual groceries—peanut butter, bananas, bread. Later on, he drove into Hoboken to leave his Strat with his guitar man there and yielded to an impulse to dine at Maxwell's and catch whatever act was playing. The staff at Maxwell's treated him like a General MacArthur returning from Korea in defiant disgrace. Chicks kept leaning over him with their tits falling out of their little tops, some guy he didn't know or had once known but long since forgotten kept him supplied with beer, and the local band that was playing, Tutsi Picnic, did not repel him. On the whole, he felt that his decision not to dive from the bridge in Washington had been a good one. Being free of the Berglunds was proving to be a milder and not at all unpleasant sort of death, a death without sting, a state of merely partial nonexistence in which he was able to go back to the apartment of a fortyish book editor ("huge, huge fan") who'd cozied up to him while Tutsi Picnic played, wet his dick in her a few times, and then, in the morning, buy himself some crullers on his way back down Washington Street to move his truck before parking-meter hours commenced.

There was a message from Tim on his home phone and none from the Berglunds. He rewarded himself by playing guitar for four hours. The day was gloriously hot and loud with street life awakening from a long winter's dormancy. His left fingertips, bare of calluses, were near the point of bleeding, but the underlying nerves, killed several decades earlier, were still helpfully dead. He drank a beer and went around the corner to his favorite gyro place, intending to have a snack and play some more. When he returned to his building, carrying meat, he found Patty sitting on the front steps.

She was wearing a linen skirt and a sleeveless blue blouse with sweat circles reaching nearly to her waist. Beside her was a large suitcase and a small pile of outer garments.

"Well, well, well," he said.

"I've been evicted," she said with a sad, meek smile. "Thanks to you."

His dick, if no other part of him, was pleased with this ratification of its divining powers.

# BAD NEWS

Jonathan and Jenna's mother, Tamara, had hurt herself in Aspen. Trying to avoid collision with a hotdogging teenager, she'd crossed her skis and snapped two bones in her left leg, above the boot, and thereby disqualified herself from joining Jenna on Jenna's January trip to ride horses in Patagonia. To Jenna, who'd witnessed Tamara's wipeout and pursued the teenager and reported him while Jonathan attended to their fallen mother, the accident was just the latest entry in a long list of things going wrong in her life since her graduation from Duke the previous spring; but to Joey, who'd been talking to Jenna twice or thrice daily in recent weeks, the accident was a much-needed little gift from the gods—the breakthrough he'd been waiting two-plus years for. Jenna, after graduating, had moved to Manhattan to work for a famous party planner and try living with her almost-fiancé, Nick, but in September she'd rented her own apartment, and in November, yielding to relentless overt pressure from her family and to more subtle underminings from Joey, who'd made himself her Designated Understander, she declared her relationship with Nick null and void and unrevivable. By that point, she was taking a highish dose of Lexapro and had *nothing* in her life to look forward to except riding horses in Patagonia, which Nick had repeatedly promised to do with her and repeatedly postponed, citing his heavy work load at Goldman Sachs. It happened that Joey had ridden a horse or two, albeit clumsily, during his high-school summer in Montana. From the high volume of Jenna's calls and texts to his cell phone, he already suspected that he'd been promoted to the status of transitional object, if not to potential full-on boyfriend, and his last doubts were dispelled when she invited him to share the luxurious Argentinean resort room that Tamara had booked before the accident. Since it further happened that Joey had business in nearby Paraguay and knew that he would probably end up having to go there, whether he wanted to or not, he said yes to Jenna without hesitation. The only real argument against traveling with her in Argentina was the fact that, five months earlier, at the age of twenty, in a fit of madness in New York City, he'd gone to the courthouse in Lower Manhattan and married Connie Monaghan. But this was by no means the worst of his worries, and he chose, for the moment, to overlook it.

The night before he flew to Miami, where Jenna was visiting a grandparent and would meet him at the airport, he called Connie in St. Paul with the news of his impending travel. He was sorry to have to obfuscate and dissemble with her, but his South American plans did give him a good excuse to further postpone her coming east and moving into the highwayside apartment that he'd rented in a charmless corner of Alexandria. Until a few weeks ago, his excuse had been college, but he was now taking a semester off to manage his business, and Connie, who was miserable at home with Carol and Blake and her infant twin half sisters, couldn't understand why she still wasn't allowed to live with her husband.

"I also don't see why you're going to Buenos Aires," she said, "if your supplier's in Paraguay."

"I want to practice my Spanish a little," Joey said, "before I really have to use it. Everybody's talking about what a great city Buenos Aires is. I have to fly through there anyway."

"Well, do you want to take a whole week and have our honeymoon there?"

Their missing honeymoon was one of several sore subjects between them. Joey repeated his official line on it, which was that he was too freaked out about his business to relax on a vacation, and Connie fell into one of the silences that she deployed in lieu of reproach. She still never reproached him directly.

"Literally anywhere in the world," he said. "Once I've been paid, I'll take you anywhere in the world you want to go."

"I'd settle for just living with you and waking up next to you, actually."

"I know, I know," he said. "That would be great. I'm just under such incredible pressure now, I don't think I'd be fun to be around."

"You don't have to be fun," she said.

"We'll talk about it when I get back, OK? I promise."

In the telephonic background, in St. Paul, he faintly heard the squeal of a one-year-old. It wasn't Connie's kid, but it was close enough to make him nervous. He'd seen her only once since August, in Charlottesville, over the long Thanksgiving weekend. Christmastime (another sore subject) he'd spent moving from Charlottesville to Alexandria and making appearances in Georgetown with his family. He'd told Connie that he was working hard on his government contract, but in fact he'd killed whole stretches of days watching football, listening to Jenna on the phone, and generally feeling doomed. Connie might have convinced him to let her fly out anyway if she hadn't been knocked flat by the flu. It had troubled him to hear her feeble voice and know she was his wife and not rush to her side, but he'd needed to go to Poland instead. What he'd discovered in Lodz and Warsaw, during three frustrating days with an American expat "interpreter" whose Polish turned out to be excellent for ordering in restaurants but heavily dependent on an electronic translation device when dealing with hardened Slavic businessmen, had so dismayed and frightened him that, in the weeks since his return, he'd been unable to focus his mind on business for more than five minutes at a time. Everything depended on Paraguay now. And it was much more pleasant to imagine the bed that he was going to share with Jenna than to think about Paraguay.

"Are you wearing your wedding ring?" Connie asked him.

"Um—no," he said before thinking better of it. "It's in my pocket."

"Hm."

"I'm putting it on right now," he said, moving toward the coin dish on his nightstand where he'd left the ring. His nightstand was a cardboard box. "It slips right on, it's great."

"I've got mine on," Connie said. "I love having it on. I try to remember to put it on my right hand when I'm not in my room, but sometimes I forget."

"Don't be forgetting. That's not good."

"It's OK, baby. Carol doesn't notice stuff like that. She doesn't even like to look at me. We're unpleasing to each other's sight."

"We really need to be careful, though, OK?"

"I don't know."

"Just a little while longer," he said. "Just until I tell my parents. Then you can wear it all you want. I mean, we'll both be wearing them all the time then. That's what I meant."

It was hard to compare silences, but the one she deployed now felt especially grievous, especially sad. He knew it was killing her to keep their marriage secret, and he kept hoping that the prospect of telling his parents would become less scary to him, but as the months went by the prospect only got scarier. He tried to put his wedding ring on his finger, but it stuck on the last knuckle. He'd bought it in a hurry, in August, in New York, and it was slightly too small. He put it in his mouth instead, probing its compass with his tongue as if it were an orifice of Connie's, and this turned him on a little. Connected him with her, took him back to August and the craziness of what they'd done. He slipped the ring, drool-slick, onto his finger.

"Tell me what you're wearing," he said.

"Just clothes."

"Like what, though?"

"Nothing. Clothes."

"Connie, I swear I'll tell them as soon as I get paid. I just have to compartmentalize a little now. This fucking contract is freaking me out, and I can't face anything else at the moment. So just tell me what you're wearing, OK? I want to picture you."

"Clothes."

"Please?"

But she'd begun to cry. He heard the faintest whimper, the microgram of misery she let herself make audible. "Joey," she whispered. "Baby. I'm so, so sorry. I don't think I can do this anymore."

"Just a little while longer," he said. "Just at least wait till I'm back from my trip."

"I don't know if I can. I need some tiny thing right now. Some tiny . . . *thing* that's real. Some little thing that isn't nothing. You know I don't want to make things hard for you. But maybe I can at least tell Carol? I just want somebody to *know*. I'll make her swear not to tell anyone."

"She'll tell the neighbors. You know she's a blabber."

"No, I'll make her swear."

"And then somebody's going to be late with their Christmas cards," he said wildly, aggrieved not with Connie but with the way the world conspired against him, "and they'll mention it to my parents. And then— And then—!"

"So what can I have if I can't have that? What's some little thing that I can have?"

Her instincts must have told her there was something fishy about his trip to South America. And he was definitely feeling guilty now, but not exactly about Jenna. According to his moral calculus, his having *married* Connie entitled him to one last grand use of his sexual license, which she'd granted him long ago and never expressly revoked. If he and Jenna happened to click in a big way, he would deal with that later. What was burdening him now was the contrast between the muchness that he possessed—a signed contract that stood to net him $600,000 if Paraguay came through for him; the prospect of a week abroad with the most beautiful girl he'd ever met—and the nullity of what, at this moment, he could think to offer Connie. Guilt had been one of the ingredients of his impulse to marry her, but he was feeling no less guilty five months later. He pulled the wedding ring off his finger and put it back nervously in his mouth, closed his incisors on it, turned it with his tongue. The hardness of eighteen-carat gold was surprising. He'd thought gold was supposed to be a soft metal.

"Tell me something good that's going to happen," Connie said.

"We're going to make a ton of money," he said, tonguing the ring back behind his molars. "And then we'll take an amazing trip somewhere and do a second wedding and have a great time. We'll finish school and start a business. It's all going to be good."

The silence with which she greeted this was disbelief-flavored. He didn't believe his words himself. If only because he was so morbidly afraid to tell his parents about his marriage—had built up the scene of disclosure to such monstrous imaginative proportions—the document that he and Connie had signed in August was seeming more like a suicide pact than a marriage certificate: it extrapolated into a brick wall. Their relationship only made sense in the present, when they were together in person and could merge identities and create their own world.

"I wish you were here," he said.

"Me too."

"You should have come out for Christmas. That was my mistake."

"I would only have given you the flu."

"Just give me a few more weeks. I swear I'll make it up to you."

"I don't know if I can do it. But I'll try."

"I am so sorry."

And he was sorry. But also inexpressibly relieved when she let him get off the phone and turn his thoughts to Jenna. He tongued the wedding ring out of his cheek pocket, intending to dry it off and put it away, but somehow, instead, involuntarily, with a kind of double-clutch of the tongue, he swallowed it.

"Fuck!"

He could feel it near the bottom of his esophagus, an angry hardness down there, the protest of soft tissues. He tried to gag it back up but succeeded only in swallowing it farther down, out of range of feeling it, down with the remains of the twelve-inch Subway sandwich that had been his dinner. He ran to the kitchenette sink and stuck a finger down his throat. He hadn't vomited since he was a little boy, and the gags that were a prelude to it reminded him of how profoundly he'd come to fear throwing up. The violence of it. It was like trying to shoot himself in the head—he couldn't make himself do it. He bent over the sink with his mouth hanging open, hoping the contents of his stomach might just come flowing out naturally, unviolently; but of course it didn't happen.

"Fuck! Fucking coward!"

It was twenty minutes to ten. His flight to Miami left Dulles at eleven the next morning, and no way was he getting on a plane with the ring still in his gut. He paced the stained beige carpeting of his living room and decided that he'd better see a doctor. A quick online search turned up the nearest hospital, on Seminary Road.

He threw on a coat and ran down to Van Dorn Street, looking for a cab to flag, but the night was cold and traffic unusually sparse. He had enough funds in his business account to have bought himself a car, even a very nice one, but since some of the money was Connie's and the rest of it was a bank loan secured on her collateral, he was being very careful with his spending. He wandered out into the street, as if by presenting himself as a target he might attract more traffic and, thus, a cab. But there were no cabs tonight.

On his phone, as he bent his steps toward the hospital, he found a fresh text from Jenna: excited. u? He texted back: totally. Jenna's communications with him, the mere sight of her name or her e-mail address, had never ceased to have a Pavlovian effect on his gonads. The effect was very different from the one that Connie had on him (Connie of late was hitting him higher and higher up: in his stomach, his breathing muscles, his heart) but no less insistent and intense. Jenna excited him the way large sums of money did, the way the delicious abdication of social responsibility and embrace of excessive resource consumption did. He knew perfectly well that Jenna was bad news. Indeed, what excited him was wondering if he might become bad enough news himself to get her.

The walk to the hospital took him directly past the blue-mirrored façade of the office building in which he'd spent all of his days and many of his evenings the previous summer, working for an outfit called RISEN (Restore Iraqi Secular Enterprise Now), an LBI subsidiary that had won a no-bid contract to privatize the formerly state-controlled bread-baking industry in newly liberated Iraq. His boss at RISEN had been Kenny Bartles, a well-connected Floridian in his early twenties whom Joey had succeeded in impressing a year earlier, when he'd worked at Jonathan and Jenna's father's think tank. Joey's summer position at the think tank had been one of five directly funded by LBI, and his job, though ostensibly advisory to governmental entities, had consisted entirely of researching ways in which LBI might commercially exploit an American invasion and takeover of Iraq, and then writing up these commercial possibilities as arguments for invading. To reward Joey for doing the primary research on Iraqi bread production, Kenny Bartles had offered him a full-time job with RISEN, over in Baghdad, in the Green Zone. For numerous reasons, including resistance from Connie, warnings from Jonathan, a wish to stay near Jenna, the fear of getting killed, the need to maintain Virginia residency, and a nagging sense that Kenny wasn't trustworthy, Joey had declined the offer and agreed instead to spend the summer setting up RISEN's Stateside office and interfacing with the government.

The storm of shit he'd taken from his dad for doing this was one of the reasons he couldn't face telling his parents about his marriage, and one of the reasons he'd been trying, ever since, to see how ruthless he had it in him to be. He wanted to get rich enough and tough enough fast enough that he would never again have to take shit from his dad. To be able just to laugh and shrug and walk away: to be more like Jenna, who, for example, knew almost everything about Connie except the fact that Joey had married her, and who nevertheless considered Connie, at most, an adder of thrill and piquancy to the games she'd like to play with Joey. Jenna took special pleasure in asking him if his girlfriend knew how much he was talking to somebody else's girlfriend, and in hearing him recount the lies he'd told. She was even worse news than her brother had made her out to be.

At the hospital, Joey saw why the surrounding streets had been so empty: the entire population of Alexandria had converged on the emergency room. It took him twenty minutes just to register, and the desk nurse was unimpressed with the severe stomach pain he feigned in hopes of moving to the head of the line. During the hour and a half that he then sat breathing in the coughings and sneezings of his fellow Alexandrians, watching the last half hour of *ER* on the waiting-room TV, and texting UVA friends who were still enjoying their winter break, he considered how much easier and cheaper it would be to simply buy a replacement wedding ring. It would cost no more than $300, and Connie would never know the difference. That he felt so romantically attached to an inanimate object—that he felt he owed it to Connie to retrieve this particular ring, which she'd helped him pick out on 47th Street one sweltering afternoon—did not bode well for his project of making himself bad news.

The ER doc who finally saw him was a watery-eyed young white guy with a nasty razor burn. "Nothing to worry about," he assured Joey. "These things take care of themselves. The object should pass right through without you even noticing."

"I'm not worried about my health," Joey said. "I'm worried about getting the ring back tonight."

"Hm," the doctor said. "This is an object of actual value?"

"Great value. And I'm assuming there's some—procedure?"

"If you must have the object, the procedure is to wait a day or two or three. And then . . ." The doctor smiled to himself. "There's an old ER joke about the mother who comes in with a toddler who's swallowed some pennies. She asks the doctor if the kid's going to be OK, and the doctor tells her, 'Just be sure to watch for any change in his stool.' Really silly joke. But that's your procedure, if you must have the object."

"But I'm talking about a procedure you could do right now."

"And I'm telling you there isn't one."

"Hey, your joke was really funny," Joey said. "It really made me laugh. Ha ha. You really told it well."

The charge for this consultation was $275. Being uninsured—the Commonwealth of Virginia considered insurance by one's parents a form of financial support—he was obliged to present plastic for it on the spot. Unless he happened to become constipated, which was the opposite of the problem he associated with Latin America, he could now look forward to some very smelly beginnings to his days with Jenna.

Returning to his apartment, well after midnight, he packed for his trip and then lay in bed and monitored the progress of his digestion. He'd been digesting things every minute of his life without paying the slightest attention to it. How odd it was to think that his stomach lining and his mysterious small intestine were as much a part of him as his brain or tongue or penis. As he lay and strained to feel the subtle ticks and sighs and repositionings in his abdomen, he had a premonition of his body as a long-lost relative waiting at the end of a long road ahead of him. A shady relative whom he was glimpsing for the first time only now. At some point, hopefully still far in the future, he would have to rely on his body, and at some point after that, hopefully still farther in the future, his body was going to let him down, and he would die. He imagined his soul, his famil- iar personal self, as a stainless gold ring slowly making its way down through ever-stranger and fouler-smelling country, toward shit-smelling death. He was alone with his body; and since, weirdly, he *was* his body, this meant he was entirely alone.

He missed Jonathan. In a funny way, his impending trip was a worse betrayal of Jonathan than of Connie. The hiccups of their first Thanksgiving notwithstanding, they'd become best friends in the last two years, and it was only in recent months, beginning with Joey's business deal with Kenny Bartles and culminating in Jonathan's discovery of his travel plans with Jenna, that their friendship had soured. Until then, time after time, Joey had been pleasantly surprised by the evidence of how genuinely fond of him Jonathan was. Fond of all of him, not just of the parts of himself that he saw fit to present to the world as a reasonably cool UVA student. The biggest and most pleasant surprise had been how much Jonathan dug Connie. Indeed, it was fair to say that, without Jonathan's validation of their coupledom, Joey would not have gone so far as to marry her.

Aside from his preferred porn sites, which themselves were touchingly tame in comparison to the ones to which Joey turned in moments of need, Jonathan had no sex life. He was a bit of a wonk, yes, but far wonkier dudes than he were coupling up. He was just terminally awkward with girls, awkward to the point of not being interested, and Connie, when he finally met her, turned out to be the one girl he could relax and be himself around. No doubt it helped that she was so deeply and exclusively into Joey, thus relieving Jonathan of the stress of trying to impress her or of worrying that she wanted something from him. Connie behaved like an older sister with him, a much nicer and more interested older sister than Jenna. While Joey was studying or working at the library, she played Jonathan's video games with him for hours, laughing congenially at her losses and listening, in her limpid way, to his explications of their features. Though Jonathan ordinarily made a fetish of his bed and his special childhood pillow and his nightly need for nine hours of sleep, he discreetly vacated the dorm room before Joey even had to ask him for some privacy. After Connie returned to St. Paul, Jonathan told him he thought his girlfriend was *amazing*, totally hot but also easy to be with, and this made Joey, for the first time, proud of her. He stopped thinking of her so much as a weakness of his, a problem to be solved at his earliest convenience, and more as a girlfriend whose existence he didn't mind owning up to with his other friends. Which, in turn, made him all the angrier about his mother's veiled but implacable hostility.

"One question, Joey," his mother had said on the telephone, during the weeks when he and Connie were housesitting for his aunt Abigail. "Am I allowed one question?"

"Depends on what it is," Joey said.

"Are you and Connie having any fights?"

"Mom, no, I'm not going to talk about this."

"You may be curious why that's the one question I'm asking. Maybe you're a tiny bit curious?"

"Nope."

"It's because you *should* be having fights, and there's something wrong if you're not."

"Yeah, by that definition, you and dad must be doing everything right."

"Ha-ha-ha! That's really hilarious, Joey."

"Why should I have fights? People have fights when they don't get along."

"No, people have fights when they love each other but still have actual complete personalities and are living in the real world. Obviously, I'm not saying it's good to fight excessively."

"No, just exactly enough. I get it."

"If you're never having fights, you need to ask yourself why not, is all I'm saying. Ask yourself, where is the fantasy residing?"

"No, Mom. Sorry. Not going to talk about this."

"Or *who* it's residing in, if you know what I mean."

"I swear to God, I'm going to hang up, and I'm not going to call you for a year."

"What realities are not being attended to."

"Mom!"

"Anyway, that was my one question, and now I've asked it, and I won't ask you any more."

Although his mother's happiness levels were nothing to brag about, she persisted in inflicting the norms of her own life on Joey. She probably thought she was trying to protect him, but all he heard was the drumbeat of negativity. She was especially "concerned" about Connie's lack of any friends besides himself. She'd once cited her own crazy college friend Eliza, who'd had zero other friends, and what a warning sign this should have been. Joey had replied that Connie did so have friends, and when his mother had challenged him to name them, he'd loudly refused to discuss things she knew nothing about. Connie did have some old school friends, at least two or three, but when she spoke of them it was mainly to dissect their superficialities or to compare their intelligence unfavorably with Joey's, and he could never keep their names straight. His mother had thus scored a palpable hit. And she knew better than to stab an existing wound twice, but either she was the world's most expert implier, or Joey was the world's most sensitive inferrer. She had merely to mention an upcoming visit from her old teammate Cathy Schmidt for Joey to hear invidious criticism of Connie. If he called her on it, she became all psychological and asked him to examine his touchiness on the subject. The one counter-thrust that would really have shut her up—asking how many friends *she'd* made since college (answer: none)—was the one he couldn't bear to make. She had the unfair final advantage, in all their arguments, of being pitiable to him.

Connie bore his mother no corresponding enmity. She had every right to complain, but she never did, and this made the unfairness of his mother's enmity all the more glaring. As a little girl, Connie had voluntarily, without any prompting from Carol, given his mother handmade birthday cards. His mother had crooned over these cards every year until he and Connie started having sex. Connie had continued to make her birthday cards after that, and Joey, when he'd still been in St. Paul, had seen his mother open one, glance at its greeting with a stony expression, and set it aside like junk mail. More recently, Connie had additionally sent her little birthday presents—earrings one year, chocolates another—for which she received acknowledgments as stiltedly impersonal as an IRS communiqué. Connie did everything she could to make his mother like her again except the one thing that would have worked, which was to stop seeing Joey. She was purehearted and his mother spat on her. The unfairness of it was another reason he had married her.

The unfairness had also, in a roundabout way, made the Republican Party more attractive to him. His mother was a snob about Carol and Blake and held against Connie the mere fact that she lived with them. She took it for granted that all right-thinking people, including Joey, were of one mind about the tastes and opinions of white people from less privileged backgrounds than her own. What Joey liked about the Republicans was that they didn't *disdain* people the way liberal Democrats did. They hated the liberals, yes, but only because the liberals had hated them first.

They were simply sick of the kind of unexamined condescension with which his mother treated the Monaghans. Over the past two years, Joey had slowly traded places with Jonathan in their political discussions, particularly on the subject of Iraq. Joey had become convinced that an invasion was needed to safeguard America's petropolitical interests and take out Saddam's weapons of mass destruction, while Jonathan, who'd landed plum summer internships with *The Hill* and then with the *WaPo* and was hoping to be a political journalist, was ever more distrustful of the people like Feith and Wolfowitz and Perle and Chalabi who were pushing for the war. Both of them had enjoyed reversing their expected roles and becoming the political outliers of their respective families, Joey sounding more and more like Jonathan's father, Jonathan more and more like Joey's. The longer Joey persisted in siding with Connie and defending her against his mother's snobbery, the more at home he felt with the party of angry anti-snobbism.

And why *had* he stuck with Connie? The only answer that made sense was that he loved her. He'd had his chances to free himself of her—had, indeed, deliberately created some of them—but again and again, at the crucial moment, had chosen not to use them. The first great opportunity had been his going away to college. His next chance had come a year later, when Connie followed him east to Morton College, in Morton's Glen, Virginia. Her move did put her within an easy drive of Charlottesville in Jonathan's Land Cruiser (which Jonathan, approving of Connie, let Joey borrow), but it also set her on course to be a normal college student and develop an independent life. After his second visit to Morton, which the two of them mostly spent dodging her Korean roommate, Joey proposed that, *for her sake* (since she didn't seem to be adapting well to college), they again try to break their dependency and cease communication for a while. His proposal wasn't entirely disingenuous; he wasn't entirely ruling out a future for them. But he'd been doing a lot of listening to Jenna and was hoping to spend his winter break with her and Jonathan in McLean. When Connie finally got wind of these plans, a few weeks before Christmas, he asked her if she didn't want to go home to St. Paul and see her friends and family (i.e., the way a normal college freshman might). "No," she said, "I want to be with you." Spurred by the prospect of Jenna, and bolstered by an especially satisfying hookup that had fallen in his lap at a recent semi-formal dance, he took a hard line with Connie, who then cried on the phone so stormily that she got the hiccups. She said she *never* wanted to go home again, *never* wanted to spend another night with Carol and the babies. But Joey made her do it anyway. And even though he barely spoke to Jenna over the holidays—first she was skiing, then she was in New York with Nick—he continued to pursue his exit strategy until the night in early February when Carol called him with the news that Connie had dropped out of Morton and was back on Barrier Street, more seriously depressed than ever.

Connie had apparently aced two of her December finals at Morton but simply failed to show up for the other two, and there was virulent antipathy between her and the roommate, who listened to the Backstreet Boys so loudly that the treble leaking from her earphones would have driven anybody crazy, and left her TV tuned to a shopping channel all day, and taunted Connie about her "stuck-up" boyfriend, and invited her to imagine all the stuck-up sluts that he was screwing behind her back, and smelled up their room with terrible pickles. Connie had returned to school in January on academic probation but proceeded to spend so much time in bed that the campus health service finally intervened and sent her home. All this Carol reported to Joey with sober worry and a welcome absence of recrimination.

That he'd passed up this latest fine chance to free himself of Connie (who could no longer pretend that her depression was just a figment of Carol's imagination) was somewhat related to the recent bitter news of Jenna's "sort-of" engagement to Nick, but only somewhat. Although Joey knew enough to be afraid of hard-core mental illness, it seemed to him that if he eliminated from his pool of prospects every interesting college-age girl with some history of depression, he would be left with a very small pool indeed. And Connie had *reason* to be depressed: her roommate was intolerable and she'd been dying of loneliness. When Carol put her on the telephone, she used the word "sorry" a hundred times. Sorry to have let Joey down, sorry not to have been stronger, sorry to distract him from his schoolwork, sorry to have wasted her tuition money, sorry to be a burden to Carol, sorry to be a burden to everyone, sorry to be such a drag to talk to. Although (or *because*) she was too low to ask anything of him—seemed finally halfway willing to let go of him—he told her he was flush with cash from his mother and would fly out to see her. The more she said he didn't have to do this, the more he knew he did.

The week he'd then spent on Barrier Street had been the first truly adult week of his life. Sitting with Blake in the great-room, the dimensions of which were more modest than he remembered, he watched Fox News's coverage of the assault on Baghdad and felt his long-standing resentment of 9/11 beginning to dissolve. The country was finally moving on, finally taking history in its hands again, and this was somehow of a piece with the deference and gratitude that Blake and Carol showed him. He regaled Blake with tales from the think tank, the brushes he'd had with figures in the news, the post-invasion planning he was party to. The house was small and he was big in it. He learned how to hold a baby and how to tilt a nippled bottle. Connie was pale and scarily underweight, her arms as skinny and her belly as concave as when she'd been fourteen and he'd first touched them. He lay and held her in the night and tried to excite her, labored to penetrate the thick affective rind of her distraction, enough to feel OK about having sex with her. The pills she was taking hadn't kicked in yet, and he was almost glad of how sick she was; it gave him seriousness and a purpose. She kept repeating that she'd let him down, but he felt almost the opposite. As if a new and more grownup world of love had revealed itself: as if there were still no end of inner doors for them to open. Through one of her bedroom windows he could see the house he'd grown up in, a house now occupied by black people who Carol said were snooty and kept to themselves, with their framed PhDs on a dining-room wall. ("In the dining room," Carol emphasized, "where everybody can see them, even from the street.") Joey was pleased by how little the sight of his old house moved him. For as long as he could remember, he'd wanted to outgrow it, and now it seemed as if he really had. He went so far, one evening, as to call his mother and own up to what was happening.

"So," she said. "OK. I'm apparently a little bit out of the loop here. You're saying Connie was at college in the East?"

"Yep. But she had a bad roommate and got depressed."

"Well, it's nice of you to inform me, now that it's all safely in the past."

"You didn't exactly make it pleasant to tell you what's going on with her."

"No, of course, I'm the villain here. Negative old me. I'm sure that's how it looks to you."

"Maybe there's a reason it looks that way. Have you considered that?"

"I was just under the impression you were free and unencumbered. You know, college doesn't last long, Joey. I tied myself down when I was young and missed out on a lot of experiences that probably would have been good for me. Then again, maybe I just wasn't as mature as you are."

"Yep," he said feeling steely and, indeed, mature. "Maybe."

"I would only point out that you did sort of lie to me, whenever that was, two months ago, when I asked you if you'd heard from Connie. Which, lying, maybe not the *most* mature thing."

"Your question wasn't friendly."

"Your answer wasn't honest! Not that you necessarily owe me honesty, but let's at least be straight about it now."

"It was Christmas. I said I thought she was in St. Paul."

"Well, exactly. And not to belabor this, but when a person says 'I think,' it tends to imply that he isn't sure. You pretended not to know something you knew very well."

"I said where I thought she was. But she could have been in Wisconsin or something."

"Right, visiting one of her many close friends."

"Jesus!" he said. "You truly have no one but yourself to blame for this."

"Don't get me wrong," she said. "I think it's very admirable that you're there with her now, and I mean that seriously. It speaks well of you. I'm proud that you want to take care of somebody who matters to you. I have some acquaintance with depression myself, and, believe me, I know it's no picnic. Is Connie taking something for it?"

"Yeah, Celexa."

"Well, I hope that works out for her. My own drug didn't work out so well for me."

"You were taking an antidepressant? When?"

"Oh, fairly recently."

"God, I had no idea."

"That's because, when I say I want you to be free and unencumbered, I really mean it. I didn't want you worrying about me."

"Jesus, though, you could at least have told me."

"It was only for a few months anyway. I was a less than exemplary patient."

"You have to give those drugs some time," he said.

"Right, so everybody said. Especially Dad, who's kind of on the front lines with me. He was very sorry to see those good times go. But I was glad to have my head back, such as it is."

"I'm really sorry."

"Yes, I know. If you'd told me these things about Connie three months ago, my response would have been: La-la-la! Now you have to put up with me feeling things again."

"I meant I was sorry you're hurting."

"Thank you, sweetie. I do apologize for my feelings."

Ubiquitous though depression seemed lately to have become, Joey still found it a little worrisome that the two females who loved him the most were both suffering clinically. Was it just chance? Or did he have some actively baneful effect on women's mental health? In Connie's case, he decided, the truth was that her depression was a facet of the same intensity he'd always so much loved in her. On his last night in St. Paul, before returning to Virginia, he sat and watched her probe her skull with her fingertips, as if she were hoping to extract excess feeling from her brain. She said that the reason she'd been weeping at seemingly random moments was that even the smallest bad thoughts were excruciating, and that only bad thoughts, no good ones, were occurring to her. She thought about how she'd lost a UVA baseball cap he'd once given her; how she'd been too preoccupied with her roommate, during his second visit to Morton, to ask him what grade he'd gotten on his big American History paper; how Carol had once remarked that boys would like her better if she smiled more; how one of her baby half sisters, Sabrina, had burst into screams the first time she'd held her; how she'd stupidly admitted to Joey's mother that she was going to New York to see him; how she'd been bleeding disgustingly on the last night before he went away to college; how she'd written such wrong things in the postcards she'd sent Jessica, in an attempt to be friends with his sister again, that Jessica had never replied to them; and on and on. She was lost in a dark forest of regret and self-disgust in which even the smallest tree assumed monstrous proportions. Joey had never been in woods like these himself but was unaccountably drawn to them in her. It even turned him on that she began to sob while he endeavored to fuck her in farewell, at least until the sobbing turned to writhing and thrashing and self-loathing. Her level of distress seemed borderline dangerous, a cousin of suicide, and he was awake for half the night then, trying to talk her out of how terrible about herself she felt for feeling too terrible about herself to give him anything he wanted. It was exhausting and circular and unbearable, and yet, the following afternoon, when he was flying back East, it occurred to him to be afraid of what the Celexa would do to her when it kicked in. He considered his mother's remark about antidepressants killing feelings: a Connie without oceans of feeling was a Connie he didn't know and suspected he wouldn't want.

Meanwhile the country was at war, but it was an odd sort of war in which, within a rounding error, the only casualties were on the other side. Joey was glad to see that the taking of Iraq was every bit the cakewalk he'd expected it to be, and Kenny Bartles was sending him elated e-mails about the need to get his bread company up and running ASAP. (Joey kept having to explain that he was still a college student and couldn't start work until after finals.) Jonathan, however, was sourer than ever. He was *fixated*, for example, on the Iraqi antiquities that had been stolen by looters from the National Museum.

"That was one little mistake," Joey said. "Shit happens, right? You just don't want to admit that things are going well."

"I'll admit it when they find the plutonium and the missiles tipped with smallpox," Jonathan said. "Which they won't, because it was all bullshit, all trumped-up bullshit, because the people who started this thing are incompetent clowns."

"Dude, everybody says there's WMDs. Even *The New Yorker* says there are. My mom said my dad wants to cancel their subscription, he's so mad about it. My dad, the great expert on foreign affairs."

"How much you want to bet your dad's right?"

"I don't know. A hundred dollars?"

"Done!" Jonathan said, extending his hand. "A hundred bucks says they find no weapons by the end of the year."

Joey shook his hand and then proceeded to worry that Jonathan was right about the WMDs. Not that he cared about a hundred dollars; he was going to be making 8K a month with Kenny Bartles. But Jonathan, a political news junkie, seemed so very sure of himself that Joey wondered if he'd somehow missed the joke in his dealings with his think-tank bosses and Kenny Bartles: had failed to notice them winking or ironically inflecting their voices when they spoke of reasons beyond their own personal or corporate enrichment for invading Iraq. In Joey's view, the think tank did indeed have a hush-hush motive for supporting the invasion: the protection of Israel, which, unlike the United States, was within striking distance of even the crappy sort of missile that Saddam's scientists were capable of building. But he'd believed that the neocons at least were serious in fearing for Israel's safety. Now, already, as March turned to April, they were waving their hands and acting as if it didn't even matter if any WMDs came to light; as if the freedom of the Iraqi people were the main issue. And Joey, whose own interest in the war was primarily financial, but who'd taken moral refuge in the thought that wiser minds than his had better motives, began to feel that he'd been suckered. It didn't make him any less eager to cash in, but it did make him feel dirtier about it.

In his soiled mood, he found it easier to talk to Jenna about his summer plans. Jonathan, among other things, was jealous of Kenny Bartles (he got pissy whenever he heard Joey talking on the phone to Kenny), whereas Jenna had dollar signs in her eyes and was all for making killings. "Maybe I'll see you in Washington this summer," she said. "I'll come down from New York and you can take me out to dinner to celebrate my engagement."

"Sure," he said. "Sounds like a fun evening."

"I have to warn you I have *very* expensive taste in restaurants."

"How's Nick going to feel about me taking you to dinner?"

"Just one less bite out of his wallet. It would never occur to him to be afraid of you. But how's your girlfriend going to feel?"

"She's not the jealous type."

"Right, jealousy's so unattractive, ha ha."

"What she doesn't know can't hurt her."

"Yes, and there's quite a bit she doesn't know, isn't there? How many little slips have you had now?"

"Five."

"That is four more than Nick would get away with before I surgically removed his testicles."

"Yeah, but if you didn't know about it, it wouldn't hurt you, right?"

"Believe me," Jenna said, "I would know about it. That's the difference between me and your girlfriend. I *am* the jealous type. I am the Spanish Inquisition when it comes to being fucked around on. No quarter will be given."

This was interesting to hear, since it was Jenna who had urged him, the previous fall, to avail himself of such casual opportunities as came his way at school, and it was Jenna to whom he'd imagined he was proving something by doing so. She'd given him instruction in the art of cutting dead, in the dining hall, a girl from whose bed he'd crawled four hours earlier. "Don't be such a tender daisy," she'd said. "They *want* you to ignore them. You're not doing them any favors if you don't. You need to pretend you've never seen them in your life. The last thing in the world they want is you mooning around or acting guilty. They're sitting there praying to Jesus that you won't embarrass them." She'd clearly been speaking from personal experience, but he hadn't quite believed her until the first time he'd tried it. His life had been easier ever since. Though he did Connie the kindness of not mentioning his indiscretions, he continued to think she wouldn't much care. (The person he actively had to hide from was Jonathan, who had Arthurian notions of romantic comportment and had torn into Joey furiously, as if he were Connie's older brother or knightly guardian, when word of a hookup had leaked back to him. Joey had sworn to him that not even a zipper had been lowered, but this falsehood was too absurd not to smirk at, and Jonathan had called him a dick and a liar, unworthy of Connie.) Now he felt as if Jenna, with her shifting standard of fidelity, had suckered him in much the same way his bosses at the think tank had. She'd done for sport, as a meanness to Connie, what the warmongers had done for profit. But it didn't make him any less keen to buy her a great dinner or to earn, at RISEN, the money to do it.

Sitting alone in RISEN's frigid one-room office in Alexandria, Joey wrote Kenny's jumbled faxings out of Baghdad into persuasive reports on the judicious use of taxpayer dollars to remake Saddam-subsidized bakers as CPA-backed entrepreneurs. He used his case studies of the

Breadmasters and Hot & Crusty chains, written the previous summer, to create a handsome business-plan template for these would-be entrepreneurs to follow. He developed a two-year plan for jacking bread prices up into the vicinity of fair market, with the basic Iraqi *khubz* as a loss-leader and overpriced pastries and attractively marketed coffee drinks as the moneymakers, so that, by 2005, Coalition subsidies could be phased out without sparking bread riots. Everything he did was at least partial and often total bullshit. He had not the foggiest notion of what a Basra storefront looked like; he suspected, for example, that plate-glass Breadmasters-style refrigerated pastry display windows might not fare well in a city of car bombings and 130-degree summer heat. But the bullshit of modern commerce was a language he'd been happy to find himself fluent in, and Kenny assured him that all that mattered was the appearance of tremendous activity and instantaneous results. "Make it look good *yesterday*," Kenny said, "and then we'll do our best here on the ground to catch up with how it looks. Jerry wants free markets overnight, and that's what we gotta give him." ("Jerry" was Paul Bremer, head honcho in Baghdad, whom Kenny may or may not have even met.) In Joey's idle hours at the office, especially on weekends, he chatted with school friends who were working unpaid internships or flipping burgers in their hometowns and showered him with envy and congratulations for having landed the most awesome summer job *ever*. He felt as if the progress of his life, which 9/11 had knocked off course, had now fully regained its sensational upward trajectory.

For a while, the only shadows on his satisfaction were Jenna's postponements of her trip to Washington. A recurrent theme of their conversations was her worry that she'd sown insufficient wild oats before committing herself to Nick. ("I'm not sure that having been a slut for a year at Duke really counts," she said.) Joey could hear in her worry the whispering of opportunity, and he was confounded when, despite the increasingly raw flirtation of their phone calls, she twice canceled plans to come down and see him, and even more confounded when he learned from Jonathan that she'd been to her parents' in McLean without letting him know.

Then, on the Fourth of July, during a family visit he was making only to be nice, he vouchsafed to his father the details of his work at RISEN, hoping to impress him with the size of his salary and the scope of his responsibilities; and his father all but disowned him on the spot. Until now, all his life, their relationship had essentially been a standoff, a stalemate of wills. But now his dad was no longer content to send him on his way with a lecture about his coldness and his arrogance. Now he was shouting that Joey made him *sick*, that it *physically disgusted him* to have raised a son so selfish and unthinking that he was willing to connive with monsters trashing the country for their personal enrichment. His mother, instead of defending him, ran for her life: upstairs, to her little room. He knew she would be calling him the next morning, trying to smooth things over, feeding him crap about how his dad was only angry because he loved him. But she was too cowardly to stick around, and there was nothing he could do himself but cross his arms tightly and make his face a mask and shake his head and tell his dad, over and over, not to criticize things he didn't understand.

"What's not to understand?" his father said. "This is a war for politics and profit. Period!"

"Just because you don't like people's politics," Joey said, "it doesn't mean that everything they do is wrong. You're pretending that everything they do is bad, you're hoping they're going to fail at everything, because you hate their politics. You don't even want to hear about the good things that are happening."

"*There are no good things happening.*"

"Oh, right. It's a black-and-white world. We're all bad and you're all good."

"You think the way the world works is that Middle Eastern kids the same age as you are getting their heads and their legs blown off so you can make a ton of money? That's the perfect world you live in?"

"Obviously not, Dad. Would you stop being stupid for a second? People are getting killed over there because their economy is fucked up. We're trying to fix their economy, OK?"

"You shouldn't be making eight thousand dollars a month," his dad said. "I know you think you're very smart, but there is something wrong with a world where an unskilled nineteen-year-old can do that. Your situation *stinks* of corruption. You smell really bad to me."

"Jesus, Dad. Whatever."

"I don't even want to know what you're doing anymore. It makes me too sick. You can tell it to your mother, but do me a favor and leave me out."

Joey smiled fiercely to keep himself from crying. He was experiencing a hurt that felt structural, as if he and his dad had each chosen their politics for the sole purpose of hating the other, and the only way out of it was disengagement. Not telling his dad anything, not seeing him again unless he absolutely had to, sounded good to him, too. He wasn't even angry, he just wanted to leave the hurt behind. He taxied home to his furnished studio apartment, which his mom had helped him rent, and sent messages to both Connie and Jenna. Connie must have gone to bed early, but Jenna called him back at midnight. She wasn't the world's best listener, but she got enough of the gist of his rotten Fourth to assure him that the world wasn't fair and was never going to be fair, that there would always be big winners and big losers, and that she personally, in the tragically finite life that she'd been given, preferred to be a winner and to surround herself with winners. When he then confronted her with not having called him from McLean, she said she hadn't thought it would be "safe" to see him for dinner.

"Why wouldn't it have been safe?"

"You're kind of a bad habit of mine," she said. "I need to keep it in check. Need to keep my eyes on the prize."

"It doesn't sound like you and the prize are having much fun together."

"The prize is extremely busy trying to take his boss's job. That's what they do in that world, they try to eat each other alive. It's surprisingly unfrowned upon. But also apparently hugely time-consuming. A girl likes to be taken out now and then, especially in her first summer after college."

"That's why you need to come down here," he said. "I'll definitely take you out."

"No doubt. But my boss has got wall-to-wall jobs in the Hamptons for the next three weeks. My services as a clipboard-holder are required. Too bad you have to work so hard yourself, or I could try to sneak you into something."

He'd lost count of the half dates and half promises she'd made since he'd known her. None of the fun things she suggested ever quite came to pass, and he could never quite figure out why she bothered to keep suggesting them. Sometimes he thought it had to do with her competing with her brother. Or maybe it was because Joey was Jewish and pleasing to her father, who was the one person she never snarked. Or maybe she was fascinated by his relationship with Connie and took a queenly relish in the nuggets of private info that he laid at her feet. Or maybe she was genuinely into him and wanted to see what he was like when he was older and how much money he could make. Or maybe all of the above. Jonathan had no insights to offer except that his sister was bad news, a freak from Planet Spoiled, with the ethical consciousness of sea sponge, but Joey thought he could glimpse deeper things in her. He refused to believe that someone disposing of the power of so much beauty could be devoid of interesting ideas of how to use it.

The next day, when he told Connie about his fight with his father, she didn't get into the merits of their respective arguments but went straight to his hurt and told him how sorry she was. She'd gone back to work as a waitress and seemed willing to wait all summer to see him again. Kenny Bartles had promised him the last two weeks of August as a paid vacation if he agreed to work every weekend before then, and he didn't want Connie around to complicate things if Jenna came down to Washington; he didn't see how he'd be able to slip away for an evening or two or three without telling Connie the kind of arrant lie that he was trying to keep to a minimum.

The equanimity with which she'd accepted the delay he attributed to Celexa. But then one night, during a routine telephone check-in, while he was drinking beer in his apartment, she fell into an especially protracted silence that ended with her saying, "Baby, there are a few things I need to tell you." The first thing was that she'd stopped taking her medication. The second thing was that the reason she'd stopped taking it was that she'd been sleeping with her restaurant manager and was tired of not coming. She confessed this with curious detachment, as if speaking of some girl who wasn't her, a girl whose doings were regrettable but understandable. The manager, she said, was married and had two teenage kids and lived on Hamline Avenue. "I thought I'd better tell you," she said. "I can stop it if you want me to."

Joey was shivering. Shuddering almost. A draft was coming through a mental door that he'd assumed was shut and locked but in fact was standing open wide; a door that he could flee through. "Do you want it to stop?" he said.

"I don't know," she said. "I kind of like it, for the sex, but I don't feel anything for him. I only feel things for you."

"Well, Jesus. I guess I have to think about this."

"I know it's really bad, Joey. I should have told you as soon as it happened. But for a while it was just so nice that somebody was interested. Do you realize how many times we've made love since last October?"

"Yeah, I know. I'm aware."

"Either twice or zero times, depending on whether you count when I was sick. There's something not right there."

"I know."

"We love each other but we never see each other. Don't you miss it?"

"Yes."

"Have you had sex with other people? Is that how you can stand it?"

"Yeah, I did. A couple of times. But never more than *once* with anybody."

"I was pretty sure you had, but I didn't want to ask you. I didn't want you to think I wasn't going to let you. And that's not why I did it myself. I did it because I'm lonely. I'm so lonely, Joey. I'm dying of it. And the reason I'm so lonely is I love you and you're not here. I had sex with somebody else because I love you. I know that sounds mixed up, or dishonest, but it's the truth."

"I believe you," he said. And he did. But the pain he was experiencing didn't seem to have anything to do with what he believed or didn't believe, what she might say now or not say. The mute fact of his sweet Connie having lain down with some middle-aged pig, of her having taken off her jeans and her little underpants and opened her legs *repeatedly*, had embodied itself in words only long enough for her to speak them and for Joey to hear them before returning to muteness and lodging inside him, out of reach of words, like some swallowed ball of razor blades. He could see, reasonably enough, that she might care no more about her pig of a manager than he'd cared about the girls, all of them either drunk or extremely drunk, in whose overly perfumed beds he'd landed in the previous year, but reason could no more reach the pain in him than thinking Stop! could arrest an onrushing bus. The pain was quite extraordinary. And yet also weirdly welcome and restorative, bringing him news of his aliveness and his caughtness in a story larger than himself.

"Say something to me, baby," Connie said.

"When did this start?"

"I don't know. Three months ago."

"Well, maybe you should just keep doing it," he said. "Maybe you should go ahead and have his baby and see if he'll set you up in your own house."

It was ugly to reference Carol like this, but in reply Connie only asked him, with limpid sincerity, "Is that what you want me to do?"

"I don't know what I want."

"It's not at all what I want. I want to be with you."

"Yeah, right. But not before fucking somebody else for three months."

This ought to have made her weep and beg forgiveness, or at least lash out at him in turn, but she wasn't an ordinary person. "That's true," she said. "You're right. That's absolutely fair. I could have told you the first time it happened, and then stopped. But doing it a second time didn't seem much worse than doing it once. And then the same thing with the third time and the fourth time. And then I wanted to go off my drug, because it seemed stupid to be having sex when I could hardly feel it. And then the counter sort of had to be reset."

"And now you're feeling it, and it's great."

"It is definitely better. You're the person I love, but at least my nerve endings are working again."

"So why'd you even tell me now? Why not go four months? Four's hardly any worse than three, right?"

"Four's actually what I was planning," she said. "I thought I could tell you when I come out next month, and we could make a plan to be together more often, so we could start being monogamous again. That's still what I want. But I started having bad thoughts again last night, and I thought I'd better tell you."

"Are you getting depressed? Does your doctor know you quit the drug?"

"She knows, but Carol doesn't. Carol seems to think the drug is going to make everything OK between her and me. She thinks it's going to solve her problem permanently. I take a pill out of the bottle every night and put it in my sock drawer. I think she might be counting them when I'm at work."

"You should probably be taking them," Joey said.

"I'll go back on them if I can't see you anymore. If I see you, though, I want to feel everything. And I don't think I'll need them if I keep on seeing you. I know that sounds like a threat or something, but it's just the truth. I'm not trying to influence you about whether to see me again or not. I understand that I did a bad thing."

"Are you sorry about it?"

"I know I should say yes, but I don't actually know. Are you sorry you slept with other people?"

"No. Especially not now."

"Same with me, baby. I'm exactly like you. I just hope you can remember that, and let me see you again."

Connie's confession was his last, best chance to escape with his conscience clear. He could so easily have fired her for cause, if only he'd felt angry enough to do it. After he got off the phone, he hit the bottle of Jack Daniel's that he was normally disciplined enough to keep away from, and then he went out walking the humid streets of his bleak non-neighborhood, relishing the blunt-force summer heat and the collective roar of the air conditioners compounding it. In a pocket of his khakis was a handful of coins that he took out and began to fling, a few at a time, into the street. He threw them all away, the pennies of his innocence, the dimes and quarters of his self-sufficiency. He needed to rid himself, to rid himself. He had nobody to tell about his pain, least of all his parents but also not Jonathan, for fear of damaging his friend's good opinion of Connie, and certainly not Jenna, who didn't understand love, and not his school friends, either—they all, to a man, saw girlfriends as a senseless impediment to the pleasures they intended to spend the next ten years pursuing. He was totally alone and didn't understand how it had happened to him. How there had come to be an ache named Connie at the center of his life. He was being driven crazy by so minutely feeling what she felt, by understanding her too well, by not being able to imagine her life without him. Every time he had a chance to get away from her, the logic of self-interest failed him: was supplanted, like a gear that his mind kept popping out of, by the logic of the two of them.

A week went by without her calling him, and then another week. He became sensible, for the first time, of her greater age. She was twenty-one now, a legal adult, a woman interesting and attractive to married men. In the grip of jealousy, he was suddenly seeing himself as the lucky one of the two of them, the mere boy on whom she'd bestowed her ardor. She assumed fantastically alluring form in his imagination. He'd sometimes dimly sensed that their connection was extraordinary, enchanted, fairy-tale-like, but only now did he appreciate how much he counted on her. For the first few days of their silence, he managed to believe that he was punishing her by not calling her, but before long he came to feel like the punished one, the person waiting to see whether she, in her ocean of feeling, might find a drop of mercy and break the silence for him.

In the meantime, his mother informed him that she would be sending him no more monthly $500 checks. "I'm afraid Dad's put an end to that," she said with a breeziness that annoyed him. "I hope it was at least useful while it lasted." Joey felt a certain relief at no longer having to indulge her wish to support him and no longer owing her regular phone calls in return; he was also glad to stop lying to the Commonwealth of Virginia about his level of parental support. But he'd come to rely on the monthly infusions to make ends meet, and he was now sorry about having taken so many cabs and ordered in so many meals that summer. He couldn't help hating his father and feeling betrayed by his mother, who, when push came to shove, despite the many complaints about her marriage that she inflicted on Joey, seemed always to end up deferring to his father.

Then his aunt Abigail called to offer him the use of her apartment in late August. For the last year and a half, he'd been on Abigail's e-mail list for the performances she gave at bizarrely named small venues in New York, and she'd called him every few months to deliver one of her self-justifying monologues. If he clicked the Ignore button on his phone, she didn't leave a message but simply kept calling until he clicked Answer. He had the impression that her days consisted largely of cycling through every number she knew until someone finally answered, and he hated to consider who else might be on her calling list, given the tenuousness of his own connection with her. "I'm giving myself the little gift of a beach vacation," she told him now. "I'm afraid poor Tigger died of kitty cancer, though not before some verrrrry expensive kitty-cancer treatments, and Piglet's all alone." Although Joey was feeling somewhat dirty about his flirtation with Jenna, as part of a more general new queasiness about infidelity, he accepted Abigail's offer. If he never heard from Connie, he thought, he might console himself by showing up in Jenna's neighborhood and asking her to dinner.

And then Kenny Bartles called with the news that he was selling RISEN and its contracts to a friend of his in Florida. Had already sold them, in fact. "Mike's going to call you in the morning," Kenny said. "I told him he had to keep you on till August fifteen. I didn't want the hassle of trying to replace you after that anyway. I got bigger and better fish to fry."

"Oh yeah?" Joey said.

"Yeah, LBI's willing to subcontract me to procure a fleet of heavy-duty trucks. Not a job for the squeamish, and a lot better bread than bread's been, if you know what I mean. It's easy in, easy out—none of this bullshit with quarterly reports. I show up with the trucks, they cut the check, end of story."

"Congratulations."

"Yeah, well, here's the thing," Kenny said. "I could still really use you there in D.C. I'm looking for a partner to invest with me and make up some of the shortfall I'm looking at. If you're willing to work, you could pay yourself a little salary, too."

"That sounds great," Joey said. "But I have to go back to school, and I don't have any money to invest."

"OK. Sure. It's your life. But how about a smaller piece of the action? The way I read the specs, the Polish Pladsky A10 is gonna do just fine. They're not in production anymore, but there's fleets of 'em standing around military bases in Hungary and Bulgaria. Also somewhere in South America, which doesn't help me. But I'm gonna hire drivers in Eastern Europe, convoy the trucks across Turkey, and deliver 'em in Kirkuk.

That's going to tie me up for God knows how long, and there's also a nine-hundred-K subcontract for spare parts. You think you could handle the spare parts as a sub sub?"

"I don't know anything about truck parts."

"Neither do I. But Pladsky built a good twenty thousand A10s, back in the day. There've gotta be tons of parts out there. All you gotta do is track 'em down, crate 'em up, ship 'em out. Put in three hundred K, take out nine hundred six months later. That's an eminently reasonable markup, given the circumstances. My impression is that's a low-end markup in procurement. No eyebrows will be raised. You think you can get your hands on three hundred K?"

"I can hardly get my hands on lunch money," Joey said. "What with tuition and so forth."

"Yeah, well, but, realistically, all you gotta do is find fifty K. With that, plus a signed contract in hand, any bank in the country's gonna give you the rest. You can do most of this stuff on the internet in your dorm room or whatever. It sure beats working the dish belt, huh?"

Joey asked for some time to think it over. Even with all the takeout and taxis he'd indulged in, he had $10,000 saved up for the coming academic year, plus potentially another $8,000 available on his credit card, and a quick internet search turned up numerous banks willing to make high-interest loans with small collateral, as well as multiple pages of Google matches for pladsky a10 parts. He was aware that Kenny wouldn't have offered him the parts contract if finding the parts were as straightforward as he'd made it sound, but Kenny had made good on all his RISEN promises, and Joey couldn't stop imagining the excellence of being worth half a million dollars when he turned twenty-one, a year from now. On an impulse, because he was excited and, for once, *not* preoccupied with their relationship, he broke his phone silence with Connie to solicit her opinion. Much later, he would reproach himself for having had her savings in the back of his mind, along with the fact that she was now legally in control of them, but in the moment of his calling he felt quite innocent of self-interested motive.

"Oh my God, baby," she said. "I was starting to think I'd never hear from you again."

"It's been a hard couple of weeks."

"My God, I know, I know. I was starting to think I should never have told you anything. Can you forgive me?"

"Probably."

"Oh! Oh! That's so much better than probably not."

"Very probably," he said. "If you still want to come out and see me."

"You know I do. More than anything in the world."

She didn't sound at all like the independent older woman he'd been imagining, and a flutter in his stomach warned him to slow down and be sure he really wanted her back. Warned him not to mistake the pain of losing her for an active desire to have her. But he was eager to change the subject, avoid miring himself in abstract emotional territory, and ask her opinion of Kenny's offer.

"God, Joey," she said after he'd explained it to her, "you have to do it. I'll help you do it."

"How?"

"I'll give you the money," she said as if it were silly of him to even ask. "I've still got more than fifty thousand dollars in my trust account."

The mere naming of this figure sexually excited him. It took him back to their earliest days as a couple on Barrier Street, in his first fall of high school. U2's *Achtung Baby*, beloved to both of them but especially to Connie, had been the soundtrack of their mutual deflowering. The opening track, in which Bono avowed that he was ready for everything, ready for the *push*, had been their love song to each other and to capitalism. The song had made Joey feel ready to have sex, ready to step out of childhood, ready to make some real money selling watches at Connie's Catholic school. He and she had begun as partners in the fullest sense, he the entrepreneur and manufacturer, she his loyal mule and surprisingly gifted saleswoman. Until their operation was shut down by resentful nuns, she'd proved herself a master of the soft sell, her cool remoteness serving to madden her classmates for her and Joey's product. Everybody on Barrier Street, including his mother, had always mistaken Connie's quietness for dullness, for slowness. Only Joey, who had insider access, had seen the potential in her, and this now seemed like the story of their life together: his helping and encouraging her to confound the expectations of everyone, especially his mother, who underestimated the value of her hidden assets.

It was central to his faith in his future as a businessman, this ability to identify value, espy opportunity, where others didn't, and it was central to his love of Connie, too. She moved in mysterious ways! The two of them had started fucking amid the piles of twenty-dollar bills she brought home from her school.

"You need the trust-fund money to go back to college," he said nevertheless.

"I can do that later," she said. "You need it now, and I can give it to you. You can give it back to me later."

"I could give it back to you *doubled*. You'd have enough to cover all four years then."

"If you want to," she said. "You don't have to."

They made a date to reunite for his twentieth birthday in New York City, the scene of their happiest weeks as a couple since he'd left St. Paul. The next morning, he called Kenny and declared himself ready to do business. The big new round of Iraq contracts wouldn't be let until November, Kenny said, and so Joey should enjoy his fall semester and just be sure to be ready with his financing.

Feeling flush in advance, he splurged on an Acela express train to New York and bought a hundred-dollar bottle of champagne on his way to Abigail's apartment. Her place was more cluttered than ever, and he was happy to shut the door behind him and cab out to LaGuardia to meet Connie's plane, which he'd insisted she take instead of a bus. The whole city, its pedestrians half naked in the August heat, its bricks and bridges paled by haze, was like an aphrodisiac. Going to meet his girlfriend, who'd been sleeping with someone else but was zinging back into his life again, a magnet to a magnet, he might already have been king of the city. When he saw her coming down the concourse at the airport, jumpily dodging other travelers, as if too preoccupied to see them until the last second, he felt flush with more than money. Felt flush with importance, with life to burn, with crazy chances to take, with the story of the two of them. She caught sight of him and started nodding, agreeing with some thing he hadn't even said yet, her face full of joy and wonder. "Yeah! Yeah! Yeah!" she said spontaneously, dropping the pull handle of her suitcase and colliding with him. "Yeah!"

"Yeah?" he said, laughing.

"Yeah!"

Without even kissing, they ran down to the baggage level and out to the taxi stand, where, by some miracle, nobody was waiting. In the back of their taxi, she peeled off her sweaty cotton cardigan and climbed onto his lap and began to sob in a way akin to coming or a seizure. Her body seemed entirely, entirely new in his arms. Some of the change was real—she was a little less arrowy, a little more womanly—but most of it was in his head. He felt inexpressibly grateful for her infidelity. His feeling was so large that it seemed as if only asking her to marry him could accommodate it. He might even have asked her, right then and there, if he hadn't noticed the strange marks on her inner left forearm. Running down its soft skin was a series of straight parallel cuts, each about two inches long, the ones nearest her elbow faint and fully healed, the ones approaching her wrist increasingly fresh and red.

"Yeah," she said, wet-faced, looking at the scars with wonder. "I did that. But it's OK."

He asked what had happened, though he knew the answer. She kissed his forehead, kissed his cheek, kissed his lips, and peered gravely into his eyes. "Don't be scared, baby. It was just something I had to do for penance."

"Jesus."

"Joey, listen. Listen to me. I was very careful to put alcohol on the blade. I just had to do one cut for every night I didn't hear from you. I did three on the third night and then one every night after that. I stopped as soon as I heard from you."

"And what if I hadn't called? What were you going to do? Slit your wrist?"

"*No.* I wasn't suicidal. This is what I was doing *instead* of having thoughts like that. I just needed to hurt a little bit. Can you understand that?"

"Are you sure you weren't suicidal?"

"I would never do that to you. Not ever."

He ran his fingertips over the scars. Then he raised her unscarred wrist and pressed it to his eyes. He was *glad* she'd cut herself for him; he couldn't help it. The ways she moved were mysterious but made sense to him. Somewhere in his head, Bono was singing that it was all right, all right.

"And you know what's really incredible?" Connie said. "I stopped at fifteen, which is exactly the number of times I was unfaithful to you. You called me on exactly the right night. It was like some kind of sign. And here." From the back pocket of her jeans she took a folded cashier's check. It had the curve of her ass and was impregnated with her ass's sweat. "I had fifty-one thousand in my trust account. That was almost exactly what you said you needed. It was another sign, don't you think?"

He unfolded the check, which was payable to JOSEPH R. BERGLUND in the amount of FIFTY THOUSAND dollars. He wasn't ordinarily superstitious, but he had to admit that these signs were impressive. They were like the signs that told deranged people, "Kill the president NOW," or told depressed people, "Throw yourself out a window NOW." Here the urgent irrational imperative seemed to be: "Wed your lives together NOW."

Outbound traffic on the Grand Central was at a standstill, but the inbound side was moving briskly, the cab was sailing right along, and this, too, was a sign. That they hadn't had to wait in line for a cab was a sign. That tomorrow was his birthday was a sign. He couldn't remember the state he'd been in even one hour earlier, heading to the airport. There was only the present moment with Connie, and whereas, before, when they'd fallen through a cosmic fissure into their two-person world, it had happened only at night, in a bedroom or some other contained space, it was now happening in broad daylight, under a citywide haze. He held her in his arms, the cashier's check resting on her sweaty breastbone, between the damp straps of her top. One of her hands was pressed flat against one of his breasts as if it might give milk. The grown-woman smell of her underarms intoxicated him, he wished it were much stronger, he felt there was no limit to how strongly he wanted her underarms to stink.

"Thank you for fucking somebody else," he murmured.

"It wasn't easy for me."

"I know."

"I mean, it was very easy in one way. But almost impossible in another. You know that, right?"

"I totally know it."

415

"Was it hard for you, too? Whatever you did last year?"

"Actually, no."

"That's because you're a guy. I know what it's like to be you, Joey. Do you believe that?"

"Yes."

"Then everything's going to be all right."

And, for the next ten days, everything was. Later, of course, Joey could see that the first, hormone-soaked days after a period of long abstinence were a less than ideal time to be making huge decisions about his future. He could see that, instead of trying to offset the unbearable weight of Connie's $50,000 gift with something as heavy as a marriage proposal, he should have written out a promissory note with a schedule for payment of interest and principal. He could see that if he'd separated himself from her for even an hour, to take a walk by himself or to talk to Jonathan, he might have achieved some useful clarity and distance. He could see that postcoital decisions were a lot more realistic than precoital ones. In the moment, though, there had been no post-, it had all been pre- upon pre- upon pre-. Their craving for each other cycled on and on through the days and nights like the compressor of Abigail's hardworking bedroom-window air conditioner. The new dimensions of their pleasure, the sense of adult gravity conferred by their joint business venture and by Connie's sickness and infidelity, made all their prior pleasures forgettable and childish in comparison. Their pleasure was so great, and their need for it so bottomless, that when it waned even for an hour, on their third morning in the city, Joey reached out to press the nearest button to get more of it. He said, "We should get married."

"I was just thinking the same thing," Connie said. "Do you want to do it now?"

"You mean like today?"

"Yes."

"I think there's a waiting period. Some kind of blood test?"

"Well, let's go do that, then. Do you want to?"

His heart was pounding blood into his loins. "Yes!"

But first they had to have the fuck about the excitement of going to have the blood tests. Then they had to have the fuck about the excitement of finding out they didn't need to have them. Then they wandered up

Sixth Avenue like a couple drunk beyond caring what anybody thought of them, like red-handed murderers, Connie braless and wanton and attracting male stares, Joey in a state of testosterone heedlessness in which, if anybody had challenged him, he would have thrown a punch for the sheer joy of it. He was taking the step that needed to be taken, the step he'd been wanting to take since the first time his parents had said no to him. The fifty-block walk uptown with Connie, in a baking welter of honking cabs and filthy sidewalks, felt as long as his entire life before it.

They went into the first deserted-looking jewelry store they came to on 47th Street and asked for two gold rings that they could take away right now. The jeweler was in full Hasidic regalia—yarmulke, forelocks, phylacteries, black vest, the works. He looked first at Joey, whose white T-shirt was spattered with mustard from a hot dog he'd bolted along the way, and then at Connie, whose face was flaming with heat and with abrasion by Joey's face. "The two of you are getting married?"

Both of them nodded, neither quite daring to say yes aloud.

"Then mazel tov," the jeweler said, opening drawers. "I have rings in all sizes for you."

To Joey, from far away, through a fine tear in his otherwise tough bubble of madness, came a pang of regret about Jenna. Not as a person he wanted (the wanting would return later, when he was alone and sane again) but as the Jewish wife he was never going to have now: as the person to whom it might actually have mattered that he was Jewish. He'd long ago given up on trying to care, himself, about his Jewishness, and yet, seeing the jeweler in his well-worn Hasidic trappings, his vestments of minority religion, he had the peculiar thought that he was letting down the Jews by marrying a Gentile. Morally dubious though Jenna was in most respects, she was still a Jew, with great-great-aunts and uncles who'd died in the camps, and this humanized her, took the edge off her inhuman beauty, and made him sorry to let her down. Interestingly, he felt this only about Jenna, not Jonathan, who was already fully human to Joey and did not require Jewishness to make him any more so.

"What do you think?" Connie asked, gazing at the rings arrayed on velvet.

"I don't know," he said from his little cloud of regret. "They all look good."

"Pick them up, try them on, handle them," the jeweler said. "You can't hurt gold."

Connie turned to Joey and searched his eyes. "Are you sure you want to do this?"

"I think so. Are you?"

"Yes. If you are."

The jeweler stepped away from the counter and found something to busy himself with. And Joey, seeing himself through Connie's eyes, couldn't bear the uncertainty in his own face. It enraged him murderously on her behalf. Everybody else doubted her, and she needed him not to, and so he chose not to.

"Definitely," he said. "Let's take a look at these."

When they'd selected their rings, Joey tried to bargain down the price, which he knew he was supposed to do in a store like this, but the jeweler merely gave him a disappointed look, as if to say: You're marrying this girl and you're quibbling with me about fifty dollars?

Leaving the store, the rings in his front pocket, he almost collided on the sidewalk with his old hall mate Casey.

"Dude!" Casey said. "What are you doing here?"

He was wearing a three-piece suit and was already losing his hair. He and Joey had drifted apart, but Joey had heard he was working in his dad's law office for the summer. Running into him at this moment seemed to Joey another important sign, although of what, exactly, he wasn't sure. He said, "You remember Connie, right?"

"Hi, Casey," she said with fiendishly blazing eyes.

"Yeah, sure, hi," Casey said. "But, dude, what the fuck? I thought you were in Washington."

"I'm taking a vacation."

"Man, you should have called me, I had no idea. What are you guys doing on this street anyway? Buying an engagement ring?"

"Yeah, ha ha, right," Joey said. "What are you doing here?"

Casey fished a watch on a chain from his vest pocket. "Is this cool or what? It used to be my dad's dad's. I had it cleaned and repaired."

"It's beautiful," Connie said. She bent over to admire it, and Casey shot Joey a frown of inquiry and comic alarm. From the various acceptable guy-to-guy responses available to him, Joey chose to produce a sheepish smirk suggesting mucho excellente sex, the irrational demands of girlfriends, their need to be bought trinkets, and so forth. Casey cast a quick connoisseurial glance at Connie's bare shoulders and nodded judiciously. The entire exchange took four seconds, and Joey was relieved by how easy it was, even at a moment like this, to seem to Casey a person like Casey: to compartmentalize. It boded well for his continuing to have an ordinary life at college.

"Dude, aren't you hot in that suit?" he said.

"My blood is Southern," Casey said. "We don't sweat like you Minnesotans."

"Sweating is wonderful," Connie offered. "I love sweating in the summer."

This obviously struck Casey as a too-intense thing to say. He put his watch back in its pocket and looked down the street. "Anyhow," he said. "If you guys want to go out or something, you should give me a call."

When they were alone again, in the five o'clock flow of workers on Sixth Avenue, Connie asked Joey if she'd said the wrong thing. "Did I embarrass you?"

"No," he said. "He's a total dork. It's ninety-five degrees and he's wearing a three-piece suit? He's a total pompous dork, with that stupid watch. He's already turning into his dad."

"I open my mouth and strange things come out."

"Don't worry about it."

"Are you embarrassed to be marrying me?"

"No."

"It kind of seemed like you were. I'm not saying it's your fault. I just don't want to embarrass you around your friends."

"You don't embarrass me," he said angrily. "It's just that hardly any of my friends even have girlfriends. I'm just kind of in a weird position."

He might reasonably have expected to have a little fight then, might have expected her to try to extract, via sulking or reproach, a more definitive avowal of his wish to marry her. But Connie could not be fought with. Insecurity, suspicion, jealousy, possessiveness, paranoia—the unseemly kind of stuff that so annoyed those friends of his who'd had, however briefly, girlfriends—were foreign to her. Whether she genuinely lacked these feelings, or whether some powerful animal intelligence led her to suppress them, he could never determine. The more he merged with her, the more he strangely also felt he didn't know the first thing about her. She acknowledged only what was right in front of her. She did what she did, responded to what he said to her, and otherwise seemed wholly untroubled by things occurring outside her field of vision. He was haunted by his mother's insistence that fights were good in a relationship. Indeed, it almost seemed to him as if he were marrying Connie to see if she would finally start fighting with him: to get to know her. But when he did marry her, the following afternoon, nothing changed at all. In the back of a cab, as they rode away from the courthouse, she wove her ringed left hand into his ringed left hand and rested her head on his shoulder with something that couldn't quite be described as contentedness, because that would have implied that she'd been discontented before. It was more like mute submission to the deed, the crime, that had needed to be done. The next time Joey saw Casey, in Charlottesville a week later, neither of them even mentioned her.

The wedding ring was still stalled somewhere in his abdomen as he breasted through the churning warm sea of travelers at Miami International and located Jenna in the cooler, calm bay of a business-class lounge. She was wearing sunglasses and was additionally defended by an iPod and the latest *Condé Nast Traveler*. She gave Joey a once-over, head to toe, the way a person might confirm that a product she'd ordered had arrived in acceptable condition, and then removed her hand luggage from the seat beside her and—a little reluctantly, it seemed—pulled the iPod wires from her ears. Joey sat down smiling helplessly at the amazement of traveling with her. He'd never flown business-class before.

"What?" she said.

"Nothing, I'm just smiling."

"Oh. I thought there was some schmutz on my face or something."

Several men in the vicinity were checking him out resentfully. He forced himself to stare down each of them in turn, to mark Jenna as claimed. It was going to be tiring, he realized, to have to do this everywhere they went in public. Men sometimes stared at Connie, too, but usually seemed to accept, without undue regret, that she was his. With

Jenna, already, he had the sense that other men's interest was not deterred by his presence but continued to seek ways around him.

"I have to warn you I'm a little grouchy," she said. "I'm getting my period, and I just spent three days among the ancients, looking at pictures of their grandkids. Also, I can't believe it, but they make you pay for alcohol in this lounge now. I was like, I could have sat in the gate area and done *that*."

"Do you want me to get you something?"

"Actually, yes. I'd like a double Tanqueray and tonic."

It seemed not to occur to her, or, fortunately, to the bartender, that he was under age. Returning with drinks and a lightened wallet, he found Jenna with her earphones in again and her face in her magazine. He wondered if she were somehow mistaking him for Jonathan, so little was she making of his arrival. He took out the novel his own sister had given him for Christmas, *Atonement*, and struggled to interest himself in its descriptions of rooms and plantings, but his mind was on the text that Jonathan had sent him that afternoon: hope it's fun looking at a horse's ass all day. It was the first he'd heard from him since calling him preemptively, three weeks earlier, with word of his travel plans. "So I guess everything's come up roses for you," Jonathan had said. "First the insurgency and now my mom's leg."

"It's not like I *wanted* her to break her leg," Joey had said.

"No, I'm sure. I'm sure you wanted the Iraqis to welcome us with wreaths of flowers, too. I'm sure you're very sorry about how fucked up everything's gotten. Just not quite sorry enough to not cash in."

"What was I supposed to do? Say no? Make her go by herself? She's actually pretty depressed. She's really looking forward to this trip."

"And I'm sure Connie understands about that. I'm sure you've gotten her total seal of approval."

"If that were any of your business, I might dignify it with an answer."

"Hey, you know what? It is totally my business if I have to lie to her about it. I already have to lie about my opinion of Kenny Bartles whenever I talk to her, because you took her money and I don't want her worrying. And now I'm supposed to lie about this, too?"

"How about just not talking to her constantly instead?"

"It's not constantly, asshole. I've talked to her, like, three times in the last three months. She considers me a friend, all right? And apparently entire weeks can go by without her hearing anything from you. So what am I supposed to do? Not pick up when she calls? She calls me for information about you. Which, there's something a little weird about this picture, right? Since she is still your girlfriend."

"I'm not going to Argentina to sleep with your sister."

"Ha. Ha. Ha."

"I swear to God, I'm going as a friend. The same way you and Connie are friends. Because your sister's depressed and it's a nice thing to do. But Connie's not going to understand that, so if you could just, like, not mention it, if she calls, that would be the kindest thing you could do for all concerned."

"You're so full of shit, Joey, I don't even want to talk to you anymore. Something's happened to you that makes me literally sick to my stomach. If Connie calls me while you're gone, I don't know what I'm going to say. I probably won't tell her anything. But the only reason she calls me is she doesn't hear enough from you, and I'm sick of being in the middle like that. So you do whatever the fuck you want, just leave me out of it."

Having sworn to Jonathan that he wouldn't have sex with Jenna, Joey felt insured against every contingency in Argentina. If nothing happened, it would prove him honorable. If something did happen, he would not have to be chagrined and disappointed that something hadn't. It would answer the question, still open in his mind, of whether he was a soft person or a hard person, and what the future might hold for him. He was very curious about this future. Judging from his nasty text message, Jonathan wasn't looking to be a part of it either way. And the message definitely did sting, but Joey, for his part, was sick of his friend's relentless moralizing.

On the plane, in the privacy of their vast seats, and under the influence of a second large drink, Jenna deigned to remove her sunglasses and converse. Joey told her about his recent trip to Poland, chasing the mirage of Pladsky A10 parts, and his discovery that all but a very few of the seeming scores of suppliers advertising these parts on the internet were either bogus or sourced from the same single outlet in Lodz, where Joey and his almost worse than useless interpreter had found shockingly little to buy at any price. Taillights, mudguards, push plates, some battery boxes and grilles, but very few of the engine and suspension parts that were critical for maintaining a vehicle out of production since 1985.

"The internet's fucked up, isn't it?" Jenna said. She'd picked all the almonds out of her own nut bowl and was now picking them out of Joey's.

"*So* fucked up, *so* fucked up," he said.

"Nick always said international e-commerce is for losers. E-anything-financial, really, unless the system's proprietary. He says free information's by definition worthless. Like, if a Chinese supplier is listed on the internet, you can tell, just from that, that it can't be any good."

"Right, I know that, I'm very aware of that," Joey said, not wanting to hear about Nick. "But truck parts should be more like eBay or something. Just an efficient way to connect buyers with sellers they might not be able to find otherwise."

"All I know is Nick never buys anything on the internet. He doesn't even trust PayPal. And he's, you know, pretty well up on these things."

"Well, and that's why I went to Poland. Because you have to do these things in person."

"Right, that's what Nick says, too."

Her somewhat slack-jawed chewing of the almonds was irritating him, as were her fingers, lovely though they were, as they rooted methodically in his nut bowl. "I thought you didn't like to drink," he said.

"Heh-heh. I've been working on increasing my tolerance lately. I've made great strides."

"Well, anyway," he said, "I need some good things to happen in Paraguay, or I don't know what I'm going to do. I spent a fortune on shipping that Polish crap, and now I'm hearing from my partner, Kenny, that there wasn't even enough to get partially paid for. It's sitting in some goat pasture outside Kirkuk, probably not even guarded. And Kenny's pissed off with me because I didn't send some other kind of truck parts instead, even though they're totally useless if they're not from the same model and manufacturer. Kenny's like, Just send me weight, because we get paid by weight, if you can believe that. And I'm like, These are thirty-year-old trucks that weren't built for dust storms or Middle Eastern summers, they're going to be breaking down, and when you're trying to run convoys through an insurgency, you do not want your truck to be breaking down. And meanwhile I've got plenty of outflow but no income."

He might have worried about admitting this to Jenna if she'd been paying attention, but she was now yanking on her onboard video screen, peevishly trying to wrest it from its stowage hole. He lent a gallant hand.

"So, I'm sorry," she said, "you were saying . . . ? Something about not getting paid?"

"Oh, no, I'm definitely getting paid. In fact, I'm probably going to end up making more than Nick does this year."

"I doubt that, frankly."

"Well, it's going to be a lot."

"Nick's in a whole different universe of remuneration."

This was too much for Joey. "Why am I here?" he said. "Do you even want me here? You've either been ignoring me or talking about Nick, who I thought you were broken up with."

Jenna shrugged. "I told you I was grouchy. But a little word to the wise? I'm not too terribly interested in your business deal. The whole reason you're here and Nick isn't is I got sick of hearing him talk about money all day and all night."

"I thought you liked money."

"It doesn't mean I like to hear about it. You're the one who brought it up."

"I'm sorry I brought it up!"

"OK, then. Apology accepted. But also? I don't see why I can't mention Nick if you're going to be talking about your woman all the time."

"I talk about her because you *ask* about her."

"I'm not sure I see the difference."

"Well, and also, she's still my girlfriend."

"Right. I guess that is one difference." And she leaned over suddenly and offered her mouth to his. First the merest brush, then a softness almost like warm whipped cream, and then full flesh. Her lips felt every bit as beautiful, as complexly animated and valuable, as they had always looked to him. He leaned into the kiss, but she pulled away and smiled approvingly. "Happy *boy*," she said.

When a flight attendant came to take their dinner orders, he asked for beef. He was planning to eat nothing but beef for the entire trip, on the theory that it was somewhat constipating; he hoped to make it all the way to Paraguay before he had to go ring-hunting in the bathroom. Jenna watched *Pirates of the Caribbean* while she ate, and he put on his head-phones and watched it with her, leaning awkwardly into her space rather than pulling up his own screen, but there were no further kisses, and the one drawback of business-class seats, as he discovered when the movie ended and they bedded down beneath their respective comforters, was that no cuddling or incidental contact was possible.

He didn't see how he was going to fall asleep, but then suddenly it was morning and breakfast was being served, and then they were in Argentina. It was nowhere near as exotic as he'd imagined it. Except that everything was in Spanish and more people were smoking, civilization here seemed like civilization anywhere. The plate glass and floor tiles and plastic seats and lighting fixtures were exactly the same, and the flight to Bariloche boarded with the rear seats first, like any American connecting flight, and there was nothing marvelously different about the 727 or the factories and farm fields and highways he could see from the window. Dirt was still dirt, and plants still grew in it. Most of the passengers in the first-class cabin were speaking English, and six of them—an English couple and an American mother with three children—joined Joey and Jenna in wheeling their Priority-tagged luggage to the cushy white Estancia El Triunfo van that was waiting for them in a no-parking zone outside the Bariloche airport.

The driver, an unsmiling young man with thick black chest hair pushing through his half-unbuttoned shirt, rushed over to take Jenna's bag and stow it in the rear and install her in the front passenger seat before Joey could even clock what was happening. The English couple grabbed the next two seats, and Joey found himself sitting toward the rear with the mother and her daughter, who was reading a young-adult horse novel.

"My name is Félix," the driver said into an unnecessary microphone, "welcome to Rio Negro Province please use the seat belts we are driving two hours the road will be bumpy in places I have cold drinks for those who want them El Triunfo is remote but lucksurious you must forgive the bumps in the road thank you."

The afternoon was clear and blazing, and the way to El Triunfo led through prosperous subalpine country so similar to western Montana that Joey had to wonder why they'd flown eight thousand miles for it. Whatever Félix was saying to Jenna, nonstop, in hushed Spanish, was drowned out by the nonstop braying of the Englishman, Jeremy. He brayed about the good old days when England was at war with Argentina in the Falklands ("our *second*-finest hour"), the capture of Saddam Hussein ("*Har*, I wonder how Mister *smelled* when he came out of that hole"), the hoax of global warming and the irresponsible fearmongering of its perpetrators ("Next year they'll be warning us about the dangerous new *ice age*"), the laughable ineptitude of South American central bankers ("When your inflation rate is a thousand percent, methinks your problem is more than bad luck"), the laudable indifference of South Americans to women's "football" ("Leave it to you Americans to excel at *that* particular travesty"), the surprisingly drinkable reds coming out of Argentina ("They blow the best wines of South Africa out—of—the—*water*"), and his own copious salivation at the prospect of eating steak for breakfast, lunch, and dinner ("I'm a *carnivore*, a *carnivore*, a terrible disgusting *carnivore*").

For relief from Jeremy, Joey struck up a conversation with the mother, Ellen, who was pretty without being attractive and was wearing the stretch cargo pants that a certain kind of mom favored nowadays. "My husband's a very successful real estate developer," she said. "I trained as an architect at Stanford, but I'm home with our children now. We decided to homeschool them, which is very rewarding, and great in terms of taking vacations when it suits our schedule, but *a lot* of work, let me tell you."

Her children, the reading daughter and the game-playing sons behind her, either didn't hear this or didn't mind being a lot of work to her. When she heard that Joey had a small business in Washington, she asked him if he knew about Daniel Jennings. "Dan's a friend of ours in Morongo Valley," she said, "who's done all this research on our taxes. He's actually gone back and looked at the record of debates in Congress, and you know what he discovered? That there's no legal basis for the federal income tax."

"There's no legal basis for anything, really, when you get right down to it," Joey said.

"But obviously the federal government doesn't want you to know that all the money it's collected for the last hundred years rightfully belongs to us citizens. Dan has a website where ten different history professors say he's right, there's no legal basis whatsoever. But nobody in the mainstream media will touch it. Which, don't you think that's a little strange? Wouldn't you think at least *one* network or *one* newspaper would want to cover it?"

"I guess there must be some other side to the story," Joey said.

"But why are we only getting that other side? Doesn't it seem news-worthy that the federal government owes us taxpayers three hundred *trillion* dollars? Because that's the figure Dan came up with, including compound interest. Three hundred *trillion* dollars."

"That's a lot," he agreed politely. "That would be a million dollars for every person in the country."

"Exactly. It's outrageous, don't you think? How much they owe us."

He considered pointing out how difficult it would be for the Treasury to refund, say, the money that had been spent on winning World War II, but Ellen didn't strike him as a person you could argue with, and he was feeling carsick. He could hear Jenna speaking Spanish excellent enough that, having taken it only through high school, he couldn't catch much beyond her repetition of *caballos* this and *caballos* that. Sitting with his eyes closed, in a van full of jerks, he was visited by the thought that the three people he most loved (Connie), liked (Jonathan), and respected (his father) were all at least very unhappy with him, if not, by their own report, *sickened* by him. He couldn't free himself of the thought; it was like some kind of conscience reporting for duty. He willed himself not to barf, because wouldn't barfing now, a mere thirty-six hours after a good barf would have been very useful to him, be the height of irony? He'd imagined that the road to being fully hard, to being bad news, would get steeper and more arduous only gradually, with many compensatory pleasures along the way, and that he would have time to acclimate to each stage of it. But here he was, at the very beginning of the road, already feeling as if he might not have the stomach for it.

Estancia El Triunfo was undeniably paradisiacal, however. Nestled beside a clear-running stream, surrounded by yellow hills rolling up toward a purple ridgeline of sierras, were lushly watered gardens and paddocks and fully modernized stone guesthouses and stables. Joey and Jenna's room had deliciously needless expanses of cool tiled floor and big windows open to the rushing of the stream below them. He'd feared there would be two beds, but either Jenna had intended to share a king-size with her mother or she'd changed the reservation. He stretched out on the deep-red brocade bedspread, sinking into its thousand-dollar-a-night plushness. But Jenna was already changing into riding clothes and boots.

"Félix is going to show me the horses," she said. "Do you want to come along?"

He didn't want to, but he knew he'd better do it anyway. *Their shit still stinks* was the phrase in his head as they approached the fragrant stables. In golden evening light, Félix and a groom were leading out a splendid black stallion by its bridle. It frisked and skittered and bucked a little, and Jenna went straight over to it, looking rapt in a way that reminded him of Connie and made him like her better, and reached up to stroke the side of its head.

"Cuidado," Félix said.

"It's OK," Jenna said, looking intently into the horse's eye. "He likes me already. He trusts me, I can tell. Don't you, baby?"

"¿Deseas que algo algo algo?" Félix said, tugging on the bridle.

"Speak English, please," Joey said coldly.

"He's asking if I want them to saddle him," Jenna explained, and then spoke rapidly in Spanish to Félix, who objected that algo algo algo peligroso; but she was not a person to be gainsaid. While the groom pulled rather brutally on the bridle, she grasped the horse's mane and Félix put his hairy hands on her thighs and boosted her up onto the horse's bare back. It spread its legs and pranced sideways, straining against the bridle, but Jenna was already leaning far forward, her chest in its mane, her face near its ear, murmuring soothing nothings. Joey was totally impressed. After the horse had been calmed down, she took the reins and cantered off to the far corner of the paddock and engaged in recondite equestrian negotiations, compelling the horse to stand in place, to step backwards, to lower and raise its head.

The groom remarked something to Félix about the chica, something husky and admiring.

"My name's Joey, by the way," Joey said.

"Hello," Félix said, his eyes on Jenna. "You want a horse, too?"

"I'm fine for now. Just do me a favor and speak English, though, OK?"

"As you like."

It did Joey's heart good to see how happy Jenna was on the horse. She'd been so negative and depressive, not only on the trip but on the phone for months before it, that he'd begun to wonder if there was anything at all to like about her besides her beauty. He could see now that she at least knew how to enjoy what money could bring her. And yet it was daunting to consider how very much money was required to make her happy. To be the person who kept her in fine horses: not a task for the fainthearted.

Dinner wasn't served until after ten o'clock, at a long communal table hewn whole from a tree that must have been six feet in diameter. The fabled Argentinean steaks were excellent, and the wine drew brays of approval from Jeremy. Joey and Jenna both put away glass after glass of it, and this may have been why, after midnight, when they were *finally* making out on their oceanic bed, he experienced his first-ever attack of a phenomenon he'd heard a lot about but had been unable to imagine himself ever experiencing personally. Even in the least appealing of his hookups, he'd performed admirably. Even now, as long as he was confined by his pants, he had the impression of being as hard as the wood of the communal dining table, but either he was mistaken about this or he couldn't stand full exposure to Jenna. As she humped his bare leg through her underpants, grunting a little with every thrust, he felt himself flying out centrifugally, a satellite breaking free of gravity, mentally farther and farther away from the woman whose tongue was in his mouth and whose gratifyingly nontrivial tits were mashed into his chest. She fooled around more brutally, less pliantly, than Connie did—that was part of it. But he also couldn't see her face in the dark, and when he couldn't see it he had only the memory, the idea, of its beauty. He kept telling himself that he was finally getting Jenna, that this was *Jenna, Jenna, Jenna*. But in the absence of visual confirmation all he had in his arms was a random sweaty attacking female.

"Can we turn a light on?" he said.

"It's too bright. I don't like it."

"Just, like, the bathroom light? It's pitch-dark in here."

She rolled off him and sighed peevishly. "Maybe we should just go to sleep. It's so late, and I'm totally bloody anyway."

He touched his penis and was sorry to find it even more flaccid than it felt. "I might have had a little too much wine."

"Me, too. So let's sleep."

"I'm just going to turn the bathroom light on, OK?"

He did this, and the sight of her sprawled on the bed, confirming her particular identity as the most beautiful girl he knew, gave him hope that all systems were Go again. He crawled to her and commenced a project of kissing every part of her, beginning with her perfect feet and ankles and then moving up her calves and the inside of her thighs . . .

"I'm sorry, that is just too gross," she said abruptly, when he'd reached her panties. "Here." She pushed him onto his back and took his penis in her mouth. Again, at first, he was hard, and her mouth felt heavenly, but then he slipped away a little and softened, and worried about softening and tried to will hardness, will connection, think about whose mouth he was in, and then unfortunately he considered how little fellatio had ever interested him, and wondered what was wrong with him. Jenna's allure had always largely consisted of the impossibility of imagining that he could have her. Now that she was a tired, drunk, bleeding person crouching between his legs and doing businesslike oral work, she could have been almost anybody, except Connie.

To her credit, she kept working long after his own faith had died. When she finally stopped, she examined his penis with neutral curiosity; she gave it a wiggle. "Not happening, huh?"

"I can't explain it. It's really embarrassing."

"Ha, welcome to my world on Lexapro."

After she'd fallen asleep and begun emitting light snores, he lay boiling with shame and regret and homesickness. He was very, very disappointed in himself, although why, exactly, he should have felt so disappointed to fail to fuck a girl he wasn't in love with and didn't even like much, he couldn't have said. He thought about the heroism of his parents' having stayed together all these years, the mutual need that underlay even the worst of their fighting. He saw his mother's deference to his father in a new light, and forgave her a little bit. It was unfortunate to have to need somebody, it was evidence of grievous softness, but his self was now seeming to him, for the first time, less than infinitely capable of anything, less than one-hundred-percent bendable to whatever goals he'd set his sights on.

In the first early austral light of morning, he awoke with a monstrous boner of whose durability he had not the shadow of a doubt. He sat up and looked at the tumble of Jenna's hair, the parting of her lips, the delicate downy line of her jaw, her almost holy beauty. Now that the light was better, he couldn't believe how stupid he'd been in the dark. He slid back under the covers and poked her, gently, in the small of her back.

"Stop it!" she said loudly, immediately. "I'm trying to fall back asleep."

He pressed his nose between her shoulder blades and inhaled her patchouli smell.

"I mean it," she said, jerking away from him. "It's not *my* fault we were up until three."

"It wasn't three," he murmured.

"It *felt* like three. It felt like five!"

"It's five now."

"Augggh! Don't even say that! I need to sleep."

He lay there interminably, manually monitoring his boner, trying to keep it halfway up. From outside came neighings, distant clangings, the crowing of a rooster, the rural sounds of anywhere. As Jenna continued to sleep, or pretend to, a roiling announced itself in his bowels. Despite his best resistance, the roiling increased until it was an urgency that trounced all others. He padded into the bathroom and locked the door. In his shaving kit was a kitchen fork that he'd brought for the extremely disagreeable task ahead of him. He sat clutching it in a sweaty hand as his shit slid out of him. There was a lot of it, two or three days' worth. Through the door, he heard the telephone ring, their six-thirty wake-up call.

He knelt on the cool floor and peered into the bowl at the four large turds afloat in it, hoping to see the glint of gold immediately. The oldest turd was dark and firm and noduled, the ones from deeper inside him were paler and already dissolving a little. Although he, like all people, secretly enjoyed the smell of his own farts, the smell of his shit was something else. It was so bad as to seem evil in a moral way. He poked one of the softer turds with the fork, trying to rotate it and examine its underside, but it bent and began to crumble, clouding the water brown, and he saw that this business of a fork had been a wishful fantasy. The water would soon be too turbid to see a ring through, and if the ring broke free of its enveloping matter it would sink to the bottom and possibly go down the drain. He had no choice but to lift out each turd and run it through his fingers, and he had to do this quickly, before things got too waterlogged. Holding his breath, his eyes watering furiously, he grasped the most promising turd and let go of his latest fantasy, which was that one hand would suffice. He had to use both hands, one to hold the shit and the other to pick through it. He retched once, drily, and got to work, pushing his fingers into the soft and body-warm and surprisingly lightweight log of excrement.

Jenna knocked on the door. "What's going on in there?"

"Just a minute!"

"What are you doing in there? Jerking off?"

"I said just a minute! I have diarrhea."

"Oh, Christ. Can you at least hand me a tampon?"

"In a minute!"

Mercifully, the ring turned up in the second of the turds he broke apart. A hardness amid softness, a clean circle within chaos. He rinsed his hands as well as he could in the filthy water, flushed the toilet with his elbow, and bore the ring to the sink. The stench was appalling. He washed his hands and the ring and the faucets three times with lots of soap, while Jenna, outside the door, complained that breakfast was in twenty minutes. And it was a strange thing to feel, but he definitely felt it: when he emerged from the bathroom with the ring on his ring finger, and Jenna rushed past him and then reeled out again, squealing and cursing at the stench, he was a different person. He could see this person so clearly, it was like standing outside himself. He was the person who'd handled his own shit to get his wedding ring back. This wasn't the person he'd thought he was, or would have chosen to be if he'd been free to choose, but there was something comforting and liberating about being an actual definite someone, rather than a collection of contradictory potential someones.

The world immediately seemed to slow down and steady itself, as if it, too, were settling into a new necessity. The first, spirited horse that he was given at the stables shucked him onto the ground almost gently, without ill will, employing no more violence than was strictly necessary to dislodge him from the saddle. He was then put on a twenty-year-old mare from whose broad back he watched Jenna quickly receding on her stallion down a dusty trail, her left arm raised in backhanded farewell or perhaps just good equestrian form, while Félix galloped past Joey to join her. He saw that it would make sense if she ended up fucking Félix instead of him, since Félix was the vastly superior horseman; he experienced this as a relief, maybe even as a mitzvah, since poor Jenna certainly needed fucking by somebody. He himself spent the morning walking, and eventually cantering, with Ellen's young daughter, Meredith, the novel reader, and listening while she delivered herself of an impressive store of horse lore. It didn't make him feel soft to do this; it made him feel firm. The Andean air was lovely. Meredith seemed a little sweet on him and gave him patient instruction in how to be less confusing to his horse. Jeremy, when the group collected for midmorning snacks by a spring at which there was no sign of Jenna and Félix, was more viciously instructive to his quiet, red-faced wife, whom he apparently blamed for falling so far back behind the leaders. Joey, cupping his clean hands to drink spring water from a stone basin, and no longer caring what Jenna might be up to, felt compassion for Jeremy. It was fun to ride horses in Patagonia—she'd been right about that.

His feeling of peace lasted until late in the afternoon, when he checked his voice mail from the room phone, at Jenna's mother's expense, and found messages from Carol Monaghan and Kenny Bartles. "Hi, hon, it's your *mother-in-law*," Carol said. "How about that, huh? Mother-in-law! Isn't *that* a weird thing to be saying. I think it's fantastic news, but you know what, Joey? I'll be honest with you. I think if you thought enough of Connie to marry her, and if you thought highly enough of your own maturity to enter into matrimony, you should have the decency to tell your parents. That's just my two cents' worth, but I don't see any reason for you to keep this so hush-hush unless you're ashamed of Connie. And I really don't know what to say about a son-in-law who's ashamed of my daughter. Maybe I'll just say I'm not a very good secret keeper, I am personally opposed to all this hush-hush. OK? Maybe I'll just leave it at that."

"What the fuck, man?" Kenny Bartles said. "Where the fuck are you? I just sent you like ten e-mails. Are you in Paraguay? Is that why you're not getting back to me? When the contract says January 31, DOD fucking means January 31. I sure the fuck hope you've got something in the pipeline for me, because January 31's nine days from now. LBI's already all over my ass because these fucking trucks are breaking down. Some bullshit design flaw in the rear axle, I hope to God you got some rear axles for me.

Or whatever, man. Fifteen tons of fucking hood ornaments, I would thank you very much for that. Until you get me some kind of weight, until we can see a date of confirmed delivery of full weight of *something*, I don't have a limb to stand on."

Jenna returned at sunset, all the more gorgeous for being dust-covered. "I'm in love," she said. "I've met the horse of my dreams."

"I have to leave," Joey said immediately. "I have to go to Paraguay."

"What? When?"

"Tomorrow morning. Tonight, ideally."

"Good Lord, are you that pissed off with me? It's not my fault you lied to me about your riding skills. I didn't come here to *walk*. I didn't come here to waste five nights of double occupancy, either."

"Yeah, I'm sorry about that. I'll pay my half of it back."

"Fuck paying it back." She looked him up and down scornfully. "It's just, do you think you can find some other way to be a disappointment? I'm not sure you've checked every conceivable disappointment box yet."

"That's a really mean thing to say," he said quietly.

"Believe me, I can say meaner things, and I intend to."

"Also, I didn't tell you I was married. I'm married. I married Connie. We're going to live together."

Jenna's eyes widened, as if with pain. "God, you are weird! You are such a fucking weirdo."

"I'm aware of that."

"I thought you actually understood me. Unlike every other guy I've ever met. God, I'm stupid!"

"You're not," he said, pitying her for the disability of her beauty.

"But if you think I'm sorry to hear you're married, you are much mistaken. If you think I thought of you as *marriage material*, my God. I don't even want to have dinner with you."

"Then I don't want to have dinner with you, either."

"Well, great, then," she said. "You are now officially the worst travel companion *ever*."

While she showered, he packed his bag and then loitered on the bed, thinking that, perhaps, now that the air had been cleared, they might have sex once, to avoid the shame and defeat of not having had it, but when

Jenna emerged from the bathroom, in a thick Estancia El Triunfo robe, she correctly read the look on his face and said, "No way."

He shrugged. "You sure?"

"Yes, I'm sure. Go home to your little wife. I don't like weird people who lie to me. I'm frankly embarrassed to be in the same room with you at this point."

And so he went to Paraguay, and it was a disaster. Armando da Rosa, the owner of the country's largest military-surplus dealership, was a neckless ex-officer with merging white eyebrows and hair that looked dyed with black shoe polish. His office, in a slummy suburb of Asunción, had shinily waxed linoleum floors and a large metal desk behind which a Paraguayan flag hung limply on a wooden pole. Its back door opened onto acres of weed and dirt and sheds with rusting corrugated roofs, patrolled by big dogs that were all fang and skeleton and spiky hair and looked as if they'd barely survived electrocution. The impression Joey got from da Rosa's rambling monologue, in English little better than Joey's Spanish, was that he had suffered a career setback some years earlier and had escaped court-martial through the efforts of certain loyal officer friends of his, and had received instead, by way of *justice*, the concession to sell surplus and decommissioned military gear. He was wearing fatigues and a sidearm that made Joey uneasy to walk in front of him. They pushed through weeds ever higher and woodier and more buzzing with outsized South American hornets, until, by a rear fence crowned saggily with concertina, they reached the mother lode of Pladsky A10 truck parts. The good news was that there were certainly a lot of them. The bad news was that they were in abominable condition. A line of rust-rimmed truck hoods lay semi-fallen like toppled dominoes; axles and bumpers were jumbled in piles like giant old chicken bones; engine blocks were strewn in the weeds like the droppings of a T. rex; conical mounds of more severely rusted smaller parts had wildflowers growing on their slopes. Moving through the weeds, Joey turned up nests of mud-caked and/or broken plastic parts, snake pits of hoses and belts cracked by the weather, and decaying cardboard parts cartons with Polish words on them. He was fighting tears of disappointment at the sight of it.

"Lot of rust here," he said.

"What is rust?"

He broke a large flake of it off the nearest wheel hub. "Rust. Iron oxide."

"This happens because of the rain," da Rosa explained.

"I can give you ten thousand dollars for the lot of it," Joey said. "If it's more than thirty tons, I can give you fifteen. That's a lot better than scrap value."

"Why you want these shit?"

"I've got a fleet of trucks I need to maintain."

"You, you are a very young man. Why you want these?"

"Because I'm stupid."

Da Rosa gazed off into the tired, buzzing second-growth jungle beyond the fence. "Can't give you everything."

"Why not?"

"This trucks, the Army not use. But they can use if there is war. Then my parts are valuable."

Joey closed his eyes and shuddered at the stupidity of this. "What war? Who are you going to fight? Bolivia?"

"I am saying if there is war we need parts."

"These parts are fucking useless. I'm offering you fifteen thousand dollars for it. Quince mil dólares."

Da Rosa shook his head. "Cincuenta mil."

"Fifty thousand dollars? No. Fucking. Way. You understand? No way."

"Treinta."

"Eighteen. Diez y ocho."

"Veinticinco."

"I'll think about it," Joey said, turning back in the direction of the office. "I'll think about giving you twenty, if it's over thirty tons. Veinte, all right? That's my last offer."

For a minute or two, after shaking da Rosa's oily hand and stepping back into the taxi he'd left waiting in the road, he felt good about himself, about the way he'd handled the negotiation, and about his bravery in traveling to Paraguay to conduct it. What his father didn't understand about him, what only Connie really did, was that he had an excellent cool head for business. He suspected that he got his instincts from his mother, who was a born competitor, and it gave him a particular filial satisfaction to exercise them. The price he'd extracted from da Rosa was far lower than he'd allowed himself to hope for, and even with the cost of paying a local shipper to load the parts into containers and get them to the airport, even with the staggering sum that it would then cost him to fly the containers by charter to Iraq, he would still be within parameters that would assure him obscene profit. But as the taxi wove through older, colonial portions of Asunción, he began to fear that he couldn't do it. Could not send such arrantly near-worthless crap to American forces trying to win a tough unconventional war. Although he hadn't created the problem—Kenny Bartles had done that, by choosing the obsolete, bargain-basement Pladsky to fulfill his own contract—the problem was nonetheless his. And it created an even worse problem: counting the costs of start-up and the paltry but expensive shipment of parts from Lodz, he'd already spent all of Connie's money and half of the first installment of his bank loan. Even if he were somehow able to back out now, he would leave Connie wiped out and himself in crippling debt. He turned the wedding ring on his finger nervously, turned it and turned it, wanting to put it in his mouth for comfort but not trusting himself not to swallow it again. He tried to tell himself that there must be more A10 parts out there somewhere, in some neglected but rainproof depot in Eastern Europe, but he'd already spent long days searching the internet and making phone calls, and the chances weren't good.

"Fucking Kenny," he said aloud, thinking what a very inconvenient time this was to be developing a conscience. "Fucking criminal."

Back in Miami, waiting for his last connecting flight, he forced himself to call Connie.

"Hi, baby," she said brightly. "How's Buenos Aires?"

He skated past the details of his itinerary and cut straight to an account of his anxieties.

"It sounds like you did fantastic," Connie said. "I mean, twenty thousand dollars, that's a great price, right?"

"Except that it's about nineteen thousand more than the stuff is worth."

"No, baby, it's worth what Kenny will pay you."

"And you don't think I should be, like, morally worried about this? About selling total crap to the government?"

She went silent while she considered this. "I guess," she said finally, "if it makes you too unhappy, you maybe shouldn't do it. I only want you to do things that make you happy."

"I'm not going to lose your money," he said. "That's the one thing I know."

"No, you can lose it. It's OK. You'll make some more money somewhere else. I trust you."

"I'm not going to lose it. I want you to go back to college. I want us to have a life together."

"Well, then, let's have it! I'm ready if you are. I'm so ready."

Out on the tarmac, under an unsettled gray Floridian sky, proven weapons of mass destruction were taxiing hither and thither. Joey wished there were some different world he could belong to, some simpler world in which a good life could be had at nobody else's expense. "I got a message from your mom," he said.

"I know," Connie said. "I was bad, Joey. I didn't tell her anything, but she saw my ring and she asked me, and I couldn't not tell her then."

"She was bitching about how I should tell my parents."

"So let her bitch. You'll tell them when you're ready."

He was in a somber mood when he got back to Alexandria. No longer having Jenna to look forward to or fantasize about, no longer being able to imagine a good outcome in Paraguay, no longer having anything but unpleasant tasks before him, he ate an entire large bag of ruffled potato chips and called Jonathan to repent and seek solace in friendship. "And here's the worst of it," he said. "I went down there as a married man."

"Dude!" Jonathan said. "You married Connie?"

"Yeah. I did. In August."

"That is the most insane thing I've ever heard."

"I thought I'd better tell you, since you'll probably hear about it from Jenna. Who it's safe to say is not very happy with me right now."

"She must be *royally* pissed off."

"You know, I know you think she's awful, but she's not. She's just really lost, and all anybody can see is what she looks like. She's so much less lucky than you are."

Joey proceeded to tell Jonathan the story of the ring, and the ghastly scene in the bathroom, with his hands full of crap and Jenna knocking on the door, and in his own laughter and in Jonathan's laughter and disgusted groans he found the solace he'd been looking for. What had been abhorrent for five minutes made a great story forever after. When he went on to admit that Jonathan had been right about Kenny Bartles, Jonathan's response was clear and adamant: "You've got to bail out of that contract."

"It's not so easy. I've got to protect Connie's investment."

"Find a way out. Just do it. The stuff going on over there is really bad. It's worse than you even know."

"Do you still hate me?" Joey said.

"I don't hate you. I think you've been a total asshole. But hating you doesn't seem to be an option for me."

Joey felt enough cheered by this talk to go to bed and sleep for twelve hours. The next morning, when it was midafternoon in Iraq, he called Kenny Bartles and asked to be let out of his contract.

"What about all the parts in Paraguay?" Kenny said.

"There was plenty of weight. But it's all useless rusted shit."

"Send it anyway. My ass is on the line."

"You're the one who bought the stupid A10s," Joey said. "It's not my fault there's no parts for them."

"You just *told* me there's plenty of parts. And I'm telling you to send them. What am I not understanding here?"

"I'm saying I think you should find somebody else to buy me out. I don't want to be a part of this."

"Joey, whoa, man, listen. You signed the contract. And this is not the eleventh hour for Shipment Number One, this is the fucking *thirteenth* hour. You cannot back out on me now. Not unless you want to eat whatever you're already out of pocket. At the moment, I don't even have the cash to buy you out, because the Army hasn't paid me for the parts yet, because your Polish shipment was too light. Try to look at this from my side, would you?"

"But the stuff in Paraguay looks so bad, I don't think they're even going to accept it."

"You leave that to me. I know the LBI people on the ground here. I can make it work. You just need to send me thirty tons, and then you can go back to reading poetry or whatever."

"How do I know you can make it work?"

"That's *my* problem, right? Your contract is with *me*, and *I'm* saying just get me weight and you will get your money."

Joey didn't know which was worse, the fear that Kenny was lying to him and that he would be screwed not only out of the money he'd already spent but out of the vast additional outlays still ahead of him, or the idea that Kenny was telling the truth and LBI was going to pay $850K for nearly worthless parts. He saw no choice but to go over Kenny's head and talk directly to LBI. This entailed a morning of being passed around telephonically by people at LBI headquarters, in Dallas, before he was connected with the pertinent vice president. He laid out his dilemma as plainly as possible: "There aren't any good parts available for this truck, Kenny Bartles won't buy out the contract for me, and I don't want to send you bad parts."

"Is Bartles willing to accept what you've got?" the VP said.

"Yeah. But they're no good."

"Not your worry. If Bartles accepts them, you're off the hook. I suggest you make the shipment right away."

"I don't think you're quite hearing me," Joey said. "I'm saying you don't *want* that shipment."

The VP digested this for a moment and said, "We will not be doing business with Kenny Bartles in the future. We're not at all happy about the A10 situation. But that is not your worry. Your worry should be getting sued for nonfulfillment of contract."

"Who—by Kenny?"

"It's a total hypothetical. It's never going to happen, as long as you send the parts. You just need to remember that this is not a perfect war in a perfect world."

And Joey tried to remember this. Tried to remember that the worst that could happen, in this less than perfect world, was that all the A10s would break down and need to be replaced by better trucks at a later date, and that victory in Iraq might thereby be infinitesimally delayed, and that American taxpayers would have wasted a few million dollars on him and Kenny Bartles and Armando da Rosa and the creeps in Lodz. With the same determination that he'd brought to grabbing hold of his own turds, he flew back to Paraguay and hired an expediter and oversaw the loading of thirty-two tons of parts into containers and drank five bottles of wine in the five nights he had to wait for Logística Internacional to forklift them into a veteran C-130 and fly off with them; but there was no gold ring hidden in this particular pile of shit. When he got back to Washington, he kept right on drinking, and when Connie finally came out with three suitcases and moved in with him, he kept drinking and slept badly, and when Kenny called from Kirkuk to say that the delivery had been accepted and that Joey's $850,000 was in the pipeline, he had such a bad night that he called Jonathan and confessed what he had done.

"Oh, dude, that's bad," Jonathan said.

"Don't I know it."

"You just better hope you don't get caught. I'm already hearing a lot of stories from that eighteen billion in contracts they let in November. I wouldn't be surprised if we get congressional hearings."

"Is there somebody I can tell? I don't even want the money, except what I owe Connie and the bank."

"That's very noble of you."

"I couldn't screw Connie out of the money. You know that's the only reason I did it. But I'm wondering if maybe you could tell somebody at the *Post* what's going on. Like, that you heard something from an anonymous source?"

"Not if you want it to stay anonymous. And if you don't, you know who's going to get smeared, don't you?"

"But if I'm the whistle-blower?"

"The minute you blow the whistle, Kenny smears you. LBI smears you. They've got a whole line item in their budget for smearing whistleblowers. You'll be the perfect scapegoat. The pretty-faced college kid with the rusty truck parts? The *Post* will eat it up. Not that your sentiment doesn't do you credit. But I highly recommend you stay mum."

Connie found work at a temp agency while they waited for the dirty $850,000 to filter down through the system. Joey wandered through his days watching TV and playing video games and trying to learn how to be domestic, how to plan a dinner and shop for it, but the simplest short trip to the supermarket exhausted him. The depression that for years had stalked the women nearest him seemed finally to have identified its rightful prey and sunk its teeth in him. The one thing he knew he absolutely had to do, which was tell his family that he'd married Connie, he could not do. Its necessity filled the little apartment like a Pladsky A10 truck, confining him to the margins, leaving him insufficient air to breathe. It was there when he woke up and there when he went to bed. He couldn't imagine giving the news to his mother, because she would inevitably perceive the marriage as a pointed personal blow to her. Which, in a way, it probably was. But he dreaded no less the conversation with his father, the reopening of that wound. And so, every day, even as the secret suffocated him, even as he imagined Carol blabbing the news to all his former neighbors, one of whom would surely tell his parents soon, he put off making the announcement another day. That Connie never nagged him only made the problem more solely his.

And then one night, on CNN, he saw the news of an ambush outside Fallujah in which several American trucks had broken down, leaving their contract drivers to be butchered by insurgents. Although he didn't see any A10s in the CNN footage, he became so anxious that he had to drink himself to sleep. He woke up some hours later, in a sweat, mostly sober, beside his wife, who slept literally like a baby—with that world-trusting sweet stillness—and he knew he had to call his father in the morning. He'd never felt so afraid of anything as of making this call. But he could see now that nobody else could advise him what to do, whether to blow the whistle and suffer the consequences or stay mum and keep the money, and that nobody else could absolve him. Connie's love was too unqualified, his mother's too self-involved, Jonathan's too secondary. It was to his strict, principled father that a full accounting needed to be made. He'd been battling him all his life, and now the time had come to admit that he was beaten.

# THE FIEND OF WASHINGTON

**W**alter's father, Gene, was the youngest child of a difficult Swede named Einar Berglund who had immigrated at the turn of the twentieth century. There had been a lot not to like about rural Sweden—compulsory military service, Lutheran pastors meddling in the lives of their parishioners, a social hierarchy that all but precluded upward mobility—but what had actually driven Einar to America, according to the story that Dorothy told Walter, was a problem with his mother.

Einar had been the oldest of eight children, the princeling of his family on its farm in south Österland. His mother, who was perhaps not the first woman to be unsatisfied in her marriage to a Berglund, had favored her firstborn outrageously, dressing him in finer clothes than his siblings were given, feeding him the cream from the others' milk, and excusing him from farm chores so that he could devote himself to his education and his grooming. ("The vainest man I ever met," Dorothy said.) The maternal sun had shone on Einar for twenty years, but then, by mistake, his mother had a late baby, a son, and fell for him the way she'd once fallen for Einar; and Einar never forgave her for it. Unable to stand not being the favored one, he sailed for America on his twenty-second birthday. Once he was there, he never went back to Sweden, never saw his mother again, proudly avowed that he'd forgotten every word of his mother tongue, and delivered, at the slightest provocation, lengthy diatribes against "the stupidest, smuggest, narrow-mindedest country on earth." He became another data point in the American experiment of self-government, an experiment statistically skewed from the outset, because it wasn't the people with sociable genes who fled the crowded Old World for the new continent; it was the people who didn't get along well with others.

As a young man in Minnesota, working first as a logger clear-cutting the last virgin forests and then as a digger in a road-building gang, and not making good money at either, Einar had been attracted to the Communist notion that his labor was being exploited by East Coast capitalists. Then one day, listening to a Communist fulminator in Pioneer Square, he'd had a eureka moment in which he realized that the way to get ahead in his new country was to exploit some labor himself. With several of the younger brothers who'd followed him to America, he went into business as a road-building contractor. To keep busy in the frozen months, he and his brothers also founded a small town on the banks of the upper Mississippi and opened a general store. His politics may still have been radical at that point, because he extended endless credit to the Communist farmers, many of them Finnish, who were struggling to make a living beyond the grasp of East Coast capital. The store quickly became a money-loser, and Einar was at the point of selling his share in it when a former friend of his, a man named Christiansen, opened a rival store across the street. Purely out of spite (according to Dorothy), Einar operated the store for another five years, right through the Great Depression's nadir, accumulating unpayable chits from every farmer within ten miles of town, until poor Christiansen was finally driven into bankruptcy. Einar then relocated to Bemidji, where he did good business as a road builder but ended up selling his company at a disastrously low price to an oily-mannered associate who'd pretended to have socialist sympathies.

America, for Einar, was the land of unSwedish freedom, the place of wide-open spaces where a son could still imagine he was special. But nothing disturbs the feeling of specialness like the presence of other human beings feeling identically special. Having achieved, through his native intelligence and hard labor, a degree of affluence and independence, but not nearly enough of either, he became a study in anger and disappointment. After his retirement, in the 1950s, he began sending his relatives annual Christmas letters in which he lambasted the stupidity of America's government, the inequities of its political economy, and the fatuity of its religion—drawing, for example, in one particularly caustic Christmas greeting, a cunning parallel between the unwed madonna of Bethlehem and the "Swedish whore" Ingrid Bergman, the birth of whose own "bastard" (Isabella Rossellini) had lately been celebrated by American media controlled by "corporate interests." Though an entrepreneur himself, Einar detested big business. Though he'd made a career of government contracts, he hated the government as well. And though he loved the open road, the road made him miserable and crazy. He bought American sedans with the biggest engines available, so that he could do ninety and a hundred on the dead-flat Minnesota state highways, many of them built by him, and roar past the stupid people in his way. If an oncoming car approached him at night with its high beams on, Einar's response was to put his own high beams on and leave them on. If some pinhead dared to try to pass him on a two-lane road, he floored the accelerator to keep pace and then decelerated to prevent the would-be passer from getting back in line, taking special pleasure when there was danger of a collision with an oncoming truck. If another driver cut him off or refused him the right of way, he pursued the offending car and tried to force it off the road, so that he could jump out and shout curses at its driver. (The personality susceptible to the dream of limitless freedom is a personality also prone, should the dream ever sour, to misanthropy and rage.) Einar was seventy-eight when an extremely poor driving decision forced him to choose between a head-on crash and a deep ditch by the side of Route 2. His wife, who was sitting in the passenger seat and, unlike Einar, was wearing a seat belt, lingered for three days at the hospital in Grand Rapids before expiring of her burns. According to the police, she might have survived if she hadn't tried to pull her dead husband out of their burning Eldorado. "He treated her like a dog all his life," Walter's father said afterward, "and then he killed her."

Of Einar's four kids, Gene was the one without ambition who stayed close to home, the one who wanted to enjoy life, the one with a thousand friends. This was partly his nature and partly a conscious reproof of his father. Gene had been a high-school hockey star in Bemidji and then, following Pearl Harbor, to the chagrin of his antimilitarist father, an early

445

enlister in the Army. He served two tours in the Pacific, emerging both unwounded and unpromoted past PFC, and returned to Bemidji to party with his friends and work at a garage and ignore his father's stern injunctions to take advantage of the G.I. Bill. It wasn't clear that he would have married Dorothy if he hadn't made her pregnant, but once they were married he set about loving her with all the tenderness he believed his father had denied his mother.

That Dorothy ended up working like a dog for him anyway, and that his own son Walter ended up hating him for this, was just one of those twists of family fate. Gene at least did not insist, the way his father had, that he was superior to his wife. On the contrary, he enslaved her with his weakness—his penchant for drink in particular. The other ways in which he came to resemble Einar were similarly roundabout in origin. He was belligerently populist, defiantly proud of his *un*specialness, and attracted, therefore, to the dark side of right-wing politics. He was loving and grateful to his wife, he was famed among his friends and fellow vets for his generosity and loyalty, and yet, ever more frequently as he got older, he was given to scalding eruptions of Berglundian resentment. He hated the blacks, the Indians, the well-educated, the hoity-toity, and, especially, the federal government, and he loved his freedoms (to drink, to smoke, to hole up with his buddies in an ice-fishing hut) the more intensely for their being so modest. He was ugly to Dorothy only when she suggested, with timid solicitude—for she mostly blamed Einar, not Gene, for Gene's shortcomings—that he should drink less.

Gene's share of Einar's estate, though much diminished by the self-spiting terms of Einar's sale of his business, was large enough to put him within reach of the little roadside motel he'd long believed it would be "neat" to own and manage. The Whispering Pines, when Gene bought it, had a stove-in septic line and a serious mold problem and was already too close to the shoulder of a highway heavily trafficked by ore trucks and due to be widened soon. Behind it was a ravine full of trash and eager young birch trees, one of them growing up through a mangled grocery cart that would eventually strangle and stunt it. Gene should have known that a more cheerful motel was bound to appear on the local market, if he could only be a little patient. But poor business decisions have their own momentum. To invest wisely, he would have had to be a more ambitious kind of person, and since he wasn't this other kind of person, he was impatient to get his error over with, to shoot his wad and begin the work of forgetting how much money he'd spent, literally forgetting it, literally remembering a sum more like the one he later told Dorothy that he'd paid. There is, after all, a kind of happiness in unhappiness, if it's the right unhappiness. Gene no longer had to fear a big disappointment in the future, because he'd already accomplished it; he'd cleared that hurdle, he'd permanently made himself a victim of the world. He took out a crushing second mortgage to pay for a new septic system, and every subsequent disaster, large or small—a pine tree falling through the office roof, a cash-paying guest in Room 24 cleaning walleyes on the bedspread, the Vacancy sign's neon NO burning through most of a July Fourth weekend before Dorothy noticed it and turned it off—served to confirm his understanding of the world and his own shabby place in it.

For the first few summers at the Whispering Pines, Gene's better-off siblings brought their families in from out of state and stayed for a week or two at special family rates whose negotiation left everyone unhappy. Walter's cousins appropriated the tannin-stained swimming pool while his uncles helped Gene apply sealant to the parking lot or shore up the property's eroding back slope with railroad ties. Down in the malarial ravine, near the remains of the collapsed shopping cart, Walter's sophisticated Chicago cousin Leif told informative and harrowing stories of the big-city suburbs; most memorable and worry-provoking, for Walter, was the one about an Oak Park eighth-grader who'd managed to get naked with a girl and then, unsure about what was supposed to happen next, had peed all over her legs. Because Walter's city cousins were much more like him than his brothers were, those early summers were the happiest of his childhood. Every day brought new adventures and mishaps: hornet stings, tetanus shots, misfiring bottle rockets, ghastly cases of poison ivy, near-drownings. Late at night, when the traffic abated, the pines near the office did honestly whisper.

Soon enough, though, the other Berglund spouses put their collective foot down, and the visits ended. To Gene, this was just more evidence that his siblings looked down on him, considered themselves too fancy for his motel, and generally belonged to that privileged class of Americans which it was becoming his great pleasure to revile and reject. He singled out

Walter for derision simply because Walter liked his city cousins and missed seeing them. In the hope of making Walter less like them, Gene assigned his bookish son the dirtiest and most demeaning maintenance tasks. Walter scraped paint, scrubbed stains of blood and semen out of carpeting, and used coat-hanger wire to fish masses of slime and disintegrating hair from bathtub drains. If a guest had left a toilet especially diarrhea-spattered, and if Dorothy was not around to clean it preemptively, Gene took all three of his boys in to view the mess and then, after egging Walter's brothers into disgusted hilarity, left Walter alone to clean it. Saying: "It's good for him." The brothers echoing: "Yeah, it's good for him!" And if Dorothy got wind of this and chided him, Gene sat smiling and smoking with special relish, absorbing her anger without returning it—proud, as always, of raising neither voice nor hand against her. "Aaaa, Dorothy, leave it alone," he said. "Work's good for him. Teach him not to get too full of himself."

It was as if all of the hostility that Gene might have directed at his college-educated wife, but refused to allow himself for fear of being like Einar, had found a more permissible target in his middle son, who, as Dorothy herself could see, was strong enough to bear it. Dorothy took the long view of justice. In the short run, it may have been unjust for Gene to be so hard on Walter, but in the long run her son was going to be a success, whereas her husband would never amount to much. And Walter himself, by uncomplainingly doing the nasty tasks his father set him, by refusing to cry or to whine to Dorothy, showed his father that he could beat him even at his own game. Gene's nightly late-night stumblings into furniture, his childish panics when he ran out of cigarettes, his reflexive denigration of successful people: if Walter hadn't been perpetually occupied with hating him, he might have pitied him. And there was little that Gene feared more than being pitied.

When Walter was nine or ten, he put a handmade No Smoking sign on the door of the room he shared with his little brother, Brent, who was bothered by Gene's cigarettes. Walter wouldn't have done it for his own sake—would sooner have let Gene blow smoke straight into his eyes than give him the satisfaction of complaining. And Gene, for his part, didn't feel comfortable enough with Walter to simply tear the sign down. He contented himself instead with making fun of him. "What if your little brother wants a smoke in the middle of the night? You going to force him to go outside in the cold?"

"He already breathes funny at night from too much smoke," Walter said.

"This is the first I've heard of that."

"I'm there, I hear him."

"I'm just saying you posted the sign for the two of you, right, and what does Brent think? He shares the room with you, right?"

"He's six years old," Walter said.

"Gene, I think Brent might be allergic to the smoke," Dorothy said.

"I think *Walter* is allergic to *me.*"

"We don't want anyone having a cigarette in our room, that's all," Walter said. "You can smoke outside the door but not in the room itself."

"I don't see what difference it makes if the cigarette's on one side of the door or the other."

"It's just the new rule for our room."

"So you're making the rules around here now, are you?"

"In our room, yes, I am," Walter said.

Gene was on the verge of saying something angry when a tired look came over him. He shook his head and produced the crooked, refractory grin with which he'd responded to assertions of authority all his life. He may already have seen, in Brent's allergy, the excuse he'd been looking for to attach to the motel office a "lounge" where he could smoke in peace and his friends could come and pay a little bit to drink with him. Dorothy had rightly foreseen that such a lounge would be the end of him.

The great relief of Walter's childhood, besides school, had been his mother's family. Her father was a small-town doctor, and among her siblings and aunts and uncles were university professors, a married pair of former vaudevillians, an amateur painter, two librarians, and several bachelors who probably were gay. Dorothy's Twin Cities relatives invited Walter down for dazzling weekends of museums and music and theater; the ones still living in the Iron Range hosted sprawling summer picnics and holiday house parties. They liked to play charades and antiquated card games like canasta; they had pianos and held sing-alongs. They were all so patently harmless that even Gene relaxed around them, laughing off their tastes and politics as eccentricities, amiably pitying them for their uselessness at manly pursuits. They brought out a domesticated side of him which Walter loved but otherwise very seldom got to see, except at Christmastime, when there was candy to be made.

The candy job was too large and important to be left to Dorothy and Walter alone. Production began on the first Sunday of Advent and continued through most of December. Necromantic metalware—iron cauldrons and racks, heavy aluminum nut-processing devices—came out of deep closets. Great seasonal dunes of sugar and towers of tins appeared. Several cubic feet of unsweetened butter was melted down with milk and sugar (for chocolateless fudge) or with sugar alone (for Dorothy's famous Christmas toffee) or was smeared by Walter onto the reserve squadron of pans and shallow casseroles that his mother, over the years, had bought at rummage sales. There was lengthy discussion of "hard balls" and "soft balls" and "cracking." Gene, wearing an apron, stirred the cauldrons like a Viking oarsman, doing his best to keep cigarette ash out of them. He had three ancient candy thermometers whose metal casings were shaped like fraternity paddles and whose nature it was to show no increase in temperature for several hours and then, all at once and all together, to register temperatures at which fudge burned and toffee hardened like epoxy. He and Dorothy were never more a team than when working against the clock to get the nuts mixed in and the candy poured. And later the brutal job of cutting too-hard toffee: the knife blade bowing out under the tremendous pressure Gene applied, the nasty sound (less heard than felt in the bone marrow, in the nerves of the teeth) of a sharp edge dulling itself on the bottom of a metal pan, the explosions of sticky brown amber, the paternal cries of *God fucking damn it*, and the querulous maternal entreaties not to swear like that.

On the last weekend of Advent, when eighty or a hundred tins had been lined with waxed paper and packed with fudge and toffee and garnished with Jordan almonds, Gene and Dorothy and Walter went out giving. It took the entire weekend, often longer. Walter's older brother, Mitch, stayed behind at the motel with Brent, who, although he later became an Air Force pilot, as a child was easily made carsick. The candy went first to Gene's many friends in Hibbing and then, with much backtracking and dead-ending, to farther-flung friends and relatives, down through the Iron Range to Grand Rapids and beyond. It was unthinkable not to accept coffee or a cookie at every house. Between stops, Walter sat in the back seat with a book, watching a feeble window-shaped patch of sunlight hold steady on the seat and then, when a right-angle turn was finally reached, slide across the canyon of the floor and reappear, in twisted form, on the back of the front seat. Outside were the eternal paltry wood lots, the eternal snowed-over bog, the circular tin fertilizer advertisements tacked to telephone poles, the furled hawks and bold ravens. On the seat beside him was the growing pile of packages from homes already visited—Scandinavian baked goods, Finnish and Croatian delicacies, bottles of "cheer" from Gene's unmarried friends—and the slowly dwindling pile of Berglund tins. These tins' chief merit was that they contained the same candy that Gene and Dorothy had been giving since they were married. The candy had gradually morphed, over the years, from a treat into a reminder of treats past. It was the annual gift the poor Berglunds could still be wealthy in.

Walter was finishing his junior year in high school when Dorothy's father died and left her the little lakeside house in which she'd spent her girlhood summers. In Walter's mind, the house was associated with his mother's disabilities, because it was here, as a girl, that she'd spent long months battling the arthritis that had withered her right hand and deformed her pelvis. On a low shelf by the fireplace were the sad old "toys" with which she'd once "played" for hours—a nutcracker-like device with steel springs, a five-valved wooden trumpet—to try to preserve and increase mobility in her ravaged finger joints. The Berglunds had always been too busy with the motel to stay long at the little house, but Dorothy was fond of it, had dreams of retiring there with Gene if they could ever get rid of the motel, and so did not immediately assent when Gene proposed selling it. Gene's health was bad, the motel was mortgaged to the hilt, and whatever small curb appeal it had once possessed was now fully eroded by the harsh Hibbing winters. Though Mitch was out of school and working as an auto-body detailer and still living at home, he blew his paychecks on girls, drink, guns, fishing equipment, and his souped-up Thunderbird. Gene might have felt differently about the house if its little unnamed lake had had fish in it more worth catching than sunnies and perch, but, since it didn't, he didn't see the point of holding on to a vacation home they wouldn't have time to use anyway. Dorothy, normally the paragon of resigned pragmatism, became so sad that she went to bed for several days, complaining of a headache. And Walter, who was willing to suffer himself but couldn't stand to see her suffering, intervened.

"I can stay in the house myself and fix it up this summer, and maybe we can start renting it out," he told his parents.

"We need you helping here," Dorothy said.

"I'm only here for another year anyway. What are you going to do when I'm gone?"

"We'll cross that bridge when we come to it," Gene said.

"Sooner or later, you're going to have to hire somebody."

"That's why we need to sell the house," Gene said.

"He's right, Walter," Dorothy said. "I hate to see the house go, but he's right."

"Well, what about Mitch, though? He could at least pay some rent, and you could hire somebody with that."

"He's on his own now," Gene said.

"Mom still cooks for him and does his laundry! Why isn't he at least paying rent?"

"That's none of your business."

"It's Mom's business! You'd rather sell Mom's house than make Mitch grow up!"

"That's his room, and I'm not going to throw him out of it."

"Do you really think we could rent the house?" Dorothy said hopefully.

"We'd be cleaning it every week and doing laundry," Gene said. "There'd be no end to it."

"I could drive down once a week," Dorothy said. "It wouldn't be so bad."

"We need the money *now*," Gene said.

"And what if I do what Mitch does?" Walter said. "What if I just say no? What if I just go over to the house this summer and fix it up?"

"You're not Jesus Christ," Gene said. "We can get along here without you."

"Gene, we can at least *try* to rent the house next summer. If it doesn't work out, we can always sell it."

"I'll go there on weekends," Walter said. "How about that? Mitch can take over for me on the weekends, can't he?"

"If you want to try selling Mitch on that, go ahead," Gene said.

"I'm not his parent!"

"I've had enough of this," Gene said, and retreated to the lounge.

Why Gene gave Mitch a free pass was clear enough: he saw in his oldest son a nearly exact replica of himself, and he didn't want to ride him the way he'd once been ridden by Einar. But Dorothy's timidness with Mitch was more mysterious to Walter. Maybe she was already so worn out by her husband that she just didn't have the strength or the heart to battle her son as well, or maybe she could already see Mitch's failed future and wanted him to enjoy a few more years of kindness at home before the world had its tough way with him. In any case, it fell to Walter to knock on Mitch's door, which was plastered with STP and Pennzoil stickers, and try to be a parent to his older brother.

Mitch was lying on his bed, smoking a cigarette and listening to Bachman-Turner Overdrive on the stereo he'd bought with his body-shop earnings. The refractory way he smiled at Walter was similar to their father's, but more sneering. "What do *you* want?"

"I want you to start paying rent here, or do some work around here, or else get out."

"Since when are you the boss?"

"Dad said I should talk to you."

"Tell him to talk to me himself."

"Mom doesn't want to sell the lake house, so something's got to change."

"That's her problem."

"Jesus, Mitch. You are the most selfish person I've ever met."

"Yeah, right. You're going to go away to Harvard or wherever, and I'm going to end up taking care of this place. But I'm the selfish one."

"You are!"

"I'm trying to save up some money in case Brenda and I need it, but I'm the selfish one."

Brenda was the very pretty girl whose parents had practically disowned her for dating Mitch. "What exactly is your great savings plan?" Walter said. "Buying yourself a lot of stuff now that you can pawn later?"

"I work hard. What am I supposed to do, never buy anything?"

"I work hard, too, and I don't have stuff, because I don't get paid."

"What about that movie camera?"

"That's on loan from *school*, moron. It's not mine."

"Well, nobody's loaning me any stuff, because I'm not a candy-assed suck-up."

"That still doesn't mean you don't have to pay rent, or at least help out on the weekend."

Mitch peered down into his ashtray as into a prison yard crowded with dusty inmates, considering how to squeeze another in. "Who appointed you Jesus Christ around here?" he said, unoriginally. "I don't have to negotiate with you."

But Dorothy refused to talk to Mitch ("I'd rather just sell the house," she said), and Walter, at the end of the school year, which was also the start of the motel's high season, such as it was, decided to force the issue by going on strike. As long as he was around the motel, he couldn't not do the things that needed doing. The only way to make Mitch take responsibility was to leave, and so he announced that he was going to spend the summer fixing up the lake house and making an experimental nature film. His father said that if he wanted to get the house into better shape to be sold, that was fine with him, but the house would be sold in any case. His mother begged him to forget about the house. She said it had been selfish of her to make such a big deal about it, she didn't *care* about the house, she just wanted everyone to get along, and when Walter said that he was going anyway, she cried out that if he really cared about her wishes he would not be leaving. But he was feeling, for the first time, truly angry with her. It didn't matter how much she loved him or how well he understood her—he hated her for submitting so meekly to his father and his brother. He was sick to death of it. He got his best friend, Mary Siltala, to drive him down to the lake house with a duffel bag of clothes, ten gallons of house paint, his old one-speed bike, a secondhand paperback copy of *Walden*, the Super-8 movie camera that he'd borrowed from the high-school AV Department, and eight yellow boxes of Super-8 film. It was by far the most rebellious thing he'd ever done.

The house was full of mouse droppings and dead sow bugs and needed, besides repainting, a new roof and new window screens. On his first day there, Walter cleaned house and cut weeds for ten hours and then went walking in the woods, in the changeless late-afternoon sunlight, seeking beauty in nature. He had only twenty-four minutes of film stock, and after wasting three of these minutes on chipmunks he realized he needed something less attainable to pursue. The lake was too small for loons, but when he took his grandfather's fabric canoe out into its seldom-disturbed recesses he flushed a heronlike bird, a bittern that was nesting in the reeds. Bitterns were perfect—so retiring that he could stalk them all summer without using up twenty-one minutes of film. He imagined making an experimental short called "Bitternness."

He got up at five every morning, applied DEET, and paddled very slowly and silently toward the reeds, the camera on his lap. The bittern way was to lurk among the reeds, camouflaged by their fine vertical striping of buff and brown, and spear small animals with their bills. When they sensed danger, they froze with their necks outstretched and their bills pointing skyward, looking like dry reeds. When Walter edged closer, hoping to see more of bitternness and less of nothing in the range finder, they usually slipped out of sight but sometimes, instead, heaved themselves into flight, which he leaned back wildly to follow with the camera. Although they were pure killing machines, he found them highly sympathetic, especially for the contrast between their drab stalking plumage and the dramatic bold gray and slaty black of their outstretched wings when they were airborne. They were humble and furtive on the ground, near their marshy home, but lordly in the sky.

Seventeen years in cramped quarters with his family had given him a thirst for solitude whose unquenchability he was discovering only now. To hear nothing but wind, birdsong, insects, fish jumping, branches squeaking, birch leaves scraping as they tumbled against each other: he kept stopping to savor this unsilent silence as he scraped paint from the house's outer walls. The round trip to the food co-op in Fen City took ninety minutes on his bicycle. He made big pots of lentil stew and bean soup, using recipes of his mother's, and in the evening he played with the ancient but still workable spring-driven pinball machine that had been in the house forever. He read in bed until midnight and even then didn't fall asleep immediately but lay soaking up the silence.

One late afternoon, a Friday, his tenth day at the lake, when he was returning in the canoe with some fresh unsatisfactory bittern footage, he heard car engines, loud music, and then motorcycles coming down the long driveway. By the time he got the canoe out of the water, Mitch and sexy Brenda and three other couples—three goon buddies of Mitch's and three girls in sprayed-on bell-bottoms and halter tops—were unloading beer and camping gear and coolers onto the lawn behind the house. A diesel pickup was idling with a smoker's cough, powering a sound system loaded with Aerosmith. One of the goon friends had a stud-collared Rottweiler on a towing-chain leash.

"Hey, nature boy," Mitch said. "I hope you don't mind some company."

"Yeah, I do mind," Walter said, blushing, in spite of himself, at how uncool he must have looked to the company. "I mind a lot. I'm here alone. You can't be here."

"Yes I can," Mitch said. "In fact, it's you that shouldn't be here. You can stay tonight if you want, but I'm here now. You are on my property."

"This is not your property."

"I'm renting it now. You wanted me to pay rent, and this is what I'm renting."

"What about your job?"

"I quit. I'm out of there."

Walter, near tears, went into the house and hid the camera in a laundry basket. Then he rode his bicycle through a twilight suddenly drained of charm and filled with mosquitoes and hostility, and called home from the pay phone outside the Fen City Co-op. Yes, his mother confirmed, she and Mitch and his father had had angry words and decided that the best solution was to keep the house in the family and let Mitch do the repairs on it and learn to take more responsibility.

"Mom, it's going to be party central. He's going to burn the house down."

"Well, I just feel more comfortable having you here and Mitch on his own," she said. "You were right about that, sweetie. And now you can come home. We miss you, and you're not really old enough to be by yourself all summer."

"But I'm having a great time out here. I'm getting so much done."

"I'm sorry about that, Walter. But this is what we've decided."

Biking back to the house in near-darkness, he could hear the noise from half a mile away. Cock-rock guitar soloing, blunt drunken shouting, the dog baying, firecrackers, a motorcycle engine sputtering and screaming. Mitch and his friends had pitched tents and built a big fire and were attempting to flame-broil hamburgers in a cloud of pot smoke. They didn't even look at Walter as he went inside. He locked himself in the bedroom and lay in bed and let himself be tortured by the noise. Why couldn't they be *quiet*? Why this need to sonically assault a world in which *some people* appreciated silence? The din went on and on and on. It produced a fever to which everyone else was apparently immune. A fever of self-pitying alienation. Which, as it raged in Walter that night, scarred him permanently with hatred of the bellowing vox populi, and also, curiously, with an aversion to the outdoor world. He'd come openhearted to nature, and nature, in its weakness, which was like his mother's weakness, had let him down. Had allowed itself so easily to be overrun by noisy idiots. He loved nature, but only abstractly, and no more than he loved good novels or foreign movies, and less than he came to love Patty and his kids, and so, for the next twenty years, he made himself a city person. Even when he left 3M to do conservation work, his primary interest in working for the Conservancy, and later for the Trust, was to safeguard pockets of nature from loutish country people like his brother. The love he felt for the creatures whose habitat he was protecting was founded on projection: on identification with their own wish to be left alone by noisy human beings.

Excepting some months in prison, when Brenda was alone with their little girls, Mitch lived in the lake house continuously until Gene died, six years later. He put a new roof on it and arrested its general decay, but he also felled several of the biggest and prettiest trees on the property, denuded the lakeside slope as a playground for his dogs, and hacked a snowmobile trail around to the far corner of the lake, where the bitterns had once nested. As far as Walter could determine, he never paid Gene and Dorothy a cent of rent.


Did the founder of the Traumatics even know what trauma was? This was what trauma was: going downstairs to your office early on a Sunday morning, thinking happily of your children, both of whom had made you very proud in the last two days, and finding on your desk a long manuscript, composed by your wife, that confirmed the worst fears you'd ever had about her and yourself and your best friend. The only remotely comparable experience in Walter's life had been the first time he'd masturbated, in Room 6 of the Whispering Pines, following the friendly instructions ("Use Vaseline") provided by his cousin Leif. He'd been fourteen, and the pleasure had so dwarfed all previous known pleasures, and the outcome had been so cataclysmic and astonishing, that he'd felt like a sci-fi hero wrenched four-dimensionally from an aged planet to a fresh one. And Patty's manuscript was similarly compelling and transformative. His reading of it seemed, like that first masturbation, to last a single instant. He stood up once, early on, to lock his office door, and then he was reading the last page, and it was exactly 10:12 a.m., and the sun beating on his office windows was a different sun from the one he'd always known. It was a yellowy, mean star in some strange, forsaken corner of the galaxy, and his own head was no less altered by the interstellar distance he'd traversed. He carried the manuscript out of his office and past Lalitha, who was typing at her desk.

"Good morning, Walter."

"Good morning," he said with a shudder at her nice morning smell. He walked on through the kitchen and up the back staircase to the little room where the love of his life was still in her flannel pajamas, ensconced in a nest of bedding on her sofa, holding a mug of creamed coffee, and watching some sports-channel roundup of the NCAA basketball tournament. The smile she gave him—a smile that was like the last flash of the familiar sun he'd lost—turned to horror when she saw what he was holding.

"Oh, shit," she said, turning off the television. "Oh, shit, Walter. Oh, oh, oh." She shook her head vehemently. "No," she said. "No, no, no."

He closed the door behind him and slid down with his back against it until he was sitting on the floor. Patty drew breath, and then drew more breath, and more breath, and didn't speak. The light in the windows was unearthly. Walter shuddered again, his molars clicking as he sought to control himself.

"I don't know where you got that," Patty said. "But it was not for you. I gave it to Richard last night to get him *away* from me. I wanted him out of our life! I was trying to get *rid* of him, Walter. I don't know why he did that! It's so horrible that he did that!"

From a distance of many parsecs, he heard her start crying.

"I never meant you to read that," she said in a keening high voice. "I swear to God, Walter. I swear to God. I've spent my whole life trying not to hurt you. You're so good to me, you don't deserve this."

She cried for some long while then, some ten or a hundred minutes. All regular Sunday-morning programming was suspended for the emergency, the day's normal course so thoroughly obliterated that he couldn't even feel nostalgia for it. As chance would have things, the spot on the floor directly in front of him had been the scene of a different kind of emergency just three nights earlier, a benign emergency, a pleasurably traumatic coupling that in hindsight now looked like a harbinger of this malignant emergency. He'd come upstairs late on Thursday evening and attacked Patty sexually. Had performed, with her surprised consent, the violent actions which, without her consent, would have been a rapist's: had yanked off her black work pants, pushed her to the floor, and rammed his way inside her. If it had ever occurred to him to do this in the past, he wouldn't have done it, because he couldn't forget that she'd been raped as a girl. But the day had been so long and disorienting—his near-infidelity with Lalitha so inflaming, the roadblock in Wyoming County so infuriating, the humility in Joey's voice on the telephone so unprecedented and gratifying—that Patty had suddenly seemed, when he walked into her room, like his object. His obstinate object, his frustrating wife. And he was sick of it, sick of all the reasoning and understanding, and so he threw her on the floor and fucked her like a brute. The look of discovery on her face then, which must have mirrored the look on his own face, made him stop almost as soon as they'd got started. Stop and pull out and straddle her chest and stick his erection, which seemed twice its usual size, into her face. To show her who he was becoming. They were both smiling like crazy. And then he was back inside her, and instead of her usual demure little sighs of encouragement she was giving forth loud screams, and this inflamed him all the more; and the next morning, when he went down to the office, he could tell from Lalitha's chilly silence that the screaming had filled the whole large house. Something had begun on Thursday night, he hadn't been sure what. But now her manuscript had shown him what. The end was what. She'd never really loved him. She'd wanted what his evil friend had. The whole thing now made him glad he hadn't broken the promise he'd given Joey at dinner in Alexandria the following night, the promise that he not tell anybody, but especially not tell Patty, that he'd married Connie Monaghan. This secret, as well as several other more alarming ones that Joey had vouchsafed, had been weighing on Walter all weekend, all through the long meeting and the concert the day before. He'd been feeling bad about keeping Patty in the dark about the marriage, feeling as if he were betraying her. But now he could see that, as betrayals went, this one was laughably small. Cryably small.

"Is Richard still in the house?" she said finally, wiping her face with a bedsheet.

"No. I heard him go out before I got up. I don't think he's come back."

"Well, thank goodness for small mercies."

How he loved her voice! It murdered him to hear it now.

"Did you guys fuck last night?" he said. "I heard talking in the kitchen."

His own voice was harsh like a crow's, and Patty took a deep breath, as if settling in for prolonged abuse. "No," she said. "We talked and then I went to bed. I told you, it's over. There was a little problem years ago, but it is over."

"Mistakes were made."

"You have to believe me, Walter. It is really, really over."

"Except I don't do for you physically what my best friend does. Never did, apparently. And never will."

"Ohhh," she said, closing her eyes prayerfully, "please don't quote me. Call me a whore, call me the nightmare of your life, but please try not to quote me. Have that little bit of mercy, if you can."

"He may suck at chess, but he's definitely winning at the other game."

"OK," she said, squeezing her eyes shut tighter. "You're going to quote me. OK. Quote me. Go ahead. Do what you have to do. I know I don't deserve mercy. Just please know that it's the worst thing you can do."

"Sorry. I thought you liked talking about him. In fact, I thought that was the main point of interest in talking to me."

"You're right. It was. I won't lie to you. It was, for about three months. But that was twenty-five years ago, before I fell in love with you and made a life with you."

"And what a satisfying life that's been. 'Nothing so wrong with it,' I believe your phrase was. Although the facts on the ground would appear to suggest otherwise."

She grimaced, her eyes still shut. "Maybe you want to just read through the whole thing now and pick out all the worst lines. Do you want to just do that and get it over with?"

"Actually, what I want to do is stuff it down your throat. I want to see you fucking gag on it."

"OK. You can do that. It would sort of be a relief from what I'm feeling now."

He'd been clutching the manuscript so hard that his hand was cramped. He released it and let it slide between his legs. "I don't actually have anything else to say," he said. "I think we've pretty much covered the main points."

She nodded. "Good."

"Except I don't want to see you again. I don't want to be in the same room with you again. I don't want to hear that person's name again. I don't want to have anything to do with either of you. Ever. I just want to be alone so I can contemplate having wasted my entire life loving you."

"Yes, OK," she said, nodding again. "But also no? No, I don't agree to that."

"I don't care if you agree."

"I know you don't. But listen to me." She sniffed hard, composing herself, and set her mug of coffee on the floor. Her tears had softened her eyes and reddened her lips and made her very pretty, if you cared about her prettiness, which Walter no longer did. "I never intended you to read that," she said.

"What the fuck is it doing in my house if you didn't intend that?"

"You can believe me or not, but it's the truth. It was just a thing I had to write for myself, to try to get better. It was a *therapy* project, Walter. I gave it to Richard last night to try to explain why I stayed with you. *Always* stayed with you. *Still* want to stay with you. I know there's stuff in there that must be horrible for you to read, I can hardly even imagine how horrible, but that's not *all* there is in it. I wrote it when I was depressed, and it's full of all the bad things I was feeling. But I've finally been starting to feel better. Especially after what happened the other night—I was feeling better! Like we were finally having some kind of breakthrough! Isn't that how you felt, too?"

"I don't know what I felt."

"I wrote nice things about you, too, didn't I? Many, many more nice things than not nice? If you look at it objectively? Which I know you can't, but still, anybody else except you could see the nice things. That you've been kinder to me than I ever thought I deserved to have someone be. That you're the most excellent person I've ever met. That you and Joey and Jessie are my whole life. That it was only one small bad part of me that ever looked anywhere else, for a little while, at a really bad point in my life."

"You're right," he cawed. "I did somehow overlook all that."

"It's there, Walter! Maybe when you think about it, later, you'll remember that it's there."

"I'm not intending to do much thinking about it."

"Not now, but later. Even if you still don't want to talk to me, maybe you'll at least forgive me a little bit."

The light in the windows dimmed suddenly, a spring cloud passing by. "You did the worst thing you could possibly do to me," he said. "*The* worst thing, and you knew very well it was the worst thing, and you did it anyway. Which part of that am I going to want to think back on?"

"Oh, I'm so sorry," she said, weeping afresh. "I'm so sorry you can't see it the way I see it. I'm so sorry this happened."

"It didn't 'happen.' You *did* it. You fucked the kind of evil shit who would leave this on my desk for me to read."

"For God's sake, though, Walter, it was just sex."

"You let him read things about me you never would have let me read."

"Just stupid sex four years ago. What's that compared to our whole life?"

"Look," he said, standing up. "I don't want to shout at you. Not with Jessica in the house. But you have to help me with that and not be disingenuous about what you did, or I'm going to shout your fucking head off."

"I'm not being disingenuous."

"I mean it," he said. "I'm not going to shout at you. I'm going to leave this room, and I don't want to see you after that. And we have a bit of a problem, because I actually have to work in this house, so it's not very easy for me to move out."

"I know, I know," she said. "I know I have to go. I'll wait until Jessie's gone, and then I'll get out of your sight. I totally understand how you're feeling. But I have to tell you one thing before I go, just so you know. I want to make sure you know that it's like being stabbed in the heart for me to leave you with your assistant. It's like having the skin ripped off my breasts. I can't stand it, Walter." She looked at him imploringly. "I'm so hurt and jealous, I don't know what I'm going to do."

"You'll get over it."

"Maybe. Some year. A little bit. But do you see what it means that I'm feeling it now? Do you see what it means about who I love? Do you see what's really going on here?"

The sight of her wild, pleading eyes became, at that moment, so crestingly painful and disgusting to him—produced such a paroxysm of cumulative revulsion at the pain they'd caused each other in their marriage—that he began to shout in spite of himself: "*Who drove me to it? Who was I never quite good enough for? Who always needed more time to think it over?* Don't you think *twenty-six years* is long enough to think it over? How much fucking more time do you need? Do you think there's anything in your writing that surprised me? Do you think I didn't know every fucking bit of it every fucking minute of the way? And love you anyway, because I couldn't help it? And waste my entire life?"

"That's not fair, oh, that's not fair."

"Fuck fairness! And fuck you!"

He kicked the manuscript into a white flurry, but he was disciplined enough not to slam the door behind him as he left. Downstairs in the kitchen, Jessica was toasting herself a bagel, her overnight bag standing by the table. "Where is everybody this morning?"

"Mom and I had a little bit of a fight."

"Sounded like it," Jessica said with the ironic eye-widening that was her customary response to belonging to a family less even-keeled than she. "Is everything OK now?"

"We'll see, we'll see."

"I was hoping to get the noon train, but I can take a later one if you want."

Because he'd always been close to Jessica and felt he could count on her support, it didn't occur to him that he was making a tactical error in brushing her off now and sending her on her way. He didn't see how crucial it was to be the first to give the news to her and frame the story properly: didn't imagine how quickly Patty, with her game-winning instincts, would move to consolidate her alliance with their daughter and fill her ears with her version of the story (Dad Dumps Mom on Flimsy Pretext, Takes Up with Young Assistant). He wasn't thinking of anything beyond the moment, and his head was aswirl with precisely the kind of feelings that had nothing to do with fatherhood. He gave Jessica a hug and thanked her profusely for coming down to help launch Free Space, and then he went into his office to stare out the windows. The state of emergency had waned enough for him to remember all the work he needed to be doing, but not nearly enough for him to do it. He watched a catbird hopping around in an azalea that was readying itself to bloom; he envied the bird for knowing nothing of what he knew; he would have swapped souls with it in a heartbeat. And then to take wing, to know the air's buoyancy even for an hour: the trade was a no-brainer, and the catbird, with its lively indifference to him, its sureness of physical selfhood, seemed well aware of how preferable it was to be the bird.

Some otherworldly amount of time later, after he'd heard the rolling of a large suitcase and the clunk of the front door, Lalitha came tapping on his office door and stuck her head in. "Everything OK?"

"Yeah," he said. "Come sit on my lap."

She raised her eyebrows. "Now?"

"Yes, now. When else? My wife's gone, right?"

"She left with a suitcase, yes."

"Well, she's not coming back. So come on. Why not. There's nobody else in the house."

And she did. She was not a hesitant person, Lalitha. But the executive

464

chair was ill suited for lap-sitting; she had to hang on to his neck to stay aboard, and even then the chair rocked hazardously. "This is what you want?" she said.

"Actually, no. I don't want to be in this office."

"I agree."

He had so much to think about, he knew he would be thinking uninterruptedly for weeks if he let himself start now. The only way not to think was to plunge forward. Up in Lalitha's slope-ceilinged little room, the onetime maid's quarters, which he hadn't visited since she'd moved in, and whose floor was an obstacle course of clean clothes in stacks and dirty ones in piles, he pressed her against the side wall of the dormer and gave himself blindly to the one person who wanted him without qualification. It was another state of emergency, it was no hour of no day, it was desperate. He lifted her onto his hips and staggered around with her mouth locked to his, and then they were humping fiercely through their clothes, between piles of other clothes, and then one of those pauses descended, an uneasy recollection of how universal the ascending steps to sex were; how impersonal, or pre-personal. He pulled away abruptly, toward the unmade single bed, and knocked over a pile of books and documents relating to overpopulation.

"One of us has to leave at six to pick up Eduardo at the airport," he said. "Just want to note that."

"What time is it now?"

He turned her very dusty alarm clock to check. "Two-seventeen," he marveled. It was the strangest time he'd seen in his entire life.

"I apologize that the room is so messy," Lalitha said.

"I like it. I love how you are. Are you hungry? I'm a little hungry."

"No, Walter." She smiled. "I'm not hungry. But I can get you something."

"I was thinking, like, a glass of soy milk. Soy beverage."

"I'll get you one."

She went downstairs, and it was strange to think that the footsteps he heard coming back up, a minute later, belonged to the person who would take Patty's place in his life. She knelt by him and watched intently, greedily, as he drank down the soy milk. Then she unbuttoned his shirt with her nimble pale-nailed fingers. OK, then, he thought. OK. Forward. But as he undressed himself the rest of the way, the scenes of his wife's own infidelity, which she'd narrated so exhaustively, came churning up in him, bringing with them a faint but real impulse to forgive her; and he knew he had to crush this impulse. His hatred of her and his friend was still new-born and wavering, it hadn't hardened yet, the piteous sight and sound of her crying were still too fresh in his mind. Thankfully Lalitha had stripped down to a pair of red-polka-dotted white briefs. She was standing over him insouciantly, offering herself for inspection. Her body, in its youth, was preposterously fabulous. Unblemished, defiant of gravity, all but un-bearable to look at. It was true that he'd once known a woman's body even quite a bit younger, but he had no memory of it, he'd been too young himself to notice Patty's youth. He reached up and pressed the heel of his hand to the hot, clothed mound between Lalitha's legs. She gave a little cry, her knees buckled, and she sank onto him, bathing him in sweet agony.

The struggle not to compare began in earnest then, the struggle in particular to clear his head of Patty's sentence, "There was nothing so wrong with it." He could see, in retrospect, that his earlier plea that Lalitha go slow with him had been founded on accurate self-knowledge. But going slow, once he'd thrown Patty out of the house, was not an op-tion. He needed the quick fix simply in order to keep functioning—to not get leveled by hatred and self-pity—and, in one way, the fix was very sweet indeed, because Lalitha really was crazy for him, almost literally dripping with desire, certainly strongly seeping with it. She stared into his eyes with love and joy, she pronounced beautiful and perfect and won-derful the manhood that Patty in her document had libeled and spat upon. What wasn't to like? He was a man in his prime, she was adorable and young and insatiable; and this, in fact, was what wasn't to like. His emo-tions couldn't keep up with the vigor and urgency of their animal attrac-tion, the interminability of their coupling. She needed to ride him, she needed to be crushed underneath him, she needed to have her legs on his shoulders, she needed to do the Downward Dog and be whammed from behind, she needed bending over the bed, she needed her face pressed against the wall, she needed her legs wrapped around him and her head thrown back and her very round breasts flying every which way. It all seemed intensely meaningful to her, she was a bottomless well of anguished noise, and he was up for all of it. In good cardiovascular shape, thrilled by her extravagance, attuned to her wishes, and extremely fond of her. And yet it wasn't quite personal, and he couldn't find his way to orgasm. And this was very odd, an entirely new and unanticipated problem, due in part, perhaps, to his unfamiliarity with condoms, and to how unbelievably wet she was. How many times, in the last two years, had he brought himself off to the thought of his assistant, each time in a matter of minutes? A hundred times. His problem now was obviously psychological. Her alarm clock showed 3:52 when they finally subsided. It wasn't actually clear that she'd come, either, and he didn't dare ask her. And here, in his exhaustion, the lurking Contrast seized its opportunity to obtrude, for Patty, whenever she could be persuaded to interest herself, had pretty reliably got the job done for both of them, leaving them both reasonably content, leaving him free to go to work or read a book and her to do the little Pattyish things she liked to do. Her very difficulty created friction, and friction led to satisfaction . . .

Lalitha kissed his swollen mouth. "What are you thinking?"

"I don't know," he said. "Lots of things."

"Are you sorry we did this?"

"No, no, very happy."

"You don't look quite happy."

"Well, I did just throw my wife out of the house after twenty-four years of marriage. That did just happen a few hours ago."

"I'm sorry, Walter. You can still go back. I can quit and leave the two of you be."

"No, that's one thing I can promise you. I am never going back."

"Do you want to be with me?"

"Yes." He filled his hands with her black hair, which smelled of coconutty shampoo, and covered his face with it. He now had what he'd wanted, but it was making him somewhat lonely. After all his great longing, which was infinite in scope, he was in bed with a particular finite girl who was very pretty and brilliant and committed but also messy, disliked by Jessica, and no kind of cook. And she was all there was, the sole bulwark, between him and the multitude of thoughts he didn't want to have. The thought of Patty and his friend at Nameless Lake; the very human and witty way the two of them had spoken to each other; the grownup reciprocity of their sex; their gladness that he wasn't there. He began to cry into Lalitha's hair, and she comforted him, brushed his tears away, and they made love again more tiredly and painfully, until he did finally come, without fanfare, in her hand.

There ensued some difficult days. Eduardo Soquel, arriving from Colombia, was picked up at the airport and installed in "Joey's" bedroom. The press conference on Monday morning was attended by twelve journalists and survived by Walter and Soquel, and a separate lengthy phone interview was given to Dan Caperville of the *Times*. Walter, having worked in public relations all his life, was able to suppress his private turmoil and stay on message and decline inflammatory journalistic bait. The Pan-American Warbler Park, he said, represented a new paradigm of science-based, privately funded wildlife conservation; the undeniable ugliness of mountaintop-removal mining was more than offset by the prospect of sustainable "green employment" (ecotourism, reforestation, certified forestry) in West Virginia and Colombia; Coyle Mathis and the other displaced mountain people had fully and laudably cooperated with the Trust and would soon be employed by a subsidiary of the Trust's generous corporate partner LBI. Walter needed to exercise particular self-control in praising LBI, given what Joey had told him. When he got off the phone with Dan Caperville, he went out for a late dinner with Lalitha and Soquel and drank two beers, bringing to three his total lifetime consumption.

The next afternoon, after Soquel had returned to the airport, Lalitha locked the door of Walter's office and knelt down between his legs to reward him for his labors.

"No, no, no," he said, rolling the chair away from her.

She pursued him on her knees. "I just want to see you. I'm so greedy for you."

"Lalitha, no." He could hear his staffers going about their business at the front of the house.

"Just for a second," she said, unzipping him. "Please, Walter."

He thought of Clinton and Lewinsky, and then, seeing his assistant's mouth full of his flesh and her eyes smiling up at him, he thought of his evil friend's prophecy. It seemed to make her happy, and yet—

"No, I'm sorry," he said, pushing her away as gently as he could.

She frowned. She was hurt. "You have to let me," she said, "if you love me."

"I do love you, but this is not the right time."

"I want you to let me. I want to do everything right now."

"I'm sorry, but no."

He stood up and zipped himself back into his pants. Lalitha remained kneeling for a moment with her head bowed. Then she, too, stood up, smoothed her skirt on her thighs, and turned away in an attitude of unhappiness.

"There's a problem we have to talk about first," he said.

"All right. Let's talk about your problem."

"The problem is we have to fire Richard."

The name, which he'd refused to speak until now, hung in the air. "And why do we have to do that?" Lalitha said.

"Because I hate him, because he had an affair with my wife, and I never want to hear his name again, and there's no earthly way I'm going to work with him."

Lalitha seemed to shrink as she heard this. Her head sank, her shoulders slumped, she became a sad little girl. "Is that why your wife left on Sunday?"

"Yes."

"You're still in love with her, aren't you?"

"No!"

"Yes you are. That's why you don't want me near you now."

"No, that's not true. That's totally not true."

"Well, be that as it may," she said, straightening herself briskly, "we still can't fire Richard. This is my project, and I need him. I've already advertised him to the interns, and I need him to get our talent for August. So you can have your problem with him, and be very sorry about your wife, but I'm not firing him."

"Honey," Walter said. "Lalitha. I really do love you. Everything's going to be OK. But try to see this from my side."

"No!" she said, wheeling toward him with spirited insurrection. "I don't care about your side! My job is to do our population work, and I'm going to do it. If you really care about that work, and about me, you'll let me do it my way."

"I do care. I totally do. But—"

"But nothing, then. I won't mention his name again. You can go out of town somewhere when he meets with the interns in May. And we'll figure out August when we get there."

"But he's not going to want to do it. He was already talking on Saturday about backing out."

"Let me talk to him," she said. "As you may remember, I'm rather good at persuading people to do things they don't want to do. I'm a rather effective employee of yours, and I hope you'll be nice enough to let me do my work."

He rushed around his desk to put his arms around her, but she escaped to the outer office.

Because he loved her spirit and commitment and was stricken by her anger, he didn't press the issue further. But as the hours passed, and then several days, and she didn't report that Richard was backing out of Free Space, Walter deduced that he must still be on board. Richard who didn't believe in a fucking thing! The only imaginable explanation was that Patty had talked to him on the phone and guilted him into sticking with the program. And the idea of those two talking about anything at all, even for five minutes, and specifically talking about how to spare "poor Walter" (oh, that phrase of hers, that abominable phrase) and save his pet project, as some kind of consolation prize, made him sick with weakness and corruption and compromise and littleness. It came between him and Lalitha as well. Their lovemaking, though daily and protracted, was shadowed by his sense that she'd betrayed him with Richard, too, a little bit, and so did not become more personal in the way he'd hoped it might. Everywhere he turned, there was Richard.

Equally unsettling, in a different way, was the problem of LBI. Joey, at their dinner together, with moving expenditure of humility and self-reproach, had explained the sordid business deal he'd been involved with, and the key villain, as Walter saw it, was LBI. Kenny Bartles was clearly one of those daredevil clowns, a bush-league sociopath who would end up in jail or in Congress soon enough. The Cheney-Rumsfeld crowd, whatever the fetor of their motives for invading Iraq, surely still would have preferred to receive usable truck parts instead of the Paraguayan trash that Joey had delivered. And Joey himself, though he should have known better than to get involved with Bartles, had convinced Walter that he'd only followed through for Connie's sake; his loyalty to her, his terrible remorse, and his general bravery (he was twenty years old!) were all to his credit. The responsible party, therefore—the one with both full knowledge of the scam and the authority to approve it—was LBI. Walter hadn't heard of the vice president whom Joey had spoken to, the one who'd threatened him with a lawsuit, but the guy undoubtedly worked right down the hall from the buddy of Vin Haven who'd agreed to locate a body-armor plant in West Virginia. Joey had asked Walter, at dinner, what he thought he should do. Blow the whistle? Or just give away his profits to some charity for disabled veterans, and go back to school? Walter had promised to think about it over the weekend, but the weekend had not, to put it mildly, proved conducive to calm moral reflection. Not until he was facing the journalists on Monday morning, painting LBI as an outstanding pro-environment corporate partner, had the degree of his own implication hit him.

He tried, now, to separate his own interests—the fact that, if the son of the Trust's executive director took his ugly story to the media, Vin Haven might well fire him and LBI might even renege on its West Virginia agreement—from what was best for Joey. However arrogantly and greedily Joey had behaved, it seemed very harsh to ask a twenty-year-old kid with problematic parents to take full moral responsibility and endure a public smearing, maybe even prosecution. And yet Walter was aware that the advice he therefore wanted to give Joey—"Donate your profits to charity, move on with your life"—was highly beneficial to himself and to the Trust. He wanted to ask Lalitha for guidance, but he'd promised Joey not to tell a soul, and so he called Joey and said he was still thinking about it, and would he and Connie like to join him for dinner on his birthday next week?

"Definitely," Joey said.

"I also need to tell you," Walter said, "that your mother and I have separated. It's a hard thing to tell you, but it happened on Sunday. She's moved out for a while, and we're not sure what's going to happen next."

"Yep," Joey said.

*Yep?* Walter frowned. "Did you understand what I just said?"

"Yep. She already told me."

"Right. Of course. How not. And did she—"

"Yep. She told me a lot. Too much information, as always."

"So you understand my—"

"Yep."

"And you're still OK with having dinner on my birthday?"

"Yep. We'll definitely be there."

"Well, thank you, Joey. I love you for that. I love you for a lot of things."

"Yep."

Walter then left a message on Jessica's cell phone, as he'd done twice a day since the fateful Sunday, without yet hearing back from her. "Jessica, listen," he said. "I don't know if you've talked to your mother, but whatever she's saying to you, you need to call me back and listen to what I have to say. All right? Please call me back. There are very much two sides to this story, and I think you need to hear both of them." It would have been useful to be able to add that there was nothing between him and his assistant, but, in fact, his hands and face and nose were so impregnated with the smell of her vagina that it persisted faintly even after showering.

He was compromised and losing on every front. A further bad blow landed on the second Sunday of his freedom, in the form of a long front-page story in the *Times* by Dan Caperville: "Coal-Friendly Land Trust Destroys Mountains to Save Them." The story wasn't greatly inaccurate factually, but the *Times* was clearly not beguiled by Walter's contrarian view of MTR mining. The South American unit of the Warbler Park wasn't even mentioned in the article, and Walter's best talking points— new paradigm, green economy, science-based reclamation—were buried near the bottom, well below Jocelyn Zorn's description of him shouting "I own this [expletive] land!" and Coyle Mathis's recollection, "He called me stupid to my face." The article's take-away, besides the fact that Walter was an extremely disagreeable person, was that the Cerulean Mountain

Trust was in bed with the coal industry and the defense contractor LBI, was allowing large-scale MTR on its supposedly pristine reserve, was hated by local environmentalists, had displaced salt-of-the-earth country people from their ancestral homes, and had been founded and funded by a publicity-shy energy mogul, Vincent Haven, who, with the connivance of the Bush administration, was destroying other parts of West Virginia by drilling gas wells.

"Not so bad, not so bad," Vin Haven said when Walter called him at his home in Houston on Sunday afternoon. "We got our Warbler Park, nobody can take that away from us. You and your girl did good. As for the rest of it, you can see why I've never bothered talking to the press. It's all downside and no upside."

"I talked to Caperville for two hours," Walter said. "I really thought he was with me on the main points."

"Well, and your points are in there," Vin said. "Albeit not too conspicuously. But don't you worry about it."

"I am worried about it! I mean, yes, we got the park, which is great for the warbler. But the whole thing's supposed to be a *model*. This thing reads like a model of how *not* to do things."

"It'll blow over. Once we get the coal out and start reclaiming, people will see you were right. This Caperville fella will be writing obits by then."

"But that's going to be years!"

"You got other plans? Is that what this is about? You worried about your résumé?"

"No, Vin, I'm just frustrated with the media. The birds don't count for anything, it's all about the human interest."

"And that's the way it'll stay until the birds control the media," Vin said. "Am I going to see you in Whitmanville next month? I told Jim Elder I'd make an appearance at the armor-plant opening, provided I don't have to pose for any pictures. I could pick you up in the jet on the way there."

"Thanks, we'll fly commercial," Walter said. "Save some fuel."

"Try to remember I make a living selling fuel."

"Right, ha ha, good point."

It was nice to have Vin's fatherly approval, but it would have been nicer had Vin been seeming less dubious as a father. The worst thing about the *Times* piece—leaving aside the shame of looking like an asshole in a publication read and trusted by everyone Walter knew—was his fear that the *Times* was, in fact, right about the Cerulean Mountain Trust. He'd dreaded being slaughtered in the media, and now that he was being slaughtered he had to attend more seriously to his reasons for dreading it.

"I heard you doing that interview," Lalitha said. "You nailed it. The only reason the *Times* can't admit we're right is they'd have to take back all their editorials against MTR."

"That's what they're doing right now with Bush and Iraq, actually."

"Well, you've paid your dues. And now you and I get our little reward. Did you tell Mr. Haven we're going ahead with Free Space?"

"I was feeling lucky not to be fired," Walter said. "It didn't seem like the right moment to tell him I'm planning to spend the entire discretionary fund on something that'll probably get even worse publicity."

"Oh, my sweetheart," she said, embracing him, resting her head against his heart. "Nobody else understands what good things you're doing. I'm the only one."

"That may actually be true," he said.

He would have liked to just be held by her for a while, but her body had other ideas, and his own body agreed with them. They were spending their nights now on her too-small bed, since his own rooms were still full of Patty's traces, which she'd given him no instructions for dealing with and he couldn't begin to deal with on his own. It didn't surprise him that Patty hadn't been in touch, and yet it seemed tactical of her, adversarial, that she hadn't. For a person who, by her own admission, made nothing but mistakes, she cast a daunting shadow as she did whatever she was doing out there in the world. Walter felt cowardly to be hiding from her in Lalitha's room, but what else could he do? He was beset from all sides.

On his birthday, while Lalitha showed Connie the Trust offices, he took Joey into the kitchen and said he still didn't know what course of action to recommend. "I really don't think you should blow the whistle," he said. "But I don't trust my motives on that. I've sort of lost my moral bearings lately. The thing with your mother, and the thing in the *New York Times*—did you see that?"

"Yep," Joey said. He had his hands in his pockets and was still dressing like a College Republican, in a blue blazer and shiny loafers. For all Walter knew, he *was* a College Republican.

"I didn't come off very well, did I?"

"Nope," Joey said. "But I think most people could see it wasn't a fair article."

Walter gratefully, no questions asked, accepted this reassurance from his son. He was feeling very small indeed. "So I have to go to this LBI event in West Virginia next week," he said. "They're opening a body-armor plant that all those displaced families are going to be working at. And so I'm not really the right person to ask about LBI, because I'm so implicated myself."

"Why do you have to go to that?"

"I have to give a speech. I have to make grateful on behalf of the Trust."

"But you've already got your Warbler Park. Why not just blow it off?"

"Because there's this other big program Lalitha's doing with overpopulation, and I have to stay on good terms with my boss. It's his money we're spending."

"Sounds like you'd better go, then," Joey said.

He sounded unpersuaded, and Walter hated looking so weak and small to him. As if to make himself look even weaker and smaller, he asked if he knew what was up with Jessica.

"I talked to her," Joey said, hands in pockets, eyes on the floor. "I guess she's a little mad at you."

"I've left her like twenty phone messages!"

"You can probably stop doing that. I don't think she's listening to them. People don't listen to every cellphone message anyway, they just look to see who's called."

"Well, did you tell her that there are two sides to this story?"

Joey shrugged. "I don't know. Are there two sides?"

"Yes, there are! Your mother did a very bad thing to me. An incredibly painful thing."

"I don't really want any more information," Joey said. "I think she probably already told me about it anyway. I don't feel like taking sides."

"She told you about it *when?* How long ago?"

"Last week."

So Joey knew what Richard had done—what Walter had let his best friend, his rock-star friend, do. His smallening in his son's eyes was now complete. "I'm going to have a beer," he said. "Since it's my birthday."

"Can Connie and I have one, too?"

"Yes, that's why we asked you here early. Actually, Connie can drink whatever she wants at the restaurant, too. She's twenty-one, right?"

"Yep."

"And this is not nagging, this is just a request for information: did you tell Mom you're married?"

"Dad, I'm working on it," Joey said with a tightening of his jaw. "Let me do this my way, OK?"

Walter had always liked Connie (had even, secretly, rather liked Connie's mother, for how she'd flirted with him). She was wearing perilously high heels and heavy eye shadow for the occasion; she was still young enough to be trying to look much older. At La Chaumière, he observed with swelling heart how tenderly attentive Joey was to her, leaning over to read her menu with her and coordinate their selections, and how Connie, since Joey wasn't of legal age, declined Walter's offer of a cocktail and ordered a Diet Coke for herself. They had a tacit trusting way with each other, a way that reminded Walter of his and Patty's way when they were very young, the way of a couple united as a front against the world; his eyes misted up at the sight of their wedding bands. Lalitha, ill at ease, trying to distance herself from the young people and align herself with a man nearly twice her age, ordered a martini and proceeded to fill the conversational vacuum with talk of Free Space and the world population crisis, to which Joey and Connie listened with the exquisite courtesy of a couple secure in their two-person world. Although Lalitha avoided proprietary references to Walter, he had no doubt that Joey knew that she was more than simply his assistant. As he drank his third beer of the evening, he became more and more ashamed of what he'd done and more and more grateful to Joey for being so cool about it. Nothing had enraged him more about Joey, over the years, than his shell of coolness; and now, how glad of it he was! His son had won that war, and he was glad of it.

"So Richard's still working with you guys?" Joey said.

"Um, yes," Lalitha said. "Yes, he's being very helpful. In fact, he just told me the White Stripes might help us with our big event in August."

Joey, as he frowned and considered this, took care not to look at Walter.

"We should go to that event," Connie said to Joey. "Is it OK if we come?" she asked Walter.

"Of course it's OK," he said, forcing a smile. "Should be a lot of fun."

"I like the White Stripes a lot," she declared happily, in her subtext-less way.

"I like *you* a lot," Walter said. "I'm really glad you're part of our family. I'm really glad you're here tonight."

"I'm happy to be here, too."

Joey didn't seem to mind this sentimental talk, but his thoughts were clearly elsewhere. On Richard, on his mother, on the family disaster that was unfolding. And there was nothing Walter could say to make it any easier for him.

"I can't do it," Walter told Lalitha when they'd returned, by themselves, to the mansion. "I can't have that asshole involved anymore."

"We already had this discussion," she said, walking briskly down the corridor to the kitchen. "We already resolved this."

"Well, we need to have it again," he said, pursuing her.

"No, we don't. Did you see how Connie's face lit up when I mentioned the White Stripes? Who else can get us talent like that? We made our decision, it was a good one, and I really don't need to hear how jealous you are of the person your wife had sex with. I'm tired, and I drank too much, and I need to go to bed now."

"He was my best friend," Walter murmured.

"I don't care. I really don't, Walter. I know you think I'm just another young person, but in fact I'm older than your children, I'm almost twenty-eight. I knew it was a mistake to fall in love with you. I knew you weren't ready, and now I'm in love with you, and all you can still think about is her."

"I think about you constantly. I depend on you so much."

"You have sex with me because I want you and you can. But everybody's world still revolves around your wife. What is so special about her, I will never understand. She spends her whole life upsetting other people. And

I just need a little break from it, so I can get some sleep. So maybe you should sleep in your own bed tonight, and think about what you want to do."

"What did I say?" he pleaded. "I thought we were having a nice birthday."

"I'm tired. It was a tiring evening. I'll see you in the morning."

They parted without a kiss. On his home phone he found a message from Jessica, timed carefully while he was out to dinner, wishing him a happy birthday. "I'm sorry I haven't returned your messages," she said, "I've just been really busy and not sure what I wanted to say. But I was thinking of you today, and I hope you had a nice day. Maybe we can talk sometime, although I'm not sure when I'm going to have a chance."

Click.

It was a relief, for the next week, to sleep by himself. To be in a room still full of Patty's clothes and books and pictures, to learn to steel himself against her. During the daytime, there was plenty of deferred office work to do: land-management structures to be organized in Colombia and West Virginia, a media counteroffensive to be launched, fresh donors to be sought. Walter had even thought it might be possible to take a break from sex with Lalitha, but their daily propinquity made it not possible—they needed and needed. He did, however, repair to his own bed for sleep.

The night before they flew to West Virginia, he was packing his overnight bag and got a call from Joey, who reported that he'd decided not to blow the whistle on LBI and Kenny Bartles. "They're disgusting," he said. "But my friend Jonathan keeps saying I'd only be hurting myself if I went public. So I'm thinking I'll just give the extra money away. It'll spare me a lot of taxes at least. But I wanted to make sure you still think it's OK."

"It's fine, Joey," Walter said. "It's fine with me. I know how ambitious you are, I know how hard it must be to give away all that money. That's a lot to do right there."

"Well, it's not like I'm behind on the deal. I'm just not ahead. And now Connie can go back to school, so that's good. I'm thinking of taking a year off to work and let her catch up with me."

"That's great. It's great to see the two of you taking care of each other like that. Was there anything else?"

"Well, only that I saw Mom."

Walter was still holding two neckties, a red one and a green one, that he'd been trying to choose between. The choice, he realized, was not particularly consequential. "You did?" he said, choosing the green one. "Where? In Alexandria?"

"No, in New York."

"So she's in New York."

"Well, actually, Jersey City," Joey said.

Walter's chest tightened and stayed tightened.

"Yeah, Connie and I wanted to tell her in person. You know, about being married. And it wasn't so bad actually. She was actually fairly nice to Connie. You know, still patronizing, and sort of fake, the way she kept laughing, but not mean. I guess she's distracted with a lot of other things. Anyway, we thought it went pretty well. At least Connie thought so. I thought it was kind of ehhnh. But I wanted you to know she knows, so, I don't know, if you ever talk to her, you don't have to keep it secret anymore."

Walter looked at his left hand, which had turned white and looked very bare without its wedding ring. "She's staying with Richard," he managed to say.

"Um, yeah, I guess, for the moment," Joey said. "Was I not supposed to say that?"

"Was he there? When you were there?"

"Yeah, actually. He was. And it was fun for Connie, because she's fairly into his music. He let her see his guitars and everything. I don't know if I told you she's thinking of learning guitar. She's got a really pretty singing voice."

Where exactly Walter had thought Patty was staying he couldn't have said. With her friend Cathy Schmidt, with one of her other old teammates, maybe with Jessica, conceivably even with her parents. But having heard her proclaim so *righteously* that everything was over between her and Richard, he hadn't imagined for one second that she might be in Jersey City.

"Dad?"

"What."

"Well, I know it's weird, OK? The whole thing is very weird. But you've got a girlfriend, too, right? So, like, that's it, right? Things are different now, and we should all just start dealing with it. Don't you think?"

"Yeah," Walter said. "You're right. We need to deal with it."

As soon as he was off the phone, he pulled open a dresser drawer, took his wedding ring from the cuff-link box in which he'd left it, and flushed it down the toilet. With a sweep of his arm, he knocked all of Patty's pictures from the top of her dresser—Joey and Jessica as innocents, team photos of girl basketball players in heartbreakingly seventies-style uniforms, her favorite and most flattering pictures of him—and crushed and ground the frames and glass with his feet until he lost interest and had to beat his head against the wall. Hearing that she'd gone back to Richard ought to have liberated him, ought to have freed him to enjoy Lalitha with the cleanest of consciences. But it didn't feel like a liberation, it felt like a death. He could see now (as Lalitha herself had seen all along) that the last three weeks had merely been a kind of payback, a treat he was due in recompense for Patty's betrayal. Despite his avowals that the marriage was over, he hadn't believed it one tiny bit. He threw himself onto the bed and sobbed in a state to which all previous states of existence seemed infinitely preferable. The world was moving ahead, the world was full of winners, LBI and Kenny Bartles cashing in, Connie going back to school, Joey doing the right thing, Patty living with a rock star, Lalitha fighting her good fight, Richard going back to his music, Richard getting great press for being far more offensive than Walter, Richard charming Connie, Richard bringing in the White Stripes . . . while Walter was left behind with the dead and dying and forgotten, the endangered species of the world, the nonadaptive . . .

Around two in the morning, he staggered into the bathroom and found an old bottle of Patty's trazodones eighteen months past their expiration date. He took three of them, unsure if they were still effective, but apparently they were: he was awakened at seven o'clock by Lalitha's very determined shoving. He was still in yesterday's clothes, the lights were all burning, the room had been trashed, his throat was raw from his presumably violent snoring, and his head ached for any number of good reasons.

"We need to be in a cab right now," Lalitha said, pulling on his arm. "I thought you were ready."

480

"Can't go," he said.

"Come on, we're already late."

He righted himself and tried to make his eyes stay open. "I should really take a shower."

"There's no time."

He fell asleep in the cab and woke up still in the cab, on the parkway, in traffic stalled by an accident. Lalitha was on her phone with the airline. "We have to go through Cincinnati now," she told him. "We missed our flight."

"Why don't we just bag it," he said. "I'm tired of being Mr. Good."

"We'll skip the lunch and go straight to the factory."

"What if I were Mr. Bad? Would you still like me?"

She gave him a worried frown. "Walter, did you take some kind of pill?"

"Seriously. Would you still like me?"

Her frown intensified, and she didn't answer. He fell asleep in the gate area at National; on the plane to Cincinnati; in Cincinnati; on the plane to Charleston; and in the rental car that Lalitha piloted at high speeds to Whitmanville, where he awoke feeling better, suddenly hungry, to an overcast April sky and a biotically desolate countryscape of the sort that America had come to specialize in. Vinyl-sided megachurches, a Walmart, a Wendy's, capacious left-turn lanes, white automotive fortresses. Nothing for a wild bird to like around here unless the bird was a starling or a crow. The body-armor plant (ARDEE ENTERPRISES, AN LBI FAMILY OF COMPANIES COMPANY) was in a large cinder-block structure whose freshly rolled asphalt parking lot was ragged at the edges, crumbling into weeds. The lot was filling up with large passenger vehicles, including a black Navigator from which Vin Haven and some suits were emerging just as Lalitha screeched the rental car to a halt.

"Sorry we missed the lunch," she said to Vin.

"I think dinner's going to be the better meal," Vin said. "Got to hope so, after what we saw for lunch."

Inside the plant were pleasant strong smells of paint, plastics, and new machinery. Walter noted the absence of windows, the reliance on electric lighting. Folding chairs and a podium had been set up against a backdrop of towering shrink-wrapped oblongs of raw material. A hundred or so West Virginians were milling about, among them Coyle Mathis, who was wearing a baggy sweatshirt and even baggier jeans that looked so new he might have bought them at Walmart on his way over. Two local TV crews had cameras trained on the podium and the banner that hung above it: JOBS + NATIONAL SECURITY = JOB SECURITY.

Vin Haven ("You can Nexis me all night without finding one direct quote from my forty-seven years in business") sat down directly behind the cameras, while Walter took from Lalitha a copy of the speech that he'd written and she'd vetted, and joined the other suits—Jim Elder, senior vice president at LBI, and Roy Dennett, CEO of his eponymous subsidiary—in the chairs behind the podium. In the front row of the audience, with his arms crossed high on his chest, was Coyle Mathis. Walter hadn't seen him since their ill-fated encounter in Mathis's front yard (which was now a barren field of rubble). He was staring at Walter with a look that reminded Walter, again, of his father. The look of a man attempting to preempt, with the ferocity of his contempt, any possibility of his own embarrassment or of Walter's pity for him. It made Walter sad for him. While Jim Elder, at the mike, commenced praising our brave soldiers in Iraq and Afghanistan, Walter gave Mathis a meek smile, to show that he was sad for him, sad for both of them. But Mathis's expression didn't change, and he didn't stop staring.

"I think we have a few remarks now from the Cerulean Mountain Trust," Jim Elder said, "which is responsible for bringing all these wonderful, sustainable jobs to Whitmanville and the local economy. Please join me in welcoming Walter Berglund, executive director of the Trust. Walter?"

His sadness for Mathis had become a more general sadness, a world sadness, a life sadness. As he stood at the podium, he sought out Vin Haven and Lalitha, who were sitting together, and gave them each a small smile of regret and apology. Then he bent himself to the mike.

"Thank you," he said. "Welcome. Welcome especially to Mr. Coyle Mathis and the other men and women of Forster Hollow who are going to be employed at this rather strikingly energy-inefficient plant. It's a long way from Forster Hollow, isn't it?"

Aside from low-level systems hum, there was no sound but the echoing of his amplified voice. He glanced quickly at Mathis, whose expression remained fixed in contempt.

"So, yes, welcome," he said. "Welcome to the middle class! That's what I want to say. Although, quickly, before I go any further, I also want to say to Mr. Mathis here in the front row: I know you don't like me. And I don't like you. But, you know, back when you were refusing to have anything to do with us, I respected that. I didn't like it, but I had respect for your position. For your independence. You see, because I actually came from a place a little bit like Forster Hollow myself, before I joined the middle class. And now you're middle-class, too, and I want to welcome you all, because it's a wonderful thing, our American middle class. It's the mainstay of economies all around the globe!"

He could see Lalitha whispering to Vin.

"And now that you've got these jobs at this *body-armor plant*," he continued, "you're going to be able to participate in those economies. You, too, can help denude every last scrap of native habitat in Asia, Africa, and South America! You, too, can buy six-foot-wide plasma TV screens that consume unbelievable amounts of energy, even when they're not turned on! But that's OK, because that's why we threw you out of your homes in the first place, so we could strip-mine your ancestral hills and feed the coal-fired generators that are the number-one cause of global warming and other excellent things like acid rain. It's a perfect world, isn't it? It's a perfect system, because as long as you've got your six-foot-wide plasma TV, and the electricity to run it, you don't have to think about any of the ugly consequences. You can watch *Survivor: Indonesia* till there's no more Indonesia!"

Coyle Mathis was the first to boo. He was quickly joined by many others. Peripherally, over his shoulder, Walter could see Elder and Dennett standing up.

"Just quickly, here," he continued, "because I want to keep my remarks brief. Just a few more remarks about this perfect world. I want to mention those big new eight-miles-per-gallon vehicles you're going to be able to buy and drive as much as you want, now that you've joined me as a member of the middle class. The reason this country needs so much body armor is that certain people in certain parts of the world don't want us stealing all their oil to run your vehicles. And so the more you drive your vehicles, the more secure your jobs at this body-armor plant are going to be! Isn't that perfect?"

The audience had stood up and begun to shout back at him, telling him to shut up.

"That's enough," Jim Elder said, trying to pull him away from the mike.

"Just a couple more things!" Walter cried, wresting the mike from its holder and dancing away with it. "I want to welcome you all to working for one of the most corrupt and savage corporations in the world! Do you hear me? LBI doesn't give a *shit* about your sons and daughters bleeding in Iraq, as long as they get their thousand-percent profit! I know this for a fact! I have the facts to prove it! That's part of the perfect middle-class world you're joining! Now that you're working for LBI, you can finally make enough money to keep your kids from joining the Army and dying in LBI's broken-down trucks and shoddy body armor!"

The mike had gone dead, and Walter skittered backwards, away from the mob that was forming. "And MEANWHILE," he shouted, "WE ARE ADDING THIRTEEN MILLION HUMAN BEINGS TO THE POPULATION EVERY MONTH! THIRTEEN MILLION MORE PEOPLE TO KILL EACH OTHER IN COMPETITION OVER FINITE RESOURCES! AND WIPE OUT EVERY OTHER LIVING THING ALONG THE WAY! IT IS A PERFECT FUCKING WORLD AS LONG AS YOU DON'T COUNT EVERY OTHER SPECIES IN IT! WE ARE A CANCER ON THE PLANET! A CANCER ON THE PLANET!"

Here he was slugged in the jaw by Coyle Mathis himself. He reeled sideways, his vision filling with magnesium-flare insects, his glasses lost, and decided that perhaps he'd said enough. He was now surrounded by Mathis and a dozen other men, and they began to inflict really serious pain. He fell to the floor, trying to escape through a forest of legs kicking him with their Chinese-made sneakers. He curled into a ball, temporarily deaf and blind, his mouth full of blood and at least one broken tooth, and absorbed more kicks. Then the kicks subsided and other hands were on him, including Lalitha's. As sound returned, he could hear her raging, "*Get away from him! Get away from him!*" He gagged and spat a mouthful of blood onto the floor. She let her hair fall in the blood as she peered into his face. "Are you all right?"

He smiled as well as he could. "Starting to feel better."

"Oh, my boss. My poor dear boss."

"Definitely feeling better."


It was the season of migration, of flight and song and sex. Down in the neotropics, where diversity was as great as anywhere on earth, a few hundred bird species grew restless and left behind the several thousand other species, many of them close taxonomic relatives, that were content to stay put and crowdedly coexist and reproduce at their tropical leisure. Among the hundreds of South American tanager species, exactly four took off for the United States, risking the disasters of travel for the bounty of things to eat and places to nest in temperate woods in summer. Cerulean warblers winged their way up along the coasts of Mexico and Texas and fanned into the hardwoods of Appalachia and the Ozarks. Ruby-throated hummingbirds fattened themselves on the flowers of Veracruz and flew eight hundred miles across the Gulf, burning up half their body weight, and landed in Galveston to catch their breath. Terns came up from one subarctic to the other, swifts took airborne naps and never landed, song-filled thrushes waited for a southern wind and then flew nonstop for twelve hours, traversing whole states in a night. High-rises and power lines and wind turbines and cellphone towers and road traffic mowed down millions of migrants, but millions more made it through, many of them returning to the very same tree they'd nested in the year before, the same ridgeline or wetland they'd been fledged on, and there, if they were male, began to sing. Each year, they arrived to find more of their former homes paved over for parking lots or highways, or logged over for pallet wood, or developed into subdivisions, or stripped bare for oil drilling or coal mining, or fragmented for shopping centers, or plowed under for ethanol production, or miscellaneously denatured for ski runs and bike trails and golf courses. Migrants exhausted by their five-thousand-mile journey competed with earlier arrivals for the remaining scraps of territory; they searched in vain for a mate, they gave up on nesting and subsisted without breeding, they were killed for sport by free-roaming cats.

But the United States was still a rich and relatively young country, and pockets full of bird life could still be found if you went looking.

Which Walter and Lalitha, at the end of April, in a van loaded with camping equipment, set out to do. They had a free month before their work with Free Space commenced in earnest, and their responsibilities to the Cerulean Mountain Trust had ended. As for their carbon footprint, in a gas-thirsty van, Walter took some comfort in having commuted on bicycle or on foot for the last twenty-five years, and in no longer owning any residence besides the little closed-up house at Nameless Lake. He felt he was owed one petroleum splurge after a lifetime of virtue, one nature-filled summer in payment for the summer he'd been deprived of as a teenager.

While he'd still been in the Whitman County hospital, having his dislocated jaw and split-open face and bruised ribs attended to, Lalitha had desperately spun his outburst as a *trazodone-induced psychotic break.* "He was literally sleepwalking," she pleaded to Vin Haven. "I don't know how many trazodones he took, but it was more than one, and just a few hours earlier. He literally didn't know what he was saying. It was *my* fault for letting him make the speech. You should fire *me,* not him."

"Sounded to me like he had a pretty good idea what he was saying," Vin replied, with surprisingly little anger. "It's a pity he had to overintellectualize like that. He did such good work, and then he had to go and intellectualize it."

Vin had organized a conference call with his trustees, who had rubber-stamped his proposal to terminate Walter immediately, and he'd instructed his lawyers to exercise his repurchase option on the Berglunds' condominium portion of the mansion in Georgetown. Lalitha notified the applicants for Free Space internships that her funding had been cut off, that Richard Katz was withdrawing from the project (Walter, from his hospital bed, had finally prevailed on this), and that the very existence of Free Space was in doubt. Some of the applicants e-mailed back to cancel their applications; two of them said they still hoped to volunteer; the rest did not reply at all. Because Walter was facing eviction from the mansion and refused to speak to his wife, Lalitha called her for him. Patty arrived with a rented van a few days later, while Walter hid out at the nearest Starbucks, and packed up the belongings she didn't want put in storage.

It was at the end of that very unpleasant day, after Patty had departed and Walter had returned from caffeinated exile, that Lalitha checked her BlackBerry and found eighty new messages from young people all over the country, inquiring whether it was too late to volunteer for Free Space. Their e-mail addresses had more piquant flavors than the liberalkid@expensivecollege.edus of the earlier applicants. They were freakinfreegan and iedtarget, they were pornfoetal and jainboy3 and jwlindhjr, @gmail and @cruzio. By the following morning, there were a hundred more messages, along with offers from garage bands in four cities—Seattle, Missoula, Buffalo, and Detroit—to help organize Free Space events in their communities.

What had happened, as Lalitha soon figured out, was that the local TV footage of Walter's rant and the ensuing riot had gone viral. It had lately become possible to stream video over the internet, and the Whitmanville clip (CancerOnThePlanet.wmv) had flashed across the radical fringes of the blogosphere, the sites of 9/11-conspiracy-mongers and the tree-sitters and the Fight Club devotees and the PETA-ites, one of whom had then unearthed the link to Free Space on the Cerulean Mountain Trust's website. And overnight, despite having lost its funding and its musical headliner, Free Space acquired a bona-fide fan base and, in the person of Walter, a hero.

It was a long time since he'd done much giggling, but he was giggling all the time now, and then groaning because his ribs hurt. He went out one afternoon and came home with a used white Econoline van and a can of green spray paint and crudely wrote FREE SPACE on the van's flanks and rear end. He wanted to go ahead and spend his own money, from the impending proceeds of the house sale, to fund the group through the summer, to print up literature and pay a pittance to the interns and offer some prize money to the battling bands, but Lalitha foresaw potential divorce-related legal issues and wouldn't let him. Whereupon Joey, altogether unexpectedly, after learning of his father's summer plans, wrote Free Space a check for $100,000.

"This is ridiculous, Joey," Walter said. "I can't take this."

"Sure you can," Joey said. "The rest is going to veterans, but Connie and I think your cause is interesting, too. You took care of me when I was little, right?"

"Yes, because you were my *child.* That's what parents do. We don't expect repayment. You never quite seemed to understand that concept."

"But isn't it funny that I can do this? Isn't it a pretty good joke? This is just Monopoly money. It's meaningless to me."

"I have my own savings I could spend if I wanted to."

"Well, you can save that for when you're old," Joey said. "It's not like I'm going to be giving everything to charity when I start making money in a real way. This is special circumstances."

Walter was so proud of Joey, so grateful not to be fighting him anymore, and so inclined, therefore, to let him be the big guy, that he didn't fight him on the check. The one real mistake he made was to mention it to Jessica. She had finally spoken to him when he'd landed in the hospital, but her tone made it clear that she wasn't ready to be friends yet with Lalitha. She was also unimpressed with what he'd said in Whitmanville. "Even leaving aside the fact that 'cancer on the planet' is *exactly* the kind of phrase we all agreed was counterproductive," she said, "I don't think you picked the right enemy. You're sending a really unhelpful message when you pit the environment against uneducated people who are trying to improve their lives. I mean, I know you don't like those people. But you have to try to hide that, not lead with it." In a later phone call, she made an impatient reference to her brother's Republicanism, and Walter insisted that Joey was a different person since he'd married Connie. In fact, he said, Joey was now a major contributor to Free Space.

"And where did he get the money?" Jessica said immediately.

"Well, it's not that much," Walter backpedaled, realizing his mistake. "We're a tiny group, you know, so everything's relative. It's just, symbolically, that he's giving us anything at all—it says a lot about how he's changed."

"Hm."

"I mean, it's nothing like your contribution. Yours was huge. Spending that weekend with us, helping us create the concept. That was huge."

"And now what?" she said. "Are you going to grow your hair long and start wearing a do-rag? Riding around in your van? Doing the whole midlife thing? Do we have that to look forward to? Because I would like to be the still, small voice that says I liked you the old way you were."

"I promise not to grow my hair out. I promise no do-rag. I will not embarrass you."

"I'm afraid the horse may already be out of that particular barn."

Perhaps it was bound to happen: she was sounding more and more like Patty. Her anger would have grieved him more had he not been so enjoying, every minute of every day, the love of a woman who wanted all of him. His happiness was reminiscent of his early years with Patty, their days of teamwork in child-raising and house renovation, but he was much more present to himself now, more vividly and granularly appreciative of his happiness, and Lalitha was not the worry and enigma and headstrong stranger that Patty, at some level, had always remained to him. With Lalitha, what you saw was what you got. Their time in bed, as soon as he'd recovered from his injuries, became the thing he'd always missed without knowing he was missing it.

After movers had removed all traces of the Berglunds from the mansion, he and Lalitha struck out in the van toward Florida, intending to sweep westward across the country's southern belly before the weather got too warm. He was intent on showing her a bittern, and they found their first one at Corkscrew Swamp in Florida, beside a shady pool and a boardwalk creaking with the weight of retirees and tourists, but it was a bittern without bitternness, standing in plain sight while the strobing of tourist cameras bounced off its irrelevant camouflage. Walter insisted on driving the dirt-surfaced dikes of Big Cypress in search of a real bittern, a shy one, and treated Lalitha to an extended rant about the ecological damage wreaked by recreational ATVers, the brethren of Coyle Mathis and Mitch Berglund. Somehow, despite the damage, the scrub jungle and black-water pools were still full of birds, as well as countless alligators. Walter finally spotted a bittern in a marsh littered with shotgun shells and sun-bleached Budweiser packaging. Lalitha braked the van in a cloud of dust and duly admired the bird through her binoculars until a flatbed truck loaded with three ATVs roared past.

She'd never camped before, but she was game for it and impossibly sexy to Walter in her breathable safariwear. It helped that she was immune to sunburn and as repellent of mosquitoes as he was attractant. He tried to teach her some rudiments of cooking, but she preferred the tasks of tent assembly and route planning. He got up every morning before dawn, made espresso in their six-cup pot, and carried a soy latte back into the tent for her. Then they went out walking in the dew and the honey-colored light. She didn't share his feelings for wildlife, but she had a knack for spotting little birds in dense foliage, she studied the field guides, and she crowed with delight when she caught and corrected his false identifications. Later in the morning, when avian life quieted down, they drove some hours farther west and sought out hotel parking lots with unencrypted wireless connections, so that she could coordinate by e-mail with her prospective interns and he could write entries for the blog that she'd set up for him. Then another state park, another picnic dinner, another ecstatic round of grappling in the tent.

"Have you had enough of this?" he said one night, at an especially pretty and empty campground in the mesquite country of southwest Texas. "We could check into a motel for a week, swim in the pool, do our work."

"No, I love seeing how much you enjoy looking for animals," she said. "I love seeing you happy, after all that time when you were so unhappy. I love being on the road with you."

"But maybe you've had enough of it?"

"Not yet," she said, "although I don't think I really get nature. Not the way you do. To me it seems like such a violent thing. That crow that was eating the sparrow babies, those flycatchers, the raccoon eating those eggs, the hawks killing everything. People talk about the peacefulness of nature, but to me it seems the opposite of peaceful. It's constant killing. It's even worse than human beings."

"To me," Walter said, "the difference is that birds are only killing because they have to eat. They're not doing it angrily, they're not doing it wantonly. It's not *neurotic*. To me that's what makes nature peaceful. Things live or they don't live, but it's not all poisoned with resentment and neurosis and ideology. It's a relief from my own neurotic anger."

"But you don't even seem angry anymore."

"That's because I'm with you every minute of the day, and I'm not so compromised, and I'm not having to deal with people. I suspect the anger will come back."

"I don't care for my sake if it does," she said. "I respect your reasons for being angry. They're part of why I love you. But it just makes me so happy to see you happy."

"I keep thinking you can't get any more perfect," he said, taking her by the shoulders. "And then you say something even more perfect."

In truth, he was troubled by the irony of his situation. By finally venting his anger, first to Patty and then in Whitmanville, and thereby extricating himself from his marriage and from the Trust, he'd removed two major causes of the anger. For a while, in his blog, he'd tried to downplay and qualify his cancer-on-the-planet "heroism" and emphasize that the villain was the System, not the people of Forster Hollow. But his fans had so roundly and voluminously chided him for this (**"grow some balls man, your speech totally rocked,"** etc.) that he came to feel he owed them an honest airing of every venomous thought he'd entertained while driving around West Virginia, every hard-core antigrowth opinion he'd ever swallowed in the name of professionalism. He'd been storing up incisive arguments and damning data ever since he was in college; the least he could do now was share it with young people to whom it actually, miraculously, seemed to matter. The loony rage of his readership was worrisome, however, and discordant with his peaceable mood. Lalitha, for her part, had her hands full in sifting through hundreds of new intern applicants and phoning the ones who seemed most apt to be responsible and nonviolent; almost all the ones she deemed uncrazy were young women. Her commitment to fighting overpopulation was as practical and humanitarian as Walter's was abstract and misanthropic, and it was a measure of his deepening love for her how much he envied her and wished he could be more like her.

On the day before the last destination of their pleasure trip—Kern County, California, home to dazzling numbers of breeding songbirds—they stopped to see Walter's brother Brent in the town of Mojave, near the air base where he was stationed. Brent, who had never married, and whose personal and political hero was Senator John McCain, and whose emotional development seemed to have ended with his enlistment in the Air Force, could hardly have been more perfectly uninterested in Walter's separation from Patty or his involvement with Lalitha, whom he addressed more than once as "Lisa." He did pick up the tab for lunch, though, and he had news of their brother, Mitch. "I was thinking," he said, "if Mom's house is still empty, you might want to let Mitch use it for a while. He doesn't have a phone or an address, I know he's still drinking, and he's about five years delinquent in his child support. You know, he and Stacy had another kid right before they split up."

"How many does that make," Walter said. "Six?"

"No, just five. Two with Brenda, one with Kelly, two with Stacy. I don't think it helps to send money, because he only drinks it. But I was thinking he could use a place to stay."

"That's very thoughtful of you, Brent."

"I'm just saying. I know your situation with him. Just, you know, if the house is empty anyway."

Five was an appropriate-sized brood for a songbird, since birds were everywhere being persecuted and routed by humanity, but not for a human being, and the number made it harder for Walter to feel sorry for Mitch. Imperfectly hidden at the back of his mind was a wish that everybody else in the world would reproduce a little less, so that he might reproduce a little more, *once* more, with Lalitha. The wish, of course, was shameful: he was the leader of an antigrowth group, he'd already had two kids at a demographically deplorable young age, he was no longer disappointed in his son, he was almost old enough to be a grandfather. And still he couldn't stop imagining making Lalitha big with child. It was at the root of all their fucking, it was the meaning encoded in how beautiful he found her body.

"No, no, no, honey," she said, smiling, nose to nose with him, when he brought it up in their tent, in a Kern County campground. "This is what you get with me. You knew that. I'm not like other girls. I'm a freak like you're a freak, just in a different way. I made that clear, didn't I?"

"You absolutely did. I was just checking."

"Well, you can check, but the answer will always be the same."

"Do you know why? Why you're different?"

"No, but I know what I am. I'm the girl that doesn't want a baby. That's my mission in the world. That's my message."

"I love what you are."

"Then let this be the thing that isn't perfect for you."

They spent the month of June in Santa Cruz, where Lalitha's best college friend, Lydia Han, was a grad student in literature. They crashed on her floor, then they camped in her back yard, then they camped in the redwoods. Using Joey's money, Lalitha had bought plane tickets for the twenty interns she'd chosen. Lydia Han's faculty adviser, Chris Connery, a wild-haired Marxist and China scholar, allowed the interns to unroll their sleeping bags on his lawn and use his bathrooms, and he provided the Free Space cadre with a campus conference room for three days of intensive training and planning. Walter's apparent fascination to the eighteen girls among them—dreadlocked or scalped, harrowingly pierced and/or tattooed, their collective fertility so intense he could almost smell it—made him blush constantly as he preached to them the evils of unchecked population growth. He was relieved to escape and go hiking with Professor Connery in the free spaces surrounding Santa Cruz, through the brown hills and dripping redwood glades, listen to Connery's optimistic prophecies of global economic collapse and workers' revolution, see the unfamiliar birds of coastal California, and meet some of the young freegans and radical collectivists who were living on public lands in principled squalor. I should have been a college professor, he thought.

Only in July, when they forsook the safety of Santa Cruz and hit the road again, were they immersed in the rage that was gripping the country that summer. Why the conservatives, who controlled all three branches of the federal government, were still so enraged—at respectful skeptics of the Iraq War, at gay couples who wanted to get married, at bland Al Gore and cautious Hillary Clinton, at endangered species and their advocates, at taxes and gas prices that were among the lowest of any industrialized nation, at a mainstream media whose corporate owners were themselves conservative, at the Mexicans who cut their grass and washed their dishes—was somewhat mysterious to Walter. His father had been enraged like that, of course, but in a much more liberal era. And the conservative rage had engendered a left-wing counter-rage that practically scorched off his eyebrows at the Free Space events in Los Angeles and San Francisco. Among the young people he spoke to, the all-purpose epithet for everyone from George Bush and Tim Russert to Tony Blair and John Kerry was "shithead." That 9/11 had been orchestrated by Halliburton and the Saudi royal family was a near-universal article of faith. Three different garage bands performed songs in which they artlessly fantasized about torturing and killing the president and vice president (*I shit in your mouth / Big Dick, it feels pretty nice / Yeah, little Georgie / A gunshot to the temple will suffice*). Lalitha had impressed on the interns and especially on Walter the need to be disciplined in their message, to stick to the facts about overpopulation, to stake out the biggest possible tent. But without the draw of name-brand acts such as Richard might have provided, the events mostly attracted the already persuaded fringe, the sort of discontents who hit the streets in ski masks to riot against the WTO. Every time Walter took the stage, he was cheered for his Whitmanville meltdown and his intemperate blog entries, but as soon as he spoke of being smart and letting the facts argue for themselves, the crowds went quiet or started chanting the more incendiary words of his that they preferred—"Cancer on the planet!" "Fuck the pope!" In Seattle, where the mood was especially ugly, he left the stage to scattered booing. He was better received in the Midwest and South, particularly in the college towns, but the crowds were also much smaller. By the time he and Lalitha reached Athens, Georgia, he was having a hard time getting up in the morning. He was worn out by the road and oppressed by the thought that the country's ugly rage was no more than an amplified echo of his own anger, and that he'd let his personal grudge against Richard cheat Free Space out of a broader fan base, and that he was spending money of Joey's that would better have been given to Planned Parenthood. If it hadn't been for Lalitha, who was doing most of the driving and all of the enthusiasm-providing, he might have abandoned the tour and just gone birdwatching.

"I know you're discouraged," Lalitha said while driving out of Athens. "But we're definitely getting the issue on the radar. The free weeklies all print our talking points verbatim in their previews for us. The bloggers and the online reviews all talk about overpopulation. One day, there hasn't been any public talk about it since the seventies. Then suddenly, the next day, there's talk. The idea is suddenly out there in the world. New ideas always take hold on the fringes. Just because it's not always pretty, you shouldn't be discouraged."

"I saved a hundred square miles in West Virginia," he said. "Even more than that in Colombia. That was good work, with real results. Why didn't I keep doing it?"

"Because you knew it's not enough. The only thing that's really going to save us is to get people to change the way they think."

He looked at his girlfriend, her firm hands on the steering wheel, her bright eyes on the road, and thought he might burst with his desire to be like her; with gratitude that she didn't mind that he was himself instead. "My problem is I don't like people enough," he said. "I don't really believe they can change."

"You do so like people. I've never seen you be mean to one. You can't stop smiling when you talk to people."

"I wasn't smiling in Whitmanville."

"Actually, you were. Even there. That was part of the weirdness of it."

There weren't many birds to watch in the dog days anyway. Once territory had been claimed and breeding accomplished, it was to no small bird's advantage to make itself conspicuous. Walter took morning walks in refuges and parks that he knew were still full of life, but the overgrown weeds and heavily leafed trees stood motionless in the summer humidity, like houses locked against him, like couples who had eyes for nobody but themselves. The northern hemisphere was soaking up the sun's energy, plant life silently converting it to food for animals, the burring and whining of insects the only sonic by-product. This was the time of payoff for the neotropical migrants, these were the days that needed to be seized. Walter envied them for having a job to do, and he wondered if he was becoming depressed because this was the first summer in forty years he hadn't had to work.

The national Free Space battle of the bands was scheduled to happen on the last weekend in August and, unfortunately, in West Virginia. The state was uncentrally located and hard to reach by public transportation, but by the time Walter had proposed changing the location, on his blog, his fans were already excited about traveling to West Virginia and shaming it for its high birth rates, its ownership by the coal industry, its large population of Christian fundamentalists, and its responsibility for tipping the 2000 election in George Bush's favor. Lalitha had asked Vin Haven for permission to hold the event on the Trust-owned former goat farm she'd always had in mind for it, and Haven, dumbfounded by her temerity, and as helpless as anybody else to resist her velvet-gloved pressure, had consented.

A grueling haul across the Rust Belt pushed their total trip mileage past ten thousand, their petroleum consumption past thirty barrels. It happened that their arrival in the Twin Cities, in mid-August, coincided with the first autumn-smelling cold front of the summer. All across the great boreal forest of Canada and northern Maine and Minnesota, the still substantially intact boreal forest, warblers and flycatchers and ducks and sparrows had completed their work of parenting, shed their breeding plumage for better camouflaging colors, and were receiving, in the chill of the wind and the angle of the sun, their cue to fly south again. Often the parents departed first, leaving their young behind to practice flying and foraging and then to find their own way, more clumsily, and with higher mortality rates, to their wintering grounds. Fewer than half of those leaving in the fall would return in the spring.

The Sick Chelseas, a St. Paul band that Walter had once heard opening for the Traumatics and guessed would not survive another year, were still alive and had managed to pack the Free Space event with enough fans to vote them on to the main event in West Virginia. The only other familiar faces in the crowd were Seth and Merrie Paulsen, Walter's old neighbors on Barrier Street, looking thirty years older than everybody else except Walter himself. Seth was very taken with Lalitha, could not stop staring at her, and overruled Merrie's pleas of tiredness to insist on a late, post-battle supper at Taste of Thailand. It became a real noseynessfest, as Seth prodded Walter for inside dope on Joey and Connie's now notorious marriage, on Patty's whereabouts, on the precise history of Walter and Lalitha's relationship, and on the circumstances behind Walter's spanking in the *New York Times* ("God, you looked bad in that"), and Merrie yawned and arranged her face in resignation.

Returning to their motel, very late, Walter and Lalitha had something resembling an actual quarrel. Their plan had been to take a few days off in Minnesota, to visit Barrier Street and Nameless Lake and Hibbing and to see if they could track down Mitch, but Lalitha now wanted to turn around and go straight to West Virginia. "Half the people we have on the ground there are self-described anarchists," she said. "They're not called anarchists for nothing. We need to get there right away and deal with the logistics."

"No," Walter said. "The whole reason we scheduled St. Paul last was so we could take some days here and rest up. Don't you want to see where I grew up?"

"Of course I do. We'll do it later. We'll do it next month."

"But we're already *here*. It won't hurt to take two days and then go straight to Wyoming County. Then we won't have to come all the way back. It doesn't make any sense to drive two thousand extra miles."

"Why are you being this way?" she said. "Why don't you want to deal with the thing that's important right now, and deal with the past later?"

"Because this was our plan."

"It was a *plan*, not a contract."

"Well, and I guess I'm a little worried about Mitch, too."

"You hate Mitch!"

"It doesn't mean I want my brother living on the street."

"Yes, but one more month won't hurt," she said. "We can come straight back."

He shook his head. "I also really need to check the house out. It's been more than a year since anyone was there."

"Walter, no. This is you and me, this is our thing, and it's happening right now."

"We could even leave the van here and fly out and rent a car. We'd only end up losing one day. We'd still have a whole week to work on logistics. Will you please do this for me?"

She took his face in her hands and gave him a border-collie look. "No," she said. "You please do this for *me*."

"You do it," he said, pulling away. "You fly out. I'll follow in a couple of days."

"*Why are you being this way?* Was it Seth and Merrie? Did they get you thinking too much about the past?"

"Yes, they did."

"Well, put it out of your mind and come with me. We have to stay together."

Like a cold spring at the bottom of a warmer lake, old Swedish-gened depression was seeping up inside him: a feeling of not deserving a partner like Lalitha; of not being made for a life of freedom and outlaw heroics; of needing a more dully and enduringly discontented situation to struggle against and fashion an existence within. And he could see that simply by having these feelings he was starting to create a new situation of discontent with Lalitha. And it was better, he thought, depressively, that she learn sooner rather than later what he was really like. Understand his kinship with his brother and his father and his grandfather. And so he shook his head again. "I'm going to stick to the plan," he said. "I'm going to take the van for two days. If you don't want to come with me, we'll get you a plane ticket."

Everything might have been different if she'd cried then. But she was stubborn and spirited and angry with him, and in the morning he drove her to the airport, apologizing until she made him stop. "It's OK," she said, "I'm over it. I'm not worrying about it this morning. We're doing what we have to do. I'll call you when I get there and I'll see you soon."

It was Sunday morning. Walter called Carol Monaghan and then drove on familiar avenues up to Ramsey Hill. Blake had cut down a few more trees and bushes in Carol's yard, but nothing else on Barrier Street had changed much. Carol embraced Walter warmly, pushing her breasts into him in a way that didn't feel quite familial, and then, for an hour, while the twins ran squealing around the child-proofed great-room and Blake stood up nervously and left and came back and left again, the two parents made the best of being in-laws.

"I was dying to call you as soon as I found out," Carol said. "I literally had to sit on my hand to keep from dialing your number. I couldn't understand why Joey didn't want to tell you himself."

"Well, you know, he's had some difficulties with his mother," Walter said. "With me, too."

"And how is Patty? I hear you guys are not together anymore."

"That's true enough."

"I'm not going to bite my tongue on this one, Walter. I'm going to speak my mind even though it's always getting me in trouble. I think this separation was a long time coming. I hated to see the way she treated you. It always seemed like everything had to be about *her*. So there— I said it."

"Well, Carol, you know, these things are complicated. And she's Connie's mother-in-law, too, now. So I hope the two of you can find some way to work things out."

"Ha. I don't care about me, we don't need to see each other. I just hope she recognizes what a heart of gold my daughter has."

"I certainly recognize that myself. I think Connie's a wonderful girl, with a lot of potential."

"Well, you always were the nice one of the two of you. You always had a heart of gold yourself. I was never sorry to be your neighbor, Walter."

He chose to let the unfairness of this pass, chose not to remind Carol of the many years of generosity that Patty had shown her and Connie, but he did feel very sad for Patty's sake. He knew how hard she'd tried to be her better self, and it grieved him to be aligned now with the many people who could see only the unfortunate side of her. The lump in his throat was evidence of how much, in spite of everything, he still loved her. Dropping to his knees for some polite interaction with the twins, he was reminded of how much more comfortable than he she'd always been with little kids, how forgetful of herself she'd been with Jessica and Joey when they were the twins' age; how blissfully absorbed. It was much better, he decided, that Lalitha had gone on to West Virginia and left him alone to suffer in the past.

After making his escape from Carol, and deducing from Blake's cool good-bye that he hadn't been forgiven for being a liberal, he drove up to Grand Rapids, stopped for some groceries, and reached Nameless Lake by late afternoon. There was, ominously, a FOR SALE sign on the adjoining Lundner property, but his house had weathered 2004 as middling-well as it had weathered so many other years. The spare key was still hanging on the underside of the old rustic birch bench, and he found it not too intolerable to be in the rooms where his wife and his best friend had betrayed him; enough other memories flooded him vividly enough to hold their own. He raked and swept until nightfall, happy to have some real work to do for a change, and then, before he went to bed, he called Lalitha.

"It's *insane* here," she said. "It's a good thing I came and good that you didn't, because I think you'd be upset. It's like Fort Apache or something. Our people practically need security to protect them from the fans who've shown up early. All those jerks in Seattle seem to have come straight here.

We've got a little camp by the well, with one Porta Potti, but there's already about three hundred other people laying siege to it. They're all over the property, they're drinking from the same creek they're shitting right next to, and they're antagonizing the locals. There's graffiti all along the road leading up there. I have to send out interns in the morning to apologize to the people whose property's been defaced, and offer to do some repainting. I went around trying to tell people to chill out, but everybody's stoned and spread out over ten acres, and there's no leadership, it's totally amorphous. Then it got dark and started to rain, and I had to come back down to town and find a motel."

"I can fly out tomorrow," Walter said.

"No, come with the van. We need to be able to camp on-site. Right now you'd only get angry. I can deal with it without getting so angry, and things should be better by the time you get here."

"Well, drive carefully out there, OK?"

"I will," she said. "I love you, Walter."

"I love you, too."

The woman he loved loved him. He knew this for certain, but it was all he knew for certain, then or ever; the other vital facts remained unknown. Whether she did, in fact, drive carefully. Whether she was or wasn't rushing on the rain-slick county highway back up to the goat farm the next morning, whether she was or wasn't rounding the blind mountain curves dangerously fast. Whether a coal truck had come flying around one of these curves and done what a coal truck did somewhere in West Virginia every week. Or whether somebody in a high-clearance 4x4, maybe somebody whose barn had been defaced with the words FREE SPACE or CANCER ON THE PLANET, saw a dark-skinned young woman driving a compact Korean-made rental car and veered into her lane or tailgated her or passed her too narrowly or even deliberately forced her off the shoulderless road.

Whatever did happen exactly, around 7:45 a.m., five miles south of the farm, her car went down a long and very steep embankment and crushed itself against a hickory tree. The police report would not even offer the faintly consoling assurance of an instant killing. But the trauma was severe, her pelvis was broken and a femoral artery severed, and she had certainly died before Walter, at 7:30 in Minnesota, returned the house key to its nail beneath the bench and headed over to Aitkin County to look for his brother.

He knew, from long experience with his father, that alcoholics were best conversed with in the morning. All Brent had been able to tell him about Mitch's latest ex, Stacy, was that she worked at a bank in Aitkin, the county seat, and so he hurried from one to another of Aitkin's banks and found Stacy in the third of them. She was pretty in a strapping farm-girl way, looked thirty-five, and spoke like a teenager. Although she'd never met Walter, she seemed ready to assign him significant responsibility for Mitch's abandonment of their children. "You could try his friend Bo's farm," she said with a cross shrug. "The last I heard, Bo was letting him stay in his garage apartment, but that was like three months ago."

Marshy, glacially scraped, oreless Aitkin County was the poorest county in Minnesota and therefore full of birds, but Walter didn't stop to look for them as he drove up dead-straight County Road 5 and found Bo's farm. There was a large field scattered with the overgrown remnants of a rapeseed crop, a smaller cornfield much weedier than it should have been. Bo himself was kneeling in the driveway near the house, repairing the kickstand of a girl's bike adorned with pink plastic streamers, while an assortment of young children wandered in and out of the house's open front door. His cheeks were gin-blossomed, but he was young and had the muscles of a wrestler. "So you're the big-city brother," he said, squinting in puzzlement at Walter's van.

"That's me," Walter said. "I heard Mitch was living with you?"

"Yah, he comes and goes. You can probably find him up at Peter Lake now, the county campground there. You need him for something in particular?"

"No, I was just in the neighborhood."

"Yah, he's had it pretty rough since Stacy threw him out. I try to help him out a little bit."

"She threw him out?"

"Oh, well, y'know. Two sides to every story, right?"

It was nearly an hour's drive to Peter Lake, back up toward Grand Rapids. Arriving at the campground, which looked a little bit like an auto junkyard and was especially charmless in the midday sun, Walter saw a paunchy old guy squatting by a mud-stained red tent and scraping fish scales onto a sheet of newspaper. Only after he'd driven past him did he realize, from the resemblance to his father, that this was Mitch. He parked the van close against a poplar, to catch a little shade, and asked himself what he was doing here. He wasn't prepared to offer Mitch the house at Nameless Lake; he thought that he and Lalitha might live in it themselves for a season or two while they figured out their future. But he wanted to be more like Lalitha, more fearless and humanitarian, and although he could see that it might actually be kinder just to leave Mitch alone, he took a deep breath and walked back to the red tent.

"Mitch," he said.

Mitch was scaling an eight-inch sunny and didn't look up. "Yeah."

"It's Walter. It's your brother."

He did look up then, with a reflexive sneer that turned into a genuine smile. He'd lost his good looks, or, more precisely, they had shrunk into a small facial oasis in a desert of sunburned bloat. "Holy shit," he said. "Little Walter! What are you doing here?"

"Just stopped by to see you."

Mitch wiped his hands on his very dirty cargo shorts and extended one to Walter. It was a flabby hand and Walter squeezed it hard.

"Yeah, sure, that's great," Mitch said generally. "I was just about to open a beer. You want a beer? Or are you still teetotaling?"

"I'll have a beer," Walter said. He realized that it would have been kind and Lalitha-like to have brought Mitch a few sixpacks, and then he thought that it was also kind to let Mitch be generous with something. He didn't know which was the greater kindness. Mitch crossed his untidy campsite to an enormous cooler and came back with two cans of PBR.

"Yeah," he said, "I saw that van go by and wondered what kind of hippies we had moving in. Are you a hippie now?"

"Not exactly."

While flies and yellowjackets feasted on the guts of Mitch's suspended fish-cleaning project, the two of them sat down on a pair of ancient camp stools, made of wood and mildew-splotched canvas, that had been their father's. Walter recognized other similarly ancient gear around the site. Mitch, like their father, was a great talker, and as he filled Walter in on his present mode of existence, and on the litany of bad breaks and back injuries and car accidents and irreconcilable marital differences that had led

502

to this existence, Walter was struck by what a different kind of drunk he was than their father had been. Alcohol or time's passage seemed to have expunged all memory of his and Walter's enmity. He exhibited no trace of a sense of responsibility, but also, therefore, neither defensiveness nor resentment. It was a sunny day and he was just doing his thing. He drank steadily but without hurry; the afternoon was long.

"So where are you getting your money?" Walter said. "Are you working?"

Mitch leaned over somewhat unsteadily and opened a tackle box in which there was a small pile of paper money and maybe fifty dollars in coins. "My bank," he said. "I got enough to last through the warm weather. I had a night-watchman job in Aitkin last winter."

"And what are you going to do when this runs out?"

"I'll find something. I take pretty good care of myself."

"You worry about your kids?"

"Yeah, I worry, sometimes. But they've got good mothers that know how to take care of them. I'm no help at that. I finally figured that out. I'm only good at taking care of me."

"You're a free man."

"That I am."

They fell silent. A small breeze had kicked up, casting a million diamonds across the surface of Peter Lake. On the far side, a few fishermen were lazing in aluminum rowboats. Somewhere closer, a raven was croaking, another camper was chopping wood. Walter had been spending his days outdoors all summer, many of them in far more remote and unsettled places than this, but at no point had he felt farther from the things that constituted his life than he was feeling now. His children, his work, his ideas, the women he loved. He knew his brother wasn't interested in this life—was beyond being interested in anything—and he had no desire to speak of it. To inflict that on him. But at the very moment his telephone rang, showing an unfamiliar West Virginia number, he was thinking how lucky and blessed his life had been.

# MISTAKES WERE MADE
## (CONCLUSION)
### A Sort of Letter to Her Reader
### by Patty Berglund

# Chapter 4: Six Years

The autobiographer, mindful of her reader and the loss he suffered, and mindful that a certain kind of voice would do well to fall silent in the face of life's increasing somberness, has been trying very hard to write these pages in first and second person. But she seems doomed, alas, as a writer, to be one of those jocks who refer to themselves in third person. Although she believes herself to be genuinely changed, and doing infinitely better than in the old days, and therefore worthy of a fresh hearing, she still can't bring herself to let go of a voice she found when she had nothing else to hold on to, even if it means that her reader throws this document straight into his old Macalester College wastebasket.

The autobiographer begins by acknowledging that six years is a lot of silence. At the very beginning, when she first left Washington, Patty felt that shutting up was the kindest thing she could do both for herself and for Walter. She knew that he'd be furious to learn that she'd gone to stay with Richard. She knew that he'd conclude she had no regard for his feelings and must have been lying or deceiving herself when she'd insisted she loved him and not his friend. But let it be noted: before going up to Jersey City, she did spend one night alone in a D.C. Marriott, counting the heavy-duty sleeping pills she'd brought along with her, and examining the little plastic bag that hotel guests are supposed to line their ice buckets with. And it's easy to say, "Yes, but she didn't actually kill herself, did she?" and figure she was just being self-dramatizing and self-pitying and self-deceiving and other noxious self-things. The autobiographer nevertheless maintains that Patty was in a very low place that night, the lowest ever, and had to keep forcing herself to think of her children. Her pain levels, though perhaps no greater than Walter's, were great indeed. And Richard was the person who'd put her in this situation. Richard was the only person who could understand it, the only person she didn't think she'd die of shame to see, the only person she was sure still wanted her. There was nothing she could do now about having wrecked Walter's life, and so, she thought, she might as well try to save her own.

But also, to be honest, she was furious with Walter. However painful it had been for him to read certain pages of her autobiography, she still believed he'd committed an injustice in throwing her out of the house. She thought he'd overreacted and wronged her and was lying to himself about how much he'd wanted to be rid of her and go to his girl. And Patty's anger was compounded by jealousy, because the girl really did love Walter, whereas Richard isn't the sort of person who can really love anyone (except, to a touching degree, Walter). Although Walter undoubtedly didn't see things this way himself, Patty felt justified in going to Jersey City for such consolation and payback and self-esteem bolstering as sleeping with a selfish musician could provide.

The autobiographer will skim over the particulars of Patty's months in Jersey City, admitting only that her scratching of her ancient itch was not without its intense if short-lived pleasures, and noting that she wished she'd scratched it when she was 21 and Richard was moving to New York, and had then gone back to Minnesota at summer's end and seen if Walter might still want her. Because let it also be noted: she didn't have sex one single time in Jersey City without thinking of the last time she and her husband had done it, on the floor of her room in Georgetown. Though Walter no doubt imagined Patty and Richard as monsters of indifference to his feelings, in fact they could never escape his presence. Regarding, for example, whether Richard should make good on his commitment to help Walter with his anti-population initiative, they simply took it for granted that Richard had to do it. And not out of guilt but out of love and admiration. Which, given how much it cost Richard to pretend to more famous musicians that he cared about world overpopulation, ought to have told Walter something. The truth is that nothing between Patty and Richard was ever going to last, because they couldn't help being disappointments to each other, because neither was as lovable to the other as Walter was to both of them. Every time Patty lay by herself after sex, she sank down into sadness and loneliness, because Richard was always going to be Richard, whereas, with Walter, there had always been the possibility, however faint, and however slow in its realization, that their story would change and deepen. When Patty heard from her kids about the crazy speech he'd made in West Virginia, she despaired altogether. It seemed as if Walter had needed only to get rid of her to become a freer person. Their old theory—that he loved and needed her more than she loved and needed him—had been exactly backwards. And now she'd lost the love of her life.

Then came the terrible news of Lalitha's death, and Patty felt many things at once: great sorrow and compassion for Walter, great guilt about the many times she'd wished Lalitha dead, sudden fear of her own death, a momentary flicker of selfish hope that Walter might take her back now, and then great sickening regret for having gone to Richard and thereby ensured that Walter would never take her back. As long as Lalitha was alive, there'd been a chance that Walter would tire of her, but once she died there was no hope at all for Patty. Having hated the girl and made no secret of it, she had no right to console Walter now, and she knew it could only seem monstrous of her to use such a sad occasion to try to worm her way back into his life. She tried for many days to compose a condolence note worthy of his grief, but the chasm between the purity of his feelings and the impurity of her own was unbridgeable. The best she could do was convey her sorrow secondhand, through Jessica, and hope that Walter would believe that the yearning to comfort him was there in her, and that he might see how, having sent no condolence, she could then never communicate about anything else. Hence, from her side, these six years of silence.

The autobiographer wishes she could report that Patty left Richard immediately after Lalitha died, but in fact she stayed another three months. (Nobody will ever mistake her for a pillar of resolve and dignity.) She knew, for one thing, that it would be a long time, possibly forever, before somebody she really liked would want to sleep with her again. And Richard, in his stalwart if unconvincing way, was doing his best to be a

Good Man now that she'd lost Walter. She didn't love Richard a lot, but she did somewhat love him for this effort (although even here, let the record show, she was actually loving Walter, because it was Walter who'd put the idea of being a Good Man into Richard's head). He manfully sat down to the meals she made him, he forced himself to stay home and watch videos with her, he weathered her frequent downpours of emotion, but she was forever aware of how inconveniently her arrival had coincided with his reawakening commitment to music—his need to be out all night with his bandmates, or alone in his bedroom, or in numerous other girls' bedrooms—and although she respected these needs in the abstract, she couldn't help having her own needs, such as the need not to smell some other girl on him. To absent herself and earn some money, she worked evenings as a barista, making exactly those coffee drinks she'd once ridiculed the idea of making. At home, she struggled hard to be funny and agreeable and not a pain in the ass, but before long her situation became rather hellish, and the autobiographer, who has probably already said far more about these matters than her reader cares to hear, will spare him the scenes of petty jealousy and mutual recrimination and open disappointment that led to her parting with Richard on not very good terms. The autobiographer is reminded of her country's attempts to extricate itself from Vietnam, which ended with our Vietnamese friends being thrown off the top of the embassy building and shoved away from the departing helicopters and left behind for massacre or brutal internment. But that is truly all she's going to say about Richard, except for one further small note toward the end of this document.

For the last five years, Patty has been living in Brooklyn and working as a teacher's aide in a private school, helping first-graders with their language skills and coaching softball and basketball in the middle school. How she found her way to this wretchedly paid but otherwise nearly ideal job was as follows.

After she left Richard, she went to stay with her friend Cathy in Wisconsin, and it happened that Cathy's partner, Donna, had had twin girls two years earlier. Between Cathy's job as a public defender and Donna's at a women's shelter, the two of them together earned one decent salary and were getting one person's decent night's sleep. So Patty offered her services as a full-time babysitter and instantly fell in love with her charges.

Their names are Natasha and Selena, and they are excellent, unusual girls. They seemed to have been born with a Victorian sense of child comportment—even their screaming, when they felt obliged to do it, was preceded by a moment or two of judicious reflection. The girls were primarily focused on each other, of course, always watching each other, consulting each other, learning from each other, comparing their respective toys or dinners with lively interest but rarely competition or envy; they seemed jointly *wise*. When Patty spoke to one of them, the other also listened, with an attention that was respectful without being timid. Being two years old, they had to be watched constantly, but Patty literally never tired of it. The truth was—and it made her feel better to be reminded of this—she was as good with little kids as she was terrible with adolescents. She took a deep ongoing delight in the miracles of motor-skill acquisition, of language formation, of socialization, of personality development, the twins' progress sometimes clearly visible from one day to the next, and in their innocence of how hilarious they were, in the clarity of their needing, and in the utter trust they placed in her. The autobiographer is at a loss to convey the concreteness of her delight, but she could see that one mistake she hadn't made about herself was wanting to be a mother.

She might have stayed much longer in Wisconsin if her father hadn't gotten sick. Her reader has no doubt heard about Ray's cancer, the aggressive suddenness of its onset and swiftness of its progress. Cathy, who is herself very wise, urged Patty to go home to Westchester before it was too late. Patty went with much fear and trembling and found her childhood home little changed from the last time she'd set foot in it. The boxes of outdated campaign materials were even more numerous, the mildew in the basement even more intense, Ray's towers of *Times*-recommended books even higher and more teetering, Joyce's binders of untried *Times* Food Section recipes even thicker, the piles of unread *Times* Sunday magazines even more yellowed, the bins of recyclables even more overflowing, the results of Joyce's wishful attempts to be a flower gardener even more poignantly weedy and random, the reflexive liberalism of her worldview even more impervious to reality, her discomfort in her oldest daughter's presence even more pronounced, and Ray's snide jollity even more disorienting. The serious thing that Ray was now disrespectfully laughing at was his own impending death. His body, unlike everything else, was greatly changed. He was wasted and hollow-eyed and pallid. When Patty arrived, he was still going to his office for a few hours in the morning, but this lasted only another week. Seeing him so sick, she hated herself for her long coldness to him, hated her childish refusal to forgive.

Not that Ray, of course, was not still Ray. Whenever Patty hugged him, he patted her for one second and then pulled his arms away and let them wave in the air, as if he could neither return her embrace nor push her away. To deflect attention from himself, he cast about for other things to laugh at—Abigail's career as a performance artist, the religiosity of his daughter-in-law (about which more later), his wife's participation in the "joke" of New York State government, and Walter's professional travails, which he'd read about in the *Times*. "Sounds like your husband got involved with a bunch of *crooks*," he said one day. "Like he might be a little bit of a crook himself."

"He's not a crook," Patty said, "obviously."

"That's what Nixon said, too. I remember that speech like it was yesterday. The president of the United States assuring the nation that he is not a *crook*. That word, 'crook.' I couldn't stop laughing. 'I am not a crook.' Hilarious."

"I didn't see the article about Walter, but Joey says it was totally unfair."

"Now, Joey is your Republican child, is that correct?"

"He's definitely more conservative than we are."

"Abigail told us she practically had to burn her sheets after he and his girlfriend stayed in her apartment. Stains everywhere, apparently. The upholstery, too."

"Ray, Ray, I don't want to hear about it! Try to remember I'm not like Abigail."

"Ha. I couldn't help thinking, when I read that article, about that night when Walter got so exercised about his Rome Club. He was always a bit of a crank. That was always my impression. I can say that now, can't I?"

"Why, because we're separated?"

"Yeah, that, too. But I was thinking, because I'm not going to live long, I might as well speak my mind."

"You *always* spoke your mind. To a fault."

Ray smiled at something in this. "Not always, Patty. Less than you might think, actually."

"Name one thing you ever meant to say but didn't."

"I was never very good at expressing affection. I know that was hard for you. Hardest for you, probably. You always took everything so seriously, compared to the others. And then you had that terrible luck in high school."

"I had terrible luck with how you guys handled it!"

At this Ray raised a warning hand, as if to forestall further unreasonableness. "Patty," he said.

"Well, I did!"

"Patty, just—just—. We all make mistakes. My point is that I do have a, ah. I do have affection for you. A lot of love. It's just hard for me to show it."

"Tough luck for me, then, I guess."

"I'm trying to be serious here, Patty. I'm trying to tell you something."

"I know you are, Daddy," she said, breaking down in somewhat bitter tears. And he did his patting thing again, putting his hand on her shoulder and then drawing it away indecisively and letting it hover; and it was clear to her, finally, that he could be no other way.

While he was dying, and a private nurse came and went, and Joyce repeatedly, with contortionate apologies, slipped off to Albany for "important" votes, Patty slept in her childhood bed and reread her favorite childhood books and combated the household's disorder, not bothering to ask permission to throw away magazines from the 1990s and boxes of literature from the Dukakis campaign. It was the season of seed catalogues, and she and Joyce both gratefully seized on Joyce's sporadic passion for gardening, which gave them one common interest to talk about, instead of zero. As much as possible, though, Patty sat with her father, held his hand, and allowed herself to love him. She could almost physically feel her emotional organs rearranging themselves, bringing her self-pity plainly into view at last, in its full obscenity, like a hideous purple-red growth in her that needed to be cut out. Spending so much time listening to her father make fun of everything, albeit a little more feebly each day, she was disturbed to see how much like him she was, and why her own children weren't more amused by her capacity for amusement, and why it would have been better to have forced herself to see more of her parents in the critical years of her own parenthood, so as to better understand her kids' response to her. Her dream of creating a fresh life, entirely from scratch, entirely independent, had been just that: a dream. She was her father's daughter. Neither he nor she had ever really wanted to grow up, and now they worked at it together. There's no point in denying that Patty, who will always be competitive, took satisfaction in being less embarrassed by his sickness, less afraid, than her siblings were. As a girl, she'd wanted to believe that he loved her more than anything, and now, as she squeezed his hand in hers, trying to help him across distances of pain that even morphine could only shorten—could not make disappear—it became true, they made it true, and it changed her.

At the memorial service, which was held in the Unitarian church in Hastings, she was reminded of Walter's father's funeral. Here, too, the turnout was enormous—easily five hundred people. Seemingly every lawyer, judge, and current or former prosecutor in Westchester attended, and the ones who eulogized Ray all said the same thing: that he was not only the ablest attorney they'd ever known but also the kindest and hardest-working and most honest. The breadth and height of his professional reputation were dizzying to Patty and a revelation to Jessica, who was sitting beside her; Patty could already anticipate (accurately, it turned out) the reproaches that Jessica would be leveling at her, afterward, and with justice, for having denied her a meaningful relationship with her grandfather. Abigail went to the pulpit and spoke on the family's behalf, attempted to be funny and came off as inappropriate and self-involved, and then partially redeemed herself by crumbling into sobs of grief.

It was only when the family filed out, at the service's end, that Patty saw the assortment of unprivileged people filling the rear pews, more than a hundred in all, most of them black or Hispanic or otherwise ethnic, in every shape and size, wearing suits and dresses that seemed pretty clearly the best they owned, and sitting with the patient dignity of people who had more regular experience with funerals than she did. These were the former pro-bono clients of Ray's or the families of those clients. At the reception, one by one, they came up to the various Emersons, including Patty, and took their hands and looked them in the eye and gave brief testimonials to the work that Ray had done for them. The lives he'd rescued, the injustices he'd averted, the goodness he'd shown. Patty was not *entirely* blown away by this (she knew too well the costs at home of doing good in the world), but she was still pretty well blown away, and she couldn't stop thinking of Walter. She now sorely regretted the hard time she'd given him about his crusades for other species; she saw that she'd done it out of envy—envy of his birds for being so purely lovable to him, and envy of Walter himself for his capacity to love them. She wished she could go to him now, while he was still alive, and say it to him plainly: I adore you for your goodness.

One thing she soon found herself particularly appreciating about Walter was his indifference to money. As a kid, she'd been lucky enough to develop her own indifference, and, in the way of lucky people, she'd been rewarded with the further good luck of marrying Walter, whose non-acquisitiveness she'd enjoyed with minimal thought or gratitude un-til Ray died and she was plunged back into the nightmare of her family's money issues. The Emersons, as Walter had told Patty many times, repre-sented a scarcity economy. To the extent that he meant this metaphori-cally (i.e., emotionally), she could sometimes see that he was right, but because she'd grown up as the outsider and had excused herself from her family's competition for resources, it took her a very long time to appre-ciate how the forever lurking but forever untappable wealth of Ray's parents—the *artificiality* of the scarcity—was at the root of her family's troubles. She didn't fully appreciate it until she pinned Joyce down, in the days following Ray's memorial service, and extracted the story of the Em-erson family estate in New Jersey, and heard about the quandary in which Joyce now found herself.

The situation was this: as Ray's surviving spouse, Joyce now owned the country estate, which had passed to Ray after August's death, six years earlier. Ray had been constituted to laugh off and ignore the entreaties of Patty's sisters, Abigail and Veronica, to "deal with" the estate (i.e., sell it and give them their share of the money), but now that he was gone Joyce was getting a daily drumbeat of pressure from her younger daughters, and Joyce was *not* well constituted to resist this pressure. And yet, unfortu-nately, she still had the same reasons that Ray had had for being unable to "deal with" the estate, minus only Ray's sentimental attachment to it. If she put the estate on the market, Ray's two brothers could make a strong moral claim to large shares of the sale price. Also, the old stone house was currently occupied by Patty's brother, Edgar, his wife, Galina, and their soon-to-be-four little kids, and was unhelpfully scarred by Edgar's ongoing DIY "renovations," which, since Edgar had no job and no savings and many mouths to feed, had so far not advanced beyond certain random demolitions. Also, Edgar and Galina were threatening, if Joyce evicted them, to relocate to a West Bank settlement in Israel, taking with them the only grandchildren in Joyce's life, and live on the charity of a Miami-based foundation whose in-your-face Zionism made Joyce extremely uncomfortable.

Joyce had volunteered for the nightmare, of course. She'd been attracted, as a scholarship girl, by Ray's Waspiness and family wealth and social idealism. She'd had no idea what she was getting sucked into, the price she would end up paying, the decades of disgusting eccentricity and childish money games and August's imperious discourtesy. She, the poor Brooklyn Jewish girl, was soon traveling on the Emerson dime to Egypt and Tibet and Machu Picchu; she was having dinner with Dag Hammarskjöld and Adam Clayton Powell. Like so many people who become politicians, Joyce was not a whole person; she was even less whole than Patty. She needed to feel *extraordinary*, and becoming an Emerson reinforced her feeling that she was, and when she started having children she needed to feel that they, too, were extraordinary, so as to make up for what was lacking at her center. Thus the refrain of Patty's childhood: we're not like other families. Other families have insurance, but Daddy doesn't believe in insurance. Other families' kids work afterschool jobs, but we'd rather have you explore your extraordinary talents and pursue your dreams. Other families have to worry about money for emergencies, but Granddaddy's money means that we don't have to. Other people have to be realistic and have careers and save for the future, but even with all of Granddaddy's charitable giving there's still a huge pot of gold out there for you.

Having conveyed these messages over the years, and having allowed her children's lives to be deformed by them, Joyce now felt, as she confessed to Patty in her quavering voice, "unnerved" and "a tiny bit guilty" in the face of Abigail's and Veronica's demands for the liquidation of the estate. In the past, her guilt had manifested itself subterraneanly, in irregular but substantial cash transfers to her daughters, and in her suspension of judgment when, for example, Abigail hurried to August's hospital deathbed late one night and extracted a last-minute $10,000 check from him (Patty heard about this trick from Galina and Edgar, who considered it highly unfair but were mostly chagrined, it seemed to her, not to have thought of the trick themselves), but now Patty had the interesting satisfaction of seeing her mother's guilt, which had always been implicit in her liberal politics, applied to her own children in broad daylight. "I don't know what Daddy and I did," she said. "I guess we did something. That three of our four children are not quite ready to . . . not quite ready to, well. Fully support themselves. I suppose I—oh, I don't know. But if Abigail asks me one more time about selling Granddad's house . . . And, I guess, I suppose, I deserve it, in a way. I suppose, in my own way, I'm somewhat responsible."

"You just have to stand up to her," Patty said. "You have a right not to be tortured by her."

"What I don't understand is how *you* turned out to be so different, so independent," Joyce said. "You certainly don't seem to have these kinds of problems. I mean, I know you have problems. But you seem . . . stronger, somehow."

No exaggeration: this was among the top-ten most gratifying moments of Patty's life.

"Walter was a great provider," she demurred. "Just a great man. That helped."

"And your kids . . . ? Are they . . . ?"

"They're like Walter. They know how to work. And Joey's about the most independent kid in North America. I guess maybe he got some of that from me."

"I'd love to see more of . . . Joey," Joyce said. "I hope . . . now that things are different . . . now that we've been . . ." She gave a strange laugh, harsh and fully conscious. "Now that we've been *forgiven*, I hope I can get to know him a little."

"I'm sure he'd like that, too. He's gotten interested in his Jewish heritage."

"Oh, well, I'm not at all sure I'm the right person to talk to about *that*. He might do better with—Edgar." And Joyce again laughed in a strangely conscious way.

Edgar had not, in fact, become more Jewish, except in the most passive of senses. In the early nineties, he'd done what any holder of a PhD in linguistics might have done: become a stock trader. When he stopped studying East Asian grammar structures and applied himself to stocks, he in short order made enough money to attract and hold the attention of a pretty young Russian Jew, Galina. As soon as they were married, Galina's materialistic Russian side asserted itself. She goaded Edgar to make ever larger amounts of money and to spend it on a mansion in Short Hills, New Jersey, and fur coats and heavy jewelry and other conspicuous articles. For a little while, running his own firm, Edgar became so successful that he showed up on the radar of his normally distant and imperious grandfather, who, in a moment of possible early senile dementia, soon after his wife's death, greedily permitted Edgar to renovate his stock portfolio, selling off his American blue-chips and investing him heavily in Southeast Asia. August last revised his will and trust at the height of the Asian stock bubble, when it seemed eminently fair to leave his investments to his younger sons and the New Jersey estate to Ray. But Edgar was not to be trusted with renovations. The Asian bubble duly burst, August died soon after, and Patty's two uncles inherited next to nothing, while the estate, due to the building of new highways and the rapid development of northwest New Jersey, was doubling in value. The only way Ray could hold off his brothers' moral claims was to retain possession of the estate and let Edgar and Galina live on it, which they were happy to do, having been bankrupted when Edgar's own investments tanked. This was also when Galina's Jewish side kicked in. She embraced the Orthodox tradition, threw away her birth control, and aggravated her and Edgar's financial plight by having a bunch of babies. Edgar had no more passion for Judaism than anybody else in the family, but he was Galina's creature, all the more so since his bankruptcy, and he went along to get along. And, oh, how Abigail and Veronica hated Galina.

This was the situation that Patty set out to deal with for her mother. She was uniquely qualified to do it, being the only child of Joyce's who was willing to work for a living, and it brought her the most miraculous and welcome feeling: that Joyce was lucky to have a daughter like her. Patty was able to enjoy this feeling for several days before it curdled into the recognition that, in fact, she was getting sucked back into bad family patterns and was competing with her siblings again. It was true that she'd already felt twinges of competition when she was helping to nurse Ray; but nobody had questioned her right to be with him, and her conscience had been clean regarding her motives. One evening with Abigail, however, was enough to get the old competitive juices fully flowing again.

While living with a very tall man in Jersey City and trying to look less like a middle-aged housewife who'd taken the wrong exit off the turnpike, Patty had bought a rather chic pair of stack-heeled boots, and it was perhaps the least nice part of her that chose to wear these boots when she went to see her shortest sibling. She towered over Abigail, towered like an adult over a child, as they walked from Abigail's apartment to the neighborhood café at which she was a regular. As if to compensate for her shortness, Abigail went long with her opening speech—two hours long—and allowed Patty to piece together a fairly complete picture of her life: the married man, now known exclusively as Dickhead, on whom she'd wasted her best twelve years of marriageability, waiting for Dickhead's kids to finish high school, so that he could leave his wife, which he'd then done, but for somebody younger than Abigail; the straight-man-disdaining sort of gay men to whom she'd turned for more agreeable male companionship; the impressively large community of underemployed actors and playwrights and comics and performance artists of which she was clearly a valued and generous member; the circle of friends who circularly bought tickets to each other's shows and fund-raisers, much of the money ultimately trickling down from sources such as Joyce's checkbook; the life, neither glamorous nor outstanding but nevertheless admirable and essential to New York's functioning, of the bohemian. Patty was honestly happy to see that Abigail had found a place for herself in the world. It wasn't until they repaired to her apartment for a "digestif," and Patty broached the subject of Edgar and Galina, that things got ugly.

"Have you been to the Kibbutz of New Jersey yet?" Abigail said. "Have you seen their *milch cow?*"

"No, I'm going out there tomorrow," Patty said.

"If you're lucky, Galina won't remember to take the collar and leash off Edgar before you get there, it's such a verrrry handsome look. Very manly and religious. You can definitely bet she won't bother washing the cow shit off the kitchen floor."

Patty here explained her proposal, which was that Joyce sell the estate, give half the proceeds to Ray's brothers, and divide the rest among Abigail, Veronica, Edgar, and herself (i.e., Joyce, not Patty, whose financial interest was nugatory). Abigail shook her head continuously while Patty explained it. "To begin with," she said, "did Mommy not tell you about Galina's accident? She hit *a school crossing guard* in a crosswalk. Thank God no children, just the old man in his orange vest. She was distracted by her *spawn*, in the back seat, and plowed straight into him. This was only about two years ago, and, of course, she and Edgar had let their car insurance lapse, because that's the way she and Edgar are. Never mind New Jersey state law, never mind that even Daddy had *car* insurance. Edgar didn't see the need for it, and Galina, despite living here for fifteen years, said everything was different in Rrrrussia, she had *no idea*. The school's insurance paid the crosswalk guard, who basically can't walk now, but the insurance company has a claim on all their assets, up to some ungodly sum. Any money they get now goes straight to the insurance company."

Joyce, interestingly, had not mentioned this to Patty.

"Well, that's probably as it should be," she said. "If the guy is crippled, that's where the money should go. Right?"

"It still means they run away to Israel, since they're penniless. Which is fine with me—sayonara! But good luck selling that to Mommy. She's fonder of the spawn than I am."

"So why is this a problem for you?"

"Because," Abigail said, "Edgar and Galina shouldn't get a share at all, because they've had the use of the estate for six years and pretty well trashed it, and because the money's just going to vanish anyway. Don't you think it should go to people who can actually use it?"

"It sounds like the crossing guard could use it."

"He's been paid off. It's just the insurance company now, and companies have insurance for these things themselves."

Patty frowned.

"As for the uncles," Abigail said, "I say tough tittie. They were sort of like you—they ran away. They didn't have to have Granddaddy farting up every holiday like we did. Daddy went over there practically every week, his whole life, and ate Grandmommy's nasty stale Pecan Sandies. I sure don't remember seeing his brothers doing that."

"You're saying you think we deserve to be paid for that."

"Why not? It's better than not being paid. The uncles don't need the money anyway. They're doing verrrrry well without it. Whereas for me, and for Ronnie, it would make a real difference."

"Oh, Abigail!" Patty burst out. "We're never going to get along, are we."

Perhaps catching a hint of pity in her voice, Abigail pulled a stupid-face, a mean face. "*I'm* not the one that ran away," she said. "I'm not the one who turned her nose up, and could never take a joke, and married Mr. Superhuman Good Guy Minnesotan Righteous Weirdo Naturelover, and didn't even pretend not to hate us. You think you're doing so well, you think you're so superior, and now Mr. Superhuman Good Guy's dumped you for some inexplicable reason that obviously has nothing to do with your sterling personal qualities, and you think you can come back and be Miss Lovable-Congenial Goodwill Ambassador Florence Nightingale. It's all verrrry interesting."

Patty made sure to take several deep breaths before replying to this. "Like I said," she said, "I don't think you and I are ever going to get along."

"The whole reason I have to call Mommy every day," Abigail said, "is that you're out there trying to wreck everything. I'll stop bothering her the minute you go away and mind your own business. Is that a deal?"

"In what way is it not my business?"

"You said yourself you don't care about the money. If you want to take a share and give it to the uncles, fine. If that helps you feel more superior and righteous, fine. But don't tell *us* what to do."

"OK," Patty said, "I think we're almost done here. Just—so I'm sure I'm understanding this—you think that by *taking* things from Ray and Joyce you've been doing them a favor all your life? You think Ray was doing his parents a favor by *taking things*? And that you deserve to be paid for all these great favors?"

Abigail made another peculiar face and appeared to consider this. "Yes, actually!" she said. "You actually put that pretty well. That is what I think. And the fact that it obviously seems strange to you is the reason you don't have any business messing with this. You're no more part of the family than Galina at this point. You just still seem to think you are. So why don't you leave Mommy alone and let her make her own decisions. I don't want you talking to Ronnie, either."

"It's not actually your business whether I talk to her."

"It is so my business, and I'm telling you to leave her alone. You'll just get her confused."

"This is the person whose IQ is, like, one-eighty?"

"She's not doing well since Daddy died, and there's no reason to go tormenting her. I *doubt* you'll listen to me, but I know what I'm talking about, having spent approximately a thousand times more time with Ronnie than you have. Try to be a little considerate."

The once-manicured old Emerson estate, when Patty went out there the next morning, looked like some cross between Walker Evans and nineteenth-century Russia. A cow was standing in the middle of the tennis court, now netless, its plastic boundary lines torn and twisted. Edgar was plowing up the old horse pasture with a little tractor, slowing to a standstill every fifty feet or so when the tractor bogged down in the rain-soaked spring soil. He was wearing a muddy white shirt and mud-caked rubber boots; he'd put on a lot of fat and muscle and somehow reminded Patty of Pierre in *War and Peace*. He left the tractor tilting severely in the field and waded over through mud to the driveway where she'd parked. He explained that he was putting in potatoes, lots of potatoes, in a bid to make his family more perfectly self-sufficient in the coming year. Currently, it being spring, with last year's harvest and venison supplies exhausted, the family was relying heavily on food gifts from the Congregation Beit Midrash: on the ground outside the barn door were cartons of canned goods, wholesale quantities of dry cereal, and shrink-wrapped flats of baby food. Some of the flats were opened and partly depleted, giving Patty the impression that the food had been standing in the elements for some time without being carried into the barn.

Although the house was a mess of toys and unwashed dishes and did indeed smell faintly of manure, the Renoir pastel and the Degas sketch and the Monet canvas were still hanging where they always had. Patty was immediately handed a nice, warm, adorable, not terribly clean one-year-old by Galina, who was very pregnant and surveyed the scene with dull sharecropper eyes. Patty had met Galina on the day of Ray's memorial service but had barely spoken to her. She was one of those overwhelmed mothers engulfed in baby, her hair disordered, her cheeks hectic, her clothes disarranged, her flesh escaping haphazardly, but she clearly could still have been pretty if she'd had a few minutes to spare for it. "Thank you for coming to see us," she said. "It's an *ordeal* for us to travel now, arranging rides and so forth."

Patty, before she could proceed with her business, had to enjoy the little boy in her arms, rub noses with him, get him laughing. She had the mad thought that she could adopt him, lighten Galina and Edgar's load, and embark on a new kind of life. As if recognizing this in her, he put her hands all over her face, pulling at her features gleefully.

"He likes his aunt," Galina said. "His long-lost aunt Patty."

Edgar came in through the back door minus his boots, wearing thick gray socks that were themselves muddy and had holes in them. "Do you want some raisin bran or something?" he said. "We also have Chex."

Patty declined and sat down at the kitchen table, her nephew on her knee. The other kids were no less great—dark-eyed, curious, bold without being rude—and she could see why Joyce was so taken with them and didn't want them leaving the country. All in all, after her bad talk with Abigail, Patty was having a hard time seeing this family as the villains. They seemed, instead, literally, like babes in the woods. "So tell me how you guys see the future working out," she said.

Edgar, obviously accustomed to letting Galina speak for him, sat picking scabs of mud off his socks while she explained that they were getting better at farming, that their rabbi and synagogue were wonderfully supportive, that Edgar was on the verge of being certified to produce kosher wine from the grandparental grapes, and that the game was amazing.

"Game?" Patty said.

"Deers," Galina said. "Unbelievable numbers of deers. Edgar, how many did you shoot last fall?"

"Fourteen," Edgar said.

"Fourteen on our property! And they keep coming and coming, it's stupendous."

"See, the thing is, though," Patty said, trying to remember whether eating deer was even kosher, "it's not really your property. It's kind of Joyce's now. And I'm just wondering, since Edgar's so smart about business, whether it might make more sense for him to go back to work, and get a real income going, so that Joyce can make her own decision about this place."

Galina was shaking her head adamantly. "There's the insurances. The insurances want to take anything he makes, up to I don't know how many hundred thousands."

"Yes, well, but if Joyce could sell this place, you guys could pay off the insurances, I mean the insurance companies, and then you could get a fresh start."

"That man is a fraudster!" Galina said with blazing eyes. "You heard the story, I guess? That crossing guard is one hundred percent guaranteed fraudster. I barely tapped him, barely *touched* him, and now he can't walk?"

"Patty," Edgar said, sounding remarkably much like Ray when he was being patronizing, "you really don't understand the situation."

"I'm sorry—what's not to understand?"

"Your father wanted the farm to stay in the family," Galina said. "He didn't want it going in pockets of disgusting, obscene theater producers making so-called 'art,' or five-hundred-dollar psychiatrists who take your little sister's money without ever making her better. This way, we always have the farm, your uncles will forget about it, and if there's ever *real* need, instead of disgusting so-called 'art' or fraudster psychiatrists, Joyce can always sell part of it."

"Edgar?" Patty said. "Is this your plan, too?"

"Yeah, basically."

"Well, I guess it's very selfless of you. Guarding the flame of Daddy's wishes."

Galina leaned into Patty's face, as if to aid her comprehension. "*We have the children,*" she said. "We'll soon have six mouths to feed. Your sisters think I want to go to Israel—I don't want to go to Israel. We have good life here. And don't you think we get credit for having the children your sisters won't have?"

"They do seem like fun kids," Patty admitted. Her nephew was dozing in her arms.

"So leave it alone," Galina said. "Come and see the children whenever you want. We're not bad people, we're not kooks, we love having visitors."

Patty drove back to Westchester, feeling sad and discouraged, and consoled herself with televised basketball (Joyce was up in Albany). The following afternoon, she returned to the city and saw Veronica, the baby of the family, the most damaged of them all. There had always been something otherworldly about Veronica. For a long time, it had had to do with her dark-eyed, slender, wood-sprite looks, to which she'd adapted in various self-destructive ways including anorexia, promiscuity, and hard drinking. Now her looks were mostly gone—she was heavier but not heavy like a fat person; she reminded Patty of her former friend Eliza, whom she'd once glimpsed, many years after college, in a crowded DMV office—and her otherworldliness was more spiritual: a nonconnection to ordinary logic, a sort of checked-out amusement regarding the existence of a world outside herself. She'd once shown great promise (at least in Joyce's view) as both a painter and a ballerina, and had been hit on and dated by any number of worthy young men, but she'd since been bludgeoned by episodes of major depression beside which Patty's own depressions were apparently autumn hayrides in an apple orchard. According to Joyce, she was currently employed as an administrative assistant at a dance company. She lived in a sparsely furnished one-bedroom on Ludlow Street where Patty, despite having phoned in advance, seemed to have interrupted her in some deep meditative exercise. She buzzed Patty in and left her front door ajar, leaving it to Patty to find her in her bedroom, on a yoga mat, wearing faded Sarah Lawrence gym clothes; her youthful dancer's limberness had developed into a quite astonishing yogic flexibility. She obviously wished that Patty hadn't come, and Patty had to sit on her bed for half an hour, waiting eons for responses to her basic pleasantries, before Veronica finally reconciled herself to her sister's presence. "Those are great boots," she said.

"Oh, thank you."

"I don't wear leather anymore, but sometimes, when I see a good boot, I still miss it."

"Uh huh," Patty said encouragingly.

"Do you mind if I smell them?"

"My boots?"

Veronica nodded and crawled over to inhale the smell of the uppers. "I'm very sensitive to smell," she said, her eyes closed blissfully. "It's the same with bacon—I still love the smell, even though I don't eat it. It's so intense for me, it's almost like eating it."

"Uh huh," Patty encouraged.

"In terms of my practice, it's literally like not having my cake and not eating it, too."

"Right. I can see that. That's interesting. Although presumably you never ate *leather*."

Veronica laughed hard at this and for a while became quite sisterly. Unlike anyone else in the family, except Ray, she had a lot of questions about Patty's life and the turns that it had lately taken. She found cosmically funny precisely the most painful parts of Patty's story, and once Patty got used to her laughing at the wreck of her marriage, she could see that it did Veronica good to hear of her troubles. It seemed to confirm some family truth for her and put her at ease. But then, over green tea, which Veronica averred she drank at least a gallon of per day, Patty brought up the matter of the estate, and her sister's laughter became vaguer and more slippery.

"Seriously," Patty said. "Why are you bothering Joyce about the money? If it was just Abigail bothering her, I think she could deal with it, but coming from you, too, it's making her really uncomfortable."

"I don't think Mommy needs my help to make her uncomfortable," Veronica said, amused. "She does pretty well with that on her own."

"Well, you're making her *more* uncomfortable."

"I don't think so. I think we make our own heaven and hell. If she wants to be less uncomfortable, she can sell the estate. All I'm asking for is enough money so I don't have to work."

"What's wrong with working?" Patty said, hearing an echo of a similar question that Walter had once asked her. "It's good for the self-esteem to work."

"I can work," Veronica said. "I'm working now. I'd just rather not. It's boring, and they treat me like a secretary."

"You *are* a secretary. You're probably the highest-IQ secretary in New York City."

"I just look forward to quitting, that's all."

"I'm sure Joyce would pay for you to go back to school and get some job more suitable for your talents."

Veronica laughed. "My talents don't seem to be the kind the world's interested in. That's why it's better if I can exercise them by myself. I really just want to be left alone, Patty. That's all I'm asking at this point. To be left alone. Abigail's the one who doesn't want Uncle Jim and Uncle Dudley to get anything. I don't really care as long as I can pay my rent."

"That's not what Joyce says. She says you don't want them getting anything, either."

"I'm only trying to help Abigail get what she wants. She wants to start her own female comedy troupe and take it to Europe, where people will appreciate her. She wants to live in Rome and be *revered*." Again the laugh. "And I'd actually be fine with that. I don't need to see her that much. She's nice to me, but you know the way she talks. I always end up feeling, at the end of an evening with her, like it would have been better to spend the evening alone. I like being alone. I'd rather be able to think my thoughts without being distracted."

"So you're tormenting Joyce because you don't want to see so much of Abigail? Why don't you just not see so much of Abigail?"

"Because I've been told that it's not good to see no one. She's sort of like TV playing in the background. It keeps me company."

"But you just said you don't even like to see her!"

"I know. It's hard to explain. I have a friend in Brooklyn I'd probably see more of if I didn't see so much of Abigail. That would probably be OK, too. Actually, when I think about it, I'm pretty sure it would be OK." And Veronica laughed at the thought of this friend.

"But why shouldn't Edgar feel the same way you do?" Patty said. "Why shouldn't he and Galina get to keep living on the farm?"

"Probably no reason. You're probably right. Galina is undeniably appalling, and I think Edgar knows it, I think that's why he married her—to inflict her on us. She's his revenge for being the only boy in the family.

And I personally don't really care as long as I don't have to see her, but Abigail can't get over it."

"So basically you're doing this all for Abigail."

"She wants things. I don't want things myself, but I'm happy to help her try to get them."

"Except you do want enough money so you never have to work."

"Yes, that would definitely be nice. I don't like being someone's secretary. I especially hate answering the phone." She laughed. "I think people talk too much in general."

Patty felt like she was dealing with a huge ball of Bazooka that she couldn't get ungummed from her fingers; the strands of Veronica's logic were boundlessly elastic and adhered not only to Patty but to themselves.

Later, as she rode the train back out of the city, she was struck, as never before, by how much better off and more successful her parents were than any of their children, herself included, and how odd it was that none of the kids had inherited one speck of the sense of social responsibility that had motivated Joyce and Ray all their lives. She knew that Joyce felt guilty about it, especially about poor Veronica, but she also knew that it must have been a terrible blow to Joyce's ego to have such unflattering children, and that Joyce probably blamed Ray's genes, the curse of old August Emerson, for her kids' weirdness and ineffectuality. It occurred to Patty, then, that Joyce's political career hadn't just caused or aggravated her family's problems: it had also been her *escape* from those problems. In retrospect, Patty saw something poignant or even admirable in Joyce's determination to absent herself, to be a politician and do good in the world, and thereby save herself. And, as somebody who'd likewise taken extreme steps to save herself, Patty could see that Joyce wasn't just lucky to have a daughter like her: that she was also lucky to have had a mother like Joyce.

There was still one big thing she didn't understand, though, and when Joyce returned from Albany the following afternoon, full of anger at the senate Republicans who were paralyzing the state government (Ray, alas, no longer being around to rag Joyce about the Democrats' own role in the paralysis), Patty was waiting in the kitchen with a question for her. She asked it as soon as Joyce had taken off her raincoat: "Why did you never go to any of my basketball games?"

"You're right," Joyce said immediately, as if she'd been expecting the question for thirty years. "You're right, you're right, you're right. I should have gone to more of your games."

"So why didn't you?"

Joyce reflected for a moment. "I can't really explain it," she said, "except to say that we had so many things going on, we couldn't get to everything. We made mistakes as parents. You've probably made some yourself now. You can probably understand how confused everything gets, and how busy. What a struggle it is to get to everything."

"Here's the thing, though," Patty said. "You did have time for other things. It was specifically *my* games that you weren't going to. And I'm not talking about every game, I'm talking about *any* games."

"Oh, why are you bringing this up now? I said I was sorry I made a mistake."

"I'm not blaming you," Patty said. "I'm asking because I was *really good* at basketball. I was really, really good. I've probably made more mistakes as a mother than you did, so this is not a criticism. I'm just thinking, it would have made you *happy* to see how good I was. To see how talented I was. It would have made you feel good about yourself."

Joyce looked away. "I suppose I was never one for sports."

"But you went to Edgar's fencing meets."

"Not many."

"More than you went to my games. And it's not like you liked fencing so much. And it's not like Edgar was any good."

Joyce, whose self-control was ordinarily perfect, went to the refrigerator and took out a bottle of white wine that Patty had nearly killed the night before. She poured the remainder in a juice glass, drank half of it, laughed at herself, and drank the other half.

"I don't know why your sisters aren't doing better," she said, in an apparent non sequitur. "But Abigail said an interesting thing to me once. A terrible thing, which still tears me up. I shouldn't tell you, but somehow I trust you not to talk about these things. Abigail was very . . . inebriated. This was a long time ago, when she was still trying to be a stage actress. There was an excellent role that she'd thought she was going to be cast in, but hadn't been. And I tried to encourage her, and tell her I believed in her talents, and she just had to keep trying. And she said the most terrible thing to me. She said that *I* was the reason she'd failed. I who had been nothing, nothing, nothing but supportive. But that's what she said."

"Did she explain that?"

"She said . . ." Joyce looked woefully out into her flower garden. "She said the reason she couldn't succeed was that, if she ever did succeed, then I would take it from her. It would be *my* success, not hers. Which isn't true! But this is how she felt. And the only way she had to show me how she felt, and make me keep suffering, and not let me think that everything was OK with her, was to keep on not succeeding. Oh, I still hate to think about it! I told her it wasn't true, and I hope she believed me, because *it is not true.*"

"OK," Patty said, "that does sound hard. But what does it have to do with my basketball games?"

Joyce shook her head. "I don't know. It just occurred to me."

"I was succeeding, Mommy. That's the weird thing. I was totally succeeding."

Here, all at once, Joyce's face crumpled up terribly. She shook her head again, as if with repugnance, trying to hold back tears. "I know you were," she said. "I should have been there. I blame myself."

"It's really OK that you weren't. Maybe almost better, in the long run. I was just asking a curious question."

Joyce's summation, after a long silence, was: "I guess my life hasn't always been happy, or easy, or exactly what I wanted. At a certain point, I just have to try not to think too much about certain things, or else they'll break my heart."

And this was all Patty got from her, then or later. It wasn't a lot, it didn't solve any mysteries, but it would have to do. That same evening, Patty presented the results of her investigations and proposed a plan of action that Joyce, with much docile nodding, agreed to every detail of. The estate would be sold, and Joyce would give half the proceeds to Ray's brothers, administer Edgar's share of the remainder in a trust from which he and Galina could draw enough to live on (provided they didn't emigrate), and offer large lump sums to Abigail and Veronica. Patty, who ended up accepting $75,000 to help start a new life without assistance from Walter, felt fleetingly guilty on Walter's behalf, thinking of the empty woods and untilled fields that she'd helped doom to fragmentation and development. She hoped Walter might understand that the collective unhappiness of the bobolinks and woodpeckers and orioles whose homes she had wrecked was not much greater, in this particular instance, than that of the family that was selling the land.

And the autobiographer will say this about her family: the money they'd waited so long for, and been so uncivil about, wasn't wholly wasted on them. Abigail in particular began to flourish as soon as she had some financial weight to throw around in her bohemia; Joyce now calls Patty whenever Abigail's name is in the *Times* again; she and her troupe are apparently the toast of Italy, Slovenia, and other European nations. Veronica gets to be alone in her apartment, in an upstate ashram, and in her studio, and it's possible that her paintings, despite how ingrown and never-quite-finished they look to Patty, will be hailed by later generations as works of genius. Edgar and Galina have relocated to the ultra-Orthodox community in Kiryas Joel, New York, where they've had one last (fifth) baby and don't seem to be causing active harm to anybody. Patty sees all of them except Abigail a few times a year. Her nephews and nieces are the main treat, of course, but she also recently accompanied Joyce on a British garden tour that she enjoyed more than she'd thought she might, and she and Veronica never fail to have some laughs.

Mainly, though, she leads her own little life. She still runs every day, in Prospect Park, but she's no longer addicted to exercise or to anything else, really. A bottle of wine lasts two days now, sometimes three. At her school, she's in the blessed position of not having to deal directly with today's parents, who are *way* more insane and pressurized than even she had been. They seem to think her school should be helping their first-graders write early drafts of their college application essays and build their vocabulary for the SAT, ten years in the future. But Patty gets to deal with the kids purely as kids—as interesting and mostly still untainted little individuals who are eager to acquire writing skills, so as to be able to tell their stories. Patty meets with them in small groups and encourages them to do this, and they're not so young that some of them might not remember Mrs. Berglund when they're grown up. The middle-school kids should definitely remember her, because this is her favorite part of her job: giving back, as a coach, the total dedication and tough love and lessons in teamwork that her own coaches once gave her. Almost every day of the school year, after class, for a few hours, she gets to disappear and forget herself and be one of the girls again, be wedded by love to the cause of winning games, and yearn pureheartedly for her players to succeed. A universe that permits her to do this, at this relatively late point in her life, in spite of her not having been the best person, cannot be a wholly cruel one.

Summers are harder, no question. Summers are when the old self-pity and competitiveness well up in her again. Patty twice forced herself to volunteer with the city parks department and work outdoors with kids, but she turns out to be shockingly bad at managing boys older than six or seven, and it's a struggle to interest herself in activity purely for activity's sake; she needs a real team, her own team, to discipline and focus on winning. The younger unmarried women teachers at her school, who are hilariously hard partyers (like, puking-in-the-bathroom hard partyers, tequila-drinks-in-the-conference-room-at-three-o'clock hard partyers), become scarce in the summer, and there are only so many hours a person can read books by herself, or clean her tiny and already clean apartment while listening to country music, without wanting to do some hard partying of her own. The two sort-of relationships she had with significantly younger men from her school, two semi-sustained dating things that the reader surely doesn't want to hear about and in any case consisted mainly of awkwardness and tortured discussion, both began in the summer months. For the last three years, Cathy and Donna have kindly let her spend all of July in Wisconsin.

Her mainstay, of course, is Jessica. So much so, indeed, that Patty is rigorously careful not to overdo it and drown her with need. Jessica is a working dog, not a show dog like Joey, and once Patty had left Richard and regained a degree of moral respectability, Jessica had made a project of fixing up her mother's life. Many of her suggestions were fairly obvious, but Patty in her gratitude and contrition meekly presented progress reports at their regular Monday-evening dinners. Although she knew a lot more about life than Jessica did, she'd also made a lot more mistakes. It cost her very little to let her daughter feel important and useful, and their discussions did lead directly to her current employment. Once she was back on her feet again, she was able to offer Jessica support in return, but she had to be very careful about this, too. When she read one of Jessica's overly poetic blog entries, full of easily improvable sentences, the only thing she allowed herself to say was "Great post!!" When Jessica lost her heart to a musician, the boyish little drummer who'd dropped out of NYU, Patty had to forget everything she knew about musicians and endorse, at least tacitly, Jessica's belief that human nature had lately undergone a fundamental change: that people her own age, even male musicians, were *very different* from people Patty's age. And when Jessica's heart was then broken, slowly but thoroughly, Patty had to manufacture shock at the singular unforeseeable outrage of it. Although this was difficult, she was happy to make the effort, in part because Jessica and her friends really are somewhat different from Patty and her generation—the world looks scarier to them, the road to adulthood harder and less obviously rewarding—but mostly because she depends on Jessica's love now and would do just about anything to keep her in her life.

One indisputable boon of her and Walter's separation has been to bring their kids closer together. In the months after Patty left Washington, she could tell, from their both being party to information that she'd given only one of them, that they were in regular communication, and it wasn't hard to guess that the substance of their communication was how destructive and selfish and embarrassing their parents were. Even after Jessica forgave Walter and Patty, she remained in close touch with her war buddy, having bonded with him in the trenches.

How the two siblings have negotiated the sharp contrasts between their personalities has been interesting for Patty to watch, given her own failures in this line. Joey seems to have been especially insightful regarding the duplicity of Jessica's little drummer boy, explaining certain things to her which Patty had found it politic not to. It also definitely helps that Joey, since he had to be brilliantly successful at something, has been flourishing in a business that Jessica approves of. Not that there aren't still things for Jessica to roll her eyes at and be competitive about. It rankles her that Walter, with his South American connections, was able to steer Joey into shade-grown coffee at exactly the moment when fortunes could be made in it, while there is nothing that either Walter or Patty can do to help Jessica in her own chosen career of literary publishing. It frustrates her to be devoted, like her father, to a declining and endangered and unprofitable enterprise while Joey gets rich almost effortlessly. Nor can she conceal her envy of Connie for getting to travel the world with Joey, getting to visit precisely those humid countries that she herself is most multiculturally enthusiastic about. But Jessica does, albeit grudgingly, admire Connie's shrewdness in delaying having babies; she's also been heard to admit that Connie dresses pretty well "for a midwesterner." And there is no getting around the fact that shade-grown coffee is better for the environment, better especially for birds, and that Joey deserves credit for trumpeting this fact and marketing it astutely. Joey has Jessica pretty well beaten, in other words, and this is yet another reason why Patty works so hard to be her friend.

The autobiographer wishes she could report that all is well with her and Joey, too. Alas, all is not. Joey still presents a steel door to Patty, a door cooler and harder than ever, a door that she knows will remain closed until she can prove to him that she's accepted Connie. And, alas, though Patty has made great strides in many areas, learning to love Connie isn't one of them. That Connie sedulously checks every box of good daughter-in-lawship only makes things worse. Patty can feel in her bones that Connie doesn't actually like her any more than she likes Connie. There is something about Connie's way with Joey, something relentlessly possessive and competitive and *exclusive*, something *not right*, that makes Patty's hair stand on end. Although she wants to become a better person in every way, she has sadly begun to realize that this ideal may very well be unattainable, and that her failure will always stand between her and Joey, and be her lasting punishment for the mistakes she made with him. Joey, needless to say, is scrupulously polite to Patty. He calls her once a week and remembers the names of her co-workers and her favorite students; he extends and sometimes accepts invitations; he tosses her such small scraps of attention as his loyalty to Connie permits. In the last two years, he's gone so far as to repay, with interest, the money she sent to him in college—money that she needs too much, both practically and emotionally, to say no to. But his inner door is locked against her, and she can't imagine how it will ever open again.

Or actually, to be precise, she can imagine only one way, which the autobiographer fears her reader won't want to hear about but which she will mention anyway. She can imagine that, if she could somehow be with Walter again, and feel secure in his love again, and get up from their warm bed in the morning and go back to it at night knowing that she's his again, she might finally forgive Connie and become sensible of the qualities that everybody else finds so appealing in her. She might enjoy sitting down at Connie's dinner table, and her heart might be warmed by Joey's loyalty and devotion to his wife, and Joey in turn might open the door for her a little bit, if only she could ride home from dinner afterward with Walter and rest her head on his shoulder and know she's been forgiven. But of course this is a wildly unlikely scenario, and by no stretch of justice one that she deserves.

The autobiographer is fifty-two now and looks it. Her periods have lately been strange and irregular. Every year at tax time, it seems as if the year just past was shorter than the year before it; the years are becoming so similar to each other. She can imagine several discouraging reasons why Walter hasn't divorced her—he might, for example, still hate her too much to put himself even minimally in contact with her—but her heart persists in taking courage from the fact that he hasn't. She has embarrassingly inquired, of her children, whether there's a woman in his life, and has rejoiced at hearing no. Not because she doesn't want him to be happy, not because she has any right or even much inclination to be jealous anymore, but because it means there's some shadow of a chance that he still thinks, as she does more than ever, that they were not just the worst thing that ever happened to each other, they were also the best thing. Having made so many mistakes in her life, she has every reason to assume she's being unrealistic here, too: is failing to imagine some obvious fatal impediment to their getting back together. But the thought won't leave her alone. It comes to her day after day, year after similar year, this yearning for his face and his voice and his anger and his kindness, this yearning for her mate.

And this is really all the autobiographer has to tell her reader, except to mention, in closing, what occasioned the writing of these pages. A few weeks ago, on Spring Street in Manhattan, on her way home from a bookstore reading by an earnest young novelist whom Jessica was excited to be publishing, Patty saw a tall middle-aged man striding toward her on the sidewalk and realized it was Richard Katz. His hair is short and gray now, and he wears glasses that make him weirdly *distinguished*, even though he still dresses like a late-seventies twenty-year-old. Seeing him in Lower Manhattan, where you can't be as invisible as you can in deep Brooklyn,

Patty was sensible of how old she herself must look now, how much like somebody's irrelevant mother. If there'd been any way to hide, she would have hidden, to spare Richard the embarrassment of seeing her and herself the embarrassment of being his discarded sexual object. But she couldn't hide, and Richard, with a familiar effortful decency, after some awkward hellos, offered to buy her a glass of wine.

In the bar where they alighted, Richard listened to Patty's news of herself with the halved attention of a man who's busy and successful. He seemed finally to have made peace with his success—he mentioned, without embarrassment or apology, that he'd done one of those avant-garde orchestral thingies for the Brooklyn Academy of Music, and that his current girlfriend, who is apparently a big-deal documentary-maker, had introduced him to various young directors of the kind of art-house movies that Walter always loved, and that some scoring projects were in the works. Patty allowed herself one small pang at how relatively contented he seemed, and another small pang at the thought of his high-powered girlfriend, before turning the subject, as always, to Walter.

"You're not in touch with him at all," Richard said.

"No," she said. "It's like some kind of fairy tale. We haven't talked since the day I left Washington. Six years and not one word. I only hear about him from my kids."

"Maybe you should call him."

"I can't, Richard. I missed my chance six years ago, and now I think he just wants to be left alone. He's living at the lake house and doing work for the Nature Conservancy up there. If he wanted to be in touch, he could always call me."

"Maybe he's thinking the same thing about you."

She shook her head. "I think everybody recognizes that he's suffered more than I have. I don't think anyone's cruel enough to think it's his job to call me. Plus I've already told Jessie, in so many words, that I'd like to see him again. I'd be shocked if she hadn't passed that information along to him—there's nothing she'd like better than to save the day. So he's obviously still hurt, and angry, and hates you and me. And who can blame him, really?"

"I can, a little bit," Richard said. "You remember how he gave me that

536

silent treatment in college? That was bullshit. It's bad for his soul. It's the side of him I could never stand."

"Well maybe *you* should call him."

"No." He laughed. "I did finally get around to making him a little present—you'll see it in a couple of months if you keep your eye out. A little friendly shout across the time zones. But I've never had any kind of stomach for apologies. Whereas you."

"Whereas I?"

He was already waving to the bar waitress for the check. "You know how to tell a story," he said. "Why don't you tell him a story?"

# CANTERBRIDGE ESTATES LAKE

There are many ways for a house cat to die outdoors, including dismemberment by coyotes and flattening by a car, but when the Hoffbauer family's beloved pet Bobby failed to come home one early-June evening, and no amount of calling Bobby's name or searching the perimeter of Canterbridge Estates or walking up and down the county road or stapling Bobby's xeroxed image to local trees turned up any trace of him, it was widely assumed on Canterbridge Court that Bobby had been killed by Walter Berglund.

Canterbridge Estates was a new development, consisting of twelve spacious homes in the modern many-bathroomed style, on the southwest side of a minor water now officially called Canterbridge Estates Lake. Though the lake wasn't close to anything, really, the nation's financial system had lately been lending out money essentially for free, and the building of the Estates, as well as the widening and paving of the road that led to it, had momentarily stirred the stagnant Itasca County economy. Low interest rates had also then enabled various Twin Cities retirees and young local families, including the Hoffbauers, to buy themselves a dream home. When they began moving in, during the fall of 2007, their street still looked very raw. The front and back yards were lumpy and furzed over with unthriving grass, scattered with intractable glacial boulders and such birches as had been spared felling, and resembled, all in all, a child's too-hastily completed school terrarium project. The cats of the new neighborhood understandably preferred to stalk the woods and thickets of the adjoining Berglund property, where the birds were. And Walter, even before the last Canterbridge house was occupied, had gone door to door to introduce himself and ask his new neighbors to please keep their cats inside.

Walter was a good Minnesotan and reasonably friendly, but there was something about him, a political trembling in his voice, a fanatic gray stubble on his cheeks, that rubbed the families on Canterbridge Court the wrong way. Walter lived by himself in a dumpy, secluded old vacation house, and although it was undoubtedly nicer for the families to look across the lake at his scenic property than for him to look at their bare yards, and although a few of them did stop to imagine how noisy the construction of their homes must have been, nobody enjoys feeling like an intruder on somebody else's idyll. They'd paid their money, after all; they had a right to be there. Indeed, their property taxes were collectively hugely higher than Walter's, and most of them were facing a ballooning of their mortgage payments and were living on fixed incomes or saving for their children's educations. When Walter, who obviously had no such worries, came to complain to them about their *cats*, they felt they understood his worry about birds a lot better than he understood what a hyper-refined privilege it was to worry about them. Linda Hoffbauer, who was Evangelical and the most political person on the street, was especially offended. "So Bobby kills birds," she said to Walter. "So what?"

"Well, the thing is," Walter said, "small cats aren't native to North America, and so our songbirds never evolved any defenses against them. It's not really a fair fight."

"Cats kill birds," Linda said. "It's what they do, it's just part of nature."

"Yes, but cats are an Old World species," Walter said. "They're not part of our nature. They wouldn't be here if we hadn't introduced them. That's the whole problem."

"To be honest with you," Linda said, "all I care about is letting my children learn to take care of a pet and have responsibility for it. Are you trying to tell me they can't do that?"

"No, of course not," Walter said. "But you already keep Bobby indoors in the winter. I'm just asking that you do that in the summer, too, for the sake of the local ecosystem. We're living in an important breeding

542

area for a number of bird species that are declining in North America. And those birds have children, too. When Bobby kills a bird in June or July, he's also leaving behind a nest full of babies that aren't going to live."

"The birds need to find someplace else to nest, then. Bobby loves running free outdoors. It's not fair to keep him indoors when the weather's nice."

"Sure. Yes. I know you love your cat. And if he would just stay in your yard, that would be fine. But this land actually belonged to the birds before it belonged to us. And it's not like there's any way that we can tell the birds that this is a bad place to try to nest. So they keep coming here, and they keep getting killed. And the bigger problem is that they're running out of space altogether, because there's more and more development. So it's important that we try to be responsible stewards to this wonderful land that we've taken over."

"Well, I'm sorry," Linda said, "but my children matter more to me than the children of some bird. I don't think that's an extreme position, compared to yours. God gave this world to human beings, and that's the end of the story as far as I'm concerned."

"I have children myself, and I understand that," Walter said. "But we're only talking about keeping your Bobby indoors. Unless you're on speaking terms with Bobby, I don't see how you know he minds being kept indoors."

"My cat is an animal. The beasts of the earth weren't given the gift of language. Only people were. It's one of the ways we know we were created in God's image."

"Right, so my point is, how do you know he likes to run free?"

"Cats love being outdoors. Everybody loves being outdoors. When the weather warms up, Bobby stands by the door, wanting to go out. I don't have to *talk* to him to understand that."

"But if Bobby's just an animal, that is, not a human being, then why does his mild preference for being outdoors trump the right of songbirds to raise their families?"

"Because Bobby is part of our family. My children love him, and we want the best for him. If we had a pet bird, we'd want the best for it, too. But we don't have a bird, we have a cat."

"Well, thank you for listening to me," Walter said. "I hope you'll give it some thought and maybe reconsider."

Linda was very offended by this conversation. Walter wasn't really even a neighbor, he didn't belong to the homeowners association, and the fact that he drove a Japanese hybrid, to which he'd recently applied an OBAMA bumper sticker, pointed, in her mind, toward godlessness and a callousness regarding the plight of hardworking families, like hers, who were struggling to make ends meet and raise their children to be good, loving citizens in a dangerous world. Linda wasn't greatly popular on Canterbridge Court, but she was feared as the person who would knock on your door if you'd left your boat parked in your driveway overnight, in violation of the homeowners covenant, or if one of her children had seen one of your children lighting up a cigarette behind the middle school, or if she'd discovered a minor defect in the construction of her house and wanted to know if your house had the same minor defect. After Walter's visit with her, he became, in her incessant telling, the animal nut who'd asked her if she was on speaking terms with her *cat*.

Across the lake, on a couple of weekends that summer, the people of Canterbridge Estates noticed visitors on Walter's property, a handsome young couple who drove a new black Volvo. The young man was blond and body-built, his wife or girlfriend svelte in a childless big-city way. Linda Hoffbauer declared the couple "arrogant-looking," but most of the community was relieved to see these respectable visitors, since Walter had previously seemed, for all his politeness, like a potentially deviant hermit. Some of the older Canterbridgeans who took long morning constitutionals were now emboldened to chat up Walter when they met him on the road. They learned that the young couple were his son and daughter-in-law, who had some sort of thriving business in St. Paul, and that he also had an unmarried daughter in New York City. They asked him leading questions about his own marital status, hoping to elicit whether he was divorced or merely widowed, and when he proved adept at dodging these questions, one of the more technologically savvy of them went online and discovered that Linda Hoffbauer had been right, after all, to suspect Walter of being a nutcase and a menace. He'd apparently founded a radical environmental group that had shut down after the death of its co-founder, a strangely named young woman who clearly hadn't been the mother of his children. Once this interesting news had percolated through the neighborhood, the early-morning walkers left Walter alone again— less, perhaps, because they were disturbed by his extremism than because his hermitlike existence now strongly smacked of grief, the terrible sort of grief that it's safest to steer clear of; the enduring sort of grief that, like all forms of madness, feels threatening, possibly even contagious.

Late in the following winter, when the snow was beginning to melt, Walter showed up again on Canterbridge Court, this time carrying a carton of brightly colored neoprene cat bibs. He claimed that a cat wearing one of these bibs could do any frolicsome outdoor thing it pleased, from climbing trees to batting at moths, except pounce effectively on birds. He said that putting a bell on a cat's collar had been proven to be useless in warning birds. He added that the low-end estimate of songbirds daily murdered by cats in the United States was one million, i.e., 365,000,000 per year (and this, he stressed, was a conservative estimate and did not include the starvation of the murdered birds' chicks). Although Walter seemed not to understand what a bother it would be to tie a bib around a cat every time it went outdoors, and how silly a cat would look in bright blue or red neoprene, the older cat owners on the street did politely accept the bibs and promise to try them, so that Walter would leave them alone and they could throw the bibs away. Only Linda Hoffbauer refused a bib altogether. Walter seemed to her like one of those big-government liberals who wanted to hand out condoms in the schools and take away people's guns and force every citizen to carry a national identity card. She was inspired to ask whether the birds on his property *belonged* to him, and, if not, what business of his it was if her Bobby enjoyed hunting them. Walter replied with some bureaucratese about the North American Migratory Bird Treaty Act, which supposedly prohibited harming any nongame bird that crossed the Canadian or Mexican border. Linda was disagreeably reminded of the country's new president, who wanted to hand over national sovereignty to the United Nations, and she told Walter, as civilly as she could, that she was very busy raising her children and would appreciate it if he wouldn't knock on her door anymore.

From a diplomatic perspective, Walter had chosen a poor time to come around with his bibs. The country had stumbled into a deep economic recession, the stock market was in the toilet, and it seemed almost obscene of him to still be obsessed with songbirds. Even the retired couples on Canterbridge Court were hurting—the deflation of their investments had forced several of them to cancel their annual winter retreats to Florida or Arizona—and two of the younger families on the street, the Dents and the Dolbergs, had fallen behind on their mortgage payments (which had ballooned at exactly the wrong moment) and seemed likely to lose their homes. While Teagan Dolberg waited for replies from credit-consolidation companies that seemed to change their phone numbers and mailing addresses weekly, and from low-cost federal debt advisers that turned out to be neither federal nor low-cost, the outstanding balances on her Visa and MasterCard accounts were jumping up in monthly increments of three and four thousand dollars, and the friends and neighbors to whom she'd sold ten-packs of manicure sessions, at the manicure station she'd set up in her basement, continued to show up to have their nails done without bringing in any more income. Even Linda Hoffbauer, whose husband had secure road-maintenance contracts with Itasca County, had taken to lowering her thermostat and letting her children ride the school bus instead of delivering and fetching them in her Suburban. Anxieties hung like a cloud of no-see-ums on Canterbridge Court; they invaded every house via cable news and talk radio and the internet. There was plenty of tweeting on Twitter, but the chirping and fluttering world of nature, which Walter had invoked as if people were still supposed to care about it, was one anxiety too many.

Walter was next heard from in September, when he leafleted the neighborhood under cover of night. The Dent and Dolberg houses were standing empty now, their windows darkened like the call-holding lights of emergency-hotline callers who'd finally quietly hung up, but the remaining residents of Canterbridge Estates all awoke one morning to find on their doorsteps a politely worded "Dear Neighbors" letter, rehashing the anti-cat arguments that Walter had presented twice already, and four attached pages of photographs that were the opposite of polite. Walter had apparently spent the entire summer documenting bird deaths on his property. Each picture (there were more than forty of them) was labeled with a date and a species. The Canterbridge families who didn't own cats were offended to have been included in the leafleting, and the families who did own them were offended by Walter's seeming certainty that every bird death on his property was the fault of their pets. Linda Hoffbauer was additionally incensed that a leaflet had been left where one of her children could easily have been exposed to traumatizing images of headless sparrows and bloody entrails. She called the county sheriff, with whom she and her husband were social, to see whether perhaps Walter was guilty of illegal harassment. The sheriff said that Walter wasn't, but he agreed to stop by his house and have a word of warning with him—a visit that yielded the unexpected news that Walter had a law degree and was versed not only in his First Amendment rights but also in the Canterbridge Estates homeowners covenant, which contained a clause requiring pets to be under the control of their owners at all times; the sheriff advised Linda to shred the leaflet and move on.

And then came white winter, and the neighborhood cats retreated indoors (where, as even Linda had to admit, they seemed perfectly content), and Linda's husband personally undertook to plow the county road in such a way that Walter had to shovel for an hour to clear the head of his driveway after every new snowfall. With the leaves down, the neighborhood had a clear view across the frozen lake at the little Berglund house, in whose windows no television was ever seen to flicker. It was hard to imagine what Walter might be doing over there, by himself, in the deep winter night, besides brooding with hostility and judgment. His house went dark for a week at Christmastime, which pointed toward a visit with his family in St. Paul, which was also hard to imagine—that such a crank was nonetheless loved by somebody. Linda, especially, was relieved when the holidays ended and the crank resumed his hermit life and she could return to a hatred unclouded by the thought that somebody cared about him. One night in February, her husband reported that Walter had filed a complaint with the county regarding the deliberate blockage of his driveway, and this was somehow very agreeable for her to hear. It was good to know he knew they hated him.

In the same perverse way, when the snow again melted and the woods again greened and Bobby was let outside again and promptly disappeared, Linda felt as if a deep itch were being scratched, the primal sort of itch that scratching only worsens. She knew immediately that Walter was responsible for Bobby's disappearance, and she felt intensely gratified that he'd risen to her hatred, had given it fresh cause and fresh nourishment:

that he was willing to play the hatred game with her and be the local representative of everything wrong with her world. Even as she organized the search for her children's missing pet and broadcast their anguish to the neighborhood, she secretly savored their anguish and took pleasure in urging them to hate Walter for it. She'd liked Bobby well enough, but she knew it was a sin to falsely idolize a beast. The sin she hated was in her so-called neighbor. Once it became clear that Bobby was never coming back, she took her kids to the local animal shelter and let them pick out three new cats, which, as soon as they were home again, she freed from their cardboard boxes and shooed in the direction of Walter's woods.

Walter had never liked cats. They'd seemed to him the sociopaths of the pet world, a species domesticated as an evil necessary for the control of rodents and subsequently fetishized the way unhappy countries fetishize their militaries, saluting the uniforms of killers as cat owners stroke their animals' lovely fur and forgive their claws and fangs. He'd never seen anything in a cat's face but simpering incuriosity and self-interest; you only had to tease one with a mouse-toy to see where its true heart lay. Until he came to live in his mother's house, however, he'd had many worse evils to contend against. Only now, when he was responsible for the feral cat populations wreaking havoc on the properties he managed for the Nature Conservancy, and when the injury that Canterbridge Estates had inflicted on his lake was compounded by the insult of its residents' free-roaming pets, did his old anti-feline prejudice swell into the kind of bludgeoning daily misery and grievance that depressive male Berglunds evidently needed to lend meaning and substance to their lives. The grievance that had served him for the previous two years—the misery of chain saws and earthmovers and small-scale blasting and erosion, of hammers and tile cutters and boom-boxed classic rock—was over now, and he needed something new.

Some cats are lazy or inept as killers, but the white-footed black Bobby wasn't one of them. Bobby was shrewd enough to retreat to the Hoffbauer house at dusk, when raccoons and coyotes became a danger, but every morning in the snowless months he could be seen sallying freshly forth along the lake's denuded southern shore and entering Walter's property to kill things. Sparrows, towhees, thrushes, yellowthroats, bluebirds, goldfinches, wrens. Bobby's tastes were catholic, his attention span limitless. He never tired of killing, and he had the additional character flaw of disloyalty or ingratitude, rarely bothering to carry his kills back to his owners. He captured and toyed and butchered, and then sometimes he snacked a little, but usually he just abandoned the carcass. The open grassy woods below Walter's house and the surrounding edge habitat were particularly attractive to birds and Bobby. Walter kept a little pile of stones to throw at him, and he'd once scored a direct aqueous hit with the pressure nozzle on his garden hose, but Bobby had soon learned to stay in the woods in the early morning, waiting for Walter to leave for work. Some of the Conservancy holdings that Walter managed were far enough away that he was often gone for several nights, and almost invariably, when he returned home, he found fresh carnage on the slope behind his house. If it had only been happening in this one place, he might have stood it, but knowing that it was happening everywhere deranged him.

And yet he was too softhearted and law-abiding to kill somebody's pet. He thought of bringing in his brother Mitch to do the job, but Mitch's existing criminal record argued against taking this chance, and Walter could see that Linda Hoffbauer would probably just get another cat. Only after a second summer of diplomacy and educational efforts had failed, and after Linda Hoffbauer's husband had blocked his driveway with snow one too many times, did he decide that, although Bobby was just one cat among seventy-five million in America, the time had come for Bobby to pay personally for his sociopathy. Walter obtained a trap and detailed instructions from one of the contractors fighting the nearly hopeless war on ferals on Conservancy lands, and before dawn one morning in May he placed the trap, baited with chicken livers and bacon, along the path that Bobby was wont to tread onto his property. He knew that, with a smart cat, you only got one chance with a trap. Sweet to his ears were the feline cries coming up the hill two hours later. He hustled the jerking, shit-smelling trap up to his Prius and locked it in the trunk. That Linda Hoffbauer had never put a collar on Bobby—too restrictive of her cat's precious freedom, presumably—made it all the easier for Walter, after a three-hour drive, to deposit the animal at a Minneapolis shelter that would either kill it or fob it off on an urban family who would keep it indoors.

He wasn't prepared for the depression that beset him on his drive out of Minneapolis. The sense of loss and waste and sorrow: the feeling that he and Bobby had in some way been married to each other, and that even a horrible marriage was less lonely than no marriage at all. Against his will, he pictured the sour cage in which Bobby would now be dwelling. He knew better than to imagine that Bobby was missing the Hoffbauers personally—cats were all about using people—but there was something pitiable about his trappedness nonetheless.

For nearly six years now, he'd been living by himself and finding ways to make it work. The state chapter of the Conservancy, which he'd once directed, and whose coziness with corporations and millionaires now made him queasy, had granted his wish to be rehired as a low-level property manager and, in the frozen months, as an assistant on particularly tedious and time-consuming administrative tasks. He wasn't doing dazzling good on the lands he oversaw, but he wasn't doing any harm, either, and the days he got to pass alone among the conifers and loons and sedge and woodpeckers were mercifully forgetful. The other work he did—writing grant proposals, reviewing wildlife population literature, making cold calls on behalf of a new sales tax to support a state Land Conservation Fund, which had eventually garnered more votes in the 2008 election than even Obama had—was similarly unobjectionable. In the late evening, he prepared one of the five simple suppers he now bothered with, and then, because he could no longer read novels or listen to music or do anything else associated with feeling, he treated himself to computer chess and computer poker and, sometimes, to the raw sort of pornography that bore no relation to human emotion.

At times like this, he felt like a sick old fucker living in the woods, and he was careful to turn his phone off, lest Jessica call to check up on him. Joey he could still be himself with, because Joey was not only a man but a Berglund man, too cool and tactful to intrude, and although Connie was trickier, because there was always sex in Connie's voice, sex and innocent flirtation, it was never too hard to get her chattering about herself and Joey, because she was so happy. The real ordeal was hearing from Jessica. Her voice sounded more than ever like Patty's, and Walter was often perspiring by the end of their conversations, from the effort of keeping them focused on her life or, failing that, on his work. There had been a time, after the car accident that had effectively ended his life, when Jessica had descended on him and nursed him in his grief. She'd done this partly in expectation of his getting better, and when she'd realized he would not be getting better, didn't feel like getting better, never wanted to get better, she'd become very angry with him. It had taken him several hard years to teach her, with coldness and sternness, to leave him alone and attend to her own life. Each time a silence fell between them now, he could feel her wondering whether to renew her therapeutic assault, and he found it deeply grueling to invent new conversational gambits, week after week, to prevent her from doing so.

When he finally got home from his Minneapolis errand, after a productive three-day visit to a big Conservancy parcel in Beltrami County, he found a sheet of paper stapled to the birch tree at the head of his driveway. HAVE YOU SEEN ME? it asked. MY NAME IS BOBBY AND MY FAMILY MISSES ME. Bobby's black face didn't reproduce well in photocopy—his pale, hovering eyes looked spectral and lost—but Walter was now able to see, as he hadn't before, how somebody might find such a face worthy of protection and tenderness. He didn't regret having removed a menace from the ecosystem, and thereby saved many bird lives, but the small-animal vulnerability in Bobby's face made him aware of a fatal defect in his own makeup, the defect of pitying even the beings he most hated. He proceeded down his driveway, trying to enjoy the momentary peace that had fallen on his property, the absence of anxiety about Bobby, the spring evening light, the white-throated sparrows singing *pure sweet Canada Canada Canada*, but he had the sense of having aged many years in the four nights he'd been away.

That very evening, while frying some eggs and toasting some bread, he got a call from Jessica. And maybe she'd called him with a purpose, or maybe she heard something in his voice now, some loss of resolve, but as soon as they'd exhausted the meager news that her foregoing week had produced, he fell silent for so long that she was emboldened to renew her old assault.

"So I saw Mom the other night," she said. "She told me something interesting that I thought you might want to hear. Do you want to hear it?"

"No," he said sternly.

"Well, do you mind if I ask why not?"

From outdoors, in blue twilight, through the open kitchen window, came the cry of a distant child calling *Bobby!*

"Look," Walter said. "I know you and she are close, and that's fine with me. I'd be sorry if you weren't. I want you to have two parents. But if I were interested in hearing from her, I could call her up myself. I don't want you in the position of carrying messages."

"I don't mind being in that position."

"I'm saying *I* mind. I'm not interested in getting any messages."

"I don't think this is a bad message she wants to send you."

"I don't care what kind of message it is."

"Well then can I ask you why you don't just get divorced? If you don't want to have anything to do with her? Because as long as you're not divorced, you're sort of giving her hope."

A second child's voice had now joined the first, the two of them together calling *Bobbbby! Bobbbbbby!* Walter closed the window and said to Jessica, "I don't want to hear about it."

"OK, fine, Dad, but could you at least answer my question? Why you don't get divorced?"

"It's just not something I want to think about right now."

"It's been six years! Isn't it time to start thinking about it? If only out of simple fairness?"

"If she wants a divorce, she can send me a letter. She can have a lawyer send me a letter."

"But I'm saying, why don't *you* want a divorce?"

"I don't want to deal with the things it would stir up. I have a right not to do something I don't want to do."

"What would it stir up?"

"Pain. I've had enough pain. I'm still in pain."

"I know you are, Dad. But Lalitha's gone now. She's been gone for six years."

Walter shook his head violently, as if he'd had ammonia thrown in his face. "I don't want to think about it. I just want to go out every morning and see birds who have nothing to do with any of it. Birds who have their own lives, and their own struggles. And to try to do something for them. They're the only thing that's still lovely to me. I mean, besides you and Joey. And that's all I want to say about it, and I want you not to ask me any more."

"Well, have you thought of seeing a therapist? Like, so you can start moving on with your life? You're not that old, you know."

"I don't want to change," he said. "I have a bad few minutes every morning, and then I go and tire myself out, and if I stay up late enough I can fall asleep. You only go to a therapist if you want to change something. I wouldn't have anything to say to a therapist."

"You used to love Mom, too, didn't you?"

"I don't know. I don't remember. I only remember what happened after she left."

"Well, she's fairly lovely herself, actually. She's fairly different from the way she used to be. She's become sort of the perfect mom, unbelievable as that may sound."

"Like I said, I'm happy for you. I'm glad you have her in your life."

"But you don't want her in your life."

"Look, Jessica, I know that's what you want. I know you want a happy ending. But I can't change my feelings just because it's something you want."

"And your feeling is you hate her."

"She made her choice. And that's all I have to say."

"I'm sorry, Dad, but that is just grotesquely unfair. You were the one who made the choice. She didn't want to go."

"I'm sure that's what she tells you. You see her every week, I'm sure she's sold you on her version, which I'm sure is very forgiving of herself. But you weren't living with her for the last five years before she left. It was a nightmare, and I fell in love with someone else. It was never my intention to fall in love with someone else. And I know you're very unhappy that I did. But the only reason it happened was that your mother was impossible to live with."

"Well then you should divorce her. Isn't that the least you owe her after all those years of marriage? If you thought well enough of her to stay with her for all the good years, don't you at least owe her the respect of honestly divorcing her?"

"They weren't such good years, Jessica. She was lying to me the whole time—I don't think I owe her so very much for that. And, like I said, if she wants a divorce, it's available to her."

"She doesn't want a divorce! She wants to get back together with you!"

"I can't even imagine seeing her for one minute. All I can imagine is unbearable pain at the sight of her."

"Isn't it possible, though, Dad, that the reason it would be so painful is that you still love her?"

"We need to talk about something else now, Jessica. If you care about my feelings, you won't bring it up again. I don't want to have to be afraid of answering the phone when you call."

He sat for a long time with his face in his hands, his dinner untouched, while the house very slowly darkened, the earthly springtime world yielding to the more abstract sky world: pink stratospheric wisps, the deep chill of deep space, the first stars. This was the way his life worked now: he drove away Jessica and missed her the second she was gone. He considered returning to Minneapolis in the morning, retrieving the cat, and restoring it to the kids who missed it, but he could no sooner actually do this than he could call Jessica back and apologize to her. What was done was done. What was over was over. In Mingo County, West Virginia, on the ugliest overcast morning of his life, he'd asked Lalitha's parents if they minded if he went to see their daughter's body. Her parents were chilly, eccentric people, engineers, with strong accents. The father was dry-eyed but the mother kept erupting, loudly, unprovoked, in a keening foreign wail that was almost like song; it sounded strangely ceremonial and impersonal, like a lament for an idea. Walter went alone to the morgue, without any idea. His love was resting beneath a sheet on a gurney of an awkward height, too high to be knelt by. Her hair was as ever, silky and black and thick, as ever, but there was something wrong with her jaw, some outrageously cruel and unforgivable injury, and her forehead, when he kissed it, was colder than any just universe could have allowed such a young person's forehead to be. The coldness entered him through his lips and didn't leave. What was over was over. His delight in the world had died, and there was no point in anything. To communicate with his wife, as Jessica was urging, would have meant letting go of his last moments with Lalitha, and he had a right not to do this. He had a right, in such an unjust universe, to be unfair to his wife, and he had a right to let the little Hoffbauers call in vain for their Bobby, because there was no point in anything.

Taking strength from his refusals—enough strength, certainly, to get him out of bed in the morning and propel him through long days in the field and long drives on roads congested by vacationers and exurbanites— he survived another summer, the most solitary of his life so far. He told Joey and Connie, with some truth (but not much), that he was too busy for a visit from them, and he gave up on battling the cats that continued to invade his woods; he couldn't see putting himself through another drama of the sort he'd had with Bobby. In August, he received a thick envelope from his wife, some sort of manuscript presumably related to the "message" that Jessica had spoken of, and he stowed it, unopened, in the file drawer where he kept his old joint tax returns, his old joint bank-account statements, and his never-altered will. Not three weeks later, he received a padded compact-disc mailer, bearing a return address of KATZ in Jersey City, and this too he buried, unopened, in the same drawer. In these two mailings, as in the newspaper headlines that he couldn't avoid reading when he went to buy groceries in Fen City—new crises at home and abroad, new right-wing crazies spewing lies, new ecological disasters unfolding in the global endgame—he could feel the outside world closing in on him, demanding his consideration, but as long as he stayed by himself in the woods he was able to remain true to his refusal. He came from a long line of refusers, he had the constitution for it. There seemed to be almost nothing left of Lalitha; she was breaking up on him the way dead songbirds did in the wild—they were impossibly light to begin with, and as soon as their little hearts stopped beating they were barely more than bits of fluff and hollow bone, easily scattered in the wind—but this only made him more determined to hold on to what little of her he still had.

Which was why, on the October morning when the world finally did arrive, in the form of a new Hyundai sedan parked halfway down his driveway, in the overgrown turnout where Mitch and Brenda had once kept their boat, he didn't stop to see who was in it. He was hurrying to get on the road to a Conservancy meeting in Duluth, and he slowed down only enough to see that the driver's seat was reclined, the driver perhaps sleeping. He had reason to hope that whoever was in the car would be gone by the time he returned, because why else hadn't they knocked on his door? But the car was still there, its reflective rear plastic catching his headlights, when he turned off the county road at eight o'clock that evening.

He got out and peered through the parked car's windows and saw that it was empty, the driver's seat restored to its upright position. The woods were cold; the air was still and smelled capable of snow; the only sound was a faint human burble from the direction of Canterbridge Estates. He got back in his car and proceeded to the house, where a woman, Patty, was sitting on the front step in the dark. She was wearing blue jeans and a thin corduroy jacket. Her legs were drawn up to her chest for warmth, her chin resting on her knees.

He shut off his car and waited for some longish while, some twenty or thirty minutes, for her to stand up and speak to him, if that was what she'd come here for. But she refused to move, and eventually he summoned the courage to leave his car and head inside. He paused briefly on the doorstep, not more than a foot away from her, to give her a chance to speak. But her head remained bowed. His own refusal to speak to her was so childish that he couldn't resist smiling. But this smile was a dangerous admission, and he stifled it brutally, steeling himself, and entered the house and shut the door behind him.

His strength wasn't infinite, however. He couldn't help waiting in the dark, by the door, for another long while, maybe an hour, and straining to hear if she was moving, straining not to miss even a very faint tapping on the door. What he heard, instead, in his imagination, was Jessica telling him that he needed to be fair: that he owed his wife at least the courtesy of telling her to go away. And yet, after six years of silence, he felt that to speak even one word would be to take back everything—would undo all of his refusal and negate everything he'd meant by it.

At length, as if waking from some half-sleeping dream, he turned on a light and drank a glass of water and found himself drawn to his file cabinet by way of compromise; he could at least take a look at what the world had to say to him. He opened first the mailer from Jersey City. There was no note inside it, just a CD in impenetrable plastic wrapping. It appeared to be a small-label Richard Katz solo effort, with a boreal landscape on the front, superimposed with the title *Songs for Walter*.

He heard a sharp cry of pain, his own, as if it were someone else's. The *fucker*, the *fucker*, it wasn't fair. He turned over the CD with shaking hands and read the track list. The first song was called "Two Kids Good, No Kids Better."

"God, what an asshole you are," he said, smiling and weeping. "This is so unfair, you asshole."

After he'd cried for a while at the unfairness, and at the possibility that Richard wasn't wholly heartless, he put the CD back into the mailer and opened the envelope from Patty. It contained a manuscript that he read only one short paragraph of before running to the front door, pulling it open, and shaking the pages at her.

"I don't want this!" he shouted at her. "I don't want to read you! I want you to take this and get in your car and warm up, because it's fucking freezing out here."

She was, indeed, shuddering with chills, but she appeared to be locked in her huddled position and didn't look up to see what he was holding. If anything, she lowered her head further, as if he were beating on it.

"Get in your car! Warm up! I didn't ask you to come here!"

It may have just been an especially violent shudder, but she seemed to shake her head at this, a little bit.

"I promise I'll call you," he said. "I promise to have a conversation on the phone with you if you'll go away now and get yourself warmed up."

"No," she said in a very small voice.

"Fine, then! Freeze!"

He slammed the door and ran through the house and out the back door, all the way down to the lake. He was determined to be cold himself if she was so intent on freezing. Somehow he was still clutching her manuscript. Across the lake were the blazing wasteful lights of Canterbridge Estates, the jumbo screens flashing with whatever the world believed was happening to it tonight. Everybody warm in their dens, the coal-fired Iron Range power plants pushing current through the grid, the Arctic still arctic enough to send frost down through the temperate October woods. However little he'd ever known how to live, he'd never known less than he knew now. But as the bite in the air became less bracing and more serious, more of a chill in his bones, he began to worry about Patty. Teeth chattering, he went back up the hill and around to the front step and found her tipped over, less tightly balled up, her head in the grass. She was, ominously, no longer shivering.

"Patty, OK," he said, kneeling down. "This is not good, OK? I'll bring you inside."

She stirred a little, stiffly. Her muscles seemed inelastic, and no warmth was coming through the corduroy of her jacket. He tried to get her to stand up, but it didn't work, and so he carried her inside and laid her on the sofa and piled blankets on her.

"This was so stupid," he said, putting a teakettle on. "People die from doing these things. Patty? It doesn't have to be below zero, you can die when it's thirty degrees out. You're just stupid to sit out there for so long. I mean, how many years did you live in Minnesota? Did you not learn *anything*? This is so fucking stupid of you."

He turned up the furnace and brought her a mug of hot water and made her sit up to take a drink, but she blew it right back onto the upholstery. When he tried to give her more, she shook her head and made vague noises of resistance. Her fingers were icy, her arms and shoulders dully cold.

"Fuck, Patty, this is so stupid. What were you *thinking*? This is the stupidest thing you've ever done to me."

She fell asleep while he took off his clothes, and she woke up only a little as he peeled back the blankets and took off her jacket and struggled to remove her pants and then lay down with her, wearing only his underpants, and arranged the blankets on top of them. "OK, so stay awake, right?" he said, pressing as much of his surface as he could against her marmoreally cold skin. "What would be particularly stupid of you right now would be to lose consciousness. Right?"

"Mm-m," she said.

He hugged her and lightly rubbed her, cursing her constantly, cursing the position she'd put him in. For a long time she didn't get any warmer, kept falling asleep and barely waking up, but finally something clicked on inside her, and she began to shiver and clutch him. He kept rubbing and hugging, and then, all at once, her eyes were wide open and she was looking into him.

Her eyes weren't blinking. There was still something almost dead in them, something very far away. She seemed to be seeing all the way through to the back of him and beyond, out into the cold space of the future in which they would both soon be dead, out into the nothingness that Lalitha and his mother and his father had already passed into, and yet she was looking straight into his eyes, and he could feel her getting warmer by the minute. And so he stopped looking at her eyes and started looking into them, returning their look before it was too late, before this connection between life and what came after life was lost, and let her see all the vileness inside him, all the hatreds of two thousand solitary nights, while the two of them were still in touch with the void in which the sum of everything they'd ever said or done, every pain they'd inflicted, every joy they'd shared, would weigh less than the smallest feather on the wind.

"It's me," she said. "Just me."

"I know," he said, and kissed her.


Near the bottom of the list of conceivable Walter-related outcomes for the residents of Canterbridge Estates had been the possibility that they'd be sorry to see him go. Nobody, least of all Linda Hoffbauer, could have foreseen the early-December Sunday afternoon when Walter's wife, Patty, parked his Prius on Canterbridge Court and began to ring their doorbells, introducing herself briefly, noninvasively, and presenting them with Glad-wrapped plates of Christmas cookies that she'd baked. Linda was in an awkward position, meeting Patty, because there was nothing immediately unlikable about her, and because it was impossible to refuse a seasonal gift. Curiosity, if nothing else, compelled her to invite Patty inside, and before she knew it Patty was kneeling on her living-room floor, coaxing her cats to come and be stroked and inquiring about their names. She seemed to be as warm a person as her husband was a cold one. When Linda asked her how it had happened that they'd never previously met, Patty laughed trillingly and said, "Oh, well, Walter and I were taking a little breather from each other." This was an odd and rather clever formulation, difficult to find clear moral fault with. Patty stayed long enough to admire the house and its view of the snow-covered lake, and, in leaving, she invited Linda and her family to the open house that she and Walter were hosting on New Year's Day.

Linda was not much inclined to enter the home of Bobby's murderer, but when she learned that every other family on Canterbridge Court (except two already in Florida) was attending the open house, she succumbed to a combination of curiosity and Christian forbearance. The fact was, Linda was having some popularity problems in the neighborhood. Although she had her own dedicated cadre of friends and allies at her church, she was also a strong believer in neighborliness, and by acquiring three new cats to replace her Bobby, who certain irresolute neighbors believed might have died of natural causes, she'd perhaps overplayed her hand; there was a feeling that she'd been somewhat vindictive. And so, although she did leave her husband and kids at home, she drove her Suburban over to the Berglund house on New Year's and was duly flummoxed by Patty's particular hospitality toward her. Patty introduced her to her daughter and to her son and then, not leaving her side, led her outside and down to the lake for a view of her own house from a distance. It occurred to Linda that she was being played by an expert, and that she could learn from Patty a thing or two about winning hearts and minds; already, in less than a month, Patty had succeeded in charming even those neighbors who no longer opened their doors all the way when Linda came complaining to them: who made her stand out in the cold. She took several valiant stabs at getting Patty to slip up and betray her liberal disagreeability, asking her if she was a bird-lover, too ("No, but I'm a Walter-lover, so I sort of get it," Patty said), and whether she was interested in finding a local church to attend ("I think it's great there are so many to choose from," Patty said), before concluding that her new neighbor was too dangerous an adversary to be tackled head-on. As if to complete the rout, Patty had cooked up an extensive and very tasty-looking spread from which Linda, with an almost pleasant sense of defeat, loaded up a large plate.

"Linda," Walter said, accosting her while she was taking seconds. "Thank you so much for coming over."

"It was nice of your wife to invite me," Linda said.

Walter had apparently resumed regular shaving with the return of his wife—he looked very pink now. "Listen," he said, "I was awfully sorry to hear your cat disappeared."

"Really?" she said. "I thought you hated Bobby."

"I did hate him. He was a bird-killing machine. But I know you loved him, and it's a hard thing to lose a pet."

"Well, we have three more now, so."

He calmly nodded. "Just try to keep them indoors, if you can. They'll be safer there."

"I'm sorry—is that a threat?"

"No, not a threat," he said. "Just a fact. It's a dangerous world for small animals. Can I get you something else to drink?"

It was clear to everyone that day, and in the months that followed, that Patty's greatest warming influence was on Walter himself. Now, instead of speeding by his neighbors in his angry Prius, he stopped to lower his window and say hello. On weekends, he brought Patty over to the patch of clear ice that the neighborhood kids maintained for hockey and instructed her in skating, which, in a remarkably short time, she became rather good at. During small thaws, the two Berglunds could be seen taking long walks together, sometimes nearly to Fen City, and when the big thaw came, in April, and Walter again went door to door on Canterbridge Court, it was not to berate people about their cats but to invite them to join him and a scientist friend on a series of nature walks in May and June, to get to know their local heritage and to see, up close, some of the marvelous life the woods were full of. Linda Hoffbauer at this point abandoned the last vestiges of her resistance to Patty, admitting freely that she knew how to manage a husband, and the neighborhood liked this new tone of Linda's and opened its doors a little wider to her.

And so it was all in all unexpectedly sad to learn, midway through a summer in which the Berglunds hosted several barbecues and were much sought after socially in return, that they would be moving to New York at the end of August. Patty explained that she had a good job in education that she wanted to return to, and that her mother and her siblings and her daughter and Walter's best friend all lived in or near New York, and that, although the house on the lake had meant a lot to her and Walter over the years, nothing could last forever. When she was asked if they might still return for vacations, her face clouded and she said that this wasn't what Walter wanted. He was leaving his property, instead, to be managed by a local land trust as a bird sanctuary.

Within days of the Berglunds' departure in a big rental truck, whose horn Walter tooted while Patty waved good-bye, a specialized company came and erected a high and cat-resistant fence around the entire property (Linda Hoffbauer, now that Patty was gone, dared to declare the fence somewhat ugly), and soon other workers came to gut the little Berglund house, leaving only the shell standing, as a haven for owls or swallows. To this day, free access to the preserve is granted only to birds and to residents of Canterbridge Estates, through a gate whose lock combination is known to them, beneath a small ceramic sign with a picture of the pretty young dark-skinned girl after whom the preserve is named.